27/4

£2·50

D1348844

The Dragon's Tail

Also by Adam Williams

The Palace of Heavenly Pleasure
The Emperor's Bones

ADAM WILLIAMS

The Dragon's Tail

HODDER &
STOUGHTON

Copyright © 2007 by Adam Williams

First published in Great Britain in 2007 by Hodder & Stoughton
A division of Hodder Headline

The right of Adam Williams to be identified as the Author
of the Work has been asserted by him in accordance with the
Copyright, Designs and Patents Act 1988

A Hodder & Stoughton Book

1

A CIP catalogue record for this title is
available from the British Library

Hardback ISBN: 978 0 340 89910 6
Trade Paperback ISBN: 978 0 340 89911 3

Typeset in Monotype Sabon by Palimpsest Book Production Limited,
Grangemouth, Stirlingshire

Printed and bound by
Mackays of Chatham Ltd, Chatham, Kent

Hodder Headline's policy is to use papers that are natural, renewable and
recyclable products and made from wood grown in sustainable forests.
The logging and manufacturing processes are expected to conform to the environmental
regulations of the country of origin

Hodder & Stoughton Ltd
A division of Hodder Headline
338 Euston Road
London NW1 3BH

To all my family

Contents

The Dragon's Tail

PROLOGUE

The Mountain Hospital,
Shandong Province 1940

On a rise above a river and a village, nestled in the fringes of the woods that sloped up towards the clouded summit of Mount Tai, a cluster of grey bungalows was surrounded by a stone wall. Once a Catholic mission, it was now a hospital, run by an unconventional Scottish doctor, Edmund Airton, who, a decade ago, had retreated to it from the world with his wife, Catherine, and their infant son. The Bishop of Jinan had bequeathed it to him, because he had seen the humanity that underlay the atheism of his old friend and intellectual sparring partner. Edmund had satisfied the expectations of his practical benefactor and built a reputation as a healer throughout the province.

They were troubled times in China, but Edmund and Catherine treated everybody who came to them whether they were Christians or Buddhists, Nationalists or Communists, with devoted and impartial attention. When they were young, they had experienced enough of war and politics to care only for the suffering of ordinary people. In their district every peasant family had, at one time or another, dragged their sick relatives up the steep path to the Airtons' gate, confident that they would find comfort and care, free of charge or obligation. A year after his arrival, Edmund had cured a concubine of the local governor, once a minor warlord, of a skin complaint that had been diagnosed erroneously as leprosy. This had earned him gratitude and protection, and no questions were ever asked subsequently about his patients. There were occasions when bandits and revolutionaries found themselves recuperating beside policemen wounded in the same gun battle: in Edmund's hands they were, by tacit consent, on neutral ground.

The Mountain Hospital, as it became known, gradually acquired the aura of a monastic sanctuary, although no god was worshipped there: funded by an American philanthropist, it had no tie to any charitable institution or religious foundation. Edmund and Catherine had cut their links with the foreign concessions, which had, anyway, dismissed them long ago as eccentrics of the wrong sort.

Their son, Harry, grew up among the bamboo forests, ricefields and water-buffalo. His first memory was of running in a crowd of village urchins to greet the travelling opera troupe that had arrived for the New Year Festival, his ears jangling with the din of cymbals, drums and screeching arias. He came to know the shop-owners, who rarely let him pass without giving him a wink and a surreptitious slice of sweet dried meat, which they snipped off with big scissors from the strips that hung on hooks, or a sugared pastry from a tray in the window. Mr Lo, the confectioner, would carefully select for him a toffee apple from a blue and white porcelain brush jar in which he displayed his creations as if they were flowers. Spoiling the son was small compensation for the kindness they had received from the father.

In the evenings, after school, Harry ran off with the village boys to fly his kite in the meadow by the riverbank. Often the fishermen casting their nets from their small skiffs beckoned him over to look at a newly caught carp, flapping in their gnarled, brown hands. Sometimes he and his friends crept into the temple, where they watched the monks intone the scriptures under the shadow of the great gilded statue of Buddha. The hall was swathed in incense, and the teeming life of the village stilled to a mysterious solitude.

From his earliest years, Harry believed there was magic in this land. It was partly the stories he heard from his Japanese grandmother, his grandfather's second wife and Catherine's stepmother. For her, every natural phenomenon was imbued with animism. Fox fairies lived near the temple grove, and when light rain poured from a sunny sky over the ricefields at harvest time, Harry knew that a monkey was marrying a badger. From the village storyteller, he heard older tales, of the creation of the gods, of the heroic Knights of the Water Margin, of the Monkey King and his journey to the west. Once, with the Taoist monk Hsiung, his father's friend, he had climbed breathlessly through the bamboo groves in the hour before dawn as the sun's red rim peeped out from behind the jagged peaks of Mount Tai, the holy mountain. The old monk had told him that this was Nu Wa, the life goddess, who had coupled with the King of Heaven to bring abundance to the earth.

Harry's special friend was the cook's son, Chen Tao. When they had first met, Harry was sitting in the hospital yard, playing with the string of wooden ducks he had been given for his sixth birthday. He was vaguely aware that a new cook had replaced Lao Tang who, at the age of eighty, had finally been induced to retire. Looking up, he had observed a Chinese boy gazing curiously at him from the kitchen door.

'I haven't seen you before,' said Harry, in his piping, well-bred voice. His Chinese was fluent, with only a touch of the Shandong accent spoken in those parts. In a household where Chinese friends and patients visited his parents at all hours, he had grown up speaking and even thinking in their language. If his tone was a little patronising, he was not aware of it: he had grown up as the lord of his little world.

'I've seen you, though,' said the strange boy, who was not in the least intimidated.

'You're the boss's son, aren't you? What are you doing?'

'Feeding my ducks,' answered Harry, surprised to be questioned.

'How can you feed wooden ducks?' The tone was sceptical.

'I pretend.' Harry shrugged.

The boy watched him, eyes protruding as he frowned. Harry felt self-conscious and wished he would go away, which eventually he did. A few moments later, he returned covering something in his hands. He walked boldly up to Harry and opened his palms to reveal three fluffy ducklings. Live ones. He must have seen Harry's delight in his face because his own lit up in a wide grin.

From that moment on, the two boys were inseparable. Their friendship was based on mutual admiration. Chen Tao was a year older than Harry, who hero-worshipped him because he was practical, capable, fearless, and knew so much more than he did. Chen Tao respected Harry's size (he was a head taller) and was fascinated by his foreignness. While Tao broadened Harry's horizons by leading him on adventures further and further away from the village and the hospital, Harry introduced his peasant friend to stories and the world of the imagination.

Together they roamed the bamboo groves on the mountain. Chen Tao knew all the paths that led to the temple on the summit and the little woodcutter's hamlet below. The woods became their private haven, where they re-enacted scenes from their favourite tales. Chen Tao, who had been brought up in poverty and whose education had been utilitarian, was unused to indulging his fantasies, but Harry's life had been filled with stories, so at first Chen Tao good naturedly took the subordinate role, playing the tiger to Harry's heroic Wu Song, when they pretended to be outlaws from *The Water Margin*, or Piggy to Harry's Monkey when they did *Journey to the West*. Gradually, however, he became more assertive. Now they spent days as the contesting heroes in Chen Tao's favourite book, *The Romance of the Three Kingdoms*, and as often as not Chen Tao was the godlike Guang Gong, with his huge spear, while Harry, marshalling his armies on the other side of the valley, became the villainous Cao Cao. Not that Harry minded. Anything the older boy suggested promised fun and excitement. The woods rang with their battle cries, or the tumble of rocks and leaves when one or other assaulted the walls of the castle they had dug into the side of a hill. Afterwards they swam in the pool under the waterfall, and tried to wash the mud off their clothes – they didn't want trouble when they got home.

To the amusement of the indulgent Edmund and Catherine, Chen Tao began to treat the Airtons as his own family. After breakfast, he would join Harry, who had been taken out of the village school when he was six, for lessons with Hsiung. The Taoist had his own eccentric way of teaching arithmetic and Chinese history, and his storytelling gave the boys new ideas for their games on the mountain. Under his influence they became Shaolin warrior monks, wrestling, kick-boxing and whirling wooden swords.

After Harry's eighth birthday their lives began to change. One evening, his father came into Harry's room and sat down. 'You're a big boy, now, Harry,' he said, 'and in a few years you'll be going home to boarding-school.'

'But this is home, Daddy.'

'I meant England, you silly fellow – well, Scotland, actually. That's where we come from. It's where your aunt Mary lives, my sister. You'll love it. There are lochs where you can fish, and in Edinburgh, where we'll send you to school, there's a beautiful old castle, just like in the King Arthur stories. You'll make new friends and learn all sorts of things.'

It was not the first time that boarding school had been mentioned and Harry was excited. He had discussed it with Chen Tao, who had agreed that it would be a splendid adventure.

'But before you go, I'm afraid you'll need to study hard. You have to pass an exam. A clever boy like you will sail through it, but we have to prepare you first. So, from next week, your mother will take over your lessons. Teaching you lessons in English, geography and our own country's history. It's not so different from the Chinese tales Hsiung's been telling you. There are wise rulers, like King Alfred, and great warriors, like Robert the Bruce and Hereward the Wake. Wonderful stories, Harry, but it will mean a few more hours' work each day so there'll be less time for games with Tao. Sorry about that, but I know you'll work hard – and enjoy it too.'

Harry told Chen Tao about this in their secret cave behind the waterfall. Chen Tao was elated. 'It's a great opportunity, Ha Li,' he said. 'My dad tells me that schooling is the best thing in the world. You know, he's made offerings at the temple in thanks for my friendship with you. I never understood why until now.' He grabbed Harry's shoulders and embraced him. 'I think it's time,' he said.

Harry was confused. 'Time for what?' he asked.

'For us to become blood brothers – to make our friendship eternal,' said Chen Tao. 'You remember – we've talked about it. It's what warriors do. It's like the oath between Guang Gong, Liu Bei and Zhang Fei in the Peach Garden. Now that we're about to learn grown-up things, it's time.'

Harry's eyes widened as Chen Tao pulled out the scalpel Harry had stolen from his father's surgery. 'You're not afraid, are you? It won't hurt,' said his friend, smiling. 'Look.' He ran the blade over his own palm. Harry saw a thread of blood, and shivered. 'Your turn,' said Chen Tao. Gingerly Harry held out his hand, screwing his eyes shut. He felt stinging and flinched, but Chen Tao clasped his fingers and squeezed their palms together. His eyes gleamed and he smiled. 'It's done,' he said. 'Our blood has mingled. It means our lives are bound together for ever.' He raised Harry's hand high. 'We'll just have to imagine the chicken's head being cut off, but we can burn some yellow paper with our birth dates written on them, and steal some of my dad's rice wine for the libation when we get home. Say the words after me: "Your life is mine, mine is yours. We swear to live and die together."'

Then he taught Harry the Triad salute and other rituals he had decided were appropriate to celebrate their bandit brotherhood. Harry loved this mumbo-jumbo, but he was surprised that Tao was so excited about him going to school.

Next morning he found out why when he turned up with his exercise books and pencils in his mother's little study off the courtyard. Suddenly Chen Tao appeared beside him. He was wearing new blue trousers, a clean shirt and clutching an exercise book with a box of pencils – the expensive one he and Harry had admired in Mr Lai's store. He gave Harry a clap on the back and a broad grin.

Harry's ears began to burn, and his face reddened. Something was very wrong, and he didn't know what to do about it.

His mother was kind. She ruffled Chen Tao's hair as she said, 'I'm so sorry, Chen Tao, but these lessons are going to be in English, which you don't speak. The subjects are for English children, about our kings and queens, and geography, the things Ha Li has to learn so he can pass the exam for boarding-school in England.'

Chen Tao stiffened. His face was set, expressionless, although there were crimson spots on his cheeks. Harry felt a pang of guilt at the dull hurt in his friend's eyes.

'I know how much you want to learn and that's wonderful,' Catherine continued, 'but these lessons are just for Ha Li. I do hope you understand.' She ruffled his hair again, then steered Harry into her study. She was smiling at Chen Tao, about to close the door, when the Chinese boy flung his pencil box and book on to the ground. His lips were twisted, his teeth bared, and his eyes blazed with jealousy and resentment. Then he turned and ran out of the yard.

That evening Dr Airton had a long talk with the cook. He apologised that Chen Tao could not take part in Harry's English lessons, then added that Harry would be learning mathematics and science from Hsiung in Chinese: Chen Tao was welcome to join those classes if he liked. The cook was grateful, bowing to Edmund and brushing his hand – but, unaccountably, Chen Tao refused. 'No,' he told Harry, when they next met. 'I'm just a peasant boy. What do I need learning for? I've got things to do in the village. I've friends there too, you know. Who wants to be stuck in a classroom?' He laughed and threw a stone at a sparrow.

Harry was concerned that his friend might still be angry with him. 'Are you sure?' he asked.

Chen Tao grinned and shook Harry's shoulder. 'Of course I'm sure,' he said.

'We're still friends?'

'We're blood brothers,' said Chen Tao. '"Your life is mine, mine is yours. We swear to live and die together." That means for ever, Ha Li. It's an irrevocable oath.'

Harry didn't know what 'irrevocable' meant, but it sounded good.

'We'll still play together, then? We'll be bandits in the mountains, when I can get away from class?'

Chen Tao's eyes were gleaming. 'Try to keep me away,' he said.

So, when Harry had time he continued to play with Chen Tao. The older boy was always available and never again showed resentment about the misunderstanding. On the contrary, he seemed to have accepted that, in addition to his lessons, Harry would sometimes be involved in activities that did not include him. 'It's all right, Ha Li,' he said once, when Harry apologised that he would be away for two weeks with his parents at the seaside in Tsingtao. 'You do your Western things, and be Chinese again when you return. I'm not you and you're not me. I have my own life too, you know. When you're at your studies, I get up to all sorts of things you wouldn't believe.'

Harry suspected he was making it up. 'What things, Chen Tao? What do you do?'

'Just . . . things,' he said slyly. 'If you can have your secrets, I can have mine.'

'I have no secrets from you,' said Harry, lamely. He still felt guilty, as if he had let his friend down. He was old enough to appreciate that the Chinese valued 'face' above all things, and he knew, too, how proud his friend was. He liked to be the leader, and Harry was generally content with that because he loved him: Chen Tao was his *gege*, his elder brother. If he wanted to pretend he had another life more interesting than Harry's, that was fine.

It saddened Harry, though, that his friend had been right: Harry did have secrets that he had never got round to telling Chen Tao. They applied particularly to the Airton family's annual visit to Shanghai, when they stayed in a big hotel, ate enormous meals in restaurants and visited his parents' friends. There was a Chinese lady, a special friend of his mother, who lived in a tall apartment block with a fat baby. She had an artificial leg and a withered arm, the result, his mother had said, of a terrible accident during the civil war, when the Nationalists had been fighting the warlords. The first time they had been there the disfigurement and her sharp, penetrating eyes had frightened him and made him wonder if she was a witch. But she had laughed, embraced him and given him a wooden tiger. On subsequent visits he had enjoyed seeing her and playing with her child. He had not told Chen Tao about them because he thought his friend would laugh at him for playing with a baby.

He had been embarrassed one summer when Catherine's friend and her daughter, who was then three years old, had come to stay with them at the hospital. Naturally, Chen Tao had been curious about the new arrivals in the Airton household, and joined Harry when the adults were talking and Harry had been deputed to look after the little girl. To Harry's alarm, however, Chen Tao had seen the opportunity to play a prank and coerced him into helping him lock her into the chicken pen. When the adults came out, alerted by her screams, Harry had had to face the music alone because Chen Tao had slunk away. He did not betray his friend, but a day later his mother had taken him aside and told him that Chen Tao must be kept out of sight while her friends were staying. She never said why, and Chen Tao did not seem to mind. 'Those superior Shanghainese,' he spat. 'They're only half Chinese anyway – bananas, with yellow skin and white inside. Class enemies. You're welcome to them.'

The incident had cast a shadow over an otherwise sunny childhood. At the time Chen Tao's inexplicable and scornful reference to 'class enemies' had struck Harry as ominous but he told himself that his friend was always coming out with strange sayings he found in the magazines he purloined from Dr Airton's outpatients' room. Eventually Harry forgot about it. There was just too much to enjoy. School in England was a year away – for ever, as far as Harry was concerned – and they had their games.

Yet here again, things had begun imperceptibly to change. They played and fought as before, but sometimes Harry felt it was no longer merely fun for Chen Tao. He had become less devil-may-care. There was a new seriousness about him, and their battle scenarios were no longer based on the old children's stories. Chen Tao pored over his magazines for pictures of modern wars. He quoted the vocabulary of present-day politics, which Harry found incomprehensible. In their new games Chen Tao liked to pretend he was head of a gang of Communist rebels hiding in the forests, while Harry was the luckless government general set up to be ambushed. Harry was happy to go along with it. It was not so different from when he had played the Sheriff of Nottingham to Chen Tao's Robin Hood, and he was still doing what he enjoyed most – playing with his best friend, in the magical China he loved. But soon Harry was taking the games more seriously too. There was no lessening of trust between the pair, but sometimes he felt that Chen Tao was challenging him in a way he didn't understand, which scared him a little.

Harry did not know it, but dark forces were gathering to threaten his idyll. Before the enigmatic Hsiung had left on a long journey from which he had never returned, he had told Harry that happiness, like everything in life, is transitory. The idea was meaningless to the boy, who believed that his golden childhood at the Mountain Hospital could never end – but when the Japanese came everything did change.

It was the spring of 1940. He was playing with his new train set on the Persian carpet that gave colour to the small sitting room when he heard a rustle of silk and saw the tall figure of his mother gazing at him from the doorway. She came in and patted the sofa. He jumped up and ran to sit beside her, snuggling into her softness. Usually the house was full of people and she would be helping his father in the surgery, or teaching at the village school, so it was rare for him to have her to himself in the daytime.

They looked out over the veranda at the bamboo groves on the mountain. The piled clouds in the sky were tinged with the pink and vermilion of approaching sunset. The slanting rays streamed through the open window, highlighting his mother's deep green eyes and auburn hair. She smelt of lilac.

But today there was an unaccountable solemnity in her face. She stroked his hand as she said, 'I'm sorry, my love, but I have bad news. I'm afraid you can't play outside any more. You know how difficult the Japanese soldiers can be, and your father and I would be worried, Harry, if you left the compound.'

He protested. Chen Tao was allowed outside. Nobody told him what to do.

She sighed. 'Chen Tao's different from us, Harry. He's Chinese.'

'But Daddy's always saying there's no difference between Chinese and English, and even Japanese, Mummy. Obah-*san* was Japanese.' Obah-*san* had gone to heaven two years before. Losing his Japanese step-grandmother had been the first tragedy in Harry's brief life.

A tear was running down his mother's cheek. 'Daddy's right, darling. Good people are the same whatever their race or nationality. You must always remember that, Harry, and be kind and good, especially to those who are weak and innocent. There are good people even among our enemies. Sometimes they need our help too.'

'Like Obah-*san*, Mummy? She was a good Japanese, wasn't she? Not like the soldiers, the Aizi.'

'The Japanese aren't really our enemies – and Obah-*san* certainly wasn't. What an idea, you muffin.' He loved it when she ruffled his hair. 'She adored you and we all adored her. Anyway, you mustn't call them by that horrible name. The Japanese would only become our enemies if there was a war here, like the one they're having in Europe.'

'But there *is* a war here, Mummy. Chen Tao told me.'

'Oh, darling, how can I explain? Japan is at war with China but not with England. Or not yet. We must all be very strong and sensible now, Harry, and not provoke the Japanese soldiers. They're already asking your father to do things for them that are . . .' She shook her head.

'What, Mummy? What are they asking Daddy to do?'

'Never mind. He's an honourable man and he won't do anything bad for the Japanese or anybody else, but they're unscrupulous and we're his family. You must promise you won't go out alone. Promise me you won't go off and do anything silly?'

When he looked into her anxious eyes, Harry wanted to promise – but outside a breeze was shaking the bamboo, he heard the oriole singing in the Siberian pine, and he knew that Chen Tao was waiting for him. He said, 'Of course, Mummy.' And as she hugged and kissed him, he felt his fingers tingle as they crossed behind his back. He hated lying to his mother, but now he had another loyalty, to the Hong Huzi, Chen Tao's name for their own rebel faction, and a meeting had been arranged for that night.

Even so, he was anxious when, long after he had been tucked into bed, he looked out of his window into the courtyard. By now Chen Tao would be crouched behind Harry's father's car, and in a moment he would raise the blue flag.

The two boys had developed a simple code, based on traffic lights Harry had seen in Shanghai. In their waterfall hideout, they had cut strips off Chen Tao's blue trousers, Harry's red scarf and his yellow pullover: if Chen Tao waved a blue flag (they had not been able to find any green cloth) it meant, 'Action, go ahead as planned'; a red flag signalled, 'Danger, expedition's cancelled'; and a yellow one meant, 'Problems, wait until the coast is clear.'

That had been shortly after the Aizi – the 'dwarf men', as Chen Tao called the Japanese – had set up their camp in the valley. Chen Tao had discovered from his magazines that the Hong Huzi, the bandit gangs who fought the Aizi in far-away Manchuria, used such signals to communicate with each other when they were creeping through forests to ambush enemy patrols or to blow up a railway line. Chen Tao had also wanted Harry to swear an oath of allegiance to the Communist Party because they had the best guerrilla fighters, but Harry had been reluctant: he knew his father disapproved of Communists. They had argued until Chen Tao had given him his twisted smile, clapped him on the back and said, 'All right, you can be a Nationalist. That's good, too, because the Nationalists and Communists are in alliance against the Aizi. Together we can be the United Front.'

Harry had not been sure he wanted to be a Nationalist – his father never had many good words for them either – but he did want to be a Hong Huzi and fight the Aizi. For several weeks, he and Chen Tao campaigned in the bamboo groves, escaping enemy pursuit, stalking the woodcutters who stood in for Aizi patrols, pretending to spy on enemy troop movements. They hid under the leaves, signalling to each other with their flags. Sometimes they practised elaborate stratagems that Chen Tao remembered from his stories of ancient battles, when he or Harry would pretend to be captured, only to give the enemy false information that would lead them into an ambush further up the track. On those occasions the woodcutters would be surprised by a little boy leaping off a rock and blazing away at them with his stick.

One day, shortly before Harry's mother had asked him not to leave the compound, Chen Tao had produced a letter, which he said contained orders from their Hong Huzi commanders. He and Harry were to make their first real reconnaissance inside the Japanese camp. Harry recognised Chen Tao's characters on the paper, and thought this was a new game, but when he said so, Chen Tao bridled. 'Ha Li, sometimes I'm disappointed in you. Don't you realise how lucky we are that the Hong Huzi have let us join their brigade?'

Harry couldn't bring himself to commit the heresy and say what was in his mind, that this was only pretend, but he felt resentful. 'You're only a year older than me,' he said. The age difference had always rankled. 'Why should you always be the leader, and tell me what we have to do? We're equal. Isn't that what you keep saying Communists are? We're friends.'

Chen Tao took his shoulders and gave him a sad smile. 'Of course we're friends, Ha Li, but these are orders. We have to trust each other, don't we?'

Harry allowed himself to be mollified. Reluctantly he had followed his friends down the path to the village and across the bridge to the old warehouse where the Aizi kept their stores. One of the Japanese soldiers had been friendly and given them sweets. Later Chen Tao threw his away, so Harry, regretfully, did too – but not before they had spotted the rickety staircase at the back of the storehouse and the broken window through which they might be able to enter. Chen Tao took Harry's wristwatch and timed the movements of the sentries. Afterwards he told Harry that he would choose a night on which there was no moon to make their reconnaissance. Harry should wait at the appointed hour for Chen Tao's signal.

As he looked out at the dark shadow of his father's car he felt again the butterflies in his stomach, and hoped that Chen Tao would not be behind the car, or that when the torch flashed, it would reveal a red flag instead of a blue one. But a blue flag was illuminated in the darkness, and he had no choice but to obey the summons. He climbed down the wistaria that covered the wall by his bedroom window and crouched in the flowerbed. He saw another flash of blue by the dispensary – the signal for him to run across the yard – and soon he and his friend were scrambling through the hole in the wall, skirting the narrow lane that led to the road and eventually to the dried-out riverbed they had to cross. Harry experienced a moment of terror when one of the sentries patrolling the bridge stopped half-way across and shouted something. He thought they had been discovered, but it was a false alarm.

Soon they were sneaking through the sleeping village, and almost stumbled upon two Japanese officers making their way drunkenly to a comfort house. Harry wanted to turn back, but Chen Tao gave him a stern look. A few moments later, they were beside the stinking honey carts, on the dark side of the warehouse, watching the Aizi guard disappear round the corner of the building.

'Right,' whispered Chen Tao. 'We have six minutes before he comes back.'

'I don't want to go,' said Harry. 'Why are we doing this? I don't know what the plan is.'

'Obey orders, that's all,' hissed his friend. 'But if you're frightened, you can stay here – and you'll never be a Hong Huzi again.' He ran towards the stairs.

The climb was interminable. Every time Harry's foot touched a plank it creaked, and he could hear his gasping breath. When he reached the top, there was a terrifying wriggle along the ledge to the open window. He was certain he would fall, or freeze with fear and be caught in the sentry's torchlight, but Chen Tao's arm snaked out of the dark window and pulled him through. His stomach lurched as he fell through blackness to land with a thump on a grain bag.

Chen Tao flicked on his torch. They were in a storage attic, built half-way across the warehouse. A ladder was propped against the side, leading to the depths below.

'You're a hero, a good Hong Huzi,' muttered Chen Tao. 'Do you have your torch and flags? Good. I'm going to climb down and see what I can find. You stay up here on guard. If you hear anything, flick your torch once. I'll see it. When it's all clear you can flash the blue flag.'

Before Harry could protest, his friend had disappeared. In the pitch blackness he imagined Chen Tao creeping along the warehouse floor, feeling his way round the crates and bales. He heard a creak as his friend prised open the lid of a box. 'Ha Li! Ha Li! There are guns!'

Then he heard the rattle of chains, and realised it came from outside the warehouse gates. Frantically he fumbled with his torch and dropped it. When he had found it again, and pressed the switch, all the lights came on at once and he saw Japanese soldiers enter the warehouse. Chen Tao was nowhere to be seen. Hopelessly, Harry clutched the red flag. There was nothing he could do.

But the Japanese had not come to look for children. They were herding in five Chinese prisoners with bent heads and bound hands. They were laughing at them and kicking them, prodding them with their rifles until they were kneeling in a ragged line on the floor.

With a shock Harry recognised two. One was Lao Zhao, who owned the pastry shop. He often gave Chen Tao and Harry sweet dumplings. He was usually such a cheerful man, but now he hung his bald head to his chest, and tears were running down his cheeks. The other was the village storyteller, Zhang Laoshi. Harry had spent hours in the square listening to his tales from the Chinese classics.

Three Japanese soldiers were carrying buckets, and another, a big man stripped to his vest, had a baseball bat. Harry watched as the Aizi placed the upended buckets over their prisoners' heads. Then, one after the other, the man with the bat began to beat them. There was a dreamlike quality to his actions as if he were performing them in slow motion. The bat would arc in a graceful curve through the air, and when it hit the side of the metal bucket, there would be a long, echoing clang, like the sound of the big gong they struck in the temple on the mountain. It seemed to reverberate inside Harry's own head, to be replaced by a louder crash as the baseball bat hit again, unleashing another hideous timpani. Harry imagined what would happen if the Japanese caught him. He seemed to feel the bucket over his own head, and anticipated the explosion when the bat struck.

He screamed.

Time resumed its normal pace. The startled Japanese soldiers were staring about the warehouse, reaching for their rifles. Chen Tao stepped out from behind a pile of crates and yelled, 'Ha Li! Run!' then scampered away as they tried to catch him. Eventually they cornered him and dragged him by the ear into the centre of the concrete floor. The big man, who had dropped the baseball bat, was raising his hand to strike him.

Harry ran.

Scrambling somehow out of the window, slithering along the ledge, sliding down the staircase so his hands burned on the banisters, slipping in the mud at the bottom, dodging the sentry, who fired his rifle into the night, then pounding through the alleys, his heart thumping, he had no idea where he was running, only that he had to get away. Soon he was stumbling across the dry riverbed, ankles twisting on the stones. Did he imagine the searchlights? At last he reached his home and banged on the compound gates. Then he was weeping in his mother's arms, his father kneeling beside him, questioning him quietly. All the time sirens were sounding from the village. His father put an arm round the shoulders of the frightened cook, then the two were in the car, and driving out of the gates.

He must have fallen asleep. The last thing he knew his mother had been lying beside him on his bed. He remembered her rocking him in her arms, and whispering, 'It's all right, darling, Mummy's here.' But he had woken alone, starlight washing faintly over his bedclothes and casting wraithlike shadows on the walls. He was terrified, thinking of Chen Tao and everything that had happened. Would the Aizi come for him too? He heard the sound of an engine. Yellow light from headlamps flashed in through his window. He sat up in bed. It must be the Japanese. Then, he heard a car door close, his father's quiet voice and Chen Tao's father sobbing.

He had to find out what had happened to his friend. He pushed off the bedclothes and crept down the stairs. There was a place behind the pillar in the hall where he could peer into the sitting room and not be seen. His father was slumped wearily on the sofa, his head in his hands. His mother moved into view and passed him a glass.

'Darling, it was useless,' he heard his father say. 'They denied all knowledge of him. They laughed at me and said no Chinese boy had been taken into custody tonight. They went through the motions. We all drove to the warehouse, which was empty. Then I was told I had insulted the honour of the Kwantung Army. Apparently, the Japanese do not make war on children. Old Chen is heartbroken and wants to go back to his home province. I think he knew all along it would be pointless trying to find his son. Chen Tao's dead or disappeared, which amounts to the same thing.'

'Did they make the same demands on you as before?'

'Oh, yes, laced with the usual threats. But I told them again, I'm neutral, and a doctor, and that interrogation centre they want me to work in is nothing but a torture chamber, flagrantly abusing the Geneva Convention and every other civilised code of conduct. Catherine, can you imagine what would have happened if they'd caught Harry? How they'd have used him to pressure me? And what they might have done to him? We must face it, darling. It's time.'

'No, Edmund, I can't bear it.' His mother began to cry.

'I know, darling. I feel the same but we mustn't delay any longer. Tomorrow we'll go to Shanghai. The British Consulate sent a circular. There's a boat leaving for England next week. They're recommending women and children evacuate. That means they think war is inevitable. We must get Harry out.' His father put an arm around her shoulders. 'Catherine, you go with him. I can't leave the hospital, but you can. Go with the boy. I'll be happier if I know you're both safe.'

'Don't ask me to do that, Edmund,' his mother said, through her tears. 'You can't run this place on your own. We have a duty to all who depend on us. The consulate did say they would have people to look after unaccompanied children and hand them over to their relatives safely. They did promise that, didn't they?'

He bowed his head. 'Yes,' he said. 'They did.'

She wiped her eyes. 'Well, there you are, then,' she said. 'We're not the only ones, are we? Anyway, you and I tried being apart once before, and we weren't very good at it, were we? In any case, whatever you say, you know I'm needed here as much as you are.' Her voice quavered. 'Oh, God, Edmund, I know I'm being foolish and selfish. Of course Harry must go. But he's so little.'

Harry rushed out of his hiding-place. 'No! I don't want to go away! I know it's my fault. I'll never do it again, I promise. Please don't send me away!'

His father and his mother put their arms around him. He knew – even then – that his life, the life he loved, was over.

In adulthood he had no recollection of what had happened in the days that followed. It seemed that at the next moment he was standing among a crowd of European children by the rail of a liner. Tall skyscrapers of a big city rose up beyond the quay, but he had eyes only for the two figures standing on the jetty, waving frantically, calling to him, although he could not hear them.

And he knew it was his own fault that he had to leave China: he had lied, and broken his promise. That was why he would never see his family again, or his friend, Chen Tao, whom he had abandoned and betrayed.

Southampton, where they disembarked, was grey, like the Atlantic, and at night searchlights crisscrossed the darkness. On the voyage, all the ship's lights had blazed at night to signify that it was neutral, but Harry could not sleep, thinking of the U-boats that prowled the black waters.

He was handed into the care of a tall, angular woman, with a severe, lined face, greying hair tied into a prim bun under her hat. 'This is you aunt Mary, dear,' said the matron, who had been looking after the parentless children on the boat. Harry clung to her apron. She detached his fingers and pushed him forward. 'Mrs Mackintosh, he's all yours,' she said. 'He's a nice little boy, but solitary. We've tried to brush up his English on the way, but he still prefers to speak Chinese. Between you and me, we found him a bit of a handful.'

The angular woman knelt down and took his hands. '*Jiuyang, jiuyang,*' she said, without changing her severe expression. 'I've heard so much about you.'

Harry's eyes widened. The formal phrase she had used was incorrect, since it was the greeting of an inferior to a superior and rarely used by an adult to children, but she was speaking *Chinese*.

She took him to tea at a Lyons Corner House before they boarded their train. It reminded him of a restaurant in Shanghai, the last time he had eaten with his parents, and he burst into tears. She hugged him.

On the long train journey up to Scotland, in a compartment full of soldiers in uniform, all available leg space filled with kitbags and rifles, she told him who she was. As a girl, she'd been in China. That was why she still spoke some Chinese. Her parents, Harry's grandparents, had been medical missionaries in Manchuria, but she had never returned there after her schooling, unlike her other brothers and sisters. She had worked as a secretary in a firm of solicitors, and when her parents had retired, she had kept house for them in Edinburgh till they died. 'So there I was, a poor spinster, alone in the world, a bit like you've been, Harry, on that long voyage – but the Lord was kind to me. He gave me, even late in life, a good, God-fearing man to be my husband. Your uncle Angus, Harry. He's a fisherman and we live on a beautiful island in the Outer Hebrides. You'll be happy there.'

Harry had never had any Christian instruction and did not know what a 'God-fearing man' was. He wondered if Uncle Angus was scared of temple statues, as he himself had once been. It was only after their ferry had disembarked them in Harris and he had got to know the grizzle-bearded man in dark Sunday best, who had been waiting for them on the pier, that Harry came to understand what it meant to be God-fearing. Also, although this realisation came gradually, after many beatings for 'lying', 'idleness' and other arbitrary crimes, he began to appreciate what was meant by hell.

When the news came one day in a letter from the Red Cross that his parents had been interned in a Japanese prison camp called Weixian, Aunt Mary was so worried that she wept.

Harry, however, took the news coolly. He ran out of the house and stood for hours on the cliff edge, looking at the seabirds and the waves crashing on the rocks. He had allowed himself to hope that he might be forgiven for his lies, that one day his parents would come and rescue him. Now he knew that that would never be. This must be the damnation Uncle Angus kept talking about. He cast his eyes up at the grey, louring skies of his own prison, and screamed in his anguish, but the cold wind carried his voice away, indistinguishable from the cry of the gulls.

* * *

To survive, Harry learnt to dissemble. The 'young heathen' dutifully studied his Bible, although he found the stories in the Old Testament not a patch on the romances he had heard in the village square, and it was some time before he grasped that the silent Sunday gatherings in the stone kirk on the promontory, so unlike the gaudy temple parades with their firecrackers, were occasions of worship. After a while, he looked forward to the services: they gave him a chance to think his own thoughts, without the danger that was ever present around the hearth at home. There, even his taciturnity might be construed as insolence, and an excuse for him to be taken to his uncle and aunt's bedroom for a beating with his uncle's buckled belt. What was worse than the pain were the prayer sessions afterwards, when his uncle made him kneel by the bed, and repeat, over and over again, the Lord's Prayer.

Even so, silence was a better policy than talking, especially about China – the most innocuous remark might lead to an accusation of lying. This also applied at school, where he was bullied and had to resort to his fists to earn respect, but the big fisher-boys were a match for any of the martial-arts tricks he had practised with Chen Tao. Harry learnt to blend, and after a year, at least on the surface, there was no discernible difference between him and the other children of the wind-lashed island. Dour silence punctuated by violence was a way of life and, for Harry, solitude was a means of survival. It allowed him to develop his own interests in what he thought of later as his secret world.

From the first, his aunt had been his ally. When she was there, Uncle Angus moderated the discipline, except when he was drunk. Then, sometimes, he turned his rage on her too, leaving her bruised and weeping while he took Harry into the other room.

There were, however, blessed intervals when his uncle was away with the boats, sometimes for weeks, and Harry, with his aunt, experienced something that approached happiness. At first it was a sharing of stories. She wanted to hear everything about his life in China. She would bring out treats – crumpets or buns – and then they would share their experiences: his adventures near the Mountain Hospital, her girlhood at the mission station with her parents, far away in the north of China in a town called Shishan. Sometimes Harry would be so excited that he babbled in Chinese, which still came more naturally to him than English.

'You know, Harry,' she once told him, 'if I were to close my eyes and listen to you, I wouldn't know that you were European. Your accent is perfect. It's a gift, and something you must cling to if you can.' She smiled. 'Come with me. I think you're old enough. I have something to show you.'

They had to climb a ladder to get into the loft. There, among the bric-à-brac, were two tin trunks. Harry held the candle while his aunt prised open a rusty catch and lifted a lid. It was filled with books. She picked one up and blew off the dust. Harry saw Chinese characters. 'This is your grandfather's library,' she told him. 'I inherited it from him and you will inherit it one day from me. He was a great scholar and taught medicine in the Chinese language. Most of these books mean nothing to me as I can't read the characters, but one day you may be able to. There are all sorts of books here, some scientific works, some stories . . .'

To Harry it was as if she had uncovered a pirate's treasure trove. 'Can I learn now, Aunt Mary?'

'I don't think there is anybody here who can teach you,' she said. 'But let me think about it. If God is kind, He will find a way to help us. In the meantime, you won't say anything about this to Uncle Angus, will you? He wouldn't approve.'

Two months later (Uncle Angus was away again with the fishing fleet) Aunt Mary came back from the village with buns, scones and a grin on her face. 'God has answered our prayers, Harry. A Chinaman – a real Chinaman – has moved to Harris. He worked on a ship and was wounded when his convoy was bombed. He can't be repatriated to China until the war's over, and for some reason he has made his way from Glasgow to here. He's setting up a tailor's shop. I talked to him, and found him to be an educated man from Tientsin. Would you believe it? That's where our family used to live. And what's more, because of that connection, he's agreed to teach you, free of charge. I'll take you to him tomorrow.'

So began Harry's education. Every day, after school he would slip away to the shop in the village where, hidden from the counter in a back room among all the tweeds, Mr Lin would put him through his lessons, sewing as he listened to Harry read, criticising the slightest infraction of tone or grammar. This was discipline that Harry enjoyed. Mr Lin, it turned out, was Professor Lin, once a lecturer of physics at a northern university, whose family had been bankrupted when the

Japanese invaded, forcing him to take a menial job in the merchant marine to support his family.

Soon Harry was reading the first book his aunt had taken out of the trunk, *The Romance of the Three Kingdoms*, stories Harry remembered from long ago in the village square. At the end of every lesson, first merely to entertain the boy after his hard study, the professor would set up little physics experiments, showing how light refracted into colour through a prism or making waves in a bowl. He soon discovered Harry had an aptitude for science, and began to teach him the theory. By the time Harry was fifteen, the texts he was using in his Chinese lessons were his grandfather's tomes on physics and chemistry.

It was not only language and science that Professor Lin taught Harry. He knew that the lessons had to be kept secret from Harry's uncle, so teacher and pupil devised ways to deceive him. Professor Lin, as a student during the warlord period in China, had been an undercover agent for the Chinese Nationalist Party, the Kuomintang, which at the time was fighting a war to unite the country. It had been dangerous work – the warlord Generalissimo Chang Tso-lin, the Tiger of the North, had ruled with an iron hand – so the young Lin had learned many tricks to avoid surveillance by the secret police. It amused him enormously, in the quiet Scottish village, to train Harry in the arts of dead-letter boxes, evasion techniques and cover stories. In the lessons, he sometimes tested Harry's knowledge of *The Art of War* by the ancient Chinese general Sunzi, a compendium of deception and guile. 'What gives an army the means to defeat an enemy?' he asked.

'Greater numbers of troops? More advanced weapons?' Harry teased, knowing the answer.

'No,' Professor Lin banged a roll of broadcloth with his scissors. 'Its spies. A good general knows his enemy as well as he does himself. It is how clever you are, not how strong, that counts.'

This was meat and drink to Harry. Once again he was a Hong Huzi. In his imagination he was back on the slopes of Mount Tai with his friend. And, more important than anything else, the secret world he shared with Professor Lin and Aunt Mary kept the flame of China alive in him.

In the summer of 1944, as the newspapers were announcing the success of the Normandy landings and the prospect, at last, of victory over

Germany, another letter arrived at their cottage from the Red Cross. The writer informed Mary Airton, with deep regret, that her brother Edmund had died of mysterious causes in the Weixian prison camp, apparently after a beating by the Japanese guards. His wife, Catherine, had succumbed to cholera. Their deaths had occurred more than a year ago, and the Red Cross apologised for the delay in informing the family.

Shortly after the receipt of this sad news, Aunt Mary caught a chill, and by the autumn she had bronchitis. In October she developed pneumonia and, as Harry held her hand and Uncle Angus drank whisky in front of the fire, she passed away.

The business connected with death anaesthetizes the initial shock. Young as he was, Harry found that his uncle's drunkenness and incapability meant he had to make the arrangements for his aunt's funeral. He dealt with the undertaker and the register office, chose the coffin, filled in the forms, contacted the solicitor who kept his aunt's will and received the many members of the community who had loved Mary and crowded into the parlour with commiserations.

After the interment he was exhausted, and only then did the full force of what had happened hit him. He spent three days wandering the clifftops, sitting for hours on wet rocks, drenched by rain, and shivering in the pale sunshine that followed the squalls.

In all those months of his aunt's illness he had hardly thought of his parents. Over the years his memory of them had faded to the point that he had almost forgotten what they looked like, but now he saw their features delineated in the scudding clouds, and grieved for them too. In the red and gold of the sunset he remembered his mother's auburn hair. In the calm sea he saw his father's taciturn face. They were suddenly very close to him, as was his aunt, but as quickly as they appeared, the mist rolled round them, their faces became insubstantial and he was left with the cold realisation that those who had loved him were gone for ever. He was alone.

As the beloved faces disappeared into the mist, he heard again the clods falling on his aunt's coffin. In a small way she had kept China alive for him. Interred with her was the hope that he would one day return. That had also been taken away from him.

He had been left with his uncle, the man who tormented him. It was a savage irony that the monster he despised and hated was now his legal guardian.

Then something inside him rebelled. China was life to him. It was only the thought that one day he would go back that had kept him going. He would not – he could not – give up his dream.

He sat on the rock and thought of his alternatives. He had lost everybody and everything that had ever meant anything to him, and things looked black. But there was one hope left to him, and he blessed Aunt Mary: she had realised that to get back to China he needed a good education. He would dearly have loved to run away, leave Uncle Angus and this island behind him, but Aunt Mary had made him promise to continue his Chinese studies. She had left money in her will, she told him, to ensure that he would be able to do so, as well as bequeathing to him all her father's books. That was a start and gave him a degree of freedom, he thought.

The rain lashed his face, and he shivered. He knew that exposure to the elements had weakened him, but inside he felt the heat of his new resolve. He would return – by God he would. And he no longer feared Uncle Angus. He saw him clearly for the pathetic man he was. He could put up with him for a few years more. He was not beholden to him. Or anybody.

Anyway, what choice had he?

When he returned home he was running a fever. For the next three days he lay, semi-conscious, on his bed. When, eventually, he felt well enough to go downstairs, he found Uncle Angus had returned to sobriety and was sitting, curiously smug, at the dining-table. 'So, you've decided to stop being a layabout and rejoin the world?' he greeted his nephew.

Harry ignored him. He was starving, and only wanted to heat some broth.

'You may be interested to hear that, while you've been lounging upstairs, Mr Brodie's been and gone.'

Harry stiffened. Mr Brodie was the solicitor whom he had contacted about Aunt Mary's will.

'He wanted to know where you were,' continued the older man, 'but I told him your presence was neither here nor there, since I'm your guardian and can speak for you.'

'Aunt Mary said she'd left me something in the will,' said Harry, the heavy saucepan in his hand. 'I had a right to be there for the reading.'

'Aye, well, poor Mary hasn't been herself for several months, has she?' said Uncle Angus, tapping his head. 'Poor creature. There was a whole lot of rubbish about money to be put aside for schooling and future university education. Oh, yes, and that you're to continue to learn Chinese.' He laughed. 'Well, of course, that's nonsense, which I think we can count as the ravings of a feeble mind.'

'What are you saying?' Harry's cheeks were burning.

'That as main beneficiary and executor of Mary's estate, such as it is, I'm in a better position to interpret what is best for you. Mr Brodie agrees with me that the clauses in Mary's will relating to you, which also contain, by the way, the bequest of several trunks of books that are heathenish in nature and only good for the rubbish pile, are not reflective of a sound mind and, moreover, legally constitute only a request rather than a binding instruction. It was his view, one with which I concur, that I am not bound in any way to honour such panderings to paganism, and I am disinclined to do so.'

Harry banged the saucepan on the table. 'I don't know about the money but those books belonged to my grandfather and are mine. Aunt Mary gave them to me. If you take them away from me, you'll be stealing.'

'If you expect further to benefit from my charity, young man, I'd advise you to treat your elders and betters with courtesy. I never said I wouldn't give you the books or deny you the money for a university education, but I expect you to earn it.' He grinned, showing broken teeth.

'What do you mean?' asked Harry, confused.

'How long have you been enjoying board and lodging in this house? Five years? There's a cost to that, as well as for your schooling, which your aunt and I have had to pay. Well, you're fifteen now, and no longer required to attend school. You can go out and work, my boy. You can pay back some of the kindness you've received by earning an honest living. I'll give you your books on credit, and I'll pay your fees if you can get into a university, but it'll be against indentured service to me. Five years you've been here. Five years you'll work for your further keep. And then we'll see.' With a sneer, he picked up his Bible. 'I'd provide yourself with some thick sweaters and boots, if I were you. The fishing fleet leaves next week.'

Harry, as his uncle delighted in reminding him, was only fifteen. He was big for his age, but no match yet for his uncle, and what benefit would it do him anyway to hurt him, which at that moment was all he desired? A stint in prison would never get him to China. Without a word, he placed the saucepan on the hob and ran out into the rain. There he wept for a while out of anger and frustration. He knew he had no choice. His future lay in those trunks of books and his uncle had the power to take them away from him. He had no money, relatives or prospects. Furthermore, there was a war on. His uncle could probably organise through his contacts in the village for Harry to be assigned to the fishing fleet. He was trapped.

His uncle was still sitting by the fire when he returned. 'All right,' he muttered, as he walked past him on the way to his room. 'But I keep the books.'

His uncle shrugged, and buried his long nose in his Bible. Harry pounded up the stairs to his room, slamming the door behind him.

It was not a bad life. There was no 'punishment' on board a rocking boat, and thankfully his uncle, on their long voyages, was too absorbed in running the ship to pay attention to his nephew's moral deficiencies. While the war was still on they did not go much further than Orkney because of the danger of submarines, but when peace came they sailed as far as Newfoundland and Greenland, seeking the cod. During the intervals off watch, Harry kept up his Chinese reading, looking up characters he did not know in the dim light of the swinging oil-lamp above his bunk. Meanwhile, he hardened physically, gaining strength in his arms and back from pulling in the catch.

By the time he was eighteen there were no more physical punishments. His uncle was scared of Harry's size and his great hands, which could smash the life from a tuna at a single blow, so he resorted to other means. He arranged for Harry to crew another boat, and when Harry returned to the cottage after two months at sea, he discovered that the trunks of books were missing from the loft.

Quietly he returned to the kitchen, where his uncle was sitting morosely by the fire. 'Where are my books?' he asked.

'I sold the heathen rubbish.'

Harry noticed the sly triumph in the man's eyes. He kicked the chair legs. His uncle fell forward, jarring his chin on the table, then slid backwards until his head was half in the grate. Harry put a booted foot on his chest and leant forward to pick up the poker. He raised it above his head. His uncle screamed. For a moment, Harry observed his terrified face, then bent the poker into a bow. He picked up his uncle by the scruff, hung the bent poker round his neck, like a noose, then released him and strode into the night.

He spent a year working at whatever jobs he could find. He drank. He was often in fights and occasionally woke up in police cells. At weekends he went to the dance hall, where his size and looks usually brought him success. Seduction came easily to him. A ladies' man, they called him. When his money ran out, and he found that the fishing-boats wouldn't take on a man with a reputation as a drunkard and a philanderer (he sensed his uncle's hand: the fishing fleet was a close community), he spent his last pence on a final binge, then enrolled in the army. He picked a regiment that was due to be posted to Hong Kong. That was as close to China as he would get, he thought.

In the event, war broke out on the Korean peninsula, and his regiment was sent to reinforce the American-led United Nations forces that were about to invade the north under General Douglas Macarthur.

It was there, in due course, that he met a field intelligence officer, fifteen years his senior. In the surly misfit that Harry had become, Captain Julian Pritchett saw someone who fitted his own particular, if eccentric, requirements.

PART ONE
Harry's Story

I

The China Lover – Korea, 1950

Julian discovered Harry Airton on a cold December day in 1950 when the United Nations' defeated army had already been driven back two-thirds the length of the Korean peninsula. For all anybody knew, the Russians were close behind the advancing Chinese forces, in which case nuclear holocaust might be a button's push away.

Hysterical rumours were drifting down to the south of whole divisions surrounded and massacred. Pyongyang had been abandoned. The Allies didn't wait to defend Seoul. Burning ammunition dumps lit the night sky had tricked the sparrows into believing it was morning. It was difficult to imagine where the retreat would stop. There were no other fortified lines between the Thirty-eighth Parallel and the sea.

Julian had not slept for forty-eight hours. He had spent the last night in his office at Pusan, sorting out which files were to be burned and which crated in the eventuality of evacuation. He was blearily contemplating breakfast when he received a phone call from 8th Army HQ ordering him to drive north to interrogate a wounded Chinese commissar whom a Highland regiment had captured near the Yalu. They had fought their way south and were now apparently in temporary quarters in a Methodist church in Taejon.

The last thing Julian needed was a drive through a hundred miles of blizzard back into the war zone. He doubted that any Allied units had captured a commissar – a position more senior than brigadier general in the politically driven Chinese Army. Even if the man *was* a commissar, Julian could hardly believe he would get anything useful out of him. Any knowledge he might have had of troop dispositions would have been overtaken by subsequent events – the front had moved two hundred miles south since he was captured – but orders were orders. Julian was the only available Mandarin speaker in the intelligence unit, he was British and British troops were involved. He dispensed with breakfast and set off in an open jeep.

It was not long before he saw the full extent of the catastrophe. The road north was clogged with refugees. He had become familiar with such sights in Europe in the aftermath of Hitler's war, when thousands of displaced persons had been escaping the Russian sectors. Here again were the carts loaded with family possessions, old men, women and children staggering through slush and mud. The clothing was different, but the expressions on the faces were the same: eyes glazed with fear, cheeks pinched with hunger, lips tight with despair and, worse, in some, a look of incipient madness. Many had dropped by the wayside, snow shrouding their bodies. The driver pushed his hand hard on the horn and they threaded their way slowly through the misery and the swirling snow.

It took them twelve hours to drive the sixty miles from the coast. As they descended from the hills, the dim lights of Taejon were welcoming, but on the horizon, beyond the Kum river, Julian could see flashes and hear the distant thump of artillery. On the outskirts of the town, military police with flashlights stopped them at roadblocks. They passed tent lines and armoured vehicles parked askew by the side of the road. Their headlights picked out GIs in parkas and frosted helmets, wandering through the sleet. Julian's driver had to stop many times to ask directions to the church.

The stocky sergeant, clean-shaven under his tam o'shanter, wearing khakis that might have been newly pressed, thumped the paving-stone in a sharp salute. 'Can you fix up a meal for my driver?' asked Julian, and the man saluted again. Julian entered the church to discover it was now a hospital. Rows of wounded men lay quietly under the pillars while medics moved among them. The Highlanders had been badly mauled, and several were being treated for frostbite.

Two officers in greatcoats appeared out of the vestry. Julian saluted, recognizing the colonel. He spoke in a quiet Morningside burr. 'Kind of you to come all this way, Pritchett. Hope it's worth your while. Not quite sure how long you have, though. It's a miracle Dr McKyntire has kept him alive so far.' He tapped his forehead. 'Sorry, I'm forgetting my manners. You must be tired and hungry after your drive. Shall I get the orderly to cook you something?'

'No, sir. Better if I see him straight away.'

'You're probably right. Major Thomas will take you to the prisoners' compound. Come in for a chat afterwards. I'd like to know who we've dragged all this way from hell and beyond.'

Major Thomas was the sort of spick and span officer who would have looked elegant in the most rumpled uniform, but his chin was covered in stubble and there was a streak of mud above his right cheek. 'What can you tell me about the commissar, sir?' Julian asked. 'Surprised you could get close enough to capture him, or that he allowed you to take him alive. Come to that, I'm impressed that you came away with any prisoners. In most retreats they're left with the baggage, or aren't taken at all.'

Thomas stiffened. 'What are you implying, Captain? We're not savages, you know.'

'I'm sorry, sir, but it's my business to ask questions.'

Thomas opened a door at the side of the church. Outside the snowflakes were scurrying. 'Forgive me, Captain, I'm a little tired. Yes, of course there were unpleasant incidents. It wasn't the time for civilized rules of war. I don't blame the men. They were fighting for their lives. Kill or be killed.' He offered Julian a cigarette, which he took, feeling a little uncomfortable to be lighting up in a church. Outside, the wind moaned as Thomas began his tale.

They had defended their hill for forty-eight hours. Through the day they hunkered down under a mortar barrage. The Chinese came for them at night. It didn't matter how many they killed. They kept coming. Out of the ground like goblins. Thomas had his men sweep the slopes with their searchlight. They would see nothing, then the beam would sweep back again and where there had been empty snow or piles of bodies there would suddenly be snarling faces, right on top of them, firing burp guns, screaming, bugling. Next thing they knew, they were in hand-to-hand combat again. Thomas had lost count of the times he had had to rally his men to counter-attack. They fought them foxhole by foxhole.

On the second night they had realised they couldn't hold on. There hadn't been orders worth anything from Headquarters. Anyway, it became academic. A mortar knocked out the only radio. It was then that the colonel had decided to retreat.

Every ridge of the mountains contained another ambush. The Chinese had infiltrated heavily behind their lines. Thomas and his men, trudging through the snow, at first made for the road. That was where salvation lay, they told themselves. That was where they'd join up with the main army. When they had traversed a ridge and seen the road below them, Thomas had frozen with horror. 'Jesus, it's like Guy Fawkes Night,' he muttered.

31

'Or a bloody shooting gallery at a fairground, begging your pardon, sir,' murmured his sergeant. 'Heads down, boys,' he called, to the men coming up behind. Thomas stared in disbelief. The Americans were trying to evacuate their armour – tanks, trucks, jeeps – and were being blown to pieces by enemy mortars. Men clutching on to the vehicles were being shot off like ninepins.

The colonel took one look at the scene and gave orders to move on. Despite the deep snow, he thought they had a better chance in open country. They headed into the forest, and that had become a nightmare of another sort.

'I could hear them all around us,' said Thomas, shivering at the memory. 'Behind the fir trees, crying out to each other in their hideous language. We were crawling up to our knees in snow. It was a deadly game of hide-and-seek. Every man knew that if we were spotted, and if there was a firefight, we would have the whole Chinese Army down on us.'

'Like the Ardennes,' murmured Julian, thinking of his own experience in a retreat.

Thomas's eyes narrowed, and his mouth opened in a snarl. 'Maybe, Captain, but we weren't in the mood for historical comparisons at the time.'

On the colonel's orders, Thomas had sent men forward with bayonets and knives to ambush patrols in the line of march. The damned thing was that the further they penetrated into the forest the more of the enemy there seemed to be. It wasn't just a small patrol here and there. The whole forest was infested with enemy soldiers. Thomas knew they did not have far to go. They had crested the mountain and the ground was sloping down to the paddies, where the colonel believed they would be invisible in the network of ditches and be able to make their escape. But the way was blocked. With a sinking heart, Thomas had reconciled himself to his fate. In this lonely forest they would have to make their last stand and die.

'What happened?' asked Julian, as Thomas fumbled for a second cigarette.

'What happened? We discovered one of our enlisted men spoke fluent Chinese.'

'A squaddy? Speaking Chinese?'

'Yes, I'm not making it up, Captain. It was Private Airton.' He pronounced the name and rank with distaste. 'Surly bugger. One of those cussed I'm-better-than-you-even-though-you're-an-officer types.

Closet socialist, I suspect, always on a charge. The men didn't like him, either. Called him a China-lover because he played the barrack-room lawyer, arguing we shouldn't have crossed the Thirty Eighth Parallel and should leave the Chinese border alone.'

'He was probably right,' Julian murmured.

'That's as may be,' said Thomas. 'Well, for all his faults, on that occasion the bastard probably saved our lives, though he scared the life out of me first.'

The silence in the forest had been shattered by a long, warbling cry. Thomas started, and looked frantically around him, his pistol shaking in his hand. He thought the Chinese were in the middle of them, that they had been ambushed – but his men were lying in the snow where they had been a moment before. Through the trees he heard answering shouts. The loud voice called again, just behind his ear. *'Bu zai zher. Wang dongbian, wang dongbian. Wo kandao tamenle!'*

Then he saw the giant figure, rifle hanging from his shoulder as he cupped his mittened hands to his mouth to amplify the sound. It was Airton – and he was betraying their position to the enemy. Thomas felt a surge of rage. He leapt to his feet, raised his pistol and pointed it at Airton's forehead. The insolent eyes turned towards him, and the man's wide mouth curved into a smile as he whispered, 'Steady, Major. I know what I'm doing. If you fire that pop gun you'll bring them all down on us.'

Thomas felt the eyes of the other men on him.

'Listen to the voices,' said Airton. 'They're moving away. I mis-directed them.'

And, sure enough, the voices beyond the trees were fainter. They heard the shuffle of bodies moving through the snow. The sounds faded down the hill.

'Put that thing away, Major.' It was the colonel's voice. 'Whatever your man said, it worked. We can move on now.'

'Yes, sir,' said Thomas, and holstered his pistol.

The colonel was looking up at the tall private. 'Now, young man, can you play that trick again?'

'Aye, sir,' was the reply.

'Then I think we'd better move you up the line,' said the colonel. 'If that's all right with you, Major?'

They ended up using Airton as point for the whole battalion. Sometimes he steered the enemy off them. At others he lured them forward so they stumbled into an ambush. It took two more hours, but as dawn was breaking, they began to hope that they were out of the trap.

Julian was intrigued. 'You didn't know one of your men spoke Chinese?'

'He'd kept his light under a bushel. Far as we knew, he was a fisherman from Harris, bloody-minded one at that.'

'He spoke Chinese well enough to convince enemy soldiers he was one of them? I find that hard to credit. I speak Chinese, learnt it at Oxford after the war, and I'm pretty fluent – but any native speaker would recognise I was a foreigner as soon as I opened my mouth.'

'I'm only telling you what I saw and heard, Captain – and this wasn't an Oxford cloister. Now, do you want to hear how the commissar was captured or not?'

The forest had been thinning, Thomas recalled, and he could see pink light through the trees ahead. A whispered command was passed back through the lines. He made his way forward, and below him he could make out tents, tanks and a pole bearing a red flag. His heart sank. Far from reaching safety, they had stumbled upon a Chicom command post. Hundreds of soldiers were milling about, but there was no point in going back. He was damned if he could see how they could move forward, though – not without a pitched battle.

He joined a knot of officers gathered round the colonel. They were already forming plans for their attack. It was a sombre gathering. None believed they stood a chance of getting through. 'Well, gentlemen, it's over the top, I believe,' said the colonel, with a wan smile. 'Any final questions?'

Thomas heard a familiar cough, and turned to see Private Airton, glowering on the edge of the circle.

'Do you want me to put him on a charge, sir?' Thomas blurted out.

'No, Major. *Nil desperandum*. I might be open to any counsel at the moment, however irregular the source. Well, man, what have you to say?'

'There could be a better way, sir,' said Airton.

'I see. And what exactly do you have in mind?'

'While you officers were talking, I made a reconnoitre, sir. Wriggled down the hill and observed the enemy camp. I think that what I saw may interest you. There are three Chinese generals down there, sir, and a command tent. I saw them go inside carrying maps and papers.'

'This is preposterous, sir,' muttered Thomas. 'He's a damned private. How would he be able to distinguish a Chinese general? They all wear the same coolie padding in that rag shop of an army.'

Airton kept his eyes at twelve o'clock as he muttered, 'In the Chinese Army, you can tell a man's rank by the soldiers' demeanour towards officers they respect.'

'Control yourself, Major,' snapped the colonel, as Thomas raised a hand. 'Let him speak.'

'It's the maps and plans, sir,' said Airton. 'If we stage an all-out frontal attack they'll destroy them. But if we could get hold of them we might discover their troop deployments and find a way to avoid their main forces. And if we're clever we could avoid a lot of bloodshed while we're at it.'

'And how do you propose we achieve that?' the colonel asked.

'We should fight them the Chinese way, sir.' He turned mocking eyes on Major Thomas. 'With intelligence. I've read a bit about how they think, sir. It's all in their classics, where they made a sort of art out of war.'

'Would you believe it, Captain?' Thomas had broken off his narrative, reliving his astonishment. 'He mentions some bloody book. *Three Kingdoms*, or something—'

'Hold on. This was a ranker and he knew about the *San Guo Yanyi*?' *San Guo*, or *The Romance of the Three Kingdoms*, was a Chinese classic that told the story of ancient battles at the end of the Han Dynasty. It was full of clever stratagems, which largely accounted for its popularity. It was not the sort of book with which Julian expected a fisherman from Harris to be familiar. He was becoming almost as interested in the extraordinary Private Airton as he was in the supposed commissar he had come to interview.

'Yes, in the bloody snow and howling gale, he was rattling on about some Chinese war manual. I thought the man had gone mad but the colonel listened to him. I'll cut to the chase. Against all our advice the colonel agreed to adopt Airton's ruse. It involved splitting our forces into three. If you'd asked me I'd have told you it was madness. Suicidal madness . . .'

Captain Sanderson had been sent off to lead a company of men with flares, mortars and a couple of Brens a mile through the forest to the east. Three other companies moved through the darkness to either side of the Chinese camp. Fifteen volunteers with Airton –

Major Thomas among them because the colonel had told him to – bandaged themselves to look like wounded men. Raising a white flag, they hobbled out of the woods towards the camp.

Thomas had expected they would be mown down on sight, and was mortified as much as relieved when he realised that Airton had read the Chinese correctly. The bandaged men were shoved and slapped, but they were taken into the enemy's camp.

'Airton put on a disgraceful performance,' he told Julian. 'He was weeping, shaking, dropping on his knees and clutching their legs – the picture of the coward in a state of funk. And all the time he was pointing in the direction of Sanderson's company and blathering away in Chinese. Then it was my turn to act – well, it didn't take much acting because I half believed Airton was giving away our real plans. The colonel may have trusted him, but I didn't. I yelled at him to shut his mouth and tried to restrain him physically. The Chinese pulled us apart, but we'd aroused their curiosity. The three generals came out – one was the commissar we're holding here. They ordered Airton into the tent, while we were left in a circle being guarded at gunpoint. It was a long wait before the generals reappeared. One – not the commissar, he was standing silently, very superior and self-satisfied, smoking a cigarette – barked a string of orders. Three-quarters of the men in the camp formed up and silently headed off in the direction Airton had been pointing, led by two of the generals and followed by the tanks on the farm track below. Only then did I relax a little. The commissar glanced at us balefully, stubbed out his fag and went back into the tent.

'Eventually they brought Airton to us. His nose was bleeding and he had two black eyes. They'd obviously given him a hell of a beating, but he was all right. He's a tough bugger. I did my part and yelled at him for being a traitor until a Chinese shoved his bayonet in my face and told me to shut up. We sat down to wait while the remaining guards shouted at us. I've never been colder or more uncomfortable. Nobody attempted to treat our supposed wounds. Uncivilised bastards. Still, it would have been tricky if they had because we had weapons concealed in the bandages. I'd seen to that,' he added smugly.

'Wasn't that a bit risky? If they'd found them it might have given the game away.'

'As far as I was concerned, Captain, this whole bloody escapade was a forlorn hope. I'd been grateful to Airton, like the rest of the men earlier, but his last performance was madness. All right. The colonel had given his say-so. Desperate times, desperate measures – but I for one believed we weren't going to get out alive, and if I was going to be sacrificed I wanted to take a few of the bastards with me. Now, do you want to hear the end of the story or not?'

'I'm sorry I interrupted,' said Julian.

Irritably, Thomas resumed his tale. An hour had passed. The men crouched under their captors' guns. Then faintly, they detected the sound of firing along the hillside. It was as if an electric shock had passed through them. That was the signal. It meant that Sanderson had engaged the enemy. Next minute there was shooting on their perimeter, as the flanking companies attacked.

Thomas and his men took the guards, pulling out their concealed knives. Thomas, already in a berserk state, did not count the cost. He lost two of his men, but at that moment he hardly cared. He wanted revenge for the humiliation of the last two hours.

When they were dead, Thomas propelled himself forward to join the men from the companies, who were running out from the trees and firing into the tents, taking out any resistance. He picked up a burp gun from one of the fallen guards and joined the fray.

It was only when there was nobody left to kill that he noticed Airton was missing. He had an impression that he had seen him fall, shot in the thigh, but where he should have been lying, there was only a bloody patch in the snow and a red trail leading to the generals' tent. Cursing, he followed it. Gun at the ready, he burst through the flaps, ready to fire at anyone he found inside.

Airton was struggling on the floor with the commissar. For a moment, Thomas stood there, confused. Then he heard Airton shout, 'Get the satchel out of the stove! He's burning the papers.'

Thomas stood there, uncertainly. The commissar was gripping a pistol in one hand and Airton was pressing it to the floor. Thomas strode forward, heaved aside the wounded Airton and cut a burst across the commissar's chest. The man's face contorted in pain. Thomas was about to finish him off when he heard a sound and turned. Airton had dragged himself to the stove and pulled out the satchel. It flamed in his hands. He was shouting, 'You stupid shite! You murderous fucking officer shite!' Thomas's gun barrel moved in Airton's direction, but he had hesitated a fraction too long. He felt the breath forced out of his body as the big private threw himself at him. He felt the Fisherman's hands on his throat. His vision faded. He was losing the strength in his arms and legs.

'Are you all right, sir?' There was a constriction in his neck but he could breathe again. Airton had been pinioned under two soldiers, and the anxious face of his sergeant was looking down into his. 'You're to put that bastard under arrest,' he croaked. 'He'll hang for this.'

Thomas paused, fingering his collar reflectively. His face was red with remembered fury.

'You arrested him?' Julian asked. 'After all that? I'd have thought the man deserved a medal.'

'Can't have rankers attacking officers, old boy,' he said. 'You should know that. Where'd the army be without discipline? Colonel agreed with me when he came in, although he seemed more concerned with getting a medic to bind up the wounds of the commissar and Private Airton. All heart, our colonel. Beats me. He looked a bit upset when he found out that the maps and papers were burned to cinders but, as he said, nobody was to be blamed. We weren't any worse off than we had been before. Anyway, it was time to get out of there. That's the end of the story, really. Sanderson got back all right. He'd set off bombs and flares on timers to keep the enemy occupied. We high-tailed it into the paddies. There were a few firefights with Chink patrols – the stretcher party, with that damned commissar, plus the wounded the colonel insisted we take along slowed us down – but eventually we made it to a road where we found American contingents with trucks and joined the retreat south. Fought another battle after Seoul, in which we lost more men, but here we are.'

'And what happened to Private Airton?'

'He's in the stockade. I put him with the Chinese prisoners he dotes on. He's still telling everybody who listens that we shouldn't be fighting the Chinese. If I was the colonel, I'd have him court-martialled for treason.'

Not for the first time Julian marvelled at the crassness of the British Army. This had been a remarkable story of ingenuity, not to mention valour, by an enlisted man under combat conditions, and Thomas, in his self-righteousness, appeared unaware of how he himself, for his petty reasons, had sabotaged a potentially brilliant intelligence coup. They might as well have been back in the Great War, thought Julian ruefully: lions were being led by donkeys.

It was still snowing as they crossed the little courtyard behind the church. Under an awning Julian saw two young prisoners who had been issued with military greatcoats. They were squatting over a Chinese chessboard. A British soldier, his leg in plaster, was stretched beside them on a mat, cupping a cigarette in bandaged hands and observing them. He was a tall, craggy, dark-haired man, with handsome features that were marred by bruises. Julian heard him advising one of the players in remarkably colloquial Chinese on how to move his cannon to avoid a chariot threatening an elephant. To Thomas's annoyance Julian paused to watch him, hypnotised by the native fluency of his Mandarin. Airton looked up and their eyes met. Airton frowned, then turned back to the chessboard.

'I told you he was a surly bastard,' said Thomas.

Julian's interview with the commissar was as futile as he had anticipated. Dr McKyntire was reluctant for his patient to be disturbed. He did not expect him to last the night and muttered that dying men should be left in peace. He led Julian into a cubicle where a dignified-looking Chinese, in his late forties but with prematurely white hair, was lying stoically, his cheeks clenched with pain. Julian tried to get through to him, promising him this and that if he would only talk to him, but he ignored him, staring fixedly at the ceiling. Only as Julian was leaving did he raise himself slightly on his elbows and shout, with as much strength as he could muster, 'May Mao Tse-tung live for ten thousand years!'

Later he drank tea with the colonel in the vestry that he had made into his office. 'You've got to admire men like that commissar,' he said.

'If he was one,' Julian said morosely.

'Anybody who believes so devoutly in a political system that he would die for it without betraying it is courageous. Of course, to me, and I imagine to you, Captain, Communism is abhorrent – but if we are to win this war, we must at least attempt to understand our enemy. I sometimes wonder, had I been a starving, maltreated peasant in China, would I too not have welcomed the socialist salvation that this Mao Tse-tung is promising? His People's Army has certainly given us a bloody nose. Say what you like, they're fine soldiers and have extraordinary pride in themselves.'

'You don't see them as brainwashed fanatics?'

'Well, anybody who believes overmuch in a religion tends to be fanatical, for that's what Communism is. The last few weeks have shown us that we're facing an entirely new and very formidable enemy. They're not like the Russians, whose Mr Stalin is an Empire-builder. Communism to him is a means to an eighteenth-century end. But these Chinese are true believers. This isn't a war about territory but a challenge to our way of life. I fear this will be a long, long war, which will stretch well beyond Korea: a new sort of war, where we will have to match our ideals and propaganda against theirs. Intelligence boys like you, my friend, are likely to be in the front line of it for many years to come. Thankfully, I'm just a soldier, and have only to concern myself about the men in my regiment.'

'Like Harry Airton?' Julian asked.

He chuckled. 'So Major Thomas told you about our black sheep?'

'I saw him in the stockade.'

'It seems rather cruel, doesn't it, that after everything that remarkable young man did for us we have the paucity of imagination to punish him for it? Armies are not very clever in how they handle square pegs in round holes. In a few days the helicopters will take out the less seriously wounded once they've finished airlifting the life-and-death cases. Airton will be evacuated to Pusan, then probably to Tokyo.'

'Is he a Communist sympathiser?'

'I don't imagine so. I think he just admires the Chinese. He's an unhappy young man, Pritchett, angry for some reason with the world – but he's talented. Perhaps those talents could be better used in another sphere. But that had already occurred to you, hadn't it?' His lined features broke into a boyish, rather mischievous grin.

Julian laughed. 'Am I so transparent, Colonel?'

'I'll put it down to tiredness after the trials of your long journey. But then, of course, I knew even before you arrived that you'd be interested in a man like Airton. That is, if he was prepared to work for you. No doubt Major Thomas told you how cussed and wilful he can be.'

'I'll think about it.'

'You do that, Captain. It would be gratifying if, just once, we could discover the right hole for a square peg. Perhaps you might find an excuse to visit Tokyo?'

'I'd already thought of that, Colonel.'

He gave another dry chuckle. 'I'm amazed, young man, that you can think clearly about anything at the moment. It's time you got off to bed. I can't guarantee a comfortable one, but in your state I doubt you care. You have an arduous drive ahead of you in the morning.'

It was another couple of months before Julian had any time on his hands. He had sent a signal to the Office in London asking them to find out anything they could about Airton, whom he had ascertained was still in hospital in Tokyo. Julian was due furlough, and next day he travelled on a transport flight to Haneda airport.

After dinner at the Imperial Hotel, and a night in which he must have sampled every delight that the clubs in the Ginza had to offer, he called in to see his technical superior in the British Embassy. There was a lot of debriefing on either side, and it was almost as an after-thought that his colleague handed Julian a package that had come through the diplomatic bag and was marked for his eyes only. Julian opened it and saw the photographs he had asked for.

'Is that package something to do with the squaddy you've been making so many enquiries about?' the other man asked when, later, they were sitting in the lounge at the Imperial, drinking cocktails. 'What is he? A Commie mole in our ranks whom you're trying to expose?'

'Now, now, Gerald, there are channels and channels. You know you're not involved in all my ops.'

'Come on, Julian, out with it. What devious scheme are you concocting?'

'You remember we talked last summer about how spectacularly ill-equipped we are to get any humint out of China – and have been since we lost our networks after the Communists took power in '49?'

'Yes,' he said, drawing on his pipe. 'And I said it wasn't the end of the world. We still have the Nationalists.'

'Exactly. And most of those Nationalist agents are blown from the moment they land, so anything that seems to be of value is probably highly suspect or what we want to hear being fed back to us by the Commies. Face it, I've got more from interrogating PoWs in the last two months than the Nationalists have given us in a year.'

'Yes, you've done a good job.'

'What if we had our own man inside their system? A Brit we could trust? Somebody whose background we'd created, whom they thought they were using against us but whom we controlled?'

41

'A double?' He sounded sceptical.

'A triple.'

'What is it you're drinking?' he asked. 'I didn't realise they served hallucinogens in a high-class establishment such as this. Or was it something you took last night?'

'I'm serious, Gerald. What if?'

'Well, if we could lay our hands on such a man, it would be the answer to a widow's prayer. But we're talking Proletarian People's Paradise here, Julian. They're as different from us as Martians. We don't even know how their intelligence apparatus operates, whether they follow the rules of the same game.'

'There's only one game. We've seen that with the Russians. How the Chinese organise themselves appears opaque to us at the moment, but that's because we don't know their trademarks yet. But in time they'll come down to the exchange with the rest of us, and it'll be business as usual – infiltrators in our trade unions, honey traps for unwary diplomats and everything else we've come to expect from the Russians, or the Germans, or the Americans for that matter. The principles and methods of intelligence-gathering haven't changed since time began.'

'So what are you saying? We need to reorganise ourselves to tackle China, is that it?'

'This is going to be a long, long war. We should be planning years ahead.'

'Grooming up? Getting hold of a secret weapon or two of our own?'

'Exactly.'

'And you think this Airton is the right material?'

'He might be. He's a rough block of granite at the moment – but I suspect there's a work of art inside if I'm a good enough sculptor to get at it.' He passed Airton's file to his companion.

Gerald flicked through it quickly and paused at the photo of Airton's mother. 'She was a beauty, wasn't she?' he said. 'What a serene face. Gorgeous hair and eyes. Do you think he remembers her?'

'I'd bet on it,' Julian said. 'She represents the world that was taken away from him, everything beautiful and fine that he associates with his childhood in Shandong. Growing up among the Chinese, with his mother the presiding deity. If anything makes sense in his sorry tale, it's his passion to return. That's why he kept up the language. Are you beginning to see why I'm interested in him?'

'I see a sad prodigy. I also see a disturbed young man. Chippy, undisciplined, in and out of fights. Look at his charge sheet. And these police reports from Scottish fishing ports – wrecking a pub here, assaulting a policeman there. Doesn't sound very tractable material to me.'

'Isn't that the hook? He's a born outsider, somebody who doesn't fit in. Hates authority. Set that against his fascination for China. If we were inventing a background for a potential double we couldn't come up with anything half as good. Don't you think he's ripe to be turned? Get him into a job where he has assets valuable to the Chinese and they'll come to him.'

'Assets? What do you have in mind?'

'I don't know yet, Gerald. It doesn't really matter what the asset happens to be, as long as the Chinese believe our man has it and is sympathetic to their cause. As I said, I see this as a long game. If the war in Korea escalates, there might be a market for military or diplomatic intelligence, in which case we could put Airton into some sensitive position in the Foreign Office. Maybe it'll be something more strategic, in which case we can work out some other identity for him.'

Gerald shook his head. '"Strategic", he says. My dear Julian, you *are* hallucinating today. May I remind you that we're talking about an uneducated fisherman from Harris, and a thuggish one at that? This is fantasy.'

'Isn't that what our profession is all about?'

'No, Julian, it's about credibility.'

Julian shrugged and gave him a broad smile. 'You've taken my point, though? You recognise the raw material we have here? He's a blank piece of paper on which we can draw. Maybe the whole thing will come to nothing. Maybe at the end of the day we'll produce just another low-grade spook, but he's promising material. That's all I'm saying.'

Gerald sighed and drained his glass. 'All right, say I accept your ludicrous hypothesis that you can Pygmalion this raw Scottish granite into something valuable for the service. Granted, too, his possible Bolshevik sympathies. Let me ask you this. Why do you think – when push comes to shove – that he won't go over to the other side?'

'Because when push came to shove in that forest he showed where his loyalty lay – and it wasn't with the Chinese. It was with us.'

'I hope you know what you're doing.'

'I'm not doing anything at the moment. Just hypothesising. I've got to get to know the man first, haven't I? Test him out – and that's where, if you'll indulge me, I might ask you to pull a few strings with the Americans. I want him assigned to Koje-do as a camp guard.'

'The island where the Yanks put their PoWs? That hellhole? For God's sake, why?'

'I'd like to see how young Airton measures up when he gets to know the enemy at first hand.'

Next day Julian visited the hospital. The recovery ward was a bright, white, cheery place. The pretty young wives of local British and American residents in their New Look frocks were arranging flowers and exchanging banter with the men – but Airton's bed was empty. Julian asked a Japanese nurse where he was. To his surprise she directed him to the burns unit. 'He often go there,' she said. 'He very, very kind man. Always help those in trouble or too weak.'

'Are we talking about the same patient?

'Yes,' she cooed. 'Ha-ree. Ha-ree Ai-ru-ton.'

She led him up the stairs and opened the door. It was like a room full of mummies, bandaged legs and arms supported by straps. Julian heard a murmur and recognised a quiet Highland voice. Airton was sitting beside a curtained-off bed, reading *David Copperfield* to the occupant. Julian slipped away.

In the end, it was Airton who found him. Julian was walking down a corridor towards the exit. Through the window he could make out Fuji, its snow cone rising out of the clouds. 'Captain Pritchett?' Airton was supporting his big frame on two spindly crutches. 'You were looking for me.'

Julian saw no reason to deny it. 'Yes, I was. We came across each other once before.'

'I recognised you. You're the intelligence man they sent to interview my prisoner.' Julian was struck by the possessive pronoun. 'Didn't get anything out of him, though, did you? Sir,' he added.

'No.'

'You wouldn't have. I could have told you that. Why are you interested in me? I've no intelligence to give you.'

'I was curious to meet you,' Julian said. 'I know about your remarkable exploits in the forest, and I heard you speaking Mandarin like a native.'

44

'Aye, well, I lived among the natives, as you call them, when I was a lad. Didn't learn to speak from books like some. Sir.'

'You must have picked up something from books. You have more than a child's vocabulary. Your missionary grandfather left you his library, did he?'

Airton laughed. It was rather a pleasant laugh, though Julian detected an underlying bitterness. 'So you *are* a spy,' he said. 'Know everything about me, do you?'

'A lot. Not everything, though. I still don't really know what makes you tick.'

'And why would you want to? Suspect I'm a Commie, do you? Starting a fifth column all of my own?'

'No. I'm curious.'

'And what if I said to you, "Bugger off. It's none of your business"?'

'You'd have every right, Private. This is merely a social call.'

'Officers don't make social calls on rankers. Sir.'

'You *are* an angry young fellow, aren't you? Are you suspicious of everybody?'

'I am of intelligence officers. You lot are a bit too devious for simple chaps like me.'

'And you're not devious, Airton? I recall a rather clever trap you engineered on the enemy camp. 'Fight them the Chinese way, with intelligence' – wasn't that what you said? And didn't you quote the *San Guo* to poor Major Thomas?'

He laughed again. 'I don't think anybody appreciated it. Bar the colonel, of course. He's a clever man.'

'And he was the only one who mattered, wasn't he? You got your way. Airton, tell me, do you sometimes think your talents are under-employed?'

'Are you wondering whether I'll agree to join your intelligence outfit, Captain?'

'I don't think I asked you to, did I?' Julian looked deliberately at his watch. 'It was pleasant meeting you, Private,' he added brusquely. 'Sincere congratulations on your remarkable piece of soldiery. I'm sorry you got into trouble afterwards. Goodbye, and good luck. I hope you keep up your Chinese. It'll probably come in handy one day, when the war's over.'

'Captain Pritchett?'

Julian turned. He saw the tension that the young man had been holding back under his belligerent manner. 'If – if you haven't come to offer me a job, what's going to become of me, sir? After I get fit again.'

'I don't know, Airton,' he said, feeling a heel. Gerald had been successful in arranging the posting he wanted and he knew only too well how unpleasant it would be. 'You're still on a charge, aren't you? I imagine your regiment will devise a suitable punishment. Shouldn't make a habit of hitting officers.'

Airton's shoulders slumped. 'You know why I did it, sir. We could have saved those papers, and preserved the life of that commissar. Major Thomas was such a fool . . .'

Julian felt for him, but spoke harshly. 'I think you were the fool, Private,' he said, and strode away. The meeting had not gone as he had planned, but neither was he disappointed. He had made his first chisel stroke in the granite.

Six months later Julian was standing on the deck of a PT boat being drenched in spray as he crossed the choppy strait between Pusan and the island of Koje-do. The laconic lieutenant in command contemplated him from behind his sunglasses. 'You going there because of the riots?' he asked.

'My visit's not unrelated.'

Three days before, in one of the Chinese compounds, prisoners had beaten up UN officials who had entered to make a routine screening for repatriation purposes. They had been trying to sift out those who wanted to go back to China and those who would have preferred to go to Formosa to join the Nationalists. Camp guards going in to rescue them had been pelted with stones and makeshift spears. Three guards and more than a hundred prisoners were killed, and at least another hundred were wounded. The inmates refused to allow medics inside to treat them until three prisoners, who had been arbitrarily identified and dragged out as ringleaders, were returned. For two nights, there had been a stand-off. The camp authorities had agreed to return two. The third had died of wounds.

The scandal was not that such a breakdown of order had occurred in a prison camp run by the UN. It was that such an event was no longer unique. This was the fourth major riot in as many months. What was unique, and had brought Julian out in a PT boat, was that a camp guard was to be court-martialled following the latest incident.

He was a British national, who had been seconded to the US Military Prison forces: Private Harry Airton.

Julian had not been to Koje-do for several months, and was alarmed by the change. In the old days it had been a pretty fishing village. That was gone, replaced by concrete and Nissen huts. The vegetation that had lined the shore was cut down, and the asphalt road that led to the compounds was lined on either side by barbed wire. Coils of it stretched off into the hinterland, creating aimless enclosures of dried yellow shrubland and desert-like patches of sand, through which the occasional tank crawled. He could smell the compounds long before he reached them.

As his jeep took him past the North Korean prison, he saw captives drilling, with home-made pikes fashioned from broom handles sloped on their shoulders, while guards watched from the other side of the wire. In one of the Chinese compounds, a political indoctrination class was going on. Inmates sat in rows on the ground, listening to a man harangue them as he wrote slogans on a blackboard. When he drove past the section in which the disturbance had taken place he saw that armoured cars had ringed off the area in which the engineering corps were working on the damaged huts. Two companies of riflemen were stationed inside the wire keeping back the prisoners, who were laughing and jeering at them. It looked as if it was the guards who were on the defensive.

He was taken to see Colonel Lantano, a slight, immaculately uniformed officer, who greeted him courteously and waved him to a seat in front of an uncluttered desk. His Italian descent was evident in the madonnas, saints and crucifixes he had chosen to decorate his walls, and there was something priestly about his thin face and the darkly shadowed eyes that watched Julian warily as he saluted. He told him that the case against Airton was cut and dried. The man had been a troublemaker since he arrived. Two nights ago he had assaulted an officer, Captain Gutierrez, who had reprimanded him for being drunk on duty. Several men, who had witnessed the scene, were prepared to testify against Airton. 'So why is this of interest to a British intelligence officer, Captain?' He gave Julian an amused man-of-the-world' smile. 'You proposing some kind of deal?'

'I'm not sure if I take your meaning, sir. I'm merely following procedure. A British national is involved.'

Lantano stared at him. Carefully he pulled a neatly folded handkerchief from his breast pocket and dabbed his forehead, then replaced it. 'You intend to interview this soldier?' he said at last.

'I'd like to, yes.'

'Well, I can't stop you, Captain. He may have his own version of events, of course. Accused often do, not that it ever does them any good because a court will believe the evidence of trusted officers, like Captain Gutierrez and Lieutenant Schiller. Now, you're an intelligence officer, experienced in distinguishing fact from unlikely fiction – especially when you consider the background of the accused. It's not the first time, I believe, that this man has struck a superior officer. In fact, Captain, I wonder why, since you have so little time on this island, you need an unpleasant interview with a man who is so certainly guilty. I'm sure my boys can give you the most excellent entertainment while you're here, which will cause you to remember your trip with pleasure.'

'Has this something to do with the deal you mentioned when I came in, Colonel?'

He laughed. 'A figure of speech, Captain,' he said. 'You're an intelligence officer, I'm sure you know what's at stake here.'

'And what is at stake, Colonel?'

Lantano appeared to Julian to be sizing him up. 'Do you know why the prisoners are staging these riots?' Julian held his gaze. 'They're looking for opportunities to show us up for brutality at the peace talks in Panmunjom.'

'Hasn't what's happened during the last few days given them ample propaganda, Colonel?'

'It was a situation that got out of control. It was regrettable, but it shows you what we're up against.'

'But what has this to do with Harry Airton?'

'Sometimes we come across a weak link, Captain. Idealistic young men who don't quite appreciate what's at stake. So, we educate them. Maybe we have to punish them a little, send them to detention for a while until they learn the facts of life.'

'You're talking of whistle-blowers, I assume.'

He sighed. 'You know what makes our army the great organisation that it is, Captain? Loyalty – to the unit, to the battalion, to the flag. This is a new kind of war. My boys are under pressure you wouldn't believe. I think the least you can expect under these circumstances is a degree of loyalty to one's comrades. You could say it's a matter of hearts and minds.'

Julian remembered the gentle British colonel in Taejon, who had also been interested in the battle of hearts and minds. He would have been profoundly shocked by the context in which they were being used today. He wondered if he should play along for a while longer to elicit more – but the man disgusted him, and he had heard enough. 'Thank you, Colonel,' he said. 'I will see Airton now. In the interests of fair play, and for my report.'

Lantano's fists clenched. 'You know this man is a Commie lover? We're at war here on Koje-do. And it's not just behind those compounds where the stinking Chinks are. Those senators back home have it right. We've got to watch out for the enemy within too. On this island we know how to deal with them, Captain. You should leave us to get on with it in our way.'

He extricated himself without undue difficulty. Lantano had detailed Captain Gutierrez and Lieutenant Schiller to escort him to the cells. The first was languid, superficially handsome and menacingly self-contained; the second was a dim bully-boy. It was the latter who maintained a vituperative attack on Airton as they drove in the jeep. Julian noticed several contradictory statements. He hoped that the tape attached to the wire inside his shirt was still running because this would also be damning evidence.

Both officers stood outside the cell door when he went inside. He didn't care if they put their ears to the keyhole. He doubted that either spoke Mandarin.

Airton had been badly beaten. His face was a mess, and he clutched his side where they had smashed his ribs. 'I thought I might see you,' he said, 'but you took your time getting here.'

'Are you all right?' Julian asked.

'I've been worse. Fisherfolk in Harris could give these pansies a lesson or two in how to inflict grievous bodily harm.' He was overtaken by a fit of coughing, but he was smiling when he looked up. He was about to say more when Julian indicated the officers outside the door. 'Speak in Mandarin,' he told him.

'I was thinking maybe you didn't get my letter,' Airton said fluently.

'I did and I've been using it to good effect. Several generals at Headquarters were stunned by your revelations and know exactly why I've come here today. You didn't need to organise such a dramatic post-script, though. I'd rather hoped you might have grown out of attacking superior officers.'

'I only hit officers who deserve it. I'd have killed those two bastards outside the door if I'd had the chance. Wish I had. I might have saved the poor fellow's life.'

'I take it this was one of the three Chinese they took out of the prison compound during the riot? The man who was reported to have died of wounds?'

'Yes, they were torturing him. They gave him the water treatment, then strung him up by the testicles to the ceiling, using a pulley contraption tied to his legs so they wouldn't rip straight off. They thought that would be amusing because that's how the Communists deal with their own in the compounds. It's not the first time it's happened. I put that into my report too, didn't I?'

'You told me they made you witness their abuses so you, too, would be complicit. But why did you intervene this time? In your letter you said you'd only gather evidence.'

'I don't know. Something about that boy got to me. Of course he was a fanatical Commie, they got that right. A political, no doubt about it. Came out with all the slogans, even when they started beating him – but he was very young and, anyway, he reminded me of someone I knew when I was a lad in China. Couldn't stand it when he started screaming, and blubbering for his mother. And Gutierrez had that cold, dead look in his eyes – I knew he wouldn't stop till he'd killed him. So I laid into him. Then they laid into me. They made me watch afterwards, holding me so I couldn't move. Gutierrez kept turning towards me, taunting me, 'Commie lover', like it was a show for my benefit. Then he shoved the hose down his throat, at the same time blocking his nostrils. Boy's stomach exploded eventually. Bastards.' He dabbed his eye on a sleeve.

'You've got a soft heart somewhere inside there, haven't you?' Julian said.

'I don't like it when the innocent suffer, or the weak.'

'You said this one wasn't innocent. He was a fanatical Commie, a political. You wrote to me that you hated them for what they did in the camps to those who didn't go along with them, and for what they've done to the China in which you grew up. Or did I misread all that purple prose about how you wanted to devote your life to combating these enemies of civilisation? Commie lover? China lover? How do I know you really can tell the difference?'

Airton rubbed his big hands together, then surprised Julian by laughing at him. 'So don't I pass? Have I failed the exam because I was sentimental about one poor sod being tortured for what he believed in? Back to square one, is it? Where are you going to send me next time? Got a worse hell-hole than Koje-do lined up, have you? Did they make you go through all this before they signed you up as an intelligence officer?'

Julian laughed too. 'As far as I recall, I still haven't indicated that a job is on offer.'

'*De bi . . . gou pi . . . hu sho ba dao . . .*' Not having the younger man's mastery of Chinese colloquialisms Julian was only able to make out the words for "mother's sexual organs" and "dog's farts" and assumed he was being gently asked to "cut the crap" or something to that effect. 'You decided to recruit me the moment you saw me,' Harry continued, grinning broadly. 'That evening back in Taejon in the snow. And you know damn well I volunteered long ago. You've been playing with me because you're a bastard and an officer. Now, how are you going to get me out of here before Gutierrez or Schiller or one of the other cunts decides to have me shot while I'm trying to escape?'

'It's arranged,' said Julian, wondering how he would ever control Airton when the younger man was working for him. 'By the way, I do have a worse hell-hole than Koje-do lined up for you.'

'Oh, no,' he said. 'You're not going to make me finish my time in the regiment?'

'No,' Julian said. 'Worse. You're going under cover.'

'To China?' He almost whistled.

'You'll get to China one day. That I promise. First you're going to university to learn some skills. I doubt we'll ever make you into a convincing gentleman, so I'm going to make you masquerade as an aspiring member of the left-wing establishment.'

'University?'

'You're not going to be much use to me unless you're educated.'

Airton shook his head, smiling. Then he frowned. 'What am I to study?'

'I don't think it matters particularly,' said Julian. 'What subject interests you?'

The reply was immediate. 'Physics,' he said.

This time it was Julian's turn to be surprised. In fact, he gaped. 'Why physics? Do you know anything about it?' His mind was spinning, as he thought of his conversation with Gerald. Strategic, he had hypothesised idly, before Gerald had accused him of being a fantasist. These days, with the Rosenberg trial on in America, there was nothing *more* strategic than physics. In Julian's world it was the Crown Jewels . . .

Airton was looking up at him curiously. 'Aye, a bit,' he said cautiously. 'Quite a lot, actually, the basic theories, laws and such things. Didn't teach those subjects to fisherfolk in Tarbert High, but I've read the odd physics textbook. Mechanical, molecular. In Mandarin, mind. Learned it along with my Chinese. Kept up by reading scientific journals, when I could lay my hands on them.'

Was it possible? Julian looked down at the young soldier almost fondly. 'You've studied molecular physics in Chinese? I'll be damned.'

Three weeks later Harry and Julian were reclining in a hot tub in one of the geisha parlours in the Ginza. Julian had noticed with wry satisfaction that the girls had competed for his companion's favours and that Harry had taken their advances as his due. Afterwards Julian had shooed the besotted creatures out of the bathhouse so he could give his *protégé* a final briefing before he took the flying-boat to England next day.

'Harry, will you stop blowing into that hot towel and pay attention?'

'Aye, sir.' Harry rolled his limbs in the steaming water, and gave Julian a mock salute.

'You seem to have got over the Calvinistic inhibitions instilled in you by that uncle of yours – you haven't displayed much in the way of moral rectitude tonight. But I suspect it's in there all the same. Tell me, have you ever been in love?'

'None of your business. Sir.' Harry grinned. Julian thought he looked his twenty-one years, and felt a moment of foreboding, then an almost paternal sense of responsibility. 'Listen, Harry. I'm unlikely to be home for several years. The Office wants me to set up a network in South East Asia. We don't much like what's going on in Indochina. The Communist insurgency against the French may not be contained within Vietnam's borders. The pundits are already talking of a 'domino theory' – Southeast Asian countries falling one by one to the Reds – and that spells trouble for Malaya. For the first few years you'll be on your own. Now, we've been over it and you know what you have to do.'

'Yes, yes. Play the socialist at college. Join the societies. Become a labour activist . . .'

'All of that – but, above all, study. You're going to be a scientist, Harry, and you must be convincing in the part. We'll fix it so you have the right degrees. We'll give you a dazzling paper for your doctorate. My colleagues will hold your hand all the way, but you must master at least the concepts and the theory. At the end of it we'll be using you where all that science you've learnt will be useful, and you must pull your weight.'

Harry sat up in the bath, eyes blazing. 'Julian, don't patronise me. I've agreed to work for you, be a scientist and I will be – a bloody good one. On my own merits, not on fake degrees given me by a bureaucrat in your pay. I don't need handholding – by you or anybody else.'

Julian laughed. 'If I'm not wrong there's a bit of the fanatic in you, Harry Airton. Maybe that uncle of yours had more of an effect on you than you recognise.'

'Isn't that the sort of man you want me to be for my cover? What did you say earlier? Moral rectitude. Isn't that the bait?' He reached into the water for the soap and began to scrub his armpits.

'Everything in moderation,' said Julian. 'Yes, moral rectitude is part of the mix, but a certain weakness is the other side of the coin. Especially for the ladies – but remember, it's got to be on my terms. That's the other hook. Remember? I'm going to enjoy developing your role, my lad. Play it right, and you and I will create the most complete and convincing background for an undercover agent that I have ever come across in all my years in the service.'

'Fuck you,' muttered Harry. 'All I want is to get back at those bastards who've ruined China.'

'You will,' said Julian. He looked at Harry's muscles moving under the smooth skin, which had the sheen of a racehorse. Well, Julian thought, there was a similarity between training an agent and training a thoroughbred. And Harry would require a long rein, he mused.

The reports Julian received from the master of Harry's college, an old friend and a recruiter for the service, could not have been more complimentary. Shortly before Harry's finals he wrote:

I don't see why you are so concerned about him. There will be no need to doctor his exam results. He would be guaranteed a first-class degree anyway, and whether you have influenced him in that direction or not, his interest in the nuclear aspects of the subject are unfeigned. Prendergast in the physics faculty boasts quite embarrassingly about 'his rough young Oppenheimer', and several other colleges are vying to poach him from me for his postgraduate year. How Airton manages to fit in the academic work on top of all his political activities on behalf of the Labour Party I don't know, but he does, and his reputation as a union activist has seriously alarmed the Vice Chancellor's Office, which complains to me with tedious regularity. I would say that what-ever future you have in mind for him is assured.

Harry did get his first, and a year later, his paper on new cooling techniques for spent nuclear rods was published to acclaim. Julian knew that he resented the input from the Office's tame boffins, but it was essential that there was enough originality in it to catch the attention of scientists overseas, and he was pleased when intelligence confirmed in due course that it had found its way, in translation, into the *Academia Sinica* in Peking. He was also the opposite of put out when he heard on the grapevine that the Office's scientist who had prepared the ma-terials for Harry was grumbling that 'The young whippersnapper had the nerve to improve on my work.'

Julian's contacts arranged for Harry to be given a job at the Windscale power station in Sellafield, where he could learn the prac-tical engineering side of the industry. Windscale was pleased to have him. A year and a half afterwards, Julian decided that the time had come for his pupil's first test.

He flew back from Singapore to co-ordinate the London end with the ministries. First he took the train to Sellafield and, on a windy beach near the power station, told Harry what he wanted him to do. The gangling soldier he had known in Korea had thickened out in the five years since he had seen him and, if anything, his manner was more surly than before. Now he looked troubled. 'You know it means betraying my colleagues?' he said, when Julian had outlined his inten-tions.

'Yes, Harry – but on a point of conscience. It's necessary. You know that.'

'They've been good to me here, accepted me for who I am.'

'So shall we call it a day?' asked Julian. 'Do you want to be a nuclear technician on this barren coastline all your life? What about China? Here, I've drafted a letter. You can polish it.'

His resignation did not create the stir: the Ministry of Defence had a process for dealing with disgruntled employees. It was the leak to the newspapers that was responsible for the rumpus. Overnight Harry became a celebrity.

'WINDSCALE SCIENTIST ACCUSES M.O.D. OF WEAPONS RESEARCH COVERUP IN CIVILIAN FACILITIES'

was the headline in the *Daily Telegraph*. The *Daily Mail* had a cartoon of Harold Macmillan trying vainly to put a lid over a mushroom cloud billowing up above Big Ben, with the words 'WINDSCALE SCANDAL' scrawled in the smoke.

Harry despised the beatniks and misguided philosophy professors with whom he found himself associating on the CND marches that followed. He took care to maintain his dignity when interviewed on the radio, stating that he regretted the publicity his resignation had caused. No, he had no idea where the leak had come from. As far as he was concerned, he had merely exerted his right as a citizen. Contrary to his contract he had been ordered to divert reactor resources into making the unstable isotopes that could only be used in nuclear bombs, and he could not reconcile this with his conscience. He deplored any embarrassment he had caused the government. Ultimately that attitude, and strong support from the Labour opposition, who saw the episode as another opportunity to attack Tory defence policy in the wake of Suez, made credible his transfer to the newly constituted Ministry of Power. It was also, as far as the beleaguered government was concerned, desirable: it showed they had no intention of persecuting an honest official. More importantly, it was a means to buy his silence. Submissively Harry accepted the offer, for which Julian had been angling from the start.

'You see, it wasn't so bad,' Julian remarked, as they sat one night in the pub close to Harry's new place of work. 'All over and forgotten. You're no longer news – except where it matters, and there we struck a bull's eye.'

'What do you mean?'

Julian reached into his briefcase and pulled out a Chinese newspaper. It was a copy of the *People's Daily*, dated a few weeks earlier, and contained an hysterical account of the whole Windscale scandal.

Harry was described as a 'man of the people, prepared to stand up to imperialist hypocrisy'.

'More to the point, we've identified you as somebody who knows the process of how to manufacture uranium 235, and that'll be the area in which the comrades will have most difficulty when it comes to converting the reactors the Russians have promised them for peaceful-energy use into military-grade facilities. It's a grain of sand on the growing pile,' said Julian. 'The first down-payment on your ticket to China.'

'Let's hope so,' muttered Harry.

Julian laughed. 'Look at your long face. It's good news, Harry. It means the game's afoot. In fact, it's about time we started training you up in the more clandestine techniques of our profession. You've a couple of months before you start at the ministry. I think you could do with a breath of sea air at the Office's training school in Portsmouth.' He observed him affectionately. 'All those devils inside you. A few weeks of unarmed combat should get them out, and then you'll be ready for the fray again.'

Julian waited another two years before he decided to turn the screw again. Meanwhile Harry had built himself a reputation in the Ministry of Power. It was tedious work. While his colleagues on the spy course were setting off to foreign parts to take on the enemy, he remained at the ministry, where for three years he regulated gas emissions, assessed new technology for coal mines, and delivered dull papers at businessmen's conferences. He never complained. In fact, he performed his functions with exemplary diligence. He was even promoted. 'My God, you're conscientious,' Julian said to him, during one of his irregular visits from Malaya. 'You're not just establishing a background, you actually are what you pretend to be. When it comes to the crunch, your cover will be so immaculate that no intelligence agency on this earth will find the crack.'

But he was still concerned. He had been pleased that Harry's self-image had been a little tarnished after his betrayal of his colleagues at the power plant. It was a useful first step into the grubby world of deception, but he was all too aware that it had not fundamentally changed the younger man. He had ensured that the service's psychologists monitored Harry closely during his training at Portsmouth. They had identified in him a deep psychological inhibition against anything that smacked of deceit, and concluded that he was suffering from inverted guilt.

Julian considered himself a practical man and tended to seek solutions to problems rather than agonising over fundamental causes. He had learnt that Harry was still finding the concept of betrayal – lying and deceit, as he saw it – difficult to stomach. He had to get him used to the idea that this would be an integral part of his work, so why not begin with Harry's cover job? He began by asking Harry to investigate certain of his colleagues, whom he said MI5 suspected of treachery. He had merely taken their names at random from a civil-service list. At first Harry was reluctant, and Julian did not push him. Instead he waited for him to come round, which, inevitably and with bad grace, he did. Julian encouraged him to peer at his colleagues' in-trays, and follow them after they went home from work. Harry hated doing this, but persuaded himself it was his duty. As luck would have it, his surveillance bore fruit and he discovered that one colleague was a member of the Communist Party, a friend, as it happened, with whom he'd taken to playing darts in the pub on Thursday evenings. He found a copy of the *Daily Worker* in the man's briefcase.

'Oh, that's very important,' Julian told him, when Harry reported it. 'The man is well known to Five, but they've never had proof until now.' Like every member of the Communist Party in England, he was indeed known to Five but they had dismissed him long ago as a harmless eccentric. However, it was technically an offence to hide involvement in a dubious political party from a government employer. The man was eventually fired, but not without another stroke of luck: he had been fiddling his expenses and diverted some of the money he'd stolen, a paltry sum, to Communist Party funds. When Harry found this out, Julian made an anonymous phone call to Accounts.

Immediately afterwards, Five treated Harry to dinner at the Savoy. Julian paid, but Harry did not know that: he came away, ears burning with praise, having been told he had helped to uncover a dangerous enemy agent.

In 1959 Julian decided that Harry was ready for his first foreign posting. It was easy to have him accredited to the embassy in Budapest as a science officer. The Hungarians had expressed interest in Britain's coal-fired techniques and it made sense to have a man from the ministry to assist the diplomats in what might be a valuable sale of technology. But, first, there was one more test that Julian had determined Harry should undergo, which was why he had invited Audrey to dinner. She was an old flame, an associate of the Service who specialised in entrapment operations, and with whom he had worked several times. After their meal, and the gymnastics between the sheets that she enjoyed, he put to her his proposal.

'You can't be serious. He's one of ours, isn't he? I'll whore for you at the drop of a hat, darling, but I like to think I'm doing it for Queen and country. A Russian or a Bulgar is fair game, but a fellow Brit? One does have standards.'

'This is for Queen and country,' said Julian. 'You'll be training a most important operative.'

'Go on.' She giggled.

Julian explained.

'You want me to *marry* him? What would my parents say? He's a fisherman!'

'A well-built one,' said Julian.

'As strong as you?'

'Much stronger – in all the right places. Come on, my love, it'll only be for a year or so. And you'll be paid handsomely. More than you'd get for a Bulgar.'

'How much more?' she asked.

They haggled for a while.

'Well, I'll have a look at him, but no promises. Anyway, what makes you so sure he'll want to marry me?'

Julian laughed. 'My dearest girl, can you think of a single red-blooded male on this planet who wouldn't leap at the chance?'

'You, for one,' she said.

'I don't have to, do I?'

'Oh, you bastard,' she said, and pulled him backwards on to the already rumpled sheets.

Julian introduced her to Harry at the Arts Club in Dover Street. They hit it off together straight away. He wasn't surprised. Audrey was chameleon-like and counter-intuitive, with an instinctive ability to size up any target within a moment of meeting him, then effortlessly become the woman he desired. She gave Harry aristocratic disdain at the beginning, challenging his prejudices, then slowly, over the evening, allowed insecurity to show. By the time Julian left them, she was gazing at Harry with wide, wondering eyes, murmuring, only slightly tipsily, how she wanted 'something real in life, something real', the implication being that Harry was the man to save her. Julian shook his head admiringly. She was such a loss to the theatre.

Next morning she phoned him. 'Why didn't you tell me he was so adorable, darling? I'm quite exhausted.'

'You'll take the job?'

'Oh, yes,' she said. 'Beats Bulgars. He's gorgeous.'

'Don't get too fond of him.'

'Julian,' she said, admonishingly, 'this is work.'

Later, Julian told Harry why they should make a spurious marriage. He described it as another operation to build his cover. Another grain of sand on the pile. He told him what would happen eventually, that it was important he should be seen by the opposition as a man recovering from a broken heart – and Harry seemed to accept his arguments. There had to be an impression of vulnerability in his background. What Julian did not tell him was that he knew he would fall head over heels for her. That, after all, was Audrey's stock-in-trade. It was why she had always been such an effective agent: she was totally mercenary, utterly ruthless and – unlike any other woman he had known – she didn't have a heart.

2

Crossing the Bridge

Hungary, October 1961

He had lost count of the bottles of Tokay they had consumed during the long lunch that had turned into dinner. When the moon rose above the pine trees and glinted on the snow crests of the distant Carpathians, Professor Galady brought out the vodka, and Harry reconciled himself to a debauch that would probably last until dawn.

The rent-a-crowd of intellectuals were scattered in little groups round the trestle tables in the overgrown yard of the *dacha*. Inevitably one of the painters brought out his guitar and began to sing 'We *shall overcome*' and other imported American protest songs about universal peace and brotherhood. On the veranda, under the vine leaves, the poet in the lumberjack shirt whose name he could never remember was quoting Akhmatova. Around him the university students lounged in their Western jeans, leather jackets and caps – the boys aping Marlon Brando, the girls Anouk Aimée. The clothes must have cost whoever was funding these exercises a fortune on the black market.

Harry looked surreptitiously at one of the girls. Her hair was cut in a tomboy fringe, her long legs were folded in a yoga position, and her brown eyes were half closed as she listened dreamily to the verse. Her full red lips were pursed mischievously under prominent cheekbones. She was Audrey to the life, which was probably why she had been chosen.

He felt a pang of pain. He always did when he thought of his wife. It had gone so well in the beginning. He had even believed they were happy in the tiny flat in Fulham, which he had rented so that they could be together while he studied Hungarian in the sitting room and Audrey painted in the guest bedroom, converted to a studio, and where, for the first time since he had left China, he had celebrated anything approaching a real Christmas. Of all the memories, that one hurt most . . .

He had woken with her weight on his legs, and her mouth working on him below. The bedclothes and blankets exploded. He saw her mischievous brown eyes, her freckled nose and her irresistible smile. She wagged a long finger in his face, on which gleamed a large ruby. 'Ta-ra!' she cried. 'Look what I found in my stocking, you sweet, adorable, profligate man, you!' She covered his face with kisses, while she expertly adjusted herself over him, screaming and laughing when they climaxed together. Then she pulled him out of bed – 'Presents! I want more presents!' – and dragged him into the living room, while he, laughing, snatched up her abandoned clothes and his dressing-gown.

She sat cross-legged on the carpet under the tree they had decorated together. Her tweed skirt was pulled up over her thighs to reveal her long, beautiful legs. One shoulder peeped out from the loose Jaeger sweater, half covered with a tangle of blonde hair. She wore nothing underneath. After she had found the car keys for the bright red Mini: in the tiny parcel he had hidden near the top of the tree, they made love again, on the floor among the shreds of wrapping-paper.

That was how he liked to remember her: a greedy child, tousled and beautiful on the carpet, tearing open the parcels of chocolates, books and blouses he had spent a month's salary to buy for her. He was still receiving invoices for the hire purchase on the car . . .

Now the girl on the veranda turned her eyes coolly in his direction and smiled. He could have her if he wanted her. Before long the artists and students would pair off into the bedrooms. 'My friend, my friend,' Galady had said, on the first occasion Harry had taken up the invitation to join what the professor called one of his weekend 'symposia' in the forest retreat, 'here we have left behind us the politics of this fractured world, the friction between East and West. In these shaded arbours we recreate the Athens of the philosophers, where older minds and younger bodies can meet in the freedom of thought. It is Arcadia. It is Lesbos, where the only entry ticket is an open mind.'

That was one way of describing a state-sponsored orgy, Harry thought, and there were times when he was certainly tempted, but he remembered Julian's warning on his last trip to London.

Julian had been triumphant, tapping the table in the Office's briefing room, as he always did when he was excited. 'Bloody right you take up the invitation! Bugger embassy rules! This means the game's on. Didn't I tell you you could always trust your uncle Julian?'

Harry had sighed. 'Aye, you were right. It seems they've spotted me.'

'Dead right they've spotted you – *and* they've fingered you as a potential wobbly. I knew they would if you followed the script – but we don't want you crossing any boundaries yet, just for them to think you might have it in you to do so. As far as the comrades are concerned, you're still a loyal British civil servant. We're still in the courtship stage, after all. You can be coy and flirtatious, but for the moment you should be hanging on to shreds of your virtue. In boudoir terms you should have taken off your stockings, but not your smalls.'

'You're shameless, Julian. Amoral, heartless, and the most cavalier spy I've ever met. I'm astonished that I'm so glad to see you.'

'That's my Harry.' Julian grinned. 'I take it I'm forgiven for Audrey then?'

'What's to forgive? You spelled it out for me, didn't you? You got the scandal you wanted.'

More fool him for believing it could have been any different, Harry thought now. He had really believed they were the ideal couple, she the bright aristocrat and society painter, he the socialist sucker who had come up in the world. He had certainly never anticipated the ruthless cruelty with which that consummate actress would perform her final scene . . .

It had begun with the infidelities, and the artfulness with which she failed to conceal them. First it was the pipe in the living room, then a man's mackintosh in the cupboard and, later, rumpled covers in the guest bedroom. Harry suspected his colleagues in the embassy. He read mockery in their smiles, and sensed they whispered about him whenever he left the room.

Audrey laughed, and taunted him for his unmanliness or his proletarian prudery, depending on her mood.

The end had been truly awful. It had come during the Queen's birthday party in the ambassador's garden. Audrey was already tipsy on champagne, or pretending to be, among a group of military attachés, lampooning his Scottish accent. 'Och, aye and a noo. Well, it was all the fishing I did as a boy, ye see. Ye can't get rid of that smell, can ye? It's manly.' Then she switched back to patrician English: 'So you see, darling, that's who we are. A perfect modern marriage. There's no John Braine novel or Osborne play that could begin to describe Harry and me. Chanel and fish oil round the kitchen sink. Imagine!

Although privately, darling, I'll tell you, Harry is more old-fashioned. Thinks he's the virile gardener and I'm Lady Chatterley. Or maybe he's convinced himself he's the lonely Long Distance Runner. He certainly takes his time, these days. Oh dear, I'm being indiscreet again. You'd better get me another glass of bubbly . . .'

Harry knew that the whole party had heard her. Even the kindly Hungarian scientist he was talking to had averted his eyes.

Eventually the ambassador told him to control his wife. Steeling himself, he moved towards her.

'Oh, my, look who's coming! Do you think I've offended the poor wee man?' She clutched the arm of the Danish air-force attaché, pretending fright. He disengaged himself. Harry noticed that he and the other attachés looked embarrassed, although they had been laughing earlier.

'You know what the most pathetic thing about him is?' Audrey continued. 'He still believes we're in love, poor darling.'

'I think I should take you home, Audrey,' he had said, as calmly as he could.

'"Home", he calls it!' She threw the contents of her champagne glass in his face. 'That's what I think of the idea of home with an emasculated boor like you, Harry Airton. Sorry, *Doctor* Harry Airton. Titles mean so much to the lower classes, don't they?'

He took her arm roughly. 'That's enough,' he said. 'You're making a scene.'

She slapped him. In the sudden silence, he picked her up and threw her over his shoulder. She was screaming, scratching, kicking, biting, laughing – yes, she had been laughing even then – as he carried her out of the garden, aware that hundreds of eyes were watching them.

Next day she flew back to London. Three weeks later he received a letter from her lawyer . . .

Well, he had compensated since then, he told himself, as he emptied the remains of the vodka bottle into his glass. He had dutifully followed Julian's script. First there had been the despairing affairs with women from other non-Warsaw-Pact embassies – Scandinavian, Austrian: secretaries, bored wives, usually one-night stands or week-long flings. He had broken them off before they went too far, hit the booze afterwards to show what a desperate, unstable man he was. There had been little acting involved. And eventually, as Julian had known they would, the comrades had spotted him . . .

Somewhat to his relief, he saw that the girl on the balcony was deep in conversation with the poet, who had an arm round her shoulders. He sipped his vodka, waiting for Galady to return from whatever errand had detained him. The other scientists, who usually stood in as his minders when Galady was absent, were nowhere to be seen. After the heavy drinking, and the serious conversation, he was pleased to have a few moments to himself. He had been drawn into giving an anti-Suez tirade today, a variation on his standard complaints about American iniquities – Indo-china, Lebanon, Bay of Pigs. He had had to be careful not to criticise the British government too overtly, while keeping up his socialist and peace-loving credentials. This time, thank God, he had been spared a rehash of Windscale. They loved hearing about the CND marches, and he always had to pretend embarrassment when they called him a proletarian hero.

'Softly softly,' Julian had told him. 'You can dip your fingers into the forbidden candy jar, but don't unwrap the sweets.'

Harry looked up and saw Galady's untidy white hair and Einstein moustache wagging mischievously, his brown eyes glistening in the lantern light. 'My friend, can you forgive me for abandoning you? I had to drive to the station to pick up another friend. He will interest you. A fellow scientist with whom you will have much in common. Indeed, he even speaks the same language.' This last arch remark came out as a giggle. 'He is now tidying himself after his long journey, but he will be with us presently.'

Harry felt his stomach muscles tighten, and a rush of exhilaration. Bloody Julian, he thought. He'd been right again. It was happening. But 'Oh, yes?' was the only response he allowed himself. 'And what common interests are they?'

'Hydropower, perhaps?' Galady grinned. 'You remember the exposition you gave on the subject at one of our sessions? Well, it attracted interest far and wide. Far and wide,' he repeated. 'I remember your words to this day – you were inspiring as well as passionate, my friend. "If we only harnessed the forces of nature, and the water that flows in God-given streams, then desert wastes would be made fertile, and mountains and forests could achieve the productivity of atomic-power stations."'

'I was drunk,' muttered Harry. 'I just think coal-powered stations are dirty and wasteful, that's all. And some of our British companies have good alternative technology.'

'You're a visionary, Harry,' said Galady. 'And that is why our guest has travelled such a long distance to meet you. From China,' he added softly.

'China?' Harry made sure he sounded surprised.

'Yes, Harry. Professor Wei Jian has come all the way from Peking.'

When the man was brought to the table, flanked by Galady's Romanian assistant and two other acolytes, Harry rose.

He looked the part. Sallow face, pepper hair, little round spectacles, bad teeth. He affected a bow-tie, and wore one of those Kremlin-style overcoats over a shabby charcoal suit. It even fitted him. He could have been any of the academicians in the delegations Harry and his colleagues had observed over the years, trawling the international exhibitions.

'*Jiuyang, jiuyang, Aitun Boshi, tingsho nin hui sho piaoliang de Zhongwen.*'

Harry replied in Mandarin: 'No, Professor Wei, you are kind to say so, but I think my Chinese is very rusty now.'

The soft eyes behind the glasses observed him closely. 'You are modest, Dr Airton. Your Chinese is fluent. I detect a Tianjin accent, perhaps?'

'My teacher came from that city.'

'Then you're a credit to him, as you were a credit to your professors at Oxford. Your master's paper on nuclear cooling rods is known even in my country. It is a privilege to meet you.'

Professor Galady was fussing with the seats. Harry noticed that the guitarists and poets had fallen silent, and some of the students were drifting towards them.

'Although I don't understand what you are saying, it's clear that the two of you are friends already,' said Galady, as he ushered them to the table. 'The meeting of minds. All you need is another bottle of vodka. Then we will leave you to your discussion.'

'Tea. Please,' said Professor Wei, in Hungarian.

'That will be fine for me too,' said Harry.

Professor Galady looked aggrieved, then grinned and shooed the students away. 'Now now, girls, pretty as you are, it's time for grown-up discussion here. There will be time for play later. You, Marysha, and Grunya,' he put an arm round the shoulders of the Audrey looka-like, 'make yourselves useful. Go to the kitchen and prepare tea for our guests. Thank you, my pigeons.' He kissed their cheeks and patted their bottoms as they slouched towards the *dacha*, dark eyes slanted over their shoulders.

'I gather you're interested in hydropower, Professor Wei,' said Harry, when they had been left alone. 'At least, that's what Professor Galady told me.'

'In China we have been harnessing the energy of water for more than two thousand years, Dr Airton. You have perhaps heard of the Dujiangyan, in Sichuan, a system to control turbulent rivers created in the Han Dynasty and still in use today.'

'I've also seen your ancient Grand Canal. I have memories of a boating holiday when I was a boy. And I'm up to date with your present hydropower projects. I should tell you that I'm impressed by your industrial and scientific achievements since your Communist Party liberated the country in 'forty-nine. Lest you misunderstand me, I should tell you clearly from the outset, I'm no Communist. Don't believe in centralised systems and all that uniformity, but credit should go where it's due and, as a working man – that's my class background, as you lot would have it – I can't deny what the Chinese working man has recently achieved. I'm a member of the Society for Anglo-Chinese Understanding in London, Professor, and I've heard the lectures and seen the films. Most impressive.'

Wei smiled. 'That is most gratifying to hear, Doctor, and I assure you I am not offended by your political beliefs. As scientists we need not bother ourselves with ideologies. Our chairman himself has told us we should seek truth from facts.'

'He's a great man, your chairman,' said Harry.

'That, too, is gratifying to hear – from a Westerner.'

Harry laughed. 'Well, you mentioned facts. They speak for themselves, don't they? Nobody can deny China's achievements.'

Wei frowned. 'Yet we have such a long way to go, Dr Airton. You were kind enough to compliment us on our hydro-projects – but their efficiency and output are low. Our technology is old. It must be improved if we are to satisfy our leaders' requirements that we build a powerful industrial society.'

'Your Russian friends aren't helping you?' asked Harry.

Wei's eyes narrowed. 'Our Russian friends? Yes. You have perhaps heard the Chinese expression '*Tong chuang yi meng*', Same Bed Different Dreams? When we founded our People's Republic we believed that our Russian brothers shared the same dream in the same bed but over the years we have become disillusioned. They are not so generous with their technology as we might have expected. Our leaders have remonstrated with theirs, but it is no use. There is a growing rift.'

'You are being very candid.'

'Only as one scientist to another, Doctor. May I be blunt? I have been authorised to ask you today about certain processes we believe your British companies possess, particularly your nationalised energy corporation, GPR, which we would like to study further.'

'I am in no position to talk about the proprietary technology of British companies,' said Harry.

'Of course not. My interest is general – theoretical,' said the Chinese. 'My understanding was that you might be . . . sympathetic. For the betterment of the working man. We have heard of your brave manifestation of conscience at Windscale.'

'I see,' said Harry. He played for a while with his cigarette lighter. 'All right,' he said, as if he had come to a decision. 'I see no harm in discussing theoretical matters of common interest to us all. What exactly do you want to know?'

'Professor Galady told me that you spoke eloquently on this subject not so long ago. Perhaps you could repeat to me some of the things that so impressed your audience.'

Once more Harry went over the lecture he and Julian had so often rehearsed. At first the man gave every indication of attentiveness, but as Harry laid on the technical detail, the shrewd eyes glazed. Harry felt again the twinge of excitement in his stomach. Professor Wei Jian was no scientist. 'So, you see,' he concluded, 'it's the small adjustment to the output process that makes all the difference. GPR heat exchangers, if you install them, could effectively double or triple your yields. It's a pity you're so tied to the Russians, Professor, or we could have helped you.'

'Perhaps one day the global situation will change,' murmured Wei. 'It is a tragedy that the nations of the world cannot co-operate for the betterment of mankind.'

'I'll drink to that,' said Harry. 'It's not my place to say so but I think we got it all wrong back in the forties. There was never any need to go to war in Korea. China, Communist or not, has never been a threat to us.'

'We have so many problems of our own, we cannot afford to be anything but a peace-loving nation.'

'Our politicians are too blind to see that. It's tragic, if you ask me.'

Professor Wei sipped his tea. 'You are an extraordinary man, Dr Airton. A top-ranking scientist who at the same time understands China so well. I hear that you lived there as a child. Have you never thought of returning one day?'

Harry sighed. 'Frankly, Professor, I've dreamt of nothing else, but it's not to be, is it, with this bloody stupid Cold War raging?'

'Tell me about your childhood, Doctor,' said Wei, gently, in the sympathetic tones of a priest probing a penitent, but the gleam in his eyes gave him away. And Harry relaxed. It had taken him ten years to prepare for this moment, and now it had come. It was the point in the interrogation when the unwitting target has been lulled into a false sense of security and is ready to reveal all.

'I grew up in a hospital,' said Harry, 'a mission station under the peaks of Mount Tai . . .'

They talked for nearly three hours. The candles had long since burnt out, but the moon had risen high above the fir trees, and washed the garden in an eerie blue light. The students and artists had sat for a long while, as the two men murmured in their incomprehensible language, but had become bored and drifted into the *dacha* to their beds. Grunya stayed for some time on the balcony, looking wistfully at Harry, until the poet in the lumberjack shirt came out with two mugs of coffee. He nuzzled his head into her shoulder and whispered in her ear. She turned questioningly towards Galady, who was smoking his pipe in a rocking-chair. He nodded dismissively and the two disappeared inside the house.

Some time towards four in the morning, when Galady, yawning, approached them suggesting it was time for bed, Harry noticed that the dark girl called Marysha was waiting in the shadows. It was she who led off the Chinese 'professor', while Harry climbed the pinewood stairs, to the attic room, where he would sleep alone until the cars arrived in the morning to take them back to Budapest.

Beijing, May 1962

It was a hot day, even for early summer. The lake around which the state leaders' houses and offices nestled so picturesquely was like a mirror reflecting the mountainous white clouds in the sky. The willow trees on its banks drooped with torpor. In the distance the Dagoba at

Bei Hai gleamed brilliantly in the sunshine. The two men being escorted along the paths of the Zhongnanhai were uncomfortable in their formal cadres' tunics, but if they were sweating, it was less because of the heat than their trepidation about the meeting to which they had been summoned.

They were both well aware of Premier Zhou Enlai's sensitivity about using Chinese women in what Westerners euphemistically referred to as 'honey-trap' operations. There was an official policy against it. It had only been because of the importance of the issues at stake that a majority of the Central Committee had voted in favour. Even so, it was conditional. No less a figure than Kang Sheng, once head of the Social Affairs Department, which supervised state security, now in charge of Culture and Education, and Chairman Mao's closest adviser and personal emissary since the 1940s, had been delegated to make an investigation. That was why Commissioner Hao, head of the Scientific Intelligence Unit of the Second Department, and his short, bulging-eyed assistant, Chen, had been called to report to him. It was not expected to be a pleasurable experience.

Chen's only comfort was that, since he himself was the junior, Commissioner Hao would bear the brunt of the questions. He was alarmed when his superior was stopped at the door, and only he was ushered into Comrade Kang's study. Every wall was lined with books and ornaments, and there was a fine carpet on the floor, but his eyes were drawn to the angular grey-haired figure bent in concentration over pages of calligraphy that all but covered a large walnut desk. When the head lifted, he saw the familiar round spectacles, the pencil-line moustache and the pallid, skull-like features of one of the most feared men in the country.

'I have been reading your Party file, Comrade. It is impressive. You have made significant contributions, first to the People's Revolution and now in the ongoing struggle against imperialism.' He consulted the paper on his desk. 'Your class background is satisfactory. You are the son of a worker. What did your father do?'

'He was a factory hand, Comrade Kang in Jiangsu.'

'An honourable profession, but he chose to work in a mill owned by foreigners. Why was that?'

'Times were hard, Comrade Kang.' He had blurted this out and immediately realised it was an incorrect response. He felt a shiver down his spine as Kang observed him.

'That was why we made a revolution, Comrade, to end such humiliations for honest people like your parents. They died, I see, unfortunate victims of Japanese aggression, and you, orphaned as a result, made your way to Yan'an to join the People's Struggle. How old were you?'

'Thirteen, Comrade Kang.'

'A young age, yet it says here you were active even then in hunting out class enemies. Who were they?'

'Intellectuals and others whose conversation revealed their anti-proletarian sympathies. I – I reported them.'

Kang made a sound that might have been a laugh. 'You were a little snoop, Comrade. But I congratulate you. For its safety, our country requires constant vigilance against our enemies, within and without the Party. There is no place for bourgeois sentimentality or mistaken personal loyalties.'

He went through everything: Chen's army service, the first intelligence operations he had been engaged in against the Nationalists, his transfer after Liberation in 1949 to the Second Department, his counter-intelligence work in Fujian, turning Taiwanese agents, and finally – by which stage Chen had developed a twitch in one knee – his present activities in connection with scientific and technological espionage.

'You were part of the operation that led to the defection of Professor Luo Mingan from MIT in the United States. That was a great coup. Professor Luo is now making valuable contributions to our rocketry research in the Fifth Ministry.'

'My part was only small, Comrade Kang. I passed a message to him in the hotel where he was staying in Milan. I was there with a trade delegation looking at shoe-making machinery. It was Comrade Hao's operation.'

'I am aware of all the details, and also that I had authorised Commissioner Hao to lead the team in Milan. You went in his stead at the last minute. You had to use the false papers we prepared for him, including his alias. Was that not risky – as well as irregular?'

'It was necessary. Just before the delegation was due to depart from Beijing, Comrade Hao developed a stomach complaint. I had been involved in some of the organisation and training beforehand and was familiar with the details of the operation so—'

'A stomach complaint, did you say?'

'Yes, gastroenteritis, Comrade Kang.'

'I see. I had been told it was something more serious.' He gave a cold smile. 'Fortunate for him, then, that you were on hand to step in and save the day.'

'It was still Comrade Hao's operation. I acted under his instructions.'

'You are modest, Comrade. You did more than pass a message. On your own initiative you also arranged for some highly compromising photographs to be taken of Professor Luo with a Swiss prostitute, which later played no small part in his decision to return to the Motherland.'

'The opportunity presented itself. I was lucky.'

'And so, it seems was Comrade Hao, who was promoted afterwards on the back of your success. I must be careful in future to observe you more closely, Comrade. You are a man who is prepared to use unconventional methods to help our country. I like that. This is apposite, is it not, to the matter in hand today? This operation, unlike the one we have been describing, was your idea.'

'Yes, Comrade, I am prepared to shoulder full responsibility, and I will be actively involved throughout. I am convinced that this British scientist, because of his earlier background in China, will be responsive to our approach.'

'The nuclear physicist?'

'Yes. Our studies of his psychology confirm deep-rooted character traits that I believe will make him an ideal target. He has a senior government role in the British Ministry of Power to which he will return after his present posting in their embassy in Hungary.'

'Are you basing your assessment of the man on the report of your agent who met him in Budapest?'

'No, Comrade Kang. I have subsequently conducted exhaustive research into his history and psychology. He is an outsider in his society. In addition he is emotionally unstable, particularly when it comes to women, which is why I have suggested a sexual trap as the principal means to turn him. Above all, he has a sentimentality towards China, on which I believe I can play effectively.'

'And you think that if you can induce him to spy on his own country, he will have valuable material to give us?'

'He has not been working actively in the nuclear industry for some years, but he retains that specialist knowledge. In his government role, he will have access to any information we require.'

'This is the key issue, is it not? As you know, when the Russians abandoned us two years ago, they withdrew all the drawings and blue-prints for the nuclear reactor they were helping us to construct. More importantly, they sabotaged our project to build a bomb. To have a bomb of our own is a vital necessity if we are to conduct our struggle against imperialism, not to mention the influence that it will give us geopolitically. Our chairman has publicly announced that our research is ongoing and that within a few years China will have atomic weapons developed by home-grown technology. The truth, Comrade, is that we are still backward in many areas of knowledge. Of course we make propaganda of self-reliance, but the truth is that all attempts to provide stable elements with the poor-quality uranium we have been able to discover have failed. We will triumph one day. That is unquestioned – the People's Revolution cannot be stopped. But we should investigate any means to accelerate the process. For that we require information.'

'I believe, Comrade Kang, that if we can persuade him to work for us, this British scientist will be in a position to accommodate us – he was once responsible for isolating the 235 isotope at Windscale.'

With a refined movement of his slender hand, Kang brought out a packet of cigarettes from his top pocket, lit one, drew in a lungful of smoke, then stubbed it out in a marble ashtray. 'I am inclined to clutch at this straw, Comrade. The situation merits it. I have read your paper thoroughly and it is convincing. Some of my colleagues find the methods you propose distasteful. Officially so do I. Unofficially you have my permission to proceed – on condition, Comrade, that you use a woman of a suitable background, I mean a *hei wu lei*, someone from the Five Black Categories – former land-lords, rich peasants, reactionaries, rightists, stinking intellectuals. To sacrifice a maiden from the Red Category would demean Chinese womanhood. If you proceed on this basis, you have my support. I will not blame you if you fail, as long as no embarrassment results for our country. I believe your chance of success to be minimal. The operation will therefore be unofficial and deniable, and in the event of failure, all evidence that it took place will be destroyed. Whatever the results, you will remove the woman once she has served her purpose. She must disappear, and you must find means to control your new agent without her. Then I may be able to persuade my colleagues to agree to my recommendation.'

'I thank you for your wise guidance, Comrade Kang.'

'You may go.' The skull-like head dropped back to the papers, the two round spectacle lenses opaque as the coins on a dead man's eyes.

Hungary, June 1962

Julian was in newspaper-correspondent cover, and arrived at the embassy in a Gannex raincoat with a trilby. Harry took him immediately to the safe room. They had not met for nearly eight months, and greeted each other warmly.

'What's so important that it brings you from your comfortable office in London?' Harry asked. 'It's not like you to come slumming into the comrades' territory. I didn't think grey uniformity was your style.'

'Oh, I don't know, Harry. Isn't Budapest the city of wine, women and song? Gypsy dancers and flowing Tokay? From your reports you appear to have been living it up.'

'Come on, what's so secret that you can't put it into a coded signal?'

Julian grinned. 'I wanted to see your face when you had a look at this.' He reached into his briefcase and pulled out a telegram.

Harry read it quickly, then slowly, and once more to be sure. His ears burnt and his chest constricted. He was rubbing his hands together, and one knee was shaking. 'This isn't one of your jokes, Julian? You're not setting me up?'

'Well,' Julian drawled, 'technically you might say I've been setting you up for the last twelve years.'

'You bastard,' Harry muttered, although a smile was broadening over his craggy features. 'You beautiful bastard. This means I'm going back, doesn't it?'

'I rather think it does,' said Julian.

Harry was holding a note from the Foreign Office. It described how the previous week the Chinese *chargé d'affaires* in London had requested information on new efficiency processes for hydropower stations that had been exhibited recently by the British company GPR at the Trade and Technology Fair in Warsaw. The *chargé* had indicated that if the British government would like to take the project forward, the Chinese government would put no obstacles in the way of accrediting a science officer to the British legation in Peking. In fact, they would appreciate it if the British Foreign Office would take steps to expedite such an appointment.

'This calls for a small celebration,' said Julian, pulling two glasses and a bottle of champagne from his briefcase. 'It's Russian, I'm afraid, all they sell here, but since we're toasting your return to your socialist motherland, it's not inappropriate. We'll drink the real stuff when you come back to London as a fully fledged Chinese spy.'

Hong Kong, August 1962

After an hour's ride through the paddy-fields, the train he had boarded at Kowloon station dropped him at a small wooden platform where a porter was punching tickets. Lowu might have been a rural station anywhere in the New Territories: Hakka women in black pyjamas and fringed straw hats were unloading pigs and chickens from second-class carriages, and farmers were gathering up produce to take to market. A less bucolic aspect of the scene was the coils of barbed wire that rolled to the horizon on either side of the railway line, and the sentries in khaki shorts and helmets who guarded the bridge beyond.

Harry appeared to be the only person crossing the border that day. He felt self-conscious as he stepped away from the throng, a suitcase in one hand and a briefcase in the other. The British corporal greeted him cheerfully. 'Travelling light, sir? Off to the trade fair in Canton, are you? Ah, you're a dip,' he said, cursorily examining Harry's passport. 'So it's Peking, then? Rather you than me, sir. Long posting?'

'Two or three years, I imagine.'

'Well, someone's got to do it. Hope you've got some edibles in that bag of yours, sir. Hear they don't have much to eat over there.'

'I'm sure I'll survive.'

'Good luck, sir. Looks like you'll need it.'

Suddenly Harry felt warmth towards the man. Now that the moment had come, he experienced a slight tremor in his legs and a hollowness in the pit of his stomach. 'Thank you, Corporal,' he said. 'I probably will.' A private had pulled open the metal mesh gate. Beyond, the bridge crossed a narrow stream. Sunlight flashed on the water, where ducks were swimming. Ahead he saw two Chinese border guards in olive green uniforms, submachine-guns hung over their shoulders and, past them, a red flag, ruffling in the slight breeze. Further away, he could see the curved roof of a train waiting in another station.

'Well, sir, you're on your own now.'

Harry turned to him and smiled. 'Don't worry, Corporal. I've been on my own nearly all my life.' He put a firm foot forward, and crossed the bridge briskly into China.

He passed the guards, who stared at him with wooden, impassive faces. One swung his gun in the direction of a small hut with a sign that read in Chinese and English: 'Welcome to the People's Republic of China. Customs and Immigration.'

Harry stepped inside. It was a bare concrete room, dominated by a huge wooden table behind which sat a bespectacled, crop-haired official who was fanning himself with a sheaf of immigration forms. Behind him, on a bunk, one of his colleagues, stripped to his vest, was reading the *Guangzhou Daily*. A radio, tuned to Hong Kong's broadcasting station, was jangling a Cantonese popular song, the music competing with the buzz of flies. Above his head hung a portrait of Mao Tse-tung. The official at the desk buttoned his collar, and stretched out a hand imperiously for Harry's passport. One of the soldiers had remained in the doorway.

Harry's linen jacket clung to his back in the heat. The man called something in Cantonese to his colleague, who put down his newspaper and loped over to the desk. Both of them stared up at Harry's face.

'It's an old photograph,' Harry said, in Mandarin, in an attempt to lighten the atmosphere, 'but you can tell it's me. Look at the long nose.'

'You do not have to speak Chinese. We speak English,' said the first official. 'Empty your bags on to the table, please. Also the contents of your pockets.'

Harry did as he was told. He could have pointed out that he was a diplomat but he saw little point. They went through every page of his novels, felt in the pockets of his spare trousers and jackets, and sniffed his aftershave. At one point they seemed to be examining the labels on his underpants. They opened every blade of his Swiss Army knife, then put it aside while they separated his socks. Finally, after half an hour, during which his legs and arms were running with sweat and he had brushed away at least a hundred flies, he was told he could repack his bags. 'Except this,' said the second official, picking up the penknife. 'You are forbidden to carry weapons into China.'

'Keep it,' said Harry, thinking that some things had not changed and this was a demand for *cumshaw*.

'You must write a description of the article on this form,' said the man.

'Is that really necessary?'

It was, as it was also necessary to itemise the amount of loose change in his pocket, his carton of cigarettes, his three bottles of whisky and his transistor radio.

It was another half-hour before they let him go. Then Harry made his way to a first-class compartment. Faces in the other carriages were glaring at him because of the delay he had caused. He stowed his baggage on the rack, and slumped into a comfortable leather seat.

He closed his eyes as a rush of emotion overwhelmed him. He was only a few hundred yards still from Hong Kong, but in his sudden intoxication, even the smell of the musty carriage was different. It was welcoming – familiar . . . He had done it. He was in China.

He sensed a presence. A female attendant, with crimson cheeks and two braids hanging from her green cap, was leaning over him proffering a tray of hot towels and oranges. As he looked into her soft brown eyes, he felt a devil-may-care sense of elation. He winked at her. 'May Mao Tse-tung live for ten thousand years.' The girl frowned suspiciously. Harry pointed outside the window at the characters on the long red banner that hung on the station wall next to a portrait of the great leader. The girl stood to attention and raised her arm in a salute to the portrait. 'Long live Chairman Mao,' she screeched.

His sense of homecoming evaporated. She turned on her heel, and sat down at the other end of the carriage. From there she watched Harry with a hostile expression for the rest of the journey.

The carriage jolted as the wheels began to turn. At the same time loudspeakers in the carriage blared martial music, followed by propaganda announcements, read by a vehement female voice: 'The force at the core leading our cause forward is the Chinese Communist Party. The theoretical basis guiding our thinking is Marxism-Leninism.'

And Harry came down to earth with a thump.

After a while, he distanced himself from the noise and looked out at the fields, where farmers were bending over green paddies. There seemed to be an air of dereliction about the landscape, or perhaps that was his imagination, jaded by the propaganda ringing in his ears.

The slogans only stopped when the train pulled into the terminus at Canton. More posters and banners were emblazoned on every building, and everywhere portraits of Mao smiled down at him. As a taxi took him through the crowded streets, the traffic had to stop for a procession of Young Pioneers to pass by: children with red cotton scarves tied round their necks, singing passionately of their love for the people of Albania.

He spent the evening alone in his Spartan hotel room, avoiding the raucous company of the foreign businessmen who were in town for the autumn trade fair, trying to make sense of his first impressions. It had been anti-climactic after his earlier excitement, depressing even, but the regimentation he had seen was only to be expected. He had read enough about it, and he was not yet disheartened. He would find traces of his China, he told himself. Somewhere it would still be there. He would spot it out of the window on the two-day train journey he would take to Peking.

He had a four-bunk cabin to himself on the train going north. The same slogans and injunctions mixed with ludicrous lectures on hygiene – how to brush one's teeth and why one should not wash rice bowls in the lavatories. He found a dial in his carriage and discovered how to turn down the sound to an indistinct murmur, but it was blaring full blast in the dining car. Here, a severe woman, wearing a white hairnet and a face mask, served him unappetising soup and bony chunks of chicken; she gave no indication that she could understand his Chinese. By the time he rolled into his bunk at the end of the first day, Harry was feeling distinctly unenthusiastic.

The country rolled by. The yellow soil of the southern provinces gave way to the red of central China. Again, he saw peasants in the fields. The first time he spotted a line of bent figures in the paddies, he felt a jolt of emotion. These were the scenes from his childhood – but there was a subtle difference. As often as not the peasants, dressed in monotonous blues and greens, rather than the colours that had brightened the landscape of his youth, were sitting in groups listening to officials in straw hats. He recalled the Party propaganda sessions behind the wire compounds when he was a guard at Koje-do. There was the same regimented uniformity.

He supposed these were the famous communes that had been imposed on the countryside in 1958, heralding the disastrous Great Leap Forward, Mao's home-grown attempt to create an industrial paradise overnight that instead had stripped the country bare, resulting in a famine in which tens of millions had starved. He had read that new policies had been introduced to alleviate the damage, but the harvests he saw in the fields still looked meagre. The vague air of lassitude seemed echoed in the cities through which he passed. He observed several large factories when they crossed the Yangtze at Wuhan, but not many chimneys were smoking. Shortly afterwards, he saw a road-building gang, regiments of forced labour – perhaps it was one of the terrible prison farms of which he had heard – in an ant column stretching to the horizon. Men and women were bent double, hauling rocks or loaded with panniers of earth like beasts of burden. By the time he turned in to sleep on his second night, he was thoroughly depressed. Everything he had read about the new China seemed confirmed.

As he lay listening to the rhythmic thump of the wheels, he thought, for the first time in many years, of Chen Tao. He wondered what might have become of him if, by some miracle, he had escaped the Japanese. Would Chen Tao, too, have been condemned to slave in some dreadful work brigade, like the ones he had seen from the window that afternoon? In which case it was perhaps a mercy that he was no more. Or would the irrepressible adventurer have found a way to beat the system and use his guile to rise through the ranks to a safe position in the hierarchy? Harry envisaged him mouthing the slogans with the others, but he liked to believe that in Chen Tao's case it would have been an act, a necessary subterfuge like the stratagems he had devised in their games. The twisted lips would still be curved in the old ironic smile. The cavalier sense of fun that had brightened Harry's childhood would still bubble in his heart . . . He smiled with affection at the thought, then felt a stab of pain, for he knew that the chances of Chen Tao having survived were minimal. Harry's scream in the loft had condemned him to execution – or worse. Over the years he had tried to numb himself to that guilt, but now, in this dark, rocking compartment, it returned with full force, as fresh as it had been on the day it had happened.

The wheels thundered to a different timbre as the train crossed a bridge. He guessed they were at the Huai river. In ten hours more they would reach Peking. He wondered what he would find there. In his present mood it seemed a hollow triumph that he had fulfilled his dream and returned. Everything he had seen indicated that the China he had loved was no more, as Chen Tao, with whom he had once shared it, was no more. He was fooling himself, he decided bitterly. He should abandon this absurd desire to look for signs that anything remained. It was a pipe-dream, nothing more. He should be concentrating on his task.

He woke on the last morning of his journey, red dawn light creeping through the cracks in the curtain. Listlessly, he opened them, and saw that the landscape had changed. The endless paddy-fields were gone, replaced by the maize of the north. Yellowing leaves covered ears of corn that glistened ruddy ochre in the early sunshine. Lines of tall poplar trees marked a road, their shadows striping the sandy path. Suddenly he saw a cart being pulled by a Bactrian camel. Two little boys, in ragged clothes but with shining eyes and wide grins, were jumping up and down, waving at the train. An old farmer, leading the camel, had a hand to his brow and was smiling.

It was only a brief glimpse – but Harry was filled with joy, and something of his old sense of purpose. He had seen in the faces of those two anonymous children a vision of himself and Chen Tao.

Perhaps it was not too late. Perhaps something did remain. If he owed anything to the memory of his friend, he was determined to find it.

3

The Trainers

Peking, October 1962

───────

Boarding the aeroplane at Canton airport, Julian realised that almost every major phase of his involvement in the Airton project had coincided with some critical episode of the Cold War. He was still smarting at his misfortune that two days after he received his accreditation to Peking the Cuban missile affair had escalated into an international crisis.

He had spent a tense fortnight, alternating dumb insolence with one master and increasingly feeble excuses to the other, both *The Times* and the Office wanted him to return immediately to London, but he excelled at slipperiness, and in the end had his way and was allowed to await developments in Hong Kong. It was a surreal place to be. On the other side of the world Russian ships loaded with missiles were heading inexorably across the Atlantic towards potential Armageddon. In Hong Kong the traders went about their business and their entertainments, the weekly races, the charity balls and their all-important appointments with their tailors. The only significance of the crisis related to fluctuations in the Hang Seng Bank Index; some were busy shoring their positions by buying bonds and gold; others were speculating wildly in the hope of an upturn – but that was Hong Kong. A unique cocktail of acquisitiveness, hedonism and wilful amnesia made it the vibrant place it was. It appeared to Julian that only the small intelligence fraternity had the dubious distinction of knowing what was really going on. They would meet every evening at the Eagle's Nest bar in the Hilton Hotel, and drink their way into oblivion.

The crisis passed. The ships returned. Life went on, but the delay meant that Julian had to reapply for his visa, so it was another month before he was allowed to purchase his tickets from the China Travel Service for the train to Canton and the flight from there to Peking. Unlike Harry, with his sentimental desire to see the Chinese countryside, Julian preferred to risk four hours in a bucketing Tupolev rather than lock himself in for a two-day train ride. He was keen, anyway, to make up for lost time. Harry had been alone in the Chinese capital for more than four months.

By the time his plane had arrived in Peking, and his taxi was threading its way through a flock of sheep that was inexplicably wandering across the road into town, he was impatient to find out what was going on and how his agent was taking the strain.

Harry knew of his arrival, but they had agreed to leave it a couple of weeks before they were formally 'introduced' at some suitable social function, where they would visibly 'hit it off'. It was important that nobody in the British Legation, except the minister, who had been briefed by the Office, should suspect that Harry and he had any previous acquaintance. Needless to say, Julian did not want any of the comrades to get any wrong ideas either.

In any case, he needed that fortnight to negotiate his way through the bureaucracy and bloody-mindedness of the various officials he had to wait on before he was allowed to establish his news bureau in the Xin Qiao Hotel. For the first few days he spent hours waiting in ministerial lobbies or sipping tea through interminable courtesies in audience halls. Then there was the whole process of selecting his staff – or, rather, his minders, because he knew their primary role was to spy on him – but finally he found himself on his way to the British legation in the back of a venerable Red Flag limousine that he had hired at an extortionate rate from the Foreign Ministry's Information Department. For the first time since he had arrived, he was able to take stock of the city he had first visited in Nationalist times, on a long vacation from Oxford after the war.

And he was not impressed. The old Qing Dynasty government offices at either side of what had once been a narrow, rather mediaeval Tiananmen Square had been pulled down and replaced with monumental Soviet-style workers' palaces, the Great Hall of the People and the History Museum, leaving between them a flagstoned emptiness, dominated by a gigantic portrait of Mao Tse-tung. The Great Helmsman beamed down in an avuncular fashion from the great gate tower marking the entrance to the Imperial Palace. At least that had been preserved, thought Julian, ruefully, as awed as he had been before by the yellow roofs that seemed to float, like a depiction of heaven in a scroll painting, to the green mound of Coal Hill in the distance.

But what caught his eye was the activity in the middle of the vast square: hundreds of young men and women, in Mao caps and blue or green tunics, were going through a complicated rigmarole with red flags. As he watched the set faces, and the exaggerated revolutionary pose, puffed chest and fingers pointing witheringly at class enemies, Julian remembered what the Reuters correspondent had been telling him in the bar of his hotel.

'There's a circus of some kind every day. Never know who the People's Wrath will fall on next, but every day, you can bet on it, there'll be a demonstration outside one of the embassies – Indian, Yugoslav, Polish or Russian, depending on whether the political venom of the week is directed against Nehru, Tito, Gromulka or Khrushchev. We Brits are particularly favoured, of course, since our mission's the general punchbag for all the Western democracies. Hardly a week goes by without a screaming mob dragging burning effigies of Kennedy, de Gaulle and even dear old Macmillan to the wrought-iron gates. Welcome to Peking.'

Julian, looking disdainfully at the rehearsing demonstrators, felt a moment of anger at what had become of the city he had loved as a young man. The car drove along Chang An Avenue, past the granite front of the Peking Hotel. Not much left of the charming old Wagons Lits hotel, he thought, remembering the elegant parties in the old days. Along either side of the boulevard, widened to accommodate tanks and missiles in the annual parade, anonymous brick workers' dwellings had replaced the charming alleys known as *hutongs*. As they passed out of the former city limits towards the new diplomatic quarter, Julian felt the worst cut of all. Blue-coated work gangs were pulling down the last remains of what had once been the beautiful city walls. Ancient bricks and blocks of masonry were being passed from hand to hand, while a loudspeaker blared exhortations and slogans. It was like watching a swarm of army ants stripping a log.

But, ever practical, he comforted himself with the thought that the demise of the old Tatar Wall, which had delighted him as a language student and dilettante Sinologist, would inspire a piece of purple prose for the paper. After all, he was here to do a job – two jobs. It didn't matter a toss what he thought of all this destruction. More important was the effect it might have had on Harry. Suddenly Julian hoped that, by now, his *protégé* was very, very angry.

That day there was no riot outside the Lego-like British Legation.

A secretary, who might have stepped out of Mayfair, asked him to sign the visitors' book under the portrait of the Queen. He passed through typical Whitehall furnishings, up the carpeted stairs, to the minister's office.

Garrard was a grey diplomat of the old school, wearing a quiet bow-tie and a three-piece navy suit. He looked up from his desk with infinite weariness, took off his half-glasses and gave Julian what he supposed was a welcoming smile.

'Travers,' he said, using Julian's cover name. 'Sit down. Sit down. Are we to be discussing *Times* matters, or . . . ah . . .' Julian watched as he fumbled among the papers on his desk, and pressed a button on what appeared to be a tape recorder. Suddenly, from loudspeakers behind him, came the clatter and hubbub of a cocktail party in full progress. 'Or – ah – other matters?' Garrard continued, putting a finger to his lips. 'We are not secure in this room. Boom microphones.' He added this in a stage whisper that hardly penetrated above the chattering voices.

Julian was inwardly rolling his eyes. He thought such amateurish precautions had gone out a decade before. 'Very sensible, sir,' he said. 'You can never be too careful.'

'Indeed.' Garrard frowned, perhaps sensing Julian's scorn. 'I am perhaps over-egging the salad, but I wanted to make the point that in future, if we are to meet in my office, we should not discuss openly – ah – the sensitive aspects of your posting here.'

'I quite agree, Minister,' said Julian.

'Then, with your permission, we should – ah – relocate to somewhere more appropriate. If you would care to come with me . . .' He switched off the cocktail party and lifted himself from his chair, rather in the manner of a spider extending its legs.

Julian followed him down white corridors, past offices where bright-faced young men, dictating letters to their secretaries or immersed in the Chinese papers, responded to his nod. Julian remembered that Desmond Garrard was a scholar of repute, who had written a learned paper on Chinese playwrights of the Ming Dynasty. He imagined that these eager first and second secretaries were Sinophiles of a similar academic cast. So might he have been once, if the Office and the Cold War had not steered him in another direction.

They passed down some steps into a dark cul-de-sac stacked with filing cabinets. Garrard fiddled with several complicated locks and wheels on a metal door that led to the Wendy Room, which could be found in all overseas embassies. It was furnished with the usual nondescript table and chairs, a tape-recorder and decoder. The minister glanced at him as they sat down. 'We can talk quietly here,' he murmured. 'This safe room is state of the art – I believe that is the current term – and – ah – safe,' he ended lamely.

'I very much appreciate your consideration, sir,' said Julian.

Garrard was fiddling with a pencil to disguise nervousness or irritation, but he produced no notebook. 'Well,' he said, 'I see from your article in the newspaper that you have settled in. Rather a provocative piece, I thought. Is there anything in particular that our mission can do to help you?'

'In which role, Minister?' Again, Julian repressed a smile.

'Well, either, I suppose. As a newspaperman you are entitled to our help. Jenkins, one of our second secretaries, acts also as our press officer. I shall introduce you, if you like.'

'I would appreciate that,' said Julian.

The minister shuffled, clearing his throat. 'I have been informed that you and our science officer are planning some – ah – activity together. I have been instructed to help you in every way I can, and I will, but I have not been made aware of the – ah – ultimate purpose of the operation or, indeed, what help you may require. I have therefore assumed there is no necessity for me to know. Would that be a fair assessment?'

'I am in a position to brief you more fully, sir, should you or I at any time think that that is required. I am under strict instructions not to embarrass the mission.'

'That, at least, is gratifying. Well, our facilities are at your disposal. I imagine that from time to time you would like to use our communication equipment and this – ah – room. Was there anything else, perhaps? Feel free to ask.'

'I won't be bothering you very much, sir. Better that I'm not seen to have too close a relationship with the mission beyond the sort of social contacts that a British reporter might be expected to have. On that score, did you receive our message that we would like us to organise a dinner?'

'So that you can meet your own man? I must say it smacks very much of the cloak-and-dagger to me, but in due course Jenkins will be inviting you and the Reuters correspondent to dinner at his apartment. I have suggested that he includes some of his other colleagues and Airton.'

'That's very kind. There is another thing.'

'By all means.'

'How is Harry Airton getting on?'

Garrard raised his eyebrows. 'As science officer? A few weeks ago he organised a most successful symposium on rare metals used in chemical processes. He took over the translation at one point and almost conducted a seminar on his own for half an hour. At one point he corrected one of the British lecturers on a point of scientific detail about nuclear isotopes, which certainly impressed the Chinese. Usually they sit mute, but Airton had them popping off their seats with questions. Colliers – our commercial counsellor – had never seen anything like it.'

'Yes, Harry's the real thing,' said Julian.

Garrard looked at him shrewdly. 'It makes me wonder why he's working for you.' He paused. 'Travers, may I ask you something in turn?'

'As I said, I will tell you everything about the operation if you wish.'

'No, I don't want to know more than I have to, but tell me this. Did you know how unhappy he is?'

Julian let the silence hang. Usually when people ask such questions they want to get something off their chest.

'You may be aware,' Garrard continued, 'that not everybody in our mission was pleased when we heard that a science officer was being appointed with a specific brief to look after the hydropower inquiry. In ordinary circumstances, a potential project for a big company like GPR would be handled by one of our commercial officers. In fact, Colliers had been quite excited by the prospect.' He pressed his long fingers together. 'Another thing, this hydropower project happens to be rather important to us politically. It's been some time since a big industrial deal has come our way, and we've never been invited into the power sector before. I don't want to bore you with the bigger picture, but this country has been going through quite a shake-up during the last few years. The Great Leap Forward crippled the economy. We don't know how many people died in the famine it caused – twenty million? More? Thank God the Chinese government seems to have come to its senses now, restored free markets, rationalised industry, that sort of thing, but it will take years to get back to where the economy was in 1958 – especially since the Russians pulled out. In any civilised country, after a disaster of such magnitude, there would be questions as to who had been responsible. Everybody knows who was, but he's a god, Travers, untouchable . . . Or is he?'

'I hadn't heard otherwise,' said Julian.

'Of course, he's still Party Chairman, father of his country, the Great Liberator of the People, but President Liu Shaoqi and the Party Secretary, Deng Xiaoping, are reversing, one by one, nearly all of Mao's Cloud Cuckoo Land economics. The old doomsayer Chen Yun, who criticised the Great Leap, is handling the country's finances. And then, suddenly, we're asked for our help in their power sector. Without the Russians, could this mean that China is turning to the West for technology? And might a geopolitical shift follow? That's why this GPR project could be so important. All sorts of things may follow, even a bit of influence for GB.'

'And you're worried that a loose cannon is handling it? Because Harry's unhappy?'

'I didn't say that, Travers. All I'm saying is that he's been put in charge of a most sensitive project, which, I'll admit, he's handling well.'

'Then what is the problem?'

'Well, he works for you, not us.'

'He works for us both, Minister.'

'Rebuke taken, Travers.' He sighed. 'Then I don't know. He's so . . . so . . .'

'Unpredictable? Cussed? Bolshie?'

Garrard gave a dry chuckle. 'Well, he's certainly not a team player, and that's unfortunate in a small community like our mission, where we make a point of getting on with each other. His general surliness and his occasional secretiveness do not endear him to his colleagues. And he's a womaniser, Travers. Airton has serious affairs, which he breaks off for no apparent reason, leaving the poor girl heartbroken. That won't do in our fragile little world. I've had the Finnish and Dutch ambassadors complaining about it. Once, it happened with a girl in one of our own sections. She came weeping into my office. In the end I had to send her home.'

'I'm sorry to hear it.'

'You misunderstand me. Whether a secretary comes or goes is neither here nor there, but we cannot afford to lose Airton. For better or worse, he's the one in charge of the GPR project. However, he is showing all the wild restlessness of a man who has been deeply hurt. I know he drinks. He sits all alone in that courtyard house of his—'

'Doesn't he live in one of the diplomatic flats?'

Garrard sighed. 'He moved out last month into a small compound off Morrison Street – or Wangfujing, as they call it now. I tried to dissuade him, but since I had already given young Peter Foxley permission to take a *hutong* house, I could hardly deny Airton the same privilege. It's an odd quirk of the Chinese security system that they will sometimes allow diplomats to find their own accommodation, even after the Foreign Ministry has spent so much money building an ugly ghetto to house us all. Some of our chaps like living among the ordinary people, and savouring what remains of the old architecture. Foxley's little courtyard is charming. It surprised me that Airton wanted one too. Despite his remarkable language capabilities, he has shown little sign of liking the Chinese. I fear he wanted a retreat in which he could indulge his own gloomy self-recriminations about his failed marriage, or whatever his problem is. And that's hardly healthy, Travers.' The sharp eyes were probing again. 'Or is there another reason of which I'm not cognisant? He received approval from the Foreign Ministry to take the house in remarkably short time.'

'Perhaps it's a sign that the comrades also recognise the importance of the GPR deal, Minister. A favour to the chosen liaison officer?'

'Perhaps,' said Garrard, drily. 'In which case it would be an encouraging precedent. Well, I've told you my concerns. You will know best what to do about them. As I said, my interests lie solely with the handling of the hydropower deal. As long as your man performs as conscientiously as he has been doing, I will put no obstacles in your way. I'll introduce you to Jenkins on the way out, shall I?'

Julian followed the minister back down the corridor, mulling over some of the things he had told him. For all he knew, Harry had good reasons for taking a courtyard house, and Garrard's comment about him not liking the Chinese was, at face value, not too alarming. Nevertheless it was a subtle change to the script. He was mentally kicking at the improvidence that had kept him away from Peking for so long when suddenly, at the end of the corridor, the man himself appeared.

His wide shoulders were constricted in a shabby tweed jacket, his flannels were shiny, and his hair was unbrushed. He was striding down the corridor, a secretary trying to keep pace with him, frowning as he scrutinised some document.

'Ah, Airton,' said Garrard, bringing Harry up short before he cannoned into him. Harry's features reflected his irritation. His eyes flicked towards Julian, but he showed no sign of recognition. 'Any more news on the project?'

'Aye, sir. They've postponed the trip again. I'm signalling GPR now.'

'Well, never mind. These things always take a while. Airton, before you go, I'd like to introduce you to Jonathan Travers, who's just opened a Peking bureau for the London *Times*. You might like to brief him one day on what you're doing. Symposia, exhibitions, that sort of thing. Travers, this is our science officer, Dr Harry Airton.'

Harry looked at Julian as if he were a traffic bollard, but grasped the outstretched hand.

'Did I hear you mention GPR, Dr Airton?' Julian asked, aware that the first and second secretaries were watching eagerly from their offices. 'Have they a project here?'

Harry scowled.

Garrard chuckled. 'Ever the questing newshound, Travers? No, but if they happen to find one, I'm sure you'll be the first person Airton will inform. We'll let him be on his way, shall we, while I take you downstairs to meet Jenkins?'

Harry nodded curtly, and strode on.

Two days later, Alan Jenkins and his wife, Annie, gave Julian dinner at their flat in one of the tower blocks where the Chinese housed the diplomatic community. They had done their best to make their home a little England, with government-issue furniture and hunting prints on the wall, as well as some African bric-à-brac they had picked up on their last posting, but the design was typically Soviet, from the creaking lift to the chilly landings. It was in keeping with the anonymous workers' housing blocks that were rising above ruined *hutongs* all over the city.

The Reuters correspondent had cried off, so Julian was the only journalist. The other guests were an assortment of diplomats and their wives, whose hospitality the Jenkinses were repaying in the musical-chairs round of dinner parties that passed for social life. There was a Swedish cultural attaché and his wife, with whom Julian's hosts shared a passion for antique-collecting. Half the dinner was spent discussing the difficulty of finding genuine Ming vases. The Jenkinses hadn't managed to locate any antiques except a flaking Qing Dynasty chair of which they were inordinately proud. There was a Dutch couple: he talked tediously about the Chinese economy, and she wobbled, giggled and knocked back her gin. There was Colliers, the commercial man, who fancied himself a wit, and his wife from the Home Counties, who was anything but. And there was Harry Airton.

The preliminaries followed the usual form, gin and tonic on the sofas, served by white-uniformed waiters, with all the laboured anecdotes that were common in any Iron Curtain country after the waiters had gone back into the kitchen. Julian played along. 'Really? They have the technology to listen in when you're at home?'

'Oh, yes, but actually it's rather useful. Our bug's behind the mirror,' Doreen Colliers explained happily. 'I make a point of talking to it every day, with marvellous results. Our Ayi's a lazy creature, you see, and she never listens to me, so every time I catch her slacking, I just go to the mirror, pour my heart out and next day she'll be busily polishing the silver.'

Julian joined in the laughter, knowing full well that if the low-level monitors who conducted home surveillance were anything like the boys who did the same job in London, they wouldn't have cared less: they'd have yawned and carried on with their card games.

He noticed the nervous eye contact between host and hostess. Alan Jenkins leant forward. 'Well, ladies and gentlemen, shall we dine?'

They shuffled through an archway for the next stage, their formal placing round a long, polished table – also standard issue – where Annie had laid out napkins, and Alan, with a flourish, produced a bottle of mediocre burgundy to wash down the compromise between an English school dinner and Eastern-bloc borscht-and-schnitzel that Party-trained cooks served British diplomats anywhere between Warsaw and Ulan Bator. Julian had seen it all before, and turned on his most unctuous charm, but all the time he was watching Harry, tense in his chair, responding monosyllabically to Mrs Colliers's chatter about hunts and hounds.

Oddly enough, it was this that gave Harry the opportunity to broach the location for their first assignation. Mrs Colliers, bored by him, turned to Julian and asked him whether he hunted, but before he could answer, Harry interrupted her. It was partly his deep, growling voice, partly surprise that he had spoken, but a sudden silence descended. 'Coincidentally,' he said, which told Julian that a message was coming, 'there is opportunity to go shooting in Peking. If you don't mind getting up before dawn, Mr Travers, I could take you with me next time I go. It's a bit of a drive but it's in one of the unrestricted areas. You wouldn't need a pass. We can borrow shotguns from the mission's armoury. The ducks rise at first light. I could pick you up from your hotel . . . If you're interested, that is.'

Julian sensed all eyes at the table were turned on him. 'I'd be delighted, Dr Airton. Thank you,' he said.

There was a burst of nervous laughter. 'Why, you're the privileged one, Travers,' said Colliers. 'Airton's never invited any of us to go shooting with him. You're a bit of a dark horse, aren't you, Airton? Wherever did you find a place to shoot in Peking?'

'Lu Gou Qiao,' said Harry. 'Marco Polo Bridge.' He reverted to his morose silence, and the conversation bubbled on.

He phoned next day, and at the end of a stilted conversation, they agreed to meet at four a.m. the following Sunday.

Harry drove Julian west down the long boulevard that intersected the city. He was a hulking shadow as he hunched over the wheel of his tiny, unheated Volga, peering ahead through the darkness. Chinese traffic regulations insisted that vehicles drove without headlights, but it was the custom for everyone to flash on their fog lamps, dazzling each other, whenever they sensed anything moving towards them – Julian supposed it was a hangover from the days long ago when they had expected Macarthur's bombing raids. It made for nerve-racking progress but Harry had picked up the technique. Meanwhile they kept up a bland conversation for the benefit of the bugs. It was all formal, surface stuff, as anybody would expect the conversation to be of two people who were getting to know each other.

After a while Harry turned south. The road was severely potholed and he had to negotiate his way past columns of trucks, parked for the night. The drivers, in padded army coats and batwing fur hats, were boiling up tea for themselves on little coal stoves in the pre-dawn chill. Sometimes they'd be hunched around them in the middle of the road, so Harry had to crawl in case he hit anybody. Julian's feet were almost numb with cold.

They arrived at Lu Gou Qiao in the half-light. There had been a heavy frost during the night, so at first Julian was only aware of white fields, shrouded in mist. He saw the huddle of a small Chinese village, with the broken remains of what had once been a surrounding wall and gateways. Almost hanging in the air was the shadowy outline of a bridge, with knobs on the balustrades, which turned out to be stone lions. It was uncannily beautiful in the dawn light.

Harry pulled the car to the side of the road. 'That's the Marco Polo Bridge,' he said. 'The place where the "Incident" happened. Japanese accused Chinese troops across the river of firing on them, and used it as their excuse to invade.'

'Before my time,' said Julian.

'The bridge is nearly a thousand years old.' Although he had turned off the engine, Harry kept his hands on the steering-wheel and was looking almost wistfully ahead. 'See those lions? Traders coming from the south would walk past them and know they were nearing the Great Khan's city. If Marco himself did come here, he'd have seen what we can see now.'

'Also before my time,' said Julian. 'Are we going shooting?'

'Aye.' Harry sighed. 'Let's get the guns.' When they were out of the car, he turned towards his colleague. In the dim light, Julian could make out weariness in his features. 'I love it here on mornings like this. It's the only place I've found that reminds me . . .' He shouldered both gun cases. A cartridge box hung from a strap round his neck. 'Follow me. There's a path that leads to the riverbed. It's steep so you may need your hands.'

For a while they walked in silence over the pebbles. Julian could hear the rushing sound of water to his right, which was presumably the river channel. Harry had said there were some lagoons and reeds ahead where they might spot duck. They passed under the great bridge. After about half a mile, light broke through the mist and they saw the pale red ball of the sun, rising in a tangerine sky.

'So, how's it going?' Julian asked eventually. They were holding their shotguns and keeping an eye open for any flights of duck, but neither man had come for the shooting. 'Garrard told me you were doing a good job on the hydropower side, that it's moving along.'

'Aye, slowly. Finally got a date for the GPR engineers to come. There are meetings scheduled for Christmas week at a research institute in Shanghai.'

'But no approach to you?'

'Not a sign.'

'You'd have signalled to me if there had been, wouldn't you?'

'Julian, I don't know what you're implying, but it's not been for want of trying. This isn't Hungary or Moscow. There are no *dachas* in the countryside where you can socialise with the comrades. It's formal meetings in conference rooms, arguing every point. Even when I spend the day in one of their institutes, and we break for lunch, my meal is served in one room and theirs in another. In the streets and restaurants, nobody talks to you in case they get packed off to a labour camp.'

'It'll come,' said Julian. 'In the meanwhile I gather you've been breaking hearts among the ladies.'

'I've made myself into a social outcast, actually. Garrard thinks I'm having a breakdown.'

'You're not taking it a bit too far? At the Jenkins party, you were behaving like a misanthrope – and what's this business about moving out of the diplomatic compound into a house of your own?'

He laughed. 'Partly to get away from all those legation women. They wanted to come round and mother me because I was all on my tod – or maybe because they wanted something else. If I'm going to be tumbling in the hay, I can do better than Doreen Colliers, thank you.'

'And the main reason?'

There was a flurry in the reeds, and two ducks flapped into the sky. Harry pulled his stock to his shoulder, and sighted, but he didn't pull the trigger. Instead he broke his gun over his arm, and ruminated for a while.

'I'm getting tired of waiting, Julian. I wanted to raise the stakes. Let the Chinese see how desperate I am. The outsider, hating his own kind. The depressive loner. Let them count the empty bottles I leave every morning in the alley. Don't worry – I pour half down the sink. And being alone in a courtyard house in the middle of Chinese town? It's a way of saying, 'Here I am. Come and get me. Make your play.' Not that anybody appears to be listening.'

Julian was not sure that this was what he wanted to hear. He knew the strain that could affect even the best agents when they were isolated in enemy territory. Perhaps, if it had been another sort of operation, and if it had not been Harry, he might have chosen this moment to send him away for a break, to Hong Kong perhaps, or Tokyo, but that was not an option. Things were finally moving on the GPR front. The worst thing he could do was criticise, or try to rein him in. So he said merely, 'That all sounds very sensible, Harry, as long as you don't overdo it. Remember, it's a subtle game we're playing.'

He heard a squawk. A covey of ducks had broken out of the mist and was flying almost directly above their heads. Harry had already snapped his shotgun shut and, in rapid succession, fired both barrels. One of the birds was winged and plummeted down in the direction of the river channel.

Harry was smiling. 'When it comes to it, I'll be subtle. Very subtle.' With his big hand, he patted him affectionately on the shoulder, then strode off to pick up his bird.

Somehow Julian wasn't reassured.

Shanghai, November 1962

Commissioner Hao, glad to shelve the responsibility, was content to let his junior handle the operation. Chen lost no time. The news that he had spent an hour alone with Kang Sheng and survived earned him prestige throughout the department, and this he used to have his way. He had no problems arranging for a message to be sent via the Foreign Ministry to the legation in London, and was easily able to persuade the ministries of Foreign Trade and Power Resources to make the hydroelectricity project a priority. More staff became attached to him as the operation grew, and the joke in the canteen, though never made to his face, was that he was inverting physics by running his own department inside the department, which was larger than the department itself. He put the manpower he had at his disposal to good use once the target arrived. He had them observe his activities on a twenty-four-hour basis, and after a few months he was satisfied that the Englishman's behaviour matched the character assessment.

Chen decided that the first phase of the operation would take place in Shanghai. He already knew whom he would use to bait the sexual trap. Kang Sheng had told him to find a *hei wu lei*, and as it happened there was a candidate in the Black Category who was ideal – in many ways. He had been careful to hide from Hao, and certainly from Kang Sheng, his personal interest in the operation. He was sure that the records in his Party file did not go back far enough to reveal the secrets of his early life. In fact, he had had the sense to fabricate his background at a time when the Communist Party had little wherewithal to check. He had known, even at the age of thirteen, that the aristocracy of the Revolution were those of proletarian origin, and opportunity had presented itself during an air-raid at the railway terminus in Wuxi. The boy cowering beside him had been killed. Quickly, Chen had rifled the corpse's pockets and discovered papers proving he had been the son of a mill worker. These he presented as his own when he arrived in Yan'an a few months later. His career had prospered ever since on the back of them. Yet for him the significance of this operation lay in the dark, hidden past that he had been at pains to cover up over the years.

He recalled the visit made by a certain Shanghai woman to the compound where his real father had worked as a cook. She had been the friend of his foreign masters and had humiliated him when she discovered that he, a lowly peasant boy, was playing with her infant daughter. He had never forgotten the look of scorn in her eyes as she snatched her baby out of his arms. He had not hurt the little girl, although she was crying. He had merely taken her into the shed because he had been curious to see how girls were different from boys – but the woman had reported him to his father's foreign master. For several days he had not been allowed near the main house, and his frightened father had punished him and told him to 'remember his place'. That girl was twenty-four now. Chen had kept tabs on her and on her mother, Professor Yu, who still taught English at Fudan University. He had always preserved the hope that he might one day get his own back on them for the insult.

If only he could do the same to the British family, who had humiliated him on more than one occasion, although they had sanctimoniously patronised him for many years, making him believe he was one of their family. They and their son had been directly responsible for all his subsequent sufferings, which he also kept secret, though not a day passed without him thinking about how he would exact his vengeance. Well, now the opportunity had come. By some miracle of Fate, all the various strands had come together. He could even justify what he was doing professionally, for the daughter perfectly fitted the profile he had devised for the woman who would be the instrument by which he would complete the primary task he had set himself, to bring about the ruin of the British scientist, whom – irony of ironies – the state itself had sanctioned him to destroy.

First he went back to Professor Yu's Party file to satisfy himself about her *hei wu lei* credentials. She had been thoroughly investigated during the Anti-rightist Campaign, and had made numerous self-criticisms. Irritatingly, several pages were missing at various crucial points of her life. Every detail of what she had been doing between 1925 and 1927 had been removed. Chen made enquiries as to why and never found a satisfactory answer, but such sloppiness was not unusual. He himself had been involved in interrogations during the period when denunciations were coming in so quickly that they were worked off their feet. It was perfectly possible for documents, taken home late at night for a struggle session next morning, to become inadvertently lost. It hardly mattered. She had once been the wife of a Kuomintang secret policeman. Her second husband, a professor, had been sent to the countryside after the Hundred Flowers Movement for criticising the government. That was more than enough to damn her.

He put the two women under surveillance to learn their habits, then chose an evening of the week when Professor Yu had no classes and both mother and daughter were at home.

Professor Yu opened the door. Clearly she did not remember him. She saw only his uniform and the armed men in the hall. She maintained an icy calm as they pushed past her, and watched disdainfully as they searched her small flat. When one pulled her daughter, in a nightgown, roughly out of her bedroom, her eyes narrowed and she bit her lip, but she said nothing, merely leaning on the stick supporting her crippled frame. After a moment, when she had satisfied herself that her daughter was not being harmed, she returned her contemptuous gaze to Chen. 'I suppose there is no point in my asking to see your warrant?' she said.

He grinned. She was a hard one, he realised. He would enjoy breaking her. He clapped his hands, and his policemen left the flat. He had only one remain, as sentry on the door. With a jut of his chin, he indicated mother and daughter should move to the study, where he followed, seating himself across the table from them. His next calculated shock was to show them his identity card from the Second Department. It meant nothing to Peng Ziwei, the daughter, who was hunched on her chair, wide-eyed and white-faced, but he could see from her mother's expression that she knew exactly what it represented and the power he wielded.

'I assume there is a purpose to this intimidation?' the mother asked him.

Without replying, Chen laid the papers, which contained the concocted new charges, on the table. They had the right seals and chops, so he was confident that Professor Yu at least would know they were official. Then he went through them point by point, outlining all the new evidence he was supposed to have discovered about her first and second husbands' crimes against the People of China and her complicity in them. The daughter whimpered occasionally and put her knuckles to her mouth, but Professor Yu listened stonily. He told her she would be formally arraigned before a People's Court, which would probably order the death penalty or at least a lifetime's imprisonment in a labour camp. The woman showed no emotion, merely asking when Chen had finished, 'Is that all?'

'Mama,' cried the girl, bursting into tears.

Professor Yu gave her a gentle smile. 'It's all right,' she murmured. She stretched out her good arm – the other was withered and hung loose in her sleeve – and patted the girl's hand, then tidied a loose strand of her own hair, as if she was composing herself for what was to come. 'It'll be all right, believe me.' She turned to her accuser. 'You do have more to say, don't you, now you've achieved your first objective of frightening us? If all you wanted to do was to arrest us, you'd have delegated it to the Public Security Bureau, but you've come yourself, an important official of the Second Department, because you want something from us.'

Chen laughed. She had not reacted as he'd expected. He wondered whether she had some intelligence background. She had read him like a true professional. Perhaps when he had been considering fabricating some espionage charge against her he had been closer to the mark than he'd thought. Still, it made the next part easier. He had always found it much more convenient to do business where there was mutual understanding.

But first he told her she should have no illusions. The documents were official and he had made no empty threat. He also reminded her that should she be condemned, and he assured her she would be, her daughter would also face punishment. In ordinary circumstances she would be sent to the countryside, but he would make certain that Ziwei faced far worse, in a *laogai* in the remotest, coldest province he could find. He was pleased to see the effect on both women. The daughter became hysterical and the mother's eyes narrowed with what he took to be rage. He rounded it off with a piece of theatre and pointed his finger accusingly as he shouted, 'Blood is on your hands, woman, and yours, Comrade Peng, for being the progeny of such a worthless scab.'

Chen had seen powerful Party officials wet their pants when subjected to this treatment, but Professor Yu glared at him, and told him he was repeating himself. 'You have chosen to rake up these long-buried cinders from my past for a reason. You don't have to demonstrate to me what you are capable of. For myself I don't care. You and your like have long ago perverted the revolution in which I once believed. This is not the society I fought to build in my youth. There, if it is treason you want, I've condemned myself with my own words. Go ahead. Have me shot. Do with me what you will. I will still never fear you – but your threats to my daughter are detestable and cruel. That is why I despise you, because you are prepared to use your power even to hurt the innocent if it helps you get what you want. Understand this. It is for my daughter's sake, not because you intimidate me, that I am prepared to agree to whatever you want me to do. Whom would you have me denounce? What new lie must I now utter? Who is the poor wretch whose life you want me to help you destroy? Tell me the name. Give me the document to sign.'

Chen enjoyed the tirade, but he had to maintain his position. 'You are a foolish woman,' he told her. 'Your own actions only demonstrated the justice of the charges against you. You can, however, be thankful that the Party is occasionally merciful even to counter revolutionaries. Yes, even those like you, if there are sincere signs that you are prepared to make amends.' He held up his hand to stop another interjection. 'I advise you to listen to me because your life and that of your daughter may depend on it. It so happens that there is a task in which your daughter – not you – can be of help. It will be an important task that will, if carried out successfully, help the Motherland protect itself against the imperialists who seek to do us harm. If Comrade Peng Ziwei is prepared to assist us, the charges against you might be dropped.'

Professor Yu spat in his face. She was shaking her fists as she screamed, 'She will only do so over my dead body!'

Chen smiled as he wiped his face with his handkerchief. Things were going very well. He watched with satisfaction as the daughter threw herself forward. 'Mama, please, please, listen to him.'

All he had to do now was remind Professor Yu for the last time that if she did not agree it certainly would be over her dead body, because he would see that she was executed for her previous and present treasons. He did not have to do anything else. Inevitably, the daughter pleaded with the mother, then told him she would do anything he wanted, as long as her mother was unharmed; and ultimately the mother did break down and weep. He even had the chance to smoke a cigarette before he judged that they had wrangled enough, and it was time to bring this satisfactory session to a close. The daughter had by then gained psychological dominance over the mother, as he had known she would, because it was his experience that you could always rely on people's finer feelings.

Next morning, punctually at nine o'clock, Peng Ziwei appeared at his office in the International Hotel. Standing by the window, looking down at the old racetrack, which was being turned into a park, he briefed her on what her mission involved, while she sat on a chair, hands in her lap, big eyes fixed on his. If she was shocked, she did not show it. He was impressed.

Of course, he did not tell her the whole background, merely that the operation concerned a dangerous foreign spy, whom they had to trap. 'In due course, your mother will have to be brought into the picture. Will she co-operate?'

'I will see to it,' she said submissively.

'Good. As for yourself, are you not a little alarmed by some of the unpleasant things I might require you to do?'

There was a long silence as she considered this. 'If it is important for the safety of our country,' she said, 'and to protect my mother, I am prepared to do anything. I – I am not a virgin.' She blushed becomingly.

Of course Chen had checked her background: he was aware of her two adolescent affairs with boys at her school, and the pathetic dalliance with a married man, one of the supervisors in the Textile Bureau, whom he had had transferred to Inner Mongolia, but he made her tell him about them in detail, not for titillation but because it was important for an operative in this kind of project to feel no lingering embarrassment about sex. Talking about it to a stranger was a first step.

Later, when he thought she was ready, he put her in the charge of a former prostitute, who taught her various alluring tricks of the profession, particularly the art of pretending to be a virgin. She hated that – he made sure that the sessions with the old harridan were intimate

– but he received satisfactory reports on her performance. He did not want to take it too far because her innocence would be her attraction. He was still hoping that the chemistry between her and the target would be natural.

That was only one part of her training. There were weeks of role-play with an actor from the film studio who stood in for the British scientist. This was to allow her to rehearse every stage of the operation. He had the sessions closely monitored by psychologists, who were expert at detecting any artificiality in her behaviour. He interspersed the operational lessons with hard ideological study courses. Of course it was fear for her mother that had impelled her to work for him, but now he had to persuade her that the cause for which she was sacrificing herself had virtue so that she would work willingly and effectively for him. His experience informed him this was quite easy to achieve with younger *hei wu leis*, who had grown up being persecuted and wanted only to prove their loyalty to the state that had rejected them. He did not care if she was a good Marxist or not. The point was to ensure that she believed she was. It was important to bolster her conviction that she was performing a patriotic duty.

He lied to her, naturally, and made her believe that, if she completed her mission successfully, he would intercede with the Party to have her and her mother's Black category status removed. The stick was necessary to ensure her initial dedication – it would be necessary with her mother throughout – but on the whole people worked better for carrots so he had no qualms about encouraging these illusions.

By the end of the year, he had everything in place, ready for the British engineers' arrival in Shanghai.

4

Old Friends

Shanghai, December 1962

A reception committee was waiting for them at the airport. Somebody had rolled out a mud-stained red carpet, which didn't quite reach the aircraft steps. In the icy wind that gusted over the runway four girls, wrapped in quilted army coats, were having difficulty controlling a flapping banner: 'WRAMLY WELCOME BIRTISH ENERGY EXPERTS TO SHANGHAI.' A photographer and his assistant hovered with an ancient box camera and a flash. Finally, a delegation of three old men, wearing thick navy blue coats and matching cotton caps, stepped forward and ceremoniously shook their hands. They introduced themselves as the deputy heads respectively of the Ministry of Machine Building Industry Shanghai Branch, the Shanghai Foreign Trade Commission and the Shanghai No. 16 Power Resources Institute. Without further ado, Harry and his charges were led to a waiting line of black sedans, and driven in convoy to their hotel.

The Cathay, renamed Peace after the Revolution, had been a luxurious Western hotel and in the old days the most famous building on the Shanghai Bund. Now the dark lobby dimly reflected its former art-deco glory. There was a bellhop in the creaky lift, wearing a white pillbox hat and brass-buttoned jacket, who greeted them incongruously in French. Each of the suites that awaited them had a spacious bedroom, a sitting room with leather armchairs and a writing desk, and a large dressing room, with a curtained-off section for the *amah*. In each bathroom there was a huge white porcelain tub, which the engineers gleefully identified as having been made by Shanks. The furnishings were musty and faded, and told of a different era.

They were served a sumptuous Chinese dinner in the old sprung-floor ballroom. Braithwaite, the senior of the three GPR men, sipped his third glass of beer, and sighed. 'Well, Harry my lad, I won't say this is being back in civilisation again, but it certainly beats bloody Peking. Don't you think so, Billy?'

Hudson, the commercial man in the team, nodded. 'Aye, Jack, nothing but the best for "Birtish experts who've been wramly welcomed".' They laughed uproariously, and even Tommy Gallagher, the willowy twenty-five-year-old technical wizard, who hardly ever spoke and rarely touched Chinese food, smiled as he dangled a second *xiao long* dumpling on his chopsticks, and pronounced it 'not half bad'.

After the meal, Harry stepped out for a walk to clear his head. He had some translations to check for the meeting in the morning. A dense fog was swirling sulphurously over the pavements. The street was deserted. There were no lights. Shadowy buildings towered gloomily above him.

He heard the chugging of an engine, the groan of a foghorn, and could dimly make out the tree-lined riverbank across the road. As he walked towards the Bund he had the strange feeling that he had been there before. On the aeroplane he had lent his *Nagel's Guide* to Braithwaite, and had half listened as the engineer regaled his companions with information about the Cathay Hotel: it was the most prestigious hotel in the Orient; Noël Coward had written *Brief Lives* in the Sassoon Suite . . . Now Harry wondered whether he himself had ever stayed there. There had been something faintly recognisable about the *amah*'s alcove. It was possible, he supposed. There had been family trips to Shanghai in his childhood.

He crossed a wide thoroughfare, also empty of traffic, and climbed some steps on to the esplanade. Looking back, he saw the silhouettes of monumental buildings curving into the haze. These had once been offices and banks, built when Shanghai had been a great mercantile city. As he gazed at the Corinthian pillars and the titanic blocks of masonry, which seemed to shiver in the swirling mist, he sensed that this was a city full of ghosts. He gazed at the shadowy buildings, comparing them with the cityscape that had been etched on his memory from the day he had stood on the deck of an ocean liner and waved goodbye for ever to his parents. Yes, his own ghosts haunted this city as well.

He froze as he heard the sound of footsteps, muffled at first, but becoming distinct as they tapped in his direction. There was purpose in their beat. It was almost a military step. This couldn't be some late-night promenader – most Chinese padded, and even soldiers wore cotton shoes. These were the clicks of leather soles. His first thought was that one of the engineers had come to look for him, but what emergency would have taken them away from their beer? He felt afraid, but of what he could not imagine. There were no rules against foreigners taking a stroll in an open city, and these were the steps of only one person. If, by any unlikely chance, the Chinese had discovered his secret role, they would come for him in a company ...

A figure was emerging through the mist. Short, stocky, like every-body else, in a padded coat. Was he raising an arm? Harry turned and forced himself to walk away at a steady pace. The footsteps behind him quickened. Ahead, he made out a lamp. There was a ferry terminal. There might be people. He walked faster. Then he heard a voice, not loud but urgent, and Harry stopped. Whoever it was had called his name in Chinese, but not in the form he used at the legation. In fact, only one person had called him by that name, and in that tone.

'Ha Li, stop, please. You'll give me a heart attack. I'm not so fit any more.' There was no mistaking the accent, and the panting laughter that seemed to bubble like the running water that had once trickled over the black rockface near a grotto, on a mountainside, among bamboo groves, so long ago.

He thought he was imagining things. He had been thinking of ghosts but he had not expected one to materialise.

His heart was pounding as he faced him in the half-light cast by the streetlamp. At first he felt insane relief. This squat, fattish, coughing man, with flushed cheeks, was a stranger, after all. He could be anybody – not the person whom, in a mad moment, he had conjured out of his imagination – but that feeling lasted only the seconds it took the man to raise his head and smile. Then Harry noticed the familiar eyebrows, slightly raised, one higher than the other, the squashed nose, the twisted tilt to the mouth that looked like a sneer until one saw the merriment in those protuberant eyes that even now appeared to be daring him into a prank for which he knew he would be punished. A man in his thirties stood in front of him – but Harry saw the boy he remembered.

'Chen Tao?' he whispered. He felt dizzy with shock and, above all, disbelief. Chen Tao was *dead*. He had betrayed him. How could he be standing there, large as life? 'Is it – is it really you?'

The eyebrows lifted comically, and the twisted smile widened. 'It's me,' he said.

Suddenly Harry felt like a little boy again: it was as if Chen Tao had played one of his clever tricks on the mountainside, ambushing him from a position he had never expected, leaving him helpless and abashed as he crowed, 'Fooled you, fooled you.'

For a long moment the two men observed each other. Harry's heart was pounding, and now that Chen had made his greeting, he appeared as overcome as Harry by the momentousness of the occasion. His expression had become solemn, and his eyes were flickering over Harry's features. 'Ha Li,' he murmured, 'you're so big, so tall.'

The voice was wondering and affectionate. He looked as he had on the day Harry had first seen him: wide-eyed and astonished as he watched a little foreign boy play with his wooden ducks. He recalled his friend's generosity afterwards, when he produced real ducklings, winning his friendship and his heart. Then Harry remembered the last time he had seen him, the desperate cry, 'Run, Ha Li, run,' and was overwhelmed with sorrow, remorse, and guilt that could never be washed away.

His eyes began to mist, and he found himself shaking.

'It's all right, Ha Li. It's me. It's really me.' Hesitantly Chen Tao stretched out his arms. In a moment the two men were embracing.

'I missed you, Chen Tao,' said Harry, clutching his friend's shoulder. 'God, I missed you.'

'I know, Ha Li. Me too.'

Then they were suddenly shy – grown men again, embarrassed by emotion. Chen Tao fumbled in his pocket for a packet of cigarettes. He took out two and offered one to Harry, who still felt shaken. 'I can't believe it's really you,' he said.

'It's me,' said Chen. 'I live in Shanghai now. I've been here, oh, eight years. It's not a bad place. Good food. Pretty women.'

It was ridiculous that they could be having a normal conversation. It seemed so anti-climactic. There were so many big things to discuss, a lifetime of guilt somehow to be absorbed, but Harry did not know where to start. Every illusion about his life appeared to have been challenged. 'I never thought I'd see you again,' was all he could manage. 'After the Japanese . . . I thought they'd . . .'

'Killed me, Ha Li?' said Chen, softly. A frown flitted over his brows. His voice quivered as he continued, 'No, the Aizi weren't so merciful as that.' Briefly, he closed his eyes, as if to erase a bad memory, but when he opened them, he was smiling again. 'It's all in the past, Ha Li. Forgotten. We should be talking about happy things, not sad.'

The brief bitterness in his tone had said it all, though, and Harry's guilt returned with double force. He remembered the beatings the Japanese had inflicted on their prisoners in the warehouse before his scream condemned his friend to a similar fate. What, then, had his friend experienced – *if he had survived*? 'Oh, Chen Tao, I'm sorry,' he said.

Chen laughed, and spoke with his old insouciance: 'Ha Li, it's past. Past. It's not important any more. Anyway, I escaped. You know me. I was a good Hong Huzi. So were you. We had great times in the mountains, didn't we? Do you remember how we scared the woodcutters? And the flags?' He shook his head. 'Blue, yellow and red. I'd forgotten them until now.'

'I've never forgotten,' said Harry.

Chen's cigarette sparked and crackled, even though it was a quality brand. Harry had noticed it had come from a packet of Presidents, the prestigious tobacco only smoked by senior cadres. It was second nature for him to observe that sort of thing now, like all the other little tricks of survival he had learnt in the Office's school. Now he watched as his friend crushed the stub under the leather sole of an expensive, hand-made Western brogue . . .

But he was not ready for those implications. Not yet.

Chen noticed that Harry had been watching him. 'Do you like my shoes?' he asked. 'Got them two years ago when I went to a trade fair in Milan.' He chuckled. 'None of us ate for a week. We were saving up our allowances to go shopping. We're not as rich here as you capitalists, Ha Li.'

'You appear to have done well for yourself.' Harry felt a deep sadness growing inside him. He did not want to ask what Chen Tao did. He wanted to preserve for a while longer the illusion that two old friends, by a miraculous coincidence, had bumped into each other on an empty riverbank in Shanghai.

A look of severity crossed Chen's features. 'It was never easy in China after you left, Ha Li. There was no more playing at being soldiers. I fought in real wars after I made my way to Yan'an. Many terrible things happened. Many great things too. Do you know how proud I was when I stood in Tiananmen Square on the first of October 1949 and Chairman Mao read out that we had become an independent republic? I cried. Yes, and I thought of you then, Ha Li, because all those dreams we had as children, you and I, when we pretended to be Hong Huzi, had been fulfilled.'

'And now?'

'China is becoming a great nation. We have made some mistakes but we are correcting them. The dreams are still being fulfilled.'

'And you're contributing, my old friend?' asked Harry. The insistent voice inside him could not be ignored. There was no room for co-incidence in the world of the spy.

'In my small way.' Those mischievous eyes flashed. 'But let us not talk politics. Not now, when we are fortuitously meeting again after so many long years.'

'Chen Tao, how – how did you find me?' Harry had to ask. The reunion of the heart was over, he recognised sadly. It was time for busi-ness – for business this must be: there were no fortuitous meetings like this in real life.

'That was easy. I was waiting in the lobby. I was going to try and catch you in your room. I thought you would have finished dinner, but I saw the doorman usher you out, so I followed you. I lost you in the fog.' He laughed. 'But I found you again.'

'No,' said Harry. 'How did you know I was in Shanghai?'

Chen was wearing a teasing expression. 'What if I said to you that I am the deputy Party secretary of the Shanghai Foreign Trade Commission? Would you believe me?'

'No, I don't think I would. That would be too . . . coincidental.'

Chen punched his arm. 'But it's true, Ha Li. Can you imagine what I felt when I saw your name on the list of negotiators who had come to discuss the hydropower project? I couldn't believe it. I still don't really believe that my old friend is in China, a famous scientist coming to negotiate with us for an important project. It was like a dream come true. If I were superstitious I would think it was Fate. Well, maybe it is,' he said, 'although as a good Communist I would have to call it Historical Inevitability.' His eyes were twinkling.

'You're involved in the hydropower project?'

'Ha Li, I'm leading it. When we come to commercial discussions, I will be the chief negotiator, just as you will be on the other side. That's why I came to warn you tonight, in case you recognised me tomorrow at your technical presentation, and said, 'I know you. You're my old friend, Chen Tao.' That would be a little compromising, Ha

Li, for both of us, perhaps. You and I, we must learn to be secretive again, as we were when we were Hong Huzis. Nobody must discover that we know each other. It will be our own undercover operation, Ha Li.'

'Undercover operation?' Harry repeated.

'Like when we tricked the Aizi long ago. We will give each other long, suspicious faces in the meetings, pretending we don't trust a word the other has said. And at the welcoming and return banquets, we will toast each other like strangers, drinking to eternal friendship and co-operation and all those other things we don't mean. Then, when your delegation has flown on to Guangzhou, you will stay an extra day or two because I will find a last-minute query in our memorandum of understanding. We will solve the problem quickly and be free to spend some time together so we can tell each other all the things that are in our hearts – everything we have wanted to say for so many years. Then we can be the United Front again. Do you remember? You the Nationalist, me the Communist. Still on different sides, but friends.'

Harry listened to Chen Tao's speech with a sinking heart. Suddenly he wished he was who he pretended to be: a civil servant posted to China, unsure of the realities here, a little naïve, overjoyed to be meeting again a friend he had thought lost. He would trust everything this plausible man was saying, persuade himself that the most unlikely coincidences do happen, and follow Chen's lead. They would meet furtively in whatever circumstances his old friend arranged. He would be very cautious, so as to compromise neither his friend nor himself. Even the naïve civil servant would know that it was not usual for a Chinese and a foreigner to have a personal relationship, that it was frowned upon, that it was even dangerous – but he would trust Chen Tao's instincts. And they would sit for hours, talking over old times, as private opportunity permitted, and the chasm that had been in his heart for twenty or more years would be filled.

And, of course, that was exactly what would happen. Harry would follow Chen Tao wherever it led him, because that had been his purpose in coming to China. It had been what he and Julian had planned for the last twelve years. He would be exactly the naïve civil servant that Chen thought him.

If it had been anybody else but Chen Tao, he thought, as tears welled in his eyes. He turned his face to the shadows, pretending he had heard a sound that had made him nervous. He didn't want the other man to see the tears. The bastards. Why did they have to use his old friend? But why wouldn't they? He had spent a decade leaving a trail for them and they had had plenty of time to bait a trap of their own.

There were still tears in his eyes when he faced his old playmate again, but they indicated only joy. Harry was smiling as he put his hands on Chen's shoulders. 'Oh, Chen Tao,' he said, 'you haven't changed in all these years. Of course I'll stay behind after the engineers go home, anything you say.'

Before he went up to his room Harry called in at the bar. Braithwaite and Hudson were drinking, while Gallagher was on his fourth plate of peanuts. It was exactly the scene he had left less than an hour ago, but now the homely picture of ordinary people enjoying themselves seemed to belong to a different period of his life. That short meeting on the Bund had changed Harry's world.

At his desk, he composed the message to send back to the legation, which included a code for the minister to pass on to Julian. He wondered if he should be feeling a sense of elation. After all, the game he and Julian had rehearsed was now afoot. Instead, he felt sad, weary and empty.

In the end he tore up the draft of the telegram, and threw it into the bin. It would be innocuous if any cleaner delivered the pieces to the Public Security Bureau next morning. All it had said was that the delegation was enjoying Shanghai. Nobody would know that that was code for 'First contact made'.

Something had stopped him sending it. He told himself there was no hurry. It wouldn't matter if he waited to report to Julian when he got back to Peking. Yet he knew that weak sentiment had stopped him, a self-deceiving desire that for a little while longer he could pretend – if only to himself – he had rediscovered a friend.

Chen Tao greeted Harry offhandedly when they arrived at the Institute, merely nodding with a disinterested handshake. He was no longer the nervy, irrepressible figure Harry had met the night before. He moved with languid dignity, his overcoat hanging loosely over his shoulders in the casual style Chinese leaders liked to adopt, while the professors from the Institute deferred sycophantically to him. His demeanour suggested a man who was comfortable with power.

He made a brief speech, welcoming foreign friends and stressing the importance of this project to Sino-British relations, then sat back and smoked a cigarette, allowing the director of the Institute to take over the proceedings, occasionally sipping his mug of tea. He did not look once at Harry. In fact, his eyes focused on a point somewhere above their heads. When the greeting formalities were over, the party moved down the corridor to the lecture room. This might have been a chance for casual conversation, but Chen ignored his foreign guests, walking ahead with the director of the Institute, who was murmuring in his ear. After perfunctorily acknowledging the clapping from the assembled professors and technicians, he sat down in his allotted place in the centre of the front row and lit another cigarette.

The director said a few words of introduction, then, glancing at Chen for approval, invited the British to commence their presentation. Jack Braithwaite was ready with his slide projector. The makeshift screen lit up with pictures of hydropower plants that GPR had built in Wales and Canada, followed by charts and technical drawings of pumps and generators.

When Tommy Gallagher introduced GPR's new heat-exchange process, the Chinese interpreter began to sweat. It had been clear all along that he was out of his depth, so Harry took over. As Gallagher chalked complicated equations on the blackboard, Harry tried to forget the squat figure swathed in cigarette smoke in the front row.

Over the next five days, Chen Tao joined in the sessions only occasionally. Once, when he was interrogating Braithwaite about some detail of the proposed energy savings, Harry was interpreting for him. There was a moment when he thought he saw the familiar twinkle in his friend's eyes – but he might have imagined it.

After a week they were ready to discuss the memorandum of understanding. Chen was present throughout as Harry, Hudson and the Chinese commercial team separated into a smaller meeting room to agree the wording. He was curt and business-like, as had been the other tough Chinese negotiators Harry had encountered in Peking. They ended up with a bland document, but Braithwaite had what he wanted: the Chinese side had invited the GPR delegation back to China to visit the hydropower station in one of the Yangtze gorges that had been chosen as the prototype for the new technology. All that was left was for Jack Braithwaite and the Institute director formally to sign the document at the banquet on the last evening, and for Harry and Chen to witness it on behalf of their respective governments.

They spent the day sightseeing. There was a river trip, a visit to a primary school, and a tour of the Shanghai movie studios where a revolutionary opera was being filmed. Pink-cheeked women soldiers, in khaki shorts and white stockings, put paid to evil capitalists, recognisable by their top hats and long papier-mâché noses, with a few balletic *kung-fu* kicks on *pointe*. The engineers found it hilarious.

They were in end-of-term spirit when they sat down to the banquet – Braithwaite and Hudson knocked back glasses of Maotai with enthusiasm – but the convivial atmosphere was chilled when Chen, who arrived late, took out the memorandum from his briefcase and laid it on the table. 'I am embarrassed,' he said. 'The Foreign Trade Commission has not approved the wording. They want you to take out the exclusivity and confidentiality clauses.'

Harry translated.

'Tell him we can't do that,' said Braithwaite. 'We're talking proprietary technology here. Anyway, they're standard terms.'

'I have already told my superiors that,' said Chen. 'They're considering the matter.'

'But we're flying to Canton first thing in the morning. Ask him how long they'll take to consider, Harry. We've already missed Christmas, so I suppose we could stay on a day or so if we have to – but bloody hell!'

'That would be inconvenient,' said Chen. 'The tickets are already booked.'

'What do you propose, then?' asked Harry. 'We can't go forward with the project without a memorandum of understanding.'

Chen appeared to consider. 'I believe the Commission will eventually agree,' he said. 'There would be no harm if the British engineers and the Institute were to sign the document first. It would not be valid until you and I countersigned – which would mean you might have to remain in Shanghai for a few days more. It would be easier, since you are a diplomat, to rearrange your ticket.'

'I could do that,' said Harry, trying to hide a smile. 'May I congratulate you on your inspired solution to our problem?'

Next morning Harry saw off the GPR team at the airport. On his return to the hotel there was a message for him from the Foreign Trade

Commission. A car would pick him up at two o'clock. Deputy Party Secretary Chen Tao was ready to sign the documents.

He spent the rest of the morning writing a note for the minister on the meetings, explaining why his return had been delayed. He said he was confident of a happy outcome in two days' time. He hesitated, then crossed that out, and wrote 'within three or four days'. Again he had an opportunity to insert a message for Julian. Again he decided to wait until he saw him in Peking.

It was sleeting when he left the hotel for the short walk to the white colonial style building at the end of the Bund where, in a huge garden compound, the British consulate had somehow been allowed to maintain its splendour. His courtesy call on the consul general, after he had handed his signal to the communications officer, developed into a full-blown curry lunch, then brandy and cigars in the drawing room, while the man's children shouted ecstatically as they watched the first snowflakes descend on the immaculate lawn. The homeliness was unreal, a world away from the espionage in which he was now, finally, engaged. He would have liked to stay longer, but twenty minutes before his meeting he made his excuses. As he stepped out into the snow, he remembered the Latin tag Julian liked to quote: 'Iacta alea est'. The die is cast. By two o'clock, he was back in the hotel lobby, ready for whatever might befall him.

He was surprised that the car drove him to the Institute, and that Chen Tao was not alone: the whole negotiating team was with him. So he's playing this formally, thought Harry. That reassured him. Chen was a professional: he was maintaining his cover for his own people's benefit as well as Harry's.

While everybody else in the auditorium clapped, Chen and Harry mounted the stage where a table had been set up for them. Chen did not glance in his direction as they each took a copy of the memorandum. He merely drew a fountain pen from his pocket and blew on the nib. They each signed and initialled one set, then exchanged documents for the other to countersign. Harry smiled inwardly when he saw Chen's illegible characters. They had not changed substantially since he had put his name on battle orders when they played games in the forest. He also noticed the thinly rolled piece of rice paper wedged against the binder. He put his hand over it as he scrawled his own signature, and transferred it discreetly to his pocket. Then Chen and he posed for a photograph, each holding a copy of the

110

memorandum. After a perfunctory handshake, Harry was shown out to the car.

Back in his hotel room, he unrolled the note: '7.00 o'clock. Xin Ya Restaurant, Nanjing Road. Top floor. Book through hotel.'

It was a well-chosen location, a prestigious restaurant open to foreigners. The hotel receptionist had not raised an eyebrow when Harry had asked him to telephone and make a booking. To be safe, he specified that it should be for one person. When he arrived, a waiter in a greasy white jacket led him up two flights of stairs to a floor of individual wooden cubicles in the traditional, and very discreet, Shanghai style. No doubt in the old days, thought Harry, when Shanghai had been a haunt of gangsters and a byword for decadence, this had been a place where tycoons had brought their mistresses.

The waiter led him to a compartment in the far corner, slightly separated from the other cubicles, and lifted the curtain. Chen Tao was already there, sitting at a table stacked with starter dishes, contemplatively sucking a chewy morsel of chicken's foot.

'Ha Li,' he said, 'sit down and eat. I couldn't wait. I'm starving. Anyway, I don't often get the chance to come to a restaurant like this. Since you're paying, I've ordered everything.'

'You haven't changed as far as your appetite's concerned.'

'Of course not. You haven't changed either, except that you've grown into a giant. But, Ha Li, how we both acted this last week! Were you impressed by how important I've become? There were times when I had to squeeze my balls to prevent myself laughing, especially when you were translating so solemnly. Don't we still make a good undercover team?'

'Are you sure it's safe for us to meet like this?' asked Harry. 'I mean, not for me – the legation would consider it quite a coup if they knew I was having dinner alone with such an important official. But isn't it compromising for you?'

Chen waved a chubby hand. 'This is Shanghai. Things are easier here than in Beijing. We're all still businessmen at heart, even though there's a new system of government that has us pretending we're not. Anyway, don't worry. I picked this restaurant because the manager owes me a favour. That waiter who brought you in is his cousin. Nobody will know we've met. China's not that different now from the old days, Ha Li. Know the right people, have the right back doors and you can

111

do anything.' He laughed. 'I've probably got more back doors than anybody in the city.'

'Now why does that not surprise me?'

'Ha Li, it's so good to see you. Now, come on, eat. We have all evening ahead of us. You and I are not children any more so we'll get very drunk together. I've ordered Wuliangye. It's the most expensive liquor in the house. Eat first, talk later, drink throughout. By the end of the evening, we will have told each other everything about ourselves, so all those years we've been apart will vanish.'

He poured the clear Five Grain spirit into two small glasses and handed one to Harry. 'Let us make our first toast. To brotherhood. Do you remember, in our grotto, when we cut our palms with your father's scalpel and mingled our blood?'

'How could I forget?' said Harry. The fiery liquid stung his throat.

'Your father was a good man, Ha Li, for a capitalist. He is the only one of you foreigners, except yourself, whom I have never viewed as an enemy. Here,' he said, pouring another glass. 'To your father, who saved my life.'

'When did he do that?' asked Harry, a warning bell ringing in his ear. 'Were you ill once? Did he operate on you? I can't remember.'

'No, Ha Li. He saved me from the Japanese. Or, rather, you did, because you raised the alarm. Your father went with mine to the Aizi headquarters and threatened the Japanese commandant. He said he would report what they were doing to the League of Nations unless they let me go. So they didn't beat me too much. He saved me. You saved me. It is a debt of thanks I can never repay. Later he gave my family money to take me to another part of China in case the Japanese remembered me.'

'I didn't know,' said Harry. This did not tally with his memory of what had happened. 'I thought you said you escaped?'

'That's how I escaped,' said Chen Tao, after only a fractional pause. 'I realise he sent you away, too, to protect you. But did he never tell you after the war? I've always wondered what became of him, and your kind mother, whether they got into trouble for helping us as they did. I hope they're both healthy now in their old age.'

'They're dead, Chen Tao. They died in Weixian, the Japanese prison camp for foreigners.'

Chen lowered his glass. 'Those Aizi,' he muttered. 'Bastards.' He shook his head, then looked at Harry, with a hint of a tear in his eye.

'I grieve when I hear that news, Ha Li, but we will still drink to your father and your mother. And to you and me, because now there is another thing we share. My parents died, too, when one of the Aizi aeroplanes bombed the village in Hebei where we were staying. That was when I went to Yan'an. Oh, Ha Li, we share so much. The Aizi made us both orphans. That makes it even more precious that we have discovered each other again. Here, *ganbei*! Cheers!'

Harry drank. He wanted to believe Chen, whose every gesture confirmed Harry's old memories of him, from his spontaneous tears to his bravura play-acting during the negotiations. But something jarred, and it had nothing to do with the game of spying that they were now playing. There were too many inconsistencies in his account of how he had escaped from the Japanese, a subject on which there was no reason to lie.

Yet in every other respect this was the old Chen Tao. And he realised, with concern, that he was responding to him as he would to his genuine friend. Perhaps it didn't matter. That was how he was meant to be responding, at least for now – but he was confused, and as the evening went on, and the Wuliangye flowed with their mutual reminiscences, his head became cloudier, and he realised he was speaking more and more from his heart. Even when he was lying, Chen drew out of him some of the truth. When he told Chen about Audrey, he related far more about how broken and betrayed he had felt than he had ever told Julian, and when Chen told him that he, too, had once been betrayed by a woman, he felt that sense of shared brotherhood that can only come when true friends reveal their innermost feelings to each other. The irony, he told himself, at some rational point in the evening, was that Julian would be delighted because everything he had said reinforced his cover, but he was alarmed that the renewed friendship was clouding his judgement and sense of purpose.

It was late, and they were the last guests in the restaurant. Only the waiter who had greeted him remained. Chen lurched back into the cubicle from the lavatory. He, too, was very drunk, or appeared to be. 'Ha Li,' he said, slurring the name, 'I have suddenly remembered something I wanted to do.'

'What's that?' Harry asked.

'I'm not going to tell you. It'll be a surprise.' He attempted to tap his nose and missed. 'Just be ready. Tomorrow afternoon. I'll get a message to you to tell you where to meet.' He looked anguished. 'You're – you're still going to be here tomorrow afternoon? You're not – not flying back to Beijing?'

'No, I'm here for two more days,' said Harry.

'Good, that's what I thought,' said Chen, cheerful again. 'Tomorrow afternoon, then. Two o'clock. I have a surprise for you.'

Harry was trying to make out the time on his watch but it was difficult because there seemed to be four minute hands. 'I think I must go to bed,' he said.

'Yes, so must I,' said Chen. 'I am a deputy Party secretary. I have responsibilities.' He uttered a long, coughing laugh.

'Here let me help you up,' said Harry.

'We will help each other,' said Chen, 'but – but you must go out into the street alone. We can't – we can't be seen, even though we're Hong Huzi and blood brothers.'

'Yes, we're Hong Huzi, old friend. Don't worry. I've got your arm.'

But the waiter in the greasy jacket had to help them both down the stairs. As Harry reeled down Nanjing Road, he turned, momentarily confused, having stumbled on the ice on the pavement. As he slipped he thought he saw a black sedan pull out of the shadows, and a figure – it looked like Chen's – open the door and slide in. That was strange, because he distinctly remembered him lurching off in the other direction towards a bus stop. A bus had arrived and when it left Chen had no longer been on the pavement. How could there be two Chen Taos?

Then he laughed. Of course there were two Chen Taos, just as there were two Harry Airtons. It was fated to be that way. It was . . . historical inevitability.

The next morning Harry dragged himself out of bed at twelve, soaked himself briefly in the tepid brown water that poured into his Shanks bath, shaved and dressed. He still felt filthy, although it had less to do with the sand from the polluted Suzhou Creek in the water system than the sour smell of the Wuliangye that emanated from his every pore. He made his way to the bar, drank two Bloody Marys, then forced himself to eat some fried rice mixed with scrambled egg. After that, he felt slightly more human, and tried to put into order some of his impressions of the night before.

After a while, he decided that his cold fear on waking had been misplaced. He had not given away anything substantial, merely played his part – rather well, he supposed. It had been encouraging that Chen Tao had brought the conversation round to women. Yes, they had talked about Audrey, and Chen had told him teasingly that a night with one of the nurses in the Shanghai Military Hospital would put him right. Some were rehabilitated prostitutes from the old days, and would still perform the old tricks for somebody senior enough, if you had the right *guanxi*. 'You go ahead,' Harry had said. 'I'd rather keep my job, thank you. If the legation found out I was playing around with a Chinese girl they'd have me straight back to London on a one-way ticket.'

There had been some positive political conversation too. Chen had talked about the economy, and how new policies were in place that would open up the country to Western technology. He had said how much he looked forward to working with Harry to build China into a world-class state through peaceful means. That was another tick in the box. If the senior trade man with whom he had spent a week nego-tiating had not talked about the hydro deal, Harry the science officer might have been suspicious. Harry the spy was also content: this was evidence that the Chinese had bought his cover.

As for his personal relationship with Chen, well . . . In future he would have to be more detached. Hangovers have a habit of helping you focus your mind, he thought, and in the cold light of day, his task seemed manageable. Or so he was thinking when a waiter came to his table to tell him there was a call for him.

It had been put through to the telephone in the kitchen, and it was difficult to hear above the yelling of the cooks, but Harry recognised the voice of the liaison man from the Foreign Trade Commission. He was calling on behalf of Deputy Party Secretary Chen, he said. Comrade Chen was concerned that it would be another day before Dr Airton could take his flight so he suggested he might like to use this extra time to visit the Cultural and Exhibition Hall where there happened to be a display of Polish power equipment that was not dissimilar to the machines currently being used in the Yangtze Gorges hydro stations. Would Dr Airton like the Commission to send a car and a guide for him? No, replied Harry, belatedly remembering Chen's last drunken remarks of the evening – something about a surprise. He would certainly follow his suggestion, but he could make his own way in a taxi.

He looked at his watch: half past one. His friend, he now remembered, had mentioned a time to meet: two o'clock. It would be tight, but he could make it.

The Cultural and Exhibition Hall had been modelled on Stalin's great Workers' Palace in Moscow, and had its like in almost every East European capital. Harry walked up the grand sweep of steps, under titanic pillars and sculptures of muscled Communist manhood wielding mattocks and pile-drivers, and stepped into a reverberating marble hall. He walked down a corridor festooned with portraits of Mao on one side and Soviet-style posters on the other (more muscles, more hammers and sickles) that pointed the way to the Exposition of Polish Scientific Achievement. The few exhibition stands in another hall contained some items of machinery, but none that Harry would ordinarily have crossed town to see. However, a milling crowd of green military greatcoats and cloth caps was besieging the hard-pressed Polish exhibitors, who were handing out leaflets and brochures.

Harry heard a familiar voice in his ear: 'They're not interested in the technology but the paper, Ha Li, which is better quality than ours. They take it to market to wrap the fish they buy.'

Chen was wearing opaque black spectacles. The fur collar of his greatcoat came up to his cap, making him almost unrecognisable. He had hardly spoken before he ducked aside, edging towards the northern entrance. Before he reached it, he turned into a narrow corridor and disappeared. Harry followed.

The corridor was empty. He felt his arm tugged from behind, and Chen pulled him into a doorway that led into another corridor with a door at the end to the outside. 'This way. It's a back entrance. I have a car there. Nobody will see us. Here.' He had picked up an enormous green army coat and a batwing fur hat from the floor. 'Squeeze into this as best you can. Tie the hat round your head, and take my sunglasses.' Harry did as he was told, and Chen appraised him humorously. 'Well, I suppose you could pass at a distance for a Shandong basketball player. They're giants like you are, but that long nose . . . You'd better hunch down in the car pretending you're asleep. That way at least you'll cover it. Don't want to give any traffic policemen the shock of their lives. You can have no idea how ridiculous you look.' He opened the door and peered briefly outside. 'Don't worry, Ha Li. You won't have to wear this disguise for long. Where we're going it'll be safe, I guarantee.'

'Where *are* we going?' asked Harry, as he crouched in the front seat of a little Volga, like his own, while Chen drove.

'I'm going to take you to see an old friend,' said Chen. 'No more questions, or you'll spoil the surprise.'

'I'm not sure this is a good idea. Anyway, what old friend? I think one is as much as I can take.'

'Come on, Ha Li, where's your spirit of adventure?'

Harry could barely see through the dark glasses and the hat that half covered his face as he leant forward pretending, as instructed, to be asleep, but he made out they were going north, and this was confirmed when they crossed the Suzhou Creek. He gave up trying to follow the route when Chen turned into a number of alleys that wound through low houses with tiled roofs. After about twenty-five minutes he pulled up in front of an eight-storey workers' apartment building. Over a brick wall there were trees and smarter, campus-like buildings beyond.

'Recognise where we are? I think you've been here before,' said Chen, smiling archly. 'That's Fudan University over there. Naturally, the person we're going to see didn't live in this building when you came here. She lived in a smarter block over the way. She had to move out during the Anti-rightist Campaign after her husband was compromised in the Hundred Flowers Movement. She denounced him, of course, and divorced him, and that's why they were lenient to her, but she is the wrong class, I'm afraid. *Hei wu lei*. Black Category, as most intellectuals are. Nevertheless, they still allow her to teach some English-literature classes, for special students, like diplomats, who have to go abroad. Do you still not know who I'm talking about?'

'I haven't the faintest idea,' said Harry, but a dim memory was stirring. There was only one person he could recall from his childhood who had lived in Shanghai. He had a sudden image of a severe, crippled woman, who had scared him, then given him a wooden tiger. He felt a little shocked. First Chen had materialised out of his past, now apparently it was the turn of his mother's friend who had given him the tiger, for that was who it must be. He had hardly thought of her in nearly thirty years, and had imagined she must be dead: little chance that she or her daughter could have survived the revolution, the Rectification and Anti-Rightist campaign and all the other horrific mass pogroms that Mao had imposed on his people in the interests of a classless society. Yet the Chinese intelligence services had dug her up too. He had the uncomfortable feeling that the opposition had penetrated his innermost thoughts. How could they know about her? Of course, she and her daughter had visited their hospital. Chen had met them and there had been some sort of row – but he was baffled by what game they were playing. Chen was explicable: he was a spy . . . but Auntie Yu – he had suddenly recalled her name – what had she to do with anything? If, indeed it was Auntie Yu to whom Chen was referring.

At the same time, he was becoming excited at the prospect of seeing her again. Now Chen had conjured back his memories, he wanted it to be her. He remembered how fond he had been of her and her daughter, what fun they had had when they had come to stay, and with the nostalgia came pain. Just thinking of her brought back images of his mother. She had been her best friend . . . He had to pull himself together, Harry realised. If their plan was to disorient him, they were certainly succeeding. He glanced at Chen, who was observing him with a cocked eyebrow.

'I think you *do* know who I'm talking about, Ha Li,' he said. 'I certainly remembered her when, a couple of years ago, I saw her crossing Nanjing Road. She's easily distinguishable. Artificial leg, withered arm – now do you know? She certainly made an impression on me when I was a child, that time she came to visit your mother at the hospital, she and her daughter. Do you really not remember? A baby whom someone locked in the chicken pen?'

Harry sighed. It was her. 'Yes, I do remember something of the sort. But why have you brought me here?'

'She was a friend of your mother, and of mine now,' said Chen. 'I thought you would want to meet her again. Don't you? We could turn back if you like.'

'No, Chen Tao, I'll see her, since you've brought me here,' said Harry. 'It was thoughtful of you. I'm grateful. You'd better remind me what she does, though. I don't remember her that well.'

Chen turned off the engine. 'She's a university professor and her name is Yu Fu-kuei. The daughter is Peng Ziwei, the child of Professor Yu's second husband, who was another professor at Fudan. He was the one the mother denounced. Her first husband died in the car accident that crippled her, but I think it was more than a car accident. If you look closely at her neck, you can see the scars of gunshot pellets. I think it was an assassination, relating to some murky gangster episode in the time of the warlords. A hit or a contract or something. All sorts of things happened in the old days in Shanghai. I did hear a rumour that she was married to a Nationalist policeman, so it's possible. No doubt it's all written up in her Party file, and maybe that's another reason she's been categorised as Black. But everyone in Shanghai has a story of some kind. I tend not to ask questions, except about people in my own department and that's only when I have to. "Live and let live" is my motto, when I can get away with it. Shall we go to her apartment? She's expecting us. Keep your disguise on until we get to the stairwell and then you can take it off. Her flat's on the ground floor.'

Chen got out of the car to check that nobody was about. At his signal Harry quickly crossed the yard, which was still covered in yellowish slush from the snowfall of the day before. Chen was already in the smelly concrete stairwell, banging on a metal door. He turned to Harry. 'Please take off that stupid hat and glasses. You'll terrify her, Ha Li. She'll think we're the secret police.'

A lock was turned, and the door opened a fraction. Chen Tao spoke in rapid Shanghainese, which Harry found difficult to follow. A woman's voice answered. The door closed again and Harry heard the rattle of a chain. With a creak of its hinges the door opened fully. A tiny grey-haired woman stood in the doorway, leaning on a stick. She was wearing smart white trousers, a green silk tunic, and, which amazed him, a string of pearls. 'Harry Airton, please do come in.' It was fluent, patrician English. 'You won't mind my calling you by your first name? I still think of you as Catherine's little boy.'

Harry remembered the smooth features, and the piercing eyes, which had not changed, after all these years. 'Madame Yu, I . . .' He was suddenly speechless.

'Madame?' She had a harsh laugh. 'You used to call me 'Auntie'. Come on, you'd better get in out of the cold. Not that my apartment, if you can call it that, is much warmer. I'm not in the position to entertain as I once used to.'

With difficulty she turned, dragging one leg behind her as she moved. Harry found himself rushing forward to assist her, but she waved him away. 'No, no, I've learnt how to look after myself. One has to nowadays. Anyway, with those big hands of yours, Harry, I'd be afraid you'd crush me. You're very tall, taller than Edmund was, though now I come to think of it, Catherine was tall for a woman. You're probably like her father, Henry Manners. I never met him, but I always heard he was powerfully built, like you. You probably inherit that black hair and dark, handsome look from him too. Quite the Heathcliff, aren't you? Come in. If you don't mind, we'll sit in my study where it's my self indulgence to keep a stove burning in the daytime.'

It was more a cubbyhole than a room, made smaller by the shelves that lined every wall. They were stacked with books, mostly in two layers, and nearly all were in English. Harry recognised the classics, and many writers he had heard of but never read: Marvell, Herrick, Webster, Tourneur, Marlowe. 'You're looking at my old friends,' she said. 'I hardly open them now – never teach them – but it is a comfort to me that they are there.'

They squeezed into the space between the table and the wall. Tea and cakes were already laid out. With her one good arm, she poured. 'I once studied English literature at Oxford. That was where I met your mother, when we were both students, long before we returned to China. She was at Somerville. I was at St Hugh's. Did your mother ever tell you that, Harry? No, I expect she never had a chance to. Poor Catherine. And you, poor boy, I often thought of you on the other side of the world, growing up among strangers. It would make your mother happy to see you now, tall and upstanding, successful, a diplomat – I think that is what Mr Chen said you were. I wish you had had a chance to know Catherine and Edmund properly, as an adult. You would have respected them, as well as loved them. They were good people. Honest, kind, above all principled.'

'I do remember them, Auntie, and I know how fine they were.' Harry was surprised. It was not the words she spoke in that rather harsh, didactic voice – a schoolteacher's voice – but something he sensed behind them. Hostility? Anger? Bitterness? He was not sure. Combined with the sensitive subject matter, so personal to him, this vague impression unnerved him. There was little warmth here.

'Of course you do. Why should you not? You must excuse me. Catherine was my closest friend and I become emotional when I think of her, especially now I am with her son. You know, the last time I saw her was on the day you left. She came to my flat that evening, all alone. I supposed it was to cry. We were very close and had no secrets. But she didn't cry much. She was heartbroken, of course, and probably even then she had a premonition of what would happen to her and Edmund, but, in that courageous manner of hers, she kept her self-control – rather better than I did, I think. And all she talked about was you. So many stories, about your adventures, mostly funny ones, so there was as much laughter as tears. I think she was trying to remember everything about you, as a way of holding you inside her, so you would always be with her. She told me how brave you had been, in your shorts and little overcoat, standing at the rail of the ship. She was very proud of you. You were the world to her. Above all, she kept repeating that you would be safe, and that was all that mattered. I'm sorry, this must be painful for you but, as her friend, I did want to tell you how much she loved you.'

'I think I knew that, Auntie,' said Harry, cautiously.

'Well, there is nothing stronger than a mother's love. Nothing.' She said this with intense passion – her voice even rose an octave – and Harry noticed that she was looking at Chen who gave no sign that he had understood anything of their English conversation. He was sipping his tea noisily and munching a piece of corn cake. Her eyes turned to Harry. They were like burning coals. 'There is no sacrifice – none – that a mother would not make for her child. For her son or her daughter. To make them safe. I – I wanted to tell you that, Harry,' she ended lamely, 'so you might understand.'

'I believe I do understand,' he said, but he was puzzled. Her over-emphasis indicated that there was a hidden message or significance in what she had said, but what it was he had no idea.

'Well, if you do, I'm glad,' she said. 'But I doubt you really do. Maybe you will remember my words in the future.'

Or perhaps she was just dotty, he thought. He recalled what Chen had told him. This was a woman who had denounced her husband. Friend or no friend of his mother, there was something chilly about her, and the eyes that appraised him were not those of a kindly aunt.

Chen Tao murmured something in Shanghainese. She responded shortly, then turned to Harry again. 'Mr Chen is asking where my daughter is. He wants this to be a complete family reunion. I told him he had to be patient. I sent Ziwei out to buy some biscuits, but she will be back shortly.'

'I think I remember her,' said Harry.

'Yes, you played with her as a little boy, although you were six years older than her. Your mother and I joked that one day you might make a fine couple. That's ironic, isn't it? But we are all pawns of history, are we not?'

121

Harry could not see any irony but he smiled politely. 'What does Ziwei do?' he asked.

'Despite her education, she's only a clerk in the Textile Bureau, where she translates English documents. Her talents are underemployed but, as Mr Chen has no doubt told you, she comes from the wrong class, so I suppose we should be grateful that she was given any job. It is her misfortune that she was not born a peasant, Harry.'

Perhaps that accounted for her bitterness, he thought. Professor Yu looked at him sardonically, a slight smile on her lips. 'There's no reason why *you* should be upset about it,' she said. 'We Chinese are content with our egalitarian society. I'm sure Mr Chen has told you that as well. Now, while we're waiting for my daughter to arrive, you had better tell me what you have been doing all these years. Mr Chen told me you were a scientist as well as a diplomat. Is that right?'

Harry began to explain, but her eyes kept flitting towards the door. The only one of them who seemed entirely at ease was Chen, who was smoking one of his Presidents. Harry noticed that Yu Fu-kuei's face had flickered momentarily in irritation as, without a word, she reached behind her for a saucer to serve as his ashtray. If Chen was one of her friends, she showed no sign of affection for him.

Harry was plodding painfully through a description of his duties at the Ministry of Power when they heard the click of the lock and the creak of the front door. He turned and saw a girl.

She was of medium height, taller than her mother, wriggling out of her army-style greatcoat. She was frowning as she balanced a bag of biscuits in one hand and struggled to shake the sleeve off the other arm. Harry's first impression was of elegance. She wore the same green tunic and baggy trousers as every Chinese, but they hung loosely on her, giving her a filly-like grace. His eyes were drawn, however, to the silver buckles on her shoes, and the pink ribbon with which she had tied her long hair into a braid. The simple adorments gave individuality to her uniform dress and, to Harry, emphasised her femininity more than if she had been wearing her mother's pearls.

The face, still flushed with the cold, was not that of a beauty. She had a snub nose, her cheeks were flat and faintly freckled, and there was a mole under her lower lip, but the wide brown eyes were attractive, and the dimples, when she adjusted her mouth into a nervous smile, were charming. She did not seem to know what to do with her delicately boned hands, which fluttered by her sides as she took a

gawky step into the study. To Harry, she seemed a picture of freshness and innocence – intelligence, too, which manifested itself in her
modest but direct appraisal of him.

He started, aware that he must have been staring at her. He was
also conscious that Yu Fu-kuei and Chen were looking at him, the one
with a wry, weary smile, the other with amused curiosity.

'She's a pretty thing, isn't she, Harry?' said her mother. 'Ziwei, this
is Harry Airton, the man Mr Chen has brought along for us to meet.
He is a diplomat, and very important, but you needn't be shy. You knew
each other when you were little. You were playmates,' she added acidly.

'I am very pleased to meet you,' said Ziwei, slowly, in correct but
heavily accented English. Hesitantly she stretched out her hand for
him to shake.

'And I you,' said Harry, taking it, noticing, as he did so, that Chen
was grinning again. 'Your mother was telling me about you,' he said,
'that you work in the Textile Bureau.' He was suddenly aware that he
was still holding her hand, and dropped it.

The girl looked amused. 'Yes, I am a translator,' she said. 'It – it is
an honour for me to meet you, Mr Airton. I have studied English, but
I have never met a real Englishman before.' It was said with such deliberation that it sounded like a rehearsed speech.

'He's not an Englishman. He's Scottish,' said her mother. 'You can
tell by his accent – it's not like his parents'. They spoke the King's
English.'

'It's the same,' said Harry, quickly, seeing Ziwei's alarm. 'The same
thing. Really it is. You haven't offended me.'

'I – I am happy that I have this chance to practise,' Ziwei continued
bravely. 'It will – it will help me with my work.' She turned quickly
and squeezed behind the table to sit next to her mother. Here she sat
demurely, although occasionally she raised her eyes to glance at Harry,
with what he thought was the same frank appraisal she had shown
when she had first come in. Although he tried to keep up a conversation with her waspish mother, he felt unaccountably uneasy.

'Ha Li.' Chen was smiling at him. 'I'm sorry to have to break up
this happy reunion, but I must get you back to the exhibition hall
before it closes. There will be more opportunities for you to meet
before you leave Shanghai. Why not extend a day or so? I can raise
another complication over the contract, or the timetable for our next
meeting.'

'I would like that, Ai Tun *Xiansheng*,' said Ziwei, suddenly, also in Mandarin. 'I would like to get to know you better.' From any other girl this might have sounded coquettish, but Harry saw, as she said it, her features transform into an eager, almost beseeching stare, and her wide eyes flicked towards Chen, as if seeking his approval.

Yu Fu-kuei was staring grimly at her daughter, but she turned and gave him a stony smile. 'Yes, Harry, we would love you to come again,' she said, 'at any time that Mr Chen considers convenient.'

And suddenly Harry knew what was happening, what lay behind all of Yu Fu-kuei's innuendo, her impassioned little statement about a mother's love, and her concern for the safety of her daughter. He realised how all too successful he and Julian had been, and how subtle had been the Chinese response, how ingeniously they had used his past to trap him.

He looked at Ziwei, so innocent, so natural, so attractive – so plausible – and somehow he kept his own broad smile as he told her mother that he would like nothing better.

On the aeroplane three days later, he wondered what Chen's next move would be. He had said in the car going back to the exhibition hall that he would be coming to Peking to report to the Foreign Ministry and to conduct further talks with Harry about the details of the spring visit to the Yangtze. He had indicated that he had ways, even in Peking, to meet Harry alone – but Harry could not see yet how he would involve Ziwei. On the drive back neither had mentioned her, of course, except for a sly little comment from Chen about the attractiveness of Shanghai women, but Harry had fobbed him off, as Chen had known he would. Harry had developed a respect for Chen's patient and devious method of operation.

Again, he had come up with ingenious schemes to get Harry alone. There had been another meal in the Xinya, this time with Yu Fu-kuei and her daughter in attendance. The mother had been bitter and silent, the girl shy, so Chen had led the conversation, recalling Harry's parents and how kind they had been to him as a boy, prompting Professor Yu, rather reluctantly, Harry thought, to describe how she had met his mother at Oxford – but he had paid little attention. He had been more interested in Ziwei. She had been wearing a grey cashmere sweater that emphasised the shape of her body. Her eyes had been shining when, occasionally, she smiled at him. As he sipped his beer, and nodded politely to the mother, he had been wondering what it would feel like to run his hands over the tactile material concealing the daughter's arm.

The next afternoon, Chen had taken him back to Fudan – again, disguised – but this time they did not go to Yu Fu-kuei's apartment. She and Ziwei were waiting at the gates of the campus, because it was Chen's idea that they go for a walk round the university park. Harry had made a pretence of being worried that they would be observed, but Chen had laughed and told him that anybody would think he was just an overseas fellow or a visiting East German professor. 'This is a university, Ha Li. Here, even big foreign devils like you can be invisible. It's safer than meeting in Professor Yu's flat. Believe me.'

On this occasion, Chen Tao made a fuss of helping the crippled Yu Fu-kuei, so Harry and Ziwei walked on ahead. Again, he felt her physical proximity – the soft, pink cheeks peeping from the collar of her greatcoat, the lustrous hair falling from her cap. She was natural and graceful, laughing shyly when he pressed her to tell him about her work as a translator, and blushing when he complimented her English. She asked him naïve questions about London: 'Is it foggy like it is in the Sherlock Holmes stories? Do English gentlemen really wear top hats and carry furled umbrellas to work?' It had been trivial conversation, but her artlessness was delightful in its way. Despite his reservations about her, he was warming to her. In fact, he liked her.

'I am very glad Mr Chen found you for us,' she told him. 'My mother has talked to me a great deal about your family and I feel I already know you. We are so cut off from the outside world. And it is good to meet an English – a Scotsman,' she corrected herself, with a smile. 'Sometimes when I read books about Britain and America I have wondered if the people who live there are really like the characters in Dickens or Melville.'

'I don't think I'm like any literary character,' he said. 'Just a dull civil servant. You must be very disappointed.'

She gave him a mischievous sideways glance. 'Mother said last night you were like your adventurous grandfather, a Heathcliff.'

He laughed. 'She said something like that to me too. Do you think I'm a Heathcliff?'

Her eyebrows furrowed as she observed him. 'No,' she said, after some consideration. 'I think you are more gentle.'

Immediately she blushed, and laughed to hide her embarrassment.

It was an attractive sound, like running water. She skipped ahead, and before Harry followed, he half turned, and saw Yu Fu-kuei's eyes glittering at him out of a stony face, and Chen's twisted smile.

Yes, Chen Tao would organise something, Harry thought, in his own time.

It pained him that Chen's friendship was a sham. Until the visit to Yu Fu-kuei's flat, he had allowed himself to preserve an illusion that the spy situation in which they found themselves was happening on a separate plane to their genuine childhood fondness for each other. It was an adult contest they were engaged in, but in essence no different from the games they had played on the mountain as boys. At the end of it there would be a winner and a loser, but their deeper friendship could be maintained. When Chen had introduced him to Ziwei, though, he had crossed a line, cynically manipulating Harry's most private feelings and loyalties, abusing his trust.

Yes, he had been shrewd. Ziwei was the ideal bait for the innocent diplomat Chen thought he was. The emotional foundations were already laid. Ziwei was no obvious siren, but she was something better: a childhood friend. Her gaucheness was certain to arouse Harry's instincts to protect her. He *had* been charmed by her – he could not deny it. His family's relationship with her family had primed him to be. If Harry the knowing spy was already attracted to her, then Harry the science officer would be head over heels.

Professionally it was a fair play – a brilliant one. In any case, Harry had no choice in the matter. This was the way the cards were stacked. He had no business to be hurt or aggrieved. He could not afford to allow his personal feelings to affect his judgement – but that was easier said than done. Chen had *made* this personal, and Harry was sure there was a reason behind it that went beyond the needs of a honey trap. It must go back to that incident with the Japanese, he thought: Chen wanted revenge. He was setting Harry up for the ultimate humiliation, for such it would be when Harry discovered that a girl he cherished from his most private past had betrayed him. This was no longer just a spy operation, Harry realised. It had become a personal vendetta, an emotional morass – and that complicated everything.

How on earth would he tell Julian?

He was amazed that in less than a fortnight he had moved from joy at rediscovering an old friend to something approaching hatred. The mischievous smile that Chen clicked on at every opportunity . . .

He loathed it now because he understood the hypocrisy behind it. He had been right all these years. The Chen Tao he had known as a child *was* dead, or as good as. He could no longer afford to feel affection, sorrow, even guilt – for this was an enemy seeking to destroy him.

But he felt enormously sad and empty. Leaning back in the seat, trying to ignore the elbow of the man beside him, who was indistinguishable in his green cloth cap and greatcoat from any of the other passengers sitting in cramped rows that stretched to the back of the plane, he felt a sudden hatred for this dull, uniform society, stripped of comfort, colour and human decency. Everything had become debased: love, loyalty, friendship . . .

He remembered Yu Fu-kuei's oblique warning when she had been talking about his parents: 'They were good people. Honest, kind, above all principled.' The words clanged in his head like a bell, and from a kirk on a far-away headland he seemed to hear another bell that had rung for a funeral with the same unforgiving rectitude as that of his dead uncle for whom it tolled. He could hear those same words in the whine of the aeroplane's engine, tugging at his soul, and another that knifed into his heart: 'Betrayal. Betrayal. Betrayal.'

And, mocking him through the dusty window, he could see ranges of mountain peaks rising out of layers of cloud as he flew over the China he had once loved.

5

The Cadres' Club

Peking, January 1963

They were a tedious three weeks for Julian as he waited for news. Most of the time he read old newspapers in the Xin Qiao Hotel. The Japanese reporters from the Kyodo news agency had asked him to spend Christmas with them, and on Boxing Day he accepted an invitation from the British Legation, who were organising a roast-chestnut party on the frozen lake at the Summer Palace. They followed it with a cricket match on the ice. That was mildly diverting – but all his thoughts were with Harry in Shanghai.

Three days before New Year, he was in the Banquet Hall at the Peking Hotel, pressing flesh with the foreign-affairs community who had gathered on the occasion of a state visit by the President of Ghana. This was the first time he had seen any of China's leaders in person, and he found Zhou Enlai, who was hosting the event, impressive. At one point the premier stopped briefly to chat to the Czech ambassador at his table, and Julian heard one of the famous 'Zhou-isms': 'How did my last meeting with Mr Khrushchev go?' he murmured. 'Not very well. He saw fit to criticise my landowner-class background, saying that his own was superior because his parents had been peasants. I was able to remind him that we had both, therefore, betrayed our class origins.'

Julian was laughing about this in the hall afterwards with one of the Tass reporters, a cynical bunch whom he assumed were all KGB operatives (he got on rather well with them) when Garrard tapped him on the shoulder. 'Travers,' he murmured, as he took him aside, 'about that problem of yours, perhaps you might like to call on me at the legation when it's convenient for you.'

So, Harry was back and wanted to meet him in the Wendy Room, Julian realised. He had been contacted.

He arrived at the legation late in the afternoon, just before it closed, and was shown up to Garrard's office. Garrard discussed Chinese politics politely while he waited for his staff to leave for the day. Only then did he take Julian to the Wendy Room. Harry was already there, reading a Chinese newspaper. Garrard left them to it.

Julian went to Harry's side of the table and shook his hand. 'Well done, Harry. After all these years, we've done it. You've done it. Congratulations.'

He had been expecting the younger man to respond in a similarly triumphant manner but he was morose as ever. 'Aye, Julian, I've been approached,' was all he said.

'Well, was she beautiful? Was she a Suzy Wong? Who was she?'

'It was a he, Julian,' he muttered. 'Fellow who's leading the GPR negotiations. Goes by the name of Chen Tao.'

Julian noted it.

'When we first met him, he appeared to be the typical, stand-offish senior cadre. Deputy Party secretary of the Shanghai Foreign Trade Commission. He seemed genuine enough. Arrogant as hell. All the professors in the Institute grovelled to him. Hardly spoke to us directly. It was only at the end, when he raised a foolish point in the memorandum that forced me to stay behind in Shanghai for a few days, that I suspected something was fishy about him, especially as the issue was resolved the very next day as soon as the engineers had left. There was a signing ceremony at the Institute. He didn't approach me even when we had our photograph taken with the memorandum.'

'There's a photo of him? Good. Do you have a copy?'

'No, but you can probably get one from GPR. They said they'd send all the photos to them via their legation in London.'

'It would be useful to have a mugshot. Go on.'

'Next thing I know he's arranged for me to have dinner with him.'

'He sent you an invitation? Come round to my place for a chat?'

'No, it was all very deniable. Later he explained to me he had to keep up the pretence in front of his own people. That was why he hadn't said anything to me at the Institute. He never communicated with me directly. Everything was done through oblique messages. When I got back to the hotel I found a note in my room saying that my booking at the Xin Ya restaurant had been confirmed for that evening. Since I hadn't made any such booking, I was naturally intrigued and went along. Didn't know whom to expect, but when I was shown into this private room at the top, there he was.'

'You mean this was a one-to-one in a public restaurant? Wasn't that compromising for you both?'

'He said it was safe because only the waiter would have seen us together and he was a friend. He was very relaxed. No longer the haughty cadre.'

'What reason did he give for this? As a science officer, the form would have been for you to turn right round, diplomatic rules, and report the matter to the consulate. Surely he'd have known that. Hope you stood on your high horse for a while.'

'Oh, aye, I went through the motions, but he just asked quietly, didn't I recognise him? Then he came out with it. Said he was a child-hood friend from Shandong days. He'd recognised me in the meetings, and wanted to renew acquaintance.'

Julian laughed. 'The old long-lost-friend ploy? Well, well. They've obviously been doing their research on you, my lad.'

'Julian, he knew everything about me. What my father did, what my mother did, what the hospital looked like. He knew the name of our dog, which I'd forgotten until he reminded me. And, what's more, I did have a friend once called Chen Tao. He was our cook's son. It didn't occur to me to make the connection during the presentations. Chen Tao's a common enough name. And there was nothing about his features that I remembered. But he was saying he was the same Chen Tao I'd known as a boy. Told me some elaborate story about what he'd been doing in China since I left, which was how he came to be where he was now.' The bitterness in Harry's voice was startling.

'You'll have to give me the detail.'

'I will. No doubt it's a pack of lies, but it was very plausible. They've done their homework, Julian. I feel soiled.'

'Now, now, Harry. All's fair, especially in our world. You're not saying this really was your old friend, are you? Childhood memories can be fuzzy.'

'That's what this man was banking on. He had every reason to think I'd be confused – but, Julian, this man wasn't Chen Tao. The Japanese killed him after some childish prank that offended them. Do you think I wouldn't remember that – even though I was only ten? He was my best friend.'

'How did this man explain it, then?'

'Oh, he was boasting about how he had escaped and run away to the countryside. Plausible again, but not true.'

'How do you know?'

Julian saw Harry's fists were clenched. His tone was venomous as he said, 'Because my parents told me he was dead, Julian. That's not something you forget.'

He must have seen Julian's shocked expression, because he immediately apologised. 'I'm sorry. It upsets me. It's a memory I'd buried. It's – it's been somewhat of a strain, the last few days. It was difficult pretending that this man was someone who had been so dear to me.'

Julian felt for him. He was also a little surprised. An agent-handler likes to think he knows everything about his Johnny, but inevitably there are secret places in a man's soul that he can never penetrate, especially with somebody as complicated as Harry. He had not meant to probe or upset him. He had merely fallen back into debriefing mode, because it was important for him to understand everything about this first approach to Harry by the opposition. 'But you did pretend?' he said. 'You went along with him and accepted that he was who he said he was?'

'Of course I didn't roll over quickly or he'd have suspected me. I made a point of being suspicious. I think it was when he mentioned the dog that I allowed myself to become convinced.'

'Then it became a joyful reunion?'

'Yes, lots of reminiscences between the many toasts.'

'OK, you can fill me in later on what he told you. What did he ask about the present you? Did he let slip he knew anything about you – your nuclear background, for example?'

'No, he was careful about that. Although we got quite drunk, he still maintained the impression that he was a foreign-trade man, and took my role as science officer seconded from the Ministry of Power at face value. At first we talked about our professional lives, then we got on to our personal histories. I gave him Audrey, broken heart and all . . .'

'Did he pursue it?'

'Suggested I find a nice Shanghai girl to cheer me up, but that was banter. The evening ended reasonably early and we agreed to meet next day, a bit of cloak-and-dagger at the exhibition hall. He'd fixed it so we could slip out of a back entrance where he had a waiting car.'

'Where did he take you?'

'To tea with a university professor at Fudan. This was also part of the Memory Lane experience. He told me this woman had been a friend of my mother.'

'Name?'

Julian noted a slight hesitation.

'She was a professor of English literature called Yu Fu-kuei and she had a daughter, Peng Ziwei, with whom I'd apparently played as a child. Before you ask any more penetrating questions, I didn't remember them but again I played along.'

'But you might have known them?'

'Aye. The professor talked about my mother convincingly, but there was nothing I didn't know or anything she couldn't have found out from other sources. I think the mother and daughter were genuine as far as it went. The place was full of English literature and they both spoke English, the mother fluently. I think they must have been who they said they were. They were both afraid of Chen, although they tried to hide it. Probably he'd forced them to go through this whole act with me. I think it was more cover-building for him, evidence that he's an old family friend. The sting, whatever it is, will come later.'

'You don't think Peng Ziwei was bait?'

Harry laughed. 'She was no Mata Hari, Julian. Charming in her way. Innocent, a bit naïve. Practised her English on me. Hope they can do better than that for a honey trap.'

'Perhaps they've calculated that innocence will appeal to you?'

'I suppose it's possible, but there were no signs that she was being made available to me.'

'None you might have missed?'

'Possible again, I suppose, but she's in Shanghai. I'm here. Next time I meet Chen will be in Peking in a month or so, and in spring we all go to Sichuan to see a hydropower plant. I suspect they'll try something here. That would be more logical.'

'So it's still wait-and-see?'

'I'm afraid so.'

Julian looked at him searchingly. 'There's nothing else you'd like to tell me? You were in Shanghai for some time. There was only this one meeting with the professor and her un-Mata-Hari-like daughter?'

'Yes, only the once. I can go into everything in more detail for the report – but I've covered the main points.'

Julian frowned. Harry was holding something back – but, then, he always had. He was still the thoroughbred to be kept on a long rein. It was nerves, he decided, reaction to his first real encounter with the enemy. Even though it had been predictable, it must have been something of a shock that the opposition had so cleverly played on his childhood memories. It would come out in the wash. Julian could be patient. Harry had handled things well up to now. All that was required was a bit of the agent-handler's equivalent of tender loving care so Harry would be in shape for the next round, when this Chen Tao came to Peking.

'Good,' he said. 'We'd better start coding a signal to London, then.'

That night, Harry sat in his armchair in his *hutong* house trying to drink away his demons, but even the half-bottle of whisky he had consumed when he returned from the legation had not assuaged his guilt for having lied to Julian.

It was the first time he had ever deceived him. It was not the risk that he might be found out – it was highly unlikely that Western intelligence had any records of a Chen Tao they could trace back to Shandong, and even if they did, it would take time for Julian to get hold of them, by which time the honey trap would be over, Harry would be 'turned' and any irregularities in the way he had achieved the objective would not matter. What troubled him was that this was the first time he had ever deceived the mentor who trusted him. Even now he was half tempted to arrange another meeting, at the river or in the park, so that he could confess his disloyalty – but he dismissed that idea as even more irresponsible. It had been his sense of responsibility that had caused him to lie in the first place, and his loyalty, for that matter. The long and short of it was that the Chinese had raised the stakes far beyond what either he or Julian had anticipated and, he believed, only he was capable of dealing with it.

The problem was Chen, and that Harry's so-called friend was playing a private game.

He had gone over it again and again, trying to put aside any emotion, and his dislike for the man, but the inconsistency remained: Chen's revelation that Harry's father had saved him from the Japanese did not ring true. He had thought long and hard about it, dredging his memory. It was plausible enough and, Harry admitted to himself, childhood memories could be faulty. His father had driven off with Chen's father and it might very well have been to plead with the Japanese . . . but there had been that false note in Chen's tone, a fractional shift in his expression, when he had said it. Moreover, it did not tally with what Harry had believed was genuine bitterness when he had broached the subject during their initial meeting on the Bund and Chen had steered the conversation to happier childhood times. 'The Japanese weren't so merciful as that,' he had said, which implied more than a couple of days in a lockup and a convenient release. Besides, it didn't tally with what Harry knew in his gut to be true.

It had come back to him, as he lay sleepless in his house in Peking on the night he returned from Shanghai. He remembered the conversation that his mother and father had had on the night after the incident, when he had crept downstairs and heard the terrible words that had heralded his own exile and everything that had happened to him since: *'Chen Tao's dead or disappeared, which amounts to the same thing ... we must face it, darling. It's time.'*

So Chen *had* lied – and about something there was no reason to lie about. He had somehow got away from the Japanese. Harry's father had *not* helped him. So why had he said it? The more Harry thought about it, the more baffling it became – and the more he was convinced that psychological undercurrents were in play that had nothing to do with the intelligence operation.

That afternoon, when Julian had come to the legation to debrief him, Harry had still been in a quandary about what to tell him. He had made his decision as soon as he saw the boyish excitement on his superior's face. Suddenly he knew there was no way Julian would be able to handle the truth. How could he tell him that the Chen Tao mounting the operation against them really was his childhood friend? He would think that Harry was losing his grip; such coincidences did not happen in the intelligence world. Even if Julian had believed it, he would have become alarmed at the potential instability of his agent under the stress of having to deal with a real childhood friend, the conflict of interest, even ultimate disloyalty. He might have pulled the operation.

And if he had told Julian Chen's true identity he would have risked losing the chance to make his decision about Ziwei. Julian would not give a damn whether Ziwei was an innocent or not: when it came to operational matters he was as amoral as Chen. But Harry had made a promise, tacit though it had been, to Yu Fu-kuei to look after her daughter. Whether he would honour it depended on what he decided about Ziwei – and he could not make up his mind. Was she innocent dupe or eager accomplice? He did not know, but he wanted to keep his options open. And he liked her, dammit. He could not get her laughing face out of his mind. He had thought again and again of her arm under the soft cashmere and how he had wanted to touch it. This was going to be far more difficult than he or Julian had ever anticipated.

He told himself he would have two more whiskies before he poured away the rest of the bottle. When he stepped out into his courtyard to deposit it in the dustbin, he found that his slippered feet were crushing fresh snow, although through the branches of the old acacia tree he saw a clear winter sky and sparkling constellations of stars.

He stood there, empty bottle in hand, staring at Orion and the Great Bear. He remembered that some of the first Europeans to come to China, the Jesuits led by Matteo Ricci, had been welcomed by the Chinese primarily as wise astronomers. The Chinese had looked to them to provide them with the secrets of the heavens and the universe. Had anything changed? The whole point of the operation on which he and Julian had laboured all these years was to convince the Chinese that he, too, could help them unlock secrets of the universe, in his case nuclear ones. The Jesuits had gulled the Chinese with phoney astrology as a hook to bring the Mandarinate to the Church. Harry and Julian were also offering fool's gold so that they could come away with China's secrets. The Jesuits had ultimately failed. So had every other Western endeavour in China. What a history, based on deceit and exploitation by all sides – and at what price? Betrayal and more betrayal.

Chen Tao's original plan had been to use Ha Li's courtyard house for the next stage, but on consideration he had realised this would be inappropriate. There were too many neighbours, and his surveillance team had informed him that on at least one occasion a colleague from the legation had come to call unexpectedly. There was also the difficulty of getting their equipment in because the British occasionally swept diplomats' residences for bugs, and the specialist devices he wanted to use were not the sort that were easily made undetectable.

For all these reasons, he had to persuade Comrade Hao to let him use one of the safe-houses the Foreign Ministry maintained for the entertainment of African government officials. They had the advantage of being geared up already for this sort of operation. Much of China's diplomacy consisted of providing beer and women to tin-pot dictators in attempting to cultivate the hearts and minds of the Third World. They were careful not to use Chinese girls but imported North Korean ones, assuming, probably correctly, that the Africans would not be able to tell the difference. Comrade Hao was at his most tediously bureaucratic, saying that this was not in the plan authorised by the Politburo. Chen spent two days persuading him that he would not get into trouble, and eventually Hao agreed to talk to his contacts.

When all was ready, Chen arranged for Ziwei to be flown up from Shanghai. He had timed his formal appointment with Ha Li for two days ahead of the Spring Festival. The day before the meeting was to take place he had one of his men slip a note into Ha Li's letterbox when he knew he was cycling home. Again, he had picked a restaurant with discreet private rooms.

'Ha Li,' he greeted him, when the big man stumbled in. 'You see? I have back doors in Beijing as well! We will be as safe and private here as we were the last time.'

Ha Li looked nervous. 'Can you be sure of that? What if one of my colleagues spots me?'

Chen was amused. His men had sealed off the whole block in preparation for this assignation. But he pretended to take him seriously, and promised Ha Li that he would find a safer place to meet in future, where nobody from his legation would ever see him. 'But for now, don't worry,' he said, pouring the Wuliangye. 'By the way, I have another surprise for you.'

'Not another old professor, please,' he said. 'I'm still recovering from the last surprise.'

'Which you thoroughly enjoyed,' said Chen, smiling.

'Yes, I did,' he said. 'Professor Yu was charming.'

'And her daughter? Did you find her charming too?'

She was an intelligent young thing, he said, then blushed and blathered on for a while about how she must have inherited her mother's intellect.

Oh, Ha Li, Chen thought, you are so transparent. 'I'm glad you liked her,' he said. 'I did too. I thought at the time that she was probably wasted in the Textile Bureau, so when I received a letter from her mother asking me whether I could give Ziwei a post in the Foreign Trade Commission, I was inclined to consider the request positively.

Of course, her class background was a problem, but I managed to get her a job in my secretariat as a translator.'

'That was kind of you,' said Ha Li.

'I thought you might be pleased.' Chen selected a morsel of mutton and chewed it slowly to demonstrate how insignificant he considered the matter. 'Actually, you'll see her at tomorrow's meeting. The interpreter we normally use is ill, so why not give her a chance to show her skills?'

Ha Li was now going through a similar rigmarole with his food.

'I'll tell you what,' Chen said, as if he had suddenly thought of it, 'I had been planning to spend a few more days in Beijing after the talks. Everything will be closed for the Spring Festival and I thought I would see some of the sights. I might try to persuade Ziwei to stay too. Perhaps one evening we could all get together to talk about old times.'

'Meeting again in a restaurant like this would be too much of a risk,' said Ha Li. But he looked wistful.

That was the moment for Chen's second brainwave. 'I know just the place. It's a sort of Cadres' Club, very discreet. Nobody will be using it over the holiday, and the few attendants will be no problem. It's the sort of place where nobody sees anything. Not even a big hairy foreign devil like you.'

They had three days of meetings in the Power Resources Ministry. Chen played his aloof Party secretary role, deliberately making things difficult for Ha Li the British diplomat, who also acted his part conscientiously, having been trained in Shanghai not to recognise him on this sort of occasion. Chen had made the same stricture about Ziwei. Since Ha Li spoke fluent Chinese there was no need for her to interpret, but Chen made sure she was sitting at the end of the line of Chinese negotiators, eyes focused on the tabletop. Ha Li made brave attempts to ignore her, but Chen noticed him steal a meditative glance at her. On the fourth day Chen expressed his satisfaction with GPR's proposal and quickly agreed the details of the coming visit.

On the night he had chosen, he picked Ha Li up in a dark-tinted sedan on a little-frequented side road off Nan Chizi. He had him sit in the back with Ziwei while he drove, and observed happily in the rear-view mirror how nervous they were of each other, squeezed up to the window at opposite ends of the seat. When they passed over the bridge between Bei Hai and Zhong Nan Hai, Ziwei, as primed, cooed excitedly at the lantern displays scattered round the shore of the lake. This gave Ha Li an opportunity to lean over her to look, and inevitably their bodies brushed together. Chen had wanted them to have physical contact, however slight, before the evening began.

The room he had selected was decorated in the Western style, with big leather armchairs and a roaring fire. He had placed discreetly erotic paintings on the wood-panelled walls, but they all made a point of not noticing them, and Chen had closed the door that gaped into the next room – but not before Ha Li had observed the big four-poster bed with its red sheets turned down. Then he made a great show of opening the Russian champagne in the bucket on the coffee-table. He could have provided French, but he thought that might have made even Ha Li suspicious.

Ziwei sat on the edge of her chair, as awkward as he could have hoped, and went through a coy pretence of refusing her glass, saying she did not drink, so Chen became jovial and tried to force her, until Ha Li, irritated but attempting to laugh, told him not to push the poor girl. He was almost as bashful as she was, but Chen continued to be hearty, getting him to toast this and that, telling Ziwei long, humorous stories about the games Ha Li and he used to play as boys.

Eventually the waiter came in to ask if dinner should be served. Chen looked at his watch. 'I apologise,' he said, 'but the Party secretary of the Commission has just arrived back in Shanghai from a business trip abroad and wants me to report to him on the course of our discussions. We booked a telephone call for half past seven so I must hurry. I'm sure it won't take long so you two start without me and I'll return as soon as I can.' He left them and went down the hall to the room in which his assistant was waiting with the tapes and headphones.

They eyed each other nervously, with cautious little smiles. It was Ziwei who spoke first. 'Those were interesting stories, Ai Tun Xiansheng.'

'Call me Ha Li, please,' he said, thinking how inappropriately innocent she looked in this garish setting.

'You must have had great pleasure living in the countryside as little boys. I – I have never been to the countryside, Ha Li. I – I am looking

forward to the engineering visit to the Yangtze Gorges. I hear the
mountains there are very beautiful.'

'You're coming with us, Ziwei? I didn't know,' said Harry. He felt
a stir of excitement in his stomach. He told himself that this was
because he now had confirmation of how and where the honey trap
would take place. Yet all he was aware of were her knees, so close to
his own.

'Deputy Party Secretary Chen Tao said he would consider allowing
me to come if he thinks my work has been adequate. It will be a great
privilege – it is already a great privilege – to be allowed to assist in
such an important project.'

'I think your work has been more than adequate,' said Harry. He
had to remind himself that this was a professional siren, even now
playing a part. 'On the last day you made some very good translations of the memorandum. I will speak to Chen Tao, if you like, and
tell him how capable you are.'

'Oh, no, that would not be appropriate,' she said, 'but you are very
kind.' She gave him a touching little smile of gratitude. 'Ha Li, may
I ask you something? Are you really such a good friend of Chen Tao?'

Harry had not expected this approach. 'Of course,' he said. 'He's
my oldest friend. Why do you ask?'

'It is not my place, perhaps, to say this, but I thought when Comrade
Chen was telling those stories he was often disparaging about you. All
his stories were really jokes about how clumsy you had been – and I
thought it was a little unfair. I'm sorry,' she added quickly, and her
cheeks reddened. 'I have offended you. I have never spoken like this
alone to a foreigner before, but it is you, not Comrade Chen, who is
really our old family friend – and I would have liked him to treat you
with respect.'

Well, well, thought Harry. What a clever line to take. Complicity
as a path to intimacy, making Chen the outsider and potential threat.
Or did she mean it? Looking into her earnest eyes he could not be
sure. 'That's sweet of you, Ziwei,' he replied cautiously, 'but I'm sure
Chen Tao intended only to amuse us. We've always had a relationship
based on challenging each other. That's what boyhood friendships are
like. Really, underneath, we're very good friends, as – as I'd like to be
with you and your mother. In fact, it may seem strange but I feel we
already are.'

'Yes, it is strange,' she said. 'I was scared of meeting you at first.

You know that in our country we are trained not to trust foreigners whom we think are imperialists and conspiring against us, especially diplomats – but at my mother's house you seemed so kind and ordinary.'

'Ordinary?' Harry laughed. 'Thank you very much.'

'I have offended you again,' she said, seeming flustered. 'I'm so clumsy. I meant it to have a good meaning. Really I did.' She reached out a hand and touched the back of Harry's, then snatched it back.

'I know you did,' said Harry, again taken off guard. 'I should apologise. I was teasing you. And it's true too. I am very ordinary.'

He had expected Ziwei to come back and say flirtatiously, 'Oh, no, I don't really think you are ordinary at all,' but she was cleverer. She said nothing. It was Harry who broke the long silence that followed. 'You remember that you said you had never been to the countryside before? It's not true, you know. You and your mother came to stay with us in Shandong.'

She looked up with the wary expression on her face of a young girl who thinks she is being teased but is flattered and curious all the same. She's reacting genuinely, Harry thought, then caught himself. No, she can't be. He himself had used a seduction ploy: no woman can resist hearing about herself. That's all it is, he told himself. 'Yes, you were a plump little baby,' he continued. 'Delightful, really, with the same big eyes you have now. And I was very unkind to you – or, rather, Chen Tao was. He locked you in with all the chickens, and you screamed in terror as they hopped and pecked around you.'

She giggled, again naturally. 'I don't remember that.'

'I'm glad,' he said. 'I've felt guilty about it all my life. Oh, there was a hell of a to-do, your mother upset, mine angry – with me. I was sent to bed early that night, although it had been Chen Tao's doing. The joke was, when you'd recovered, all you wanted to do was play with the chickens, and I spent the rest of your holiday trying to steer you away from them in case I was punished again.'

She was laughing, quite spontaneously. 'I do like chickens. When I was little, my father kept a cockerel for me as a pet. I used to feed it on the balcony of our flat.'

'It was horses you liked when you stayed with us. You had a little cloth toy of a circus horse, and you always got excited watching my mother and father go riding in the mornings. Once my father put you up on my pony, with me sitting behind you, holding you tightly – I was terrified you'd fall off – and then the *mafoo* walked us round the yard. You shrieked with pleasure and fear. I can still hear you.'

'You remember all that, Ha Li? About me?'

'Oh, I remember all sorts of things . . .'

If she's an actress, he thought, she's a damned good one. He was enjoying her company . . .

When Chen returned to the room he found them relaxed and comfortable, chuckling over the comic plots of old Charlee movies. It was still permitted for the Western silent films to be shown because they were judged to be politically neutral and, in Chaplin's case, socially correct because they showed the evils of capitalism. Ha Li and Ziwei, however, had instinctively found a common point of reference that they enjoyed. After making his apologies (they looked disappointed, if anything, when he returned) he let them lead the conversation. He did not have to do any work. They were no longer tongue-tied. Eventually it was he who pleaded tiredness, reminding Ziwei that they had the Great Wall to climb in the morning.

Both looked crestfallen. Chen Tao allowed fifteen seconds of silence, then added, his tone dripping with regret: 'You know you can't come with us to the Wall, Ha Li. We'd be too conspicuous in such a public place.'

'No, of course,' said Ha Li, while Ziwei bowed her head, looking embarrassed.

'I have it,' said Chen Tao, slapping his hand. 'There's a cadres' lodge in the Fragrant Hills, with private access to the gardens and hill slopes there. Public's not allowed in but occasionally we can take favoured diplomats from Eastern Bloc countries sightseeing. You could pass as a Hungarian, Ha Li. You told me you were fluent in that language, and anyway who's to know the difference? We could go there and spend all day together.'

'I don't think it would be a good idea.'

'Of course it would. Plum blossom in the snow. It'll be lovely.'

'It's February, and bloody cold. I doubt there'll be any blossom.'

'We can look at the pine trees then, and the pagodas. Don't be so negative. Comrade Peng, you'd like to go, wouldn't you?'

'Very much,' said Ziwei, lifting her eyes, and gazing at Harry.

'Then it's settled,' said Chen. 'Now all we have to do is think up a plan to pick you up, Ha Li, without being spotted.' He knew Ha Li would not take much persuasion. He could see from the glances he was giving Ziwei that he was already besotted.

Chen dropped him within walking distance of his home and took Ziwei back to the dormitory he had found for her. Then, because it was not late and he had booked the safe-house for the night, he telephoned one of the nurses he knew (he had not been lying to Ha Li about those friends of his) and had a pleasurable evening on the red sheeted double bed, having first taken the keys of the observation room from his assistant, whom he sent home. He ordered French champagne and a plateful of oysters. He was in celebratory mood. Everything was going as he had planned. After two or three days in each other's company – it would all be very decorous, old friends getting to know each other again – their affection would ripen naturally. He was confident that, when they made their visit to the Yangtze in a month's time, they would be like two swollen apples on a tree, and he, the patient gardener, would have only to snip with his secateurs to make them fall.

One day on the mountainside became two, then three. They had the whole park to themselves – Harry wondered how Chen Tao had arranged it, because this was a playground for very senior cadres, a leaders' retreat that dated back to Kuomintang days, with sumptuous brick lodges linked by paths to old temples. Chen Tao pleaded work and took over the desk in one of the guesthouses to sort through his papers (preparing for the next GPR visit, he said.) He joined them for lunch, served by silent waiters, as discreet as those in the Cadres' Club, but otherwise Harry and Ziwei were left free to roam.

They explored the park. It was a freezing morning and the bare shrubs and denuded branches of the maple trees were covered in hoar frost, as if the forest had crystallized in the night. Even the perennials – the golden larches and Chinese pines, the clumps of green bamboo, and the firs that rose to the summit of the hill – were glistening in a sheen of ice. Their boots scrunched over the last fall of snow that had hardened on the paths. 'It's beautiful,' breathed Ziwei, her breath momentarily hiding her face above the scarf that wrapped her chin.

'No sign of plum blossom,' said Harry.

She lightly punched his arm with her glove. 'It's a sort of blossom,' she said. 'An ice garden in bloom.'

He laughed. 'Yes, we can imagine it's blossom if you like,' he said.

She skipped forward, and her foot slid on the path. She giggled as she righted herself. Harry thought, even in her unshapely overcoat, that she had the grace of a young animal.

Later, they sat wrapped in their greatcoats admiring the icicles that hung from the ornamental grottoes and the hump-backed bridge, with its lions and marble balustrades that crossed the frozen lake. To their left was a red-pillared pavilion and on the hill, above the fir forest, rose a tall green and ochre pagoda. Harry was charmed by Ziwei's extraordinary mixture of naïveté and intelligence as she told him about her life in a Chinese university as the daughter of an English professor. She chuckled as she described her favourite books, English and Chinese, and clapped her hands when she realised that he was familiar with the Chinese classical tales. He asked her what she wanted to do with her life, and she told him that she wished she could do well in her trading corporation so that one day they might allow her to act as an interpreter on a delegation abroad. 'I want to go to Paris,' she said suddenly, 'and visit Notre Dame cathedral. Do you remember? The book by Victor Hugo?'

'I don't think there's a hunchback there now,' he said.

'In my mind there always will be.' She sighed. 'Tolling the bells. Falling hopelessly in love with a woman he will never attain, but being true all the same. That's a bit like our life here, Ha Li. What did your Oscar Wilde once say? That he was lying in the gutter but looking up at the stars? The stars in heaven for us are, of course, a state of Communism and that is why we are content to bear our hardship now, knowing that our revolutionary struggle will ever bring us closer to them.'

'That's what you believe?' he said.

In the play of pale sunlight, he was not sure if he imagined the amused twinkle in the clear eyes that she turned towards him, or the light mockery in her voice when she replied, 'That's what we all believe, Ha Li: that one day all the peoples of the world will be equal and united.'

'And everybody all the same?' he said.

He felt a touch of electricity as she brushed the back of his hand. 'No,' she said. 'Not the same. I would like foreigners to remain different from us.' She lifted her chin and smiled as she indicated the lace-work of hoarfrost in the tangle of branches that hung above their heads. 'Blossoms are not the same. Look, on that bush it's like a spider's web, but on the branches it's soft, and furry like buds.'

'It's still hoar frost,' said Harry.

'Yes, but it's not the same. That is why the world is so colourful. We can be ideologically united and remain different – as you are.'

'And what makes me different?'

'You are kind,' she said, then added, 'to listen patiently to the nonsense of a silly girl like me.' She got up and hugged herself. 'It's still freezing,' she said. 'Shall we walk for a while?'

Harry looked up at her. Was her guilelessness feigned? He could not believe it was anything but natural. She bubbled with life and humour and – for two whole hours, he realised – he had forgotten they were spies.

In the afternoon they climbed to the peak and were rewarded with a view of the plain and the purple summits of the Yanshan in the far distance. They lingered on the downward path. Ziwei suddenly exclaimed with delight, as they entered the first clump of trees after leaving the rocky crags. 'Do you smell it, Ha Li?'

'Smell what?'

'A fragrance. Lemony. No, spicy.'

Harry sniffed. 'I don't think so,' he said.

'Perhaps I'm only imagining it,' she said, with a crestfallen expression in her eyes, 'but for a moment I really thought I smelled flowers.'

Harry looked at the white waste around him. 'I think we should be content with the hoarfrost,' he said.

'No, look! Look!' Ziwei was stumbling and slithering through the snow. In a tangled thicket of bare branches, she turned and gazed up at him with a triumphant expression. Her mitten was hanging from her arm, and her pink fingers were holding a ragged, leafless branch, but hanging the length of it were clusters of thimble-size golden flowers.

'That's amazing,' he said.

'It's *meihua*, plum blossom,' she said.

'It doesn't look like any plum blossom I've ever seen,' he said.

'But we call it *lamei*, sacrificial plum. I don't know why.'

He looked at the pale yellow flowers tinged with gold and purple at the centre. 'Hold on. I think I know what this is. It's called wintersweet. I've heard of it. It's a flower that blooms in the deepest winter, but people say it heralds the spring, with hope, love, good things to come.'

Her expression had become solemn. 'There was snow on the ground when I arrived in Beijing. It was the heaviest I've ever seen in my life, and – and I've never known such a biting wind as we felt on the peak just now, but this flower is growing so prettily. It's as if it doesn't realise the world is frozen.'

'Nature's pretty redoubtable, Ziwei,' he said.'

'Hope, love,' she repeated his earlier words. 'That's a beautiful thought.' She suddenly appealed to her tall companion, who was reaching out to break off the branch for her. 'No, 'let's leave it growing. Don't – don't cut it, Ha Li. I think it may be unlucky.' She was smiling shyly.

With alarm, Harry saw a tear in the corner of her eye. 'Is something wrong, Ziwei?' he asked.

'No,' she said. 'I'm just happy. 'And – and I liked what you said about seeing signs of spring in the coldest winter. This is like a holiday for me.'

'And for me,' he said softly. He reached for her mittened hand. 'Come,' he said. 'It's getting on. Chen Tao will be wondering what's happened to us.'

When they descended Chen was pacing. 'I thought you were lost,' he said, 'and I'd have to spend the night clambering over rocks looking for you. Can you imagine what trouble I'd have got into if you'd had an accident? And the expensive tea I arranged for you in the Autumn Maple Pavilion would have gone entirely to waste. There's still time, I suppose,' he grumbled. 'We don't have to leave until six.' Flushed and exhilarated after their walk, Harry and Ziwei grinned at each other, like schoolchildren being admonished for a prank. Then, as Chen shook his head grumpily, Harry laughed and Ziwei giggled, her arm lightly coiling round his own, as if to acknowledge their complicity. At that moment Harry felt he could have taken her in his arms and kissed her.

Later, lying in his bed at home, he wondered if he had been bewitched. He saw only sparkling eyes raised to his against a background of hoarfrost and heard her innocent laughter as she teased him. He could not recall a conversation with a woman that he had enjoyed as much. He was no longer sure what he thought of her, except that he wanted to spend more time with her. In the car driving back he had been conscious of her presence only a finger tip away, and had felt an overwhelming sadness that their day together was ending – so when Chen dropped him in the Minzu car-park, where Harry had left his Volga, and said, 'Same time tomorrow?' he had felt a burst of joy in his heart, which had nothing to do with the professional task in which he was engaged.

Their last day they spent visiting temples. They were locked but Chen had given them a pass to show to the soldiers guarding them, and they were let in. Under the gilded Buddhas, Harry remembered the shrines of his childhood, and Ziwei laughed when suddenly, out of buried recesses in his memory, he recalled the names of some Bodhisattvas and their disciples, peering contemplatively from recesses in the walls.

'It is so strange, Ha Li,' she said. 'You know more about Chinese traditions than I do.'

'Well, you know more about English literature than me,' he retorted.

'That was my education,' she said. 'From my mother.'

'Well, there you go,' he replied. 'I got my education from a Taoist monk. We're a topsy-turvy pair, aren't we?'

In the shadows cast by the temple eaves, she observed him with a puzzled frown. 'My mother told me how close we were as children. Is it possible that lives can be linked, as if by Fate? I feel very comfortable with you, Ha Li, even if you are a foreigner and so much older than me. As if you were my *gege*, the elder brother I have never known.'

And Harry felt a moment of ridiculous hurt. He did not want this attractive young woman to think of him as a *gege*. He knew now that he wanted more.

'Chen told me that you were not like other foreigners,' she said, 'that you grew up here as a Chinese, and have always wanted to return. Now I think I see what he means. It is as if a part of you has perhaps never left.'

'Now you're being silly,' he said. 'I'm a Scotsman, as your mother said. Just look at my long nose.' But even as he made light of it, he saw why he felt so at ease with this girl. It was as if he had been propelled back in time. He had spent his life seeking his lost China, and now on this mountainside, amid the temples, he had found it again, or something like it, and more than the mountains and the temples, it was personified by this slight girl with flat features and curved eyes, who had so effortlessly got under his skin.

When he got home he could not sleep. He went over and over the events of the day. After that conversation in the temple, as they had descended the path, she had been curiously silent and occasionally he caught her giving him what appeared to be worried or at least puzzled glances out of the corner of her eye. Once, when they were taking a short-cut over some boulders, he had held out his hand to help her down. She jumped, and her body brushed his. He looked down into her face, suddenly close to his, and saw a tremor of fear in her eyes. She bit her lip, then flinched away.

He replayed that scene several times over the next few days. If she had been a temptress, an Audrey, wouldn't that inadvertent contact have been something to linger over? But she had been startled and confused, and afterwards there had been tension between them, as if the reality of their situation had hit her – as, indeed, it had him. They had been clumsy and polite all the way back to the lodge, and afterwards, in the car, they had been silent.

Yes, he did know how he felt about her now, but did she feel the same about him? Had they both so lost themselves in their roles that their feelings for each other had become real?

Or was this all part of an act? When he thought this, he hated her, even though he was relieved because if she was a professional then the honey trap, when it came to it, would be so much easier to go through – but, try as he might, he was unable to believe that anybody *could* put on such an act, at least to convince him, who knew the game. He knew very well, and it alarmed him, that there were times during the last few days when *he* had not been acting. He had never met a woman who reached so deeply into his emotions – not even Audrey, for whom the attraction had been primarily sexual. Sex he could handle, but love? And if it was reciprocated?

What the hell was he to tell Julian? He could only lie again, re-assure him he was on top of things, while he worked out in his own mind what to do.

The demonstration, an anti-American one, was still going strong outside the British Legation when Julian arrived. During a political rally in Kentucky, President Kennedy had made a mocking reference to China's pretensions to becoming a nuclear power and had galled the comrades by throwing back in their faces Mao's habitual charge that America was a 'paper tiger'. Julian saw several paper tigers being burnt, as well as the US flag and effigies of John Kennedy, Lyndon Johnson and Robert McNamara.

The young men and women shouted at him as he approached the gates, haranguing him with slogans, but it was only for show. They laughed good-naturedly when he gave them a V for victory sign, and let him through. Inside, he met Jenkins, who told him the minister was prepared to give him a statement, and in a while he was following the shapely legs of the Mayfair secretary up the carpeted stairs.

'Ah, Travers,' Garrard said, looking up from his desk. 'I think the coast will be clear since it's impossible to work with this racket going on, and most of the staff are outside watching the show. Airton is waiting for you down the corridor. And my statement for your paper on this – ah – disturbance, is "no comment". You may embroider that as you like.'

During the last few weeks Julian had been mildly irritated with Harry. He had cried off both appointments they had made to go duck shooting, pleading fever. He had been haggard and unkempt when they did meet – an 'accidental' encounter on the Great Wall. He had been truculent and uncommunicative. Admittedly, there had been little operational to talk about. The Italians were taking an inordinate amount of time checking their records of Chinese trade delegations to Milan. That seemed the obvious lead to finding the name of the real agent who called himself Chen Tao. The British databases had revealed nothing and neither had the CIA's.

As for Professor Yu Fu-kuei, the British Council had quickly established that there was an English literature lecturer at Fudan University of that name, but it had not taken them anywhere. Her former husband, a secret policeman called Yang Yi-liang, emerged in some ancient Shanghai files. He had been a warlord police chief who had gone over to the Nationalists, had played a bloody part in the crackdown on the Communists in 1927 and been assassinated a year later, as Chen had described to Harry. For what it was worth, Chen Tao's story was corroborated but, again, it added nothing to Julian's knowledge, beyond confirming how thoroughly the opposition had prepared their operation.

They were really no further forward than they had been when he had last interviewed Harry in the Wendy Room. When they met on the Wall, he had wanted to monitor his state of mind as they waited for the next approach – and he had not been encouraged. The Chinese manipulation of Harry's past had got to him. He had spoken with cold anger as he stood by a parapet: 'Stop trying to mollycoddle me,

Julian. I'm going to do this, but in my own way. I'll deliver. I've got the measure of this Chen Tao, and there's nothing you can do to help me now. I'm afraid you'll just have to trust me.'

When a man tells you to trust him it usually indicates that you should not, but Julian acknowledged there comes a point when you can do no more for an agent than send him into the field and hope he returns safely. They parted, with little resolved, and his anxiety intensified.

Today, however, as Julian stepped again into the Wendy Room, a different Harry greeted him. He was cheerful, clear-eyed, and obviously bursting to tell him what had happened after his last meeting with Chen. 'You won't believe it, Julian. They took me to a bordello for Party cadres. You were right. They're trying to match me with Ziwei. They have her in the trade talks now, and she'll be going to Sichuan with us when the GPR engineers come. God, they're bastards, Julian, and she's a professional. To think I nearly fell for that innocence!'

He towered above Julian, a lopsided grin on his face, rubbing his hands.

'Hold on, Harry. Slow down,' Julian said, laughing. 'I really don't know what's worse – you in the depths of misery, or this unstoppable jolly giant.'

'Oh, I'm unstoppable, all right. You can bet on that.'

Julian thought back to the boy soldier in the prison cell at Koje-do, coughing and spitting blood. 'I believe you are,' he said.

6

Clouds and Rain

Sichuan, March 1963

Harry did not see Chen Tao or Ziwei until they met again at the ferry pier in Chongqing, where they gathered to board the boat that was to take them two days' upriver to the hydroelectric plant. Chen was being fawned over by the local power-bureau officials and ignored him, but Ziwei gave him a shy smile when Harry lent her a supporting arm up the gangplank.

'Better watch out, Harry. Looks like she fancies you.' Jack Braithwaite had decked himself out for the expedition in plus-fours, a belted tweed jacket, sturdy boots and a deerstalker, which he had tied under his chins so it framed his cheery red face. With Hudson in a mackintosh, gum boots and a fishing hat, and Gallagher coming up behind in a black-hooded anorak, the three might have been some eccentric walking party on the moors, a world away from the bustling activity of a Chinese river port.

Harry, shivering in his worsted suit, which was already damp from the drizzle, looked back at the pier, where bare-chested coolies in conical straw hats were hurling bales of provisions over the deck rail, and others, straddled by buckets balanced on poles, moved rhythmically up and down perpendicular stone steps that disappeared into the fog. The city itself, built on a high cliff promontory at the confluence of two rivers, was invisible except for the wraith-like outlines of tiled roofs. Groups of turbaned peasants, waiting for their ferry, squatted by cloth bundles, eyeing the foreigners and smoking long pipes. The air stank of rotting vegetables and sewage. In the midday gloom, it was a Victorian traveller's sepia photograph of old China come to life, seemingly untouched by the regimentation Harry had become used to in Peking – but he knew the commissars were watching. These peasants were not heading back to sleepy ancient villages, but to communes where this evening they would attend political classes. Mao's writ ruled here as rigidly as it did in Tiananmen Square.

'She's a pretty young lass,' said Braithwaite.

'Aye,' said Harry, catching sight of Ziwei's pink hair ribbon as she disappeared to the lower decks. 'She's the interpreter for the commercial meetings.'

'Did you hear that, Billy?' Braithwaite clapped Hudson on the back. 'Speaks English and'll be in your commercial talks. You'd better put on one of your bright bow-ties, my lad. Think he stands a chance, Harry?'

'I very much doubt it.' Leaving them to their laughter, he stepped inside the iron superstructure to look for his first-class cabin.

It was a journey through fog, their vision restricted to shadowy banks, violent yellow whirlpools and the tossing waves of the river. On the second day rocks and sandbanks became more frequent. For hours at a time a crewman would stand by the bow with a long pole, shouting the depths to the pilot, who steered the small ferry along channels that only he knew. Sometimes the water hurtling through the narrows was so violent that even a sturdy craft such as this – one of the old pre-war passenger steamers – bobbed and shook while the engines and propellers screamed. There would be consultation then between the pilot and the captain, shouts to the shore and ropes cast to lines of waiting river porters – Harry counted fifty, sometimes more. While these human pit ponies strained with the cable along thread-like pathways hacked out of sheer precipices, Harry could hear them singing, a deep-throated dirge. It was a ghostly sound in the mist.

The three engineers came out on deck to watch the fun, but otherwise spent their time in the day cabin, sitting round the clamped-down dining-table, drinking beer and playing Scrabble – they had discovered an ancient set in one of the wardroom cupboards. Harry had borrowed a military greatcoat from a steward and did not join them. Except at mealtimes, and at night when the steamer moored in quiet water by the shore, he stood alone by the rails, letting the rain beat his face and trying not to think of Ziwei.

He would replay his conversations with her, and read artifice into her every utterance: if he did not, he knew, he would be unable to go through with what he had to do. Julian had told him that they would send a professional temptress – an Audrey – to trap him, and he acknowledged that this must be so. He told himself that he would not succumb a second time. Once bitten, twice shy. The proverb ran round his head. Ziwei could only be Chen Tao's willing accomplice. Logic told him so. She was a spy, as he was. Those wide, innocent eyes, those soft red lips, the pink bloom on her cheeks were the superficial shine of inwardly rotten fruit. The brush of her hand – that sweet, impulsive gesture – was the sting of a nettle. Her chuckling laugh, her apparent frankness, her boldness were snares to trap him. He had been trained to perceive it, and did. Her charm, her innocence, her spontaneity were the dewdrops hanging on a shimmering web in the sunlight to catch an unwary insect for Chen, the yellow and red spotted spider, to gobble. Well, Harry would be happy to play that fly because he in turn concealed a hook to snare his old friend. That was his mission.

Or so he tried to tell himself.

But deep inside he was unsure, as he had been since he'd left Shanghai, and was even more so after three days with Ziwei in the Fragrant Hills. He had not forgotten the enigmatic words of her mother, Professor Yu. What if Ziwei had been forced to play a role she detested? He would replay the conversations, and see her remarks in a different light. He recognised that at times she must be acting, as he was when he was with her, but he admired her bravery, intelligence and skill, performing a task that must be abhorrent to her – and, through it all, to maintain such naturalness and grace.

'Ha Li.' He jumped. 'Ha Li, am I disturbing you?' He swung round. Ziwei was beside him. She had tied a scarf around her head, and her slim body was lost in a huge green padded overcoat, like his own. She was looking up at him quizzically. 'I – I was worried about you,' she said. 'The whole ship has been talking about how you stand here every day by yourself. Deputy Party Secretary Chen gave me permission to come and talk to you in case you are troubled.'

He has sent you, he thought bitterly. Wearily, he put on a smile. 'I'm not troubled in the least, Ziwei. I'm happy standing here. I love this wild, wet scenery. It reminds me of Scotland. Home,' he said.

She nodded thoughtfully. 'Is your home very beautiful, Ha Li?' she asked softly.

'I lived on an island in the western sea. It's a windtorn piece of the world and as often as not it's raining, but sometimes the sun comes out and lights up the headlands. When we were fishing close to shore, we'd see seals and kestrels. On a day like that there's nowhere on the planet you'd rather be.'

'You were a fisherman?' Her lips were parted and her eyes wide.

'Aye, I fished. Sometimes way into the Atlantic, sometimes as far away as Greenland. I never finished school, you see. Had to work on my uncle's boat. It wasn't a bad life. Hard sometimes, but you were living with nature. You'd be rocked by a violent storm one day and find yourself surrounded by whales the next. Haven't lived till you've seen whales, Ziwei.'

'Whales.' She sighed. 'It must be wonderful to see whales.' She gazed at the river, as if she expected a great tail to lash out of its depths. 'You must have been very frightened.'

'No – awed by their size, moved by their majesty, amazed by their beauty, but not frightened.'

'I don't think I will ever see whales,' she said, in a tiny voice. 'That would be a dream.'

'Dreams can come true,' he said, 'if you really want them to.'

'No, Ha Li,' she said sadly. 'I do not believe in personal dreams. Not since I was a child. In China, we are not . . . encouraged to have dreams of our own. It would be considered bourgeois.'

'The Party can't rule the heart.'

She did not answer. He watched her profile as she leant against the rails, the slightly pointed chin, the round curve of the cheek, and a wisp of hair blowing from under her scarf. There was a smile on her lips when she turned to him, and a mischievous expression in her eyes. 'You are right. Even the Party cannot stop me dreaming about whales if I want to, Ha Li, though I may have to think of them as revolutionary ones.'

He laughed, and she pushed him lightly on the arm. 'Are you joking with me, Ha Li? Were you really a fisherman who sailed to Greenland over the Atlantic Ocean?'

'I was,' he said. 'I've caught cod near the Sargasso Sea.'

'*Captains Courageous*,' she said suddenly. 'You were like the boy in *Captains Courageous*.'

'You've read it?' He was amazed.

'My mother read it to me when I was a girl, to help me practise my English. I have never forgotten that boy who was lost at sea, and rescued into a new world. As I've told you, I have read many of my mother's books – Kipling, also Dickens and Thackeray and Jane Austen. When I was twelve I wanted to be like Elizabeth Bennet.'

'You're amazing,' he said.

She was looking at him curiously. 'Ha Li, I can see you as a fisherman – you are strong – but Comrade Chen said you were a scientist and an important diplomat. He never told me you were a . . .' She seemed embarrassed.

'A worker?' He grinned. 'I've been a worker and a soldier in my time. *Gong, nong, bing.* Workers, farmers, soldiers – the three favoured categories in this country. I've never farmed, but I have been the other two. And now I suppose I'm an intellectual. But classes and categories don't mean much in my country – or not formal ones. You can be whoever you want to be.' She was watching him, eyes wide, but now that he had started he couldn't stop. 'Ziwei, you once said you thought Chen Tao was unfair to me. Well, I think your country's been unfair to you. You're decent, you're capable, you're clever. If I were the Chinese government I'd be promoting you on your abilities, instead of keeping you in a backwater.'

He felt a constriction in his chest. Somehow, he had forgotten his role and spoken from the heart. Now he had hurt her.

She had turned away from him to look out over the water. When she turned back her expression was solemn – stern, even. 'Ha Li, I think you are very kind,' she said, 'but you must not say things like that. It—' Her voice broke. 'It confuses me. Sometimes you, too, can be unfair. I have to go,' she said.

'To report to Chen Tao?' he asked harshly, and cursed himself.

Her cheeks crimsoned. He noticed the effort with which she forced herself to remain composed. 'Of course, Ha Li. He will want to know that his friend is well.'

'His friend?' he asked. 'Not yours?'

Her lips were quivering now. 'Mine too,' she said, then turned and walked back along the deck, head held high – but after two or three steps, she bent forward and ran the rest of the way towards the stairs. He wondered, as she clattered down, if it was really a sob he had heard or the moan of the wind.

He hunched on the rail and stared at the shoreline. The vessel passed a big, pointed rock. Behind it, he saw a small fishing skiff, with a man and a boy straining at the sail. The frail craft bobbed up and down in the ship's wake, their thin silhouettes appearing and disappearing behind the yellow waves.

*　　*　　*

Just after it had got dark, the ferry moored off a small jetty. Harry and the GPR men disembarked and a jeep drove them for four hours along a muddy road. During the latter stages of their journey, the weather cleared and the moon rose above the mountains, turning the water silver. In its faint light they made out a dam at the top of the gorge and, beside it, the spiky shadows and chimneys of a power station. They turned on to a track that wound upwards through a forest. The three engineers were asleep, oblivious of the bumps, when Harry saw a gate ahead, military guards, and a neat garden compound beyond.

He woke at dawn and, feeling restless, went for a walk. There were about ten other concrete and marble bungalows similar to his own behind hedges of hibiscus and bougainvillaea. A larger building, he concluded, was the dining-hall and recreation centre. These luxurious government guesthouses had been built for senior cadres around the country, and foreigners were rarely allowed near them. The cloud cover was low, but occasionally it would shift and he could make out the jagged peaks of the mountain range that surrounded the compound. The air smelt of ozone and pine, with a faint, sulphurous underlay. Below, the tops of fir trees protruded from the mist. A damp stone path led up from the garden to another clearing in which he could make out several concrete huts. As he climbed towards them the smell of sulphur became stronger, and he realised they were bathhouses. The site must have been chosen because of the hot springs.

He stiffened when he heard someone call his name. Chen Tao, a towel over his shoulder, was hurrying up the steps. 'Do you like this place, Ha Li? It is a special privilege that we are allowed to stay here. You scientists and engineers are so important.' He laughed. 'Actually, this compound was built by the district government when they thought Chairman Mao was coming to see the hydro dam. He never did and they were criticised for the expenditure – but since it's here we might as well use it.' He slapped Harry on the back. 'I've been missing you, my old friend. On the boat I couldn't find an opportunity to speak to you. Too many eyes and ears.'

'I was wondering where you were,' said Harry.

Chen sighed. 'In my cabin doing my homework on all those technical papers. I'm a trade man, not a scientist, but since I will have to lead the talks, I needed to refresh myself – if that's the right word for it. I'm going for a dip in the sulphur bath and to have a quick massage. The waters are good for the liver and rejuvenating for certain other parts of the body, which is probably why this place is so often full of very old generals with pretty young nurses and secretaries, never their wives.' He guffawed. 'Don't worry, Ha Li, it is perfectly respectable, and we have it to ourselves.'

'It's a beautiful spot,' said Harry. 'I'd forgotten what the real China looks like, locked up in Beijing.'

'That's one of the reasons I chose it,' said Chen. 'See those bamboo groves, and the mountains, don't they remind you a little of our old home? You see what a sentimentalist I am.'

'You? Sentimental?' He smiled. 'But there are some similarities.'

'If only we had time,' said Chen, 'there's a fine walk up to the peak, and a small temple, like the one we had on our mountain. Wouldn't it be wonderful? We could explore, pretending we were still Hong Huzi, but instead we'll be crawling round pumps and valves, talking about heat exchangers.' He paused. 'Ha Li, there's no reason why you shouldn't go. I have to be present for all the meetings and site inspections, but there is nothing to stop you.'

Harry laughed. 'You're suggesting I play truant?'

'You're only needed for the commerical discussions. These first three days will consist of our engineers taking yours round the plant, then giving presentations on the Russian technology we use, with which you're familiar anyway. I've replaced that first useless interpreter we had with an old professor who speaks fluent English, so you're not needed to translate.'

'It's tempting, but I couldn't leave Braithwaite and the others on their own.'

'All right – come today to start them off, then tell your friends you have a headache. No one will miss you, I promise. I'll give Ziwei the day off too. Why not? We must look after our important foreign guests, after all, and since the commercial discussions won't have started, my people will understand that she can be spared.' He looked at his watch. 'I must hurry if I'm to have my bath. Think about it, Ha Li.'

Harry could not remember a more tedious day. He and the three GPR engineers had been forced to sit through nearly eight hours of lectures from the Chinese hydro-technicians, at cramped desks a mile away from the plant they had come to inspect.

'Harry,' Braithwaite had complained after the assistant chief engineer had read notes on the first principles of hydropower generation, 'can't you tell that Chen fellow we know all this? We're engineers. We only have to look at the power station to understand what it's all about.'

'Sorry, Jack, it's the way they do things here.'

'You mean we've got to shut up and put up? Bloody hell. Open our legs and think of England?'

Harry glanced at Ziwei, who was sitting at the furthest end of the room. Her eyes were as glazed as everybody else's, including Chen's.

The assistant chief engineer was back at the podium, adjusting his spectacles. The new interpreter announced, 'Gentlemen, your attention, please. Comrade Yan is going to talk to us about the historical development of the power industry in south-west China.'

Braithwaite groaned, put his deerstalker on his head and tied the flaps round his ears.

The next day Harry made his excuses to the engineers, who drove off for the day's talks, leaving him alone on the steps to the dining-hall. Whatever Chen intended would take place today, he thought. Would Ziwei invite him to her bungalow or suddenly turn up in his? He thought of the thriller Julian had once given him, about a secret agent who finds a Russian seductress in his bed, dressed in nothing but a black choker. The night before he had tossed and turned, alternating from guilty fantasies of taking her to his bed and disgust that he could contemplate it. Eventually he had fallen into a weary fatalism, the state he was in at the moment.

In a while he and Ziwei would be performing their appointed roles. There was no turning back for either of them.

He turned to meet his temptress, but when he went back into the dining-hall, where he had left her, he saw not a siren but a girl draped in a long plastic raincoat, wearing a sensible cloth cap and walking plimsolls. 'Oh, Ha Li,' she chided, 'are you not ready? Chen Tao said we were going to climb to the top of the mountain today. I have sandwiches and even boiled eggs.'

This was no Tanya Romanova waiting for James Bond, thought Harry, and he was surprised because he felt only relief.

The steep path beyond the bathhouses was a mudslide and sometimes a stream. When it was not raining, moisture from the wet leaves dropped on to their heads and trickled down their backs. Ziwei's plastic rain-coat became so torn she abandoned it, and they were soon soaked to the skin. For most of the walk, they were inside the low-hanging clouds, so there was no view.

As they helped each other over obstacles, they talked. She wanted to hear more about Harry's life in Scotland, and described something of her own childhood in a city. Many of the incidents she related concerned her father, an impractical, absent-minded man whom she had adored. After a time they forgot the rain, and Harry realised, to his surprise, that he had not felt as relaxed in anybody's company for years.

About noon they paused in a meadow that separated two clumps of firs. The mist had lifted and one of the peaks was briefly in view. It reminded Harry of his day with Hsiung when they had climbed Mount Tai, and he began to think of his parents. He had never discussed them with anybody before, but the intimacy that had developed between him and Ziwei that morning made it natural for him to do so now. When he told her how they had died in a Japanese camp, his voice was emotionless.

She took his arm. 'You were young to suffer such tragedy,' she said. 'My mother told me that you were exiled to England as a little boy. I wondered how you managed to bear it.'

'One learns to bear anything in time.'

'Yes,' she said thoughtfully, releasing him, 'but it must have been hard for a child to understand. When my father was taken away, I was twenty.'

'That's also very young,' he said.

The rain glistened on her cheeks. 'I think I was luckier than you, Ha Li, although of course my heart still breaks sometimes when I think of it, and I cannot help being angry when I imagine him suffering alone at the end. It is difficult to explain but my father made it easier for us to bear. We had an evening alone together, he, Mother and I, before they came to take him away. That was when he told my mother to denounce him. I had never seen my parents quarrel before, but eventually he persuaded her. And then he became so happy. That's the only word I can use to describe him. He was more light-hearted than I'd ever seen him. He made both of us giggle when he described what sort of farmer he was going to be, as you did, Ha Li, when you told me funny stories about what I was like when I was little.

'At the end of the evening, before we went to bed, he explained to us that he would never be sad because he would always remember us as we were that evening, a happy and loving family. Just by holding on to that memory, he said, he would be with us whenever he wanted to be, and we would be with him, and nothing could hurt him. He was a philosopher and always enjoyed teasing me with confusing concepts, but I think I understood then, for the first time, what he meant by saying that time is a single, perpetual moment. He ensured that we, too, had a good memory of him. It was his gift to us as he said goodbye.'

She looked at him seriously. 'Perhaps that doesn't make sense, Ha Li, but I think you *can* squeeze everything that is important into a single moment, and that makes whatever happens before or afterwards meaningless. It is a way of dealing with pain. It can help you go through some of the terrible things that happen to you as well as some of the unpleasant things you have to do to survive. I – I am not always strong, but when I think of my father that night, it sometimes steadies me a little.'

'We all stumble eventually on ways to get through life, Ziwei,' he muttered inadequately. 'The system here perhaps makes your life more difficult than mine.'

'There are ways to comfort ourselves, but I have also been thinking of what you said to me on the boat, Ha Li. You mentioned decency. Do you think that one can remain decent yet be made to do terrible things? You are a good man,' her voice cracked, 'and I doubt that you have ever been in any situation that calls for deceit, but it is common in China.'

He thought how bitterly ironic this was. If he could believe the implication behind what she was saying, she had cast him in the role of an innocent, but he (or he through Julian) had set this trap in the first place. He felt an enormous rush of pity and affection for her, but he could see no way of showing it without tearing his cover, destroying the operation and, for all he knew, endangering her. 'Come on,' he said, somehow managing a cheerful tone. 'It can't be far to that temple Chen Tao told me was up here.'

'Let's hurry. I'm cold!' she cried. She snatched his hand and began to pull him up the meadow towards the treeline. Once he was moving, she flung a mischievous smile over her shoulder, dropped his hand and ran, arms swinging awkwardly. Laughing, he loped after her and it became a race to the top.

Twenty minutes later they found the ruined temple and huddled together for warmth under its broken timbers to eat their sandwiches. Afterwards they walked back down the mountain. They parted at the bottom, then went to their separate bungalows to wash off the mud.

Half-way through the morning discussions at the hydro-plant, Chen Tao received an urgent message to phone Beijing. He was not concerned. Commissioner Hao was always fussing about something or other. As soon as his superior started speaking, however, he realised that something had gone very wrong.

With some smugness, Hao told him how yesterday he had been summoned to the Zhong Nan Hai to report to Kang Sheng on the progress of the operation. Chen gathered there had been developments on the nuclear front – an explosion in one of the prototype reactors or something equally disastrous, which had set back the whole programme – and the whole Politburo was demanding action and, above all, information. Even more alarmingly, the prime minister had been making his own enquiries about who was being used as bait in the sexual sting. Zhou Enlai's sensitivity about honey traps had always been an obscure threat to the operation. Now Chen discovered that Kang Sheng had misled his colleagues all along and told them they would be using a foreign girl.

'Of course I spoke up for you,' said Hao, over the crackling line. Chen could hear satisfaction in his voice. 'But Comrade Kang is not happy with your procrastination. The orders now are that you bring this project to a conclusion within six weeks.'

Chen did not need Hao to tell him his career was on the line. As far as the operation was concerned, the new deadline was achievable but only if everything went to schedule. He no longer had the luxury of fail-safes and counter-strategies in the event of any upsets or hitches. In military terminology, it meant that everything now depended on a successful first strike. In other words he had the three days that remained at the guesthouse for Ziwei to seduce Ha Li.

He was optimistic that she would. Her friendship with Ha Li had already developed to the point at which he believed it required only a little effort to tip them into bed. The idyllic conditions were perfect for the necessary romantic tryst. If all went well, the temple, with its childhood connotations for Ha Li, would do the trick. He had the bathhouse as fall-back. As long as he managed to manipulate them into spending time together, he was sure that chemistry would do the rest. Three days should be ample time.

Or so he comforted himself, but over lunch the idiot plant director told him that all the rooms were prepared for the British engineers in the power station's hospitality building. Chen stared at him and asked, with icy politeness, what possible reason on earth would induce them to move to that hovel? Then he found out that three months ago the People's Liberation Army South-western Command had scheduled a strategy meeting in the government guesthouse, which would start in two days' time. Did the honourable deputy Party secretary not know? No, Chen told him, the honourable deputy Party secretary did not know, and why had the turtle's egg of a plant director not told him earlier, if he had known beforehand?

There was little point in taking it out on a nonentity like him. Chen knew that one of the flaws of their system was that all departments operated in secret boxes, trying to keep news from their superiors. By rights the PLA General Headquarters in Beijing should have known about this when he had checked through the Second Department, but provinces always went their own way, especially the military satrapies. He spent the whole afternoon telephoning anybody influential he could find in the province. He even considered calling Commissioner Hao, to ask him to make a plea to Kang Sheng, but after the morning's phone call he realised that that would be pissing in the wind. By the time the meetings closed in the late afternoon he had accepted that he had lost his three days. Everything now depended on Ziwei's success at the temple.

'Well? What have you to report?' he asked her, when she appeared in his bungalow.

'It is going very well. We considerably deepened our emotional intimacy today,' she said. She looked like a Young Pioneer standing to attention in class, waiting for a merit badge to be pinned on her tunic.

'Really?' said Chen.

'Oh, yes, Comrade,' she bubbled on. 'He was very revealing about personal details of his life. He treated me like a dear friend. And – and I found many admirable qualities in him too, which will make it easier to seduce him.'

'That's the point of our expensive operation, is it? For the two of you to become friends?'

She frowned, as if puzzled by his remark. 'Those were your orders,

Comrade,' she said, 'to establish an emotional intimacy that would later become a physical one. Or – or so I thought.'

'My orders, Comrade, were for you to take him up the mountain today and fuck him in that temple.'

She stiffened, her face paling in shock.

'Well, why didn't you? The observers told me you did not even attempt it.'

'The – the atmosphere did not seem appropriate,' she stuttered. She raised her head. Her eyes were appealing. 'I'm sorry, Comrade, it just . . . It wouldn't have been right.'

'Wouldn't have been right?' Chen was conscious that his voice had risen in pitch. 'Are you questioning my orders?'

'No, Comrade,' she said quickly. 'But . . . but—'

'But what?'

'I – I wonder if we are mistaken about him,' she cried. Her body was trembling although she looked Chen directly in the eyes. 'Ha Li's a good man, Comrade. He is kind and considerate. He was once a worker, a fisherman, and – and he loves China. I know he does. It was the way he spoke about his childhood and serving the common people. I – I cannot believe he is our enemy or has evil intentions against us.'

Chen spoke icily: 'You want me to call off the operation because you think Ha Li is a good man?'

She blushed. 'No, Comrade Chen. Only I worry – perhaps we have been mistaken. You told me that this operation was to trap a dangerous spy, but – but Ha Li seems to be an innocent scientist, honest in every way. I wonder – I wonder if the spy you are seeking is perhaps another man.'

Well, he had had a bad day. Chen liked to think of himself as a man of temperate character, but something snapped. He rabbit-chopped the side of her belly, and then as she crouched, winded and terrified, on the carpet, he pulled off his belt and beat her with the buckle. 'You *hei wu lei* bitch! Do you think you know Ha Li better than I do?'

He pulled her up by the collar. She was staring at him, opening and shutting her mouth like a newly caught fish. He told her very quietly that she should be grateful he had given her only physical punishment. The next time she showed such disobedience she would be put on a train to a labour camp in Qinghai and her mother would be shot. Then he pushed her backwards on to the bed, and told her to strip.

She was so traumatised – perhaps she thought he intended to rape her – that it took the threat of another blow to make her do as she was told. When she was naked Chen ordered her to turn on her side. He had been careful, even in his anger, to direct all his strikes at a small area on her hips and side. The black and red swellings were commensurate with an injury from a fall, except for a couple of welts that clearly showed the mark of a belt. That was unfortunate and he cursed his lack of self-control. There was only one thing to do. He told her not to cry out, or he would reconsider his leniency to her, and gave her three more blows with the edge of the marble ink mixer from the desk to blur the swellings from the strap and to make the bruise look as if it had been made by a jagged stone. Then he ordered her to put on her clothes.

'Now you have a choice,' he told her, and explained what he wanted her to do. 'Do you understand, Comrade Peng?'

'Yes, Comrade,' she whispered.

'You realise that if you fail tonight there is nothing I can do to protect you or your mother?'

'Yes, Comrade. I'm sorry, Comrade, for letting you down today. Thank you, Comrade.'

He looked at her with disgust. The abjectness of these *hei wu leis* when you disciplined them was pathetic. 'Then get out of here and prepare yourself.' He looked at his watch. There was much to do before dinner, when he would have to inform the British engineers and Ha Li of the change in plan.

His mind full of affectionate memories of their walk together, Harry had been looking forward to seeing Ziwei when he entered the dining-hall, but she was not there. Harry wondered why. It was not like Chen Tao to hide her. He usually flaunted her at every opportunity. Had she caught a chill on the mountain? He imagined her lying feverish in her bungalow, sheets drawn up to her child-like face, cheeks flushed. No. If she wasn't here it was because Chen had ordered her not to come.

Just after they had started dinner, Chen came up to the table Harry was sharing with the GPR engineers. He had brought with him the old professor who had been doing the technical interpretation. He was polite and formal as usual, the senior cadre graciously giving some of his time to his foreign guests, but Harry noticed unfamiliar tension and a cold expression in his eyes that might have been anger or irritation. Through the interpreter he promised Braithwaite that they would have the whole day tomorrow to inspect the plant. He asked if one day would be enough. Braithwaite said that would be fine. Chen said he was pleased because there had to be a change in the schedule. A senior military delegation was visiting the district in two days' time so they would have to leave the guesthouse earlier than intended. He regretted this but proposed that the wrap-up discussions planned for the last two days should now take place on the boat back to Chongqing. The experts from the hydroelectric station could accompany them, he said. Braithwaite, clearly delighted to be leaving earlier than scheduled, agreed.

Chen turned to Harry, but again spoke through the interpreter. 'Dr Airton, we were worried about your headache.' Harry said he was feeling much better now. 'Nevertheless,' said Chen, 'I have consulted with the doctor at the nearby army base on your behalf. He tells me that at this altitude chills can be dangerous. He has selected some medicines for you. He advises that you should also take advantage of the hot springs here. I have therefore ordered one of the bathhouses to be prepared for you after dinner. You are to soak in the sulphur pool for an hour, then a medical masseur will come to treat you.'

'That's very kind of the Deputy Party Secretary,' said Harry, 'but there is no need to go to such trouble for me.'

'Deputy Party Secretary Chen insists,' said the interpreter, his anxious look revealing his nervousness.

'I see,' said Harry. 'In which case tell him I'd be delighted.'

When he left, Braithwaite rubbed his hands together. 'That's a spot of luck. If we can change our flights we might be able to get home in time for Easter. I think another drink's in order, lads.' His eyes twinkled. 'Don't envy you, though, Harry. Looks as if you're to be punished, old son. I've heard of these Chinese masseurs. If I know Deputy Party Secretary Chen you're in for an excruciatingly painful half-hour or more. That'll teach you to go off for the day with pretty interpreters.'

Harry took the ribbing in good part, but throughout the rest of the meal he wondered what this session in the bathhouse portended. Chen Tao, at the other end of the room, looked up only once, and Harry was surprised to see that for once he had dropped his guard: he appeared to be staring at him with venomous hatred.

The bathhouse was empty when Harry entered, but he noticed that one of the beds had been turned down and that candles, matches, moxibustion bottles and a case of acupuncture needles waited on a shelf. In the bathroom beyond, there were two large wooden tubs, with submerged stools to sit on. Both were brimful of water. One was cold, for rinsing, the other hot. The fug was almost as dense as the mist that had enveloped him on his walk up the mountain. There was an overpowering stench of sulphur.

Not knowing what was expected of him, Harry drew the cotton curtains across the windows in the bedroom, and took off his clothes. Wrapping a towel round his waist, he returned to the bathroom, closing the door. There was no lock. Nor had there been one on the outside door, only a keyhole without a key. He immersed himself in the water, lowering his limbs by stages because of the scalding heat. On the stool, the water came just below his shoulders, so he dispensed with it and settled into a position where his chin was just under the surface. His eyes were closed and he had probably dozed a little, when he felt a brush of cooler air on his forehead. He started and saw a figure standing silently in the steam. It was another second before he recognised Ziwei.

She was dressed in the floppy tunic and trousers in which he had first seen her at her mother's flat. She had tied her hair into two loose braids that hung below the cloth cap that was pulled tightly over her forehead. She was silhouetted in the doorway, one knee bent, accentuating the filly-like grace he so admired. Her arms hung loosely at her sides. Her head was half turned and the light from the bedroom caught the perspiration on her cheek, which glistened.

Through the steam it was difficult to make out her expression. Her plain, flat features were drained of their usual vivacity, and the wide brown eyes appeared to contemplate him with sad serenity.

At first Harry just stared at her. There was something magnificent about the slender girl in the Mao suit. He recalled the opera he had seen in Shanghai: the female soldiers dispensing justice to evil capitalists. The crudeness of her presence in his bathroom seemed iconic, a tableau in a morality play, personifying in stark contrast all the forces – historical and political – that had brought them to this point of no return.

He wondered why she didn't move. Long moments passed when the only sound was the drip of the overflow on to the duckboards and the gurgle through the pipe – but perhaps it was only a few seconds. For form's sake he covered his arousal with the flannel he had been resting his head on.

He heard her take a deep breath before she stepped forward with a deliberate stride. Even so, she hesitated before resting her hands lightly on the edge of the tub. The proximity of those slim, white fingers to his flesh, the faint sound of her breathing, the contours of her body under the damp tunic, the sweat on her throat and her upper chest, the swell of a breast under her half-open tunic tantalised him. He had to exert all his self-control not to reach out for her.

She seemed to be experiencing a similar tension. Although she was still looking at him with the same sad, fixed expression, she was trembling, and Harry wished he could take responsibility, but he had to let her make the moves, and appear to resist, when all he wanted to do was take her in his arms. 'Ziwei,' he muttered, 'what are you doing here?'

She leant forward and brushed a finger across his lips. One of her braids dangled forward to tickle his exposed shoulder. She was looking searchingly into his eyes as her palm stroked his cheek. It took him an effort to move her hand away. Even so he could not resist kissing a knuckle. 'You're very beautiful, Ziwei, but – but I'm a foreign diplomat. We – we shouldn't be doing this.'

She kissed the back of his hand. When she looked up, there were tears in her eyes, although she tried to smile. 'Please, Ha Li,' she whispered. 'No words or – or it will be too difficult for me. Remember what we said on the mountain today about a moment of infinity? If we tell each other we love each other, can we not believe it for one night? Like . . . like the dream of whales.'

She gave him a long, beseeching look, lip quivering, hands fluttering by her side. Then she took another deep breath, closed her eyes and tore at the remaining buttons on her tunic. Almost angrily, she cast it aside. A tear rolled down her cheek as she kicked off her shoes. Her loose trousers fell to the duckboards. She wore no underclothes or socks. Her arms were hanging loosely by her sides when she raised her head and opened her eyes.

'You know this is madness, Ziwei. I'm very fond of you, and you're beautiful, but this isn't the way. Come into the other room. Get dressed, and we'll talk about it.'

But he did not avert his eyes from the strong thighs tapering to slender calves, the narrow waist and rounded hips, the wispy black triangle of hair that led the eye up the slope of belly and ribcage towards her breasts, and the thin arms hanging awkwardly by her sides.

Then he saw the livid marks on her side and hip.

He stared at her in horror. He knew what caused bruises like those. He had examined himself in the mirror often enough after his uncle had given him the belt strap. Like his uncle, whoever had done this to Ziwei had also been skilful, concentrating the blows in one place so the injury might seem the result of a fall or a scrape, but not to Harry. He shivered.

'Please don't find me ugly, Ha Li,' she whispered. 'The bruises will go in a week or two. I wanted to be perfect for you, but I fell on the steps.'

It could only be Chen Tao's doing, but why?

'I love you, Ha Li,' she said, and began to cry.

This is mad, he thought. There was no way he could go through with this. Forgetting any sense of modesty, he got out of the bath, and knelt beside her. She had slumped to the floor, crouching with one hand on the side of the tub, the other covering her face as she moaned, 'I love you . . . I love you . . . Please.'

She looked up at him with blazing eyes, her forehead and cheeks flushed from the steam. Suddenly Harry realised she was terrified. 'Ziwei,' he said firmly, 'you must get up and get dressed. This is wrong.'

The words that came out of her mouth were almost incoherent. 'No . . . no . . . we must . . . You don't understand, Ha Li. There is no other chance. Please . . . Look what I'll do to please you . . . Let me . . .' She threw herself at him and he felt the wet softness of her breasts against his skin as she kissed his cheeks, his mouth and neck. He felt her fingers fumbling below. It took all his strength to push her away. He held her by her shoulders. 'Ziwei. Stop this,' he said.

He felt her shoulders slump, and watched her face become haggard with despair. Her eyes, which had burned with passion a moment ago, now looked at him dully. He felt an overpowering sense of pity for her. He held her to him and kissed her damp forehead. Then, with his lips close to her ear, he breathed, 'Ziwei, can you please tell me what the hell is going on?'

'No, Ha Li. It doesn't matter any more.'

'Is it so important I make love to you?'

A spark of hope lit her eyes. She flung her arms round his neck and kissed his ears, his chin.

'You know this is madness, Ziwei?'

167

'The whole world is mad, Ha Li, but – but give me tonight to remember. Kiss me. Please, please.'

He kissed her, then carried her to the next room, where he laid her on the bed. He went to the light switch and paused. She smiled sadly, and turned her head. He switched off the light anyway. It wasn't Harry's responsibility to help Chen Tao, not after he had beaten and terrorised Ziwei. Anyway, for the moment this had nothing to do with the man. As far as Harry was concerned it was a private pact between him and Ziwei, another time out of time. In the darkness he sat beside her, stroked her, then leant over her and kissed her, savouring the hot burn of her lips and the touch of her tongue. Her body shuddered slightly when he entered her, and she gripped his shoulders.

Afterwards they lay with their bodies entwined. He felt the comfortable press of her breasts on his chest, the warm touch of her thigh on his. He had never come across another woman in his life who fitted so naturally against him. He peered at the face next to his on the pillow. Perhaps he only imagined the smile, but he heard it in her voice, in the softness of her tone, as she whispered, 'Ha Li, Ha Li.'

'What is it?' he murmured, his lips on her forehead, her flat little nose, her cheek, her chin.

'Nothing, my lovely Ha Li,' she continued, after their lips had touched and briefly lingered. 'Nothing, except you have made me very happy. I will never forget this moment whatever bad things happen in the future.'

'No bad things will happen. I won't let them,' he said, and for a fraction of a second he believed it.

Her arms reached behind his head and pulled his cheek against hers. Then their lips touched and they kissed again. He felt a delicious, wet heat below and began to harden again.

'Wait,' she said. Her voice was unutterably sad.

He felt the dampness of a tear on the cheek pressed to his. 'What?' he murmured, continuing to move, as she was also moving.

'I – I want to see you, Ha Li,' she said. 'I – I want to turn on the lights.'

He felt her hand brush down his cheek. 'Please,' she whispered. 'Forgive me.'

He held her for a moment longer, feeling intensely sad, as if he was bidding farewell to a friend. But he knew this had to be. He tried to keep any bitterness out of his voice when he said, 'What's to forgive?

I want to see you too.' He rolled off her. He felt her move away from the bed. The room seemed to blaze with light, although there was only one bulb in the ceiling. In its intrusive glare he saw her standing by the switch as she gave him a heartbreaking smile. Then he noticed the smudge of red on her thigh, and blood on the sheets. He knew it had not been her first time, that she had used some whore's artifice – but it no longer mattered. He did not care about betrayal any more. He would play his part if that was what she wanted.

'You were a virgin,' he said. 'I didn't know.'

'You did not hurt me, Ha Li. You have to believe I wanted this – more than anything in the world.'

'I do,' he said. 'I wanted it also.'

She nodded.

'Come back to bed,' he said. 'It's cold.'

As she walked towards him he thought she resembled a woman ascending a scaffold.

But they went through with it, and they found some comfort. It did not matter, thought Harry. Ziwei had been right. They had already squeezed everything important into a single moment the first time – or well enough, all imperfect things considered.

It was an unnecessary irony, he thought later, when he made his lonely way back to his bungalow, that the mist had cleared and every peak was silhouetted perfectly under the bright stars.

7

Dreaming of Whales

Sichuan, March 1963

The girl was nearly hysterical. Her clothes were soaking and she shivered in front of him. 'It's – it's done,' she whispered.

Chen felt a surge of heat that started in his cheeks and went down through his belly and loins. He closed his eyes, savouring his moment of triumph – but there was a hard expression on his face when he turned to her.

'I did everything – everything you ordered,' she said. 'It was – it was disgusting.'

'It was a job,' he said. 'For the Motherland.' He peered into her frightened eyes. 'Disgusting? Is that what you found it? Really? A few hours ago you were telling me this was a good, kind man.'

'He – he was repulsive,' she said, her eyes widening. 'You were right all along, Comrade, he is an enemy of our people.'

Chen knew when a woman was lying, or trying to ingratiate herself. He viewed the trembling figure in front of him with contempt. 'I will judge tomorrow when I see the film how disgusting you found him,' he said. 'Then I will decide whether or not you obeyed my orders.'

She began to sob. She fell to her knees and clutched his legs. 'My mother! You promised, Comrade – if I did what you wanted, you would drop the charges . . .'

'How dare you touch me?' he said. 'Get out. It is you I find disgusting, Comrade Peng. Go back to your bungalow and take a bath. Wash away the dirt. If that really is what is troubling you. Here.' He passed her a bottle of sleeping pills. 'Take one of these. It should calm your emotional state. Remember, this operation is not yet over. You must still appear attractive to your lover. Tomorrow, when I have studied the film, I will review what I will do about you and your mother.'

As she left, he realised that from now on he must factor in her inherent unreliability – but that was a small problem since the film

170

had been taken and was even now being developed. He had succeeded, against all the odds.

Later that night, tossing restlessly on his bed, he went over the details of the operation: how he would use the film, selecting the most salacious stills, the words he would use when he confronted Ha Li with the evidence, how he would use his success to denigrate Commissioner Hao in front of Kang Sheng – for that was also important, if not more so. As a precaution, he had fabricated evidence of Hao's obstruction of this operation, but he was certain that Kang would more readily believe his innuendo. Kang had spoken contemptuously of Hao, so he knew he would be sowing seed on fertile ground – but the stillness of the night is the realm of personal fears, and he knew full well that if he was plotting against Hao, he could be certain that his superior was also conniving against him. So he worried, which drove sleep further away.

When eventually he did drop off, it was only to wake again barely half an hour later, because he had been visited by the old nightmare that always came to him in times of stress. The details were never the same, never logical, but it always ended up with him in front of a Party tribunal, confessing his guilty secret, the one he had tried to cover up since his childhood. With sleep now banished and with cold sweat on his brow, all the memories came back of what the Japanese had done to him after Ha Li betrayed him. The Japanese, the damned Japanese, whom once he had convinced himself were his friends . . .

It had started with a fascination for the weapons carried by their soldiers – the rifles with their long bayonets, and the great swords carried by the officers. In the boring hours when Ha Li had been at his lessons he had spent his time loitering near their barracks.

At first he had shared the contempt that all the Chinese felt for the foreign interlopers, but gradually, as he got to know the sentries, he found that they were not the fearsome creatures he had imagined. Many were friendly, clearly homesick, and all too happy to talk to a boy whom they imagined admired them. They would answer his questions patiently in their terrible Chinese and sometimes give him presents of dried seaweed, sticky round riceballs or Japanese sweetmeats. One sergeant took a particular liking to him, telling him he reminded him of his own son. He even allowed Chen to play with his revolver and his sword.

Chen found he liked them too. They were real warriors, who had fought in campaigns throughout China, and were totally unlike the make-believe Hong Huzi he and Ha Li pretended to be in their games. Of course, he never told Ha Li that, because he knew he would never understand.

Another thing was that they treated him with respect – which the villagers never did. They were jealous of what they believed was the privileged position Chen's family had with the great foreign family in the hospital. Little did they know.

Over the months Chen took some pleasure in the double life he was leading. At home, and with Ha Li, he pretended to be the Aizis' greatest enemy, but secretly he was their friend.

One day he followed a platoon into the village. There had been an ambush by insurgents of a Japanese truck and they were looking for Chinese patriots. The village schoolteacher was a suspect. They stopped outside his house and the officer banged on the door. When it remained unopened, the officer shouted a command and the soldiers broke it down – but Chen, who was a little distance away, noticed the teacher scrambling over the roof to the house next door, where he crouched behind the tiles to keep out of sight.

Shortly afterwards the Japanese finished their search of the premises and came out, disappointed. They were about to march back to their barracks without their arrest, when Chen's friend, the sergeant, spotted the boy in the crowd. Carefully, so that nobody else would see him do it, Chen rolled his eyes upwards at the roof where the teacher was concealed.

The sergeant, who was a clever man, made no acknowledgement but spoke to his officer, who immediately ordered his men into the house next door where, subsequently, they found the teacher and dragged him away. The next day when Chen visited the barracks, the sergeant took him in to see the commandant and he came away with half a tael of silver as a reward.

That was the beginning. It was a new game, much more exciting than the ones he played with Ha Li. He became a real spy, reporting on villagers whom the Japanese suspected of being involved in insurgency, and they trusted him, arresting several of those he named, each time giving him a greater reward.

Later in life, he sometimes wondered what had prompted him to become an informer. He assumed that, even so young, he had instinctively understood that power is a god to be courted, empowering in turn those who flatter and serve it. That knowledge, as an adult, had brought him to where he was today, serving the Party and using his position for his own ends. The tragedy was that when he was eleven, though he might have grasped the principle, he had not mastered the subtleties. He did not know what he learnt later from bitter experience: that those in power can never be relied upon to return the loyalty you give them, and should certainly never be trusted. It was this *naïveté* that brought about his downfall.

When one day the Japanese commandant explained his plot to embarrass the foreign doctor, instead of being eager to please him, he should have been circumspect and calculated the consequences – but he had been eleven, and for years he had been smarting under the humiliations the Airton family had inflicted on him. He had never got over the rejection – the mortifying loss of face – when Ha Li's mother had denied him the education she was giving Ha Li. He had taken pains to conceal the hurt to his pride, but ever since he had nursed a sense of grievance against the parents and envy of his more fortunate playmate. So when the Japanese offered him revenge and the advancement the Airtons had denied him, he welcomed the opportunity.

He had brought Ha Li into the trap he had helped to design. He was confident, when he pointed out his hiding-place to the Japanese, that his companion would be captured. His shouted warning was supposed to reveal his friend's whereabouts to the soldiers. How was he to know that Ha Li would not remain in the loft, quivering with fear and indecision, wetting his pants and crying like a baby? Ha Li had always been his snivelling, cowardly follower, whom he had despised even as he led him along, revelling in the certainty that the spoiled, privileged foreigner was his dupe. Instead he ran, and through the incompetence of the Japanese – not Chen's, for Chen had loyally served his masters – he escaped. And Chen was punished for it. The commandant, instead of rewarding him, ordered him to be spirited away in case he reported their own bungling. He was put into hell.

They threw him into the back of a truck. This was after the man with the baseball bat had beaten him. He lay there through the long, cold night, shivering and shaking over the mountain roads. Sleep came, but he was woken by a kick in the ribs. He cowered against the cabin of the truck, watching the guards in terror as they played cards round an oil-lamp.

They took him to an officers' brothel in Jinan. The Korean comfort women, sewing their dresses in the day room, glanced at him with scorn. The soldiers who had brought him threw him into a cell without food or water. Hours later he heard the sound of a *samisen*. Guests were being entertained. He was dragged to the bathhouse and washed in scalding water. They put a kimono on him and rouged his cheeks. The first night he was the plaything of a fat colonel. He struggled when the man laid him on the *tatami*. A corporal was ordered to hold him down. He had never felt such pain, even during the beatings. Afterwards the colonel allowed the corporal to take his pleasure too . . .

Over the months he learnt to dissemble. If he pretended to enjoy it, he was sometimes rewarded with extra rice. He became a favourite of the fat colonel, but two months later he was posted to the north. The Korean comfort women took their revenge on the pampered boy. He was accused of stealing. Sanctioned by the *mama-san* they tortured him for a night and a day, tying him naked to a post in the yard and beating him with light canes. He would never forget their laughter, and the look of amusement on the faces of the officers who passed him on the way to their assignations.

Then he was taken to a house that served the common soldiers.

For six long months. Sixty years, a lifetime, would not be enough to clean himself of the shame and defilement he had endured when he was the common plaything of an Aizi barracks . . .

That was his unspoken secret, which the Party must never discover; if they did, he would be tainted. The Party was unforgiving. Even victims of foreigners were contaminated by association. He would be reclassified as *hei wu lei* and never trusted again.

He could not take his revenge on the Japanese, but he could on Ha Li. When he had seen his name on that transcript from Budapest, Chen had almost wept with gratitude. He had conceived his plan almost at that very moment. He had enjoyed every stage of the subsequent operation.

He knew there were many proverbs about revenge. 'Ten years are never too late for a worthy man to exact his vengeance.' The hero, Gou Jian, who had taken his revenge on the King of Wu, 'slept on woodpiles and tasted gall'. There were also the moralists who wrote that a desire for revenge only keeps open old wounds. Lying in bed, knowing that, a short walk up the hill, the man he blamed for his misfortunes was unaware of the trap that had closed on him, he could think of only one proverb that fitted, and that was not even a Chinese one. It was so simple as to be almost banal, but it reflected the feeling in his heart: 'Revenge is sweet.'

Just thinking about what he would do to Ha Li was sweet enough. He anticipated the look of horror on his face when he confronted him with the evidence that would destroy him. It would be sweeter yet because, even at the peak of his vengeance, he would watch him wriggle while he gave him what he would grasp as a way out. He would be able to enjoy Ha Li's humiliation for years to come, tormenting him even as he praised him and urged him on to yet more betrayals of everything in which he believed. And the sweetest part of all was that Chen would be serving his country while gratifying his own private vengeance.

And tonight he had delivered the first dagger thrust, and soon he would twist it into Ha Li's heart. And revenge would be – well – sweet . . .

What he had not counted on, however, was the incompetence of Technician Huang and his assistants: the film he was shown next morning was a travesty.

They had not been able to photograph anything with clarity in the sulphur room because the two-way mirror through which they were filming the bathroom had misted. They produced a clear sequence of a naked male carrying a naked female to the bed, but neither Ha Li nor Ziwei was identifiable because the camera angle had been too low. There was an adequate shot of Ziwei lying naked on the bed, but by then Ha Li was not in the picture. Apparently it had not occurred to Technician Huang that Ha Li might turn out the lights before he and Ziwei had sex. The technicians had decided to switch to a low-light film, but by the time they had done so Ziwei had turned the lights back on. The film of the second lovemaking was therefore over-exposed. The only evidence Chen was left with was a few tender, but fully clothed, farewell kisses caught on camera, and some rumpled sheets covered with chicken's blood, hardly material on which he could build a honey trap.

What haunted him was that he had only six weeks to bring this operation to a successful conclusion. Chen's original intention had been to allow the hydro project to follow a normal commercial course. The GPR engineers would have returned to England with their on-site findings, finalised their formal proposal and followed it up with contract negotiations in Beijing in four or five weeks' time, during which he would have had ample opportunity to do his business with Ha Li – but now he could not afford to let them leave. Otherwise there would be no excuse to bring Ziwei to Beijing. If he could manipulate her and Ha Li into bed at the Cadres' Club, there might yet be a chance to get his film in time. If not . . . The consequences were too terrible to think about.

Harry lay rigid on his bunk, trying to concentrate on the sound of the river that was gently rocking the ferry, hoping that the murmur of the water would send him to sleep, but all he could think of was Ziwei. He knew she must be in her own bunk somewhere below him and wondered if she was thinking of him. Was she relieved that it was over?

He hoped so. She had to put him behind her and get on with her life. He no longer doubted that her feelings for him were genuine. He could tell if a woman was pretending. Audrey had given him lessons in that, and Ziwei was no Audrey, whatever Julian said: that first time, in the dark, had told him so.

And now she had given Chen Tao what he wanted, he had no hold over her. She could get back to her dreary life in the Textile Bureau where she would be safe.

He had only seen her once today, from a distance, getting into her jeep with her colleagues to drive to the boat. The mountain peaks around them were still touched with pink, like the ribbon she was wearing again in her hair. She had seen him too. She had smiled at him, then lowered her head to climb into the vehicle.

He wondered if he would ever meet her again. Not alone, he thought. Chen Tao must have more than enough damning material on film. No, he thought sadly, the next private visit would come from Chen, who would presumably show him the evidence and dictate his terms. He doubted it would happen before they returned to Peking. Chen would not risk any abnormal behaviour on Harry's part while the three British engineers were still around.

It had been tiresome today to go through the motions of being the attentive civil servant as the engineers examined the plant. He wanted to put the charade behind him, to end the whole nasty business of blackmail and recruitment so that he could start the real work he had been preparing for. Then he could begin to exact his revenge on the evil system personified by Chen Tao. In the long years that he would ostensibly be spying for the Chinese, every item of information that Julian and his team gave him to hand over would be tainted. Each piece of plausible intelligence would steer the Chinese imperceptibly in a false direction, and eventually they would see the effects, in the continuing failure of their nuclear and weapons industry, in the malfunctioning of their missiles and rocketry, in the problems they encountered in the chemical and any other sector they asked him to spy on. Eventually he and Julian would have expert insights into their overseas intelligence networks and operations, and the disinformation they were preparing would have their effect there too. Each snippet of falsehood would be another nail in the coffin he was preparing for his one-time friend. He looked forward to the day when he could slam the lid.

He looked at his watch: three twenty a.m. Four more hours until breakfast. He might as well get up now, go on deck and wait for the dawn. It would be preferable to lying sleepless in this claustrophobic cabin.

He had just stepped off his bunk when he saw the door handle move.

His first thought was that it must be Chen, but it was Ziwei. She closed the door behind her and stood with her back to it, breathing quickly. She covered her mouth with her hands and giggled. 'Ha Li, are you always going to greet me naked?'

'I don't wear pyjamas,' he muttered, caught off-guard. He fumbled for a blanket. 'What are you doing here? Anybody could have seen you come in. It's dangerous.'

She stepped towards him and hugged him, then rested her head on his chest. 'Oh, Ha Li, I don't care any more. I just want to be with you.' And she began to kiss him again.

He felt the warmth and firmness of her body through her light cotton tunic. Why was Chen allowing this? It didn't make sense. Not now. Had she come without his permission? That really would be dangerous. He had to tell her to leave before they were found out – but she had pulled away the blanket and was fondling him. He looked down into her wide eyes. Oh, why hadn't she stayed away? It would have been so much easier.

But she was here.

He took her hand and led her to the bunk where he sat while he undressed her, kissing each part of her as it was revealed. Then he picked her up and laid her on the sheets, climbed up beside her and took her in his arms.

She was here, he marvelled, as the slow amnesia of lovemaking began. It did not matter how or why or what the consequences would be but, for this moment, she was here.

Chen had finished one packet of Presidents and smoked half of another before he saw Ziwei emerge. He handed her her greatcoat. A bitter wind was funnelling down the deck and he did not want her to catch cold. As she fumbled with the long sleeves he caught her expression in the light of the ship's lantern. It was one of cold scorn. He reached out and pinched her cheek, pulling her towards him with his fingers and nails. She yelped, struggling to retain her balance while her arms were straitjacketed in her coat. 'How did it go?' he asked.

'I obeyed your orders,' she said sullenly. 'Isn't that what you wanted?'

He twisted her flesh until tears of pain stood in her eyes. 'You know I have only to send a telegram and your mother will be charged. Let me ask you again, how did it go?'

'We made passionate love, Comrade,' she whimpered. He twisted again. 'I – I enjoyed it, Comrade.'

'And he?'

'He – is in love with me.'

'And you?'

'And I with him. Please stop hurting me.'

'Say it again.'

'I love him, Comrade.'

He released her. 'Good,' he said. 'You see how much easier it is if we are truthful with each other? Now get back to bed. You may miss breakfast but I want you at the meeting at nine o'clock.'

He smoked another cigarette to calm myself. Then he went down the corridor and stood outside Ha Li's door. He tapped on it. The door opened almost immediately. He noticed the look of disappointment on Harry's face. 'ChenTao,' he said. 'I was asleep. What time is it?'

'It's nearly five, Ha Li. I thought you might like to join me for a short promenade on deck so that we can watch the dawn come up. It's a clear morning so the mountains will be beautiful. And there's something important that you and I need to discuss. Don't worry. Nobody else is awake so we will be unobserved.'

'Ha Li's look of alarm was heartwarming.

When he came out a few moments later Chen pretended to be solicitous. 'Ha Li, don't you have an overcoat? It's cold in the mornings. Here, take mine, although it will be like a short jacket on you, you are so tall.'

'I'll be fine,' he said. 'Look, what's this about?'

'Oh, Ha Li.' He leant on the ship's rail, sighing and shaking his head. 'You sometimes try the patience of a friend.'

'I don't know what you mean,' he said, a belligerent tone in his voice.

He would try to bluff it out. Chen was going to enjoy this. 'Don't you?' he asked.

'No, I don't,' Ha Li growled. 'I have no idea why you got me out of bed at such an uncivilised hour of the morning. I was having a good night's sleep.'

'A *very* good night, but little sleep, I think, Ha Li.'

Even in the shadowy light of pre-dawn Chen could see his terror. 'What are you trying to say?' His voice was shaking.

'I saw her, Ha Li,' he said gently. 'I saw her go into your cabin and come out again, more than one hour later. I don't think you were in there discussing matters of translation, my friend.'

Ha Li stiffened and looked out rigidly over the water. The first pink in the sky caught his face and Chen saw his cheek twitching.

He continued, in the gently ironic tone he had chosen to adopt, 'I suspected something was wrong at the guesthouse when the masseur told me that Ziwei had passed on your instructions that he was not to attend you. It struck me as odd. Why had you not said so directly to me in the canteen? And how come Ziwei had been the messenger? I told myself that it was possible you had bumped into her on the pathway while you were going to the bathhouse. I wanted to believe that because the alternative was – well, problematic. Of course I knew that the two of you were family friends. I'd even encouraged you to be together, but I never dreamt that your relationship had blossomed into anything dangerous.' He dropped that word in deliberately, and had to hide a smile when he saw Ha Li start. 'I could not sleep tonight for thinking about it, which is why I was on deck, quietly smoking a cigarette or two, when I was amazed to see Ziwei creeping from the lower quarters towards the stairs. She didn't see me and I'm sorry, Ha Li, but I followed her.'

He was still staring at the water, his fists clenched on the handrail.

'My old friend, if you had this strong desire to play with your snake, why didn't you tell me? As I said, I know women who could accommodate you – but this girl, she's from the official classes. She works in a trading corporation. She's junior, of course, and a *hei wu lei,* but even so. She works for me. You have put me in a very difficult position.'

'Couldn't you just close one eye?' His face was hard and impassive, but his voice trembled.

'Ha Li, I have already closed both. What choice do I have? You are my oldest friend, and I am fond of Ziwei too. I don't want to get either of you into trouble. But you are a foreign diplomat, and she should have known better. You know that the laws of our country specifically forbid fraternisation with the enemy, because that, I'm afraid, is what our government would consider it. I should be locking her up for the most severe disciplining, and I should report you, Ha Li, to the Ministry of Foreign Affairs.'

'Would it help if I were to tell you that it will never happen again?' His eyes were pleading.

Ha Li, Chen thought, you don't know how pathetic you sound. 'I simply wouldn't believe you,' he said. 'I saw Ziwei's face when she left your cabin. It was radiant. I've never known anybody look so happy. She's in love with you, my friend. Are you with her?'

He was silent, hanging his head.

'There you are,' said Chen. 'Who in their right mind would trust lovers' promises? You or she would find a way to see each other again, and in time you would be caught. The internal security in our country is vigilant. Even I'm scared sometimes, but at least I have contacts and relationships. Maybe I can protect you.'

Ha Li's eyes widened with surprise and hope. 'You would help us?'

Chen gave what he hoped sounded like a bitter laugh. 'Have you left me any choice? Of course I'll help you, though I think you're both mad. I think I must be too.'

'But why would you risk it, Chen Tao? You have your senior position to look after. It would be dangerous for you too.'

'You should be glad I have it, although I'd have preferred it if you had considered that before you fell in love with each other. Never mind that now. We haven't much time. The others will wake soon. I'll protect you as far as I'm able. I'll organise means for you to meet. However, there are one or two things I'll want from you in return . . .'

Ha Li's eyes narrowed. 'I'm not going to betray my country, if that's what you're getting at.'

Proud, stupid Ha Li, thought Chen. He could not know what he had just given him. But he put a chilly tone in his voice when he replied: 'Is that how you see me? As another Communist official after a diplomat's secrets? I know that you're trained in your service to be suspicious of anybody in the Communist bloc but, Ha Li, that remark was offensive, and you have disappointed me a little. I had hoped that you and I had a special relationship unaffected by our respective systems.'

'I'm sorry,' he said. 'I'm not myself. It's been a shock, and I'm a little scared.'

He sounded so abject that Chen almost felt sorry for him. 'I understand, and I forgive you. Perhaps I didn't make myself clear. What I intended to do was to *request* that in order to help me you will promise me two things. One, you will no longer behave as idiotically and irresponsibly as you have been doing, because it will be dangerous for you both. There will be no more midnight trysts on this boat. In the meetings, when you see Ziwei, you will treat her with polite formality. If I consider it safe, and if there is a suitable occasion, I may send her up to talk to you by the rails, as the two of you did on the voyage here, but you will not touch each other, or otherwise draw attention to yourselves. Is that clear?'

'Yes. But Ziwei, will she—'

'Leave Ziwei to me. I will make sure she understands this too. Believe me, Ha Li, it is for your own protection.'

Ha Li gave an abject nod.

'Good. My second request is, trust me, and be patient. I promised I would bring you together again. It will probably be in Beijing, perhaps even in that house I took you to before. I'll have to find some sort of excuse for Ziwei and me to come to Beijing. You may have to be patient unless . . .'

'Unless what?' he croaked, sounding half scared, half hopeful.

'Last night I received a telegram from the Ministry of Foreign Trade informing me that our leaders want the contract to be concluded earlier than I had anticipated. I suspect that the reformists, like Chen Yun and Deng Xiaoping, want to steal a march on their more radical colleagues by announcing quickly that a co-operative project has been established which would clearly benefit the infrastructure of our country. Whatever the reason, it's good news – for GPR but also for you two, because we may all be gathering again very soon. I'm considering asking the British engineers to remain in Beijing for a while longer, to complete their proposal in the next week or so, working with our own engineers, while we start the contract negotiations in parallel.'

Ha Li was rubbing his hands nervously. 'I don't know, Chen Tao. Braithwaite and his team will probably have to return to England to correlate their findings with others back home. It may take them more than a week to prepare the proposal.'

'I'll make it clear to them that the urgency is dictated by our Politburo. I'm sure that greed will concentrate their minds on the task. You can put in a word to persuade them.'

'All right,' he said. 'That may work.'

Chen was delighted. Ha Li had probably not realised it yet but he had committed his first little act of betrayal. He had put his love life before his duty to his project. He gave a hearty laugh and slapped his shoulder. 'Trust me,' he said. 'If your British engineers agree to what I'm proposing, that undisciplined snake of yours will be drinking in the jasmine pool again before the week is out.'

Ha Li gave a sickly smile. 'I – I don't know how to thank you.'

'You can thank me by being careful, and patient, as long as this voyage lasts.'

'Chen Tao?' He was still rubbing his hands anxiously. 'What will happen after the negotiations are over?'

In six weeks, Chen thought triumphantly, Ha Li would be on his payroll, the disloyal bitch would be on her way to a labour camp, and he, if he played his cards right, would have Commissioner Hao's job, but all he said was, 'Don't worry, I'll find a way for you to continue seeing each other, I promise. Now, Ha Li, you must get back inside. I hear the crew moving. Go. Hurry.'

Harry paced the narrow space in his cabin. He could not understand Chen Tao's motives. If the man had his evidence, and he must have, why send Ziwei in to see him again? Why extend the honey trap to Peking? Why this creaky pretence that he was Harry's friend and protector?

It would make more sense to get the GPR men back to England They would only be a complicated encumbrance. If the hydro project had been Chen's cover for his operation, there were any number of ways to cancel it without arousing the British government's suspicions. He did not need the engineers in Peking to do so. If, as Julian speculated, the Chinese wanted to go through with the GPR deal, it would still be more sensible to create a breathing space so that they could go through the necessary blackmail. Harry could be primed and in place when the GPR men returned. Hurrying the contract made no sense. And Chen did not need the affair between Ziwei and Harry to continue. All he had to do now was reveal his photographs and his identity as a member of the Chinese intelligence services.

There must be a practical reason why he was allowing them to continue their liaison in Peking. Did he not believe that the blackmail threat would be enough? Did he think he could sugar the pill with the promise that Harry's beloved would be available if he did as he was told? If so he must believe that Harry was a naïve, lovelorn fool.

Harry caught a glimpse of his unshaven, haggard face and his staring eyes in the mirror above the basin. Perhaps Chen had cause to think that.

Even now his heart was beating faster at the prospect of being alone with Ziwei. Perhaps Chen would allow them some sort of relationship in the future. Perhaps Harry could insist, when he agreed to work for the Chinese, that Chen smuggle her to Hong Kong, Macao, or an Eastern-bloc country, even somewhere in the Middle East, which was neutral in the Cold War. They would forget the reality of their condition, plan for the future when he was released from his commitments . . .

Disgusted with himself, he doused his head under the cold tap, picked up his razor and began to shave, cutting himself. The pain made him think clearly again.

He was not a squaddy whose furlough had been extended. He was a British spy with a job to do. Yes, of course he was thrilled that he would see her again. He had no illusions about what she felt for him or he for her. Even if she was Chen's puppet, the strings were cut when they were in each other's arms – but that was the problem. She was in Chen's power, and the longer their affair continued and the more entangled they became, the more dangerous it would be for her.

But what could he do? If he tried to discourage her, the operation would be compromised, and Chen Tao would place all the blame for the failure of the mission on Ziwei, with horrific consequences for her.

As the ship's bell rang for breakfast, Harry made a decision. There was a way to protect Ziwei and perform his mission. The operation demanded that he continue his affair with her. He would not be able to influence the way she felt about him, but he could change the way he felt about her. He had compromised the operation by allowing himself to become infatuated. He would now force himself to behave in the way he should have done from the very beginning, coldly, coolly and ruthlessly. Ziwei would become another target for seduction, like the others in the past. He would flatter her, do whatever had to be done, but it would be a mental exercise. Meanwhile he would focus purely on the operation. He would steel himself against pity. If she became an emotional wreck, like his earlier victims, so be it. That would be preferable to the vengeance Chen would inflict on her if the operation were to fail. But there would be no need for him to punish Ziwei. Harry would make sure that everything went like clockwork. From now on, he would be Chen's most loyal pawn, and he would remain so, until the recruitment process was complete and he could turn the tables. Presently, his love for Ziwei was a weakness, endangering them both. He would serve her best by treating her as his most dangerous enemy.

As he was preparing to leave his cabin, he remembered another of Julian's truisms. It had been after a long debriefing in London and they had gone to an Italian place off St Martin's Lane to relax. Like many restaurants in the area, its walls had been covered with photographs of theatre people. Julian, swirling Tancredi in a huge wineglass, had observed them sardonically and said, 'We're no different from them, Harry. Actors, that's all we spies are. Only difference is that we perform on a larger stage and there's no audience. But we go out and give the same cock-and-bull. And we do it bloody professionally. Our survival depends on it. That's what you'll be doing, Harry, when you eventually get to China.'

* * *

184

Chen Tao was brisk and business-like when the two sides gathered in the day room at nine o'clock. Ziwei was sitting on a stool in a back row, placed modestly among the junior technicians rather than with him and the senior Chinese engineers at the table. Harry, in his new mood of resolve, found that he could look at her without emotion. Once, when their eyes met, she smiled at him and he smiled back, but he felt nothing.

There was no more time-wasting. Chen pushed the agenda forward at a spanking pace. Gallagher had some minor queries about the operational systems of the plant but the information he required was sensitive, and Deputy Chief Engineer Yan at first tried to prevaricate. Chen ordered him to answer the questions. By lunchtime the GPR team had all the information they required. When the meeting resumed in the afternoon, only Chen and the professor attended on the Chinese side. Again Chen came straight to the point, and in ten minutes it was over. He asked them to think carefully about what he had said, and to give him their answer before the ferry reached Chongqing. Then he and the professor left.

For several minutes, the engineers were silent. Then Braithwaite turned to Gallagher. 'Think we can do it, boy?' he growled.

'There are no technical issues, Jack. I could prepare something in ten days.'

'You'll work all night if you have to. The man said a week. Billy, what about the pricing?'

Hudson drew on his pipe. 'It depends what extras Tommy's proposing, but pricing's standard. I'd say there's no problem, Jack. Till Tommy gets back, we can usefully go over the standard clauses in the contract. Arbitration, *force majeure*, exclusivity.'

'It looks as if it's all settled then,' said Braithwaite. He clapped Gallagher on the back. 'You're off back to Blighty, you lucky bugger, leaving Billy and me to sample yet again the delights of Peking. I suppose the bright side is they're serious and want to conclude the deal.'

Chen Tao had correctly assessed the GPR men's greed, concluded Harry ruefully. It had been easy, he thought, as he drank a beer with them. They were already toasting the success of the project that they had convinced themselves was in the bag. When Braithwaite started to rib Hudson about the promotion he would receive when the deal was signed, Harry decided to leave them to it. He wanted to be alone, but if he had read Chen's hints correctly, Ziwei would probably be coming up on deck shortly to look for him, as she had done before. He told himself he had no wish to see her, but Chen would expect him to be eager, so eager he would be.

He walked up and down for a while. Through the windows of the bridge, he saw the pilot, one eye on his charts, the other on the water, giving instructions to the helmsman, who was expertly steering the ship through the treacherous channels. Harry recognised one of the narrows where, on the voyage up, it had had to be dragged by porters, but there was no need for that on the journey downstream. Once the pilot had positioned the ferry correctly, the fast current carried them through. A few days ago, the rocking acceleration might have exhilarated him, but today he was irritated by the distraction: all his thoughts were focused on the uncomfortable meeting that was about to occur.

Sure enough, about a quarter of an hour after he had taken up his old position at the rail, Ziwei was beside him. She was trembling and her face was flushed. He noticed a new bruise on her cheek, and felt a burst of rage against Chen Tao, but, controlling himself, he gave her what he hoped was the lover's smile she expected to see. Then he leant forward, took her shoulders in his hands and kissed her forehead. She broke away, flustered. 'No, Ha Li, we must be careful in case anyone should see us. Chen Tao told us there should be no – no touching, although all I want is for you to take me in your arms.'

'It's all I want to do too, Ziwei,' he said. 'You look ravishing in this afternoon sunlight.'

'There has not been much sunshine since we have been together, Ha Li,' she said, dropping her eyes.

He made a move towards her. 'It'll be all right, my darling,' he said. 'I promise. We'll find a way.'

'You're not angry with me?' she said, in a small voice. 'When – when Chen Tao came to my cabin after he'd spoken to you, I feared you would never want to see me again.'

'But why?' he asked, taken aback. He really was surprised. Then he added, 'I can't bear being apart from you.'

'I thought – I thought . . .' Her shoulders were shaking. 'I thought you would never forgive me for having put you in danger.'

'Oh, my darling, I think it was a good thing that Chen Tao saw us

together. We now have a powerful protector. He can help us, Ziwei.'
Then: 'Please don't blame yourself.'

She was gazing up at him quizzically. 'You really believe we can
trust him, Ha Li?' she whispered. There was ice in her tone.

'I do trust him,' he said firmly. 'He's our friend. I know him. But
I don't want to talk about him now.' He reached out and pulled her
to him. The curtains were drawn in the cabins close to them, and their
position made them invisible to the upper and lower decks. She struggled, then relaxed. 'Yes, hold me, Ha Li. I'm so scared – and ashamed.'

'Don't be,' he murmured, kissing her hair. He released her and,
lifting her chin, kissed her lips. He felt her respond. All the time he
was watching the deck. He counted thirty seconds and withdrew.
'Chen Tao's right, my darling, we mustn't take any risks on this ferry.'

Woodenly, she stepped back. She looked as if he had hit her, and
he felt a pang, but she murmured, 'You're right. It's dangerous, although
for a moment I no longer cared.'

'Listen, my love.' He held her eyes. 'There's no reason for you to
be scared, and certainly no reason to be ashamed. That's nonsense.
We have to be strong, that's all. It's difficult now, but soon we'll be in
Beijing together. Then we'll find a way.' And he added, 'Having found
you, I'm not going to lose you, whatever obstacles the People's Republic
or the British Foreign Office throw at us.'

She was shaking her head. He had to distract her before she did
anything stupid, like warning him about the honey trap. 'Look,' he
cried, waving his arm over the rail.

'What? What, Ha Li? I see nothing.'

He grinned. 'My mistake. I thought I saw a whale pop out from
behind that wave.'

'That's not funny, Ha Li,' she said.

'No, it's not,' he said. 'I'm sorry. But I wasn't entirely joking. We
must remember that whale and believe that one day we'll see it together.'

'That was a dream, Ha Li.'

'You told me that if we could make ourselves believe in something
it *can* come true.'

'You're so much stronger than I am,' she said. 'I was watching you
this morning, in the meeting. It might have been that Chen Tao had
never spoken to you.'

'I looked strong because I'm full of hope. I sense there's a way
forward. You must be strong too, and – and trust me, Ziwei.'

'Oh, Ha Li, if only you knew . . .'

'No,' he said harshly. 'Don't say it. Please, Ziwei, we must hope now, and believe in it.' Somehow he managed a laugh. 'Or else,' he said.

'Or else what, Ha Li?'

'I'm not going to be able to resist. I'll grab you, and kiss you, and hold you in my arms and never let you go, and I won't care if the whole ship's crew comes out to watch us, because that would be as mad as despairing, when everything's going right for us.'

It was with enormous relief that he heard her quiet laugh. 'I sometimes think you *are* a little mad, Ha Li.'

'I am,' he said. 'Mad as a March hare, and so are you, and so is Chen Tao, and so are both our governments, and the whole world, but it doesn't matter, Ziwei, not at this moment, because you're standing next to me, and the rest of the universe can go hang, because we're untouchable.'

'Oh, Ha Li,' she whispered. She reached hesitantly to stroke his shoulder. 'If I'm not to tell you what is in my heart, what are we to do?'

'I know what's in your heart,' he said, 'and you know what's in mine. Isn't that enough for now?'

'But do you?'

'Yes,' said Harry, firmly. 'I've never been clearer.'

'So we will stand by each other's side and say nothing. Is that what you want, Ha Li?'

'Until we reach Beijing and are really together. For now, we must be patient and strong. For me, just knowing you're by my side is enough. Is there anything more that we need right now?'

'We could look out over the waters of the Yangtze and search for whales,' she said, as she gazed at him.

'Yes,' he said. He felt like choking. 'We can search for our whales.' And somehow he responded to her smile with a confident one of his own.

'I love you, Ha Li,' she said. 'I did not want to at first, but now I cannot help myself.'

'And I love you, Ziwei.'

'Really?'

'Really.'

They did touch, discreetly. First their fingers entwined as their hands rested side by side on the rail. Gradually they drew closer together and they felt the gentle pressure of each other's limbs. They also, fleetingly, kissed when Ziwei decided it was time for her to go.

Harry's hands were shaking when he fumbled for his cigarettes and lighter, but the cigarette drooped in his mouth and eventually blew away. He gazed fixedly at the mountain peaks that were slowly passing, seeing nothing of them. He was aware only of the emptiness in his heart.

There was a reception at the minister's residence on the night Harry returned. Garrard had organised it for Julian as a favour. He had been reluctant but Julian told him he would persuade the Office to fund the expenses, and that had mollified him. The ostensible reason for the gathering was that a left-wing academic from London's School of Oriental and African Studies was in town, having finished a month's fieldwork in one of the showpiece communes. Julian had interviewed him for *The Times*, and been quietly amazed that somebody apparently intelligent could be gulled into believing the propaganda he was fed, but these people believed what they wanted to believe, and through them the comrades spread their poison into the unsuspecting West. Since a party was being held, no eyebrows would be raised if invitations were extended to the returning GPR engineers (there were now only two; one had flown directly from Chongqing to Canton, and onwards, via Hong Kong, to the UK). Meanwhile, Julian would have a chance to chat to Harry on his own.

He was talking to Harry on strictly professional lines, in keeping with their respective covers, when Molly Garrard, presumably instructed by her husband, came breezily up to them, complaining about the fug in the drawing room: would they mind it if she opened the french windows by which they happened to be standing? That gave them the opportunity to slip out of the crush on to the veranda and from there into the shadows of the enormous trees that flanked the expansive lawn. They ostentatiously lit two cigars. That, if anybody enquired, was an adequate reason for them to have gone outside. The form at the Garrards' cocktail parties was well known to be 'cigarettes if you must, but no heavier tobacco'. Julian, conscious that long-range microphones might be focused towards the legation, asked Harry if, by any chance, he had heard, while he was in Chongqing, of a new PLA-run radio station that was broadcasting in the south-west. It had been reported in *Xinhua* quite recently, so it was a natural question for a journalist to put.

'As it happens I have,' he answered.

Julian's heart was beating in his throat with his excitement. The innocuous phrase had told him that the honey trap had taken place.

'I tuned into the channel in my hotel room,' Harry continued. 'It had very clear reception.'

So the comrades had filmed the lovers in bed. 'Hear anything interesting?'

'Not really. Same old propaganda you get listening to the Central Broadcasting Station. Party speeches, that sort of thing.'

Interesting and unexpected. He had expected the sting to take place in Peking, but Harry had been approached already. 'Nothing to get excited about, then?' Julian prodded him. 'It wasn't specifically a military channel? Voice of the South-west Command?'

Julian had thought he would dismiss the idea, which would have meant that everything had gone smoothly, and that the blackmail process had begun, but Harry did not answer immediately. Eventually, he said, 'I can't honestly tell you, Travers. Might have been. Don't know. Good as my Chinese is, I found the Sichuanese accent of the speaker I was listening to pretty much impenetrable, so I switched off after a few seconds. Sorry, can't help you, I'm afraid.'

So there were complications. 'Well, I didn't think there would be much in the story,' Julian said. 'Wishful thinking, really. You know how we correspondents are always looking for potential cracks in the system. Think I'm wasting my time?'

'Oh, no, any lead's worth pursuing,' he said. 'Never know where it'll take you. That's the line I adopt in my scientific work. The path to knowledge is ever circuitous, but if you trust patiently in your common sense, you'll reach your destination sooner or later.'

Julian laughed, relieved. Whatever complication had occurred, Harry was still confident that the project was on course, and he was on top of the situation. Chen Tao was still leading him in the direction they wanted to go. That was good enough for now, although Julian was dying to hear the whole story. The main point was that the honey trap had started. The Chinese had taken the bait. 'I never knew you were a philosopher, Dr Airton,' he told him. 'Look, these cigars are damned good, but it's bloody cold out here. I'm going to keep the second half of mine for tomorrow after work. Shall we continue our conversation inside?'

'I think that would be a very good idea,' he said, having acknowledged that he would be in the Wendy Room the next evening. When they rejoined the party they saw that the Garrards had already positioned themselves by the door to say farewell to their guests. Julian did not linger. He had much to think about.

8

The Safe House

Peking, April 1963

As they were clearing up their papers after the second day of commercial talks, Chen Tao walked over to the British side of the table and asked Harry if he could remain behind. There were matters related to the government-to-government guarantees that he wished to clarify.

'Didn't we go over all of that yesterday?' asked Harry. It had been a long day, and the strain of being in the same room as Ziwei, pointedly ignoring her, had worn him down.

'I wish to clarify a few points,' said Chen.

'I'll have to tell my colleagues,' said Harry. 'They're expecting me to drive them back to their hotel.'

Chen shrugged.

Braithwaite was not concerned. 'That's all right, lad, take your time. Billy and I'll walk. Hotel's only a few blocks away, and we could do with the exercise. See you for a drink later?'

Harry glanced at Chen. 'I'm tied up this evening. Paperwork at the legation, then bed – I'm tired.'

'Aye, I'm knackered too. Think I'll turn in early myself, unless Billy here has plans to drag me round the steamy nightlife of this thrilling city. He's always gets excited after a happy day discussing contracts, don't you, Billy?'

Hudson, who was putting his spectacles into his top pocket, beamed amiably. 'That's right, Jack. Bring on the dancing girls.'

'Tell me if you find any,' said Harry. 'I never have.'

'Now, why does that not surprise me?' said Braithwaite.

Chen waited until the two GPR men had left the room. Most of the Chinese had already hurried out to catch the ministry bus. Ziwei had left with them, giving Harry a troubled glance as she reached the door. One or two foreign-trade officials, however, were still clearing their papers, irritating Chen, although he tried not to show it. To break the silence he was forced to spend several minutes going over yet again the sort of guarantees he expected the British government to supply. Harry took the hint and told him he had sent a cable to London incorporating all of Chen's terms and was expecting a favourable reply.

One by one the other officials left, until only a bald accountant remained. He was now checking his notes, occasionally underlining sections of his precise characters. Frustratingly, he showed no inclination that he wanted to leave. Chen lost patience. He leant over the table. 'Lao Zheng,' he said softly, 'don't you have a home to go to?' The accountant saw something in his eyes that made him tremble. He brushed his papers into his plastic briefcase, then, bowing and muttering apologies, he backed out of the door.

Chen turned to Harry. 'You see the sort of arseholes I have to deal with every day. I believe in our system passionately, Ha Li, but that doesn't mean I love every one of my comrades. Especially when they appoint ignorant farmers as my financial advisers.'

'I take it you didn't keep me here to discuss the merits of Communism – or the contract, for that matter.'

Chen laughed and shook him by the shoulders. 'Ha Li, Ha Li, it's good to see you alone again. I've been longing all day to tell you. I've fixed it.'

'Fixed what?' Harry was careful to put a note of nervousness in his voice.

Chen chuckled. 'Come on, Ha Li. You look as scared as a schoolgirl meeting her lover in the bushes. Nobody will disturb us. I've squared everybody so you and Ziwei won't be observed. You can be alone together until dawn if you want.'

'What do you mean, "squared everybody"?'

'The attendants, of course, at the club I took you to last time. At seven this evening, I'll come for you. You wait for me at Nan Chizi, same place as before. You'll recognise my car. I'll pick you both up again in the morning, too. Spend the whole night there, if you like. I imagine that snake of yours will want plenty of nourishment after it's lain idle all these impatient days and nights, and if I read the look on little Ziwei's face correctly when I told her the good news, her jasmine pool is already bubbling at the prospect of being filled. Oh, I'm sorry, Ha Li.' There was a look of mock concern on his face. 'I've offended you by being crude.'

'No, it's not that. I'm – I'm just worried whether it'll be safe.'

'Trust me, Ha Li. I wouldn't suggest it if it wasn't. Who do you think would get into most trouble if you were found out? Me. You think I'd be foolish enough to endanger myself? Or you? Or Ziwei? Come on, Ha Li, we're friends. Why do you think I'm doing this for you? It's because I know you'd do the same for me.' He laughed. 'Maybe, one day, I'll ask you to return the favour. If ever I'm sent on a trade delegation to London and fall in love with one of your English girls, would you consider helping out your old friend as I'm helping you?'

'Of course.' Harry allowed himself to be soothed. 'We're friends, and I owe you already more than I can ever repay. But . . .' Chen watched him with narrowed eyes, as Harry shuffled indecisively. 'I don't know. If the legation found out, I'd lose my job. I'd never work in government again. They'd never understand.'

'They won't find out. How could they?' He was no longer smiling. 'Well, it's up to you. All I can say is that Ziwei will be disappointed, but that's not my concern.' He picked up his briefcase. 'Makes it easier for me. No more headaches trying to set up love nests for you.'

'You're sure Ziwei's happy with the arrangement? She wants to see me?'

'You know her better than I do,' said Chen, scooping papers into his briefcase. 'But since you ask, I'd say she does. She's in love with you. If you decide not to see her again, you'll break her heart. But it's all right. I'll send her back to Shanghai. If that's what you want.'

'I don't want that,' murmured Harry. 'I – I couldn't bear not to see her again.'

Chen put his hands on Harry's shoulders again. 'Be a man, Ha Li. That's what she thinks you are. I guarantee that you'll both be safe. On my honour as your friend.'

Harry nodded.

'Good. Then I will pick you up in my car at seven. Now I'd better be off. If we continue discussing government-to-government relations much longer, even my dozy subordinates will become suspicious. Anyway, I have to drive to some remote suburb to pick up Ziwei from her dormitory.' His wicked grin had returned. 'Courage, my friend. You're a lucky man. My nurses give me pleasure from time to time, but never love.'

* * *

Julian decided not to tell Harry what he intended, calculating it would only worry him, and he had enough on his mind.

It had often struck him that in their business luck had a way of finding you if you were only receptive and recognised it for what it was. Julian had had no idea of the windfall that would come to him as a result of the strange party he had attended on Christmas Day at the Kyodo news agency. One of their correspondents was a man who went by the name of Tadeyama. There was something familiar about him. The grey hair above a young face, the watchful eyes, the shy smile – somewhere, he was sure, he had seen this man before and, as a matter of routine, cabled London to check up on him.

When he decoded the message that was returned through the lega- tion, it came back to him. He remembered the spooks conference he had attended three years before in Tokyo. Umegaki – that was his real name – had been a speaker at the seminar before they broke off into separate workshop sessions. He had given a workmanlike presentation on the Party's role in co-ordinating and assessing raw information gathered by the Chinese military departments involved in espionage, with some good case studies. Julian had vaguely noted his name as somebody he might contact in the future – and now, after he had confirmed that Umegaki was Tadeyama and, like him, had been sent on an undercover mission to Peking, he recognised an opportunity.

He got London to do the liaison with Tokyo. They did not tell them the whole story, merely that an operation was under way which, if successful, would sabotage China's equivalent of the Manhattan Project (the nuclear threat terrified the Japanese so at this their ears pricked). They also told them the operation would yield A-grade product over some years. The upshot was that Tadeyama received instructions from his masters in the Defence Intelligence Agency to give Julian assistance if he requested it, no questions asked. It had occurred to Julian that, with his long nose and straw-coloured hair, he would always stick out in a crowd, but an Oriental, if the need arose, might be able to pass himself off as Chinese.

And that was why the two were parked in an alley opposite Harry's *hutong*. They were in a small van, one of the fleet of local vehicles the Japanese embassy used for their more dubious activities. They were partly obscured by a heap of coal on one side and a pile of cabbages on the other. They couldn't see Harry's house, but Tadeyama was sure they would spot him leaving, either in his old Volga or on foot. Julian remained in the back, keeping his head down. Occasionally, feeling cramped or cold, he would peer through the glass panel that separated him from the driver's seat. He saw nothing but a dark Peking thoroughfare, like any other in this picturesque section of the old town. The few shops he could make out through the bare branches of the plane trees were boarded up. Nobody was about, except the occasional cyclist hurrying home and a few thickly wrapped locals making their way to the noodle stall on the corner. It had been a long winter this year. Streaks of yellowed snow were still visible here and there on the edge of the pavements. If spring had come early, what they were doing would have been impossible because Peking residents tended to live on the street, but in this weather they would all be at home, having dinner, hunched round the stove.

Julian took comfort from what he could see of Tadeyama behind the wheel. He was partly obscured by the thick fur collar of his PLA greatcoat and the protruding earflaps of his hat. He looked every inch a local. Earlier he had slouched along the *hutong* and noticed a parked car some distance away from Harry's gate. 'Maybe we are not the only ones on surveillance duty this evening. Travers-*san*?' He raised a questioning eyebrow at Julian, when he returned.

'Busy neighbourhood, Tadeyama,' said Julian, keeping a straight face, but he felt a shiver of fear. He wanted to be the hunter tonight, not the hunted.

'Apparently so.' Tadeyama's expression remained enigmatic. Julian could feel his nervousness and displeasure. If the Japanese decided to abort the operation, there was nothing he could do about it. Now he appeared to be considering the risks. At last he shrugged. 'It is manageable. We will continue,' said Tadeyama. 'but for now we stay out of sight.'

Julian breathed a sigh of relief and looked for something to cover the cold metal floor of the van, mentally preparing himself for what could be hours more of cold, discomfort, boredom – and fear.

'Lie flat, Travers-*san*,' hissed Tadeyama – it might have been twenty interminable minutes later. Julian started, and caught a glimpse of a cyclist moving towards them down their alley. The man was wearing a blue military greatcoat and a peaked cap. He pressed his cheek against the metal, heart pounding. Tadeyama had already leant his head against the steering-wheel, pretending to be asleep. He heard the rattle of a bicycle. He froze as it stopped next to them. Heavy footsteps crunched the ice on the road – oh, God, he thought, the local cop. Then he heard the creak of a gate opening, and there was silence. 'It's all right, Travers-*san*. Only a resident going home. Not police. Railway worker.' Julian relaxed, but it was several minutes before he stopped shaking.

He was wondering how much further into his pockets he could stick his freezing hands when Tadeyama tapped on the window. Harry was leaving. Julian caught a glimpse of his tall, angular frame, hands thrust into the pockets of a tweed jacket, walking purposefully northwards. The only concession he had made to the cold was a knitted scarf round his neck. He was scowling. That's Harry, he thought – the eager lover – but Julian's fear, and Tadeyama's full attention, was focused on the entrance to the alley from which Harry had emerged. Their immediate danger lay here, if the observers parked in the *hutong* decided to follow too.

Tadeyama waited. 'They're probably staying put,' said Julian. 'Radioed ahead to say he's left.' Tadeyama nodded, but kept his eyes on the entrance to the *hutong*, and it was two minutes later that he judged it safe enough to pull the car out into the street. Thankfully, Harry could still be seen, several hundred yards ahead. Tadeyama crawled until he saw Harry turn into an alley that led to Wangfujing. Here he made a U-turn and ducked into another alley parallel to the one Harry had taken. By the time Harry had emerged into the more crowded thoroughfare of Peking's main shopping street, they were waiting for him. He was still walking north, and continued to do so until the Dongsikou turning, where he headed west towards the old Imperial Palace. They followed. At the next intersection he turned south along Nan Chizi, in the direction of Chang An Avenue and Tiananmen square.

The snatch took them by surprise. Suddenly Harry crossed the road. It was empty of traffic. At the same time, in the distance, they saw a Red Flag limousine, approaching from Chang An Avenue. When it passed Harry, it braked to a stop. The back door flew open, and Harry got in.

Tadeyama put his foot on the accelerator. They passed the Red Flag as it was gathering speed. Julian saw a blur of blacked-out windows and polished metal. Tadeyama drove down the road in the opposite direction to which their target was going. Julian wondered what he was contemplating, but as they reached the arch at the intersection with Chang An Avenue, he made another dangerous U-turn, so violent that Julian was thrown against the door panel. He heard the horn of a startled taxi-driver who had had to move out of the way, but they were already off in high-speed pursuit. Even so he had several worried seconds when he could make out nothing ahead, but at last he saw the tail-lights and found his composure again. By Jesus, he thought, this man is good.

After that it was easier. They kept a safe three hundred yards behind, following the Red Flag as it drove west past the high crenellated walls of the palace. It turned right under the shadow of Coal Hill, and through a maze of smaller roads that eventually led them to the vicinity of the Drum Tower. Tadeyama dropped back to a five- or six-hundred-yard distance when the Red Flag turned north along the narrow, tree-lined road flanking the Hou Hai. By then Julian had guessed that their destination would be one of the grand mansions that lined this lake in secluded splendour behind their high walls; they housed several state leaders, including Sun Yat-sen's widow, Song Qingling, who was known to host parties for favoured foreign guests in her palatial home. It would make sense that a bordello for leaders would be located somewhere in this prestigious neighbourhood.

But he was wrong. There were more turnings. As they threaded their way through the *hutongs* on the west side of the lake, Tadeyama had to use all his skill to remain unobserved. It was a cat-and-mouse process because they could risk turning into each alley only when their target's tail-lights had turned into another, and there was every chance that they would lose it. It was on a straight road, however, that the Red Flag eventually stopped. They saw it ahead of them, idling, as its driver waited for the PLA guard to pull back the sheet iron gates that opened into the courtyard of a gabled brick house.

Tadeyama drove past casually. They had found Chen Tao's mysterious club. Tadeyama would easily find it again. It was the only Western-style house around.

'You think your surveillance teams can manage something?' Julian asked, as the Japanese drove him back to his hotel.

'Difficult,' said Tadeyama, 'High walls. Maybe not impossible.'

'Dangerous?'

Tadeyama gave him a slanted glance. Julian noticed an ironic smile and a twinkle in his eye. Tadeyama turned back to the road, and Julian realised his hands were still shaking. He needed a large brandy. He wondered if he was getting old.

This time Chen had taken no chances. He had spent much of the previous night personally testing the cameras in every variation of light conditions. He had two assistants lying stark naked on the bed throughout. He didn't care how embarrassed they were. He wanted to assure himself that every intimate gesture between Ha Li and Ziwei would be caught. Only when the film was developed and after the raw cuts had been shown in the projection room was he satisfied. Then he let everybody go home. He intended to snatch a few hours' sleep, and stretched out – why not? – on the bed on which tonight the lovers would perform. He had no desire for any company, although the house would have provided it if he had asked.

And now the moment of retribution had come – or nearly. He watched the two lovers in the mirror above the dashboard. He had adjusted it so he could observe them. They seated themselves a distance away from each other at first, as they had the last time, but it was not long before they began to hold hands. Imperceptibly they moved closer together so their bodies touched, and finally Ha Li put an arm round her shoulders, and she leant her head against his chest. All the while, they wore long, solemn faces, as if they were going to a funeral rather than a tryst. Chen supposed they were embarrassed that he was in the car, or on Ha Li's part, it might have been the crippling shyness and self-restraint that tends to overtake English people when they become intimate; at least, that was how they behaved in the movies Chen had seen. If he had been Ha Li, he thought, he would have been pawing the bitch, but then, how would he know? He'd never been in love.

He knew why Ziwei was upset. When he had collected her from her dormitory, she was wearing the red cheongsam that he had had specially measured for her. Her hair was piled up on her head. Her cheeks were rouged, she had applied lipstick and eye-shadow and she smelt pleasantly of the French perfume he had purchased at great expense from the Friendship Store. It amused him on this, her last night with Ha Li, to dress her as a bride. He also hoped her new exotic appearance would arouse Ha Li, because Chen needed sex tonight, not the tender twitterings of lovebirds. She had given Chen a nervous smile, as if she was seeking his approval.

Shortly before they picked up Ha Li, he had drawn up in the fore-court of the Peking Hotel. He turned off the engine and, after another long moment of silence and suspense, told her that he had reported her indiscipline and her lapse of patriotism to his superiors. She had to clutch the armrest of the car for support.

'Their verdict was the same as mine,' Chen continued. 'By losing control of your feelings, not to mention your better judgement, in allowing yourself to fall in love with your target, an enemy of the Chinese people, you have nearly compromised our operation.' He paused. 'It is my superiors' view, as it is my own, that this has been tantamount to a counter-revolutionary act for which you and your mother deserve immediate punishment.'

By now she was shaking with terror. From his briefcase, he with-drew the stamped documents ordering her mother's arrest and Ziwei's own deportation to a labour camp. This time they were official. He pointed to Commissioner Hao's chop, then the date. 'These orders are already effective,' he said.

He waited, allowing all the implications to penetrate her stunned mind – but not for too long. He didn't want her to lose control of her bowels and spoil her new dress. It was time to change gear. 'You may be wondering why you haven't been arrested,' he said, fractionally soft-ening his tone.

Her head jerked up, her eyes widening with desperate hope.

'It may surprise you, but I've pleaded for you. Not for your sake, of course, but for the sake of the operation. You should consider your-self fortunate that the Party, in its mercy, has agreed to give you another chance. A last chance,' he added.

She mumbled something incomprehensible. Perhaps she was attempting to thank him. He gave her a hard stare. 'You are lucky that you have not already been sent away. And so is your mother that she is not in gaol waiting execution – but that may yet happen unless you can persuade me that this clemency is justified, which means that, from now on, you must do exactly as I instruct you. Any deviation of any kind and I will implement the orders of the Party. Tonight you are being given the responsibility – the privilege – of helping me to trap an enemy of our country. It will involve you having sex with him. Sex,' he emphasised. 'You will not be making love. This is work, Comrade Peng, not pleasure, although you must make him believe that that is what he is getting. Your body no longer belongs to you. These documents, unless I revoke them, make you the property of the state and the people. The revolution demands that you manipulate your body in the most humiliating and explicit manner you can devise. If I am not satisfied by your performance, if I do not get what I want on film, these orders will have immediate effect. Your mother will be dead within the week, and you will live many long years in a labour camp until you too die, of exhaustion and despair.' She was gazing at him with the eyes of a patient under hypnosis.

'Are you clear about your alternatives, Comrade Peng?'

'Yes, Comrade Chen,' she whispered.

'Then you undertake tonight to put aside your love for this man, if such it is, and do what your country expects of you? You will conquer your emotions and treat this enemy of our people with the dispassion and ingenuity that a whore uses to please her client?'

She blanched when he said that word, and her lip trembled. He picked up the documents from the dashboard and dropped them into her lap, page by page. A single tear ran down her cheek, and she lowered her head in shame. He waited, listening to the shivering of her breath. Slowly she raised her chin. There was dull resignation in her eyes, but he saw with satisfaction that the set of her features had hardened. 'Yes, Comrade Chen. Tonight I will be Ha Li's whore.'

'Good.' He put the documents back into the briefcase and turned on the engine. Five minutes later Ha Li was in the car. Chen watched them in their clumsy embrace, feeling all the contentment of a film director whose actors have been primed for their most crucial scene.

Harry wondered if Chen Tao ever intended to leave them alone. He was obnoxiously cheerful and offensively facetious, like a boorish guest overstaying his welcome at a wedding. Making sly innuendoes about the pleasure in store for them, he fussed about the suite. He pulled the curtains tighter. He moved a vase of orchids from the dining alcove to the coffee-table. He inspected the bathroom. He checked the bedroom. He positioned two pairs of slippers by the bed. He smoothed the creases on the sheets. He insisted that he share with them a bottle of champagne 'to put you both in the right mood', and kept up a flow of chatter as they consumed it.

This time, Harry observed, Ziwei drank. She finished two glasses, one after the other. He had noticed already how stiffly she had first reacted to him in the car. She was smiling at him now but not with her eyes. It was as if she were steeling herself for something terrible she had to do. He wondered what was troubling her. He did not think her feelings for him had changed. His certainly hadn't for her (if anything they had intensified – despite all his resolutions to remain detached, he was counting the moments before he could hold her in his arms). Yet she looked scared, as she had in the bathhouse, and that struck him as odd. Chen must have coerced her again, he thought angrily. The sooner this was over and she was out of the man's power, the better – even if it meant that he and Ziwei might never see each other again. Was that what was troubling her? Did she have an instinct, or some knowledge, that this would be their last night together? But why? He had still not penetrated Chen Tao's motives for extending their affair after he had his film but, granted that he had done so, it would seem pointless if it were only for one night.

Something was not right and he could not put his finger on it. When Chen had got out of the car briefly to order the guard to open the gates of the underground car park, she had kissed his cheek, and murmured, 'Ha Li, remember that I love you.' When Chen returned, her head was back on Harry's chest, as it had been when he left them. The stolen kiss had also struck Harry as odd. They would be naked together very shortly, and Chen would almost certainly be watching them, so why her anxiety to disguise a kiss?

But then again, since that morning on the boat, there had been little that had not struck him as odd. He still had no clear idea what his enemy was intending. Julian had speculated that Chen wanted more than just film of them in bed together. Perhaps he intended to terrorise Harry. Chen might arrange for the police to make a raid on the club, have the lovers arrested in bed together, 'turn' Harry with maximum intimidation in a security cell. Was that how this evening would finish, and did Ziwei know? Might that account for her mood tonight? Yet Harry doubted instinctively that Chen would do that. It seemed so unnecessary. The result would be the same whether Chen terrorised him or not and, more than that, such crudeness would be out of keeping with the whole operation, which had been subtle and understated up to now.

But, tonight, even Chen was behaving oddly. Dressing Ziwei like a Wanchai bar-girl was hardly subtle. He had read Harry better when he had allowed her to wear the green tunic and baggy trousers, the pink bow and the buckles on her workaday cotton shoes. And the expensive Chanel . . . She smelt like Audrey.

Perhaps Chen Tao, the ignorant peasant, knew no better. Perhaps he considered this the height of sophistication, like the cheap champagne he was slurping. Harry studied the man. There was an excited gleam in Chen's eyes. He was fidgeting in the big leather armchair like a child. Why was he so excited? He had his film.

Or did he?

Harry froze.

And then it made sense. Harry felt the blood rush to his cheeks, and he looked at Ziwei, who was still gazing at him, wearing her fixed, false smile. That smile . . .

Oh, God, he knew that smile. He had seen it before, and it had caught his sympathy then, as it nearly caught him now. The first time he had suspected Audrey of infidelity, she had looked just as broken, just as stunned, as innocent . . .

He leant back in his chair, feeling suddenly very tired. Flashing through his mind, he replayed the scenes – the conversation on the boat with Ziwei before they reached the hydro-plant, the walk up the mountain, the reminiscences about her father, which had touched him so deeply, the bruises on her side that had aroused his pity and anger, the lovemaking in the dark when she had persuaded him that this really was a time out of time, the night in the cabin, the subsequent pitiful conversation on the deck when they had disobeyed Chen's orders and kissed, even that final deceitful kiss tonight in the back of the car . . . And now this alluring picture of hurt womanhood, innocence in gaudy clothes, appealing for his protection, his sympathy for her plight . . .

And he realised he'd been wrong about everything. Audrey was an amateur compared to this one. Subtle? He had not even penetrated the surface of the subtlety.

Games within games, and he, like a star-struck fool, had been tricked at every turn – but, of course, Chen knew him inside out, or thought he did. Like a virtuoso, he had played on his emotions to keep him disoriented: first, his guilt, 'No, the Aizi weren't so merciful', then his sentiment – mutual commiseration over dead parents, a visit to an old family friend. That had been the softening up. Then had come the stage-managed introduction of the daughter, if she really was Yu Fu-kuei's daughter – the old woman was his mother's friend, no doubt of that, but she might have been terrorised into playing the part of a bitter parent; all that innuendo about protecting the innocent had again been manipulation. Chen Tao wanted to arouse Harry's sympathy, his sense of honour, before casting himself in the role of villain, the ogre who somehow had control of the pretty girl – at the same time reminding Harry at every turn of the competition that had existed in their own relationship from the very beginning. He wanted Harry unconsciously to imagine himself the protector of the girl. How otherwise could Chen guarantee that he would fall in love with her? The bruises on her body were the final touch . . .

And the girl herself? So gauche, so natural – well, so had Audrey been. He should have listened to Julian.

Suddenly he saw the whole distorted picture. Everything up to now had been foreplay. Plausible Chen Tao. Innocent Ziwei, playing Chen against him to draw his sympathy. It had been a patient wearing-down of his defences and suspicions. The ruthlessness of it! Had she lain there passively while Chen beat her with the belt, then with a rock to half disguise the marks? Had they paused to examine their handiwork in the mirror? And had she given Chen helpful suggestions on where to hit her next? The mind boggled. Those two were a superior act. There was no doubting it.

The fact was that Chen had not taken any film of them in the bath-house. Why should he have bothered? That had been a warm-up. He was after bigger box office than first-time lovers tenderly making love. He wanted a spectacular, and this club or bordello was the setting he had chosen.

Harry had had enough of this pansying around.. If violent love-making was what Chen and Ziwei required, that was what they would get. If Ziwei could stand a beating with a belt and a rock on the way to her Oscar, she could withstand Harry's fury when he had his way with her. If they were going to do it, let them, while he was in the mood.

Chen Tao was in the middle of a story, a twinkle in his eye. Harry cut him short. 'My friend,' he said, 'I hate to interrupt you, but there's an old English expression: two's company, three's a crowd.'

Chen Tao looked startled, then laughed. 'Forgive me, I have been inconsiderate.' He stood up. 'It's only that I'm so happy for you both. A handsome man and a beautiful maiden. The one bold and virile, the other . . .' He placed a hand lightly on Ziwei's shoulder. 'No, don't shy away,' he said. 'I was about to compliment you. Don't you think she looks like a bride tonight, in this elegant red gown? I know she'll please you.' His finger coiled momentarily in her hair.

'Yes, Comrade Chen, I will please Ha Li, if I can.' The smile remained, but her voice wavered, and a bubble of a tear appeared in her eye.

What an actress, thought Harry. 'Thank you, my old friend,' he said.

'I'm going,' said Chen, raising his open palms. 'I'll be back at five.' He paused at the door to wink at Harry.

Harry contemplated Ziwei. She was staring miserably at the floor. 'I've never seen you look so beautiful,' he said.

She looked up, again attempting to smile, although her eyes were still tragic. 'Do you really think so, Ha Li? I'm glad it pleases you. Chen Tao gave me the dress and the perfume. I – I was not sure whether you would like it.'

'It suits you,' he said. 'But do you know what I'm thinking now?' He knelt beside her and lightly brushed her forehead with his lips. 'I'd rather see you out of it.'

'Ha Li,' she said tenderly, although there was an attractive blush on her cheek, 'you embarrass me.'

'I don't see why,' said Harry. 'Didn't you say last time that I usually greet you naked? Maybe we should do it the other way round. This time you can strip first.'

She gave a soft laugh, but her eyes searched his sadly. 'It's true, Ha Li. You were naked. And so beautiful, although I know I startled you, but if you wish, this time I will take my clothes off for you.' She raised herself from her chair and edged past him, moving towards the bathroom.

'No,' said Harry, preventing her. 'Do it here. Where I can see you. Please,' he added. 'You're so beautiful.'

She turned, frowning. 'Of course, if that's what you would like.' She reached for the embroidered button that attached the side of her dress to her shoulder. It separated from the loop, and she paused, with the corner hanging. 'But – but I'm a little shy, Ha Li. Will you – will you not kiss me first? To give me a little courage.'

He stepped towards her and lifting her chin, kissed her on the lips. She responded passionately, moving her body close to his and pressing herself to him. With his lips he pressured her mouth open and put his hands on her breasts, feeling the swell under the silk. She gasped as he pushed his tongue roughly against hers, and with a jerk pulled her head away. Her brown eyes widened. 'I'm sorry, Ha Li. I was choking a little.' She ran a hand down his cheek. 'Ha Li, you're acting a little strangely tonight.'

'Am I?' he said, taking her hand and kissing it. 'It's only because I'm so thrilled we're together again, Ziwei, all alone, just you and I, with the long night ahead of us. I love you so much.'

'Do you? Oh, do you?'

'Of course I do, my darling,' he said. 'Now, those clothes.'

'Can we – can we not take our clothes off together?' she asked. 'I would feel more comfortable.'

'No,' said Harry, kissing her eyes, feeling the grease and powder of her makeup on his lips. 'You first, my darling. I really want to see you as you are. Won't you do that for me?'

'Yes, Ha Li.' Again she frowned, as she looked at him quizzically. 'I love you, Ha Li. I will do anything for you.'

'Anything?'

'Yes,' she said. 'Of course.'

'I like the sound of that,' he said. He sat down in an armchair. She stood hesitantly, then, lowering her head, began to unloop the buttons at her sides. Harry watched.

When she was naked, Harry leant over the table and picked up the champagne bottle. 'Good,' he said. 'There's a little left. I feared that greedy Chen Tao had drunk it all.' He grinned at her. She was trembling, covering herself with her hands. Still keeping his eyes on her, he brushed the glasses, the fruit bowl and everything else off the coffee-table, vase, orchids and all. The oranges and pears thudded on to the carpet, and there was a tinkle as one of the champagne glasses broke.

'Ha Li.' It was a startled yelp. 'What are you doing?'

'What am I doing?' he said softly. 'We have a long night of love ahead of us, Ziwei. What did Chen Tao say? Something about champagne getting us in the mood? Oh, don't worry about the mess. There are attendants to clear it up.'

'I don't understand you, Ha Li. I'm a little frightened.'

'My love,' he said. 'My love. You don't have to be frightened of me. I'm your Ha Li, remember, and I love you. Trust me. I'm thinking only of your pleasure, and mine.' He placed the bottle on a chair. He kissed her, running his hands down her sides, lingering on her thighs. He bent her backwards, then lifted her and carried her to the coffee-table, where he laid her down. She stared at him, stunned or scared. Slowly, he poured the champagne so it trickled on to her breasts. The foamy liquid ran in rivulets along the line below her ribcage to her belly button. He parted her legs and emptied the last dregs over her crotch. Then he lowered his head.

After a while he heard a moan. He looked up. She was smiling nervously at him. Substituting two exploring fingers for his mouth, he knelt forward and kissed her lips, which were warm. He moved down and licked the last of the champagne from her nipple. As his fingers penetrated, fold by fold, and touched her deep inside, her back arched. She flung her arms round his neck. 'Ha Li, I told you once that I thought you were a little mad.' Passionately, she kissed his cheeks and chin.

'And I said the whole world was mad,' he murmured in her ear. 'But that doesn't matter, does it? Not to us.' He felt her lips, her tongue, her teeth worrying his neck.

'Now, now, easy does it. You mustn't be impatient. That was only for starters.' He smiled as he extricated his hand, feeling the stickiness on his fingers. He wanted to say, 'You see, I can whore too.' Instead, he looked down at the body he had once loved. It was still so beautiful, even if she was rotten inside, but he steeled himself. He did not feel any emotion. He felt barely aroused. He had a job to do. That was all. For that matter so did she. 'I'm going to carry you to the bed now,' he told her. 'It's your turn to watch me take off my clothes. Then our night can really begin. Our lovemaking,' he added. 'In our private paradise.'

'I do love you, Ha Li.' It sounded like a sob.

'Oh, I know that,' he said. 'You said you would do anything to please me.'

'I – I will,' she said, her brown eyes peering. He lifted her up. 'But – but you'll be gentle with me? You – you won't hurt me?' she whispered.

'Hurt you?' he said, looking down into her deceitful features. It was still the face he had adored – the mole, the little snub nose – as fresh and innocent and intelligent as on the first day he had seen her, although now she had skilfully fashioned her expression into a perfect representation of apprehension and alarm. 'Hurt the woman I love? The idea.'

*   *   *

In the decadent West, thought Chen Tao, there were people who paid good money to watch the sort of show that was taking place below him. In his own country it was only the privileged who had the chance, but as he stood next to the cameraman above the mirror that gave them a fish-eye view over Ziwei and Ha Li on the bed, he became certain that he had obtained, within the first hour, more than enough obscenities to build a museum archive. His difficulty would be to choose which stills to blow up from the wealth of material.

He almost felt sorry for Ziwei, who had certainly taken heed of his instructions, and was offering her body up for indignity upon indignity with commendable application. Some of the positions in which Ha Li and she ended up in were frankly perverse, although they gave him ample ideas for his next encounter with one of his nurses; sooner rather than later, he decided, as the evening went on. She certainly made the cameraman's work a joy – Young Liu must imagine he was in paradise. After a while, he allowed him to set the camera on automatic while he went to the bathroom.

It was Ha Li who surprised him. He had imagined that he would be shy and conservative and require leading on but, if anything, he was more imaginative than Ziwei. That initial business with the champagne bottle, although it was a difficult shot into the next room, astounded him. He had lined the champagne glass Harry was using with aphrodisiac powder as a precaution, and he imagined that Ziwei's beautiful costume had also inspired him, but he was forced to conclude, after some hours' observing them, that it was in the nature of the man. The many surveillance operations he had conducted over the years had often revealed unexpected aspects of a target's personality. It was remarkable what effective masks people presented to the world, especially in China's regimented society. Naked in bed, you saw the man for what he really was. The bullying Party cadre became gentle and considerate, an aspect he would never dare show to his colleagues. Conversely, the retiring intellectual behaved like a ravening beast. Watching others' sexual encounters rarely aroused him, but it never failed to intrigue.

Tonight he was both aroused and intrigued. Ha Li penetrated Ziwei's jasmine pool from underneath, from the side, from behind. They did it standing, sitting, and once he seemed to be steering her legs like a wheelbarrow, as he literally pushed her up the bed, all the time keeping his position inside her – that was certainly a still Chen wished to blow up, for his own future reference if nothing else. She used her tongue on him, he again on her, sometimes together with their heads buried between each other's legs, other times lying passively while the other administered. Those occasions were the nearest either came to having a rest.

The microphone picked up Ha Li's voice. He kept telling her he loved her and he sounded sincere enough, but the expression on his face was what Chen would have described as cold – but that was the interesting aspect of what you observed when watching another man's sexual performance. Despite his surface nature, romantic, idealistic, trusting, everything on which Chen had played to bring Ha Li to this point, Chen realised that, hidden in his psyche, perhaps only half realised, there was probably a cruel side to him. There was an element of ruthlessness in the way in which he was now humiliating Ziwei, even if it was only unconsciously. At any rate, the results were everything Chen had wanted. He was also excited about this other side of Ha Li and wondered how he would make use of it in the long revenge he was planning. It would be useful, too, when Ha Li came to spy for him, and that was the beauty of the retribution he had designed. His own objectives fitted perfectly with those of his country.

Eventually Ziwei told him she wanted to go to the bathroom. When she came back she had the lubricant Chen had given her. She had hated this part of his instructions, and her scared, tearful face was a picture. Harry frowned. 'Is that really what you want?' he asked.

Chen thought she might not go through with it, but with a tear running down her cheek, she said. 'I thought it would please you, Ha Li. Tonight . . . I want to do everything to make you happy.'

'And you think that will make me happy?' he said.

'I have offended you,' she said. 'I am sorry.'

Chen noticed the relief on her face, because she thought Ha Li might be refusing her, but it became stony hard as she heard Ha Li say: 'No, it doesn't offend me in the slightest. How could anything you desire offend me? You'd better turn over, then. My love.'

Chen's film was complete.

There was a message from Harry's secretary in Julian's office. His copyreader had taken the call. Dr Airton had sent an apology, Mr Ren told him, in his precise English. He wanted to cancel the duck shooting on Sunday because of other engagements. Perhaps Mr Travers could try calling later today to arrange another time, but Dr Airton was very busy, so the secretary couldn't be sure whether he would be available. Julian thanked Ren gruffly and asked for the press cuttings.

He quickly scanned the *People's Daily*, and found a standard speech by President Liu Shaoqi on foreign policy. He immediately phoned the legation, requesting an interview with the minister later that morning or early in the afternoon. It was hardly a matter on which he needed the minister's opinion but, sure enough, shortly after his superior secretary had put the phone down on him, Garrard himself rang, and told him he would be delighted to see Julian at noon.

Julian then wrote a short note. 'Operation requires use of safe room and communication facilities late tonight, probably post-midnight. Can you arrange?' He hid it deep in his wallet and had the driver take him to the legation. While Garrard and he waffled on about foreign policy, he passed it to him. Garrard looked over his half-spectacles, and nodded. 'Travers,' he said, 'is this story of yours urgent?'

'I'm afraid it is. I'd like to get off copy tonight.'

'Listen,' Garrard said, 'I apologise, but there are a couple of points I have to check with London before I can give you my formal comment. The problem is I'll be tied up in a dinner at the Belgian Embassy. It's irregular, I know, and asking a lot of you, but could you come round to the mission, at, say, eleven or just after, and I'll give you my comment then – assuming that's still in time for your deadline, Travers?'

'That would be fine. Thank you, sir.'

Julian had arranged to meet Tadeyama at the International Club where a foreign correspondents' lunch was going on that day. It was the usual boozy affair. The object of such meetings was to listen to talks given by interesting visitors, but since hardly any came, they had become an excuse for weekly gossip and drinking. Ostensibly to clear their heads afterwards, the two men decided to take a stroll together in the nearby Ritan Park. In an isolated spot in one of the ornamental rock grottoes, they began to confer.

'Any chance?' Julian asked.

'Still difficult,' said the Japanese. 'The house is heavily protected.'

'As in impossible or just difficult?'

Tadeyama gave his charming, boyish smile. 'Nothing is impossible, Travers-*san* – but it may be challenging. Fortunately we have friends who can provide access to house opposite. There we can install long-range microphone, and direct it towards window of room in which your friend will be. Naturally he must first indicate to us which one it is. If room is on other side of house then, of course, it will not work.'

'That will be difficult to establish. Harry's not in on this, or we could tell him to open a curtain, but I'd prefer it if, for now, he was unaware.'

Tadeyama smiled. 'Then it is you, Travers-*san*, who are creating difficulties, but do not worry, we will think of something if we can.'

'You can be ready by tonight?'

'Oh, I think so, Travers-*san*. Our sister signals organisation, Chobetsu, has agreed to work closely with my own department on this project. American spy plane, U2, leave Japanese base and fly over north China daily. US owe Chobetsu big favour – never mind what – so we have requested, on no questions basis, slight diversion of today's flight, enabling us to get visual feed of courtyard. It would be useful, no? Since it is outside area, we have already found ways to monitor for sound.'

'I didn't expect you to go to so much trouble.'

'It is no trouble, Travers-*san*.' He bowed politely. 'We are allies. By the way, we also found means to put listening device in car belonging to Mr Chen Tao.'

'Good God! How did you manage that?' Julian was amazed.

'Luck, Travers-*san*. We followed him this morning to Ministry of Foreign Trade, and by good fortune my colleague noticed his car and driver leave. My colleague has two cars. One stays, one follows Chen's car, and when it is parked in Friendship Store – Chen's driver is buying whisky – my colleague walks by and puts magnetic listening device under chassis. It is called 'initiative', I think. Am I right?'

'You are indeed, Mr Tadeyama. That was a brilliant coup.'

'Thank you – but so far, I regret, we have heard nothing of interest, although our device is functioning. Mr Chen broke up trade meetings early today and drove to guesthouse where he spent two hours. Last time I checked, two hours ago, he was on his way back to Ministry of Foreign Trade. Oh, yes, he did ask a subordinate, when he got in car first time, if all the films had been developed. Had they come out clearly? He appeared pleased by positive reply. Does that signify anything to you?'

'Yes, it does. Thank you,' said Julian, his mind still boggling over the U2.

'We have also ascertained true function of this house and to whom it belongs. It is an establishment run by Ministry of Foreign Affairs, a department in charge of entertainment of foreign visitors, particularly from Third World. I believe it is a sort of brothel, Travers-*san*. I thought that might also interest you. It makes me speculate on what sort of operation you are conducting, although it would be indelicate to ask under terms of our co-operation. However, I will offer you my hope that the result will be sweet . . .'

Julian laughed. 'It is a pleasure working with you, Mr Tadeyama. Please pass my thanks to everybody involved. By the way, I don't expect anything to happen before dark. I will make sure you can find me in the Xin Qiao Hotel before eleven o'clock, after which I will be in the legation safe room.'

'If I discover anything important I will find means to contact you. Good hunting. Is that not what is appropriate to say in these circumstances?'

Julian had nothing to do now but wait. On his return to the Xin Qiao he went through his office into his private room and stretched out on the bed, mulling over what Tadeyama had said. Blast it, he would have to let Harry in on the monitoring, and risk his annoyance. There was no other way to identify the window. Julian tried his office only to be told by his secretary that he was not there, so he called his *hutong* house, the first time he had done so.

'Dr Airton?' he said, when an irritable voice answered.

'Aye.'

'Apologies for calling you at home. This is Travers, from *The Times*. Look, I'm sorry to bother you,' Julian continued, 'but it's rather urgent I see you. I was wondering if you could meet me for a drink at the bar of the Peking Hotel tonight around six.'

'Why?'

'It's about GPR. Their deal.'

'I told you, they don't have a deal. There's nothing I can discuss with the press.'

'I don't quite believe that, Dr Airton. I saw the excitement at the legation the other night, and I've been making one or two enquiries of my own since. Look, I'm planning to do a story anyway, a speculation piece. Unless . . .'

'Unless what?'

'Unless I could be guaranteed an exclusive when there is more definite news. I'm sorry if that sounds a bit bald . . .'

'It sounds like blackmail, Mr Travers.'

'So we might talk about it? Over a friendly drink.'

'All right. Six, then.' He hung up.

Julian called the Kyodo news agency. 'Mr Tadeyama? Can I trouble you a moment? During lunch I was talking to Pichugov – you know, the Tass reporter – about President Kennedy's announcement this week that he plans to visit Berlin in the summer. Well, Pichugov was speculating that the Soviet Union's reaction, in an attempt to forestall negative publicity about the Berlin Wall, might be to encourage the *lifting of some travel impediments* between East and West Germany. It would be a *window opening up*, a *drawing back of the* Iron *Curtain*, which only a short while ago seemed unthinkable.'

'Yes, Travers-*san*. This is most interesting, but how can I help you?'

Julian could imagine the smile at the other end of the line. 'Well, Mr Tadeyama, bearing in mind Kyodo's unique global perspective, if a window can be opened, would Kyodo have a positive view on potential reaction from behind the Bamboo Curtain?'

'This is difficult question to answer, Travers-*san*. We cannot be sure. However, if what you indicate is true, then I expect my news agency would regard this as very positive step towards facilitating better communication between nations. I will certainly check for any such signs. Thank you for informing me.'

Good man, Tadeyama, thought Julian. He lay on his bed and picked up a novel, but he could not concentrate. He turned on the radio and listened to mindless propaganda until it was time to leave for his assignation with Harry.

9

The Sting

Peking, April 1963

It took Harry nearly the full quarter-mile walk from the Peking Hotel to his meeting-point in Nan Chizi to calm himself. What the hell was Julian playing at? Organising an unnecessary and, frankly, dangerous meeting in a public place before what promised to be the most crucial event of the whole operation was not the way to get a field agent into the right frame of mind.

Harry had been nervous enough already. He had spent the whole day disciplining himself into a calm enough state to put the events of last evening into perspective. He had got over his fury that Ziwei had hoodwinked him. He regretted the punishment he had inflicted on her in bed. It had been excessive, even if he had provided Chen Tao with the material he wanted. She was, after all, just an enemy doing her job, and if she was whoring for her country so was he. Anyway, thank God that part of it was over.

Tonight he had to play the part of a diplomat whose life was about to be ruined. If he made a single false move, everything he had worked for would go to waste. It was a challenge for which he would require all his training, his instincts and his full concentration.

He did not need the distraction of Julian's pointless surveillance operation to be explained to him in laborious code over cocktails. All those variations of a repeated phrase: 'I want you to help me open the curtains.' All right, it might be useful to have a recording of the sting, but why hadn't Julian told him two nights ago in the safe room? If infuriated him that Julian had been spying on him. How else had he discovered the club's location? He must have followed the Red Flag last night. How cavalier and irresponsible. If Chen Tao hadn't been leering at the lovers in the back seat, he might have spotted the tail.

His mood hardly improved when he reached the dark, secluded spot for the pick-up. It was neither secluded nor dark. The District

214

Committee had chosen this section of the street for a '*Weisheng*' meeting. Red banner posters had been stretched between the bare branches of the trees under a string of lightbulbs, and a crowd of bored onlookers was listening to an old woman with an armband lecturing them on the community work that was expected of local residents. Harry walked past until he had found another spot out of range of this unexpected illumination, but it was not ideal, for every few seconds he was passed by people on their way to the meeting, each of whom gazed up in surprise at the tall foreigner.

The first time the Red Flag appeared, two old ladies had chosen a position right next to Harry for a long gossip. Chen slowed down, but on seeing the unwanted company he immediately accelerated away to circle the block. When he came back, a section of the Zhong Nan Hai Guard, whose barracks were not far away, were marching past on some kind of training drill. Chen circled again.

The next time the car appeared, Harry was being edged off the pavement by a crocodile of tiny Young Pioneers, whose teacher was leading them in a revolutionary song. Chen Tao's tail-lights disappeared for the third time. Harry grinned inanely at the children, who stared up in stupefaction at the monstrous alien.

Eventually the Red Flag stopped. The back door opened, and Harry leapt inside to find Chen Tao alone. He would have been prepared to go through the act with Ziwei again, but was glad he did not have to. Her absence could mean only one thing. They had passed the first stage and were into the second. The sting was on.

However, in a nervous tone, he asked, 'Where's Ziwei?'

Chen laughed, but did not answer until he had turned past the northern walls of the Forbidden City and was heading towards Bei Hai. 'Is that snake of yours lonely already, Ha Li?' he said. 'Patience, my friend, she's waiting for you at the club.' He let out a mock-sigh. 'Are you upset, Ha Li, that you'll see her in ordinary clothes this evening and not the gorgeous costume she wore for you last night? I don't suppose you care. I suspect that you and she look forward to dispensing with costumes when you're together.' He made a fast turn by Coal Hill. 'But don't despair. I'm sure she'll be wearing the perfume I gave her. I know how much that excites you, my friend.'

'How do you know that, Chen Tao?' asked Harry.

Chen turned away briefly from the windscreen. There was a malicious gleam in his eyes. 'I guessed,' he said.

Ziwei was not waiting for them in the room. On the coffee-table stood two bottles of White Horse whisky, and two tumblers. In Harry's world, the hard stuff came out for business, not love. 'Where is she? Do you think something's happened to her?'

'Don't worry,' murmured Chen. 'Women are always late. It's in their nature. Look, Ha Li, they've laid out whisky for you. How unromantic – but since Ziwei's not here yet, why don't we help ourselves to a man's drink? And do stop pacing. Why are you fiddling with the curtains? Please sit down. You're making me giddy.'

With bad grace, Harry made his way to one of the armchairs and perched on the edge of the seat. Chen cut the wrapper on the bottle with a penknife he took from his pocket.

'You really think she's all right?'

'Ha Li, it's undignified for a man always to be panting after a woman's skirt.' He laughed. 'Relax. Perhaps she caught the wrong bus. You know how muddled women can be, especially when they're daydreaming about their lover.' He poured three inches into Harry's glass, a little less into his own. 'Chairs,' he said. 'Isn't that your English toast? Oh, please, Ha Li, stop looking so miserable. She'll be here soon enough. In the meantime you and I can have a little talk. I've been jealous lately of Ziwei, occupying all of your time and your thoughts.'

'I'm sorry,' said Harry. 'You know how grateful I am – how grateful we both are – for the help you've given us.'

Chen smiled. 'I'm sure that when you have an opportunity to help me in return, you will.'

'What sort of help do you have in mind?'

'Oh, I don't know,' said Chen. 'How about the English lady when I get to London? Did you think I meant something else? You're not suspicious of me again, are you, as you were on the boat?' He chuckled. 'You thought I wanted you to betray your country. As if I was a spy!' He slapped his thigh. 'Oh, Ha Li, what am I to do with you?'

Harry laughed with him. 'You must have thought me very stupid.'

Chen was still laughing, but his features hardened. 'In any case, it's a bit late for you to start worrying now about betraying your country. You've been doing it all your life, and you probably weren't even aware of it.'

'You'll have to explain that to me,' Harry said. 'Is it another joke?'

Chen was lighting a cigarette. 'It is a sort of joke, Ha Li,' he said softly. 'As your friend, I would call it a tragic one. Since we're having a heart-to-heart talk, and since you're indeed my friend, let us be honest with each other. I might start by telling you how I would analyse your interesting character.'

'Go on. This should be amusing.'

'No. Tragic was the word I used,' said Chen. 'You're a bit of an enigma, my friend. You're not a happy man. Deep in your heart, you're perplexed and confused.'

'Oh, really?'

'On the surface, you would be considered in your society a talented success, with a bright future in your scientific ministry, but you do not act like a man at ease in any society. You live alone, and you drink far more than is good for you. You told me about your wild, despairing affairs and the woman you married in a failed attempt to enter the upper-class establishment. Your marriage fell apart, because it was based on a false premise from the start. With similar mixed motives, you serve your government loyally because you think it your duty to do so, but actually you loathe the capitalist system it represents.'

'And what evidence have you to support that?'

'Oh, from things you've said, your behaviour . . . newspaper articles in our archives. As a youth you were thrown out of the army, you were a labour activist at university, your left-wing ideals, the so-called Windscale affair, in which you informed on the illegal activities of your own government. China is not so cut off from the rest of the world that we don't hear of these things, and as a senior official I have more access than most.'

'So what are you getting at?'

'Merely that you're an outsider in the country of which you happen to be a citizen. They have been successful in bringing you into their fold. The capitalist system is good at that. Perhaps you try to persuade yourself that you're doing good and fulfilling your noble potential, but I doubt you believe it inwardly. You rage at the inequalities of the system you serve.'

'I wouldn't give you high marks for psychoanalysis. I don't think I'm the miserable fellow you're describing, and if you really had been watching me these last few days, I don't think you'd have found anybody happier.'

'Because of Ziwei,' said Chen, 'and, though I may be flattering myself, also a little bit because of me. In these last few weeks you've found friendship and love. I have had great pleasure seeing the care-free boy I once knew struggling out of the shell in which he has lived most of his life. And why is that, Ha Li? It is because, for the first time since you were a child, you are among your own people. You may have the gigantic, ugly features of a foreigner, but your heart is Chinese. China is your real country. Unlike your own class-ridden society, ours is free and equal, and we would welcome you to help us fight the oppression you have suffered all of your life.'

'I'm feeling a little dizzy,' said Harry, leaning back in his chair. 'Tell me I only imagined what you just said.'

'No, Ha Li, you did not. If you doubt me, just think what you were doing barely twenty-four hours ago in this very room. I see it as being, in its way, a celebration of your joyful reunion with the land of your birth. I think you love Ziwei, but she represents something else to you too. She is the China you dreamed of rediscovering.'

'I should leave,' said Harry, standing up. 'I don't like the way this conversation's heading.'

'No, you should stay and consider what I've been saying to you, for your life is at a crossroads now. I'm not asking you to betray your country. What I'm offering, as a friend, is a chance for you to serve your real country. I would like you to see it as a great opportunity.'

Harry strode towards the door and tried the handle. It was locked. He walked over to a window and dragged aside the heavy curtains. The panes were screwed down into the wood. He picked up a jade horse and smashed it against the glass. The horse broke. All the time, Chen watched him impassively. Harry returned to his chair and sat down, running his hands through his hair.

Chen sighed. 'I didn't think I'd be able to persuade you, not imme-diately, but as a friend – and I am your friend – I tried. Here.' He poured whisky into Harry's glass until it was full.

'I'm British, not Chinese, and I'm not a traitor. I'm going to report this,' he said. 'I don't know what you're hoping to achieve, Chen Tao. You can't keep me here. I'm a diplomat. I have immunity, and you're coercing me, or attempting to, into doing I don't know what, and it's pathetic. It's laughable. It's . . .' Shakily, he reached for the whisky glass. 'Look, I'll view all this as a joke, but I should go now. You can make my excuses to Ziwei. We'll . . . meet again tomorrow as if nothing has happened.'

'Ha Li, I had hoped it wouldn't come to this. It would have been so much better if I could have persuaded you out of friendship. Will you not reconsider?'

'To spy on my country? Do you know how ridiculous that sounds? If that's what you're suggesting, the answer is no. Never. Who do you think I am?'

'It would be better if you started wondering who I am,' said Chen. He reached into his briefcase and pulled out a large manila envelope. 'I had been hoping to avoid this,' he added, as he began to withdraw from it ten large black-and-white prints. One by one, he laid them on the coffee-table. 'I could show you many more, equally shocking. I have more than three hours of film. You and the girl were enthusiastic, to say the least, and quite, quite uninhibited.'

Harry sat rigid. He had rarely seen porn more explicit, even in Budapest, where German magazines from the Reepersbahn were a late-night feature of the *dacha* parties he had attended.

'In these two pictures, you are actually breaking specific laws of our country. I wouldn't be surprised if your own country also imposes a ban on such acts. That would be a matter for your minister to decide, were I to send this package to him.'

Harry rose to his feet, fists at his sides. 'If you think I'll react to cheap blackmail like this, Chen Tao, you're wrong. Publish and be damned.'

'The choice is yours,' said Chen, 'but I urge you to reflect on your position. By consorting with a Chinese girl you have disobeyed the regulations of your service, not to mention the laws of the People's Republic of China. You will be dismissed from the Foreign Office and also the Power Ministry, from which you are seconded. It will be a dishonourable discharge. You will never find employment again in your civil service. You are unlikely to find a job in any of the industries in which you have expertise. We will make clear to the GPR representatives and to your government why such a promising deal has been cancelled, for cancelled it will be, and your behaviour will be given as the cause. Your career will be ruined.

'Now, you may decide, in your perverse Western way, that a greater dishonour lies in submitting to blackmail. Perhaps you think you can leave Britain for another country, and start your life again. That, too, will be impossible. You see, I haven't yet come to the criminal charges that will be laid against you, which will ensure you a long prison sentence, perhaps for life. You have probably guessed by now that I work for the intelligence services. We spy on your country as your country spies on us. You would be surprised how often we're rewarded with success. We have friends in the wider intelligence world who help us from time to time. Some are from neutral countries who will do favours for both sides, if it profits them. The publicity after your dismissal will lead one of those countries to alert the British to the fact that they have discovered through their channels that we, the Chinese, are in possession of certain sensitive information that could only have been passed to us by you, Ha Li. When your government hears of this, they will be unforgiving.

'Understand what I'm saying, my friend. The evidence in front of you will already have destroyed your career. The evidence of treason that we will supply will take away your freedom. You may try to tell your government that the charges are fabricated, but after seeing the photographs, will they believe you? They will think that we trapped you long ago and that you were already working for us. They will assume that the reason we sent the photographs was to punish you, perhaps because you were extorting more payment from us. Naturally we will provide them with evidence to support this conclusion. There is a bank account in Switzerland, opened several months ago in your name, which already contains a sizeable sum, and there will be other clues. The more you protest, the guiltier you will sound. You will be put behind bars. They may even hang you.

'Again, you may take a noble stand, and face prison or death, consoling yourself that you are innocent – but you would be forgetting one thing. Little Ziwei, whom you say you love. She has already committed treason as far as we are concerned. I'm sure that her motives were pure and patriotic when I brought her into this operation, but her subsequent passion for you was not. She will be sentenced to death, Ha Li. We'll probably execute your mother's friend, Professor Yu, too. I will do this, Ha Li – unless you agree to work with us.'

'You bastard.' He crumpled into the back of his chair, wringing his hands behind his knees and rocking in as pathetic a manner as he could devise, but inside he felt triumphant. The smug look on Chen's face convinced him that he had no suspicion other than that Harry was the broken man he appeared.

Chen solicitously refilled his glass with whisky, and again after Harry had gulped it down. 'Take your time, Ha Li. It's understandable that you are upset. Here, use my handkerchief and wipe your eyes.'

Several heavy breaths later, Harry pointed a trembling finger at the photographs and asked, 'Does Ziwei know anything about this?'

'She has probably guessed,' said Chen. 'I doubt that she has blinded herself to reality as much as you have, although I'm sure that her feelings for you are sincere. I've been quite moved on occasion over the last few weeks. It has been like watching a romantic drama from the Shanghai studios, although it's one that I fear can never be shown without censorship. You are a great lover, my friend. I compliment you.'

'You won't . . . do what you said you would to Ziwei? She's innocent, Chen Tao.'

'I will if you don't co-operate,' said Chen. 'I don't bluff. But you can prevent me by agreeing to do what we require of you.'

'And what is that?' Harry whispered.

Chen was silent, frowning. 'Ha Li, I'd like you to forget for a moment the photographs, the threats, the blackmail. Think over what I was saying earlier. The last thing I want is for you to be destroyed, or to suffer. You have it within you to be loyal to our cause. Over time you will understand that what I'm doing now is merely wielding a rod over an unruly child in whom I know there is high potential for good but who needs a shock to realise what is in his best interests. I do not wish you to see this as an attempt by us to attack Britain. It is really a way of assisting you to help the country you love, which is China. So, it may surprise you when I tell you that, for now, it is not what we expect you to do for us that is important but what you will allow us to do to help you.'

'I don't understand,' said Harry.

'Ha Li, as a science officer in the British Legation, you are shortly to achieve a triumph that will rebound to your credit, and earn you the thanks of your government. In a few days' time, the technical expert will return from England with proposals for the hydro deal, and we will begin intense negotiation over the pricing.'

'Is that all this is about? You want me to give away our bottom line?'

Chen slapped his knees. 'No, Ha Li. I want you to take over the commercial negotiations on the British side from their financial man, Hu De Sun. I want you to be the one who negotiates so forcefully with us that we have no choice but to give way on the exorbitant prices your side will demand. We want all the credit to go to you for having stood up to us. Your reputation will grow within your service. Probably, after this triumph, you might ask if you can return to your Power Ministry where, in the wake of your magnificent success, promotion will be guaranteed. Afterwards you will rise steadily into new areas of responsibility and authority. Wherever we can we will assist you. There will be new energy deals. Perhaps our co-operation will extend to other areas, but you, Ha Li, will be the man who masterminds it all. We will be helping each other. The more your influence grows, the more you will be in a position to help China. The more loyally you serve your government's interests, the more you will be aiding the country you love.'

'There must be more to it than that.'

'We will sometimes ask you to remember your old friends,' said Chen. 'We may require your help and advice where they will assist our research into new areas of technology, in areas where our own knowledge is not so advanced. You may be in a position to give us the little bit of extra intelligence we need.'

'In other words, to spy for you?'

'To share knowledge, Ha Li. Science is a free gift of Nature that should be shared among all the nations of mankind. You are already assisting us with hydro energy. We might ask you to share some of your knowledge in other areas . . . nuclear, for example. The peaceful aspects, of course. It will help China grow and prosper. Yes, you will technically be spying because of the regrettable Cold War your government – not ours – has imposed on us, but you will really be acting as a back door for knowledge, which, in a just and fair world, should be exchanged anyway. I envisage a long, happy relationship consisting of mutual self-interest. Isn't that what friendship is about?'

'I can't give you nuclear secrets.'

Chen sighed. 'I had not intended to go into grubby details this evening, but I wasn't lying when I told you there is already a Swiss bank account in your name. What we will be asking you to provide for us will probably incur little risk, since the sources will be at your disposal, but we will certainly be mindful of your trouble and reward you accordingly.'

Julian's words echoed in his mind: 'By the way, Harry, when the Chinks do offer you money, you take it. None of your high moral sensibilities, please. The Office can always do with the extra funds.'

He thought moral outrage might be more appropriate. 'I won't spy for money,' he muttered. 'What – what you said earlier, about conscience, where I stand regarding China and my own society, and free scientific exchange, maybe ... maybe that's something we can discuss, but – but I won't do it for money.'

'Of course not, Ha Li,' crooned Chen. 'Nor would I want your services if they were mercenary but, as Marx himself said, 'To each according to his due.' I think our government would be offended if they were not able to extend a generous token of appreciation to a loyal worker who is helping our cause.'

'How generous?' asked Harry, spilling a little of the whisky he was pouring into his glass.

'At least as much as the British government is already paying you. With bonuses, much more. You could become rich.'

Harry drained his glass. He hunched forward in his chair, and his foot tapped the carpet. He shook his head from side to side. 'I – I can't do this, Chen Tao. Please, please, find somebody else.'

'Think of Ziwei, Ha Li. I have told you what will happen to her if you do not co-operate, but if you do, I will personally guarantee that her career in the Ministry of Foreign Trade will blossom. One day she may even be posted in an embassy overseas. It can be arranged that her postings coincide with yours. A good agent will certainly be entitled to a reward for good behaviour. Listen to your heart, Ha Li. This is your true motherland. Come home to us and help our cause.'

Harry decided to play for time. He doubted that Chen would give him any, but he would be surprised if he did not ask. 'This is all a bit shocking. Can I have a week to think about it?'

Chen picked up the photographs one by one, and put them back into the manila envelope. He took a stick of rice paste from his pocket and sealed the envelope. With his fountain pen he wrote on it in English: 'For His Excellency, the Minister, Mr Desmond Garrard, CMG, British Legation, Peking'.

'That is the reality, Ha Li.' He flapped the envelope in his hand. 'The time for your decision is now.'

Harry knew that Julian would have advised him to plead: 'Be pathetic. Fall on your knees if you have to. Show him what a whipped cur you are.' But there was a smugness in Chen Tao's face that stuck in his craw. It was the same arrogant look he had worn when he ordered Harry around as a boy. 'Give me a day, then,' he said. 'Just a day. You've always said we were friends, that we're Hong Huzi. Blood brothers. You've convinced me I have no choice, and you're right about what I feel for China, but I don't like to be forced. Give me just one day to see if there is a way out for me.'

'A way out?' Chen sneered. 'You think you can get the better of me?' He laughed and, unbelievably, shrugged. 'All right, Ha Li, let me indulge you, as I did when you were small – but whenever you challenged me then, you never succeeded in defeating me. I will give you until tomorrow morning, at nine o'clock, when our meetings resume. You can give me a signal. If it's not the one I expect, then within five minutes your minister will receive this package because I will have a man outside the legation waiting to deliver it. At the same time Ziwei here and her mother in Shanghai will be arrested. That is the reality. Do you still wish to play games?'

'I just want this one night to consider my position. I've already accepted that there probably isn't a way out, but I won't forgive myself if I don't consider all the consequences before agreeing to such a drastic step. I'll probably go back to my office in the legation. I can think there.'

'You can go where you like, of course, but if you imagine that you can make a plea to your colleagues, I would not advise it. They will come to the conclusions I outlined a few minutes ago when they discover the evidence we have planted. You might as well face it, you're trapped.'

'I realise that, Chen Tao.' He tried to inject humility into his tone, although he felt like crowing.

'All right, I'll await your signal.' He looked at Harry and grinned. 'Wear the same blue tie you're wearing now and I'll know you agree. Remember our flags? Since you insist on childish games, we might as well use a childish signal. Hong Huzi!' He said the words with contempt as he unlocked the door. 'Come, Ha Li, we've said all we have to say. One of my men is waiting to drive you home. You can do what you like with your life and Ziwei's. The choice is yours. For her sake and your own, make the right one.'

Harry whistled as he ran up the legation stairs. The guard, a stocky ex-paratrooper, who still looked military in his civvies, watched him curiously. This was not the usual Dr Airton, who was universally disliked in the legation for his bad temper. Harry strode down the upstairs corridor and was still grinning when he entered the safe room, where Julian and Garrard were waiting for him.

'Well, Travers,' said Garrard, 'it looks like your man is bringing you good news. I hope that the same can be said for the GPR deal.'

'The contract's in the bag, sir,' Harry reassured him, 'and on our terms.'

'I see,' said the minister. 'Well, I won't ask you how you know that. If that's the case, it *is* good news – very good news indeed. Is there something I can report formally to London?'

'Not yet.'

'Ah. Then I'll leave you two to your skulduggery. I hope you won't be too long, Travers. If you need me, I'll be in my office. By the way, Airton, you're the duty officer tonight but I'll stand in for you until I'm relieved.'

Julian had sat down again. He waited until the door had closed on Garrard, then said, 'Go on, Harry, tell me that expression on your face means what I think it does.'

'Aye, Julian, it happened, exactly as you said it would thirteen years ago. You're now talking to a grade-one Chinese spy. We did it, Julian.'

'My God.' Julian ran a hand through his hair.

Harry flung himself into a chair. 'For once in my life I feel on top of the world.' He grinned. 'But I thought you'd have known already. I opened the curtains for you.'

'A friendly agency was helping out. They should deliver the tapes soon. I wasn't spying on you, by the way. I wanted to be in a position to know what had happened – in case anything went wrong.'

'And I got arrested, you mean? So you could skedaddle out of the country before they picked you up too?' Julian's face showed outrage, but he blushed too. Harry laughed. 'I'm teasing you, Julian. It was a sensible precaution. Thankfully unnecessary. Chen Tao suspects nothing. He and Ziwei are probably congratulating each other on their great coup as we speak.'

'Ziwei?'

'Aye, one of the most difficult parts of the sting was listening to him threaten me with Ziwei's execution if I didn't do as I was told, and trying to act as if I cared. At the end of the day, he thought that was his major lever on me. Not the blackmail or the concocted spying charges, but my fear for Ziwei's life.'

'He fell for the broken-hearted lover, then?'

'Hook, line and sinker.'

'Well, well, so he really followed up all the clues we'd built into your cover?'

'The lot, Julian. Windscale, seductions, Audrey . . .'

Julian shook his head. 'I wouldn't be surprised if one day this operation will be a textbook case study at our training school. Who'd have thought we'd get so far?'

'We've come a long way, Julian. We never deviated, did we?'

Julian laughed. 'Well, there were one or two hiccups along the way.'

'Oh, aye? What were they?'

'At one point I thought you'd fallen for Ziwei. You kept telling me what an innocent she was. I was worried she'd got to you.'

Harry nodded sadly. 'She was good. There was a time I almost believed she was Chen's dupe, and she did get to me for a while, until I saw how hand in glove she was with him.'

'They played on your weaknesses. We all have them. No cover story, however good, can ever truly convince unless it's based on underlying reality. At the end of the day, the character of the agent dictates what it will be. Your love of China, your romantic soul – they're inside you, and Chen Tao saw them. I knew he would. It's what ultimately made you so plausible. There were times when I believed you weren't being entirely honest with me, but I let it pass. I knew you had to work these things through. Deep down I trusted your instincts.'

Both men were silent for a moment. Suddenly Julian slapped the table. 'Before I get down to debriefing you, I've got some good news of my own, or I think it's good news. It may relieve a nagging doubt, if you still have one.'

'What's that?' asked Harry.

'Chen Tao, your so-called boyhood friend. He never was. The Italians eventually matched our photograph with a passport copy of the man who was with that trade delegation in Milan. His name was Liao Fangqi. Obviously it was a cover name, but it rang a bell with the CIA. They'd come across the alias before, and had already identified it as that of a man they knew as Hao Aijun, who's in charge of the Second Department section responsible for scientific espionage. Hao Aijun's a real name, rank commissioner. A year or so ago the Taiwanese, through some complicated operation they were conducting illegally via Hong Kong, came across an Inner Party document that mentioned this Hao in the same context and passed it to the Yanks. It's all in the files in London, and they've checked and double-checked. So we can be pretty clear that that's the man you're dealing with. So you can relax, Harry. Chen Tao's almost certainly Hao Aijun, who was not the son of a doctor's cook in Shandong but a long-term spook, born to army parents in Chengdu in 1927.'

Harry did not have to pretend confusion. He knew exactly who Chen Tao was. Through some intelligence muddle, Julian had mixed him up with a colleague, perhaps his superior. He chose his words carefully. 'I thought I told you he was pretending.'

'Yes, but in such a way that I decided you believed he was your friend but weren't telling me. So I wrongly suspected you.' Julian grinned. 'Anyway, it doesn't matter. I'm just saying these are the sorts of strains inevitable in a psychological operation like this. The pressure gets to us. We all head down the wrong track sometimes. The important thing is to work it out and deal with it, as you did, Harry, so successfully. We should be celebrating. I haven't brought any champagne, but I do have a couple of cigars. Wendy Room rules can go hang. Let's smoke them while you tell me every glorious detail about your triumph.'

It took Harry an hour to go through the whole conversation. Julian and he had just begun the process of transcribing the report that would be coded for London when Garrard came back. 'Still at it? You know it's past one? I've come to tell you that your Japanese man has arrived. He's downstairs with Sergeant Ryan. Do you really want me to bring him up to this room? It would be highly irregular.'

A few minutes later Tadeyama came in. He bowed to Harry as Julian introduced them. 'You were resourceful, Dr Airton,' he said. 'The manner in which you opened curtains alarmed us, but then we realised you had staged tantrum – is that right word? – deliberately in order to do so.'

'Did you get the recording?' asked Julian.

'We were able to pick up two men talking, but reception was faint. I think you will have to ask your technicians to augment and isolate signals. If urgent, of course, we can do it for you in Japanese Embassy, but I imagine Dr Airton has already informed you of what transpired.'

'No doubt your technicians will do so anyway with your back-up copy, Mr Tadeyama.'

'Back-up copy?'

227

Both men grinned, then Tadeyama frowned. 'We have, however, other recordings, and a section of magnified camera footage from the U2 flight earlier in the day. We transcribed it because we thought it might be of interest to you. Our sister organisation, Chobetsu, noticed an incident happening in courtyard. We asked Tokyo to process and, just recently, coded signal was transmitted to our embassy. One of my colleagues replayed it on television set, then recorded it on his cine-camera. It is poor quality, but may I borrow your projector?'

It was only a short piece of film and, as Tadeyama had said, the image flickering on the screen was by no means clear, but it was enough to break Harry's heart. He had a premonition as he watched the gates open to let a black Red Flag drive into the courtyard and park next to an army truck. He had already guessed what was about to happen when he saw a squad of armed soldiers moving towards it, and recognised the driver of the Red Flag, a cigarette in his mouth, as he got out, stretched, then pointed to the rear door. Strangely, the figure whom the soldiers pulled out of the rear seat, struggling, kicking, and obviously screaming in terror, was not particularly recognisable, except that it was wearing a hair ribbon and a flash of sunlight gleamed on a shoe buckle. It was bundled into the back of the army truck, three soldiers jumping in behind.

'Curious,' said Julian. 'Mean anything to you, Harry?'

Harry was silent.

'It will become clearer when I play you sound tape,' said Tadeyama. 'I have brought recorder.' He extricated a small tape from a plastic container and wound it on to the spool. 'This conversation was recorded in Mr Chen Tao's car, in which, as I told Travers-*san*, we placed listening device yesterday morning. Excuse me while I wind forward to relevant section.' He peered at the moving dial, and pressed the stop switch. 'Conversation is in Mandarin, a language you both understand. The film I showed you was recorded at about one fifteen yesterday afternoon. What you are about to hear starts at three minutes past one. There is earlier conversation, which you can listen to at leisure, but this short sequence is indicative of what is happening. Male speaker is Mr Chen Tao, other is a young woman. At twelve thirty-two they left Ministry of Foreign Trade together. I believe there is a third person in the vehicle, perhaps soldier or policeman, but he does not speak.'

After a few seconds Harry could hardly bear to listen and began to pace the room.

The sharp scream drowned the man's voice initially, but it was clearly Chen's and the woman was almost certainly Ziwei. This was confirmed when she began to repeat, over and over: 'But you promised. You promised. You promised . . .'

Chen's voice was cheerful when he replied: 'I never promised you anything, Comrade Peng. I merely said that I would consider leniency.'

'But I whored for you. I did what you asked.'

'It was indeed a spectacular performance for which I, and no doubt also the state, are grateful. While you spend the rest of your days in a labour camp, you may think back to last night and consider that, despite your earlier crimes, on this one occasion you served your country, and that knowledge may assist your re-education and reform. However, you did so unwillingly and only under coercion and threat. That you belatedly repented and did your duty does not excuse the fact that you fell in love with and nearly betrayed our operation to an enemy agent.'

Ziwei was overcome by a fit of sobbing. Only one word, 'innocent', repeated several times, was clear.

'You see, you are saying it again. What arrogance! How dare you question an operation sanctioned by the Party? It is not for you to judge whether Ha Li is innocent. It hardly matters if he is or is not, if the state has decided that he is our enemy. Comrade Peng, even now you are revealing your guilt. You are putting your personal feelings before those of the people and the Party. Your misguided love for this man has caused you to commit treason by word and deed. You are lucky you have been condemned only to life imprisonment. You deserve to be taken to a field and shot like your mother.'

The screams now became hysterical, and there were other ominous noises, indicating a struggle. Then there was a slapping sound, perhaps a hard blow to a face, presumably Ziwei's. This stopped the screaming, which was replaced by the sound of gasping, then sobbing.

Chen's voice was peremptory: 'That's enough. No, there's no need to gag her. I want to hear what she has to say. Comrade Peng, do you deny that you continue to love this man? That your passion for him is stronger than your devotion to the Party?'

There was silence, for at least twenty seconds.

Chen's voice was dripping with sardonic irony: 'You see? You will not deny it even now. Even to beg for your mother's life and your freedom. Who knows? I may yet be merciful.'

Ziwei's voice, now pitched low, was icy and defiant: 'I would deny it if I thought you were capable of mercy but I know you are not. So I will say that I continue to love Ha Li Aitun and I always will, even if . . .' Here, her voice broke, and she continued, in a small, pathetic and, to Harry, heart-rending tone: '. . . even if I think he no longer loves me. So do with me as you will, Chen Tao. I no longer care, but please . . . spare my mother. She is harmless. She is innocent . . .'

There was renewed sobbing and Tadeyama pressed the stop switch. 'There is not much more,' he said quietly. 'Car stops, and girl, seeing they have arrived at gates of compound, begins to scream again. It is distressing.'

'Thank you, Mr Tadeyama,' said Julian. He glanced towards Harry. 'Was there anything else?'

'No, Travers-*san*.' He was also looking at Harry with an expression of sympathy. 'If you would kindly open door for me, guard the minister left outside will let me out. We will meet tomorrow for drink at International Club, perhaps?'

'Yes, let's have lunch, and a walk together afterwards.'

'I will leave these tapes and film here.'

He nodded at Julian, as Harry opened the door. Julian turned towards Harry. He spoke harshly: 'There's nothing we can do for her. You must put what you've heard out of your mind.'

'Easier said. What's your next piece of comfort, then? "Win some, lose some"?'

'No. I'm probably as shocked as you are. This was never what I anticipated. Look, I think I know how you're feeling, but you must be hard now. I realise that anything I say will sound melodramatic or pompous, and certainly callous, but I'll say it anyway because it's true. What we've heard justifies everything we're doing. This is the system you and I have set out to destroy. We can only do that by going on. You can't save her but you can avenge her. That's the only comfort I can give, and you know I'm right.'

'Avenge her?' Harry began to thump his fist gently against the wall. 'Didn't you hear what Chen Tao said, Julian? He's sending her to a labour camp and shooting her mother. It was over and done with seven hours before I met him. All the time he was talking to me he knew.

Can you imagine Ziwei surviving in a camp? You told me once what you'd seen in Belsen. That's what it'll be like.'

'You've *got* to put this behind you. This is a war, Harry, in which horrible things happen. Grit your teeth, do your duty.'

'My duty?'

'It's hard, I know,' said Julian. He made a movement towards Harry, as if to put a hand on his shoulder, but thought better of it. For a long while, the two men stood side by side, a gulf between them.

Eventually Harry turned. 'Aye, I don't have a choice, do I? Don't worry, Julian,' he said gently. 'I'm not going to crack up on you. I'm a little angry, and a little sad, but you know me, I'll get over it. I'll bury my feelings and get the job done. Tomorrow I'll sit across the table from Chen Tao and give him the signal he wants. Will you excuse me now? Sorry to leave you with the transcription and coding, but I'd like to be by myself for a while.'

'You don't want to sit here for a bit longer? I'm sure Garrard could rustle up tea or something stronger. And I'll be here.'

'I'm best alone.' He took a heavy step towards the door, and paused. 'Make my excuses to Garrard – I'm in no mood to play science officer tonight. I'll meet you here tomorrow evening, shall I? There'll probably be more to report.'

Julian gave him a slap on the back. 'You've done a marvellous job, Harry,' he said.

Harry leant forward and embraced him fiercely. 'Thanks, Julian. You've been a good friend to me over the years. I won't forget it.'

He had decided what he was going to do before he left the legation. He felt calm as he cycled back slowly to his *hutong* house.

On the way, he stopped by the rubble of the old city walls. On his left one great bastion was still standing. It was the observation tower that a Ming emperor had built for the Jesuits. On its roof, the ancient bronze astrolabes were silhouetted against the night sky. This tower and some of the great gatehouses were all that remained of the Tatar Wall. Some bureaucrat must have given an order, Harry thought, and so, for that arbitrary reason, this old monument had survived the destruction. The system is not invincible, he thought. Something always remains.

It occurred to him that this would have been a perfect night for the Jesuits, had they still been around, to make their astronomical observations. There was no moon, and every constellation was glittering in the velvet dome above his head. There they were: Orion, the Bear and, to the west, a soft wash of light: the Milky Way in all its diamond-spotted splendour. Suns with planets whirling round them at colossal speeds, at infinite distances away. Always moving. Never changing. Violence and heat that would vaporise the earth's strongest metal reduced to a pinprick in the sky, an insignificant atom of an insignificant galaxy in a universe of galaxies larger than this. So what did that make the earth and everything happening in it?

There was a tranquillity in the old city tonight, thought Harry. The darkness had obliterated all the modern excrescences, the flags and the workers' hovels, the portraits of Mao, Marx and Engels. Standing here now, by the old Jesuits' tower, an emperor of the Ming Dynasty would still recognise where he was. One day these new emperors, with their red flags and stars, would go the way of the others. It was only a matter of time before they were replaced by another dynasty, for that was the way of things – but Peking would remain, as China would remain. History itself was merely repetition. What the inhabitants of a particular time chose to do with themselves might vary in form but not in substance from what their predecessors had done before them. There had been tyrants and mass persecutions before. Madness visited every generation. For that matter, there had been spies in the past as there were spies today.

He cycled on, down a deserted Chang An Avenue. Ahead was the shadow of one of the modern city's landmarks, the sprawling Peking Hotel, with its gleaming new Soviet wing. Behind it, Harry could make out the darker, hazier shadow of the Imperial Palace, with its stacked roofs and towers, reflecting the glory of centuries past. Nothing he, or Julian or Chen Tao could do would ever affect what was fated to happen. To imagine that they could was as futile as to believe that humankind could alter the course of the stars. The Jesuits could have told him that four hundred years ago.

There was only one thing that Harry wanted to change now, and that was a small thing in the scales of the universe. He had lost interest in the greater game he had been playing for almost thirteen years. Since he had heard that tape, his mission had shrunk to a much smaller target.

He wanted only to make amends for a betrayal. It affected one other person, a girl who had loved him, and who was being punished for it after he had abandoned and abused her. It was irrelevant in the big picture, which Chen Tao, Julian and their like believed they could influence. It mattered only to him. In cosmic terms, it was an interplay of two atoms, but they were important to him, because he was one and Ziwei the other. Whatever chemical or electrical process bound atoms together was impelling him to do something about it. In human terms they loved each other, although he had lately been blinded to it. Ziwei was threatened, he had been largely responsible and had to save her. Being a scientist, and analysing the alternatives, he thought he had found a way.

Spying was a rational business, like any other. It came down to human mechanics. He should know. Over the last several years different people with different agendas had pulled him in all sorts of directions. It was time to stop now – or, rather, it was his turn to pull levers of his own. Things had gone too far. It did not matter what spies did to each other: that was their professional risk. This time, however, innocents were being hurt, and that stuck in Harry's craw – especially when one of the innocents was Ziwei and the other her mother, to whom he had made a promise, which he had broken. Also he had made a promise to his own mother – to protect the weak. It was time to make amends.

Strangely, sleep came to him quickly. There was no point in dwelling on his guilt, or torturing himself with remorse for having treated Ziwei like a whore the last time he saw her. There would be time for that later. It was more important that he slept, because tomorrow he had something important to do. For her.

He woke early. Sunlight was pouring through the lattice windows and, for the first time in months, he heard a bird singing. From the street outside he heard the call of the man who ran the breakfast stand: '*Youtiao, mantou, doujiang.*'

He did his exercises, shaved, then put on his best suit. He left the tie until last. The blue one he had worn the night before was hanging over his chair. In his cupboard, there were several others. He remembered his games with Chen Tao on the mountain. He could hear his old friend explaining it to him as if it was yesterday. 'A blue flag means action, go ahead as planned. A red flag means danger, expedition's cancelled. A yellow one means problems, wait until the coast is clear.'

Harry did not look in the mirror after he had tied it. He went out into the yard, leather shoes crunching on the gravel as he walked to the shed where he kept his bike.

He cycled out into the *hutong* and from there to the main road. It was pleasant in the cool of the morning, when only a few sweepers were on the streets. He looked up at the sunlight sparkling through the branches of the trees that lined the road, and saw the clean pale green of a budding leaf. That's good, he thought inconsequentially. Spring is coming.

IO

Endgame

Peking, April 1963

'What is this, Ha Li? Some kind of joke?'

Chen Tao was furious, as he had been from the moment that Harry had entered the conference room with Braithwaite and Hudson. He had fidgeted in his chair until the coffee break. Harry smiled amiably at him while he translated Hudson's explanations of payment terms and deposits related to shipping schedules. With Ziwei gone, there was no other interpreter on the Chinese side so Harry had filled in. Just before the coffee break was due, Harry noticed that Chen was whispering to one of the senior Chinese engineers. He had a grim smile on his face as he announced the end of the first session. 'I regret, gentlemen, that our interpreter is absent. She has had to return to Shanghai and a new one is being found. This presents me with a difficulty. For the rest of the day I will need to consult with Dr Airton about government matters, and he cannot do two things at once. This means that we must postpone the commercial side of the discussions until tomorrow. I am sorry.'

'Not again,' fumed Braithwaite, gathering his papers. 'Fine help you are, Harry. You're meant to be assisting, not delaying us.' This time the Chinese side also left promptly: the pedantic accountant was first out of the door. Harry and Chen were left sitting at either side of the table, facing each other.

'It's no joke, Chen Tao,' said Harry, calmly. 'You remember the old code, don't you?'

'Yes, yes,' growled Chen. 'I told you to put on a blue tie and you're wearing a yellow one. Why?'

'It's your code, old friend. I thought it would be clear enough. After all, you're the one who keeps telling me what a happy childhood we had together, and how fresh it is in your memory.'

'You realise I just have to pick up that telephone and the photos will be in the legation with your minister?'

235

'Of course. You explained yourself very clearly last night. You also said that Ziwei and her mother will immediately be arrested, but you can hardly do that, can you?'

Chen glared at him. 'Are you trying to bluff me, Ha Li? Are you still pretending you've found a way out, and that you can beat me? I gave you a deadline. It's overdue.' He got up and walked to the phone, picked up the receiver and spoke to the operator. 'Put me through to Comrade Dong.' He turned to Harry, who was contemplating him with a smile. 'You're very stupid, Ha Li. I have you trapped, and unless you say something quickly before my officers come on the line you will regret for the rest of your life this pathetic attempt to confound me.'

'You're taking it very personally, aren't you? "Beat me"? "Confound me"? For an intelligence officer, you're behaving rather emotionally. There should be no personal vendettas in this game. It's strictly business, after all.'

Chen pointed a shaking finger at him. 'I'm warning you for the last time. You should treat this seriously, Ha Li.' There was the sound of another voice in the receiver. Chen shouted: 'Then look for him, you dolt.'

'Temper, Chen Tao. That's not like you. What's become of my jolly old friend? I was saying, by the way, when you interrupted me, that you can't arrest Ziwei and her mother . . . Well, maybe you can arrest her mother, but certainly not Ziwei, because you have already done so, at one fifteen yesterday afternoon. You loaded her into an army truck. Presumably to send her off to the labour camp to which you have condemned her.'

Chen's face paled. Another voice was on the line. He hesitated, then mumbled, 'Comrade Dong, it's nothing. I just wanted to check that your men were in position . . . Good. I'll call you later.' He put down the phone. 'Are you still bluffing me, Ha Li?'

'Well, you should know. You either arrested her yesterday afternoon or you didn't. I happen to know that you did, and that you treated her with unnecessary cruelty in the car on the way to the Ministry of Foreign Affairs' guesthouse, which you were trying to pass off as a cadres' club for your operation.'

Chen sat down, glaring at Harry. He picked up a pencil and began to twist it. It snapped. He ran a hand over his forehead, which was beaded with perspiration. 'You might have found out about the house from an African diplomat,' he said. 'The other is guesswork. You somehow saw Ziwei in my car and drew the wrong conclusion. You were following me yesterday afternoon.'

'I don't think so, Chen Tao. You have my house under heavy surveillance. There's always a car or a van parked in my *hutong*. I'm sure your men reported to you that I was at home all day. And, anyway, if I'd known that Ziwei had been arrested and on her way to a labour camp, I'd hardly have reacted in the way I did last night when you were threatening me with her death on one hand and promising me everlasting happiness with her on the other. Not if I was the innocent honey-trap victim you thought I was. It must be obvious to you that I used other resources.'

'Something made you suspect,' said Chen, 'so you foolishly alerted your intelligence people to what was happening. That will not save you when I bring my evidence to bear. It will certainly not save the women. You do not intimidate me with your threats. You will bring down retribution on your own head the faster.'

'As far as I was aware I have made no threats of any description. I've merely stated a few facts. Look, I understand this must be a terrible shock to your pride.' Harry smiled, as he repeated Chen's words of the previous evening. 'You looked so triumphant last night I almost felt sorry for you. I do sympathise. I was feeling pretty triumphant myself. But we should be looking at things in a more rational way, you and I, if we're to co-operate. I know it will take time for you to recover from your loss of face.'

'Why should I be suffering from loss of face?' There was venom in Chen's tone.

'Call it what you like, but I've been running rings round you ever since I came to China. Before that, even. Budapest – that's probably when you found out about me. The stooge I met at the *dacha* was surely one of your men, and it was his report of our conversation that gave you the idea for your big operation. Energy? Hydropower? Ring a bell? I must say, you've been a dream to work with, predictably following up every one of our leads and suggestions. And very subtly and intelligently too, if I may be allowed to inject a note of praise. I loved your choice of bait. It was psychologically penetrating of you to go for a plain, innocent girl instead of a tart. But the beating you gave her was unncessary and reflects a weakness in your character.'

Chen was sitting rigidly in his chair, consternation evident in his slack jaw. 'What are you saying, Ha Li? That you knew about the honey trap from the very beginning?'

'Of course. I was the one who designed it. Haven't I made myself clear? We set you up. For the last six months you've effectively been working for the British Secret Intelligence Service.'

'You're lying.'

Harry shrugged, and Chen's cheeks went crimson. He looked as if he wanted to hit him. He closed his eyes and took a deep breath. 'All right, Ha Li, but why? If this is true, what motive do you have for telling me this? Yes, if true, it would be a shock, and loss of face, perhaps – but do you think that by fooling me you have some sort of hold on me? That you can reverse the sting, and threaten me into working for you?'

Harry laughed. 'Of course not. You've only been doing your job. It may not help your career along if anyone finds out how you've been hoodwinked, but that's not strong enough to blackmail you. No, the object of our exercise was simple: to have you believing you'd recruited a tame British scientist into your intelligence service. You'd send me home and I'd spy for you. I'd do everything, in fact, that you asked me to do for you last night. You've fallen for a simple double or triple operation, depending on how you look at it – because, of course, the intelligence we manufactured for you would be tainted, designed to do the maximum damage to your weapons and nuclear programmes and, over time, hurt your economy and intelligence networks. There's nothing complicated about it. We and the Russians have been playing this game back and forth for years. If you'd had a bit more experience in the way the big boys play, you might even have spotted it.'

Chen reached into his pockets for a cigarette and lit it. His eyes narrowed. 'If – if this is as you say, Ha Li, then you are deliberately betraying what has been, from your point of view, a magnificently successful operation. You have also, by admitting you're a British spy and saboteur, compromised yourself by putting yourself in my power. And if you have accomplices in Beijing, we will surely find them and break up your network, which must be a sizeable one if you found a way to spy on my own activities, as you described earlier. Why would you be so foolish as to do this? Unless you have some other mysterious purpose, which, frankly, I cannot see.'

'Do you mind if I have one of your cigarettes? I forgot my own when I left this morning. Perhaps I was too absorbed in choosing what tie to wear. Thank you.' Harry leant over and took a light from the Chinese. 'How are you going to find out about our network? It's obviously well-concealed if you haven't managed to discover it already. Plan to send me to one of your torture chambers? Give me the water treatment, death by a thousand cuts and all of that?'

'There are more subtle ways of inducing information. However, we must be careful how we treat you, Ha Li, because you have diplomatic immunity.'

'Glad you spotted that one,' said Harry. 'Look, I think you can see from my manner that I'm sane and rational. And I'm not frightened of you. I'm aware that you have some grievance against me. I presume it's to do with that incident with the Japanese or another resentment relating back to our childhood. Perhaps you'll tell me one day. Perhaps not. In any case, I've apparently put myself in your power, and that means I must have a good reason for doing so. I'm coming to you now, as one professional intelligence agent to another, with a proposition that I think will be to your advantage, and my own. Now, are you prepared to talk business on that basis?'

'What if I disagree?'

'You won't, because you're curious, but you must have recognised already that we're at stalemate. What you proposed last night won't work any more, and I've blown our own operation. Your blackmail can't work now. All the effort you put into setting up a honey trap and all the state funds you used to effect it have been wasted. The British government's hardly likely to take any notice of dirty pictures since we sanctioned the set-up in the first place. That whole phoney spying rigmarole won't work either, although SIS will be interested to know what information you've stolen from them. Of course, I can't stop you persecuting two innocent women, but that's a chance I'll have to take. Also, frankly, I don't give a damn about the GPR deal and, I suspect, neither do you.

'As to your telling them that I've betrayed our operation, nobody will believe you. They'll think you found the listening device in your car – that's where it is, by the way. They'll assume the coincidence and the timing of this discovery alarmed you, and you eventually worked out all by yourselves that something fishy was going on. You won't find out who's helping me because I won't tell you and, as you admitted, you can only go so far in torturing a diplomat. You can bump me off,

I suppose, but again, much good it will do you. So you see, the downside is limited for me. No promotion because no successful operation, but my life goes on. So does yours. I doubt your intelligence services are as forgiving as mine, though, and you'll get into trouble for what they'll see as your failure. Fair assessment?'

'Go on,' said Chen, through gritted teeth. 'What is your advantageous proposition?'

'All right. What if, as far as our respective intelligence services are concerned, our operations have both been successful, at least on the surface?'

'After what you have told me, how can that be? Are you suggesting that I allow you to give false information to my government? That I commit treason?'

'Obviously not,' said Harry. 'You'll be getting bonafide information from me. As far as the SIS is concerned, they'll still think we're leading you astray, but I'll be letting you know where the deliberate errors are in our planted material so your scientists can compensate. You'll also be getting real information from me on scientific matters, intelligence matters, whatever you want. Think about it. Think about the implications for your own career. You've not recruited an idealistic scientist. You've found yourself a spy who's also a scientist. You've hit a treasure trove. It's not a double or a triple operation. It's a quadruple one. Any intelligence service would be salivating at what I'm offering you.'

'So you'll really be spying for us? You'll commit treason for your country voluntarily?' It was Chen's turn to laugh. 'Am I expected to believe I convinced you last night that China is your spiritual home?'

'No, Chen Tao, I loathe your country – at least, I hate this present regime. The more I've seen of it the more I detest it. It's evil, but I'll spy for you all the same.'

'I see,' said Chen, coldly. 'Why? For money? That's all you capitalists seem to worship.'

'I'll take your money. Why not? But more than you were offering last night, because I'll have to hand over a convincing amount to my service, if they're to believe the sting's still on. I'll take a more modest sum for myself to be deposited in another bank I choose – but to answer your question. No, I'm not doing this for money, or power for that matter, which is all you crave. I'll do this for you on one condition and one condition only.'

'And what's that?' Chen sneered.

'I want Professor Yu Fu-kuei and her daughter, Peng Ziwei, released from prison and put on a plane to a non-Communist country. I'm not particular about where. You have the world to choose from.'

Chen's eyebrows rose in astonishment. 'That's ridiculous, Ha Li. I thought we were talking business and I was almost prepared to listen to you, but this is childish. They're only women, and they would be dangerous to us, especially if we enter into such a deal as you propose. Much better they're liquidated. They know too much. In any case, they're condemned. The orders have been issued. Take as much money as you like, but forget those women, Ha Li.'

'You should hear yourself, and then you might understand why I despise you and all you represent. It's up to you, of course. I can't stop you hurting or killing them – but if you want me to help you, you'll find a way to get them out of China. I don't expect Ziwei will want to see me again after what happened the other night. In any case, if I went anywhere near them, it would compromise what I'll be doing for you. All I want to know, every month, is that they're safe. You'll send photographs of them, holding a newspaper of a recent date, against a background that is clearly not in China. It must be convincing evidence, Chen Tao. I'll know if you've faked it. As long as I have that, I'll do anything you want of me.'

'But why, Ha Li? Don't tell me you really love this girl.'

'Business is business, but it should be conducted between professionals, who know what is at stake. You have abused innocents, and I, since I set up this operation, feel partly responsible. I don't expect you to understand. You work for a system in which human beings are ciphers to be manipulated in the interests of the state. That is why I believe ultimately you will lose this Cold War. One day the people will stand up and there will be a settling of accounts. Until then there's not much to be done, except resist you. This operation has failed, but there'll be others. For now all I'm doing is squaring my conscience by trying to save two innocent individuals who don't deserve to be punished.'

'You're mad.'

'Then there's no deal, is there? Where do you think you'll end up, my old friend, when they promote you sideways after your failed operation? Xinjiang, perhaps? Tibet? I imagine Commissioner Hao's already gunning for you. He'll relish the opportunity to bring you down if he finds out your apparently successful operation's been a disaster. I know your dog-eat-dog system.'

'What – what name did you refer to?'

'Hao. Hao Aijun. Aijun means "love the military", I suppose. One of the pathetic revolutionary sobriquets you inadequates like to use to give spurious meaning to your pathetic lives.'

This time Harry had the satisfaction of seeing Chen tremble. 'What makes you think that the name of my superior is Hao?'

'I guessed,' said Harry, sweetly. 'Incidentally, it was also his usual alias that you used to do the Milan job a couple of years ago. Basking in reflected glory, were you? Or trying to pin the blame on your boss if something went wrong?' He sighed, and reached for another of Chen's cigarettes. He lit it with his own lighter. 'Look,' he said, 'just think about the opportunity I'm offering you. You'll be serving your country as well, because I'll be able to give you far more intelligence than you dreamt of when I started this deal. All you have to do is fiddle a bit of paperwork to make two *hei wu leis* disappear. I can't advise you how, you know your own system better than I do. Just do it, and I'll start co-operating. You want advice on nuclear reactors? I've probably got the knowledge and practical experience to give you several useful tips while I'm in Beijing. You'll smell of roses from day one. But, first, you'll have to convince me Ziwei and her mother are out of the country.'

'What if you give me affidavits as to who your accomplices are in Beijing first? As a gesture of good faith,' said Chen.

'Thought you might ask that. I've no objections, although you'd be wise to leave them in play if you want them to believe the honey trap's worked. I'll tell you exactly who they are, and how we've monitored your operations, the moment you give me proof that the women are abroad.'

'That is not acceptable,' said Chen. 'A guarantee of your good faith first. Who are your accomplices?'

'Sorry, Chen Tao, no deal. The women must be freed first. That's the bottom line.'

'Their punishment has been authorised by the state,' said Chen. 'It will not be easy for me to change a decision of the People's Court. Even if I could, it would take several days to release them and organise what you want.'

'You're a Hong Huzi, my old friend. You'll think of a way. I don't mind waiting. I'll be occupied with the discussions at GPR. Have you forgotten? You can always get hold of me to pass me the evidence I need. Then I'm yours to command.'

'I'll have to consult my superiors. They may not agree. How do I know I can trust you unless you give me some proof of your willingness to work for us?'

'You can do what you like,' said Harry, wondering if he had pushed it too far.

'No, Ha Li, you don't understand. If I go to my superiors I must give them something solid, or they won't allow me to co-operate further – even if I want to. Ha Li, I need those names to help you get what you want as much as to help me.'

Harry had a vision of Ziwei being hustled through the barbed-wire gates of one of those desolate encampments in Qinghai that he had seen on satellite photographs. It would be so easy to write Julian's name on a piece of paper and pass it to Chen. What Chen had asked was not unreasonable, and Julian knew the risks. He was a Cold War warrior. Every soldier faces the chance of falling on the battlefield.

He couldn't do it. He knew that, if he were to succeed, he must maintain the dominant hand over Chen. If he allowed Chen any leeway, he would demand more, and excuses would be made. His only chance of saving Ziwei was to stand firm now, even if he knew that by doing so he might lose her altogether.

He remembered his childhood again, the games with his old friend. It had always been a battle of wills, Chen Tao taunting him, pushing him, challenging him, always so plausibly, and he had always given way.

He stood, and picked up his briefcase.

'What are you doing, Ha Li?'

'I think we've said all there is to say. You have my terms. I'm going back to the legation. I have work to do.'

'You think I'll let you go, after what you've told me? That you're an enemy spy?'

'No, Chen Tao, I offered to be *your* spy. If you want me, you know what you have to do. If you don't want me, well, I don't care what you do. We'll face the consequences together, shall we?'

He paused at the door. 'If you're not proposing to have me arrested in the meanwhile, I'll see you at the commercial meetings tomorrow.

Tell you what, if by then you've decided to go along with what I require, why don't you put a blue handkerchief in your top pocket?'

'Wait,' said Chen. Sweat was pouring down his face.

'Yes?'

'There – there's no need for that. I agree to your terms,' he said.

'Good,' said Harry. 'I'll await your evidence of the women's safe arrival in a neutral country.'

Somehow he kept a steady pace as he walked through the concrete and marble corridors. He passed the PLA guard by the pillared entrance, trying not to observe too closely the helmet and rifle. He reached the great gates of the trade ministry compound, where more guards waited, checking the papers of those coming in and going out. He waited in line, his pass in his hand. Through the window of the hut, he saw the officer inside talking animatedly on the phone. The man put down the receiver, and grunted an instruction to the guard at Harry's side. The blood was pounding in Harry's ears and he didn't catch what the man said, but he was looking into Harry's face with an angry expression. The guard by his side stood to attention – and, sloping his rifle, ran off towards the steps of the ministry. The surf noise in Harry's ears subsided and he heard the officer shout, 'And remember to bring the vinegar with the lunchboxes.'

A few moments later, Harry passed through. As he reached the wall where he had left his bicycle, he had to push both hands against the bricks for support. His legs were jelly. His shirt was clammy against his body, despite the cool air. He was not sure whether he wanted to retch, or to shout in exultation. In the space of half an hour, he had betrayed his country and saved the woman he loved. Maybe. If only he could keep his nerve for the next few days.

He did not go back to the legation. He went home, where he showered again and changed into a clean shirt.

He drank two glasses of whisky, put on two sweaters and his thick tweed coat, then went outside. He did not have to wait long. He spotted a car idling towards him at about twenty kilometres an hour. He judged the distances, then reached into his pocket for his cigarettes and lighter. Concentrating on flicking his lighter, and without looking where he was going, he stepped into the road.

Even though he had left enough space for the driver to slam on his brakes, the vehicle must still have been moving at nearly fifteen kilometres an hour when it hit him. He felt a terrible regret that he had miscalculated, then everything went into slow motion, and he saw himself rolling over the bonnet, bouncing on the windscreen and landing, with another bone-jarring crump, on the pavement. He lay there panting, only vaguely aware at first of the crowd clustering round him in a circle, staring. The driver was kneeling beside him, shouting something, while the crowd shouted back.

Harry felt an excruciating pain in his stomach and left shoulder. There was a cold trickle down his cheek and his head was ringing. Gingerly he stretched his arms and legs. He knew he had to move before the police came. It was painful, but he managed to stand. He raised his hands and smiled at the fascinated faces around him. 'Look,' he said, 'I'm fine. I'm not hurt – and it was my fault. I don't want to get anybody into trouble.' He patted the driver's shoulder. 'It wasn't your fault, Comrade,' he said. 'I'll tell you what. I was looking for transport anyway. I'll pay you to show there are no hard feelings.' He leant forward and whispered, 'Listen, I'm a diplomat. I'm afraid you'll be blamed if we don't disappear.' The frightened man nodded, opened the rear door for him and got in quickly, shaking off the restraining arms of people in the crowd, who felt they were being cheated of their fun. The driver, sweat pouring down his bald head, had to push the car through the mass, and hands scrabbled at the windows. 'Take me to the British Legation,' said Harry. It was uncomfortable, with the jolting suspension, but he kept his lips and teeth tightly compressed, and only uttered a groan when they had reached the legation and he had paid off the relieved driver.

Of course they made a fuss when he came in bleeding from his cut temple. He had to explain over and over again what had happened, insisting he was all right. Jenkins ran off to get the legation nurse, who treated him in her surgery. There were no internal injuries beyond a broken rib. His heavy coat had protected him. The bruises on his belly were perfect, as were the dislocated shoulder, the black eye and the gash on his head.

Garrard himself came in after the nurse had finished with him, and peremptorily ordered him home to rest. He asked if Harry wanted the legation to bring charges against the driver. Harry told him it had been his own carelessness, and he was fine. He just wanted to get back to work. He could still write with his right hand, even if the left was in a sling. The GPR report was crucial and, he added significantly, so were other things. Garrard gave him an irritated look, and murmured, 'So be it. I hope this accident really was an accident. I don't like this. I don't like it at all,' then added louder, for the benefit of Colliers and Jenkins, waiting outside the door, 'Well done, Airton. That's the industrious spirit I like. You're showing a lot of grit.'

Harry had no report to write. He had nothing to do, during the long afternoon, except wait for Julian to arrive in the Wendy Room.

'The bastards,' said Julian, after he had examined the bruises. 'They beat you with iron bars?'

'Among other things. I had to tumble down the stairs a couple of times as well. And there were the usual slaps and punches to the face as well.'

'Chen Tao did this?'

'One of his goons. Chen did the interrogation.'

'You're a bloody diplomat, for God's sake. This could cause an international incident, if it came out.'

'The legation believes what I told them. It was a car accident. That's what Chen ordered me to say. Apparently it happened just outside my *hutong* as I was crossing the road. I'm sure they've fixed it by now so that every bloody resident in the street will corroborate it if we pressed enquiries. But don't worry, Garrard won't. I've persuaded him I don't want a fuss.'

'But what could possibly induce Chen or Hao, or whatever his name really is, to do such a thing to you? I thought we had him by the balls. He'd turned you. You'd agreed to work for him. What made him suspicious?'

'You did.'

'He knows about me?' Julian staggered back, his face drained of colour.

'Not yet. But he found the listening device in his car. He showed it to me when he was beating me up. They're not fools, you know. Look at the timing. Doesn't take a genius to link the coincidence of a piece of incompetent bugging by agencies unknown to the most important intelligence operation going on. Are you honestly surprised?'

'Jesus, I must warn Tadeyama. I take it the whole operation's off. Bloody hell.' He punched his fist into his palm. 'Presumably you kept up your cover under the beating? Well, you're trained for that sort of thing. Jesus, it breaks my heart. After all these bloody years.'

Harry said nothing.

'I suppose I'd better start thinking about contingencies. It'll take them some days to put a coherent picture together. I may be able to get out before they work out why you and I so often went duck shooting together. You'll probably be all right. You have diplomatic immunity. Presumably that's why they didn't keep you in custody. They'll expel you, of course, and there'll be the usual tit for tat. No way we can avoid a diplomatic row. I'll warn Garrard about the photographs in case they send them. They probably won't, though. It'd put them on the wrong foot, wouldn't it, as they complain to the United Nations and God knows who else about how they're victims yet again of capitalist espionage?'

'That won't happen,' said Harry.

'Maybe not. There's egg on their faces as well. They may just want to bury the whole thing. I'd still better warn Garrard, though.'

'I told you, Julian, that won't happen. They have other plans.'

Julian stopped pacing and gave Harry a puzzled look. Harry calmly returned his gaze. 'How do you know that?'

'Because they told me, Julian.'

'They told you?' Julian's voice was now icy. 'You'll have to explain that, Harry.'

'They turned me,' said Harry, gently.

'I know they turned you. But that's all over now.'

'No, Julian, I mean they turned me this morning. They really turned me.' He gave a sad smile. 'I told them everything.'

Julian, stunned, clutched for a chair and sat down. 'They – they only gave you a light beating. Did they have Pentothal?'

'They didn't need it. I told them voluntarily. I didn't give them your name or Tadeyama's, but I promised I would, if they in turn came up with the right terms of employment for me. This morning I gave them only chapter and verse about our operation. How we planned it all after I was recruited into the SIS in Korea. Oxford. Windscale. My cover as a nuclear scientist, which, by the way, I also confirmed was a real one. I *am* a nuclear scientist, and through the Ministry of Power I can still get access to what they want. I told them how we would plant false information. I told them the lot, Julian.'

'Harry, that's treason. Why – why did you do it?'

'Because after they'd been beating me up for a bit, and produced the surveillance device, I knew the game was up. Frankly, I didn't see the harm in it. At least it stopped them punching me.' He grinned. 'I thought you told me last night you trusted me, Julian?'

'I did. I'd be happy to see you hang now, though.' His face crumpled. 'Harry, I still don't understand why you confessed.'

Harry leant forward in his chair. 'Because I didn't want all those years of my life to go to waste. Because I want to hurt the bastards. Because I want my revenge for what they're planning to do to Ziwei and her mother.'

'Oh, my God,' said Julian.

'Aye,' said Harry, his eyes twinkling. 'It's taken time enough for you to work it out. Are you slowing down on me? It's probably all the cigars and champagne.'

'The car accident? Yes – of course. Chen Tao rigged it to cover for you. Because you told him you'd spy for him not as a blackmailed legation science officer but as a member of SIS?'

'Exactly,' said Harry. 'They wouldn't have let me go so quickly if they only suspected I was an enemy spy – diplomatic status or none. But they did because I gave them a better offer. One no intelligence agency on earth would in their right mind refuse.'

'You clever bastard – you've set up a quadruple, haven't you? Or is it a quintuple? Jesus, it's going to be complicated.'

'It widens the area of activity, though, doesn't it? And opportunity.'

Julian's fingers were drumming the table. A slow smile was forming on his face. 'You think we can get away with it?'

'It's worth a try, wouldn't you say?'

'They trust you?'

'They're businessmen and can see a good deal. My conditions were realistic enough to make them think the turn was genuine.'

'Money, presumably?'

'Lots. Incidentally, it's money for me rather than the Office. You'll get the sums they were talking about last night – but, Julian, I'll hang on to the rest.'

Julian waved a languid hand. 'My dear fellow,' he said. 'Was there anything else?'

'There was,' replied Harry. 'But I'll keep that to myself for the moment. It's personal.'

'You're being unusually enigmatic. It also sounds as if you're – negotiating with me.'

'Life's about negotiation, Julian, and mutual benefit where you can find it.'

'I remind you that you work for me and the British government.'

'That's not entirely true, Julian. Not any more. Technically I work for the Chinese government now. Alternatively you could say I'm working for both China and the UK, so that could equally well mean I work for neither. That I'm self-employed.'

'I see,' said Julian, after a long pause. 'Harry against the world, is it?'

'I told you last night, didn't I? I'm a solitary bugger. I work better alone.'

'And I'm to believe that, as an independent consultant to two secret services, you'll somehow resolve your conflict of interest in favour of Britain rather than China. Don't you think that might be rather difficult for the Office to swallow without some pretty hard-and-fast guarantees?'

'There are no guarantees in our line of work, Julian. Anyway, who ever trusts a consultant or a middle man? I'm sure you'll put measures in place to protect yourself until you can confirm that my actions justify my hire. I think one favourable sign is that I've come forward and told you all this. I could have kept quiet about it and you'd have been none the wiser, until you belatedly discovered that all your secrets had been given to the Chinese. What would I be then? Fourth man? Fifth man? Sixth man? I forget where we are, with so many moles operating in our service for the KGB. At least you know about me. Anyway, what are you worrying about? If you ever suspect me, you can put me in gaol for life.'

Julian laughed. 'My dear, complicated Harry. How boring my life would have been without you. Are there any other surprises you have in store for me? I didn't like the sound of that "for hire" you slipped in just now. Are you telling me you expect more from us than HM's wages, to go alongside what the Chinese are going to secrete in your private bank account?'

'Aye, once my services merit it. I realise you'll need to be convinced, as much as the Chinese will.'

'Then, to line your retirement, we'll have to be specially careful to make sure that the false-false-false information we give you to hand over to the comrades is convincing.'

'I'd appreciate that,' said Harry.

'You know I'll have to clear this with the Office, and probably higher up as well?'

'You can be persuasive, Julian, when you want to be – but I don't think you should be worrying about that now. If I were you, I'd be taking steps to clear out of Peking. Tadeyama as well. Within a few days they'll be questioning your nocturnal call on the legation last night and, as you know, I promised to tell them about our intelligence network here.'

'So you weren't joking?'

'I might have to tell them, once you're gone, that there was a junior runner in the operation who posed as a journalist called Travers. Of course, he wasn't the brains behind it all. The mastermind, I think, will be somebody in the legation itself. Don't you think Colliers is a shifty fellow?'

'Very,' said Julian. 'Spot him a mile away. All those witticisms of his – must be secret codes. Do you think it's a husband-and-wife team? I'd love to hear the comrades trying to make sense of her huntin', shootin', fishin' tales.'

'Doreen?' said Harry. 'A-grade spook, no doubting that.'

Suddenly the two men didn't have much to say to each other. Harry was rubbing his hands. Julian's fingers were drumming the table.

'You'll look after yourself, Harry? You know how dangerous what you're proposing is? If they ever suspect you're two-timing them, there'll be no diplomatic niceties. They'll liquidate you. The strain of a double life is bad enough, as you've found. The pressure of a triple or quadruple life is not something to take on lightly.'

'I'll play it by ear, Julian. I know what I'm doing. Only difference for a while will be that I'll be having furtive assignations with them rather than you. Otherwise it'll be GPR meetings and science-officer work as normal. It's in their interest to keep things steady until I'm back in England and I really get to work – when *we* get to work, that is.'

'You're a remarkable man, Harry, and a brave one.'

Harry dropped his head. 'No, Julian, I'm a normal one. For the first time I know what I want. It's modest – but I think I've found a way of getting there. There's a little bit of complicated business to do first.'

'Good luck,' said Julian. 'I'm not going to ask about the personal condition you're demanding from the Chinese. I might be able to guess.

If I'm right, I take my hat off to you as a man. If you need me, I'll help you when the time comes.' He paused. 'I'd better go,' he said. 'I feel the onset of this amazingly painful toothache. I think I'd better negotiate an exit permit so I can visit my dentist in Hong Kong.'

'That would be a very good idea,' said Harry. 'Sooner the better.'

'Until London, then?'

'See you in Piccadilly,' said Harry.

The two men shook hands. Harry saw Julian to the end of the corridor, and watched him clatter down the stairs in his Gannex raincoat and trilby.

He left shortly afterwards. He had to wait some time before a texi came, and the drive was painful, with his injuries, but he didn't mind the discomfort.

The taxi sped by the ruins of the city walls and the Jesuits' tower where the astrolabes stood out starkly against the sun, sinking into the smoke that rose from the millions of coal briquettes over which families were cooking their dinner. The outlines of the buildings shivered in the haze. Soon their shapes would be indistinguishable altogether in the dusk, but the same smoke would rise from the same cooking fires in the morning, and life would go on.

Harry, too, would have to take each day at a time. Chen Tao was bound to raise more problems. He would anticipate and deal with each one until he had his way.

His course was set. It would work, or it wouldn't. Harry, not Chen Tao or Julian, was calling the shots. If the gods were kind, Ziwei might one day find it in herself to forgive him. He was optimistic – as far as a dour fisherman from the islands can ever be – that, this time, everything would turn out for the best.

I I

The Best-laid Plans

Peking, April 1963

A strong wind was gusting across the water as Kang Sheng's secretary led Chen Tao along the familiar path by the Zhong Nan Hai lake. Waves lapped against the bank like snapping dogs. The bare branches of the willow trees shook like fettered patients in a lunatic asylum. The concrete office buildings that rose up behind the state leaders' villas seemed to be the high walls of the prison in which he would soon be incarcerated. He had no doubt that the only reason Kang had summoned him was to gloat over his fall.

Two days had passed since the double catastrophe. The first shock he might have surmounted – indeed, he knew that Ha Li had offered him an opportunity, and despite the bruise to his pride, he was already calculating how it might play to his advantage. It was when he returned to his headquarters that he realised another blow had fallen, which changed everything.

The door to his office was sealed and a soldier stood guard outside. He demanded identification papers. After examining them he told Chen to report to Acting Commissioner Ren. This turned out to be a svelte young man in an expensive blue Mao suit, who had taken over Commissioner Hao's office. The room was packed with boxes of confidential files, which he was examining one by one.

'Chen Tao,' he murmured, checking a list on his desk. 'Yes, you are the agent in day-to-day charge of Operation Red Flag. That project is suspended by order of the prime minister, pending the result of our investigation.' He wore the expression and used the severe, cold tone that Chen had adopted a thousand times when he added. 'That means you also are under investigation, Comrade.'

Chen told him he reported to Kang Sheng, and demanded an explanation of why the prime minister's office was interfering in secret operations. Ren coolly produced a document countersigned by Kang authorising the investigation. Chen knew there was little point in blustering: he accepted his orders that he should continue with the hydro negotiations until further notice. An escort would take him to and from his apartment, but otherwise he would be under house arrest.

It was galling to have to sit opposite Ha Li's mocking smile during the sessions. Of course he could say nothing to him about what was really going on – Chen did not know himself. He had the humiliation of having to wear a yellow handkerchief in his top pocket, indicating he was still working on Ha Li's demands. Ha Li's calm rattled him – he was no longer the man Chen had thought he knew.

It was no relief when his summons to the Zhong Nan Hai came on the third afternoon. He had no doubt what it portended. As he walked down the path, he determined to tell Kang everything. It was a slim chance, but perhaps the fact that he had discovered a British plot and been able to turn a spy might save him.

Again, he found himself ushered alone into Kang's presence. Again, he found himself standing in front of the desk, sweating while he was interrogated. As those snake's eyes examined him, he felt that his carefully thought-out arguments were as insubstantial as the blue cigarette smoke that curled round the skull-like face.

When he had finished, Kang laughed. 'It's a pity that you did not discover the true identity of this scientist earlier. Even three days ago, I might have been able to use such information. It's now irrelevant.'

'But the chance of discovering nuclear secrets . . .'

'You have no need to concern yourself with that. The foreign ministry has been diligent behind our backs. We have had another defector, it seems, from America. Our consulate in Los Angeles has recruited a certain Professor Sang, whose knowledge of the industry exceeds that of your Englishman. He arrived last night bursting to reveal his secrets.'

'That is very good news,' Chen said, 'but this British agent we have turned can also—'

Kang raised his hand. 'No buts, Comrade. It is, as you said, good news, and I was the first to congratulate Comrade Zhou Enlai on the coup by his department. We now have all the resources we need to build our bomb. It should be ready in two years. Yet you look despondent, Comrade. Are you not proud that at last we have the means to become a world military power, fulfilling the goals of our revolution?'

Chen knew he was mocking him, but suddenly Kang tired of the game. He rose from his desk, and gestured towards a set of armchairs.

As he stepped from behind the desk, Chen noticed how frail he was. His authority seemed to lie only in his immaculate tunic and crisp trousers. For the first time, he appeared human, and old.

'Sit down, Comrade Chen,' he said. 'You have served me faithfully in your way, and you deserve an explanation.'

Wearily he leant his head against the soft leather of the chair. 'Revolution is constant struggle,' he sighed, 'so our chairman has ordained, and he is right. Do not think that the purges against unreliable elements are restricted to the masses. Even in the Politburo there are Enemies of the People. Our chairman is shrewd and patient. He watches and waits. There will come a time when there is a reckoning against counter-revolutionaries like Liu Shaoqi and Deng Xiaoping. It is a matter of time.

'It is in this context that you must see the action by my colleague, the prime minister. He is ever anxious to prove his loyalty, and he saw an opportunity to ingratiate himself with our chairman. First, he made his stinking carcass sweet by producing his own answer to our nuclear problem. This has emboldened him to attack the intelligence services because it has always vexed him that he never was able to control them. He therefore feared them. Your honey trap has given him a weapon because you used a Chinese girl as the bait.'

'It was in the interests of the state, Comrade Kang.'

'Yes, yes. You don't need to persuade me. I authorised your actions, but I also warned you of the risks. I told you that in the event of failure the whole operation must be deniable.'

'Our operation did not fail. Or, rather, we have the means to make an even greater harvest from it.'

'You don't understand me, Comrade. Since the intervention of our premier, it will be necessary to prove that, contrary to the hopes of this investigation team, no such operation was ever sanctioned. With the assistance of Commissioner Hao, I have made sure that there is nothing in the records to prove that it was. If I am to protect the department it must be clear that no honey-trap operation officially ever took place.'

'But that is impossible, Comrade Kang. I have had a staff of fifty people working on it for the last six months.'

'Yes, there was a most irregular misuse of resources towards unsanctioned activities. That will be attested to by independent witnesses and observers whom, no doubt, the prime minister's spies will discover –

attendants at that spa in Sichuan, for example – but, as I told you, Commissioner Hao has destroyed any actual evidence that can reveal what the operation was about.'

'But – but surely they will discover that the files have been tampered with.' Chen could not believe the foolhardiness of this action. 'It will confirm their suspicions. It will all come out into the open. We even used a foreign-ministry guesthouse. Their own people will be able to corroborate that a honey-trap operation took place.'

The skull grinned. 'Perhaps Commissioner Hao should have considered that when he burnt the files,' he said.

Chen's heart lightened. Some instinct told him he was saved.

'Yes,' said Kang, reaching languidly into his top pocket for his cigarettes. 'I imagine that the investigating team will be curious as to why he committed such sabotage, and will draw the conclusion that he was seeking belatedly to hide the proof of his guilt. Personally, I was shocked when you loyally brought to my attention your misgivings about your superior's actions and your suspicions that this so-called honey trap was all along a cover for Hao's treason. How devious are our enemies, and how perceptive you were to have seen through them.'

'I sent you such a report?'

'Assuredly. It was the basis of my own explanation to the Politburo two days ago. Hao's elaborate exercise was to trick us into believing that he had recruited an agent in the British scientific establishment when in fact he was preparing a channel whereby, unsuspected, he would be able to communicate intelligence about our own military secrets to the imperialist powers. You, like the rest of us, were duped at first, and served his plan conscientiously. Fortunately you saw through it in time and were able to warn us. I would advise you to remember these details when it comes to your turn to be interrogated.'

Chen blurted out his thanks.

'You can thank me by continuing to serve me as efficiently as you have done up to now. The situation requires a scapegoat. By rights it should be you since this was, in fact, your operation not Hao's, but the interests of the state are better served by those who are capable and, for the moment, I have judged that the buffoon who is your master is more expendable. Do not make me regret that decision, Comrade Chen, otherwise evidence of your complicity will surface, and your head, too, will roll. Do you have any further questions?'

Chen asked him what he should do to wind down the operation, in light of the fact he had discovered that an enemy spy ring had been operating.

'I leave that to you,' he said. 'My advice would be to scare them so that they leave the country forthwith. By the way, tomorrow you will receive official orders to cancel the hydroelectric project. It has served its use and we do not desire co-operation with imperialists. You will see, in a year or so, a change in our government. Our chairman, as I told you, is preparing to reveal the pseudo-Khrushchevs and closet rightists who are perverting our revolution. Meanwhile I suggest that you use the cancellation of the project to embarrass this now inconvenient science officer so that his own people deal with him. You have my permission to release the blackmail photographs to the British minister, although unofficially they do not exist, as that will further discredit him. It should serve as a warning to any other spies who are involved in this operation, urging their hasty departure.'

'And the women?' Chen asked.

Kang drew on his cigarette. 'The girl is now on her way to a camp. Commissioner Hao has destroyed the files concerning her. She has entered the category of the disappeared and therefore no longer presents a problem. As to her mother . . .' He paused. 'The mother may remain where she is.'

'Would that not be dangerous? She knows about the operation.'

'Do not presume to question my decisions, Comrade,' came the hissing reply. 'The mother remains where she is, and you are to have no further contact with her. Need I repeat myself?'

'No, Comrade Kang.'

The cold eyes examined him. 'So, Comrade Chen, perhaps you have learnt something from this débâcle?'

Chen had no idea what answer was expected. He felt he was being tested. He recalled what Kang had said to him in his first interview and repeated it: 'For its safety, our country requires constant vigilance against our enemies, within and without the Party. There is no place for bourgeois sentimentality or mistaken personal loyalties.'

Kang smiled, but did not reply. He rose uncomfortably from his seat and moved back to his desk, from which he withdrew a canister of film.

'I believe this is yours,' he said. 'I found it diverting, but decadent. Tell me what you intend to do with it?'

There was sweat on Chen's brow when he withdrew the spool. He cast it on to the fire where it began to melt and smoke.

Kang nodded. 'You and I will see more of each other, Comrade Chen, when you take up your disgraced superior's position. As you say, we have many enemies within our country. Together we will hound them. May Chairman Mao live for ten thousand years!'

From the grate came a bitter-sweet acid smell. The spool was a burning wheel. Chen thought of ancient Buddhist pictures of sinners caught on the wheel of fate in the fiery kingdom of hell, and he saw Ha Li's face in the smoke. He felt a moment of sadness and regret. Then he steeled his heart.

Outside, the red flag of the People's Republic fluttered over the audience hall of the Zhong Nan Hai. Tomorrow, when he went into the hydro meetings for the last time, he would carry a handkerchief of similar crimson hue: the colour of blood, the colour of sacrifice, the colour of the relentless revolution that had been the extinction of Ha Li's hopes.

Julian was not able to save him, although he tried. He argued extenuating circumstances but the Office blamed Harry for the failure of the operation. They wanted a scapegoat because their chief had been embarrassed in the Joint Intelligence Committee. The Foreign Office had used the whole sorry episode to exact their revenge. It was couched in suitable mandarin terms. 'Regrettable misuse of funds', 'misguided adventurism', 'cavalier disregard of national interest'.

The arrival of the photographs on Garrard's desk on the day that the Chinese broke off the GPR negotiations was evidence enough to hang the Secret Intelligence Service. Their chief had been ambushed, and had no argument to stave off the criticism. It happened before Julian arrived back in London. He was fortunate that he was able to keep his own job.

His departure from Peking had been surprisingly easy. He received an exit visa as soon as he asked and next day was on a plane to Hong Kong. Tadeyama had also managed to leave the country without mishap. Harry had to spend a month in his *hutong* lodgings before the legation got rid of him. His last days in China were spent in the sort of Coventry that only well-bred Englishmen can devise. Julian doubted he cared. His brave attempt to assert control over an uncontrollable situation had failed. He was a broken man.

Julian met him at the airport. It was a glorious spring day. He had rented a cottage on the downs to debrief him. They drove through avenues of bridal blossom decking the narrow Sussex lanes, but the atmosphere in the car was the winter they had left behind in China.

Harry was curiously gentle. Even his granite features had softened. His eyes gazed out of the window. Their blankness revealed his despair.

They sat on garden chairs near the flowerbeds. A chestnut tree waved in the slight breeze. Harry's teacup looked tiny in his massive hands.

'I thought we could go over your story this weekend,' Julian told him. 'It'll be a sort of prep before the official interrogations begin on Monday.'

'That's good of you, Julian.'

'I'm your friend. Probably the only one.'

'I know,' he said.

'They'll be hard on you. There's no going back to your former existence. Braithwaite and Garrard between them have blackened your name with the Ministry of Power. That means a job in industry is out, too. The closed ranks of the establishment have behaved entirely predictably.'

'It doesn't matter.'

'No – I expect not.'

They sat in silence. A nervous bluetit hopped on to the table where the uneaten sandwiches lay. Neither man waved it away.

'You couldn't have saved her,' Julian said. 'It's honourable that you tried.'

For a moment Harry's eyes narrowed with their old angry spark, but they dulled. 'Aye,' he muttered.

'What do you think you'll do? You know that if I can help in any way . . .'

He did not reply.

'When this is over, I can probably pull a few strings with the Colonial Office. Who knows? Somewhere in one of the old Dominions they might be crying out for scientists and engineers of your experience. You can have a new life, Harry, if you pull yourself together. You're wounded, but the spirit inside you still burns. I'm sure of it.'

'Aren't you here to interrogate me, Julian?' he said harshly. 'Hadn't we better get on with it?'

That little exchange was about the closest Harry allowed Julian to come to him. On Monday morning Julian drove him to Portsmouth and handed him over to the inquisitors.

He saw Harry once more. He was staying in a YMCA near the docks. His ship for Canada was due to leave the following day. Julian was appalled by the stubble on his cheeks, the shaking hand and Harry's tramp-like appearance. He could smell the whisky on his breath. 'Harry,' he said, as they sat in a nearby pub. 'This isn't you.'

'I'll be all right.' Somehow he managed a smile. 'I won't be drinking when I reach Canada. Or not so much. A New Year resolution,' he added. 'Promise.'

'I'm glad to hear it. You must look after yourself. You'll have to brush up your act a bit if you're to wow one of those British Columbian farm girls. It's clean living and apple cheeks out there, you know.'

He looked back with haggard eyes. 'If I get a job that'll be enough.' He sipped his beer. 'What are you up to now? Still on the China desk?'

'I can't talk about that, I'm afraid, Harry. You know the rules.'

'Aye,' he said, and laughed bitterly. 'You and your rules.'

'I'm sorry,' Julian said.

Suddenly Harry grabbed his hand in a crushing grasp. There was a wild look in his eyes. 'Julian, if you hear anything – anything – about Ziwei, you'll tell me, won't you?'

'My dear chap,' Julian said, withdrawing his hand, 'of course. Like a shot. But – I'm afraid the chances are slim. Conditions in those camps, as far as we know, are . . .'

'I'm not a child, Julian. I know the odds. I've told myself she's already dead. I have to live with that . . . but . . . but . . .'

'Miracles happen?'

'Sometimes. I have to believe that, Julian. You . . . You never know.'

'No.' Julian's heart went out to him. 'You're right. You never know, old fellow.'

Harry's eyes seemed to lighten, and there was a flash of the old lopsided grin. '"Old fellow"? Somehow I never got used to those superior upper-class mannerisms of yours, though you've been a good friend. We've come a long way from Koje-do, haven't we?'

'Aye,' Julian said. 'That we have.'

PART TWO
Ziwei's Story

12

Tranquil Streams

Laogai 873, Liao River, 1966

The file of women on the dike cast silhouettes on the rice paddies as the sun came up behind them. Their conical straw hats and wicker baskets, the company flag shimmering at the end of a pole and, at the tail of the column, the rifle barrel of their guard were elongated on the soup-like surface of the water.

It was almost a clear day, although wisps of cloud still hung over the Black Hills fifty kilometres away. In living memory those mountains had been dank forests, bandit haunts, but the demand for timber in the first stages of national reconstruction in the 1950s had denuded them, and during the starvation that had followed the Great Leap Forward, peasants had stripped the bark off the remaining trees. Now only rocks and stumps remained and, of course, the tin mines, where prisoners like themselves slaved until they dropped. Ziwei was more fortunate. She had been assigned to an agricultural battalion.

Soon the women reached their work-station. There had been silence until then, except for the buzz of insects and the chatter of crickets – no birdsong: Mao's campaign to rid the country of sparrows had seen to that – but as they climbed down into thigh-deep water, they heard squeals and shouts. Another company, a mixed-sex one, was over the dike, obviously a Laojiao intake, fresh to the fields.

Ziwei grinned at Lan Ying, her friend. You could always tell the new arrivals by how they reacted to the mosquitoes . . .

The prisoners who constituted the Tranquil Streams Brigade were divided into three categories. The majority, like Ziwei, were condemned criminals, 'bad elements' and 'class enemies', expiating their crimes through 'Laogai', the abbreviation for Reform through Labour and the name by which the camps themselves were known. In the summer, they wore regulation black-cotton pyjamas, in winter the state's benevolence extended to padded coats and fur hats (necessary in this northern borderland where temperatures fell regularly below minus thirty degrees centigrade). The state also provided them with hoes, spades and other tools for their work. They even received a salary, which was sometimes, after fines, enough to buy tobacco from the canteen. Tobacco was the currency of the camp, essential for bartering pins, needles, thread, soap, enamel cups, cotton rags to use during menstrual periods and any other valuable that could not be acquired by ingenuity or theft. Meals were free, but issued strictly according to work quotas: those who fulfilled their tasks or exceeded them received heavy rations, those who did not received light ones. The differences between heavy and light rations were only a few extra *wo-wo-tou* – the corn cakes that provided their staple diet – and a double ladling of turnip soup, but that, in the mathematics of survival, was an equation of life and death. All feared illness, because everybody knew that a rest in the infirmary meant quarter rations, which did not bode well for recovery and usually led to a transfer to Camp 848 in the Black Hills – the depository for the old, the sick and the infirm, from which there was no transfer until one's allotted time to 'meet Marx'.

The Reform through Labour prisoners were divided into platoons and companies on an arbitrary basis – common criminals were mixed with 'stinking intellectual' rightists and 'antisocial' deviationists (all by definition were counter-revolutionaries) – but there was a strict division of the sexes. Since her arrest four years ago, Ziwei had not spoken to a man, except camp guards, interrogators and the capos in charge of their work duties, and only then in reply to questions or orders.

In her company there were two other ex-prostitutes (as she was also designated), two school-teachers (who had expressed rightist views during the Hundred Flowers Movement), a former 'landlord' from Shanghai (she had run the mansion inherited from her capitalist father as a boarding-house), an actress (who had been condemned for her 'bourgeois lifestyle') and three common criminals: an embezzler, a pickpocket and an extortionist. Their official team leader was the actress, Lan Ying, who had mastered the ideological dialectic necessary to run the evening 'study sessions' and knew how to flatter their capo, Crook-backed Wang, who accompanied them to their work details and meted out punishments; but all acknowledged that the real leader of the group was the pickpocket, Xiao, in her early twenties, who resembled and had the acquisitive instincts of a vulture. Her ability to forage had kept them alive during the last winter.

The Laogai prisoners did not envy the other two categories of inmate in the camp: what was the point? The 'freed prisoners' who had completed their sentences were allowed to set up 'homes' within the barbed-wire confines as 'civilians' but were still subject to camp rules. They were allowed infrequent visits to the nearby city of Shishan, but hardly any had family there. They could cultivate their own vegetable patches, but only in the short hours between work and study details – in practice, they were subjected to the same backbreaking toil as the prisoners and on much the same rations. They received some privileges: on May Day and National Day the first ten rows of the cinema were reserved for them when a revolutionary film or ballet was shown, but that was small compensation for the fact that their 'freedom' was prison by another name. They were allowed to marry, but only to ex-Laogai prisoners like themselves. Naturally those still undergoing Reform through Labour were not allowed to have anything to do with them.

Ziwei and her teammates, secure, at least for a while, in the solidarity of their group, tended to despise these 'lost ones' and sometimes dreaded the expiry of their own sentences, still way off in the future. The freed men and women were walking symbols of perpetual exile. At least while Ziwei and her team were still subject to the rigours of prison discipline, they could sometimes allow themselves to dream that one day they might return to a normal life, but when they saw – on their way to the paddies, or gathering outside the canteen – a group of 'free prisoners', only different from them in that they were not wearing black, they could not avoid the truth that, for them, the day would never come.

The third section of the camp was reserved for transients, city hooligans and malcontents who had not committed a crime worthy of being categorised as counter-revolutionary but whom a district magistracy, a police station or sometimes only a street committee had condemned, without trial, to three years Education by Labour or 'Laojiao'. If Ziwei had not, after four years of prison, become a hardened veteran, she might have pitied these unfortunates, most of whom were in their teens and unprepared for the same brutal regime as the Laogai prisoners. The previous winter the burial ground had been filled with them. However, in Tranquil Springs, there was no room for finer human feelings. Whenever a platoon of Laogai passed a platoon of Laojiao coming in the opposite direction along the dikes, they would spit at each other and shout their mutual scorn: 'rightist shits' and 'stinking ox demons' from one side, 'whimpering Mummy's boys' and 'pampered sons of bitches' from the other, until Crook-backed Wang or one of the other capos restored order, blowing their whistles and firing their rifles into the air.

If anything, the sufferings of those undergoing Laojiao provided amusement for the old lags. In a society stripped of gradations, those who knew how to cope were infinitesimally higher on the Darwinian scale than those who didn't and could comfort themselves with a sense of superiority.

The mosquitoes were a case in point. In these swamplands and alkali flats, turned by a decade of blood and sweat into something that was only now beginning to resemble farmland, the insects that emerged from the rice paddies were not the flimsy irritants that broke through holes in sleeping nets and disturbed a citizen in his bed: they were metallic monsters the size of a girl's little finger. The inmates, now numbed to the vocabulary of revolution, named them after the days when the authorities raised work quotas arbitrarily to match incomprehensible political campaigns taking place in the rest of the country. They were 'rockets' and 'sputniks' depending on their size and the agony of their sting.

It was a mark of how long one had been in the Laogai, the equivalent of a merit badge, that after a while one could treat their attacks with the indifference of a grazing cow to a cloud of midges. Any Laogai prisoner, before they even came to the farm, had spent at least a year in prisons, interrogation centres and transit camps, where they had already become used to the constant accompaniment of lice, flies and all the other creepy-crawlies that thrive on damp flagstones or in concrete cells. Starvation did the rest. When their flaking skin itched anyway from malnutrition, and their whole being was focused perpetually on the gnawing pain in their concave bellies, a sting even from a sputnik was barely to be noticed, and the whine of wings around their heads or the black clouds of insects around their eyes were little different from the spots that appeared in their vision, or the wind sound that constantly echoed in their eardrums.

It was diverting, therefore, to watch Laojiao teams enter the paddies for the first time.

'Look at them dance,' said Lan Ying, observing them as she stretched and rubbed her back after an hour groping under the surface of the murky water for weeds. 'Some rather fine steps there. We could have used them in our ballet troupe.'

'Why don't you write a revolutionary opera about it?' murmured one of the teachers, a forty-year-old with white hair called Meichuan. 'You could call it Taking Mosquito Swamps by Strategy.'

'They might want me to dance in it, and I don't think my legs are what they were, what with the scabs and the oedema.'

'Silence,' shouted Crook-backed Wang from his position on the dike. He was sweating under his shirt, which he had erected into a tent using his rifle and stick as props. 'I'm watching you.'

The women giggled, as Lan Ying flashed him her movie-star smile. 'When is he not?' she said, as she bent to her work again.

Ziwei, too, had been smiling at the Laojiao boys and girls as they flapped vainly at the buzzing swarms around them. Tomorrow they would arrive with their pyjama legs and shirtsleeves tied. Some would have spent the night agonising whether to cut cloth from their blankets to make a veil to tie under their hats, knowing that if they did so they would no longer be able to cover their bodies at night. She could have told them that it would be useless whatever they did. The stings of sputniks and rockets could penetrate any material, night or day, and if they cut their blankets they would regret it in the winter.

She bent down until her nose was just inches above the water, and reached into the murk below, Soon her fingers were sliding through the human excrement that had been used to fertilise the paddies, expertly feeling the difference in texture between the weeds and the precious rice shoots, pulling the former as near to the roots as she could reach and flinging the stinking mass into the basket slung over her shoulder.

The stench of shit no longer bothered her: an assignment in the pig pens last autumn had inured her to it, and as for eating with fingers that were impossible to clean, diarrhoea, like hunger, was a facet of existence, and even allowed for: experienced hands welcomed the trips to the latrines as a permitted way to take a few moments off work. Anyway, if it wasn't shit it was mud: Meichuan had once joked that, in their viscous existence, if the sky rained dung their lives would be complete.

Today Ziwei was not thinking of shit. It had showered the night before, a welcome cooling after four weeks of burning sunshine, and when they woke before dawn, it had been to a clattering chorus of frogs. It was with some excitement, therefore, that they had set off to work after roll-call, and each member of their team had a forage bag hidden under her shirt. Shortly after they had started weeding, Ziwei heard behind her a satisfied grunt from the pickpocket, Xiao. She had caught one.

After that, Ziwei and the others began to examine the ripples and bubbles on the surface of the water more closely. Frogs were not difficult to catch if you were prepared, and if you could clench your hands at the right moment to grasp the slippery movement – if you could react fast enough – that would be protein for the day: meat, and the nightmare of Camp 848 staved off for another twenty-four hours.

So far she had been unlucky, but it was still early in the day, an hour off the mid-morning rest. She could be patient. Her fingers moved automatically under the water, but her eyes were alert to any tell-tale change on the surface.

At last Wang blew his whistle. The women dragged themselves out of the water and lay down where they could on the bank. The chance to straighten their backs was blissful, but inactivity meant a return of fiendish leg itches caused by immersion in the poisonous paddy, as well as the even more familiar stomach pangs. They had already used up any energy that the morning gruel had given them. There were still two hours before lunch.

The two ex-prostitutes were whispering as usual about men they had had. Ziwei settled her straw hat over her face. Xiang, the older one, prodded her with her foot. They loved to tease her. Ziwei suspected resentment under the good humour.

'Come on, Ziwei, Lao Wang's half asleep. When are you going to tell us about your clients?'

'Yes, Xiao Peng,' whispered the other. Lin had served in an illegal brothel for muleteers and was full of stories. 'You must have confessed all your juicy experiences to the interrogators. Why do you spare your friends? Confess and we'll be lenient, hide the truth and suffer the consequences.'

The two ex-prostitutes giggled. The formulation Lin had just used was written in all the interrogation cells.

'Why are you so superior, Ziwei? If you persist in such unreconstructed attitudes we may have to struggle you.' That was another formulation, used in self-criticism sessions. 'You know you're one of us.'

'Leave her alone.' As usual Pick-pocket Xiao had only to grunt, but the two ex-prostitutes were immediately silenced. Relieved, Ziwei turned on her side, but Xiang's words, 'You know you're one of us' reverberated in her head . . .

She heard the accusation during her first interrogation in the holding centre at Zhangjiakou, the city she was taken to, after a seven-hour ride in a bumping truck, on the day that Chen Tao had handed her over to the military.

They hauled her out of the truck in the prison yard, and she caught a glimpse of barred windows in blank brick walls. Then they pinioned her, pushing her head down, and prodded her along concrete corridors to the commandant's office. The men left. Two female guards strip-searched her, then made her put on prison clothes. When the men returned, they were holding manacles and chains.

The commandant made a speech full of slogans. Dazed by the unbelievable things that were happening to her, Ziwei gathered that she would be kept here for interrogation and self-criticism until her 'case' was resolved. First, though, she would be allowed a period to 'collect her thoughts'. Stumbling under her heavy chains – the metal rod that linked her ankles made even shuffling painful – she was thrown into a solitary confinement cell and the metal door slammed, leaving her in darkness.

She was there for ten days. It was her first experience of hunger and cold. On that first evening, after she had wept for hours, the door opened and a warder, without speaking to her, laid two bowls on the concrete floor. One contained water, the other corn mush. She asked him how she was expected to eat with her hands still cuffed behind her back. He did not reply. When he returned half an hour later the bowls were in their original positions, untouched. He took them away. Next day she found a way to kneel so she could lap the contents of the bowls.

When the warder returned, he inspected the cell with a torch and saw the muck on the floor. It was not only the spilt food. Manacled, there was no way she could unloose the string on her trousers. Humiliatingly, she had soiled herself in the night, and excrement and urine had spilled down her legs on to the floor.

'It is your duty to keep your cell clean,' he said quietly, pointing at the bucket. 'Your meal privileges are suspended for the rest of the day.'

'But how am I to do it? How can I?' she cried, shaking her chains.

He slammed the door.

Eventually she realised that, to relieve herself, she had to stand in the bucket.

It was two days before they came to empty it. Then they hosed the cell, and her as well. It took hours for her wet clothes to dry on her shivering body. The stench remained, and the shame.

It was through trial and error, and many wretched nights, that she found a way to squat on the straw mat in a position that would allow sleep. On the tenth night she was woken by a torch shining into her face, and soon she was shuffling along concrete corridors again, and across a courtyard to a wooden hut in which sat three men with papers in front of them.

The middle one, who had thick horn-rimmed spectacles and brush-like grey hair, spoke in a patient and even kindly tone. 'What is your name?'

Head bowed, she told him.

'And your profession?'

'I am a translator,' she said, 'in the Shanghai No. 3 Textile Bureau, and lately for the Shanghai Foreign Trade Bureau.'

'Yes, we have a record of that. And what else do you do?'

She looked at him blankly. Was she expected to tell him about Chen Tao and the honey trap? The commandant had told her to be honest in interrogation, repeating some slogan about confess all and we will be lenient.

'I – I had an assignment.'

To her surprise the burly man on the left, in policeman's uniform, laughed. 'Not just one, it seems,' he said, in a thick peasant accent.

The man with the brush hair gave him an irritated look. 'It is for the prisoner to answer the questions, Comrade. What assignment was this?' he asked Ziwei.

Stumbling with exhaustion, Ziwei tried to explain. She and her mother had been contacted by the Second Department. A man called Chen Tao had blackmailed them into working for him. He said there was a spy he wanted to trap, a foreigner. It was her duty to sleep with him, but she had discovered that he was not a spy, only an ordinary scientist, and Chen, because he thought she was disloyal, had had her arrested and threatened to shoot her mother . . .

The brush-haired man raised his hand. 'Do you realise, Comrade Peng, what a serious position you are in? Do you really wish to waste our time with fantasies taken from spy literature for children? Do you think that our own security services behave like the Kuomintang? We are here to help you, but if you lie to us, you will only force us to send you back to the solitary cell again until you are prepared to tell the truth. Don't have any illusions.' He picked up a heavy dossier. 'We know all about you, but we're giving you a chance to confess voluntarily. If you do, it may alleviate the severity of your sentence.'

'I – I am telling the truth, Comrade. It was Chen Tao . . .'

Again he raised his hand. 'I will not allow you to speak in this way about a senior official. To accuse falsely a member of the Communist Party is a counter-revolutionary act, equivalent to sabotage of the state. I urge you to consider carefully what you say. Let us do away with pretence. You know why you were brought here. It is time for you to confess. In all your pack of lies, there was one kernel of truth: you slept with a foreigner. Some would call it an act of treason and espionage. In your case, it was bourgeois greed that impelled you. He had access to the fancy clothes and perfumes in the Friendship Store so you seduced him and betrayed your country for money and gain.'

He nodded at his other companion, a thin young man in a cloth cap who had been taking notes. From under the table he produced a brown-paper parcel and began to untie it. 'Was it worth it, Comrade Peng? Was it really worth it – for this?'

The paper parted, and one by one the young man lifted out and displayed the red cheongsam that Chen Tao had given her, the necklace he had also made her wear, the bottle of perfume and, lastly, casual reminders of a life she would never know again, a pink ribbon and a pair of buckled shoes.

He shook his head as Ziwei gaped at him. 'I suppose it is not surprising. Bad blood will out. Your record at school was one of rebellion and resentment when you supposed you were unfairly treated because of your disgusting *hei wu lei* background.'

'I never—' she started.

The man banged the dossier. 'We have your teachers' reports, Comrade Peng, and denouncements from loyal citizens in the Textile Bureau, who have spontaneously written to us about your life of crime and antisocial behaviour. Your secret life, Comrade Peng, consisting of greed and debauchery, to support your and your mother's lavish and ideologically incorrect lifestyle.' He paused. 'We even have self-criticisms of some of the men to whom you sold your body.'

The man in the police uniform chuckled. 'Going right back to when you fucked members of the basketball team in the high-school showers to get their Mao badges.'

Brush Head banged the table. 'That's enough, Comrade Dai – unless you wish to take over the responsibility for this interrogation?'

The policeman looked abashed. 'Sorry, Comrade, I was merely pointing out that the accused's life of prostitution began well before she left school.'

'Then in due course she will confess it, as well as her other crimes. There is a procedure here.'

'Yes, Comrade, in future I will . . .'

But Ziwei had risen from her chair, and despite the chains weighing them down, she raised her arms behind her back, clenching her fists. 'These are lies!' she screamed. 'Don't you see, Comrade? Don't you see that Chen Tao is fabricating my background? I was never a – a prostitute.'

Brush Head opened the book. 'Do you deny, Comrade Peng, that on the fourth of February 1961, after a New Year Festival celebration at the Textile Bureau canteen, you and Engineer Tao Linfang of the Machinery Department had a tryst in the People's Park, at night, in bushes opposite the International Hotel? And that on the next day he, a married man, bought you a leather coat and a fur cap as payment for your services?'

'You are sprinkling truth to pepper a dish of lies,' she shouted. 'Yes – yes, we did! We did do that, but it was not – prostitution. It was a love affair, Comrade.'

Brush Head was smiling. 'You are trying to defend prostitution with the greater moral crime of adultery?' His voice was gentle when he continued. 'I understand, Comrade. Believe me, I understand. It is natural to try to hide unpalatable truths, but see what you have done just now. You are still making excuses for your behaviour, but you have confessed to the salient point. That is good progress. In time, when you begin to understand the error of your ways, you will find confession easier. This is the path of self-education that our generous state is offering: the opportunity to repent your crimes and reform yourself. Yes, Comrade Peng, even you – a prostitute, a bad element who deserves to be thrown into the dustbin of history – are being given a chance to turn your back on a hideous past and joyfully rejoin our ongoing revolution to reconstruct our motherland.' He turned to his companions. 'We should encourage and congratulate our errant comrade on this first brave step she has taken towards the truth.'

Joined by the others, he began to clap. She was amazed to see a tear in his eye.

And that was the moment – under the smiles of her three interrogators, the slapping of their hands ringing in her ears – when Peng Ziwei realised the enormity of what Chen Tao had done. He had seen to it that she no longer existed. Her own personality as well as her freedom had been taken away from her. If she was to survive it was in the character that Chen Tao had created for her.

Lying on the dike, waiting for the whistle that would signal the command to return to back-breaking labour, Ziwei felt another prod of a foot.

'You can attempt to clothe yourself in virtue, Younger Sister, and pretend that you are reformed,' it was Xiang again, whispering maliciously, 'but you know you stink inside like the rest of us. We are all guilty here.'

Guilty? Yes, that was true, she thought. They had all, in one way or another, betrayed and been betrayed. Such was the system.

For those first few months in the holding centre, she felt that only her love for Ha Li kept her alive. Her mother would be dead by now – arrested in her home, condemned in some hidden secret police cell, probably executed immediately afterwards in a closed prison yard with a bullet in the back of her head. There would have been no public trial or parade through the streets with a placard round her neck: Chen Tao would have kept her murder quiet to protect his secrets. In her solitary cell she had thought of little else, but afterwards, in an effort to preserve her sanity, she tried to blot those images from her mind. Following her first interrogation, after cleaning her up and giving her new clothes, they had put her into a cell with fourteen other prisoners awaiting sentence. As she lay squeezed against the others on the *kang*, the sleeping platform that occupied three-quarters of their cell space, Ziwei tried to banish nightmare and hunger by imagining Ha Li holding her in his arms.

There was little time to think of him during the day. With no labour to be done in the holding centre, the guards kept the prisoners occupied by constantly reviewing their own and their companions' 'crimes'. They were roused before dawn, and given their breakfast – no more life-sustaining than the corn mush Ziwei had received in the solitary cell. Then there was a flurry of activity and inspections, as each prisoner performed their allotted tasks, some to empty the night bucket into the 'honey cart' in the yard, others to water and polish the earthen floor of the cell, the rest to brush and dust, and all to fold and refold their blankets until the guards were satisfied. Then a 'study session' began. One of the prisoners was deputed to read an article from the *People's Daily* and, sitting in a ring on the *kang*, each prisoner was invited in turn to 'comment', receiving criticism from their companions if their statements were deemed to be 'ideologically incorrect'. Lunch followed – corn mush or vegetable soup (more soup than vegetable) with the addition of a dried *wo-wo-tou*. Then the self-criticisms began.

It took several sessions before Ziwei could bring herself to reveal that she was a prostitute. She tried to cloud the issue with vague suggestions of immorality. She admitted that she had trapped a man into adultery. This was accepted with approving nods and sententious moralising, before the ball was passed to the next self-accusant, a murderess, whose crimes were much more interesting – but clearly the cell leader, a former Party secretary of her factory who had been accused of corruption, had been tipped off by one of the interrogators, who received a daily report of these sessions. One afternoon she broke the routine by announcing, in a high-pitched tone, 'Comrades, I'm ashamed to report that one of our number has been lying to us.'

They looked at each other with scared faces. They knew what this portended. There was relief when the accusing finger pointed at Ziwei.

Her hands were tied behind her back. She was forced to kneel on the floor below the *kang*, with her forehead touching the earth. One of the other prisoners lifted her arms upwards. It felt as if her shoulders were being pulled out of their sockets. She was forced to maintain this position until the end of the 'struggle session' four hours later, by which time she was almost fainting with pain.

First there was the by now all-too-familiar formula: 'Confess and we'll be lenient, hide the truth and suffer the consequences.' One by one, her fellows joined in the chant: 'Confess. Confess. Confess.'

'I've told you! I've told you!' she shouted, as the prisoner holding her arms twisted them viciously.

'Liar, liar,' came the chorus. A girl of her own age, a young factory worker of *hei wu lei* background like herself, who was inside for writing 'bourgeois poetry', leant over the *kang* and spat in her face. 'Counter-revolutionary bitch,' she screamed. Shocked, Ziwei lifted her head and saw that the girl's pretty features were contorted with hatred.

'Cow ghost and snake demon,' yelled another, as Ziwei's cheek was pressed into the earth. 'Bad element of the worst category', 'stinking revisionist', 'pampered daughter of the bourgeoisie', 'cuckoo that soils the nest' – the standard slogans came out in the highest pitch. Ziwei was accused of worshipping the 'Four Olds' – old ideology, culture, customs and habits. She was a proponent of the 'Three Shams and Three Realities' – sham anti-imperialism but real capitulation, sham revolution but real betrayal, sham unity but a real split. Many were obviously quoting the first formula that came into their heads, but they did it with venom and hysteria that, to the cowering Ziwei, seemed as if they might explode at any moment into physical violence.

'Confess, confess,' was the continued chant, after these outbursts of loathing.

After an hour Ziwei tried, but every time she opened her mouth, there was a catcall of imprecations against her, and her face was pushed further into the dirt. Some of the women were already hoarse with shouting. The screaming reverberated around the narrow concrete walls of the cell and inside Ziwei's head. Meanwhile she felt her hands and arms grow numb.

After three hours the Party secretary called a halt. Ziwei could hear the women panting as they settled back on the *kang*. 'Are you going to confess now?' the Party secretary asked sternly.

'Yes.' It was a whimper. Ziwei felt her eyelids encrusted with grit from the tears that had mixed with the dirt on the floor.

'What were you? What are you?'

'A – a prostitute,' whispered Ziwei. 'I'm a whore – a whore.'

There was a satisfied intake of breath.

'Finally she admits it,' said the Party secretary. 'Now, what do we think of whores, comrades?'

The screaming began again, accompanied by a shower of spittle. It ended only when the warder rattled the door, telling them to clean the cell before dinner.

Chewing miserably on her *wo-wo-tou*, her shoulders and arms still burning with pain, Ziwei found herself sitting on the *kang* next to the young poet who had called her a counter-revolutionary. The girl gave her a friendly smile. 'Aren't you drinking your *congee*?' she asked. 'Here, pour some into my bowl if you don't want it. I'm starving today. Struggle sessions are so tiring, don't you think?'

The next day Ziwei was called to her second interrogation. Brush Head said he was pleased with her progress, and told her to begin writing her formal self-criticism.

Three weeks later, there was another struggle session, this time of the murderess: illiterate and uneducated, she had consistently failed to show proper political appreciation during the study sessions. This time Ziwei screamed with the rest of them. As the young poet, Guimei, told her, on the day she gave Ziwei a *wo-wo-tou*, 'in exchange for the *congee* last time': 'You've got to go along with it. If it's not you, it's somebody else. It's just survival of the fittest. Bastards,' she added, under her breath.

The Party secretary snapped, 'What's that you said?'

The girl smiled sweetly. 'Only that I would die for an egg right now.'

That was when they became friends. As the weeks passed into months, they helped each other, in the evenings, compose their self-criticisms. Guimei, with her creative talent, was expert at writing in the accepted manner. She had an inexhaustible memory for quotations from Mao Tse-tung. 'Put one of those in, and they can't argue.' She grinned. They began to exchange confidences. One evening, when the Party secretary was dozing on the other end of the *kang*, Ziwei told her about Ha Li.

Her friend looked at her with a frown. 'You love him?' she asked.

'I can't help it,' said Ziwei.

'Forget him.'

Ziwei started. Guimei's face was as contorted as it had been during the struggle session – not with anger but concern.

Guimei took her hand. 'Listen to me, Elder Sister. There is no world outside now. There is only us, here. If you even think of another life, or start wishing you could go back to your old one, you're weakening yourself. Only one thing matters and that's survival. So forget Ha Li. Forget love and any other fine feelings. They'll find out and use them against you.'

'They can't stop us feeling,' said Ziwei.

'They can,' said Guimei. Her eyes were staring urgently out of her thin face. Ziwei had observed the deterioration of her looks over the preceding months. The once plump girl, who had joked about *congee*, was skeletal. So, she imagined, was she. Guimei was the mirror of herself. They were all mirrors of each other, more shadowy by the day on their starvation rations.

'What about my feelings for you?'

Guimei spoke harshly. 'If by denouncing you I can find a way to reduce my sentence, I will do so.' Her fingers tightened on Ziwei's knuckle. It was like being held by a bird's talon. 'And you must do the same. If you ever get the chance, denounce me.'

Ziwei pulled away. 'We're friends. I trust you. I've – I've told you about Ha Li,' she said.

'You shouldn't have. Don't worry. I won't use it against you. I don't need to. My interrogations are going well enough. I've given them all they want. I – I only wanted to warn you because you've been good to me here. Forget that he ever existed. For your survival.' Her shoulders began to shake. 'I'm going to survive,' she said. Her voice came out indistinctly through her sobs. 'I am. I am.'

Ziwei put her arms around her, not caring if the others saw them. Guimei shook her off and began to unfold her blanket. 'Forget him,' she hissed.

After that Guimei avoided her, brushing past her during the morning tidying, positioning herself away from her during the study sessions. Three days later, Ziwei was called for another interrogation. This time Brush Head's usually kindly features were knitted into a grim frown. 'I'm disappointed in you, Comrade Peng. Your self-education up to now has been positive, but you have regressed.'

'I have been studiously honing my political understanding and frankly and freely confessing my former errors,' said Ziwei.

'No, Comrade Peng, you have been drawing sensational attention to yourself by spreading details of that nonsensical spy story with which you tried once to bamboozle us. Do you deny that you attempted to spread a tissue of self-exonerating lies to Comrade Shi Guimei? Fortunately, Comrade Shi is making better progress than you on how to become a responsible citizen and has informed on you.'

There was no way to bluff it out. Ziwei could only bow her head and beg his pardon, but Brush Head had already prepared the chains, and she spent a winter month freezing in solitary.

During that month, after her anger had died down, she realised she owed a debt to Guimei, who had taught her a valuable lesson. Perhaps it was the cold that kept her teeth chattering and her whole consciousness directed on the pain in her wrists and ankles, where the manacles bit into the flesh, or maybe it was just the hunger in her belly from which there were no distractions – but this time she did not think much of Ha Li, and if she did, he appeared only as a vague memory of a previous existence, which really, as Guimei had said, had no relevance to her present condition. Every minute, every second, she had to concentrate on one thing: staying alive. She found Guimei's words reverberating in her head. 'I'm going to survive. I am. I am.'

Whatever it takes, she told herself, I, Peng Ziwei, am also going to survive this, and anything else that happens to me. I am strong, she told herself. I will not allow myself to rely on anybody ever again. And I will survive this. I will.

The whistle blew. Grumbling, the women stretched, then slithered one by one down the bank into the paddy, finding their former positions and bending to reach for weeds.

The sun had risen higher and the surface of the water had become a mirror. As she leant forward, Ziwei saw her reflection – the drawn, leathery cheeks of somebody who might have been in her twenties or her fifties, the desiccated lips that set her mouth into a rodent snarl, the thin neck that looked as if it might snap at any moment, and the protuberant but shining eyes of someone in an advanced state of hunger. It was a familiar reflection. She had long got used to it. In a world of semi-skeletons, she did not look much different from anybody else.

But today, because she had been thinking about Guimei, she remembered that long ago hers had been the first face she had ever seen transformed by starvation. As a ripple crossed the surface of the water, a trick of the light seemed to show her another face, once even more familiar, fleshier, with dimples, and a full head of hair surmounted by a pink bow.

It was the ripple she found more interesting. Her hands darted below the surface, feeling for movement. Nothing. She continued to weed.

Guimei. She had not thought of her in a year. When they had let Ziwei out of solitary, they had moved her to a different cell. Guimei had been assigned to a Laogai camp long before Ziwei finished the screening process and received her own sentence.

But she did see her once again. There had been a cholera epidemic in a neighbouring camp, and the inmates had died like flies. Ziwei's team had been transferred there temporarily to help with burial details. In a pile of bodies, Ziwei had recognised her friend.

She bore her no ill will. She remembered only that once she had been kind to her, and had given her good advice. A long-submerged image of Ha Li also flickered for a moment in her mind. Guimei, lying there, had temporarily reminded her of him. It was only because she was trying to recall what she and Guimei had once quarrelled about. She could barely remember the details of his face, and that she had once loved him seemed strange to her. The image passed, almost as quickly as it had materialised. There was too much to do. The authorities were keen to get the infected bodies underground as soon as possible. So were Ziwei and her team. They had been given plastic overclothing, gloves and masks, but none was confident it would afford any protection.

Ziwei's job was to lay the lime. She watched as Xiang and Lin between them threw the bodies into the pit. Guimei was among the last, and Ziwei could see her pallid features clearly as she descended with the bucket. Some gesture seemed necessary. She climbed quickly out of the pit and gathered a bunch of wild flowers. She laid them on Guimei's chest. Then she poured the lime. Xiang and Lin, who had been waiting with shovels, teased her about her sentimentality.

But Ziwei was thinking of the irony. Guimei, who had taught her about survival, had not survived. She had.

By heaven she had, she thought angrily, as she snapped a weed and threw it into her basket.

Ziwei was moved to a transit camp after she had completed her confession to the interrogators' satisfaction. The trial was a pro-forma: there was no other verdict but 'guilty' and she had been trained by then to accept it with thanks. Brush Head wept a tear and shook her hand, urging her to continue her political studies and self-reform. He might have been a schoolmaster awarding certificates to a passing-out class.

While she waited for her sentence, she was given her first experience of hard labour. To the outside world the transit camp was a plastics factory, and the raincoats manufactured there were sold to great profit. Ziwei vaguely remembered once having bought one. She recognised the label. She had had no idea then that they were produced by slave labour.

The cell in which she lived with twenty-four others was not unlike the one at the holding centre, but the wooden *kang* served as bed and work bench. When they were roused in the morning and had completed their cleaning chores, the *kang* was dismantled and re-erected as the workbench. Then the studding machines were brought out, one for each prisoner. Each raincoat had four plastic buttons. It was a simple process. Position the plastic sheet. Insert the pellet. Pull down the lever. A battery generated enough heat to melt the plastic so the button stud melded with the sheet. Wait while it sizzled, then lift the lever, insert another pellet and repeat the process three more times before laying the raincoat on the pile. Each prisoner was given a target of two thousand raincoats a day. Except on rocket and sputnik days, when targets had to be exceeded, one thousand five hundred was considered acceptable, and the prisoner who achieved that amount was allowed heavy rations. One thousand entitled them to light rations. Any number below that brought punishment rations. It was a good Pavlovian system designed to guarantee the output required.

Except that some of the prisoners were incapable of doing it. They starved.

Ziwei took a month to earn herself light rations, and after three was regularly overtaking the fifteen hundred mark and relishing the extra *wo-wo-tou*, sometimes supplemented with a potato. She used to compete with her neighbour next-but-one on the workbench, the once famous actress, Lan Ying, who was equally dextrous with her fingers. 'Dearest,' she once told her – it was her style to affect dangerous mannerisms, one of the reasons Ziwei liked her, 'my hands can do anything. Believe me, if you've gone through the rigours of traditional opera training, as I have, anything else is a doddle.'

The tiny, birdlike woman between them was another matter. On a good day she might complete seven hundred raincoats, but usually she was pushed to get through five hundred. Nothing – not a struggle session in the evening study group, not even a spell in solitary confinement – could induce her to increase her pace. She was inarticulate when it came to her turn for self-criticism. 'I'm sorry,' she'd grunt, bowing her head, but there was a fiery glint in her beady eyes. 'I'm bad.' She would glare defiantly at the other women around her who,

one after another, would drop their gaze, sympathetic despite themselves. Only Dr Liu, a pharmacist who had stolen milk powder from
her hospital, adulterating what was left with cornflour and causing
the deaths of three infants, was unforgiving. 'You have nimble fingers,
Xiao. You're a pickpocket, aren't you?' she would taunt. 'It's not that
you can't do it. You're like the worst of the imperialist agents, deliberately sabotaging our production quota. You are an unreformed
counter-revolutionary. Even quarter rations are wasted on parasites
like you.' The cell leader had no option but to let her rant on. She
was speaking the vocabulary of revolution, which was sacrosanct, even
though everybody in the cell loathed her for her hypocrisy. Pickpocket
Xiao remained impassive. 'Sorry, I'm bad,' she'd say, glaring at the
floor.

Ziwei and Lan Ying would sometimes catch each other's eye on the
workbench, and shake their heads. As the days went by, Xiao seemed
to perform her task in slower motion, a dreamy, faraway look on her
face. One day she got through only three hundred raincoats. She
swooned as she tried to rise from her seat, and Lan Ying had to hold
on to her while the others were transforming the workbench back into
a *kang*.

The next day Ziwei could hardly bring herself to raise her eyes from
her work. She believed that Pickpocket Xiao was attempting a form
of suicide. She would not be the first to give up. Ziwei was saddened.
During the self-criticism sessions, there had been a spark of character
in the dour criminal that had impressed her.

She was surprised, therefore, when the piles of work were taken
away at the end of the day, that Xiao's was larger than usual. A glance
at the tag told her that the other woman had completed eleven hundred
pieces. She was at last eligible for light rations.

Lan Ying's pile, on the other hand, numbered eight hundred. Ziwei
stared at her, but Lan Ying shrugged. 'Bad day, dearest, maybe my
period's coming early this month.' She winked. 'Anyway, I could use
a change in diet. All those *wo-wo-tou* – so boring!'

That evening, Xiao was congratulated for showing the first signs
of a reformed work attitude. For once, Dr Liu was silenced. Lan Ying,
meanwhile, was criticised for idleness. She took the verbal abuse with
equanimity. Only Ziwei noticed the barely repressed smile.

The next day Ziwei, very carefully so that no one could observe
her, laid every third raincoat on Xiao's pile. At one point in the

afternoon, she caught Lan Ying's eye. They grinned – it was the first time since her incarceration that Ziwei felt anything approaching lightness of heart. She returned to her work, picking up her pace. At the end of the day, all three women had produced numbers barely over a thousand, but it was enough to qualify all three for light rations. During the study session, when she, like Lan Ying, was also admonished, she felt happy. Between them they had defeated the system.

Xiao's health slowly improved with the increased rations. In a fortnight she was back to her upper limits of production – not enough in itself to qualify for light rations, but supplemented by surreptitious additions from Lan Ying and Ziwei's piles, enough to make her quota. Meanwhile, Lan Ying and Ziwei, working at 'sputnik' pace, had brought themselves up to the heavy-ration mark again. In addition to the piecework, they would also slip Xiao a *wo-wo-tou* when the others' backs were turned.

Xiao did not express gratitude as such, although her eyes burnt perhaps more brightly when she looked at either of her companions. One morning, in the exercise yard, to which they were allowed access three times a week, she passed a paper pouch to Lan Ying, nodding also at Ziwei, before hurrying away. Lan Ying pocketed it quickly. Later, in the latrines, Ziwei and Lan Ying examined their trove: thirty-seven cigarette butts. It was a fortune, which could be traded in the prison's black market.

Lan Ying knew exactly how to proceed. She had already started flirting with one of the guards, who was an opera fan and had recognised her from one of her movies. The cigarette butts were more than enough to buy a wristwatch, and one of their cellmates, who was always scrounging tobacco, had one to sell. It was the beginning of a virtuous circle. In exchange for the wristwatch, the guard supplied goods, some to eat, others to barter. The three would meet in the latrines to chew tomatoes, aubergines and sometimes meat – dried pork or chicken drumsticks. Xiao, whom the others discovered was a scavenger of genius, always had a new supply of butts, and in the summer, when weeds grew in the exercise yard, she would add edible roots and mint. They called themselves the Three Crows.

There was another big difference between the holding centre and the transit camp. In the holding centre, while the regime was tough, the warders treated the prisoners with exemplary politeness. Torture, such as there was, was of the mind. In the transit camp, the gaolers were drawn from the peasants in the surrounding villages, and a harsher, more unpredictable regime prevailed. Sometimes prisoners could play this to their advantage. A few guards were corruptible, as Lan Ying had found. Others, though, were sadists. Any infraction of cell discipline was an excuse for extra punishment, which was usually a spell in solitary. Ziwei once failed to fold her bedroll in the required manner, and Dr Liu brought this up in the evening study session. She was sentenced to a week's 'disciplining'.

The hunger and cold in the cell were the same, as was the weight of the chain, but in the day-time the guards would sometimes bring her out for their version of a 'thought-reform session'. The methods they used were imaginative and had their slang names. 'Riding a Donkey Back to Front' was one of the milder tortures. She was made to crawl on all fours around the floor reciting quotations from Mao Tse-tung while the heaviest guard sat on her back, beating her buttocks with chopsticks. 'Lotus-wrapped Egg Roll' was harder. She had to kneel down, lean forward so that her head was tucked between her legs, resembling as much as possible a ball, while the guards amused themselves by rolling her round the room. Then she had to stand up suddenly and recite a quotation. The inevitable nausea and dizziness would usually make her sway and sometimes collapse – and the process was repeated. 'Martial Arts Practice' involved kicks to her back if she failed to recite a quotation exactly, and there were other forms of beating. What she hated most was 'Embracing the Cassia-blossom Vase', which involved wrapping her arms around a full toilet bucket for up to six hours and remaining motionless – even when the guards were relieving themselves on top of it, as they made sure they did frequently. The guards could get away with this. Their charges were prisoners awaiting sentence: there was no gentle Brush Head to complain to if prisoners' rights were being abused.

Here, too, the ultimate penalty was also imposed for 'serious crimes'. All the inmates, male and female, would gather in the factory yard while the prisoner was sentenced. The first man Ziwei saw executed was a homosexual, who had seduced one of his cellmates. He knelt on the stage as the commandant read the charges. A moment after the sentence was announced, a prison guard with a pistol stepped forward and fired into the back of his head. His brains splattered over the first row of crouching prisoners in the audience.

Two months later, there was another execution. A prisoner had found his way into the kitchens and stolen a sack of onions, which he buried behind the latrines, retrieving some of his treasure each day. After that, the Three Crows realised the risks in what they were doing – but they did not stop. Lan Ying argued that they had protection from the prison guard she had charmed. Xiao muttered that she didn't care, and Ziwei realised that those few tomatoes and slices of biltong now meant the difference between life and death. Going back to standard rations, heavy or light, without the extra nourishment to augment them, was not to be borne. They did, however, take precautions, especially to avoid Dr Liu, whom they had identified long ago as their cell snitch, and who took satisfaction from reporting on her fellows and subjecting them to punishment.

It was perhaps inevitable that their luck would run out, and they were right: it was Dr Liu who discovered them.

Foolishly, when the three of them were in the latrine one evening dividing their latest loot, they allowed their excitement to get the better of them – here were six slices of roasted mutton! Lan Ying, who was on watch, failed to see Dr Liu approach through the yard.

She was the picture of self-righteous anger, standing with one hand pressed to her puffed-up chest, the other pointing an accusing finger at the criminals she had brought to light. 'So, I have tracked you deviationists to your lair,' she cried. 'Oh, I have observed you,' she continued. 'I saw your sabotage of the work schedules, how you sought to steal extra food by fiddling the numbers of this creature's piecework – but I kept quiet. I knew your sabotage would not end there, and I have patiently tracked your sinister activities until today, when I have caught you red-handed, crowing over your ill-gotten gains. Perverts,' she spat. 'Degenerates! Bourgeois bloodsuckers! Counter-revolutionaries who can never be reformed!'

Ziwei was shaking with fear. Lan Ying, however, strode forward and faced her. 'Elder Sister Liu, we are prisoners like yourself. We bear you no ill will. We will even share what we have with you.' She proffered a slice of mutton.

Saliva actually dribbled down Dr Liu's chin. It was probably the first piece of meat she had seen in a year – but she knocked it savagely out of Lan Ying's hand. 'You think you can bribe me?' Her lips were snarling with hatred. Her eyes blazed. Then she laughed. 'Enjoy your ill-gotten gains. Eat them quickly, because I'm calling the guards. This will be your last meal before your execution . . .'

It seemed to Ziwei that the projectile that hit the woman on the chest had materialised from thin air – but it was Xiao. She was tiny – skin and bones – but the force of her leap knocked the bigger woman backwards. Her head banged against the concrete wall of the latrine and, stunned, she slid to the ground, moaning.

'Quickly, Lan Ying, help me. Ziwei, stand by the door and keep watch.' It was the longest sentence Ziwei had ever heard Xiao speak but there was no denying the authority, or the urgency.

The latrine consisted of planks laid over a pit. Xiao lifted one of the planks and threw it aside, leaving a larger opening. She grabbed Dr Liu's wrists and began to pull. Lan Ying had hold of her legs.

'What are you doing?' hissed Ziwei.

They ignored her. Dr Liu, recovering from her daze, had begun to struggle, but her head was already hanging over the lip of the pit.

'Push,' ordered Xiao, 'but keep hold of her ankles.' Still holding Dr Liu's hands, she jumped backwards into the pit. The body toppled after her. The legs began to kick furiously and there was the bubbling sound of a voice spitting and shouting through the ordure at the bottom.

'Keep her body still, Lan Ying, so I can push her head down,' said Xiao, unnervingly calm.

'You're murdering her!' cried Ziwei. 'You've got to stop!'

'Shut up,' snapped Lan Ying, straining to keep Dr Liu's kicking legs in her grasp. 'Xiao's right. If we don't kill her, she'll have us killed. I can't do this on my own. Help me hold her legs.'

Her ears burning, though all the blood in her veins ran chill, Ziwei stepped towards the struggling pair. Closing her eyes, she clutched a leg, hearing grunts from below and the splash of liquid. The leg kicked in a last spasm and became a dead weight. Weeping and panting, she clung on.

'All right, drop her in,' came Xiao's instruction. 'I'll position her so it looks natural.'

'Natural?' whispered Ziwei.

Lan Ying's voice was hard. 'She drowned herself. She couldn't take prison life any more. It happens all the time.'

There was a sucking sound, and a scrabbling noise as Xiao climbed out of the pit. She was covered from head to foot in shit.

'Lan Ying, take the food outside and bury it. Then go and find Officer Cai.' That was the name of the guard who had assisted them with their trade. 'At this time of night he should be in the kitchens, supervising the collection of the food for our cell. Tell him that there's been an accident, that you and I discovered a body. He'll find me down in the pit, trying to bring her to life. Hurry.' Lan Ying nodded and left.

'You did well, Ziwei,' Xiao said. 'Now go back to the cell and pretend nothing's happened. Be as surprised as the rest when you hear the news.'

'Your – your clothes? They'll give us away.'

'That's why we need Officer Cai,' she said. 'He'll give me clean ones.' She laughed. It was the first time Ziwei heard her do so. 'He may recommend me for a commendation too. It's not everybody who's prepared to go into a shit pit and give mouth to mouth to a drowning victim – especially a bitch like Dr Liu. Now go.'

There was an investigation, but Officer Cai's report left no doubt of the circumstances for, as Lan Ying told Ziwei, these things happened all the time.

There were no repercussions, except that Ziwei had crossed another psychological barrier, and the unquestioned commander of the Three Crows had ever since been Pickpocket Xiao.

They continued to play the black market, but soon they received their sentences: Lan Ying, seven years, Xiao ten and Ziwei twenty. An ordinary prostitute would have got seven but Ziwei had slept with a foreigner, which was technically treason.

Fortunately they were all in the same batch to be released into Reform through Labour, and Lan Ying's subsequent blackmail of Officer Cai over his unwitting complicity in Dr Liu's murder ensured that they remained together, as they had until this day.

It's not just extra rations that keeps you alive, thought Ziwei. It's comradeship, people you can trust, people who know as much about you as you about them. Friendship in the Laogai is identifying those who don't threaten you and preserving their secrets while they preserve yours – and there is nothing closer or more precious.

She heard a splash, and a grunt from behind her. Turning she saw Xiao fumbling inside her shirt. The bitch, thought Ziwei, she's caught another.

By mid-afternoon she was beginning to be worried. She knew Xiao would share her catch if she asked her – she always did – but Ziwei did not like obligation to go too far. It would be better if, for once, she also made a contribution. Anyway, she was concerned about Xiao, who, unlike Lan Ying, was not physically strong. She had visibly weakened over the last month of drought when outside pickings had been low. It would be better if she ate the two frogs she had caught herself. Lan Ying had one by now. Ziwei could tell from the smug smile she cast over her shoulder.

They were there, she was sure of it. She could hear them croaking – but no ripple or bubble disturbed the surface. Despite the heat of the sun on her back, she was beginning to feel a chill. She had long ago used the energy from the lunchtime soup. Her arms and legs were shaking, and her fingers were numb. The pain in her back and neck was almost stronger than the ache in her belly. She needed that extra protein. Suddenly all meaning of existence for Ziwei had narrowed down to the necessity of finding a frog.

Mechanically she felt for the weeds, snapping them and throwing them over her shoulder. Her fingers moved automatically: despite the lack of sensation in them, they still functioned, as her body functioned, by some remote command instilled by hundreds of hours of routine.

This is a rice shoot. Leave it alone. This is a weed. Pull it. This is a weed. This is a rice shoot. Rice shoot. Leave. Weed. Pull. Leave. Pull. This is a rice shoot. This is a weed. Here's another weed – it must be, it's soft and slithery, even though it's thicker than the other . . . An electric current of energy ran through her body as comprehension exploded in her numbed mind. This weed was *moving*!

Her fingers became pliers. Whatever it was, it was struggling, slipping from her grasp. She tightened her grip, squeezing, strangling. Her nails dug into flesh – tough, springy flesh. It was no frog. She didn't know what it was, except that it was meat. It was coiling, elongating. Heavens, was it a snake? Was it poisonous? She didn't care. If it was a snake it must have a head. It was stalemate otherwise. No force on this earth would induce her to release her grip. On the other hand, she had to kill it if she was to eat it.

She toppled into the murky water. Underwater – no, heaven help her, under the shit – her mouth found her hands, and her teeth closed on the slippery thing she was holding. She slid them along its moving surface, and when she judged it was the right place, she bit. She had already swallowed water, excrement, vegetable matter – who knew what? – but now she tasted something warm and sweet: blood. Then she felt cracking bone. At last the movement stopped.

She had no time. Her lungs were bursting. She was drowning – but the bag was out of her shirt, open, and the long, fat object squeezed inside. She felt hands on her arms, pulling her up. Frantically, she pulled the cord tight and pushed the bag inside her shirt – then she was gasping air, blinking at the concerned faces around her. Lan Ying was banging her back. Water and slime dribbled from her mouth.

'What happened, Sister?'

'I must have fainted,' she said. 'I'm fine now. Really.'

'You need a rest,' said Meichuan.

'No, I'm fine. Really I am.'

A rifle shot cracked the air. Crook-backed Wang was standing on the dike, glaring at them.

'You lot, get back to work!' he shouted. 'I'll cut your rations if you don't. This isn't a tea party . . . Lan Ying, is Peng Ziwei shamming?'

'No, Comrade Wang, she had a fainting fit. She's all right now.'

'Then she can continue working, and see if she feels better on light rations tonight. That'll apply to all of you if you don't complete your quota.'

As Lan Ying hovered, her face still showing her concern, Ziwei tapped her chest and winked. She had a glimpse of Xiao, who had remained at her place. Her eyes were glinting, and her lips twisted briefly into what, for her, passed as a smile.

There's no fooling Xiao, thought Ziwei, as she bent down happily to her weeding, feeling the heavy weight around her neck. What it is to have comrades!

In the free hour between dinner and the evening study session, the Three Crows feasted on eel – delicious, oily eel, with frog meat for afters. They roasted it on a fire in the burial grove behind the hut.

Ziwei was feeling as comfortable as a well-fed cat when she took her place on the *kang*. She found it difficult to concentrate on the newspaper article Lan Ying was reading aloud. Her mind was still full of the taste of meat.

But slowly the words of her friend and team leader penetrated. Lan Ying was reading from an inside article. Half of the front page of the paper was devoted to a portrait of Mao Tse-tung, waving his arm.

Beside him was a grinning Marshal Lin Biao. Photos below showed Tiananmen Square, full of shouting, screaming people, most of them very young and all ecstatic. In big red letters the headline read: 'Chairman Mao Congratulates the Launching of the Great and Glorious Proletarian People's Cultural Revolution!'

During the study session, each in turn came out with the expected adulatory slogans, coached patiently by Lan Ying, but in the latrine afterwards Ziwei muttered to her 'This use of the word revolution is new. Do you think there's something more to this than all the usual campaigns?'

'I don't know,' said Lan Ying, frowning. 'I think it's serious.'

'Won't affect us,' grunted Xiao, puffing on her cigarette.

'Why do you say that?' asked Lan Ying.

'We're the dead, aren't we? This is an outside-world thing.'

'You're probably right,' said Lan Ying. 'We may get a few more sputnik days, though, so we can show our solidarity. More hell from Crook-backed Wang.'

'You can deal with him,' said Xiao.

Ziwei was bored. She didn't want to talk about politics. She could still feel the eel inside her. 'Who cares?' she said. 'They've just given a grand name to another campaign. It'll be over in a few months.'

She felt tired. She wanted to lie down on the *kang* and relive her battle with the eel. It had been a perfect day.

13

Hugging Marx

The Cultural Revolution,
Laogai Camp 873, Liao River, 1966–7

Xiao's prediction proved right. An invisible wall appeared to insulate the inhabitants of the Laogai from the turbulence that affected the rest of the country. Every prison had its grapevine, though, and during hurried conversations with freed prisoners, who had recently visited Shishan, news of what was happening leaked out. Ziwei and her team-mates marvelled at the chaos that had overtaken China.

Ziwei heard about the mass demonstrations by 'Red Guards' – schoolchildren and students, many in their early teens, who had a mandate from Mao himself to spearhead his new revolution. They rampaged through their schools and universities, attacking the 'Four Olds'. Teachers and university professors were paraded in dunces' caps through the campuses and subjected to violent struggle sessions. Their homes were ransacked and their books burnt. A freed prisoner told Ziwei that two professors had been beaten to death at the Shishan Engineering Institute, and one had committed suicide by jumping from an upstairs window.

Ziwei recalled the quiet campus at Fudan where she had grown up, and tried to imagine this new, terrible type of student screaming down the corridors, with flags, cudgels and drums. She tried to comfort herself that her mother had been spared this new form of horror, but then the image of Fu-kuei lying in her cold grave broke the hard shell she had created around herself. That night she wept herself to sleep.

The violence did not end in the campuses. In an attempt to 'purify' the party of corrupt officials, who had deviated down the 'pseudo-Khrushchev bourgeois-revisionist line', mobs of Red Guards stormed government offices. Lan Ying heard from one of the guards that, in neighbouring Heilongjiang province, teenagers had dragged out the Party secretary, the provincial governor and the mayor of Harbin to subject them to hours of 'trial'. The Party secretary, who sported a Mao-style haircut, had been 'barbered' with pliers, the tufts stuffed one by one into his mouth, and all three had been beaten until they confessed to an extraordinary list of crimes. There were rumours that the campaigns might be turned against the leaders of the country. President Liu Shaoqi and Politburo Party Secretary Deng Xiaoping were being openly criticized.

It was hardly credible.

The newspapers Ziwei's group were given for their study sessions were generally censored of any news concerning actual atrocities committed by the Red Guards, but panegyrics on Mao or venomous articles by the radical propagandists Zhang Chunqiao and Yao Wenyuan, both members of the 'State Cultural Revolutionary Committee', which now seemed to be the only authority in the country, made not-so-veiled attacks on rightist targets at various levels in the Party. The purpose seemed to be to raise the pitch of hatred and hysteria, undercutting the very pillars of the administrative establishment. Reading between the lines, Ziwei and her friends, who had at first dismissed the rumours as exaggerated, began to appreciate that, on the contrary, such was the madness unleashed that anything was now frighteningly possible.

'Lucky we're here,' grunted Xiao, as the three laid straw over the wheatfields in preparation for the coming winter. The wind was strong enough to drown their voices from Crook-backed Wang.

'You have to be joking,' said Lan Ying.

'You'd rather be out there? With the Red Guards?'

'I think I could look quite striking in a tunic and armband,' said Lan Ying. She aped a heroic pose. 'Give me a wooden rifle and I could pose as one of Jiang Qing's Red Detachment of Women.'

'They're having fun now,' said Xiao, sourly. 'Vicious kids out of Teacher's care. Wait till they turn on each other. What happens then?'

'What?' asked Lan Ying.

'You think old Mao can control them once they've had a taste of their own power? You think those party cadres being attacked won't set up Red Guards of their own? All I'm saying is, if it comes to civil war, I know where I'd rather be. Right here.'

'That's nonsense,' said Lan Ying. 'It'll never come to that. There's the army, for a start.'

'And whose side will it be on?'

'You, there! Team Three. Yes, you, you stupid tarts!' Crook-backed Wang was directing his megaphone at them. 'Got a death wish?'

The women started. They had been so absorbed in their discussion that they had not noticed that they had edged near the side of the field. Lan Ying's foot was almost touching one of the red marker flags that denoted the boundary. Another metre and the guards would have had liberty to shoot them. Suicides who chose that route to end their sufferings, either beyond the boundary markers or by the barbed wire, were described in prison slang as 'hugging Marx', which was why Lan Ying called cheerfully as the three of them shuffled backwards: 'Sorry, Officer Wang. No hugs for you today.'

'I'm watching you,' was the reply. 'Mind what you're doing, and less of your cheek.'

'I tell you, that man will make a pass at me one day. I'll lay you any odds.' Lan Ying grinned, coquettishly placing a stalk in her mouth. Waving at him as she turned away, she began to sing a lilting snatch from the revolutionary opera they had been dragooned to sit through on the National Day holiday. It was a song about a country girl who hides revolutionaries in her father's home:

> *'There are so many uncles in my house, who come on urgent*
> * business.*
> *Really they're not my relatives, but to me they're closer than kin.*
> *Daddy and Grandma sometimes say, 'My dear, we can guess your*
> * little secret,'*
> *But I think they have shining red hearts, like Daddy's.'*

Ziwei cast a glance at Crook-backed Wang wondering how he was taking the erotic *double-entendre* implicit in Lan Ying's song. But he was sitting grumpily, looking obviously in the other direction. Again, Lan Ying seemed to have got away with it.

At least the uncomfortable conversation about the Red Guards seemed to be over, but Ziwei could not hide her alarm. For all Lan Ying's *savoir-faire*, it was Xiao's gut instinct she had come to rely on. On the other hand, she had a premonition that their little world was not as invulnerable as Xiao thought to violent and unpredictable forces blowing in the land.

Three days later, when their company returned from labouring in the fields, it was to find a pile of little books waiting for them on the *kang*, each in a red-plastic jacket embossed with a portrait of

Chairman Mao. There was one for each, and their pay for that month was to be docked as a 'contribution' in return for this 'gift from the People'. The books, when they examined them, turned out to be a synthesis of all Mao's famous sayings, compiled by his 'trusted comrade in arms' and anointed successor, Marshal Lin Biao. Under threat of cut rations, they were given the three months left of the year to learn its content by heart. In addition to Mao's famous sayings, with which most of them were familiar, they had to memorise Lin Biao's testimonials to his leader: 'Long live Chairman Mao, great teacher, great leader, great supreme commander and great helmsman' and, to Ziwei's incredulity, 'Every sentence of Chairman Mao's is truth, and carries more weight than ten thousand ordinary sentences.' Veneration for Mao Tse-tung as a leader had been instilled in them since their schooldays, but this was something new. He seemed to have taken on the status of a god.

'Well, if that's the new script, we'll just have to learn it,' said Lan Ying. The Three Crows were smoking in the burial ground in their free hour before the study session. They were enjoying the last warmth of an October sunset. In a week or so the cold winds from Siberia would begin to cut deep, and it would be uncomfortable to be out of doors. 'If all we have to do is parrot clap-trap like this, it'll at least make the study classes easier to run. Looks like it's back to kinder-garten, girls. Repeat after me . . .'

'You shouldn't joke about it,' said Ziwei. 'The people out there believe all this.'

'That Mao's an immortal?' Lan Ying snorted. 'He's an old man who dribbles, shakes and farts. You've seen him on the newsreels.'

'He's a murderous bastard,' grunted Xiao. Lan Ying laughed.

'Don't say that,' whispered Ziwei. As the shadows lengthened on the unmarked graves, there was a sudden gust of cold wind that scat-tered the fallen leaves. Suddenly she felt afraid.

Lan Ying was shaking her shoulders. 'What's got into you, dearest? You look as if you've seen a ghost.'

'We – we should be careful. That's all,' Ziwei murmured.

'You goose, have you forgotten where we are? We're in the Laogai, darling. Can you think of anything *worse* that could happen to us? Anyway, you're with Xiao and me. We'll look after you, won't we, Xiao?'

But Xiao didn't answer. Her eyes narrowed to angry slits as she stared towards the distant Black Hills, purple in the dusk. 'He's a murderous bastard,' she repeated. 'He'll be the death of us all.'

The three women smoked in silence. They all felt the chill now.

The first snow fell in early November. It stayed on the ground only a morning, but there was little warmth in the pale sun that broke through the mist. The Siberian winds blew constantly. By the middle of the month the prisoners, hurrying to lay the last of the straw covering on the fields in the eight hours of daylight they had available, were grateful for their army coats and hats. In December the earth began to freeze and they were taken off farming duties. The lucky ones were given jobs indoors, sacking grain for the winter sales, but Ziwei and her company were made responsible for taking the plough horses to the meadow, where they had to huddle from the wind as best they could until Crook-backed Wang decided the animals were exercised enough; only then were they allowed to lead them home. Invariably they arrived late for the evening meal.

In this weather there was no question of going to the burial grove for their customary evening smoke. Ziwei and Xiao sat disconsolately on the *kang* with the rest of their company, listening wearily to the ex-prostitutes squabbling, the two teachers discussing chess moves, and the extortioner complaining about her corns. They missed Lan Ying's company, but she had explained that, as team leader, she was now being called to a daily meeting 'to learn the latest clap-trap', as she put it, 'before I regurgitate it to you'.

Ziwei was sometimes worried about her friend's blithe indiscretions: this was a world in which informers were always listening – but Lan Ying obviously felt herself to be invulnerable, and would brush off Ziwei's warnings with a joke. Certainly, whatever discussions she was having with the other team leaders seemed to uplift her spirits. When she came into the classes, her eyes were shining and her cheeks were sometimes pink – but Ziwei thought it strange that the content of the study sessions seemed little different from the old ones. If Lan Ying was learning anything new, she was not regurgitating it to them.

It was also strange that Lan Ying seemed to have found a new trading source. She remained mysterious about it, although sometimes she would dig the imperturbable Xiao in the ribs, as the Three Crows tramped back from the meadow, saying, 'You see, I can forage too – and I know how to trade what I've found. Better than you.'

And that was true: Xiao had never been able to get them cans of bully-beef, or on one occasion, unbelievably, a jar of preserved pineapple, and the pouches of grain she shared out dribbled through their fingers like gold. Xiao would say nothing, only narrowing her eyes and pursing her lips, but Ziwei would press her friend, 'Come on, Lan Ying, what's your secret?' and Lan Ying would laugh merrily, but not reveal a thing.

One evening, as they waited interminably for the study session to begin, Xiao complained of stomach cramps and spent an hour in the latrine. Sitting on her own, Ziwei felt more bored than ever.

The next evening, Xiao whispered to her, 'Pretend you have the shits too. Get your coat and follow me.'

It was snowing heavily, but Xiao did not head in the direction of the latrines. Steering into the blizzard, she led Ziwei to the stables where, an hour earlier, they had been feeding the horses. 'Keep quiet,' hissed Xiao.

Ziwei heard the moan as soon as she stepped inside. She knew immediately whose voice it was. She put her mittens to her mouth, too stunned to move. Xiao had to pull her arm violently to get her to crouch behind the water barrel. From their hiding-place they could see wisps of hay falling through cracks in the floor of the loft. There was no doubt about what the two bodies above them were doing, and Lan Ying's heavy breathing was as familiar to them as their own, as were her whispered endearments: 'Oh, darling – darling' and 'My treasure – yes, yes, yes.' Crook-backed Wang contented himself with grunts, and the occasional 'Whore, oh, you whore, you beautiful, beautiful whore.'

Xiao pulled her arm again, and signalled that they should leave.

Outside in the whirling snow Ziwei, suddenly furious, grabbed Xiao's thin shoulders. 'How long have you known about this?'

'Since last night for sure, but I've suspected for some time.'

'Shit!' Ziwei cried, into the darkness. 'Shit, shit, shit, shit, shit.' She felt tears freezing on her cheek. 'We've got to do something to stop her.'

Xiao was silent for a long time. 'There's nothing we can do,' she said quietly. 'She's got the death wish. Like the ones who go to hug Marx.'

'We can't do nothing,' Ziwei almost screamed.

Xiao was watching her with hard, inscrutable eyes. The feathery snow on her lashes and earflaps made her look more like a bird of prey than ever. 'No, we can't do nothing,' she said.

It took Ziwei a few moments to realise what she was implying, and when she did she no longer felt the cold. She stared at Xiao. 'You can't mean it,' she whispered. 'Lan Ying's our friend.'

'They're bound to be caught. They have the madness on them. They don't care about risks any more. You've seen it happen before.'

'She's our friend, Xiao.'

Xiao's face twitched, and her eyes misted. 'Yes, I know,' she said, and bowed her head – but when she looked up, her face was hard again. 'And that's why they'll come after us. Everybody knows we're a team. They'll find out about the loot Crook-back's been stealing for her, and somebody will report that we've shared it. You think people don't resent us even though they're afraid of us? If Lan Ying goes down, we do too. Ziwei, what else can we do?'

She wanted to yell, shout, tear at the mud-brick buildings around her – but when she spoke, she was amazed that her voice could be so calm. 'When do you propose we do it?'

'Now,' said Xiao. 'We can't afford to delay. I – I nearly went last night, when I found out, but – but . . .' She wiped a hand over her eyes. 'Better if it's the two of us,' she said. 'I don't want to lose you too.'

Ziwei took her hand, and then she hugged her. For a long moment they stood rocking in the snow. A distant memory came back to her: Guimei's words, in a cell long ago. 'Come on, then,' she said. 'Let's get it over with.'

Their heads hunched against the snow, they walked to the gate, and Ziwei, in as strong a voice as she could manage, asked if they could be given an audience with the commandant.

They had no means of knowing it but, for the prison authorities, their denunciation could not have come at a more convenient time. Cultural Revolution politics within the security ministries had finally reached Tranquil Springs. It was a new commandant who received them. He was a tall, handsome man in his early forties, dressed in an immaculate Mao suit. Politely, he offered them cups of scented tea and quietly took notes.

'Thank you, Comrades,' he said, when they had finished. 'You have shown true revolutionary spirit in drawing this to our attention. It will be remembered when we review your cases.' He folded his spectacles into his top pocket. 'There are to be changes in this camp. You have been unfortunate to be supervised for too long by a corrupt and deviationist cadre. The monstrous crime you have uncovered is typical of the cancer of bourgeois rightism that my predecessor has allowed to flourish unchecked in this correctional establishment. No longer.' He stood up, stretching his arm. 'Long live Chairman Mao! A long life, a long, long life to him!'

Ziwei and Xiao were left under guard in his office while he organised the arrest. As they were waiting, a freed prisoner brought them buns filled with meat and vegetables. They stared at the steaming pile. Neither could bring themselves to eat. Catching Xiao's eyes, Ziwei saw tears in them – but by then Ziwei was so filled with horror at what she'd done that she was beyond tears. She had a memory of her mother telling her the Jesus story, and of how the Christian God was betrayed by his disciple for thirty pieces of silver.

They heard Lan Ying and Crook-backed Wang through the thin door when they were taken to the interrogation cells. Lan Ying was singing, but they could not make out the words.

The commandant himself took them back to their cell, and praised them in front of their bewildered companions, urging the latter to study their heroic example. That night the others huddled close together, distancing themselves from Ziwei and Xiao on the *kang*. The next day there was no banter as they made their way to the meadow at dawn with the horses.

The ex-prostitutes, Xiang and Lin, never dared tease Ziwei again. They were too afraid of her. When Ziwei was appointed team leader, there was no dissent. Under the new camp regime, even more time was allotted to political study. Ziwei led the discussions and everybody responded, having hurriedly learnt the right phrases from their books. Ziwei discovered one day that she had a new nickname: 'The Little Red Guard'. Only Xiao perhaps knew that her heart was breaking inside – but a distance had grown between the two friends. They hardly ever talked to each other now.

A month after Lan Ying's arrest, Ziwei and Xiao were called again to the commandant's office. 'Your former companion has signed her confession,' he told them, 'and tomorrow she and her lover will face trial. Your evidence will naturally be read out. I want you therefore to be sitting in the front row.' They nodded. They had been expecting it.

He drew on his cigarette, contemplating them. 'The accused has now submitted herself to the People's Justice and acknowledged that her crimes were committed with no accomplice besides her fellow accused. In the early stages of her interrogation, she made many contrary accusations, however, some against the two of you. Is there anything you would like to tell me?'

Ziwei and Xiao shook their heads. Again, they had anticipated this.

'Anything about a former prisoner in your transit camp by the name of Liu?'

'There was a member of our work team called Liu,' said Ziwei. 'She committed suicide. There were no suspicious circumstances,' she added.

'Quite so,' said the commandant. 'It would confuse the issue at this stage of proceedings if our two chief witnesses were to be considered anything but model prisoners. It is my hope that you will continue to be model prisoners, helping us reform this camp on correct ideological lines. If you behave, your future is bright. I would not like to be . . . disappointed.'

'No, Comrade,' said Ziwei, echoed sullenly by Xiao.

'Good, we have an understanding, then,' he said. 'Do you have questions?'

'Are we to take an active role in the trial tomorrow?' asked Ziwei. 'Besides having our depositions read out.'

'No. If you sit in the front row that will be enough. This is an important event, Comrades,' he added. 'It will turn a shining light on the corruption of the past. The prisoners' righteous anger against worms such as these saboteurs of self-education and reform must be given an outlet. The case has also attracted publicity in the outside world. I am taking a precedent from other cities and have invited a contingent of the Shishan Red Guards to conduct the struggle. I expect you, from the front row, to lead the response with the right enthusiasm.'

As they passed through the barbed wire back to their compound, Ziwei turned to her friend. 'We were wrong, Xiao, you and I.'

Xiao's eyes narrowed, but she said nothing.

'There *are* worse things than staying alive.'

Xiao's mouth twitched. Then she hurried away. Ziwei followed with heavy steps, as if her feet were manacled with chains.

* * *

The next morning loudspeakers ordered all the prisoners in the camp to remain where they were after roll-call. A big stage had been erected during the night. Behind it hung an enormous portrait of Mao Tse-tung, and on either side, in large white letters on a red cloth background, two banners, one of which read, 'Bombard the headquarters! Expose and denounce corrupt Party officials', and the other, 'Punish severely all deviationists who take the capitalist road.'

As Ziwei and her team were ushered to reserved positions in the front row, she saw unfamiliar figures strutting or lounging on the platform. Most were young, many in their teens, although the ones they seemed to defer to were older, in their late twenties and early thirties. They wore padded jackets and trousers similar to those of the prisoners below them, squatting in rows, hunched under their fur collars to avoid the sleet that whipped down from a grey sky. What differentiated the men on the platform were their red armbands: the characters for 'Red Guard' and 'Shishan Tiger Rebels Brigade' were sewn on to the cloth. When they glanced at the prisoners, it was with contempt.

The loudspeakers blared Mao's anthem, 'The East Is Red', and the prisoners shuffled to their feet. The Red Guards began to clap, so they did too. The commandant ascended the platform, flanked by his staff. He lowered his spectacles and observed the crowd. Then he raised both arms in the air and shouted, 'Long live Chairman Mao and the Great and Glorious Proletarian People's Cultural Revolution!' The prisoners dutifully roared the slogan in reply. The commandant sat down and studied his notes. A line of freed prisoners filed in carrying baskets, which they deposited at the feet of those in the front row. Inside were eggs and what looked like rotten cabbages. For most prisoners, the first response was 'Food!' but they knew it had not been brought to be eaten.

There was a half-hour pause while the prisoners froze. Even the Red Guards were stamping their feet, looking irritably at the commandant, who was imperturbably correcting his speech with his fountain pen. Unlike everybody else, he was not in a greatcoat and fur hat. He was dressed in the neat Mao suit that Ziwei and Xiao had seen him in before. Apparently, the cold did not disturb him. Eventually, he looked up and nodded.

One of the Red Guards began to thump a kettledrum. Through the curtain at the back of the stage, their feet and hands manacled,

Lan Ying and Crook-backed Wang tottered on to the stage. Their necks were weighed down with placards, on which were written, in jagged, deliberately ugly characters, their names, which had then been scratched through with red ink. Above was a list of their crimes: 'bourgeois criminal element and counter-revolutionary', 'capitalist roader, deviationist and counter-revolutionary'. They were flanked by Red Guards, some of whom were brandishing rifles, the others forcing their charges' heads down, as they pushed them along. The Red Guards on the stage kicked or spat at them as they passed. When they had been brought to the front, they were lifted on to chairs, on which they had to balance themselves, while again their heads were forced into a bowing position, and there they hung, staring straight down into the audience.

Although she was shouting slogans and imprecations with the rest, taking her cue from the Red Guards, Ziwei felt tears running down her cheeks. Her friend was barely recognisable. She was thinner than she remembered. Her eyes and cheeks were swollen with bruises, and her gashed lips were bleeding. Her hair, which even in prison she had fussed over, was hanging in limp strands over her forehead. Mercifully, her eyes remained closed. Crook-backed Wang, at her side, looked in a worse state than Lan Ying. One of his arms hung at an odd angle by his side. It had been dislocated from the shoulder.

'See before you the Enemies of the People!' the commandant was shouting, raising his arms for silence. 'They are disgusting spectacles, but even more disgusting are the crimes they have committed against you, Comrades. Look at this man, who once held a responsible position in the Communist Party! They called him a model prison warder – but it was a sham. All the time he was following the capitalist road, and instead of looking after you, as he should have done, he stole your food to give it to his whore.'

'Capitalist roader! Thief! Criminal!' The Red Guards led the screaming imprecations that followed this revelation.

'And then look at this whore, whom the generosity of the state forgave for her former crimes, allowing her to expiate them, like you, by Reform through Labour. See how her disgusting black blood, her loathsome bourgeois habits and cravings, her greed, her stinking sexual appetite brought her into a conspiracy to defraud you – her fellows and comrades. These are the degenerates who stole your grain to line their love-nest. These are the stinking imperialist offal that leech on the People's Welfare. These are the criminals, the counter-revolutionaries, the monsters and demons, whom we have come to condemn today.'

There might have been a time when Lan Ying would have laughed superciliously at the mixed metaphors being used to attack her, thought Ziwei, while she mouthed, 'Bourgeois imperialist,' and the other slogans, but today the ruined face above her barely showed comprehension as it twitched with the effort that Lan Ying had to make to stand upright in her contorted position.

The commandant's speech lasted more than an hour. By the end of it Ziwei was barely listening, although at one point the commandant mentioned her name and that of Xiao, praising them for their revolutionary consciousness in helping bring the crimes to light. Lan Ying's eyes flickered open briefly, but there was no recognition in their dull brown depths, although she was facing Ziwei.

The crowd roared the set responses. The Red Guards cavorted on the stage. One was brandishing shears, winking at the audience like the clown in an opera.

The terrible denunciation was coming to an end. 'So, Comrades, you have heard their confessions. How do you find them?'

'Guilty,' shouted a Red Guard, and the cry was taken up by the prisoners, including, to her shame, Ziwei.

This was the moment the Red Guards had been waiting for. One came forward with a bucket full of ink. With a brush, he painted the faces of the bowing couple, then splattered their clothes. The Red Guard with the shears positioned himself behind Lan Ying, and, laughing, began to chop her hair. He did not stop until she was bald and bleeding. Now Ziwei could see that Xiao, too, had tears running down her face.

A youth leant over the stage and screamed at them, 'Are you reactionary sympathisers? What are you waiting for? You have the baskets in front of you, don't you?'

So Ziwei and Xiao threw eggs and rotten cabbage leaves at their friend. At the bottom of the basket were clumps of pig manure. They threw those as well. The screaming of slogans lasted long after lunchtime and well into the afternoon.

The sky was already darkening when the two condemned were escorted through the squatting ranks of prisoners to the waiting truck. Hanging over the tailgates, with placards round their necks, they were paraded through the small village that had given the name 'Tranquil Springs' to the camp. The villagers lined the streets and cheered.

Ziwei and Xiao, as accusers, were given the privilege of following in the truck behind. It also contained the execution squad, who were giving a last-minute check to their rifles as they bounced along the dirt roads. They were all too aware of the two women prisoners, squatting with their backs to the cab, heads lowered, sunk in their own misery, and made bawdy jokes to cover their nervousness and embarrassment.

When they came to the stone quarry near the dam, the commandant was already there, waiting for them by his car with the other officials.

The sleet had turned into a light snow, and the sandy earth was already covered with white patches.

Nobody said anything. They wanted to get it over with.

Lan Ying tripped on her chains as she descended from the truck, and fell on to her side in the mud. Ziwei and Xiao were standing close by. In an involuntary response, they ran forward to help her to her feet. Lan Ying was still dazed after her treatment, but when she saw Ziwei and Xiao, the eyes in the blackened face brightened, and the broken mouth and teeth opened painfully in a smile. She tried to raise her manacled hand as if to brush Xiao's face. That was when Ziwei fell on to the ground and began to sob.

Lan Ying and Crook-back were led to slightly rising ground near the cliff that had been hacked out of the quarry. They were helped to a kneeling position with their backs to the executioners.

'I can't watch, Xiao. It's us aiming those rifles,' Ziwei whispered.

'No – it's the system. The fucking system.' Xiao, white-faced, was staring down the valley. Ziwei closed her eyes. She felt Xiao urgently grip her arm. 'Listen, she's singing to us.'

Ziwei strained her ears and over the wind she heard the faint lilt.

'. . . Oh, dear Grandma, listen to my tale . . .'

They heard the rattle of bolts being drawn.

'. . . Really, they're not my relatives but to me they're closer than kin . . .'

'Oh, Lan Ying,' whispered Ziwei. 'Forgive me.'

'. . . we can guess your little secret But I think they have shining red hearts, like—'

The rifles fired. Then all was quiet. Thick flakes of snow were falling.

The commandant rubbed his hands, and whistled. 'Lend me your coat awhile, Comrade,' he said to his driver. 'Damn, it's cold.'

Two nights later Ziwei lifted herself from the *kang*. She smiled at Xiao, who was lying on her side, watching her. 'It's all right. I have to go to the latrines,' she said.

It was a clear night. Stars sparkled in the sky. There was – what was it called? – Orion. Ha Li had pointed it out to her one evening as they stood together on the side of the boat. So long ago. She couldn't remember when she had last thought of Ha Li. She hoped he was well, wherever he was, on the other side of the world.

It was a beautiful night. She was fractionally annoyed when she approached the end of the line of huts and a pool of light from the guard tower dazzled her briefly, but the searchlight moved on, and the stars came out in the sky again.

She wondered what Lan Ying would say to her, whether she would be angry.

She would find out soon.

With a deliberate step she walked across the open space between the huts and the boundary line. She knew where it was, although the stones were now covered with snow. Ten more steps should take her safely into the forbidden zone before the searchlight swept again. She might even get close enough to touch the barbed wire.

A weight crashed into her back and she was knocked over into the snow. She looked up and saw Xiao, standing above her, clenching her tiny, talon-like hands.

Ziwei tried to get up. Xiao pushed her back. 'You stay on this side of the line,' she hissed.

'You can't stop me. I'm finished. I want to die. I – I can't live with myself,' Ziwei panted as she tried to wrestle with her friend.

'You must go on. Otherwise all we've done is wasted.' Xiao pushed her down again. 'You're the decent one. Not like me. Not like Lan Ying. Don't you understand? You have to live, Ziwei. Live.' Suddenly she cocked her head to one side. The beam of the light was approaching. She straightened, and smiled. 'For me, Ziwei. Also for Lan Ying. Live,' she whispered. Then she punched Ziwei hard on the jaw.

For a moment Ziwei, stunned, found herself on all fours in the snow, spitting blood from a broken tooth. She blinked in the sudden dazzling light. She heard shouts. Dazed, she looked around for Xiao.

She saw a tiny figure running towards the barbed wire. Xiao's greatcoat flapped around her like wings. She stopped, just short of the wire, and turned, lifting one arm. It might have been a wave. She was still smiling.

A shot cracked the air. Xiao fell to her knees, slumped on to her side, and with a final jerk, rolled over on to her face.

There was the crunch of boots in the snow and Ziwei felt rough arms pulling her to her feet. As they dragged her away, she turned her head for one last look behind her, and saw only a greatcoat lying on the ground. It was as if the little bird it had once enveloped had slipped from its folds and flown away.

She spent the next two months in solitary confinement. The commandant doubled the usual sentence, offended by the erratic behaviour of two women whom he had characterised as 'model prisoners'. It had set back his plans.

With one already gone, he perhaps wanted to get the other off his books. Solitary in Tranquil Springs in mid-winter – in a chicken cage in a converted cowshed barely closed off from the elements – was usually, at best, a ticket to Camp 848. But Ziwei had made a pledge to the shades of Lan Ying and Xiao to survive; they were with her throughout and at the end of her confinement, the camp doctor, somewhat to his surprise, judged her fit to return to work.

Mercifully, they put her in another work company. The women there, of course, knew about her, and despised her. This was a company of criminals who liked to deal justice to their own. After lights out Ziwei found herself receiving much the same sort of treatment as she had once suffered at the hands of the guards when she was doing solitary in the transit camp. She even found herself on some nights "Embracing the Cassia-blossom Vase'. She did not care. She preferred even this sort of company to the fellowship of her old work team, who would have brought back too many memories if she had stayed with them. Nor did she think she had the courage to look into any of their faces. Eventually, her passive attitude bored the team leader, who began to pick on somebody else. Ziwei was ignored but tolerated. As far as the others were concerned, she was a shadow in the cell. That was acceptable, even welcome. She had lost the desire for companionship. Who could replace her friends?

By spring the Cultural Revolution had turned in on itself. In almost every city in China rival gangs of Red Guards, all apparently pledging fealty to Mao but some supporting the old establishment, others sheer anarchy, fought it out in the streets. Workers organised their own revolutionary militia – also calling themselves 'rebels', also claiming to be supporting Mao Tse-tung. It was an escalation of violence, as Xiao had once feared. In some provinces youths broke into military arsenals and stole guns. Then it became open warfare.

In an attempt to re-impose some sort of order, Mao sanctioned the military to become involved. In future a tripartite committee of workers, soldiers and radical students would rule in each city. The idea did not catch on. Divisions were too deep to be patched over. In any case, not every army unit owed loyalty to Marshal Lin Biao. In Wuhan, People's Liberation Army factions fought each other, using tanks and cannon. The navy had to be sent up the Yangtze to try to impose peace, but that intensified the conflict. An intervention by Zhou Enlai averted civil war – but the commander of the Wuhan forces received only a token reprimand. Clearly the army, of whatever faction, was to be treated with kid gloves.

Prisoners in the Laogai found it difficult, with their limited access to information, to make out what was going on – so they got on doggedly with their tasks. In early spring male prisoners broke the frozen earth with pickaxes. Women's companies were given the job of transporting topsoil that had been brought to the train depot from other parts of the country to enable the first planting to go ahead. It took four women to push and pull each cart the two miles over the hill. Ziwei learnt what it was like to be a mule. Then there was the ploughing and the planting of the wheat – all backbreaking labour. After that a month was devoted to mending dikes. Ziwei was always given the hardest tasks, but she did not complain. Most days she earned her rations.

Meanwhile, the political courses intensified and there was the now customary daily worship of Mao and his 'Thoughts', The criminals in her company at last discovered a use for her. Ziwei had learnt enough from Lan Ying to keep abreast of the dialectics. Imperceptibly at first, then more openly, she led the study sessions, always careful to give face to the team leader, a condemned thief who could hardly read. She never acknowledged Ziwei's help, but Ziwei knew she was grateful.

Now more than ever, in this increasingly politicised camp, their survival depended on the right revolutionary responses. By April, when it was time to clear the rice paddies to prepare for the early-summer crop, the camp was already on its third change of management. The handsome commandant, who had presided over Lan Ying's trial, had been purged in February. His successor was in post for less than a month. The newest commandant was a former commissar in the Heilongjiang Military Command, a Lin Biao man, who imposed an even tighter regime than before, rotating capos on a regular basis, reviewing prisoners' rations (always downwards), reassessing the work quotas (always upwards). Prisoners no longer talked about sputnik days or rocket days. With the military now overtly in control, Ziwei had hoped for a more relaxed regime, but it was the opposite: hardly a month went by without a trial, and several prisoners each week made the one-way journey in the back of a truck to the stone quarry where Lan Ying had met her end.

And as spring turned to summer, Ziwei began to notice a higher and higher intake of new prisoners. It was to be expected, she realised. Those who had been arrested in the first purges of the Cultural Revolution had gone through the process of confession and sentencing, and were starting their Reform through Labour. They were a new sort of prisoner too. It was not just *hei wu leis* being brought in now, but also those of 'good' family background: the Communist governing class, purged commissars, factory directors, Party officials. They were kept apart from 'common' criminals like Ziwei in a new barracks that the first contingents built for themselves, as were the younger intellectuals and students from 'rebel' factions, who had taken their anarchistic ideas too far. These latter prisoners brought with them their 'Red Guard spirit' – at least in the early days – and marched to the fields, shouldering their hoes like rifles and singing revolutionary songs. It was rumoured, however, that for both these categories of 'politicals', the camp regime was even stricter than the one imposed on the older inmates. Ziwei shuddered to think what their rations might be. Their own had been reduced almost to starvation levels. Spring was hardly over and the older lags in Ziwei's cell were already muttering about how they would survive the next winter.

With Xiao gone, Ziwei had to rely on her own skills to forage. She sometimes caught a frog. There was no opportunity now for a roast in the evening, as the Three Crows had enjoyed in the past. When she was unobserved, she would pull it out of her pouch and eat it raw. She discovered by trial and error that the skin came easiest off the head, the rest following, leaving the meat. It was disgusting, but it provided protein. Usually she made do with roots and insects. Anything to stay alive – for what purpose, she was not sure. At first it was because of her promise to Xiao, and that was still important to her – a lifetime of guilt would not be enough to pay her debt to her two friends – but as day followed day in the monotony of hard labour, it was impossible to keep even loved ones in mind: all her energy was necessary just to get through the task – prisoners could only afford to live in the present.

Gradually, she realised, she was no longer thinking of Xiao and Lan Ying – or only rarely, when something reminded her of things they had done together last year, or when something ridiculous happened and she found herself saying, 'Oh, that will amuse Lan Ying.' Even the details of their faces were growing dim, as had Ha Li's, as had her mother's beforehand. Her promise to Xiao was sacred but, she realised, it was no longer what gave her the will to keep going. It was something else – obstinacy, pride, she did not know, and a feeling, sometimes a certainty, that there was meaning in everything that had happened to her, even while logic told her there couldn't be. There was certainly no rational reason to imagine that she would even survive the winter, let alone reach the end of her twenty-year sentence – but that did not lessen her determination, and as conditions around her worsened, she felt an even stronger urge to keep going.

It was an unforgiving summer. While the newspapers boasted that in the rest of China there would be a record harvest, the valleys on the lee side of the Black Hills were inflicted with drought, interspersed with sudden destructive rainstorms, and for two dreadful weeks in July the sky was darkened with an invasion of locusts. Naturally, the prisoners feasted on them, but once their bellies were full, they became aware of the implications: a bad harvest was now inevitable, and that meant even shorter rations in the winter ahead. By August, the usually damp soil was powdery and dry, and without wind there was no cooling in the evening or at night.

One morning, just after roll-call, while her company waited their turn to be ordered out to the fields, Ziwei saw two open trucks, crammed with a new intake of prisoners, being driven through the barbed-wire gates at the further end of the yard. Their destination was clearly the barracks on the other side of the compound that contained the 'politicals', but because the prisoners were already beginning to file off to the fields, there was a logjam, with much shouting, whistle-blowing and the hooting of horns. Eventually, the trucks had to reverse, and do a circuit of the compound to reach the gate on the other side, but there they reached another logjam, because the companies in that section, including Ziwei's, had been given their orders to move.

Ziwei had to leap aside as the first truck skewed to a halt. Making her way round it she glanced curiously at the prisoners in the back. They were all male, and mostly elderly, in the usual prison garb, with the shaven heads of those fresh out of transit camp and, as with most new prisoners seeing the Laogai for the first time, they showed a mixture of reactions – some staring out with horror or fascination, others with heads bowed, absorbed in their own misery. There was something about them, in the way they held themselves, the arrogant manner in which some were still throwing back their shoulders, that Ziwei immediately recognised. These were Party men and, by the looks of them, senior officials.

One man, younger than the rest, was resting against the tailgate with his arms folded. She could see only the back of his cropped head, and he was thin, like all of them, but the loose folds of skin on his neck indicated that he had once been plump. Her first impression was that, unlike his companions, he was relaxed. He reminded her of a farmer, leaning on his gate, contentedly counting his pigs. Then she noticed that his right hand was holding his left wrist, and his left arm was twitching uncontrollably. His shoulders were shaking too.

As she watched him, he turned his head. She saw twisted lips, a flat nose and bulging eyes, which were staring wildly, either in anger or fear. He was looking directly towards her, but he showed no indication of recognising her, or even seeing her, lost as he was in whatever thoughts were troubling him – but she knew him immediately. Her blood ran cold, for this was a face she remembered in every detail, usually in her nightmares.

As she stopped, stunned, the truck began to inch forward. The rest of her team were now about twenty feet away from her, making for the gate, but she remained, hypnotised to the spot The truck picked up speed, and the dust it raised obscured the man, but she still looked after him, transfixed – until her capo ran back and shouted at her, pushing her shoulder. He continued to shout as she ran to join her fellows, but she was oblivious to what he was saying. Printed on her mind was that face, which she had thought she would never see again – and she shook with fear, remembering the last time she had seen it, in the back of a car while she pleaded for her mother's life.

It was only after two hours' hard labour, shoring up the crumbling banks of the dikes, that she regained enough calm to realise there was no need to be afraid of him any more: unbelievable as it seemed, the once terrifying Chen Tao was just another prisoner in the same Laogai camp as her.

He had been equalised – as they all had. The Cultural Revolution had levelled all distinctions. There were no longer persecutors and victims. They were all the same.

The harvest was as bad as they had expected. Naturally the prisoners were blamed. One or two team leaders were given exemplary trials and shot.

When the cold winds began to blow in November, prisoners died in large numbers. One morning Ziwei woke to find that her neighbour on the *kang* had passed away in the night. She had been snuggling next to a dead body. By December, only seven of the original thirteen in her company were still alive, but new contingents of prisoners kept arriving, and the dead were replaced by women whom the capos could work hard until they, too, weakened on punishment rations, which were common to all.

As far as the camp regime was concerned, no concession was made to the famine. The prisoners continued to work, continued to study, until they dropped.

Even so, the conditions for ordinary prisoners in the camp were considered better than those for the 'politicals'. Watching the burial parties issuing from its gates, the prisoners would wonder how such skeletal figures had the strength to pull the carts. The cruel joke was that the 'politicals' had discovered new levels of 'revolutionary economy': those on the point of death were delegated to the burial details in the hope that they would share the graves they were digging for their fellows. Wags would refer to the politicals' barracks as 'Camp 848 – Tranquil Springs Branch'.

But really their own situation was not much better. There was the same stink of death on both sides of the barbed wire.

Three days before the new year, Ziwei found a squirrel. There was a shortage of firewood in the camp, and her team had been delegated to haul timber from a copse on the other side of the dam. In the afternoon the sporadic snow of the morning developed into a full-scale blizzard, and they had to huddle together to keep even barely warm. There was no question of returning until the blizzard abated.

That day Ziwei had a bad bout of diarrhoea. It scared her. If it turned out to be dysentery she knew it would be fatal. She had a headache, and it took every effort to move her limbs. She had been excusing herself behind bushes all morning – and now, huddled with the others, she felt the urge again.

'Well, you can't do it here,' grunted the capo, 'but keep in sight. My fingers aren't frozen enough to prevent me firing my rifle.'

Her head swimming, she pushed through the snow, her arm outstretched, feeling for the bark of a tree against which she could rest her back. She hadn't the strength to squat. Somehow, with her numbed fingers she released her trouser cord. Afterwards, she had to wait until she got her breath back – and it was as she was leaning forward, groaning, preparing for the walk back to the others, that she saw it.

A heavy branch, overloaded with snow, had cracked off, and fallen. Some miracle had trapped a squirrel underneath it. Its back was broken but it was still alive.

Ziwei felt a surge of energy, enough to strangle it and deposit it in her forage bag, where its weight under her greatcoat comforted her for the rest of the afternoon, and – who knows? – might even have kept her alive during the nightmare trudge, hauling logs, back to the camp.

In the evening she collapsed, but she had already buried her treasure in the deep snowbank next to her hut. During the night she was delirious. Next day, after a doctor had examined her, she was excused work – although that meant she received no rations. She did not care. She lay alone on the *kang* thinking of the squirrel, and how she would make a soup of it: a meat broth, full of fat. The thought gave her strength, and by the evening she thought she was well again – or what passed for well under their starvation conditions. That night she slept soundly, although she made a pretence to her companions that she was worsening, and next morning that she was still in a state of delirium. Her calculation was correct. After trying to rouse her, her teammates left her on the *kang*. A guard came to check. The doctor was called but did not bother to examine her. She heard him mutter to the guard as he left: 'This one isn't "Playing Dead Dog". I doubt she'll make it through the day.'

With all the prisoners at work, the camp was deserted, and she had no trouble retrieving her pouch with the squirrel. Nobody observed her as she made her way to the burial grove. It was no longer in use. The dead were buried in pits now. It was the first time she had come here since Lan Ying and Xiao had died. Now she thought of them warmly. They would approve of what she was doing today. She scrabbled under the snow and located the fallen headstone under which was still concealed – or so she hoped – the old wok Xiao had stolen for their feasts. It was still there – rusty, but usable – and she still had in her pocket a box of matches from her last visit to the store. Silently, as she gathered twigs and branches, she thanked the shades of her old friends.

While the snow melted in the pan on top of the small fire, she used a sharp stone to scrape off the squirrel's skin and fur and remove the guts. When a small amount of water was boiling, she topped it up with more snow. It was slow work, since the animal had frozen, but she had all day. She cut the carcass into gobbets, and dropped them into the wok.

When she smelt the cooking meat, she began to weep. Then she realised she had left her bowl in the hut. Of course, she could have waited until the wok cooled, and sipped from that, but she felt she was sharing this feast today with her ghosts – and Lan Ying had always maintained the highest standards. Ziwei had determined, in her honour, that she would enjoy this bounty of the gods in proper style – so, throwing in a few more handfuls of snow and leaving the meat cooking, she made her way back to the huts, keeping a careful watch for guards. Luckily, she heard the voices before she was seen, and quickly pressed her back against the wall.

A man, obviously a capo, was shouting, 'On your feet, you bastard, and pick up those buckets or I'll make you slurp from them. You're not in your comfortable office now, sending others to hell-holes like this, you shrivelled turd. It's your turn, and I'm going to see that you work until you drop. Tired, are you? Think cleaning shit-holes is too good for you? Well, there are three more latrines to empty after this one, so you'd better get on with it.'

And then she heard the hateful voice – weak, hardly audible, but never to be forgotten. 'All right . . . All right . . .'

'All right, what?'

'All right . . . Officer . . . Comrade . . .'

The capo laughed harshly. 'I'm not your comrade, scum. There's the latrine. There's the pit. I'll come back in an hour and I want it emptied by then, or it'll be the worse for you.'

Ziwei heard the guard's whistle as he strode off, then the shuffle of dragged feet and the clank of a bucket as Chen Tao entered the latrine.

Ziwei ran across the yard and along the alley to her hut, her emotions turbulent in her breast. 'I am not,' she told herself, 'going to let that man affect me again – and he's not going to spoil my feast.' But there were tears of anger running down her cheeks as she retrieved her bowl. 'Murderer!' she spat, thinking of her mother. 'Murderer! Bastard!'

When she reached the yard, it was empty. Thank heaven, she thought, he's still inside. I won't have to see him. I'd rather forget he even exists . . . but half-way across the yard, she froze.

With heavy steps, bowed under a bamboo pole from which were hung two buckets of excrement, Chen Tao stepped out of the latrine.

She was shocked because he was almost unrecognisable. There was hardly any flesh on him. His head looked enormous above the thin neck and shrunken shoulders. The eyes in the drawn face were more bulbous than ever, but dulled, with the blankness that indicated the last stages of malnutrition. Ziwei thought she was looking at a walking corpse. He groaned as he pushed one foot in front of the other for a few paces, then sank to his knees in the snow. He tried to unyoke himself from the buckets, but one spilt. Then he toppled forward on to his face and lay still.

Afterwards, she couldn't understand why she did it. She knelt beside him and lifted his shoulders. His head flopped forward. She dragged him to the side of a hut and leant him against it. The eyes opened a fraction. 'Wait here,' she said harshly. 'Do you understand?'

The head nodded.

She returned to the grove. The squirrel stew was almost ready. There was a delicious smell. She wanted only to sit there and eat . . . She put the bowl on the snow, lifted the wok by its handles and poured in the thick liquid. There was enough for two bowlfuls, perhaps three.

She had just finished pouring when one of the handles snapped. The wok fell upended on to the ground. She lifted it and saw a thin pile of bones with the remains of the stew draining into the snow. 'Damn,' she whispered. And then she had to make a terrible choice. She could easily have drunk the soup in the bowl herself – she wanted to from the depths of her hungry soul – but instead, she said, 'Damn' again and, with her hand over it to keep it warm, walked as fast as she could back to the compound. She gave the bowl to Chen Tao, having slapped his face twice to wake him. She even held the bowl steady as he sipped, and upended it so he could drain the last drops. When it was all gone, she took the bowl back from his hands.

'Are you strong enough to get back to work?' she asked coldly.

'Yes . . . I think so . . . Thank you,' he said.

'You know who I am?' she shouted. She felt an urge to throttle him.

'Yes,' he said. 'Thank you.'

She walked away, cheeks burning with anger, sorrow, regret – and incomprehension that she had given the soup that might have kept her alive to a man she hated.

She sifted through the bones to see if any meat remained. There were a few thin strands. She gnawed each bone, whether there was meat on it or not. Then she licked the few blobs of frosted gravy on the wok, before burying it. Even as she ate the leavings she felt hungry, thinking of the hot bowl of soup she had held in her hands.

That afternoon, she lay on her bunk, cursing her stupidity. Why had she done it? It was not as if Chen Tao was the only one dying of hunger in the camp. They all were. And he was her enemy – the man who had murdered her mother.

Yes, her action had been incomprehensible.

That evening, when the others returned from the fields, they all expressed surprise that she was up and about.

'But you're recovered! It's amazing,' said Lao Yang, one of the stupider women in her group. 'Are you really not ill any more?'

'Do I look it?' snapped Ziwei.

'So you'll be back to work tomorrow, then?' continued the woman, unabashed.

'That's why we're here, isn't it?' Ziwei rolled over on to her side angrily, trying to ignore the rumbling in her empty stomach. 'Damn,' she muttered, as she thought of how Lan Ying and Xiao must be laughing at her, in heaven or wherever they were.

14

A Touch of Mango

Cultural Revolution, Iron Man's Glade, Black Hills, 1969

Ziwei thought it must have been at least five hours since they had left Tranquil Springs. For the last three hours they had been climbing, and through the gap in the truck's tarpaulin she caught glimpses of rocky crags and bare hillsides. They must already be high in the Black Hills.

Their driver was a young soldier, who appeared to think that every pothole in the road was a challenge to his skill and the vehicle's worn-out suspension. Behind her, in the cab, she could hear him laughing. Apparently he had not discovered the gears.

It might have been tolerable if Ziwei had not been wearing hand-cuffs. She knew they would be taken off when they reached their destination, but for the moment they stopped her securing any hold in the bouncing vehicle. One particularly violent crash threw her upwards and her head hit the metal hoop supporting the tarpaulin. Stars flashed behind her eyes and she felt as if she was flying, before she was hurled down again and collided with her fellow prisoner on the floor. Their guard had also been jolted off his stool, and while he flailed for a hand-hold, the AK47 round his neck lurched alarmingly in their direction.

After seven years, Ziwei was used to men pointing guns at her, and usually she didn't care, but now she found herself praying that this one had remembered to put on the safety catch. At least he was good-natured. That was something to be grateful for. He helped them up and offered them cigarettes from a crumpled packet in his pocket.

'Thank you, but I don't smoke,' said the other prisoner. He leant forward and added in a conspiratorial whisper. 'But I see you have the true revolutionary spirit, Comrade. You may kiss my hand, if you like.'

The young soldier started. His brows knitted with anger and he obviously thought the bound, bespectacled prisoner was mocking or

315

insulting him. Frantically Ziwei shook her head, raising her eyes upwards. The young man noticed and looked puzzled. 'Technician Li's hand's touched one of the mangoes,' whispered Ziwei.

'Mangoes? What mangoes?' Then, as realisation hit him, the soldier's face blanched and he backed away a step. '*Those* mangoes?'

Ziwei nodded, attempting by her smile to indicate that this was dangerous ground.

Even the prisoners in Tranquil Springs knew about the mangoes. They had seen pictures of them in the pictorial magazines, being carried on flowery floats in great processions. Their provenance had been blasted from every headline and poster. Last summer, about the time Mao Tse-tung was ordering the army finally to round up the Red Guards and send them to the countryside, he had received a delegation of Pakistani foreign ministry officials, who had presented him with a box of the fruit. Following that meeting, he summoned his trusted bodyguard, Wang Dongxing, and ordered him to send it to the PLA and Workers Activists Group, who had been despatched to Tsing Hua University to ensure that the right proletarian values were being maintained on the campus.

Subsequently these 'gifts from the Great Helmsman to show his appreciation of the workers' became holy relics. They were sealed in wax, placed in glass caskets and transported on special trains for the edification of other workers all over the country. Tens of thousands of adulatory people gathered in the streets of every city to watch them go by.

Technician Li's claim to fame was that when a mango had arrived in his hometown of Qiqihar he, as a model worker, had been one of those privileged to oversee its transfer from the original case to a larger, crystal one that was to be carried in the parade. He had touched the mango. He had touched Mao. And that, in his own view and that of many others, made him in turn untouchable.

For by now the fruit not only represented Mao. The mangoes had become extensions of Mao himself. They *were* Mao and were treated with the same veneration. Everybody had heard stories of foolish people who had spoken about them derogatorily. In the summer heat mangoes, even cased in wax, rot and, not long into their tour, the treasures had obviously shrivelled. Woe betide any innocent who commented on the fact. A freed prisoner told Ziwei that when one of the mangoes reached Shishan, an elderly man in the crowd had casually remarked that, disappointingly, it resembled a sweet potato. For this heresy, he was arrested, taken to the football stadium and shot in the back of the head.

'I don't let just anybody kiss my hand,' said Li, amiably. He was still probably only in his thirties, although his hair was prematurely grey. He looked more like a clerk than a worker. His prison garb was neatly pressed, and his features retained a pink freshness, extraordinary to anybody who had spent any length of time in the Laogai. 'Only those who are pure in heart and who have devoted themselves to the revolution and sincerely honour our great chairman's Thoughts deserve that privilege.' He turned, still smiling, towards Ziwei. 'I wouldn't let this woman touch my hand. She's convicted of immorality and, besides, is a *hei wu lei*.'

'Quite, quite,' muttered the guard. Quickly he lit Ziwei's cigarette, then retired to his stool, where he sat with his back to them, gazing abstractedly out of the tarpaulin, although he occasionally gave them a worried glance over his shoulder.

'You do understand?' Li asked Ziwei, with a note of apology in his voice. 'I do have a responsibility.'

'Oh, yes, I very much understand,' said Ziwei. 'I'm quite unworthy to touch your hand.'

Technician Li nodded his satisfaction, and relapsed into silence.

Ziwei focused her mind on what lay ahead. Frankly, she could have done without the distraction of a lunatic like Li, but if that was the price of freedom, it would be worth it.

If it really was freedom . . .

She was still a little confused. Earlier that morning, when she had seen the reed roofs of the compound, the barbed wire and the fields disappear behind them, she had felt afraid. After five years of living at Tranquil Springs she simply could not imagine any other form of existence.

It had happened so suddenly . . .

'Sit down, Comrade,' the new commandant had muttered, without looking up from the papers he was studying.

Ziwei, who had no idea why she had been summoned to his office, examined him nervously. She knew he had been a soldier – a general or at least a senior colonel, though it was difficult to tell from his uniform because the Cultural Revolution had abolished all rankings.

He had the rough features and leathery skin of somebody in the favoured peasant-worker-soldier class, and his accent was broad Hebei, but he was no brute like his predecessor. His arrival had coincided with a restoration of old rations and reduced work schedules, and for three months now there had been no arbitrary trials or executions. He had also been more visible in the camp, inspecting the work in the fields and occasionally upbraiding a capo, never a prisoner. For no other reason than that he seemed disinclined to shoot them, the camp inmates had taken to him favourably and nicknamed him Grandpa Zheng. Looking at his grey head bent conscientiously over his reports, there was something about him that reminded her of Brush Head. She had to catch herself. However civilised he appeared, he was there to enforce the system and was as dangerous as any of his predecessors.

He looked up with tired eyes. 'Thank you for waiting, Comrade. There is always endless paperwork, all of it urgent.' He opened a file. 'Peng Ziwei, Prisoner 873/2956, aged thirty, female, former prostitute, sentenced January 1965 to twenty years' Reform through Labour. Is that correct?'

'Yes, Comrade,' she whispered. He grunted and continued to run his eyes down the file. 'There are commendations here for the manner in which you have conducted the political reform classes in your group. You have shown "ideological correctness in your judgements", "revolutionary fervour" and here it says you have "assisted culturally less endowed prisoners on the path to re-education and reform". You have been team leader for how long?'

'Nine months, Comrade. I replaced Prisoner Hao Lansan, who died of . . .' She stopped, recalling that it was taboo to state that anybody had died of hunger. The previous January they had been reduced to eating grass.

'It was another bad winter, Comrade,' he said gently. 'There was a scientific reason for the drought. For the last three years, a weather shift reduced precipitation over the Black Hills with low wheat yields as a consequence. My predecessor was correct to have introduced the policy of "lower rations to be substituted by gourds and greens". This year the rain pattern has returned to its usual levels, however. You have been eating better lately?'

'Yes, Comrade,' said Ziwei.

'You have received tomatoes and fruit?'

'We are all very grateful, Comrade.'

'Good,' said Grandpa Zheng. 'Let us hope that renewed levels of energy lead to higher production levels.' He returned to his notes.

'In December 1966 you reported a flagrant abuse of camp discipline conducted by one of the camp guards, which involved a sexual liaison with one of your fellow convicts. For this meritorious act you were named a 'model prisoner', but a few weeks later you were sentenced to solitary confinement and the title 'model prisoner' was rescinded.'

Ziwei hung her head. 'Yes, Comrade.'

'We are reviewing all the events that took place in the camp during the tenure of the disgraced Commandant Yin. There were many incorrect decisions made at that time. The death of the prisoner Xiao Er and your subsequent detention has also come under re-examination. It seems you were unfairly treated, Comrade.'

Ziwei stared. A positive review of a punishment was unprecedented. Was this a trap?

'Camp Guard Fang, who was on duty that night, reported that you struggled physically with the prisoner, Xiao, before she made her fatal escape attempt. The evidence to me suggests that you were trying to prevent her suicidal action. Every death in this camp impacts on productivity, Comrade, so, again, it appears that your instincts to save your friend were ideologically correct, deserving commendation not punishment. On that basis I have decided to reinvest your status as 'model prisoner' and backdate it to January 1967.'

Ziwei's mouth dropped open. She could almost taste the extra food rations – but there had to be a catch. There was always a catch.

Grandpa Zheng closed the file and leant back in his chair, observing her severely. After a pause, he continued: 'I have also recommended, Comrade, that subject to certain conditions, which I will elaborate, you should be released from Reform through Labour altogether. This morning I received authorisation, from a very high level, for your release.'

Now she really thought she was hallucinating. 'Release? You mean – out of the Laogai?'

'Conditionally,' he said. 'The usual sentence for prostitution is seven years, which, taking into account time spent in holding and transit camps, you have now served. I am aware of the special factors that earned you a longer sentence, but your exemplary conduct in this camp provides a reason why, in this case, the state can be merciful. You will be placed in the category of 'a prisoner freed from labour reform and

319

labour education'. You will be monitored, however, and any deviation of behaviour may result in your original sentence being reimposed or extended.'

Her shoulders shook and her eyes misted. The commandant leant over and gave her a handkerchief. He looked embarrassed. 'You may celebrate your good fortune later, but first you must listen carefully. There are other conditions.'

She sniffed into his handkerchief, and saw him frown. He bowed his head, folded his arms, then leant forward and looked earnestly into her eyes. 'May I be candid with you, Comrade? The fact is we need help.'

'Help?'

'Two years ago a directive came from the agricultural ministry that large tracts of territory in the Black Hills, which as you know is now a wasteland, should be converted into farms. If the task had been approached scientifically, using the apparatus of state labour camps like this one, it might have been easier, but political considerations – the need to find accommodation for the large numbers of former Red Guards and other student 'volunteers' who have been sent to the countryside – led to a decision that the Black Hills should be designated for them. For a year now, young men and women from the cities have been billeted on villages in the hills, but none has any experience of agriculture, let alone any knowledge of how to survive in the harsh conditions that prevail there. They have been dying like flies.'

'I'm sorry to hear that,' said Ziwei, confused as to why he was telling her this.

'Yes, it has all been very wasteful,' he continued. 'We should not criticise the peasants who might have been expected to help them. They have a hard enough life surviving as it is, and some of them, I regret to say it, are – unreconstructed individuals. Whatever the whys and wherefores, the situation has become a scandal and, to put it bluntly, we've been asked to lend a helping hand. We all accept that in the interests of national reconstruction, the Black Hills experiment should be a success, but it is also necessary to keep up production levels in the Tranquil Springs brigade. There are few able-bodied men I can spare, and even fewer with the right ideological credentials. You, Comrade Peng, who have experience of farming in this region and who, as a "model prisoner", can be trusted, do possess the credentials and the skills, and now, with your release, the freedom – to volunteer.'

'I – I have a choice?' asked Ziwei. This must be the catch.

'Yes, Comrade Peng, you have a choice – but, as I said earlier, your release does not preclude your devotion to the revolution from being re-assessed, and should you decline this offer to help the People, I doubt it will look good on your record. In other words your choice is limited.'

'I am grateful wholeheartedly for the honour of being considered for this revolutionary task,' said Ziwei. 'I readily volunteer.'

'Good,' said Grandpa Zheng. 'It will not be easy. Conditions up there are – well, you will find out.'

'What am I supposed to do when I get there?' asked Ziwei, not sure where 'there' was.

'Help the students with their agricultural tasks, give them advice, steady them. Oh, yes, and look after Comrade Li.'

Ziwei raised her eyebrows questioningly. The commandant sighed. 'Comrade Li was a model worker in an automobile plant in Qiqihar. He was given a – special privilege. It showed how highly he stood in the Party's favour. Sadly the privilege went to his head. He adopted an arrogant and unrealistic attitude, which alienated his work colleagues. Also his efficiency as a worker fell and he became increasingly careless. There was an industrial accident for which he was responsible, and two of his workmates were crushed to death. It is a tragic story.'

Very, thought Ziwei, but no more remarkable than the stories of many others who had ended up in the Laogai. She wondered what Grandpa Zheng was leading up to.

'He was tried, of course, and sentenced, and that is why he is here, but he is unsuited to the sort of work we do, and his presence among the other inmates creates . . . complications. Disciplining him is also difficult for my staff.'

'This – this privilege he received . . .' Ziwei broached the subject delicately.

'Yes, it was a very great privilege indeed.' Grandpa Zheng gave a derisory chuckle. 'That is the problem. I'll let him tell you about it when you meet him.' He placed his hands flat on his desk. 'There it is. I'm sorry, Comrade, you will not receive your graduation in a formal rewards and punishment ceremony before the rest of the camp. That is because your release is conditional and made under special circumstances. Best you do not talk to your comrades about it. They will be

321

given to understand that you have been transferred to another camp. You and Comrade Li will leave as prisoners, and your new status will come into effect only when you reach Iron Man's Glade, which is the village I'm sending you to. I'm told the place is named after a famous bandit who made his lair there in Qing times. I do not think you will find any forest glades there now – or anything else, for that matter. Don't expect too much – but I thank you for volunteering, Comrade.'

'And I will be serving the revolution by doing so?' She was worried that she might have let too much irony drip into her remark. It was quite obvious that her 'release' had been prompted more for the bureaucratic convenience of Grandpa Zheng and the camp authorities than because of any merit or favour to be bestowed on her.

But he smiled. 'Yes, Comrade, that is exactly what you will be doing. Long live Chairman Mao.'

Iron Man's Glade hardly constituted a village. Ziwei's first thought, when the truck stopped and the friendly soldier uncuffed them, was that they were being deposited on an empty hillside – but gradually, through the dusk, she made out shadowy figures observing them from a distance and smoke rising from dwellings that at first she had thought were caves or animal pens.

The young guard cupped his hands: 'Who's the head man here?' he shouted, and his voice echoed round the crags.

A lantern approached them. In its light, she saw the coarse features of a bearded man in his mid-forties. The closeness of his eyes, the beetle brows and thick band of contiguous eyebrow made her think he was inbred. 'I'm the Party secretary. Name's Gao,' he grunted. 'We don't have head men any more, not since we became a commune. Who are you and what do you want?'

'Volunteers for you,' said the soldier.

'More mouths to feed, you mean,' was the surly response. Gao moved closer and held up the lantern to examine her. She did not like the way his eyes lingered on her body. He barely glanced at Li. 'Pretty poor specimens,' he said. 'The woman's skin and bones and the man looks as if he's never done a day's work in his life. Run out of student volunteers, have you? This lot are old.'

'Comrade Peng has done hard labour in the Tranquil Springs brigade for five years,' said the soldier. 'She's a model worker.'

'Yeah?' The lantern lifted and Gao took a closer look at her.

Slowly he nodded. 'Five years, eh? From everything I've heard, most are lucky to survive two. Know how to handle a hoe, woman?' he asked.

'My name is Peng Ziwei and you can call me "Comrade",' she said. 'And, yes, I can handle a hoe, and a spade, and dig a dike too. I've built sturdier prison cells with my own two hands out of mud than those hovels on the hill you seem satisfied with.'

'Well said, Comrade,' whispered Technician Li. 'That is a correct proletarian response. Shall I tell this man about my—'

'No, Comrade,' she said hurriedly. 'Not yet.' She turned back to the bearded man, who was eyeing her with a slow, gap-toothed grin, his eyes glinting with newly kindled interest. 'Have I made myself clear?' she continued, wondering if she had pushed him too far. 'I'd be grateful if you would take us to where the students are billeted.'

'In time,' Gao said. 'First I've got to sign some delivery documents from Soldier-boy here. Receipt of – what was it, now? One saboteur and one whore – have I got that right?' He laughed harshly. 'Sorry, that'd be one reformed whore, wouldn't it? I do beg your pardon. You're freed now, aren't you? But we're only poor peasants, you see, and sometimes these distinctions are a bit complicated for simple folks. Not that we care overmuch either way. Here, whoever you are, it's work and be fed, starve otherwise. And it's my Party committee that controls the granary and the communal canteen. Have *I* made myself clear – Comrade?'

'Perfectly,' she said, shaking with anger.

Fifteen minutes later they were following Gao up a stony goat track, trying to keep pace with the pool of lantern light as he strode quickly on short legs.

'Perhaps I should tell him about the mango,' panted Li. 'He's been very rude. He hardly behaves like a peasant-farmer-soldier cadre at all.'

She wanted to scream at him to shut up, but she said softly, 'Later perhaps, Comrade, if he demonstrates proper ideological understanding.'

'I suppose you're right,' he said, sounding disappointed.

'You can tell the students when we get to the hut,' she said.

'Yes, they'll be very impressed – but I don't think I'll let them kiss my hand, not until they've convinced me of their ideological purity.'

'No, that would be inappropriate,' she puffed, weighed down by her own small suitcase, and Li's leather valise, which, strapped to her back, was grinding against her spine.

The students' billet was a converted goat-shed stacked with three rows of bunk beds. In the dim light cast by Gao's lantern, Ziwei could make out rumpled blankets, books, clothes and other personal possessions they had been allowed to bring with them, scattered untidily over the straw mattresses and on the earth floor. Although nobody seemed to be inside, the place stank of sweat and dirt. The mud walls were covered with cuttings from newspapers and magazines: many pictures of Mao, others of combine harvesters, rockets from the space programme, marching soldiers and the all-too-familiar slogans. The paper was peeling and torn. Such squalor in any of the camps Ziwei had lived in for the last few years would have earned the whole hut a term in solitary.

Gao, chuckling to himself, moved down the narrow alley between the bunks, and at the far end prodded a shadowy hump on the lower bed. There was a faint groan. Ziwei glimpsed a sweaty forehead and staring eyes.

'Still alive,' he said. 'So it looks like one of you'll have to sleep on the floor tonight, but don't worry, he won't last. They never do when the TB gets to this stage. You'll be comfortably accommodated soon enough. The bed above him's free. Girl in it died last week. Which of you wants it?'

Li gave Ziwei a shifty glance, then hurried forward and put his bag where Gao was pointing. He came back for his briefcase. He climbed up and began to arrange various articles he took from his bag, ignoring the sick boy in the bunk below him.

Ziwei dropped her case by the door. 'Where are the others?' she asked.

'Eating round the back. It's suppertime. You can go and look for them if you like, but I doubt they'll have left anything for you. Their work was a shambles today so they're on light rations. Still, work hard tomorrow and you'll be fed. We start before dawn here – fields are two miles off, other side of the cliff – so I'll expect you up at four.'

He turned, swung his lantern and thrust his face close to Ziwei's. His breath was acid with alcohol. The close-set, piggy eyes were examining her again with the same heavy interest he had shown earlier. She took a step backwards but was blocked by the end of the bunk. In the lamplight she could see the gap-toothed grin and the grey tip of his tongue. He was lifting his hand, extending calloused fingers towards her cheek – then seemed to think better of it, and in a moment he was out of the door and his lantern was bobbing down the path.

In the sudden darkness she heard a complaint from Li. 'Didn't he leave a light? I haven't unpacked yet. A fine Party secretary, he is.'

She wanted fresh air. She was shaking a little, but she managed to control her voice: 'I'm sure the students will have a light, Comrade. We should go and look for them. You were going to tell them about the mango. Remember?'

Stumbling in the dark, they found a sheep pen, looked over the crumbling earthen wall and saw shadows hunched around a small fire. Heads turned and stared at them. Two figures stood up – one male, one female, both pitifully thin. The girl seemed the more confident of the pair. In the flickering light, Ziwei could make out two thick braids hanging from a Mao cap pressed over her forehead. She wore a tight tunic that showed a well-shaped figure, and the oval face was good-looking, if drawn. There was something of Lan Ying in the loose limbs, the casual way she positioned her hips and folded her arms – but her set lips and intense, glinting eyes showed only condescension and hostility. The young man next to her had broad shoulders and muscular arms. Long hair spiked out above a cloth headband, and he wore a sailor's striped vest. Unlike the girl, he was observing them curiously. A half-smile was playing on his lips and his eyebrows were tilted questioningly above not unfriendly brown eyes. They were a handsome couple – but what most impressed Ziwei was how young they were.

Before she had a chance to introduce herself and Li, the girl spoke. She had a Shanghainese accent like Ziwei's, but she spoke in the shrill, overbearing tone that Ziwei had heard so many times on loudspeakers and newsreels. This one must have been a Red Guard, she thought, remembering Lan Ying's trial. She was even pointing an accusing finger.

'We know who you are and what is your background. You are the Laogai prisoners who have been sent to help us. You should know that we did not request this and I have written a complaint to that effect. We are a true revolutionary unit and we do not welcome in our ranks scabs and counter-revolutionaries who have betrayed the People.'

Ziwei chose her words carefully. 'I understand you are all volunteers with an important task to undertake, but it cannot be an easy one. Any kind of farming is difficult in this environment, and I believe you have faced terrible hardships. If an older person, with some experience . . .'

But she got a quotation screamed back at her: 'All revolutionaries – all young revolutionaries – should face the world and brave the storm. Revolutionaries cannot grow up in hothouses. They must grow up braving storm and stress."'

'That's very true, Comrade,' murmured Ziwei, 'but I think Chairman Mao also said that one should "overcome one's weak points by learning from each other's strong points", and that if necessary one should "make the old serve the present and the foreign serve China". I am aware of who I am, and I humbly seek your pardon, but I do have skills that could be useful to you. I – I am mindful also that our great chairman once said: "The students have too heavy a burden, which affects their health, and therefore they cannot make use of what they have learnt." I saw your comrade in the hut, and I grieve for him. Perhaps – perhaps I can use my experience of labouring in a production unit in harsh conditions to alleviate some of your suffering, to reduce the risk of misfortunes happening to us in the future.'

'Are you a doctor?' said the young man. He spoke in an attractive Sichuanese burr. 'Are you saying you can save Lao Meng?'

'Not if he is already in an advanced stage of TB,' said Ziwei, aware that the girl was looking at her venomously, but she also noticed that some of the other students had joined them and were listening to her intently. 'If you will allow me, I might be able to teach you ways to protect yourselves from some of the worst effects of hunger, heat and cold. It is probably that which is killing your friend. I am no doctor, but in the Laogai we learnt how to survive.'

She saw one or two nod, and thought she might be reaching them. Then, behind her, she heard Li clear his throat. 'I can probably cure him,' he said brightly. 'I could offer him my hand. It has touched the mango, you know.'

Her heart sank. She had forgotten him – and from the angry looks on the students' faces she could tell that what he had said confused them. Like the soldier on the truck, they were wondering whether they were being mocked. It was potentially disastrous, but she had to play along. It was sink or swim together. 'I should tell you that Technician

326

Li is a model worker,' she said, 'and – and I believe some of you can guess which mango he is referring to.'

'Chairman Mao's mango?' The young man's expression was sceptical but his eyes had widened. The other students were now looking nervous as well as confused. One, a slight boy in spectacles and a straw peasant's hat, said cautiously. 'I've heard stories of cures. If it really was one of the mangos.'

'Zhang Hong, what do you think?' the strong young man asked the strident girl who, for the first time, seemed to have lost some of her confidence, her sharp eyes moving backwards and forwards between Ziwei and Li. 'If it can save Lao Meng . . . It may be worth a try . . .'

'You're the captain of our platoon, Xing Min. I will abide by your decision,' she muttered. 'But we should be cautious of "those who sell dog meat under the label of a sheep's head". Do you trust them?' she whispered.

'No, but they're here. We have to accept them, and if – if one of them's touched . . . a mango, well, we can't—'

'If he can save Lao Meng . . .' called one of the girls in the throng.

Technician Li inclined his head politely, then in a reedy voice he began to sing: 'Beloved Chairman Mao, the red sun shining in our hearts . . .'

They looked nonplussed, then one of the students took up the tune, echoed by the others:

'*How many words so deep in our hearts we long to say to you,*
How many warm and fervent songs we wish to sing for you . . .'

Li raised his palm upwards, as if he was holding high the mango. He began to walk slowly towards the path that led to the students' dormitory. The students followed, singing:

'*Millions of red hearts excitedly beating,*
Millions of smiling faces turn to the red sun . . .'

The girl, Zhang Hong, gave Xing a sour look, then followed the others, adding her voice angrily to the refrain:

'*From our hearts we wish you beloved Chairman Mao long life,*
A long life, a long, long life . . .'

The voices disappeared down the path. Only Ziwei and the boy, Xing, remained.

'Is there some soup left?' asked Ziwei.

Xing looked irritated. 'You're asking us to share our rations with you?'

'No, for the boy in the hut – Lao Meng, or whatever you called him.'

'It's not permitted to feed him because he didn't work today or yesterday. We are under revolutionary discipline here, and there are penalties if we break the rules.'

'Whose rules?' snapped Ziwei. 'Gao's? Where do you think you are? In Party school? Here we can make our own rules. Bring what's left in the pot. What's in it? Turnips?'

'Yes,' said Xing, uncertainly. 'And we've added some roots we picked. Well, grass, actually. The village has been short of grain these last few months. Maybe after the harvest the situation will improve, but for now they asked us to help them by tightening our belts.'

'And you don't think it's odd that villagers like Gao are fat and you look like scarecrows?' She scrutinised the tall boy. Suddenly she remembered the title of a fairy story her mother had read her as a girl. *The Babes In The Wood.* She could hardly believe such innocence. 'Here,' she said, reaching into her shirt and extracting her forage bag. Hurriedly, before she had left Tranquil Springs, she had filled it with what she could from the cache she had built up for herself in the spring. There were three potatoes, a duck's egg, a paper package of millet, some salt and, most precious of all, the result of heavy bargaining, five strips of dried beef. In Laogai terms it was a fortune, and even here the boy's eyes widened. 'Put it all into the pot and add some water. Keep the thick leavings from the turnip soup. Make a stew. We want to save your friend, don't we? If it really is TB, we're sunk, but more likely, if all you've been eating is grass, it's a wasting disease and fever. With luck, it may be curable.'

'But the mango? The hand that's touched the mango?'

She looked up from the fire, and smiled acidly. 'Let's just make doubly sure, shall we? In case the Chairman's magic isn't working today.'

She regretted it as soon as she had said it. The boy leapt back like a startled rabbit, looking left and right in case anybody had heard her. Then his face softened and he gave her a delightful grin. 'Is that real beef?' he asked. 'Can I – can I taste a sliver to be sure?'

'I won't tell.'

That's one in the bag, she thought, as she stirred the pot. Now there were seventeen more to win over. She had counted them: eleven boys and seven girls, ranging from late teens to mid-twenties. Children, she thought, then realised that they were only a few years younger than she was – but that was a lifetime's difference after the Laogai.

Lao Meng recovered. Afterwards, the students were divided over whether the touch of Li's hand or Ziwei's stew had saved him, but if they had doubts they kept silent. Formally, the hut adopted the ideological line imposed by their Party secretary, Zhang Hong, who, Ziwei noticed wryly, had opportunistically changed her tune from the suspicious manner in which she had greeted them in the sheep pen. It obviously suited her that the grace of the Great Helmsman, transmitted through the mango, had cured their comrade. It was also a snub to Ziwei, whose competence the girl viewed as a threat to her authority.

Ziwei was happy to go along with that: it solved the problem of what to do with Technician Li. In his status as prophet, he was looked after. He would hold court from his top bunk in the evening, allowing those he favoured to kiss his hand – usually it was the student whom that day Zhang Hong had chosen to share rations with him. She had taken on the role of Li's amanuensis. She had commandeered the bunk below him from Lao Meng, interpreting his utterances and subtly controlling access to the great man, thus increasing her own influence in the hut over that of Xing, their platoon captain.

Again, Ziwei was content with that. For the moment, the novelty of having a revolutionary icon in their midst helped the students to overlook Technician Li's incapability of doing a day's work in the fields (hence the extra low ration he was apportioned by Party Secretary Gao, who had no time for anybody lying in the sunshine chewing a grass stalk, however blessed) and his presence, at least initially, inspired them to work cheerfully, which Ziwei saw as positive.

She could easily put up with the nightly criticism, and sometimes full-blown struggle sessions, that Zhang Hong inflicted on her. She would meekly confess her crimes and acknowledge her disgusting class background, and take whatever humiliating penalties the Shanghai girl meted out. Cleaning the latrine or rising early to bring up the water from the stream at the bottom of the cliff was light duty compared to what she had undergone during the previous seven years. As the summer progressed, Zhang Hong's screaming denunciations, echoed by a complaisant Technician Li, were no less venomous, but after-wards, curling up on her straw mat by the door, Ziwei realised that most of the others in the hut were joining in unenthusiastically, and some, not only Xing, appeared ashamed.

What was more important to her was that the measures she had imposed on the group's working style and living conditions – always after patient explanation and quiet example – were having some effect.

She had been shocked that first day when she had seen the stony fields on the higher slopes that the volunteers had been given. The peasants from Iron Man's Glade were working in fields lower down that were well irrigated by a system of drains from a mountain spring. To water their field, the students had to carry buckets up and down a half-mile footpath, with much time-wasting and to little effect. Picking up and sniffing a handful of earth, Ziwei was satisfied that the soil was good enough, but without adequate watering in the hot summer months, she foresaw a dismal harvest – and, besides, the ground was hardly broken for the planting, despite the energetic but unskilful efforts of the students with mattocks and spades.

That first afternoon, Ziwei asked Xing if she could have a rest. Pausing between swings of his mattock, he merely shrugged. Already three of the girls, exhausted, were lying by the side of the field. There were no capos here to enforce discipline.

She headed up the path with the intention of finding the spring. Gao and two of his cronies were watching the students' antics with amusement. 'Five years, was it, and you're slacking already?' he called after her. 'Lucky if you get a *wo-wo-tou* for supper tonight!'

Ziwei spent three hours exploring the slopes.

During the long walk back to the goat-shed, she told Xing her plan. He was sceptical. 'There aren't enough of us,' he said.

'Yes, there are. You can divide your forces. You and the other strong ones, eight or nine of you, are doing all the hard work anyway, and you've got to keep at it if you're to get the earth turned in time. It won't make any difference if the rest of us go off, and the work I'm proposing even the girls can do.'

He looked uncomfortable. 'They might not agree,' he said.

'You're the platoon captain. They'll listen to you. Get Zhang Hong on your side. Make it her idea. I don't care how you do it, but if we don't find a way to water that field, we won't get a crop, and Gao will have an excuse to starve us during the winter.'

330

'You really think we can do this?'

'There's an underground stream that flows not a hundred yards away from the western end of the field. It's a matter of digging and making drainage channels. How do you think the villagers water their fields?'

'Then why didn't they tell us?'

She gave him a scornful glance. 'Haven't you worked it out?' Suddenly she grabbed his arm, and nodded at the paler skin colour above his wrist. 'Who did you sell your watch to? Gao? One of his cronies? And what for? A few extra *wo-wo-tou*?'

He jerked his arm. He looked furious, and for a moment she wondered if he would strike her. Then he dropped his head. 'A chicken leg. I was hungry. I told the others I'd lost my watch. I feel ashamed.'

She spoke gently: 'You think some of the others haven't lost their watches too? And other precious possessions? Listen, Xing. These villagers, yes, they're worker-soldier-peasants, but they're not revolutionaries. They don't care about you. If anything, they see you as prey. They don't want you well fed. That's their lever. When the winter comes, and it gets really bad, they'll ask for more.' Again, she grabbed his arm, and roughly turned him. At the end of the file, two of the girls were walking with tightened shoulders and fixed, nervous expressions, while three young men from the village dogged their footsteps, teasing them. 'What happens when those girls get really hungry?' she said.

'I should report your counter-revolutionary attitude,' he said.

'No. Think about what I've been saying, then tell me if it doesn't make sense. Do you want me to quote Mao? 'A leaf before the eye shuts out Mount Tai.' 'Seek truth from facts.' All that. Come on, Xing, you can be a revolutionary and clear-sighted at the same time.'

Slowly, he nodded. He gave her a grin. 'I'll talk to Zhang Hong,' he said, and strode away from her.

Gao and the other villagers were sceptical when the students split into two groups. They laughed at the girls who thought they could discover a well. That first day they didn't even bother to cut the rations. It had been too good a jape.

The next day, when water bubbled out of the turf, Gao grabbed Ziwei by the arm. 'Is this time-wasting your idea?' he growled. She slipped from his grasp and continued digging. 'If you miss the planting it'll be you I blame,' he shouted. 'There are severe penalties for sabotage.'

In a week they had water reaching the field. Xing, whom Ziwei had taught what to do, supervised the construction of the irrigation channels. On the day they filled, Technician Li, who had somehow acquired an umbrella to ward off the sun, strolled along the banks, occasionally dipping his hand in the water to bless it.

That evening, when the students climbed down to the canteen to gather their rations, they found that they had been cut by half. For the first time, Xing stood up to Gao and complained. 'We have adopted scientific practises to increase the yield. You have no right to penalise us,' he shouted.

'You and your big words,' grunted Gao. 'As I see it you've wasted two weeks making mud-pies. It's already time for planting and you're behind schedule. If you finish it in time, then and only then I will raise the rations.'

It became a revolutionary struggle. The next morning the students were in the fields by dawn and did not leave until after the sun had gone down. They sang rousing songs as they defiantly drank their grass soup in the sheep pen, Technician Li complacently conducting them. They ploughed. They planted. On the third morning, Ziwei noticed they were flagging. These students did not have the experience of Laogai lags to keep themselves going on nothing. She took Xing aside. 'Give me four volunteers,' she said. 'Make it your order, your idea – they still don't trust me – and I'll see you get food tonight.'

'We can't spare anybody,' he protested, but she persuaded him.

That evening even Xiao would have been proud of her. From their forage bags, the four beaming students produced roots, yams, wild berries, grasshoppers, frogs and even, to Ziwei's surprise – she had had no chance to forage in this way under the capo regime but the trap she had devised worked – a hare. That night they feasted.

In the end they finished planting their wheat before the villagers in the fields below them had fully planted theirs.

Making the best of it – he had lost enough face and his only option now was to be generous – Gao supplemented their full rations with corn cakes, a leg of pork and a jar of rice spirit.

That evening there was no study session. Ziwei slipped away, and sat by herself on an outcrop that jutted over the edge of the cliff, looking at the silhouettes of the mountains and the stars. She heard footsteps behind her, and prepared to make room, thinking it must be Xing – but then she smelt vinegar and alcohol. It was Gao and he was swaying as he looked up at her from the path, a bottle in his hairy hand.

'If you even attempt anything, I'll scream,' she said, as calmly as she could. 'They shoot even Party secretaries for attempted rape.'

He laughed and squatted on his haunches, some feet away from her outcrop. 'Fancy yourself, do you?' he muttered. His teeth glinted in the depths of his beard. 'I haven't come to rape you. I've come to congratulate you.' he said.

'You should be congratulating the student leaders,' she said.

'Those scum? No.' He tapped his nose, then drank from the bottle. 'It was your doing. You're wasted on this lot. Do you know that? Someone like you . . . deserves better.'

She turned her head away.

'You're not pretty like some of those student girls, but you're a woman. Tough. Clever. Capable. You stood up to me when you arrived. I liked that. Fatten you up a bit and you'll breed. I don't care if you were once a whore. Shows you're experienced in other ways than farming. Guess you can please a man. Listen, I'm doing well as Party secretary. There's no private property nowadays, but I run the place. You'll never be short of pork or grain if you're with me.'

She stood up. 'I'm going back to the hut. Will you let me pass, please?'

He did not move. 'You probably think you're too good for the likes of me. City girls, they're all the same. Keep telling us how much they respect us for being shit-ignorant peasants, but really they despise us. Long for the day they can crawl back home to Mummy – those who survive, that is.' He spat a gobbet of phlegm over the cliff edge. 'But as a released Laogai you're here for life. You won't do better than me.'

'Are you going to let me pass?'

He shuffled to his feet. 'Yeah, if that's what you want. But you'll think on what I said?'

She had to squeeze against a rock to get by him on the narrow path. As she did so, he dropped the bottle, which smashed, and grabbed her shoulders, pushing her against the stone. Pulling her head backwards by her hair he pressed his lips to hers. She felt the scratch of his beard and smelt his breath. His tongue was pushing against her teeth. She opened them a fraction, then bit. He jerked backwards and she scratched his cheek. He let her go and she tried to run, but he grabbed at her collar, which tore. She heard him laughing behind her.

'You won't do better than me, whore. When the winter's here, you'll come round. You all do.'

Despite all Ziwei's efforts to remain in the background, most of the group now realised that the practical changes Xing was bringing to their lives had been her idea. They had her to thank for their well-watered wheat shoots, which were rising higher than the villagers'. It had been her suggestion that they build a vegetable terrace on the bare hill slope, so it was to her that they owed the cabbages and greens, which now made a welcome addition to their meals.

It had also been Ziwei's prompting that caused Xing one day to organise a rat hunt in their hut. That had been the first of many measures to tackle the squalor to which they had allowed themselves to become accustomed.

Ziwei sometimes thought it was ironic that, through Xing, she was promoting Laogai hygiene routines, but it was undeniable how popular the weekly hunt had become. It did not take even the most squeamish long to appreciate that rodent meat could supplement the low rations Gao had found excuses to re-impose, and the clearance of pests significantly reduced the number of fleas. Louse-cracking sessions, floor-cleaning rosters and other basic sanitation measures followed, and most of the students now took pride in the tidiness of their bunks and their own appearance.

They were no longer the intimidated scarecrows Ziwei had met when she arrived. They sang to and from work, grinning at Gao and his cronies if they came across them, shouting, 'Long live Chairman Mao,' and other slogans. Gao would scowl, and sometimes spit as they passed, but besides cutting their rations further there seemed nothing he could do – and, as the summer went on, even the rationing did not disturb them because they were learning to make do on their own.

Foraging was now a daily part of their existence. Xing had re-organised the work unit into sections, some to work in the fields, some to forage, and others to remain behind to wash clothes and conduct other chores at the hut. It did not impact on their productivity except to strengthen it – and the extra provisions the 'hunter team' provided compensated for the cut rations of 'slackers', as Gao dubbed anybody who did not work in the fields. Nobody went without. Xing insisted that everyone was contributing in their own way to their communal welfare, and everybody shared whatever bounty they had. Some days their traps and snares brought in more meat than they could eat.

Although his prestige was growing, at no time did Xing challenge Zhang Hong, who maintained her role as political leader. On Ziwei's urging, Xing was careful always to seek her approval for any new work practice he sought to introduce, couching his proposal in Maoist slogans, quietly provided by Ziwei, which Zhang Hong had to acknowledge. He was also careful to get the sanction of Technician Li, who could be persuaded to anything after assiduous flattery, even when Zhang Hong initially opposed him. Then Zhang Hong was trapped; how could she argue against Mao's anointed? Little by little their lives improved and, inevitably, the more intelligent students began to question whether they really owed their present good fortune to Li and his mango-blessed hands or to Ziwei and Xing's hard work.

The first indications of 'regime change' were jocular. One evening in mid-August the students returned from their field where heavy ears of wheat were nodding on thick yellow stalks, promising a good harvest to come. As usual Zhang Hong chose the 'volunteer' who would share his soup with Technician Li that day. Xiao Pan, a former astrophysics student from Nanjing, poured his ration into Li's bowl with good grace, but instead of returning to his position by the fire, he remained squatting beside Li, watching him as he drank.

'Yes?' said Li, disconcerted, while Zhang Hong looked up suspiciously from her seat beside him.

'I've never seen a mango,' said Xiao Pan, respectfully. 'Can you describe it to us?'

'It is beautiful like the rays of light that emanate from the sun rising in the east,' said Li, licking his spoon.

'It's the colour of an orange, then?' asked Xiao Pan. 'Or pink, like a peach, perhaps. There are both those colours in the sunrise.'

'It's – something in between,' said Li, clearly irritated that he was being cross-examined while he was trying to enjoy his meal.

With a grin, Xiao Pan's friend, Lei Qingjiang, leant forward. 'The sunrise also has traces of red in it, and that's very appropriate because it's the colour of revolution. It would be strange if the mango did not reflect that. Are there no traces of red in the skin of a mango?'

'Yes, there are some traces of red,' said Li.

'It's like an apple, then?' said Xiao Pan. 'Not a green one, of course. That's the colour of Kuomintang counter-revolutionaries. A red apple?'

'You are tiring Comrade Li,' said Zhang Hong, frowning.

But new questions were coming from all round the fireside.

'And how big is the mango, Comrade Li? If it's coloured like an orange or a peach, is it as big?'

'It is not a large fruit,' said Li, 'but that in no way reduces its power.'

'Not large?' One or two sighed. 'We imagined it must be as big as a melon.'

'Or at least a pineapple.'

'Then how small is it, Comrade Li? Is it the size of an apricot?'

'Or a plum?'

'Or a walnut?' somebody called. It was at this point that Zhang Hong stood up and angrily called a halt. Back in the hut, she imposed a particularly vicious struggle session on Ziwei, but the students' mood had changed after the incident round the campfire. At first, they mechanically repeated Zhang Hong's accusations, but their hearts were not in it. Zhang Hong paused, perplexed. 'Comrades,' she said, 'we have a duty to reform this *hei wu lei*.'

'I think you're being very unfair to her. She's a good person.'

Every head turned. It was the smallest girl in their group. Like Xing, Yao Fengfeng was Sichuanese and had become a Red Guard at high school, but there was nothing combative about her. She was shy and rarely spoke. During the last few weeks she had become close to Ziwei, who had done her best, in as motherly a way as she could, to comfort her in her homesickness. Ziwei was as surprised as the rest by her vehement outburst.

Zhang Hong turned on her with an angry glare, but Fengfeng bravely held her ground, although she was trembling and her cheeks had gone bright red.

'Comrade Peng Ziwei works harder than all of us, and we all know how she has been helping Xing. You shouldn't pick on her.'

In the silence that followed, Technician Li tittered. 'No kisses on the hand for her any more.'

'I don't care.' Fengfeng burst into tears, and sank down and clutched her knees, sobbing.

Xing got up from his seat on a bunk and put a hand on Zhang Hong's shoulders. She was shaking with rage. 'Let's call it a day, Zhang Hong,' he said. 'Everybody's very tired.'

'You heard her.' Zhang Hong was almost spitting. 'She is defending a counter-revolutionary, and she has been impolite to Comrade Li. She should be struggled.'

But one by one the students were turning into their bunks, some brushing past Zhang Hong rudely, not caring if they jostled her. Xing sighed, and helped Fengfeng to her feet. 'Get some sleep,' he told her. 'It's an early start tomorrow.'

Only Zhang Hong and Technician Li were left standing. Ziwei, from her kneeling position, reached for her straw mat and unrolled it in her usual place by the door, but just as she was gathering her bag to make a pillow, she felt it snatched away from her. The sick boy she had cured, Lao Meng, had picked it up and also her bedroll. 'You've been uncomfortable long enough,' he muttered. 'Take my bunk. That would only be right,' he added more loudly, looking at Li out of the corner of his eye. 'I should have thanked you earlier. Your soup saved my life.'

'Comrade Zhang,' Li stuttered. 'Comrade Zhang, you're not going to let that pass? He's – he's denied the mango, the touch of my hand.'

Zhang Hong stared at him. Ziwei was amazed to see that her face was quivering with hatred. With a moan, she ran to her bunk, where she curled up and began to sob.

Technician Li was left blinking behind his spectacles, his mouth opening and closing, until Xing reached up and turned down the oil lamp, leaving the hut in darkness.

In the end it was Ziwei who shared her rations with Li – the little she could spare, because she knew she had to preserve her strength.

Nothing was ever said. No one dared, even now, commit the heresy of challenging the mango openly, but both Technician Li and Zhang Hong were ostracised. There were no more study sessions or struggles. Xing, and Xing alone, was their unchallenged leader.

For a fortnight, Technician Li did not leave the hut. When it was Ziwei's turn to do the washing roster, she would sometimes look in to see how he was. Invariably he would be sitting on the bunk, staring at his hand, a stricken expression on his face.

In the evenings she would talk to him quietly when she brought him a bowl of gruel or a slice of rabbit meat, trying to persuade him to come out and work with the others, but he only shook his head.

One afternoon, Ziwei, Zhang Hong, Yao Fengfeng and Xiao Pan were cutting newspapers into squares to put on the spike for the latrine. It was raining, so they had brought the spike into the hut. While Zhang Hong remained silent, the others were chattering away about their hometowns. The subject, as usual, was food, and Fengfeng and Pan were arguing the merits of Sichuan and Huadong cuisines. They had all but forgotten Li, sitting on his bunk at the end of the hut.

'I'm not scared of hot spices.' Pan was grinning. 'It's only that I've never eaten a Sichuan dish I've liked.'

'You should come to Chongqing,' said Fengfeng. 'Oh, my mouth waters just thinking about it. What I could do with a hotpot now!'

'I know your hotpots – red with chillies, full of cooked offal. Disgusting.'

Fengfeng slapped his arm playfully. 'You wouldn't say that if you'd tasted it in the restaurant Xing used to work in.'

'Xing?' asked Ziwei. 'You mean our captain? I didn't know he worked in a restaurant. I thought he was just another Red Guard out of high school.'

'Oh, no.' Fengfeng laughed. 'Xing Min's a master chef. Didn't you know? He's so modest. Before the Cultural Revolution, he won prizes for his cooking. They called him the infant prodigy. He was even selected to work in a restaurant in Beijing. It was his big opportunity, what he'd always dreamt of – but then, well, all our lives changed, didn't they?'

'He does cook rabbit well,' acknowledged Ziwei, 'but I never guessed he ... Zhang Hong, whatever is the matter?'

Their Party secretary had gasped, and her face was ashen. She was staring at the neatly cut square of paper in her hand. She had been poised to place it on the spike, but now it was hanging in mid-air. Slowly she turned the page round, and they saw that she was holding an almost perfect portrait of Mao Tse-tung. She had inadvertently cut it out from the front page.

The colour drained from Pan and Fengfeng's cheeks too, as they realised the horrific implication of what Zhang Hong had so nearly done.

'It's all right,' murmured Ziwei. 'You spotted it in time. There's no harm done. We'll paste it on the wall. Nobody needs know this happened.'

There was a shout and a thump and they saw that Technician Li was rolling on the floor between the bunks where he had jumped and tripped. There was a wild expression in his eyes as he righted himself and ran towards them. They stared, frozen in surprise. He snatched the portrait of Mao from Zhang Hong's hand. He held it high. Saliva was dribbling from his open mouth and his eyes were rolling behind his spectacles; one of the lenses was cracked from his fall. Then, before they could do anything to prevent it, he rammed the portrait on to the spike. He stepped back, panting, his eyes shining with glee, and giggled. The spike was protruding neatly from one of the Great Helmsman's nostrils. As they stared at him, still with shock, he seemed to come to his senses and noticed their presence.

'It's not true,' he whispered confidentially. 'None of it is true.' He gave a ghastly smile and raised his hand, the one that had touched the mango, and, with all his strength, slapped it palm down over the portrait. The spike came out through the flesh, and blood spattered Mao's face. 'None of it's true!' he screamed. With the spike still impaling his hand, squares of newsprint falling behind him, he ran out of the hut into the rain.

The others were too stunned to move, but Ziwei raced after him. She tried to snatch the hem of his tunic, but she was too late. He teetered for a moment on the edge of the cliff, as if at the last minute he had changed his mind. Then he stepped into the void.

A wailing 'None of it is true,' echoed from the rocks. Afterwards she heard only the patter of the rain.

Ziwei had told the other three on no account to mention the details of how Li had killed himself, but inevitably the story got out, even though she had climbed down the hill and removed the incriminating picture of Mao before the villagers discovered the body. For a week there was a black, moody atmosphere in the hut. The more superstitious were worried about the insult to Mao. Others began to blame themselves for turning their backs on Li. After all, he had touched the mango. To her credit, Zhang Hong said nothing. Ziwei thought she might use the incident to try to regain her lost authority, but when Xing called a meeting, Zhang Hong was the first to give him her support.

'Comrade Xing Min is correct,' she said, after he had spoken. 'Now there is nothing – nothing – more important than redoubling our efforts to bring in the harvest. That is all we should concern ourselves with. Everything in the past, all our mistakes – my mistakes – we should put behind us. Long live Chairman Mao, and all obedience to his loyal follower, and our own leader, Comrade Xing!'

There was something magnificent in the way she stood there, eyes glittering in her sad, oval face, her slim body poised like a ballet dancer's, raising Xing's arm.

'He is our captain, and we will support him with all the strength in our bodies.'

She was like a high priestess, anointing a king.

That was the end of her ostracism. After the meeting, several students patted her shoulder, smiling and congratulating her, but she remained aloof, and retired shortly afterwards to her bunk, where she turned her back on the rest of the hut. Ziwei felt for her. She was a proud Shanghainese intellectual and had lost face. And she was only twenty years old.

During those anxious weeks, Xing came into his own. He was everywhere, exhorting, joking, cajoling, encouraging. He led the scything, singing scabrous Sichuanese folk songs to cheer them when they were exhausted. He helped the girls bundle sheaves when their fingers were numb and bleeding. He used his great strength to heave the hay cart from an irrigation ditch, when the others had despaired of moving it out of the sticky mud. Stripped to the waist, he ran like some archaic hunter-god through the smoke, holding a burning torch above his head and shouting triumphant slogans when it was time to burn the stubble in the field. The students cheered, and joked that he had somehow absorbed the power and energy of the legendary bandit, Iron Man Wang, who had given his name to the village.

Eventually the day came when all that had to be done was done. The students had scythed and stooked the wheat stalks and now were ready to carry them over the mountains to the village to add to the pile on the threshing floor outside the abandoned temple.

It was one of those evenings when the shadows and colours of the landscape were as finely etched as a photographic plate and you could see for ever. Humping her heavy load on her shoulder, Ziwei looked down at the plains, and could easily make out the faraway line of the Liao river, and even the dam at Tranquil Springs. She heard a heavy tread behind her, and Xing was at her side, sweat pouring from underneath his headband, and glistening on his bare shoulders as he balanced two of the heaviest stooks.

'Beautiful, isn't it?' he panted.

'Yes, it's a fine view,' she said.

'No, not just the view. Life itself is beautiful. Just living.' He laughed. 'I don't think I've ever been happier.'

'You've inspired these students,' said Ziwei. 'I'd never have thought it possible to build such a strong, confident team in such a short time, and achieve so much. With this fine crop, you've guaranteed our rations for the winter.'

He gave her a long look. 'No, Ziwei, it was you. We'd never have achieved anything without you, and I've never even thanked you. It was you who made it all possible. It wasn't just Lao Meng you saved. I can't express what I owe you – what we all owe you.'

She felt the sting of a tear in her eye, and tried to change the subject. 'You're the remarkable one, Xing,' she said. 'What's this Fengfeng's been telling me about you being a master chef? Such modesty.'

He laughed. 'Oh, that. It's all in the past. I'm a farmer now.'

'Fengfeng said you were invited to work in a restaurant in Beijing.'

'I was hoping one day I could manage one,' he said. 'Bring real Sichuanese food to the capital. I had it planned. I'd dreamt about it all my life. Not just food, although that would have been the main thing, I was going to make the restaurant special, unique, with Sichuan folk artists performing for the diners, the rooms decorated with traditional art. A boy's dream. Silly, isn't it?'

'It's good to dream,' she said quietly. 'I once dreamt of seeing whales.'

'Whales?' He guffawed. 'Then you're madder than I am. No, we're farmers now, and that's good too. Come on, let's get the pace up a bit. I can't wait to see Gao's face when we pour out our golden grain.'

'You've done well,' grunted Gao, after the grain had been threshed and weighed. 'A decent enough crop for your first year. No doubt you'll do better next.'

Xing's eyebrows rose merrily, and he pointed to their mound, which was fractionally higher than some of the others around it. Xiao Pan, the astrophysicist, had brought out the camera that was his prize possession and which he had refused to barter even at extremities of hunger, and was photographing his comrades, who had arranged themselves behind their golden pile, laughing and catcalling. Even Zhang Hong had a wry smile, as she was dragged to the front row to kneel with the other girls. 'I think, Party Secretary Gao,' he said, 'you'll find we've done rather better than some of you villagers have done, and we're not "singing different songs on different mountains" either. We incompetent city boys and girls have been working under the same conditions as you.'

'Don't quote Mao at me, boy. As I see it, this is only half your crop. Where's the rest?'

Ziwei felt a premonition of alarm.

'What do you mean?' said Xing, frowning.

'I see only grain here. Where are the cabbages and the beetroot from that other field you planted on the slope? I don't recall you asking permission from the commune or getting planning authority to farm there, but I'll let it pass if you bring in the produce.'

'That's our vegetable patch,' said Xing. 'It's our own.'

'It's communal land, boy. Everything here belongs to the commune, share and share alike. Now you mention it, I've heard tales that you've already started eating those vegetables. Some might call that stealing from your neighbours, in the same way as you've been poaching from the commune's game supply. We've spotted your traps on the mountainside. Caught some nice juicy hares, have you? But that's all right with me. It's all accounted for, you see. All's fair in our little hamlet. Everybody gets the same rations through the year – and if you bright city boys and girls have decided to use most of them up in the summer when the sun's shining, there'll be less for you in the winter, won't there? What else is there? Oh, yes, the water charges for that nice scientific irrigation scheme of yours, also built without permission. We'll be taking that into account too.'

'What are you saying?'

Ziwei saw that Xing had clenched his fists.

'What am I saying? It's payback time, boy. You've had your little holiday, and now we're taking back what's ours.' He nodded at the students kneeling in front of the grain pile, being photographed. 'You're not such a heroic leader after all, are you? Certainly not a wise one. Shall you tell them or shall I? That from now on, and through to spring, they're going to be living on turnip soup – because you and that Laogai bitch fooled them into squandering their rations.'

Ziwei tried to hold Xing back, but he was much bigger than she was, and there was no controlling his rage. He managed to plant two punches on Gao's face before six villagers pulled him to the threshing floor where he was pinioned, his face pushed into a pile of grain.

There was a moment when she thought that the shocked students would try to help him, but she screamed at them to stand where they were.

Gao had not moved or tried to avoid the blows. Now he calmly spat out a broken tooth, followed by blood and spittle, which dribbled over his beard. 'Take him to the lock-up, lads,' he said. 'Can't have people attacking Party secretaries.' All the time he had been gazing calmly at Ziwei. 'Don't worry, Comrade, we'll give him a fair trial.'

'Why are you doing this?' she said, in a low voice. 'If you don't give them rations in winter, they'll starve.'

'You're the clever one,' he said softly, leaning towards her. 'Maybe by rights it should be you in the lock-up. You're their real leader, not that fool. Maybe you should take on a bit of responsibility yourself. I told you once how you can help your precious charges – but don't leave it too long. Snow comes early in these altitudes.'

'You can't get away with this,' said Ziwei. 'If you bring Xing to trial, your extortion and blackmail will come out and you'll be investigated. Let Xing go. Otherwise we'll write a petition.'

'A petition? I'm quaking.' He ran a stubby finger across her cheek. 'I run this place, woman. Don't forget that. And they love me out there. Sunshine comes out of my arse. I'm the real thing, a peasant cadre, Mao's boy. I'd remember that, if I was you.'

Abruptly he turned his back on her and raised his voice, addressing the villagers: 'There's been sabotage of production here, comrades, and counter-revolutionary activity, which we will investigate. This man's guilty. There may be others. But don't worry, your committee's been vigilant and we've nipped the evil plot in the bud.' Turning to the stunned students, he added: 'As for you, you've abused the privileges of guests, stealing unlawfully from the commune. Be grateful that we continue to tolerate you. I expect proper working habits from now on and revolutionary discipline. If we find any other bad elements like this one, they'll be punished. Now get back to your hut. There's no rations for any of you tonight, but from tomorrow you'll be on light ones, until we're satisfied with your reformed behaviour. Then we may consider giving you more.'

Xing was led away. That evening the villagers held their harvest festival. The students could hear them singing, as they sat round their fire in the sheep pen contemplating their empty bowls.

* * *

Zhang Hong wrote a petition. Xiao Pan volunteered to take it down the mountain, using back paths. He was caught before he had gone a mile and, after being beaten, was ignominiously brought back to the hut, the petition confiscated. Gao used that as an excuse to arm the local militia, 'to restore discipline and counter deviationist threats'. From then on villagers with rifles guarded their hut and accompanied them to the fields. Life was little different from the capo regime of the Laogai, the only difference being that they were officially free citizens. There was no more foraging. They were denied access to their vegetable patch, which had been taken over by the villagers. With only turnip soup as rations, they began to starve.

Their only hope now was Xing's trial, which, as Ziwei had told Gao, was bound to attract publicity – but there was no trial. One evening in mid-October, a group of villagers brought Xing's body to the hut. There were red weals round his neck. He had hanged himself in his cell, or so they said, and the students had no evidence to refute that. Gao allowed them to take a half-day off work to bury him. Xiao Pan and Lei Qingjiang carved a headstone, and they left him under a makeshift mound on the hillside, with a view over the plains.

When the funeral was over Ziwei, to Gao's amusement, did not join the other students in the fields. She sat on her rock above the precipice, nursing her grief and an overwhelming sense of guilt. She cursed the fate that had made her the instrument of destruction for those she loved: Lan Ying, Xiao, and now Xing. The sun had already set when Zhang Hong and Fengfeng came to find her.

'Don't blame yourself, Elder Sister,' pleaded Fengfeng. 'Come back to us. We need you.'

'I cannot protect you. I was wrong to try,' she muttered. 'It would have been better if I had never come here. Leave me. Please.'

The tall Shanghai girl had been watching her silently. Her voice, when she spoke, was brittle and cold: 'Xing would not agree. He looked up to you. Do you think he would be impressed if you were to give up on us now we've had a setback?'

'A setback? Is that what you call it? Xing's dead, Zhang Hong. Murdered. Because of me.'

'And the rest of us?'

'You lead them, Zhang Hong. You did before. You don't need me. You're tougher than I ever was.'

'That's really what you want me to go back and tell the others?'

'Oh, Zhang Hong, don't you see? I failed you. What more do you want of me?'

Zhang Hong's voice was steely. 'Is the pride you instilled in us so shallow in yourself? Come, Fengfeng, we were mistaken. This woman is just another browbeaten *hei wu lei*. It looks as if we're on our own again.'

Fengfeng tried to plead, but the other girl pulled her roughly away. Ziwei heard her weeping down the path.

She stared into the darkness. Zhang Hong's accusatory tone rang in her ears, and gradually her self-pity turned to shame. Zhang Hong had been right to reprimand her. She felt helpless, but the others were more helpless than her. They needed to believe in her, even though she herself knew there was nothing she could do. It was a savage, savage irony: now she had become their mango, as useless as Technician Li's, which she had displaced. Oh, but Zhang Hong had been clever to play on what remained of her pride. Wearily she made her way back to the hut, where she found the students sitting disconsolately on their bunks. As one, their eyes turned to where she was standing in the doorway.

She did not know what to say.

Zhang Hong stepped towards her. 'Comrade Peng,' she said, 'we were wondering where you were. We have to decide what to do with Xing's effects. Some want to divide them, others say we should send them back to his parents, but that means talking to the Party committee. We thought you might have an idea on what would be best. Another thing, the work roster for tomorrow . . .'

Ziwei found herself involved again in the minutiae of decision-making, dealing one by one with her charges' problems and complaints.

Later, when they were trudging back from the sheep pen after their meal, Zhang Hong came up beside her. 'Thank you,' the girl murmured.

'For what?'

'For coming back to us. I didn't mean what I said earlier. We value you, Ziwei.'

'Thank you in turn,' said Ziwei. 'You're a good psychologist.'

The two women walked silently together.

'It's blacker than it's ever been, isn't it?' said Zhang Hong. 'Worse than before. Gao will continue to persecute us, won't he?'

'Yes,' said Ziwei.

'And there's nothing we can do to stop him, is there?'

'I don't think so. We're effectively his prisoners. It will be difficult when the winter comes.' She paused. 'Not all the others have your strength and will, Zhang Hong. It will be particularly hard on the other girls. They will be – tempted. When you're starved, you become selfish. You have to be to survive.'

Zhang Hong turned to face her, eyebrows knitted. 'Every person for themselves, is that it? You're saying our group will gradually fall apart?'

'It may. I'm sorry. Of course, I'll do all I can to try to prevent that happening. We'll try together,' she added, attempting to take Zhang Hong's hand.

Zhang Hong remained aloof, continuing to observe her. 'And you? In the Laogai, did you give in? Were you selfish?'

Ziwei sighed. She had a vision of Lan Ying and Xiao, then Chen Tao slurping her squirrel stew. 'I – I tried not to be,' she said.

'I will never give in,' said Zhang Hong. Straightening her shoulders, she quickened her pace, and left Ziwei walking slowly behind.

The moon was half visible behind the clouds. It looked sickly and pale, a premonition of the deadly winter that was approaching. Ziwei felt a cold trickle of fear run down her spine.

By the end of November the mountainside was two feet thick in snow. There was no heating in their hut, and Gao did not allow them a stove. The windows froze inside and out, and the cracks in the mud walls let in snow as well as wind. They tried as best they could to sleep, wearing all their clothes, as well as their greatcoats and fur hats, and in the morning they had to break several inches of ice before they could reach the remains of their soup. Lao Meng, the boy who earlier in the year Ziwei had saved, was the first to die, of pneumonia, weakened by malnutrition, but others followed, including the astrophysicist, Xiao Pan. His friend, Lei Qingjiang, carved a headstone for him, noting all his academic qualifications. Next morning, when they woke, they found that Lei's bunk was empty. They found him stretched out on his friend's grave, covered with a blanket of snow. They buried him with Pan. After that, there were no more headstones.

None of the girls died, and there was an obvious reason for that. When the temperature fell to minus ten degrees centigrade, the farmers from the village began to call, with rice cakes and cornbread under their thick padded coats. The girls were resistant at first, and even a few fights broke out between the boys and the farmers, but by

December, when the temperature regularly reached minus thirty and they spent all day huddled together listlessly for warmth, it was accepted practice that the girls would leave the hut after supper, arriving back sheepishly in the morning to share with their comrades the presents they had been given by the farmers. Only Ziwei and Zhang Hong refused to partake, either in the nightly assignations or in the other girls' extra food – even when once little Fengfeng fell on her knees and, weeping, pleaded with them to take at least a *wo-wo-tou*. Zhang Hong had her pride, and Ziwei blamed herself, feeling it was she who had brought down Gao's vengeance upon them. Not that anybody accused her of it. Most thought they had been jinxed by their own rejection of Technician Li.

In January, Zhang Hong came down with a fever. Ziwei, of course, knew the symptoms – the diarrhoea, the headaches, the luminescent eyes. She begged her to take Fengfeng's food, but she brushed it aside weakly. It was not long before she had the listless look that Laogai prisoners called 'the death mask' and was slipping more often into unconsciousness. The gurgling from her lungs also indicated the onset of pneumonia.

For an afternoon, Ziwei sat by her bedside, holding her limp hand.

By evening, she had made her decision. When the girls were shuffling to their feet to trudge down to the village, she joined them. The guard outside laughed, but the remaining male students hardly noticed her absence. They were absorbed in their usual tedious debate, with only a pretence that it was a joke, about the most effective form of suicide.

She asked to be directed to Party Secretary Gao's house.

It was a large, rambling shack, with at least four rooms, and in each were a stove and a *kang*. To Ziwei, it seemed as hot as a greenhouse. Gao was sitting in his underclothes, whittling at an apple. His heavy eyebrows hardly rose. 'I knew you'd come,' he said. 'There's a pan of *congee* on the stove, woman. Fill yourself up first.'

'No,' said Ziwei.

He grinned. 'That hot for it, are you?'

'No, you're not touching me tonight.'

He put down his knife and the apple, and observed her impassively. 'Then why've you come?'

'If you want a woman for your house, there's a price.'

'Go on,' he murmured.

'There's a dying girl in the hut. I want her carried down here by your villagers, wrapped up warm so she doesn't expire of cold on the way down. I want you to give her a bed, hot food and medicine. She'll stay here until she recovers. No, she'll stay longer than that. She'll be my companion, at least until the weather gets warmer, so I can look after her.'

'What if she dies?'

'Then you get nothing. I won't agree to be your woman unless she survives.'

He began to cut the apple into quarters. 'All right,' he said.

'That's not all.'

'Go on.'

'You give an order that full working rations be restored to the other students. You'll show me how much you have in the granary and the village stores, and I'll decide how much they get to eat.'

'It's the committee that fixes winter rations.'

'I decide how much, and that goes for the spring and the rest of the year as well. From now on they eat as well as the villagers.'

'Is that it?'

'No. There's more. The students are to be moved to proper heated accommodation. Until you can fix up a house where they can live together, you can billet them with families, but they leave that draughty goat shed tonight.'

'All right,' he said. 'Anything else?'

'No, those are my conditions.'

His lips curled into their wide, gap-toothed smile. Suddenly he slapped the table. 'For God's sake, woman, take off that fur hat and coat. You make me cold just looking at you. And eat the *congee*, and anything else you can find. It'll take me time to organise everything.'

'Bring that girl down now. Or there's no deal.'

He raised his hands. 'I'm going. I'm going.' Chuckling, he lifted his heavy body from his seat. 'Women!' he said. 'We haven't started our arrangement yet and she's hen-pecking me already.'

Whistling to himself, he picked up his sheepskin and put on his snowboots. His step was jaunty as he half danced towards the heavy padded curtain that covered the door to the outside. Without another glance at her, he walked into the night, and soon Ziwei heard him banging on doors and shouting orders.

She slumped on to a stool, and put her head into her hands, but she could not resist the temptation and, after a moment, with scrabbling fingers, she lifted the heavy pan of *congee* from the stove and poured some into a bowl. She shovelled the contents into her mouth and licked the bowl clean. Then she did the same again, and again.

Afterwards her blank eyes moved slowly around the room, from the bare wooden beams supporting the thatched ceiling to the polished mud floor, from the cupboard to the shelves stacked with canned meat and fruit, from the stove to the rack on the wall where Gao kept his hunting rifle. In pride of place above the *kang* hung a portrait of Mao Tse-tung, surrounded by stiff portraits of Gao's parents and grandparents.

It was an ordinary peasant's cottage, cleaner and more comfortable than most, perhaps, but for Ziwei it was more forbidding than the worst solitary cell she had experienced in the Laogai. That afternoon she had realised the consequence of the decision she had taken, but now she accepted the crushing reality: that this would be her home for the rest of her life.

15

Wild Geese at Loushan Pass

Cultural Revolution, Iron Man's Glade, Black Hills: 1975–7

Struggling to make sense of the contradictory course of the Cultural Revolution, Ziwei sometimes felt that she had stumbled into the pages of *Alice* – but her childhood reading had not prepared her for anything as surreal as the counter-currents in Mao's Looking Glass world. Here Tweedledum *purged* Tweedledee, Humpty Dumpty fell off the wall and was put together again, composing riddles couched in political double-talk, and the Jabberwocky that stalked China was dangerously unpredictable.

In 1971 they discovered that Chairman Mao's 'closest comrade in arms', Marshal Lin Biao, had been a traitor all along. In Iron Man's Glade, they fearfully removed the former hero's portrait from their homes and tore fading posters off the village noticeboard that praised 'Mao's chosen successor', replacing them with new ones that attacked the reinvented monster's 'bourgeois revisionism'. Two years later they found out that the United States was not in fact the Great Aggressor: on the contrary it was their ally against Soviet Russia, which was no longer their 'kindly elder brother' as it had remained, at least in propaganda terms, these many years, but now, suddenly, was more imperialist than the Americans. Ziwei who, at Gao's insistence, had taken over the political classes in the village, had a complicated three hours trying to explain to the farmers why the Great Helmsman's meeting with President Nixon had been a revolutionary proletarian action.

She was having a similar problem today because Deng Xiaoping, the former Party secretary, who had been struggled and imprisoned as a 'pseudo Khrushchev' and 'capitalist roader' of the worst possible kind, had now been restored to all his old titles and was running the economy.

'Does that mean Liu Shaoqi's coming back too?' asked old Heng Ye, still referred to as the cobbler, although he hadn't mended a pair of shoes in twenty years. Some of the younger villagers, squatting at Ziwei's feet in the outhouse that they still called 'the struggle hall', from the brief period when the Red Guards had descended on the hamlet, tittered loudly.

'No,' explained Ziwei, patiently. 'Liu Shaoqi, if he's still alive, is still the worst of all capitalist roaders and pseudo-Khrushchevs and, what's more, he's a closet Confucian. So was Lin Biao, by the way, as I've already explained.'

'Oh, yes, I remember now,' He stroked his long white beard, clearly confused. 'I'm sorry, but I still don't understand. I thought this Deng was once as bad as Liu, and Lin Biao was the one who put them both in gaol. Or is my memory playing tricks again?'

Ziwei was exasperated. Little Yanqing was pulling at her hand, demanding attention, and she was desperate to end this session or she would not have time to take the clay-baked chicken off the fire before Gao returned from his Party conference in Shishan, demanding his supper. Looking at the blank, leathery faces gazing up at her, she knew that there was nobody who could help her. 'It's like this,' she said, realising that she was skirting massive, and possibly dangerous, political error. 'Everybody thought Deng Xiaoping was Chairman Mao's enemy when he was, in fact, his friend, in the same way everybody thought Lin Biao was Mao's friend when he was actually stabbing him in the back.'

She wiped Yanqing's face with her sleeve and gave her a chalk so she could draw on the blackboard. With a few more slogans and a rousing song, she thought, she might just be able to end this session. 'Now, are there any more questions before we go for our dinners?'

A Shanghainese voice drawled from the back. 'so you don't think, then, that this new 'Criticise Confucius, Criticise Lin Biao Campaign' is a veiled attack on Deng Xiaoping's conservative policies by the more radical elements gathered around Jiang Qing?'

She spotted the grinning face of Zhang Hong, who was leaning against the doorjamb, chewing a cornstalk. Ziwei felt a flush of affection. She hadn't seen her friend since the planting season. At the same time, she was irritated by Zhang Hong's mischievous question, wondering how she could possibly explain such a heretical concept, even though it was almost certainly the Machiavellian reality, to her simplistic audience – but she need not have worried. All the heads were turned towards the door, smiling and nodding at the new arrival, and laughing as Zhang Hong picked up Yanqing and kissed her, while the little girl, who had propelled herself from the blackboard as soon as she heard her auntie's voice, noisily demanded a present.

Ziwei clapped her hands. 'Since we are honoured by the presence of Comrade Zhang of the Student Volunteers Platoon,' she called, over the hubbub, 'perhaps we can ask her to sing one of her revolutionary songs?'

Zhang Hong made a face at her, but put Yanqing back on the ground, still holding her hand, then flung her plaits over her shoulders and, in her clear, strong voice, began to sing Mao Tse-tung's poem, 'Loushan Pass', adapted to an old folk melody:

'Cold is the west wind;
Far in the frosty air the wild geese call in the morning moonlight,
In the morning moonlight
The clatter of horses' hooves rings sharp,
And the bugle's note is muted.'

The farmers nodded silently, and a few tapped the rhythm as they listened to the haunting song of exile, endurance and rebellion.

'Do not say that the strong pass is guarded with iron.
This very day in one step we shall pass its summit,
We shall pass its summit!
There the hills are blue like the sea,
And the dying sun like blood.'

Ziwei smiled affectionately, as she clapped with the others. Zhang Hong had filled out after several years of healthy diet, and despite the sun-lashing and the weather-beating that had hardened her, her skin retained a pink, youthful glow. She was no longer the gaunt beauty Ziwei had first encountered when she came to Iron Man's Glade.

'How's it going in the fields?' she asked her, as they walked back towards her house. Little Yanqing was running ahead with the straw doll Zhang Hong had made for her, showing it to every passer-by.

'It's hard work, but we're getting there. The new lot are pulling their weight at last. In fact, they think they're veterans like us. Your vegetable terraces are thriving. They climb right up the hillside to the crags. Two of the aeronautical students are designing a water-wheel to get irrigation to the upper slopes.'

'That's wonderful,' said Ziwei. 'And how are all my old friends? Have you seen anything of Fengfeng, since . . . ?'

'Zhang Hong shook her head. 'No, I don't think the pig farmer she married welcomes our visits, and she herself – I wouldn't say she's ashamed but . . .'

'You can say it,' said Ziwei, 'because it's true. Poor Fengfeng. I feel for her.' She gave Zhang Hong a sharp glance. 'And how are you coping?'

'Me? I'm fine. Why do you ask?'

'You ended our political session on a sombre note. That's a sad song – or I find it so. You're usually more upbeat.'

Zhang Hong smiled. 'You never stop worrying about us, do you? That's why we all love you. Did you know that the young ones have started to call you Mother Peng? I tell them never to say that to your face.'

'Why ever not? I *am* a mother now, and I certainly feel old.'

'You're not old,' said Zhang Hong. 'None of us is,' she added bitterly.

'There. I'm right. Something is troubling you.'

Zhang Hong frowned. 'Well, if you want to know, I've been thinking more and more of home recently. Maybe – maybe there's an end in sight.'

'Really? It seems uncertain to me. Deng comes back. Now there's this new campaign to get rid of him again. Isn't it just the wheel turning? Black is white. White is black. What's new?'

Zhang Hong's pale grey eyes had hardened to glittering stone. She clutched Ziwei's arm, and leant close to whisper in her ear: 'Mao's dying. That's what's new.'

Ziwei felt a shiver down her spine. Nobody was in earshot but she, too, found herself whispering; 'What on earth makes you say that?'

'When was the last time you saw a recent picture of him in the paper? A year ago? Two? And do you remember how decrepit he looked? You think the old Mao would have brought an enemy like Deng back? But he had no choice because Zhou Enlai's ill too. Never leaves hospital. Somebody has to keep this country running, and Yao Wenyuan, Zhang Chunqiao, Wang Hongwen and the other fanatics around Jiang Qing can't do it. All the Red Queen knows about is perpetual revolution, and probably even Mao realises we couldn't survive another 1966.'

'Zhang Hong!' gasped Ziwei, looking right and left to see if anybody had heard her. But her friend carried on regardless.

'Deng's a threat to all of them. Don't you see? He talks sense not ideology. And he knows how tired we are of politics. This isn't just another campaign, Ziwei. It's a succession crisis. It's about who's going to take power when the old man's dead.'

'Zhang Hong, be careful whom you say that to.' She shook her head. 'How you've changed.'

'I've grown up. You helped me. I'm not the indoctrinated Red Guard any more and,' she added, 'I'm not going to waste my life stuck up a mountain with peasants.'

Immediately the words were out of her mouth, her eyes widened with alarm. 'Oh, Ziwei, I'm sorry. I didn't mean to say anything to hurt you. I know your situation is different from ours.'

'That I'm married to a peasant with a peasant's child, and as a released Laogai prisoner I'll never be allowed to leave here?' She spoke coldly but, after a moment, she smiled, and touched Zhang Hong's cheek. 'It's all right. I've accepted it. Long ago. Old Gao's not as brutish as he once was. He'll do as I tell him usually. And I have a daughter, a beautiful daughter. Amazing how beautiful, when you consider who her father is. She's my world now.' She turned a bright face to the younger woman. 'That doesn't mean you shouldn't hope for something different, and you may be right, the people are tired and change might be in the air. Who knows?' She sighed. 'Please, please, go on hoping that one day you'll find yourself back in Shanghai so you can finish your studies at Fudan. That's where you were, wasn't it? I love Fudan. Oh, how I remember those beautiful French parasols and camphoras shading the Swallow Garden in summer. There was one old tree where you could kneel down and make a wish. I used to—'

Zhang Hong sprang back, astonished. 'You know the Fudan University campus? I – I thought you . . .'

Ziwei laughed merrily. 'You thought I was a common-or-garden prostitute?'

Zhang Hong blushed, but nodded.

'Well, I wasn't – or not until recently. No, that's unfair. Gao loves me, in his way. I shouldn't be bitter. Anyway, as you know, there was no other choice.'

Flustered, Zhang Hong hung her head. 'Your – your sacrifice for us . . . None of us can ever forget—'

'Please.' Ziwei embraced her. 'I've done a lot of things I'm ashamed of, but that was one decision I'll never regret. Seeing you, as you are now, healthy, happy, like a younger sister to me, makes it worthwhile, and I wouldn't have Yanqing otherwise, would I? There really is no point in worrying about what might have been. Anyway, I was about to tell you the story of my life, mundane as it was. You see, I wasn't what they accused me of being. Once upon a time, long ago, I was a little girl who grew up at Fudan. I wasn't a student. My father was a philosophy professor and my mother was a professor of English, and they were very happy times.'

'Your mother was a professor of English?' Zhang Hong was more stunned than ever.

'Oh, you wouldn't have known her. She passed away at about the same time I was taken to the Laogai. I doubt they even remember her now at Fudan, with all these worker-peasant-soldiers running the place, but in her day she was considered China's expert on sixteenth-century English prose and poetry – Shakespeare, Marlowe, Milton, Marvell . . .'

'What was her name?' Zhang Hong was staring at her.

'Yu Fu-kuei.'

Zhang Hong gasped, and ran a hand over her forehead.

'Whatever's the matter?' Ziwei asked.

'Auntie, Auntie, what's wrong?' Yanqing had returned. She was clutching her mother's tunic and gazing at Zhang Hong with big, worried eyes.

Zhang Hong made an effort to smile, and ruffled the little girl's pink bow. 'Nothing. I'm fine,' she said. 'Just a little tired, perhaps, after the planting. Nothing that should worry a sweet little thing like you. What a pretty girl you are.'

Yanqing preened, cheered by the compliment she took as her due. 'Auntie, that song you sang, was it about me?'

Zhang Hong laughed, despite her odd mood. 'Why should you think it was about you, you funny creature?'

'Because you sang about wild geese,' said the little girl. 'That's what my name means, doesn't it, Mummy? A *yanqing*'s a kind of wild goose, isn't it?'

'That's right, darling. I named you after the flocks of geese that were flying over the plains on the day you were born.' Ziwei felt a momentary pang. She had never forgotten the windy morning on which she had climbed to the old outcrop near the goat shed with the then unnamed Yanqing on her back, and how she had sat there, seeing the bleakness of her life unfolding before her. She had so nearly taken that one easy step into the void, as Technician Li had done a year before, but she had heard a faint honk in the sky and seen the skein of geese flying towards the south. Their beauty had moved her, and brought her back from the brink; the madness had gone, and she had held the tiny infant to her cheek and wept. Later she had raised her eyes to the fleeting grey clouds, and told herself that whatever hardship, whatever exile, whatever suffering was her fate, she would endure, so that one day her baby would grow up free, unlike her mother and grandparents, but like the birds now disappearing into the mist. And she remembered how later that evening, when Gao had returned drunk, she had stood up to his abuse, though he hit her, and she had pressed the point of the kitchen knife into his throat, and told him her daughter's name, and made him swear that he would never lay hands on either of them ever again. 'Yes, darling,' she said now. 'You're my little wild goose, and one day you will fly with silver wings . . .'

'. . . to the ends of the earth,' finished Yanqing, contentedly.

'I'm sorry, Ziwei, I have to go.'

'Oh, no, Zhang Hong, so soon? You've been working too hard. Look at you. You're suddenly so pale. I'm worried about you. Stay for dinner. Gao won't mind. Actually, I don't care if he does. He'll probably have been drinking in the truck coming up the mountain and will collapse into his bed as soon as he gets—'

'No, I can't,' said Zhang Hong. Ziwei saw that her hands were trembling. 'The others, they're expecting me back. We have a meeting.'

'Well, make sure you don't say any of those things you've been saying to me.'

'No, I'll be careful. Sorry, but I do have to go. Goodbye, Yanqing. Be good and help your mother.'

'Goodbye, Auntie. Thank you for the present and for singing about me.'

How very strange, thought Ziwei, as she watched the young woman hurry away. Her nerviness probably had something to do with this new political campaign, she mused, turning people's lives upside-down again, and exciting them to foolishness. When would it ever end?

She sighed, and clutched Yanqing's hand tighter. She had other things to worry about. She had enjoyed her free week while Gao was away at his Party meeting, although that had probably been about the new campaign too, and he would arrive back not just drunk but stirred up to inflict new mayhem on his fellow villagers if he could see an advantage for himself in doing so. He was tamer now, but it was always a weary battle keeping the brute in him checked. Sometimes being afraid of her was not enough – she might have to go to his bed again. The prospect disgusted her, but it had always been the carrot she had employed when the stick did not work. She would do what she had to do. She would protect her students, protect the village, protect her precious Yanqing. Life would go on.

The new campaign flared into the usual nationwide fury. In Beijing, Deng Xiaoping was purged and sent back to the countryside. In Iron Man's Glade some mean-spirited wretch denounced Heng Ye, the cobbler, for his remarks about Liu Shaoqi, and it took all Ziwei's persuasion and a gift of the old man's chickens to prevent Gao struggling him. The whole episode had upset the octogenarian, however, and he died before the winter was over, but by then everybody's attention was focused on another, bigger funeral in the capital.

Ziwei wept when she saw the black-bordered front page of the *People's Daily*, and the photograph of the beloved prime minister, Zhou Enlai, who had succumbed to cancer. She felt personally bereft, as if a favourite uncle had died – and also fear, because Zhou, through the worst of the Cultural Revolution's excesses, had managed to preserve a modicum of sanity and order and now there was no one left to protect them. That afternoon she had the struggle hall draped in black crêpe, and surprised herself by her passion when she read out the official obituary to the farmers, many of whom were weeping too. Only as she was coming to the end of the tribute did she notice her husband, with one or two of his acolytes, standing in the doorway. He was scowling at her.

As soon as she had finished, he strode into the hall. 'That's enough,' he shouted. 'Everybody home. There'll be no political meeting.'

'What do you mean?' She was astounded. 'We were each going to make our personal statements of appreciation.'

'You've read out the official statement. That's it,' he said. 'Otherwise I'll consider it fomenting counter-revolution. The man's dead. It's a pity, but that's the end of it. There'll be no trouble in my village.'

There were murmurs from some of the farmers, but when they saw

Gao's armed militia outside, they realised there was nothing they could do but obey. Sheepishly, they filed out of the struggle hall. 'Now you,' said Gao. Holding her head high, although she was shaking with rage and incomprehension, Ziwei followed.

'Zhou Enlai was our prime minister. How dare you disrupt our mourning?' she rounded on Gao when, late that night, he returned home. He ignored her and picked up a jug of rice wine from the shelf.

'Answer me!' she screamed.

He looked at her with his piggy eyes, and she saw he was drunk already. 'Don't question me, woman,' he said, 'or it will be the worse for you. Wife or no wife, I'll not abide counter-revolution in my household.'

'What counter-revolution?' she cried. 'Why do you have your militia picketing the village? We were paying our respects to a great leader.'

His eyes narrowed slyly, and he tapped his breast pocket. 'Some of our other leaders don't seem to think he was,' he sneered. 'I've orders here to preserve the peace. No unruly mob sentiment, it says, so I'm making sure there isn't any. Now, leave me to my drink.'

'Whose orders? Jiang Qing's? Wang Hongwen's? Are the radicals from the old Cultural Revolutionary Committee taking over the state already?' She slammed the door behind her, and wept herself to sleep on her cot.

The news came in gradually over the next month. There had been an unprecedented disturbance in the capital. When the Red Queen – it could have been no other; everybody knew Jiang Qing's hatred for Zhou – vetoed a state memorial service for him, the ordinary people of Beijing, in ones and twos, then in huge crowds, gathered with bouquets and placed them at the foot of the Martyrs' Memorial in Tiananmen Square. Jiang Qing sent her bully-boys in the night to clear the square, but the significance of this protest shook the country.

Gao and his cronies redoubled their militia patrols in Iron Man's Glade, and he used the opportunity to gaol several 'counter-revolutionary sympathisers', as he called them, letting them go only after he had extorted payment from them. Ziwei, who had not spoken to him since that night, kept out of his way, but she remembered Zhang Hong's remark about the people being 'tired'. Oddly, Gao's excessive clamp-down did not dampen her spirits. If stooges of the revolution, like her husband, had been impelled to react as they had to something as natural and spontaneous as public grief over the death of a revered statesmen, it could only mean one thing: they were scared.

And there was another thing: whispered conversations in the market suddenly broke off when she drew near. People were gathering in huddles, poring over the newspapers as they only did during political campaigns: it was as if they were looking for a sign, to explain the sense of uncertainty that now seemed to have overtaken their lives. One day, when she arrived late for her political class, she heard two of the farmers in deep discussion about the Chairman's health. A few months ago, when Zhang Hong had whispered her suspicion that Mao was dying, it had been like heresy, but now it was on everybody's lips.

She sensed that, for most of the villagers, the prospect of change was as much to be feared as welcomed. Those of her own age and younger had not known a world without Mao, and even the older ones had lived with revolution for so long that they could not imagine anything else, but for her the flame of hope she had nursed in her breast after the news of the protests grew into an all-consuming fire, although she was careful not to mention it to anybody.

She wished she could have shared her thoughts with Zhang Hong, but she rarely saw her friend now. It was usually Zhang Hong's deputies who came to the village, while she remained in the students' brick compound that had long ago replaced the goat shed. Ziwei knew the young woman had responsibilities as the students' leader, but she was also saddened because she suspected that Zhang Hong's avoidance of her might have had something to do with the young woman's indiscretions when they last met. She accepted it philosophically because she understood only too well the climate of fear that a political campaign brings in its wake, causing friends to suspect friends. She even persuaded herself it was for the best, if for no other reason than that Gao might have spotted them together and remembered his old grudge that after his marriage to Ziwei the students were no longer his to control – but she missed her, especially now, because there was nobody else she could trust.

When they heard the news that a huge earthquake had destroyed the city of Tangshan, not so very far away, and killed a quarter of a million people, the villagers in Iron Man's Glade saw this as the sign they had been looking for. The awesome catastrophe evoked, even for the most unsuperstitious, the traditional portents that signalled the end of a dynasty. The electrical storms that burst above the mountain peaks in the height of summer appeared that year to be external manifestations of the tension in ordinary people's homes.

Ziwei was not superstitious, but her husband was. She took a secret delight in passing on the rumours that were going from village to village in the Black Hills. 'Did you hear that a cow gave birth to two-headed calves in Six Stones Hamlet?' she asked him, as she served him his breakfast. 'Do you think it means something terrible is going to happen?'

He glared at her, picked up his cap and sidled out of the door.

'Did it really, Mama?' asked Yanqing. 'Can a cow really have two heads?'

'Of course it can't,' she said. 'I was only teasing your father. You mustn't believe old wives' tales.'

Old wives' tales or not, something was about to happen. In her gut she was certain of it.

The problem was she could not decide whether the death of the old man would be the liberation she hoped for, or whether, if Jiang Qing and her like took power, there would be greater purges than there had ever been before.

When Mao actually did die, later that autumn, it seemed at first that her fears rather than her hopes were more likely to be fulfilled. Gao, instead of crumbling at the news, seemed revived by it. He set about the arrangements for the memorial ceremony with furious energy, sending out his militia to make sure that everybody was dressed appropriately in mourning. He ordered a pavilion to be set up in the square on which to place the wreaths he insisted every household prepare. He spent the day closeted with his committee, and when he came home he did not touch his liquor.

On the morning of the memorial ceremony, he reached over the breakfast table, and suddenly twisted Yanqing's cheek in his thick fingers, making her scream. 'What are you doing, you monster?' cried Ziwei, hugging the crying child.

'Monster?' He chuckled. 'Is that what I am to you now? Well, woman, let me tell you what I'm doing. I'm making my daughter weep, as she should be doing on the day we say farewell to our Great Helmsman. I'll be expecting tears from you too. I'll be looking for them when I make my oration. You're my wife, and from now on you'll behave like one. He was a great man, our leader, and we owe him respect.'

'You disgust me,' she said.

'I'll remember you said that,' he said softly. 'Be careful, wife. There's a new lot coming into power soon, who won't be as forbearing as our chairman's been these past few years. Seems he forgot his own warnings. Remember, in 'sixty-seven, when he told us, "Signs of counter-revolutionary restoration are everywhere, beginning at the top, all the way to the bottom"? Well, those who replace him can't afford to be soft. They're people who think the revolution's run out of steam and needs to get going again. Maybe it's time to root out the evil elements all over.'

'These are your new instructions from the Red Queen, are they?'

He rose to his feet and straightened his tunic. 'Be a wife and mother. That's all I ask,' he said. 'Then I'll continue to protect you, won't I? And maybe also your precious students – if you behave.' He leant over to ruffle Yanqing's hair. She shied away from him, pressing her face into her mother's breast. Ziwei felt tears of anger welling in her eyes. 'There, you're crying at last,' he said, with a smile. 'It's not so difficult, is it?'

Gao got the mourning he desired. The presence of his militia round the square encouraged at least a pretence of weeping, and Ziwei, who was watching with a stony face, saw many pinching themselves to induce watering eyes – but the hysteria Gao had generated was such that most villagers were carried away by genuine emotion, although whether they were sobbing for Mao or because his death had created a vacuum in which they could no longer see their future, she could not tell. As Gao droned on with his tribute, the wail from the crowd rose in crescendo and echoed in the crags.

Over the following days, the atmosphere of unease intensified. People began to watch each other, competing to keep up their semblance of grief, if only for the benefit of Gao's men loitering on the street corners.

It got too much for Ziwei. One afternoon, with Yanqing following her and a bundle of provisions on her back, she climbed the old goat track to the students' compound, convinced that, if not all the students, at least her old friends, like Zhang Hong, must be as relieved by the old man's death as she was – but although everybody was glad to see her and welcomed her warmly, she soon realised they were more preoccupied than the villagers. Zhang Hong was cold and reserved. Finally, on Ziwei's urging, she agreed to have a cigarette with her on the outcrop, overlooking the plain, while Yanqing chased butterflies on the path. Her friend's views were the opposite of what Ziwei had expected.

'So what if the old man's gone? Jiang Qing's still in control. She saw Deng off and now she's got the power to turn the whole country into one of her damned revolutionary operas. It'll be more of the same, Ziwei.'

'That's what my husband believes. He's terrorising the village already,' said Ziwei, glumly.

'Well, there you go,' said Zhang Hong. Angrily, she threw her cigarette butt over the precipice. There was a catch in her voice when she continued. 'I was stupid enough to see a ticket home – but now we'll never leave this place. Never.' Her face hardened and she looked at her watch. 'I haven't time to talk to you. I've got to organise a party of volunteers to help me fix the irrigation ditches. I've got to go.'

'Won't you stay and smoke just one more cigarette with me – for old times' sake?' asked Ziwei. She was startled when she saw Zhang Hong's face. It was the same mask of hatred that she had shown Technician Li on the night the other students had rejected them.

'No, you be mother to the others. I'm too busy. I have to go.'

Ziwei trudged slowly down the path back to the village with Yanqing, wondering what she could possibly have said or done to make Zhang Hong turn against her. The initial elation she had felt at Mao's death had vanished. If somebody as politically astute as Zhang Hong was depressed, there seemed little hope – but now that was overshadowed by something even more painful: she had confirmed that she had lost her friend.

Four days later, Ziwei was woken by shouting. She recognised the voice. It was one of Gao's committee members, who had been in Shishan, delivering some of the commune's vegetable crop. Pulling her padded jacket over her shoulders, she ran out of the house in time to see him leap off the truck before it had started to negotiate the final ascent to the village. He was running towards the village noticeboard on the edge of the square, waving a newspaper and shouting, 'They're overthrown! They're overthrown!'

Ziwei clustered with the others and read the headlines. For a moment, she felt dizzy – the news was too momentous to comprehend, but there it was, in bold banner characters: 'People's Government Restored'.

The smaller characters told the story. She found herself reading them over and over to those too illiterate to make them out: there had been a *coup d'état* in the capital. Jiang Qing and the other members of the Gang of Four, as her clique was now called, had been arrested. Hua Guofeng had established a new Politburo, consisting in the main of pre-1966 conservatives, like Li Xiannian, Ye Jianying and Chen Yun.

'What's going on here?' She heard her husband's angry bark. He had come from his office with three of his militia.

She tore down the sheet from the noticeboard and thrust it into his hands. Irritated, he pulled his glasses from his top pocket and began to read. Then she had the satisfaction of seeing his face go ashen and the paper fall from his grasp. He turned to his militiamen, as if for support, but one had picked up the newspaper and was reading the headlines. He backed away.

Gao was swaying. He had placed one hand on his temple. His gaze was confused, unfocused. 'I must call the committee,' he muttered. 'We must discuss this new development.'

Now all the villagers were moving away from him. The ring around him widened. Ziwei stepped into it. 'Come home, husband, you're not looking well,' she said.

'I do have – a headache,' he said.

She put him to bed and went back to join the celebrations that were starting in the square. When she came into his room in the evening with a bowl of soup, he turned his face to the wall.

The next morning's headline made Ziwei's heart flutter, and she had to clutch the table to steady herself. Deng Xiaoping had been called back to Beijing. It was only then that she became truly aware of the unbelievable implications.

With the moderates back in government, the Cultural Revolution was over.

When she went into Gao's room to tell him the news, she found that he had had a stroke in the night. He was conscious – his eyes were rolling – but he could not move. The doctor, when he arrived that evening from Shishan, said he would probably live but that he was unlikely to recover the use of his limbs or his speech.

It took a full year for all the paperwork to be completed. Some of the students, whose families were better connected to the new regime, received earlier dispensations, and left the village quietly, but most of the young volunteers, including Zhang Hong, had no contacts on high, and waited through the long months, alternating hope and despair. The harvest had been collected, fittingly a good one, before the rest of the students' cases were reviewed.

For some months now, Ziwei had been busy in her role of acting Party secretary. A delegation from the village had come to her house when it became clear that her husband would never recover. She had tried to refuse the position. She explained that she had a sick husband and a child to look after, and if her husband was indeed to be prosecuted – there were rumours that the government would be investigating village heads for corrupt practices during the 'years of turmoil' – she would have to defend him because he was incapable of walking, let alone talking; besides, everybody knew she was a *hei wu lei* and a released felon, and therefore quite unsuitable for a Party post. They told her that that sort of thing didn't matter any more; it had been her ideas that had brought prosperity to the village in the preceding years, working behind the scenes and manipulating Gao, and if she turned her back on them they would not know what to do.

So Ziwei found herself in the uncomfortable position of sitting next to the still-estranged Zhang Hong on the night before the students were to depart. Ziwei had arranged for the threshing square to be tented over with matting so they could combine the traditional harvest festival with the village's farewell to the volunteers. Naturally she was chairing the event, and Zhang Hong, as leader of the students, was guest of honour on her right.

They had eaten the suckling pig, roasted in the middle of the tent, as well as the huge starting plate of vegetables and meats, fashioned, somewhat ironically, Ziwei thought, into a portrait of the Great Helmsman. Even though most people believed that it was really Deng Xiaoping calling the shots, Hua Guofeng was still the titular head of government and he had instructed that veneration for the deceased great leader be strictly maintained – but Ziwei was amused by the gusto with which the students, and even some of the younger villagers, tore away the chicken and pork slices that constituted Mao's face, and munched them, ironically calling quotations from his *Little Red Book* as they did so. Then they set to on the cabbage and carrot that constituted his tunic and cap.

She hated making speeches – she lacked the politician's ability to please all parties – and she found herself in a tangle of her own making when she tried, on the one hand, to praise the villagers for bringing in a record harvest, on the other to give the tribute that she felt was the students' due, because it had been their inspiration and effort that had assisted the outcome; not that this implied, she was at pains to point out, that she was not entirely confident that the farmers on their own would not do just as well next year. By this stage she had come out in a sweat.

She felt easier when it came to thanking the students for their individual contributions, telling them how much they would be missed and wishing them good fortune as they started new lives in their hometowns. She was careful to eulogise Zhang Hong, who had led them through good times and bad, and was relieved to see several villagers nod their agreement.

To finish, she asked everybody to remember Xing Min, Xiao Pan, Lao Meng, Lei Qingjiang and all the other boys and girls who had laid down their lives for the prosperity of the village. 'We'll be losing many friends when the trucks go off tomorrow,' she said, 'but these others will remain. I promise – I swear – that we will look after their graves, for they are our family now. They have earned with their blood the right to be known as the children of Iron Man's Glade. They are our children, our kinsmen. They are . . .' She came to a mumbling stop, and sat down abruptly, embarrassed by the tears welling in her eyes.

The students were the first to drum on the tables, but most of the villagers followed suit, and this was before they started to cheer. It seemed to go on for ever, and Ziwei sat through it, mouth open, stunned, humbled and amazed that these people should be manifesting such warmth to *her*.

Zhang Hong stood up and raised a hand. Slowly the applause subsided. Her eyes were glittering in her solemn face as she turned to Ziwei. She waited until she had everybody's attention.

'Comrade Peng Ziwei has made a moving speech that has expressed much that is in our hearts.' Ziwei had a sinking feeling in her stomach:

Zhang Hong was using the Red Guard's declamatory pitch that she had heard on that first night in the sheep pen. 'Comrade Peng Ziwei has been generous with her thanks. We honour her that she has mentioned those friends and comrades who are no longer with us today, acknowledging their sacrifice.' She paused and her cold eyes ranged over the audience. 'But Comrade Peng has not been entirely honest or correct when she was making her tributes, and for that we must criticise her.'

There were angry murmurs, and one or two of her fellow students stood up, as if to challenge her – but Zhang Hong raised her hand again to silence them.

'She has not once mentioned the name of the person who has been most responsible for our welfare, the one person above all others whom we must thank for bringing us to where we are today, the one person whose courage, steadfastness, sacrifice, generosity, intelligence, skill, endurance and love have touched every person in this assembly, and brought us through terrible years of suffering without harm. I would go so far as to say that without this person to help us when we needed it, many of us would not be alive today, including myself.' She was now looking directly at Ziwei, and those closest suddenly realised that the fierce glitter in her eyes was tears. 'Of course, Ziwei, I am talking about you.'

There was a roar of approval, and more table-beating, but again Zhang Hong held up her hand.

'We came here, ignorant boys and girls from the city, to learn from the wisdom of the peasant classes, and over the years, it is true, our lives have been transformed by what you villagers have taught us. Working with the good people of Iron Man's Glade in the fields, through all weathers and calamities, we now have an understanding of the hardships that are your daily existence, and we have learnt to adapt and even to turn into farmers like yourselves. Over the years we have become friends, and we will miss all of you when we return to our cities, thinking of our days here with nostalgia.'

This prompted a clap from the villagers. Zhang Hong waited before continuing.

'But, comrades, that is only part of the story. I started my words by accusing Comrade Peng of dishonesty, so I must be honest myself. We have all seen and experienced, over these last ten years, extraordinary contradictions. I might say that the very reason we came here was part of a contradiction, for such, with hindsight, was the whole social experiment that thrust city dwellers into your lives, in the belief that opposites could mix. That the experiment did not work at the beginning is something we tend to overlook today, although the graves on the hillside are mute witnesses to the truth of what I'm saying. I largely blame ourselves – yes, we students who, full of revolutionary ardour, believed we could perform miracles, and expected you to accommodate our fantasies, not realising that our arrogance and strident ignorance, far from binding you to us, repelled you. I was perhaps the most arrogant, the most ignorant of all who came here with such unrealistic expectations, the most insufferable and vain. Why should you have helped us, when such was our pride and conceit that our every attitude suggested we knew it all already?

'Well, you responded in kind. Our innocence and comparative wealth proved a terrible temptation, and you are human and flawed in your way as we are in ours. You starved us for gain. And that was another lesson, if only we had had the wit to understand it. Adversity brings out the worst in people, not the best. It is uncomfortable to dwell on these truths, and I don't wish to make what is a sad occasion sadder by recalling the evils of those early days – but if we don't face up to our mistakes, how can we progress?

'The truth was that the social experiment was a disaster. We despised you while praising you. You preyed on us while pretending to help us. And we began to die.'

There was silence now in the audience, and many angry frowns, but Zhang Hong startled everybody by opening her arms wide, as if in a gesture of surrender or a plea for mercy.

'I'm not criticising you. If anything, this is a self-criticism, for we brought it down on ourselves. Oh, we can blame the political environment, the mistakes of our elders, the madness that was then overtaking our country, but that will not do – because ultimately, and this is perhaps the most valuable lesson we have learnt, we are responsible for our own actions. I, Zhang Hong, the conceited Red Guard, am responsible for my own actions and my own mistakes, and somehow, over whatever years remain to me, I must learn to live with myself, for I did terrible things.

'But we were lucky in Iron Man's Glade, probably uniquely in this country,' her piercing voice had almost reached screaming pitch, 'because we were saved from our mistakes – in my case undeservedly

– and yes, we can be proud, because the social experiment was ultimately a success. We did become a single community, peasants working harmoniously with city folk. And how did it happen? And why? It was because we were given a helping hand when we had all but despaired. This woman – this great woman, whom the world still calls a released convict, a bad element, a counter-revolutionary – chose to sacrifice herself for all of us, peasants and students, although many of us had done her nothing but harm.'

She turned to Ziwei. Her body was poised, her arm outstretched. She had probably prepared another rhetorical gesture, but her shoulders began to shake, and she murmured, 'I'm sorry – I can't go on. Thank you, Ziwei. Thank you – and forgive me.' Wiping her eyes, she stumbled out of the tent.

There was desultory applause, but most of the audience were confused about whether they had been insulted or praised, and were muttering together, even as they clapped.

Ziwei stood up. 'We will continue the celebrations. There is food and drink for all. I will return in a moment – but please excuse me, while I . . .'

Nodding and smiling at the bewildered faces gaping after her, she hurried after Zhang Hong. She found her leaning against the wall of the struggle hall, smoking. She did not look up, but stared defiantly at the cliffs that reached to the moonlit clouds.

'Well,' said Ziwei, 'I don't think anybody was expecting a speech quite like that. It was well delivered, I can say that for it. And it was embarrassingly flattering about me.'

'At least for once I was honest and sincere.' Zhang Hong pronounced the words scornfully. 'I've extracted enough self-confessions out of others in my time. It's about time I took the medicine myself.'

'Weren't you still being a little accusing? Not that it matters much. Thankfully, most of what you said went right over our dear farmers' heads. You're still the Shanghai intellectual, it seems, despite all these years pulling grain.'

Zhang Hong lowered her eyes to face her. They glinted in the moonlight. 'Don't you see, Ziwei? I was making my apology to you. I was asking for your understanding, not theirs.'

'Don't be ridiculous. If you're still worrying about all that struggling you and Li subjected me to in the goat shed, forget it. It was water off a duck's back after the Laogai. I knew exactly why you were doing it too. It wasn't personal. Anyway, it was years ago, and since then you've become my dearest friend. And if you're referring to these last months of . . . estrangement, well, I can't say I understand it, but I do know things have been difficult for you, and – it doesn't matter. What's important is we've found each other again, before it's too late, and we part friends.'

'Ziwei?' The voice was wooden. 'There's something else I've never dared tell you. I – I wanted to. I even tried to once or twice, but I was too cowardly. I was thinking of writing to you after I left, but I knew I'd never be able to look myself in the mirror again unless I confronted you face to face.' She had become so stiff that she was almost standing to attention. 'It's about your mother.'

'My mother?' Ziwei laughed. 'What on earth has she to do with anything? She died when you were still in high school.'

'She didn't.' It came out as a hoarse whisper. 'She taught me English literature in my first year at Fudan. I was her prize pupil.'

'You must be mistaken,' Ziwei gasped. She felt a chill run down her spine. 'You must be thinking of someone else.'

'One good arm. Crippled. Sharp eyes. Tongue like a whiplash. Expert on Shakespeare and Milton. No, Ziwei, I'm talking about your mother, Professor Yu Fu-kuei.'

'That – can't be. Please, stop this – this joke, or whatever it is. It's not funny. She died in 1963. After I was arrested, the Second Department took her away and shot her. She was killed for the same reason I was put in the Laogai, although as far as the world knows, she probably just disappeared and they hid the evidence, as they fabricated my past so I would be forgotten too.' Her voice was hard now, and angry. 'I'm telling you all this to show you how offensive I find whatever cruel game you're playing – and I'll ask you this just once. Drop it – or, by heaven, we won't be friends in the future.'

'I swear to you I'm not lying. I didn't know she was your mother until you told me you were raised in Fudan University. I haven't a clue about the Second Department. They're – they're spies, aren't they? But if you think they or anybody else shot her, you're wrong, because it was she who was my tutor in Fudan when I went up in 1965. She treated me kindly, said I reminded her of her dead daughter.' She put her head in her hands. 'She must have been talking about you. She loved me because she thought I was like you, and – and—' Her voice cracked into a long drawn-out moan. 'I betrayed her. My best friend's mother. How can I forgive myself?' Her back slid down the wall, and her head bowed over her knee as she sobbed.

It took Ziwei a long time to regain her self-control. Then she, too, squatted with her back to the wall. She lit two cigarettes and gave one to Zhang Hong. 'Smoke this,' she said. 'Calm down, then tell me what happened.'

Zhang Hong had loved Shakespeare ever since, at the age of twelve, she had seen a production of *Romeo and Juliet*, performed by a Russian military troupe, which had visited her father's barracks as part of a cultural exchange. She had been angry, however, after taking up her place at Fudan, when she was told she had been assigned as a pupil to Yu Fu-kuei. As the daughter of a veteran Long Marcher, a colonel who held the post of political commissar of a section of the Shanghai garrison, Zhang Hong had felt that her Red credentials might be sullied if she spent time with a woman who was notoriously *hei wu lei*, and what was more, had not even been a formal member of the faculty since the anti-Rightist movement – but her interest was literature, and eventually she had been persuaded that Professor Yu was the only expert in her chosen area of study.

On the first day when she appeared at the professor's tiny, book-filled flat, she had been cold and aloof, but had been chastened when Professor Yu, far from being intimidated, had laughed at her, making her feel small. After only half an hour, through acerbic questioning, the professor had established how little she knew, and in the next half-hour had captivated her with quotations from Shakespeare and Milton, explaining ideas and meanings Zhang Hong had never conceived.

Over the course of that semester, they had become friends. Professor Yu allowed her to borrow any book she liked from her extensive library, and sometimes the tutorials went on late into the evening, and over suppers that Professor Yu cooked for her in her little kitchen.

'You're a bright student, Zhang Hong,' said Professor Yu one evening. 'You're a bit cold and self-centred, but that's the other side of the coin to determination and ambition. You could become the best student I've ever had if you persevere.'

'*Could* become?' asked Zhang Hong.

'You're a proud one.' The professor gave her haughty laugh. 'You still have a long way to go, young lady, but you have the aptitude and the intellect, and one day you might have the heart to be a Shakespearian scholar.'

'The heart?'

'Yes, the heart. Shakespeare writes about human love and passion. His plays are not just about ideas. But you grew up, like my own daughter, in a world where politics have monopolised passion. I feel for your generation. In an ideal world there would be a better balance.'

This last remark disturbed Zhang Hong. There was in it implicit criticism, which confused her. 'You have a daughter?' she asked, wanting to change the subject.

The old woman smiled sadly. 'I had a daughter. She'd be a little older than you if she had not passed away.'

'I'm sorry,' said Zhang Hong.

'It's odd how tragedy works,' said Professor Yu. 'The mind can come to terms intellectually with loss, but the heart, like an uncontrollable puppy, still yearns for an object of affection to replace the person who is gone. You are very different from my lost daughter, but your presence in my flat provides me with deep solace, reminding me of somebody dear to me. Oh, I have embarrassed you. I didn't mean to. Put it down to the sentimentality of a lady advanced in years. I assure you it will in no way influence the rigorousness of my tuition.'

She laughed, and Zhang Hong laughed too, but nervously, for again she felt a vague discomfort. Such genteel candour smacked of bourgeois values, but she continued to visit. The tuition was so interesting.

For the same reason, she put aside her worries that her political-study teachers might consider much of what the professor was telling her to be heretical, or that the humanistic values of the Renaissance, in the light of the tenets of Marxism, Leninism and Mao Tse-tung Thought, could be viewed as subtle, individualistic and vaguely subversive. But Professor Yu was adept at drawing parallels. She compared the imagery in Elizabethan pastoral poetry to Mao Tse-tung's verse. The stoicism, praised by philosophers like Montaigne, she compared to the endurance and fortitude of early revolutionary heroes. She even described Shakespeare's history plays as socially progressive works, the common soldiers in *Henry V* revealing the author's love of the proletariat. She said this with a wry smile and a faint twinkle in her weary eyes. Zhang Hong was by now too intoxicated to care, so absorbed was she in the new world of ideas that Professor Yu was opening up for her. She was careful, however, never to mention these out-of-hour studies to her fellow students. She had begun to view the sessions as her secret life.

Meanwhile, Zhang Hong was becoming actively involved in university politics. During the spring of 1966 the students had begun to realise that important events were happening outside their campus. With excitement, they read the increasingly outspoken articles in the *Shanghai Daily*, written by the journalist Yao Wenyuan, which attacked the corruption and revisionism of Rightists in the higher echelons of the Party. It rapidly became clear that the articles had the sanction of Mao Tse-tung himself. They would meet in excited groups to discuss them. She found she was making excuses more often to Professor Yu, and weeks went by when she did not visit her. Academic studies, even those as interesting as hers, seemed unimportant in the context of the threat that the Communist old guard posed to the country.

In the early summer, Zhang Hong was elected by her class to be one of their representatives at the mass rally of students to be held at Tiananmen Square in Beijing on 18 May. It was the first time she had left Shanghai, and it was a thrill to board the train with hundreds of others, and pass through the countryside, waving red flags out of the window. When the farmers in the fields sometimes waved red flags in return, cheers rang down the length of the train.

Nothing had prepared her for the size of the crowd gathered in the square. There must have been at least a million young people from all over the country. She lost all sense of her own identity as, with one voice, the throng chanted over and over, 'Long live Chairman Mao,' and she screamed her devotion as loudly as any of the others. When the moment came and, far away, she saw the beloved figure waving at them from the great rostrum, she found herself weeping with joy. She imagined that a purifying light was coursing through her limbs, and nearly fainted with joy when, over the tinny loudspeakers, she heard his voice exhorting students like herself to rise up and assist him to launch a Great and Glorious Proletarian People's Cultural Revolution. 'To make revolution is no crime,' he told them. 'To rebel is justified. Overthrow the rulers of hell and let the little devils free.'

On the train ride back, as part of their new determination to be Red Guards, she and her companions subjected each other to self-criticism. Hers had not been a savage session. In fact, the young man in charge, a graduate from Jiaotong University, who had also studied English literature, had been kind and humorous, but he identified many of her ideas as reactionary. She had ended up after dark in a top bunk with him. Having taken her virginity – this was the first purge, as he put it, of bourgeois convention – he spent much of the rest of the night, between kisses, attempting to clear her mind of its errors, focusing particularly on her recent education. Shakespeare, he explained, far from being the humanist that Professor Yu had made her believe, had been a paid scribe of the aristocratic classes; his plays were subtle propaganda, designed to entrap the working class into believing that their station in life was to serve kings. In the history and Roman plays, revolutionaries like Bolingbroke on one hand and Brutus on the other were condemned because they overthrew tyrants. 'In Shakespeare,' he said, 'the "time is out of joint" when the natural order is disturbed, but Chairman Mao teaches us that we must destroy order to find freedom and a just society.' When she tried to counter with some of Professor Yu's arguments, he ridiculed her. *Henry V*'s brave soldiers were imperialist cannon fodder. Montaigne's stoicism was the philosophy of slaves. To compare decadent Elizabethan verse with a line of Chairman Mao's poems was an insult. 'Face it, Zhang Hong,' he said, as the dawn light drifted into the compartment, 'your *hei wu lei* teacher has been feeding you poison – but you are very lovely, and I think I should purge you once more to get those pretty ideas out of your head for good.' She allowed him, deliciously, to do so, and when they were finished, she scrambled into her clothes before the students in the other bunks woke. For the rest of the journey, her body glowed with the memory of lovemaking, but her mind was planning vengeance on the woman who had attempted to pervert her mind.

When she returned to Fudan University, she was wearing a Red Guard arm band blessed by the Chairman. She was no longer Zhang Hong the student. That life was over. Now she was an avenging Fury, with a mission from the Great Helmsman himself to smash the Four Olds. And she had one target in particular in mind.

She led the attack on Yu Fu-kuei's apartment. She pressed the professor's head to the table so she could witness through her window the burning of all her books on the enormous bonfire they had lit outside. She placed the dunce's cap on her head and smeared her face with ink from the pot on her writing desk.

Since she was a cripple, they requisitioned a child's play-cart and made her kneel in it, her hands bound behind her back. Zhang Hong walked beside it, shouting accusations as her comrades dragged Yu Fu-kuei through the campus.

'Cow ghost and snake demon, stinking revisionist . . .' She had all the slogans.

They pulled her up the concrete stairs to the English department on the third floor. In the faculty head's study they struggled her for a day, beating her if she raised her head or tried to speak, which she attempted only once, whispering to Zhang Hong, 'Why do you hate me so?' Zhang Hong spat in her face and lashed her with her belt.

The next day they took her to the sports stadium. The whole student body had turned out and every row in the amphitheatre was filled with young men and women, and many of the faculty – those who had not been struggled yet – shouting anti-imperialist slogans. Zhang Hong was holding two Ming vases that Yu Fu-kuei had shown her in her flat, the last remaining items of a once larger collection. It had been during a discussion they were having on beauty and Plato's perfect forms, and the professor had used their slight imperfections as an illustration to prove that if there truly was a perfect form it could only be found in heaven. Zhang Hong now smashed them on the stone slabs, crushed the shards, and made her former tutor kneel on them. Then she led the denunciation. 'Do you confess?' she screamed. 'Do you admit that you were a fifth columnist of the imperialists with a mission to inculcate into students your bourgeois ideas?'

In the afternoon, because Professor Yu had kept stonily silent, refusing to confess, Zhang Hong called for assistance. She stood by, hands on her hips, watching, as two of her male comrades beat the woman with broomsticks.

That night Professor Yu dragged herself to the window of the faculty head's study, where they were still incarcerating her, and threw herself out of it – but she landed in the flowerbed and only broke a leg, her good one. In the three weeks afterwards, while she was in hospital, Zhang Hong came daily with the other Red Guards to criticise her as she lay helpless in bed. When they considered she was recovered enough, they took her back to the stadium. Again Yu Fu-kuei refused to speak, and this time metal-tipped cudgels were brought out.

By lunchtime, she was unconscious, but Zhang Hong gave no order for her comrades to desist. There was something fascinating about observing a fellow human being beaten to death. Thinking of the poison with which the professor had tried to flood her mind, Zhang Hong steeled her heart against mercy . . .

Ziwei sighed and hung her head. During Zhang Hong's monologue she had sat like a stone, registering the details impassively, even of her mother's torture, because she was hoping that the horrific tale would end with the miraculous news that her mother was still alive. Now she felt empty. She supposed it was shock, or some self-protective mechanism. She knew that the grief would hit her soon, as well as anger, and possibly the madness she had resisted for nearly fifteen years. 'Oh, you evil girl,' she said sadly. 'Wouldn't it have been kinder if you'd got on the truck tomorrow and left me in my ignorance?'

'I considered that. It was how I selfishly justified my cowardice in not telling you earlier. I was weak. I tried to persuade myself that if I remained silent I could cling to the friendship between us. You know, it's the only thing that means anything to me in my life here. Not that it did any good. In my shame I found I couldn't face you. That's why I must have appeared cold.' Zhang Hong sounded exhausted. It was as if she were forcing herself to utter each sentence.

'So now you've told me, is your conscience clear? You expect me to sympathise with you? Forgive you?'

'No, Ziwei, there's no salvation for me. I accepted that long ago. Nor is there any point in asking for your forgiveness. It is right that from now on you should hate and despise me, and I deserve nothing less. Ziwei, please believe me, I'm not telling you this to salve my conscience. I would have spared you the knowledge if I could.'

'So why have you decided to torture me now, as you tortured my mother? Is this more of the honesty that you trumpeted in your speech? Your parting gift?'

'No, Ziwei. You told me your mother was dead. I – I couldn't go away without telling you that it wasn't true. I had to break the illusion you've been living under – whatever the cost to myself.'

'You're extraordinary, as well as being despicable. You really think I feel better knowing she died in agony, humiliated and brutalised by you? That she didn't receive what I had at least comforted myself into believing had been a mercifully quick death by a bullet – and that instead she lived on, mourning her daughter and nursing a viper who'd betray her? And murder her all the same?'

Zhang Hong was staring at her. 'No. No, I – I never said we killed her. She was saved. Rescued. Oh, Ziwei. I've misled you. The whole point of my confessing all this was to let you know that when I left Shanghai she'd been rehabilitated and was teaching again at the university. She might still be alive now. You might find her again.'

The hope that flared again was even more painful than the earlier disappointment. If fifteen years in the Laogai had taught her anything, it was that miracles don't happen. Even if earlier, in a moment of weakness, she had indulged the belief that they did, having listened to Zhang Hong tell her how her mother had been cudgelled as she lay unconscious on the ground, she understood now there could be no happy outcome. In those days the Red Guards had been ravening wolves and would never release their prey until they had worried them to death.

'Stop it, Zhang Hong! Stop it! You've already told me you killed her. You can't pour spilt water back into a pot with wishful thinking. Just go, please. I can't take any more.'

'But it's true!'

'How can it be true? Why would anybody rescue her? Who had the power in those days to stand up to the Red Guards?'

'I don't know,' said Zhang Hong. 'A squadron of armed soldiers forced their way into the amphitheatre, and circled your mother on the ground. We were furious and a fight nearly broke out, but one produced a document from the municipal government with your mother's name on it, saying the interrogation was to be transferred to Party Headquarters. They took her away. We protested afterwards, but we never found out why she was being protected. There were rumours that Zhou Enlai had had a hand in it. He was visiting Shanghai at the time, but that seemed nonsensical to me. Who knows? Many incomprehensible things were happening then. I was disappointed, but my comrades had other faculty members they wanted to bring down. Our troop of Red Guards left Fudan shortly afterwards. For the next year, we were involved in all sorts of political activities. We continued to do – terrible things. I – I forgot your mother, but in the summer of 1968, a day or so before we were due to board the train to come here, I went back to Fudan and I saw her.'

'You saw her?' Ziwei stood over the girl, clenching her fists. 'Zhang Hong, if you're lying to me . . .'

'She was in a wheelchair. I suppose that the leg she broke in the fall never mended. She was propelling herself along near the arches while a student walked behind her carrying her textbooks. I'm sure she saw me. She passed right by me, but there was no change in her expression, even when she looked at me. It was as if I didn't exist. The awful thing was that she still had the same ironic smile that I couldn't rub off her face during all the struggling. It's – it's never stopped accusing me . . .'

She broke down completely, throwing herself forward into the mud, her back arched in a paroxysm of anguish as she made low moans, her fists beating the ground. Through her grunts and sniffs, Ziwei heard her gasp, over and over, 'I'm sorry . . . I'm sorry . . .'

Ziwei slumped with her back to the wall of the struggle hall, and folded her arms around her knees. She fumbled for a cigarette, but the packet slipped from her shaking fingers. The moon had broken out from behind the clouds and illuminated the huts. From the tent came the sound of drunken singing. Eventually, Zhang Hong crawled to her knees, sniffing, and wiped the mud from her tunic and her braids. 'I'd better go,' she said.

'No,' said Ziwei, thinking how much she looked like Lan Ying. She had been thinking a lot about Lan Ying and Xiao during the last half-hour. 'The packet's on the ground somewhere. We might as well enjoy the cigarettes. They're Presidents. It's probably our last chance to be alone together.'

They smoked in silence.

'I'll check at Fudan as soon as I get to Shanghai. If she's not there, I'll find her and get word to you,' muttered Zhang Hong.

'Thank you,' said Ziwei. 'I'd appreciate that.'

'Will they allow you to visit?'

'I don't know,' said Ziwei. 'I'll have to apply to the commandant at Tranquil Springs. It may be possible if the commune here vouches for me.'

'Will you – will you see me if you come to Shanghai?'

Ziwei turned and studied her. 'I don't know. I think it will take me some time to forget what you've told me.'

Zhang Hong nodded.

Ziwei sighed. She drew on her cigarette and threw away the butt, then leant her head back against the wall, closing her eyes. 'Let's give it time,' she said eventually.

Zhang Hong stared at her.

There were tears running down Ziwei's cheeks when she continued: 'You were right when you said we're all responsible for our actions.

We all have blood on our hands – but that doesn't cleanse the individual shame and guilt. It never will. We just have to find ways of living with it.'

'You can say that because you've never harmed anybody,' said Zhang Hong, bitterly. 'I've always envied you. You're a saint.'

'No, Zhang Hong, you don't know me. I survived, which means others died. I have to live with that. We're really no different, you and I. Perhaps you're luckier than I am. Your victim lived.' She stood up. 'Come on, we'd better go back to the party. They'll be wondering what's happened to us.'

'You'll go in with me, in front of all of them, after what I've told you?' Zhang Hong gasped.

Ziwei's tone was wooden. 'Why not? You've given me joyful news. My mother, whom I thought was dead, is alive. One day Yanqing will meet her grandmother. Isn't that something to celebrate?'

The next morning, the whole village gathered early to watch the students load their possessions on to the three waiting trucks. It was a sombre crowd. Many had hangovers from the night before, and most were troubled and disoriented because over the last ten years the students had become part of their community and their lives, and the village would not be the same after they left.

Zhang Hong led the file of students down the goat track, holding Yanqing's hand. The little girl had pleaded with her mother to be allowed to climb up to the students' compound before breakfast to make her own special farewell to her favourite auntie, and Ziwei hadn't the heart to refuse her.

The students were also in low spirits, any joy at returning home for the moment dispelled because the time had come to say goodbye to their friends. As they passed through the villagers, there was much quiet backslapping and the occasional embrace, but not much was spoken. It had all been said.

There was one tragicomic incident that caused a momentary burst of mirth. The students had loaded their bags, and were preparing to climb on to the trucks, when all heads turned at the sound of two voices shouting at each other, one male, one female. It was Yao Fengfeng and the pig farmer. Fengfeng had a cloth bundle over her shoulder and was trying to shake off the hand of her husband, who was cursing her and trying to pull her back, but he could not prevent her reaching the trucks. She hurled on her bag and wriggled up over the tailgate, holding on to the supports and kicking at the pig farmer's scrabbling hands.

Ziwei and Zhang Hong looked at each other. A professional decision had to be made. Fengfeng's application to leave had not been approved, pending a divorce that her husband would not give her.

'Shall we make her come down?' Zhang Hong asked.

'No, let her go. I'll see the paperwork is approved,' said Ziwei.

'Thank you,' said Zhang Hong.

The angry pig farmer was eventually led away by his friends, and Fengfeng scuttled towards the cabin end of the truck, piling bags in front of her as a barrier and darting menacing glances in all directions.

One of the drivers hooted his horn. It was time for the students to leave.

Ziwei and Zhang Hong looked at each other. The lips of the proud Shanghai student were quivering. 'I'll never forget you,' she said. 'I'll write when I have news of your mother.'

Ziwei nodded.

'Well, it's goodbye, then.'

'Yes,' said Ziwei.

Hesitantly, Zhang Hong extended her hand. Ziwei looked at the open palm and at the tears in the girl's eyes. Impulsively, she stretched out her arms. Zhang Hong stumbled forward and laid her head on Ziwei's shoulder. The two women clutched each other, rocking from side to side, then Zhang Hong broke away and clambered on to the truck, wiping her eyes. She raised an arm in the Maoist salute, and shouted, 'Long live . . . Long live our comrades in Iron Man's Glade!' The others took up the cry.

The drivers started their engines and the trucks full of waving students inched away. Some of the village children, including Yanqing, ran after them until the vehicles accelerated, then bumped out of sight, dust floating above the bare rocks.

'Yanqing,' Ziwei called, and saw the little girl turn and run back. She scooped her in to her arms, and began to run herself in the direction of the goat track.

'Where are we going, Mummy?' The child looked frightened.

'We have to hurry,' panted Ziwei. 'I can't carry you any further. Will you try to keep up with me? We must run fast.'

They passed the graves of Xing and the others, which had now become almost invisible under grass although, as she scrambled by,

Ziwei noticed that the departing students had left fresh bouquets of wild flowers where the headstones protruded. They reached the top and skirted the compound to take the narrow path between the rocks to the old outcrop that looked over the plain. Ziwei helped her daughter climb up beside her.

Far away, on the road that wound below them, they saw the dust of the trucks. Faintly, above the noise of the wind, came the sound of singing. It was another revolutionary song, praising Mao. What other songs did this generation know? thought Ziwei, as the tears ran down her cheeks. They would perhaps learn new ones when they reached their destinations. One day there would be new songs. She felt a tug on her hand. Yanqing's brown eyes were looking up at her. 'Do you think Auntie's singing that wild-geese song about me?'

'Probably, darling.' Ziwei sobbed as she hugged her daughter.

'Can we go and visit her one day? In Shanghai.' Yanqing stumbled on the name. It was a strange word to her.

'I don't know, darling. I'll see – I'll see if maybe one day we can arrange it. If – if we do, you can meet your granny too.'

'Granny? I didn't know I had a granny.'

'You have, my dearest, you have – but let's not talk about that until after we finish waving goodbye to Auntie.'

Yanqing giggled. 'You are silly, Mummy. We're far too high up for Auntie to see us here.'

But she continued to gaze down, as did her mother. Together they watched until the dust faded into the haze. Then, slowly, the two walked down to the village, which, for Ziwei, seemed now to be as desolate as a tomb.

16

The Market Gardener

Shishan and Shanghai: 1984–6

In the early 1980s, Deng Xiaoping, among his Four Modernizations, had abolished the communes. Each farmer was allocated land and told that, once state quotas had been fulfilled, he could sell any excess produce. Ziwei worked hard on the patch allocated to the Gao household, but there was little left after the government inspectors had gathered their share of the wheat crop. While villages close to towns benefited from their proximity to the markets, the farmers in Iron Man's Glade, isolated in the Black Hills, grumbled that there was hardly any difference from the old system.

Ziwei would listen sadly to their complaints as she queued to receive the few *kuai* she earned for a month's work. 'At least in Mao's days we knew we were no worse off than anybody else,' said Lao Jing, one of Gao's committee members who had since become her friend and sometimes helped her work Gao's field. 'Don't know what the revolution was about if it means the rich get richer and we're left to starve.'

'Things will get better,' she said, only half believing it, for she knew that life as a peasant was as hard as it had ever been.

'I don't see how, unless they start some new revolution. I'm going to have to sell my sow if I'm to get the family through the winter, and then where will we be?'

'I'll think of something,' she said.

He raised his eyebrows sceptically, and patted her shoulder. 'You're a good woman, Ziwei,' he said, 'and over the years you've done your best to look after us, but nobody expects you to do anything this time. It's our fate, that's all. The emperor's in heaven, and we farmers are in pigshit. Always were. Always will be. That Mao.' He spat. 'Sometimes I wish he'd never sold us those dreams.'

381

'We're better off with Deng,' she said.

'Tell that to my pig.'

One morning, after she had tended Xing's grave, Ziwei climbed up to her old outcrop for a solitary cigarette. She was in a melancholy mood because she had just put her fourteen-year-old daughter on to the weekly bus. Now the Spring Festival was over, Yanqing would be living in a dormitory in Shishan, where she was to attend high school, and Ziwei would not see her for four months.

It was the first time they had been separated. Mother and daughter had clung together until the bus driver had thrown away his cigarette and told them gruffly he would leave with or without her. 'I don't have to go, Mama,' Yanqing kept saying, through her tears. 'I can stay here with you. I wouldn't mind. Really.'

But Ziwei knew she did not mean it. 'You must go,' she said. 'For your grandmother, for me, for yourself.'

Yanqing had nodded and kissed her. 'I'll think of you every moment of the day, Mama. I promise.'

'Hurry. Go,' Ziwei whispered, and pushed her away.

Now all she could think of was Yanqing's face as she had last seen it through the dusty back window of the bus, the shy smile, the eyes shining with resolution and triumph as she set off on her adventure. At that moment, Ziwei had felt flushed with pride, but her heart was breaking.

It was for the best, she told herself. All these years the hope that one day – somehow – Yanqing would escape the exile that had been her own fate had kept her going. That was why she had spent the evenings telling her the old histories and stories her mother had read to her as a child, as well as what she recalled of the mathematics and geography she had learnt at school, dredging her memories of the half-forgotten world of books and conversation that had existed before the Laogai. Yanqing had absorbed it, yet Ziwei's patient tuition had not been enough. In this China, it was not intellectual aptitude but luck and, increasingly, contacts that determined a person's future. Ziwei had had to draw on all her favours to get the village committee to nominate Yanqing for one of the few places the Shishan Middle School offered poor peasants, and that had incurred more debts, but she didn't mind: any sacrifice was worthwhile to give Yanqing the precious start in life that might – just might – take her on to university and freedom.

She desired nothing else – but she had not calculated the cost to herself. Now her daughter was gone, she felt bereft at the thought of returning to her empty house and her invalid husband.

She sat on her rock and smoked, thinking of what might have been. Her thoughts strayed to her mother in faraway Shanghai. That was another knife in her heart. It pained her that she could not fulfil her obligations as a daughter. Yu Fu-kuei was old and ill, and there was no one to look after her.

In all these years, she had received permission only twice to visit her mother. The first time had been eighteen months after Zhang Hong's revelation that she was alive. It took that long for Ziwei to receive a permit to travel, and the ten days allocated to her, taking account of travel, left them barely five days together. She recalled how excited she and Yanqing had been as they shared a hard-class bunk on the long train journey down – and how bittersweet had been the subsequent reunion.

Even the smell of the hallway was familiar, although the fading Maoist slogans on the peeling paint were new. Yanqing was chattering as Ziwei leant over her, brushed her hair and adjusted the pink bow for the tenth time since the bus had dropped them at the Fudan stop. 'Will she like me, Mama? Granny's very, very old, isn't she? Will she be cross like Granny Liu in the village?'

'No, she'll love you, darling,' Ziwei murmured, and steeled herself to ring the bell.

'Can I sing her the wild-geese song? Will that make her like me?'

'Yes, of course you can,' said Ziwei, as her shaking finger pressed the button.

There was an interminable wait. There was no sound through the door, and Ziwei felt a chill. What if something had happened to her? What if her mother had not received her letter? Or moved? Her seven-year-old daughter became bored and began to skip up and down the concrete steps. 'Yanqing,' she called, the severity in her voice betraying her fear, 'come here.'

Then she heard a faint voice. She had to press her ear to the door to make out the words: 'Push. It's open.'

She pulled down the handle and the door opened with a squeak of hinges and the clang of metal. She peered into the darkness, and felt her first shock: the flat seemed empty. There were none of the old furnishings and decorations she remembered, only blank walls, and the shelves in the study, illuminated by a low-wattage bulb, were bare. As she stood there uncertainly, Yanqing's head pressed to her back, the door to her mother's room opened. At the same time the lights turned on in the sitting room, and she saw a figure in a wheelchair, slowly propelling itself towards her. Then she felt her second shock: she did not recognise this woman.

She was thin, almost skeletal, with wisps of grey hair on a mottled brown scalp. A thick padded jacket was hanging loosely over her shoulders, and a blanket covered her knees. The pallid face was etched and crisscrossed with so many lines it resembled the shell of a walnut. Only the piercing eyes, sunken in bruised sockets, were those of the mother she remembered, as well as the thin lips that were curving into a smile. 'Ziwei? Is it really you?' The voice was a dry croak. 'What have they done to you? Your beautiful skin and your shining hair . . .'

'I'm a peasant now, Mama. It's – it's hard in the fields . . .' She wanted to throw herself into her mother's arms but she was paralysed.

She heard the soft, sardonic laugh. 'Who'd have thought it? My daughter a peasant. A *gong nong bing*. Respectable at last.' With an effort, Fu-kuei raised her good arm. 'Come in. Don't just stand there. You know your way around. I've been boiling the kettle. Oolong. Don't suppose you've had that for a while.' She wheeled herself towards the kitchen.

'I'll do it, Mama,' said Ziwei.

'I'm crippled, but not incapacitated.' She paused and turned a severe face towards her daughter. 'You do drink tea, do you? You can get it on your mountainside?'

'Yes, Mama,' said Ziwei. Fu-kuei grunted and the wheelchair disappeared into the kitchen. Ziwei helped the fidgeting Yanqing out of her coat, and adjusted her bow yet again. 'Now be good,' she whispered, as she listened helplessly to the clatter her mother was making.

'Her face is all cracked, Mama,' whispered the little girl, gazing at her with round, puzzled eyes.

There was a crash from the kitchen as a pan fell to the floor. Ziwei had to stop herself running to help. She looked around the almost empty room and saw two chairs near the dining-table. It was the table her father had bought, the only piece of furniture she recognised. 'Sit down quietly,' she said, 'and wait for Granny to come back with the tea.'

Fu-kuei emerged holding a damp rag to a teapot balanced on her knees. 'The cups are in the cupboard,' she said. Ziwei opened it hurriedly and saw three enamel mugs, obviously purchased during the Cultural Revolution. One bore a portrait of Mao, another a faded picture of a mango, with the slogan: 'We will not eat them. We will give them to the worker activists.' As she put them on the table, she felt a lump in her throat and tears welling in her eyes.

'I'm sorry I can't serve you in a fitting style,' her mother murmured, as she flung sticks of dried leaf into the mugs.

'It's all right, Mama. I'm just so pleased to see you.'

Her mother paused and examined her. 'They haven't really changed you,' she said, 'though you're thin and tanned – and strong. Indeed like a peasant.'

'I learnt to survive, Mama,' said Ziwei, unnerved by the bitterness in her mother's tone. 'It wasn't so bad.' She watched anxiously as Fu-kuei lifted the heavy teapot and began to pour. Water spilled on to the table.

'And what are you staring at, little one?' Fu-kuei had put down the pot, and turned to Yanqing, who was gaping at her with wonder and some fear. She smiled and Yanqing pressed herself backwards in her chair. 'Am I so terrifying? Look.' She reached under the blanket and produced a cloth doll with a painted face and ragged clothes. 'If you're my granddaughter, the pretty farmer's girl I've heard so much about, this is for you.'

'Give your granny a kiss,' said Ziwei, as Yanqing snatched the doll and darted out of reach. 'Thank her properly.'

'She's a pretty thing,' said Fu-kuei. 'At least something good's come out of all these years. Aren't you going to take your tea?'

Ziwei and her mother leant forward at the same moment. Their fingers touched round the hot mug, and, startled, their eyes met, even as their hands flinched away. Ziwei's began to plead, and Yu Fu-kuei's lips quivered as her expression changed from one of alarm to fear. Slowly, a tear welled in the corner of her eye. Ziwei grabbed her mother's hand and held it tight. Their fingers began to twine. They stared at each other. Suddenly Ziwei gave a gulping sob and and threw her arms around her, pressing her cheek to her mother's, kissing the wrinkled forehead, and hugging the frail body to her. 'I've missed you, Mama, I've so, so missed you.'

Her mother's hand was brushing her hair. 'I know, my baby, I know.'

The old woman squeezed her daughter's hand, then gently disengaged her own. 'Give me time,' she said. 'It's a bit of a shock. The dead don't often get a chance to meet again. Sometimes I think Mao never intended any of us to survive his madness.'

'I know a song by Chairman Mao, Granny,' said Yanqing, suddenly. 'It's about my name.'

The moment was over. Fu-kuei's eyes glittered with savage irony. 'It's all right, Ziwei,' she said, when Ziwei hushed Yanqing anxiously. 'Let's hear my granddaughter sing a song by Chairman Mao. After all, that's whose children we are. Let us give thanks to the Great Helmsman that he spared us.'

'Oh, Mama.' Ziwei buried her face in the blanket. 'Oh, Mama.' And Yanqing began to sing, oblivious of her grandmother's stony gaze.

No, it had not been the rapturous homecoming for which she had hoped, thought Ziwei, as she lit another cigarette. The wounds were still too fresh, the hurt too deep, and, she realised with sorrow, some gulfs of time and experience could never be bridged, even between those who loved each other.

Eventually they had settled on a routine. Ziwei shopped, cooked and cleaned the dust of neglect from the flat, while Fu-kuei watched her granddaughter playing, slowly softening to the little girl's charm. There were times when Ziwei was jealous of her daughter. The old woman would listen patiently to Yanqing's prattle, admired her drawings, served her the best morsels of the food Ziwei cooked, sang old songs to her and allowed her to push the wheelchair round and round the room – but after that first time when they had embraced uncomfortably, she tended to ignore her own daughter. They spent little time talking, except about mundanities.

Ziwei was hurt and puzzled, wondering how she had offended her. She could understand why her mother would be disappointed that her daughter, for whom she had such high hopes, had become a farmer's wife – but surely she must understand that that was because of the times in which they were living. It had not been Ziwei's choice. She believed her mother still loved her: there were moments when her reserve appeared to soften, and she would gaze at Ziwei with a sad smile, and once she had stroked her hair – but within minutes Fu-kuei would say something caustic.

Eventually Ziwei decided Fu-kuei's bitterness had little to do with her. They had both suffered during their long separation, and she guessed that the experience had shrivelled her mother's heart. Perhaps the shock of Ziwei's presence, coupled with her ignominious circumstances, as her proud mother would see them, were reminders of dashed hopes, or she still blamed herself for not being able to protect her daughter and had transferred her impotence and anger into coldness. And it wasn't surprising that she was damaged. Wasn't she herself by her own experiences? When it came to it, neither Fu-kuei nor Ziwei could bring themselves to tell each other what had happened during the long years when they had thought the other was dead. It was easier just to dote on little Yanqing.

Ziwei came away at the end of the trip with only a vague idea of how her mother had been spared Chen Tao's vengeance and survived the attack of the Red Guards. Once she had pressed her, asking how she had escaped execution, but Fu-kuei had only become irritated. 'Why do you want to bring up the past all over again? Who knows why anybody did anything in those days?'

'They – they told me you were shot,' said Ziwei. 'I lived for years thinking you were dead. Of course I want to know.'

Fu-kuei's face quivered with emotion. 'They told me you were dead too,' she said. 'Do you think I cared any more whether I lived or died? In fact, when the reprieve arrived, a day before the execution was to take place, I thought only that I would not be following you and grieved the more.'

'Oh, Mama.' Ziwei clutched her hand.

'Yes, I wanted to die.' She shook her head. 'I don't know why they spared me. At the time I thought it was only another malicious torture by Chen Tao. I sat in the bus on the way home, thinking that when I got back, and people asked me where I'd been, I would tell them what had happened so the authorities would rearrest me, but when I got home I found nobody had even realised I'd been gone – and then I fell ill. I lay for months in bed, and some neighbours were kind to me, feeding me in my delirium. When I recovered it seemed invidious to involve them, as I would have done had I spoken to them about what had happened to me. So I just carried on, keeping silent, living my half-life. I suppose you think that was cowardly.'

'No, Mama.' Ziwei kissed her. 'I'm just so sorry about what happened to you.'

'You shouldn't be. It was worse for you.'

'No, I was fine,' said Ziwei, and realised that she was equally incapable of talking about her own sufferings: Ziwei had no desire to tell Fu-kuei about the Laogai or what had happened to her afterwards. Nor did Fu-kuei feel inclined to question her, certainly not about 'her pig-farmer husband', as she had referred disparagingly to Gao on the only occasion she had mentioned him.

By mutual consent they put aside the past, focusing on the uneasy present.

After three days, however, the claustrophobia caused by all that was unspoken was taking a toll on Ziwei's nerves. It was partly to get away from the brooding atmosphere that she eventually acceded to Yanqing's insistence that they look up 'Auntie Zhang Hong'.

They met in the Lao Fangzi restaurant in the old Chinese city. Although Yanqing was happy enough, guzzling dumplings and other treats, it was a stiff meeting between the two adults. The old intimacy was absent, and only the embarrassment of their last days together remained. Both were haunted by the spectre of what Zhang Hong had done to Fu-kuei, although neither mentioned it. Zhang Hong showed little interest in hearing about Iron Man's Glade: she had moved on with her life. Instead, she enthused about her job in a foreign bank.

'Everybody's working for foreigners, these days, Ziwei,' she said. 'You wouldn't believe what high salaries they pay. Nobody I know works for a state corporation any more. You should consider getting a job for Yanqing in a foreign company when she's old enough. It would be an excellent career move. If I haven't been sent abroad by then, I'll be happy to put in a word for her at my bank. I'm personal assistant to the German chief representative, and I'm learning so much about commerce, management – all sorts of things. You really should consider it.'

Ziwei listened to her boasts without saying a word. The monthly salary Zhang Hong had mentioned was three times what she herself earned in a year in Iron Man's Glade, but it was not that which depressed her. It was the artificiality of her old friend, and something else that hovered behind her efforts to be friendly. It was not only Zhang Hong's obligation to Ziwei that hung over them like a shadow: Ziwei sensed she despised the peasant Ziwei had remained and which Zhang Hong had once been. They were both relieved when the meal ended. Ziwei thought that they were unlikely ever to meet again.

That had been the last day she had spent with her mother. In the evening, after Yanqing had gone to sleep and Fu-kuei was sitting in her wheelchair watching her daughter pack, Ziwei put aside her misgivings and asked her directly about the second episode in which she had suffered: the beating by the Red Guards that had left her more crippled than she had been before.

Again, Fu-kuei tried to change the subject. 'Why spoil our last evening by going into that? What happened to me wasn't unique. Others suffered much worse that I did.'

'Oh, Mama, they hit you with cudgels. I know about it. Zhang Hong confessed to me.'

'Well, if your friend told you, why ask me? It was long ago. Forgotten.'

'Nothing's forgotten, Mama.' For the first time, Ziwei's temper snapped. 'Everything that happened to both of us has been hanging over us like a cloud since Yanqing and I arrived. You and I can't think of anything else. We can't get it out of our minds – the guilt, the horror. It's poisoned us. And this I do need to know, because it's baffled me ever since Zhang Hong told me about it. Who rescued you and why? The Red Guards were a law unto themselves in those days. Uncontrollable. What happened to you was unprecedented.'

Fu-kuei sighed. 'Why do you persist? Don't you see it doesn't do anybody any good to rake over coals? Anyway, it's dangerous to ask all these questions. Some things are better left unknown.'

'Dangerous? Things better left unknown? Mama, the Cultural Revolution's over. We, too, must get over it.'

Her mother glared at her, then her shoulders slumped. 'You don't know them,' she murmured, in a small voice.

'I don't understand. Don't know who?'

'Look, maybe somebody thought they owed me a favour,' said Yu Fu-kuei. 'Maybe they recalled a service I did way back in pre-Liberation times. Some day I might tell you a bit about it, but please, not now. I'm still recovering from the joy of seeing you alive and well, and meeting for the first time my darling grandchild. It's not the time to talk of sad things. I'm sad enough that you're both going home tomorrow. Don't, I beg you, make it worse. Please.'

And there Ziwei had to leave it. There had been no further opportunity to go into the subject again, and this was not something they could discuss in the weekly letters that they subsequently exchanged

– long, loving letters (at least on Ziwei's side), but almost entirely devoted to Yanqing and necessarily bland for the censor.

Two years later, Ziwei and Yanqing visited Shanghai again, during the Spring Festival, but their time with Fu-kuei was pitifully short on this occasion too. Ziwei was relieved that her mother had mellowed a little towards her, but she was still acerbic and critical. This time they avoided anything that might remind them of Chen Tao, Ha Li, the honey trap or any other sad memories; and the Laogai, from the selective anecdotes Ziwei told her mother, might have been a place where girls lived healthily in the countryside, supplementing their diets with eccentric dormitory feasts. The truth, of course, reverberated loudly in what was unsaid, but neither wanted to tear at half-healed scars.

Ziwei knew, of course, that sensitivity about the past was not unique to them. The whole country had entered a state of wilful amnesia. When people in apartment blocks and factories had to live or work side by side with others who had once persecuted or been persecuted by them, discretion meant survival. The icy fingers of the Cultural Revolution continued to grip people's hearts, and reserve had become second nature to a nation in which the neighbourhood committees still had the power to report on suspicious activities. Neither had the government lost the habit of launching sudden new political campaigns, using the language of previous decades. Thankfully, these days, they were short-lived and usually restricted to newspaper editorials and workplace study classes, without serious prosecution after self-criticisms had been made. Nevertheless, for a people who had become inured to terror, the same double standards of what you thought and what you said applied, if only for self-preservation. Ziwei had come to realise that the estrangement that existed between her mother and herself was not unique. Every family in the country was dysfunctional to some degree, each seeking to keep out of sight, if not out of mind, the skeletons of the past.

So they settled for what they had. They took comfort in being quietly together as a family, celebrating the Chinese New Year with a semblance of normality, laughing as Yanqing let off the fireworks at midnight, and sharing meals at the dining-table that remained from Ziwei's childhood.

That had been two years ago, and all her applications to travel since had been refused. Over the years she had kept up the weekly correspondence with her mother, but the news lately had not been good. Fu-kuei had been suffering recently from a kidney problem – Ziwei suspected it might have been damaged during the beating. Although Fu-kuei had been too proud to mention it, Ziwei knew that treatment existed if she could only afford it – dialysis, or even a transplant – but neither mother nor daughter had any money. There was nothing to be done except bear the pain: Ziwei had evidence of this in the deteriorating handwriting, and every new letter brought her only further sorrow.

There was also the increasing impoverishment of the village to worry about. In the old days, when their problems had been largely political, she had always found a way to help, but, with the breaking down of the commune system, harsh economics ruled, and she was in the same straitened situation as everybody else. Nobody blamed her or took her to task. She shared their hardships – but, even so, it preyed on her mind that there was nothing she could do.

And today she had lost her daughter. In her black mood it seemed that for the last twenty years, ever since she had been sent to the Laogai, she had been like a mouse dodging a trap – which seemed now finally to have snapped shut on her.

Her fingers fumbled for a cigarette, the last in her packet and she had no money until next week to buy more. As she lit it, she felt a moment of utter despair.

Imagining the bus with her daughter and her hopes winding down the mountain, looking out over the far horizon to where the Liao river undulated to the sea, she thought again of the city where she had grown up, the dreams and aspirations she had harboured when she was Yanqing's age, the tragedies that had overtaken her family, and exiled her. With the ash drooping on the cigarette in her hand, she began to weep.

It was a misty day but as she was making ready to return to her house, wearily itemising the chores she still had to perform, a ray of sunshine happened to illuminate the hill slope at the other side of the mountain, and Ziwei had a view of the fields where the students had once grown vegetables. The terraces were overgrown now. After their departure, there had not been enough hands to cultivate them. Ziwei gazed at them for some time – then suddenly thought of Gao's hoard. By the time the sun had set over the mountains, she had worked out a plan.

She had not touched the ill-gotten gains that Gao had extorted as Party secretary although, as a loyal wife, she had kept his secret. Now she had a reason to use his savings, and justified it to herself because it would be of benefit to the village. That evening she opened the pit under the *kang*.

The villagers were happy enough to sell her their shares in what they viewed as wasteland. It surprised them that the abandoned terraces were worth anything and they were even more pleased when she offered them good wages for time spent restoring and working them. She told them that she had taken out a loan to secure the finance, and they believed her because they trusted her. They had no reason to be dissatisfied because, after six months, Ziwei shared the profits she received from selling the vegetables in the Shishan markets. It was like the old days, when the village had prospered. More importantly to Ziwei, she had enough money left over, after she had paid for her mother's operation, to buy a truck.

Soon she signed contracts with the other hamlets in the Black Hills and took responsibility for delivering their produce, using her growing fleet of vehicles. In a year she had become the major supplier to the county capital of vegetables and fruit, fresh game and Chinese medicinal herbs. In due course she opened a shop.

The major benefit to her was that she now had a valid reason to move out of Iron Man's Glade: she wanted to be closer to her daughter. Arguing commercial necessity, and after much petitioning (with several bribes), Ziwei secured permission from the camp in Tranquil Springs to alter her *hukou* (the word embraced residence permit and much else) so that she could live in Shishan. The formal condition was that she would have to make a monthly report of her activities. Informally there was also an understanding that this would be an undertaking that by then, with the burgeoning business, Ziwei could well afford to make. She opened her shop in the old section of the city, in what had once been the main square when Shishan had been a walled town. The building she bought was located opposite the Confucian temple, which had been reopened and was now a popular tourist spot, so she benefited from the extra custom. The house also had a history: in Qing Dynasty times it had been a notorious brothel. Appreciating the irony, she branded her canned products 'Heavenly Pleasure' and they sold well. Soon she was receiving orders regularly from as far afield as Shenyang, Changchun, Harbin and other north-eastern cities. Ziwei became rich.

To give her husband face, she maintained her company's head office in the village, appointing him titular chairman, although she made sure that she left behind a capable manager to look after her interests. Gao had not been prosecuted. The government had decided that, on the whole, it was better to try to forget the past. In any case, the trial of such an invalid, shrunken both physically and mentally, would have had no useful propaganda effect. Despite the doctor's prognosis, he had recovered some of his faculties, but on the days that he was rational, he drank. Otherwise he lay silently on his *kang*. Ziwei made sure he was well fed and adequately looked after, but was otherwise content to let him be. Even Yanqing, who still retained some affection for him, had recently, on her holidays from school, tended to treat him with the casual regard that one might bestow on a dog, a cat or another favoured pet. Essentially, she had grown up without a father.

So, neither missed him. Mother and daughter, reunited, lived contentedly in their small apartment on the top floor of Ziwei's shop, above the canning works that occupied the second floor. Ziwei some- times joked that she had taken over the old madam's quarters and was becoming a fearsome madam herself. Yanqing occupied the room beside hers, and they converted the others into an office, a study and a kitchen-dining room. After so many years in the Laogai, Ziwei had become used to a frugal existence, but she enjoyed cooking delicacies for Yanqing, now she could afford them. Every morning, Ziwei would walk with her daughter to her high school before starting the day's work. She tried to avoid business banquets in the evening so that she could spend time with Yanqing. Unconsciously she had adopted the life she had once shared with her own mother. After her homework, Yanqing sat down with her mother for her real studies, and together they devoured the English books that Ziwei had been able to find in the many second-hand markets that sold antiques and ornaments that citizens had hidden during the Cultural Revolution.

It was not a bad life, but it was still exile, and the Cultural Revolution still cast its shadow over people's hearts.

Once, shortly after the end of the 1984 Spiritual Pollution Campaign, Ziwei witnessed a ludicrous manifestation of Cultural Revolution mores when she and Yanqing were ordered to attend a song-and-dance performance at the new Shishan football stadium. The municipal government was honouring a group of British engineers who had come to implement a technology transfer contract with the Shishan petro-chemical works. When they arrived, blinking, on the podium, it was to find a crowd of forty thousand people, waving British flags and screaming thanks to these friends from overseas who were assisting with the reconstruction of their city. Ziwei, who was not far away from the podium, recognised the types: they were not great industrialists, statesmen or world leaders, but simple men from the English provinces, not unlike the GPR engineers – Braithwaite, Hudson and Gallagher – whom once she had escorted to Sichuan. What they made of this 'spontaneous' adulation, she could only guess, but she was ashamed of the sycophantic excess of her leaders, disgusted by the memories of the mass movements the rally recalled and, above all, she felt supreme indifference. What was more, she was sure her feelings were shared by every member of the audience. That did not prevent her waving her flag, screaming, and encouraging her daughter to do the same. It was safer, and they had all been programmed to obey the authorities and blend with the crowd.

One other thing surprised her about that evening. Seeing the British engineers had brought back memories of Ha Li, of whom she had not thought for years. That night she lay in bed trying to conjure what he looked like, but all she could recall was his height and black hair. She tried to remember what it had been like to have sex with him – and nothing stirred. That saddened her. After all, it had been he who was responsible in a way for everything that had happened in her life since then. Had she not one fond memory? She rolled over. He was dead to her. It was better that way. She no longer cared.

Mao's cold winter might be over, but it was taking many years for people's minds to thaw. Even Ziwei's prosperity and the money she now sent Fu-kuei had not been enough to bridge the gulf between herself and her mother. Though Ziwei, through bribes, was able to arrange permission to visit Shanghai more often, the sensitive subject of what had happened to them during those lost years was never raised.

At least on one of her visits (alas, without Yanqing, who was busy with exams), Ziwei had the wherewithal to do something about Fu-kuei's poverty and, against her mother's objections, she took her to the No. 1 Department Store off the People's Square, and bought her a new set of furniture, a modern kitchen, bathroom fittings, curtains, radiators and an air-conditioner to replace the antiquated electric fan. Just before she left, she brought out the huge parcel she had been keeping mysteriously in her room.

'What's this? More luxuries?' asked Fu-kuei, acidly. 'I really don't know why you've gone to all this trouble for me. You're wasting your money, you know. You'd be much better keeping it to bribe some official to give my granddaughter a job when she finishes high school.'

'I've enough for that, Mama,' said Ziwei, patiently. 'Anyway, she's going to university. In Beijing.'

'A peasant's daughter? You're dreaming.'

'Mama, just open the parcel. I think this is something you'll like.'

'It's too bulky,' she grumbled, 'and with my arthritis I can hardly use my hands any more.'

'Well, I'll open it then,' said Ziwei.

Her mother sat on the sofa, feigning indifference, as Ziwei stripped away the newspaper wrapping, but when she solemnly handed her the first volume, Fu-kuei gasped, and her voice cracked when she saw the title: 'It's Spenser's *Faerie Queen*.'

'Yes, Mama,' Ziwei had tears in her eyes, 'and here's Milton's *Paradise Lost*.'

'It's a new edition.' Fu-kuei was overcome. 'Oxford University Press. How? Where did you . . . ?'

'I ordered them, Mama, with the help of an American businessman I met at a banquet in Shishan. He arranged for them to be sent. Look!' she said excitedly. 'There are more.'

Volume by volume, Ziwei withdrew a complete English edition of Shakespeare's plays, Malory's *Morte D'Arthur*, the poems of John Donne, Marvell and Ralegh, *The Oxford Book of Sixteenth Century Verse*, Jacobean drama, Pope, Dryden, Tennyson, Florio's translation of Montaigne, and, in Italian, the poems of Dante, Tasso and Ariosto. From the bottom of the box came a set of Jane Austen and, lastly, the books her mother had read to Ziwei as a child: *Captains Courageous*, *Alice in Wonderland* and *Through The Looking Glass*.

'My darling, my daughter,' Fu-kuei sat with the books piled on the sofa and the floor around her, tears rolling down her shrivelled cheeks, 'you shouldn't have. You shouldn't . . .'

'Oh, Mama, Mama, I so love you,' wept Ziwei, resting her head on her mother's knees, and Fu-kuei stroked her hair and murmured the endearments that had been locked until now in her frozen heart.

But, again, they did not talk about the past, and on the train north Ziwei shrugged. Perhaps it was for the best. It was easier to look forward than back. At least, she comforted herself, she and her mother had rediscovered their love for each other.

Meanwhile she devoted her energies to Yanqing's education. She had remembered what Zhang Hong had told her about the sort of jobs foreign companies offered, and she was determined that her daughter would have the English language and the university education that would make her eligible for such a career. To be a secretary was nothing much, but it was better than the fate of most girls at her high school, the pinnacle of whose hopes was to be assigned to a production line in one of the factories that belched smoke over the miles of anonymous workers' blocks in the industrial wasteland that Shishan had become, or otherwise be sent back to their farms.

She wanted her daughter to live the life that she herself had been denied. That meant Yanqing must pass the exams to secure a place at a university in Beijing or Shanghai. As far as Ziwei was concerned, nowhere else was good enough.

She had money and, as a prominent businesswoman in Shishan, some influence with the local education board: she had sponsored the construction of primary schools in the city suburbs. Using back doors was second nature to her, and she was careful to cultivate the right officials, but she was painfully aware that her influence did not extend beyond the boundaries of her insignificant township. Her one attempt to sponsor a scholarship to Peking University, in the hope that her daughter might benefit from it, had been a failure. The major universities were already wallowing in the attentions of wealthy Hong Kong and overseas Chinese, eager to make high-level political contacts and reap honorary degrees, so a letter from an unknown provincial was superciliously rejected.

Reluctantly, she had to accept that Yanqing must rely on her own academic merits. The girl's English was nearly fluent. Ziwei had bought her a short-wave radio, and every evening she listened to the BBC, as well as tuning in to the television programme *Follow Me*, which had an audience of tens of millions, and had given its unknown young English presenter, Kathy Flower, probably the highest ratings in the world. But that was the problem. Every family in China wanted their child to learn English, and the competition for the few prestigious university places was daunting. The English-literature lessons that Ziwei gave Yanqing in the evenings now took up most weekends. Fu-kuei coached her by letter from Shanghai, setting her essay questions and recommending further reading. Ziwei made friends with more foreign businessmen in Shishan, then persuaded them to send her the required titles from bookshops abroad. At the same time Yanqing had to keep up with mathematics, science and other subjects at school. The pressure on her was enormous, and sometimes she rebelled.

'Why, Mother? Why do you make me go over all this again and again and again?' she screamed. She was drooping with tiredness at two in the morning, but Ziwei had insisted she read again the storm scene in *King Lear*, which she had already learnt by heart.

'Because this is an important part of the play,' said Ziwei, who was also exhausted.

'It's a couple of madmen on a heath,' moaned Yanqing. 'They're just raving.'

'And isn't it symbolic?' pressed Ziwei. 'Isn't the whole world mad, and human beings reduced to their bare elements? Doesn't that tell you something about what happened in our country not so long ago?'

'That's your world, Mama, not mine. You were in the Laogai, not me. I want to live my own life, not make up for yours.'

'And how will you lead any sort of life if you don't get a place at university?' snapped Ziwei.

'I don't care about university!' Yanqing screamed, and hurled the book to the floor.

On these occasions, Ziwei's heart ached with sympathy, but she steeled herself to be firm, reminding Yanqing that this was the one chance she would ever have to better her life. Inevitably, the resentment resulted in some estrangement between mother and daughter, but Ziwei, knowing the stakes, was relentless, and bullied Yanqing until she had her way.

And her efforts paid off. When Yanqing received her examination results, it was perhaps the happiest day of Ziwei's life.

Yanqing returned from school wearing a shy smile. Without a word, she reached into her satchel and handed her mother a piece of paper. She made a pretence of foraging in the kitchen cupboard for the dried noodles, but she was watching Ziwei from the corner of her eye, and laughed when she saw her mother's expression. 'Not bad, are they?'

she murmured, and chuckled as Ziwei had to steady herself against the kitchen table. 'Maybe you'll allow me to go to bed early from now on.'

'Oh, Yanqing, my brilliant, brilliant daughter, can you ever forgive me?' Ziwei was shaking.

Yanqing bounded across the kitchen, the noodles spilling over the sideboard where she had dropped them, and lifted her mother into the air. 'I'm going to Beijing,' she yelled. 'Beijing! Thank you, thank you, thank you! I owe everything to you!' And, laughing and crying, mother and daughter whirled around the room.

The results could not have been better. She had come first or second in nearly every subject, and her delighted teachers assured her that she would win a place at a university in the capital. In the end it was not one of the most prestigious campuses that Ziwei had hoped for but that was only a minor disappointment. For her penetrating essay on Shakespeare's *King Lear* and her all-round ability in English, Yanqing was awarded a scholarship to the Beijing Foreign Languages Institute.

That night, after the banquet she had arranged to celebrate her daughter's success, Ziwei slept easily. Her daughter had a future.

The following morning she received a telephone call from Shanghai. It was a Dr An, from the Huadong Hospital. Alarmingly, it was the most prestigious medical establishment in the city, reserved for senior army officers, high-ranking Party cadres and municipal leaders.

'Yes,' she said cautiously. 'This is Peng Ziwei.'

'I have bad news for you,' he said, over the crackling line. 'Your mother has had a severe stroke, which we believe will be fatal. I have sent a team of nurses to monitor her on a twenty-four-hour basis in her apartment, but we fear she may not live for many days.'

'Oh, no,' Ziwei gasped, and then, ridiculously, because it was the first thing that came to her mind: 'I was about to write to her with good news.'

'I see,' said the doctor. 'Well, I suggest you come quickly and deliver your message in person.'

Ziwei, struggling with grief and the implications of what he had said, almost despaired. 'I – I can't leave here.'

'Really? This is very urgent. We have checked the timetable. There is a train leaving Shishan tonight at ten o'clock, which should bring you into Beijing before dawn. We have taken the liberty of reserving you a soft sleeper. The ticket will be waiting for you at the station. There is a connection to Shanghai at nine thirty a.m., which will get you here some time in the afternoon. Again, a ticket has been reserved.'

'You've – you've reserved tickets? I don't understand, but – but it isn't so simple. My *hukou*. I would need permission and that usually takes weeks or months. I am a—'

'We know your status,' said Dr An, impatiently. 'The Tranquil Springs Re-education Camp has been informed, and a travel pass will be issued to you at your home in the next couple of hours. You should make immediate preparations.'

This was beyond her comprehension. Suddenly she had a vision of Fu-kuei on her deathbed. 'My mother . . . my mother . . . is she . . . ?'

'She's comfortable. We're doing everything we can for her. For now, all you have to do is prepare for your journey. I'm sorry. This is a bad line. I'll see you tomorrow.'

'But why is she receiving such privileged treatment?' she asked, but too late: he had hung up.

Yanqing had been watching her anxiously. 'What is it, Mama?' she asked. 'You're shaking.'

'I've bad news – terrible news. Your granny is dying, and I have to go to Shanghai immediately.'

'But how can you?' the girl asked, frowning.

'I don't know,' Ziwei whispered, as tears fell down her cheeks. 'It's been arranged.'

Ten hours later she found herself in the unaccustomed luxury of a soft sleeping compartment in a train heading south, but she could not sleep. She was unnerved by grief, frightened and confused. She could not help thinking of the enigmatic conversations she had had with her mother when she had pressed her about the mysterious assistance that had saved her from execution and beating by the Red Guards. Again she was baffled. Who *were* the people helping her, and what secret was her mother taking to her grave? With the numbing sense of impending loss, she felt a more bitter sorrow. Her mother was dying and, Ziwei realised, she had never really known her. And she had no idea what mystery awaited her in Shanghai.

17

Yangtze Gorges

Shanghai and Beijing: 1986–7

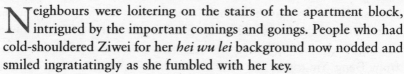

Neighbours were loitering on the stairs of the apartment block, intrigued by the important comings and goings. People who had cold-shouldered Ziwei for her *hei wu lei* background now nodded and smiled ingratiatingly as she fumbled with her key.

She could barely recognise her old home. White-garbed nurses were padding around purposefully. Machines clicked and whirred, and her mother's bedroom had been transformed into an oxygen tent.

A tall, young doctor, alerted by one of the nurses, stepped out, unclipping his mask and peeling off his gloves. 'Are you the daughter?' he asked curtly. 'I'm An. We talked on the telephone. Good. All the arrangements worked smoothly, then.'

'I want to see my mother,' she said firmly.

'We're examining her now and administering medication. We won't be long.'

'But how is she?'

'Doing as well as can be expected. We're concentrating on keeping her comfortable. Morphine,' he added. 'Better she rests. She's semi-comatose.'

'You mean I can't talk to her?'

'She has lucid moments. Be patient.'

'I demand that you tell me what's going on. Who are you? Why are you here? Why is she getting this special treatment?'

He observed her curiously. 'You don't know?' he asked.

'No, I don't,' she said, trying to keep her temper. 'She's an ordinary teacher. She's poor. She can't afford . . .' She waved a hand. '. . . this. This is the sort of attention state leaders get.'

'Well, if you don't know, neither do I,' said Dr An. 'I just have my orders.' For the first time he had dropped his professional air. 'Look,

400

I must go back. I'll be about another thirty minutes and then you can go in to her. You must be tired after your journey and probably still in shock. I'll have one of my nurses make you a pot of tea – and, while you wait, I suggest you look through some of those letters on the table. After you're read them everything might make more sense to you.'

The table in Fu-kuei's study was covered with flowers and among them lay several imposing envelopes, all addressed to her mother. Ziwei caught her breath when she saw the national emblem embossed in gold on expensive paper. Nervously she opened the first. It contained a simple message: 'The nation wishes you a speedy recovery from your illness.' The address at the bottom, in red print, was that of the Zhong Nan Hai, and the letter had been signed by the Prime Minister, Zhao Ziyang. With shaking hands, she opened another. It was handwritten, from Deng Yingchao, the widow of Zhou Enlai, who thanked her mother for 'services that have put you for ever in our debt and in our hearts'. There were letters from veteran Politburo Standing Committee members, Li Xiannian, Peng Zhen and Song Ping, another from the up-and-coming Li Peng, and there was even a short note signed by Deng Xiaoping's secretary. It described her mother as an 'unsung revolutionary hero and martyr'.

When she sat down for her tea, Ziwei was dazed and more than a little afraid.

Fu-kuei was unconscious when Dr An allowed Ziwei in to see her. She was breathing heavily through an oxygen tube that had been inserted in her mouth. In fact, the frail body was an appendage of tubes and wires, and on the shelf above the head of the bed a cardiogram showed the faint beat of her heart. Ziwei, however, saw only the sharp-featured face, which had shrunk to the bone, the skin almost translucent, and the slick of hair, no longer grey but pure white. The lip and cheek were twisted by the stroke. It was the familiar mask of death that she had seen in the Laogai. Until then she had preserved some hope that, despite what Dr An had said, her mother might recover, but now experience told her the end was imminent. She sank on to the chair that Dr An proffered, stroked the withered hand that lay on the sheet and wept.

'The nurses will come in and out from time to time, but no one will disturb you here,' said Dr An. 'I'll be back later tonight to see how she is. If you need anything, call Nurse Hu.'

'I want to say goodbye to her,' moaned Ziwei. 'There's been so much unsaid.'

'When the morphine wears off, she may come round for a while, and you'll be able to talk. It's difficult for her to speak after the stroke – but perhaps you will find a way to communicate. I'm sorry,' he added, hovering. 'I have other patients at the hospital.'

'Thank you,' she managed. 'You've been very kind.'

She began the lonely, heart-breaking vigil.

The machines whirred.

It was in the early hours of the morning that Fu-kuei stirred. Ziwei was alone in the room. She started awake, and saw her mother's eyes, contemplating her. Her mouth twisted further when she attempted to smile. She was trying to speak, but Ziwei could not distinguish the words.

She leant forward and kissed Fu-kuei's forehead. 'It's all right, Mama, I'm here. Don't talk if it's an effort. Just relax. I'm with you.'

Slowly her mother's head shook from side to side. The eyes glinted and her hand slowly rose, her finger pointing to the side table. It took Ziwei a moment to realise that she was indicating a notepad and pencil. She held the pad steady while, with difficulty, her mother scratched out some characters: 'No sorrow. Happy to leave this life join your father. Happy you here, my beautiful baby.'

'I know, Mama, I know,' murmured Ziwei, through her tears.

Again the old woman shook her head. Wincing, she tore off the first sheet on the pad, and the pencil moved once more, spelling out, this time in English, 'Important when doctors go look behind wall.' She sank back, panting, but after a moment, she had recovered enough strength to continue: 'Dr Johnson, where you played. Destroy note.'

The old eyes stared at Ziwei intensely. Ziwei was baffled ... Then, suddenly, she remembered: she had been a small child, playing with her dolls on the floor of her parents' study while they worked. She had been learning the alphabet and was trying to make out the names on the lowest shelves of books, and she remembered her triumph, when she proudly announced, 'Bos Well's Liffee of Der Jon Son.'

'Well done,' her father had cried. 'Aren't you clever, you funny child? But it's not Liffey – that's a river in Ireland, although I'm sure Boswell and Johnson liked a sip of its famous water now and again – this word is pronounced "Life", and "Der", by the way, is "Doctor".' For a long time she had puzzled over how 'D' and 'R' could possibly be pronounced 'Doctor', and why people would want to drink river water, which, if it was anything like the Huangpu or the Suzhou Creek, was smelly and brown, but she never forgot the episode, and neither did her proud parents, who would often tease her about her mistake. It had become a family joke. But now she realised she had been given a code. Her mother had hidden something behind the wall where she used to keep her Boswell. Why she had no idea.

But, at the moment, it was the last thing she cared about. She only wanted to relieve her mother's anguish. All this writing had tired her out. She put her hand over Fu-kuei's, and squeezed it. 'I understand, Mama. I'll do exactly as you say. Whatever it is you've hidden behind the study wall, I'll find, and I promise to keep it secret.' She was relieved to see Fu-kuei's face soften. The eyes opened wider, and she gazed fondly at her daughter, as if she was trying to memorise each feature. The mouth opened again, but this time, though the words were distorted, Ziwei made out the meaning: 'I love you.'

'And I love you, Mama,' she sobbed. 'So much. I'll be so lonely when you're gone.'

She felt her hand lightly squeezed.

'I've so much to say. About Yanqing, who sends her love. She's passed, Mama. She'll begin English Literature studies in Beijing next year.'

The eyes closed, and the head, resting on the pillow, nodded. Fu-kuei looked composed, almost content. Her fingers curled round Ziwei's. She soon fell asleep.

Finally Ziwei dozed. When she woke, daylight was flooding in from the sitting room. The nurses were busy around the bed, although they had not touched her mother, who was lying in exactly the same position as she had been in when she fell asleep. She looked calm, and at peace. A fluttering hair on her forehead, disturbed by the swish of a nurse's skirt, even gave the illusion of life. The green line on the cardiogram above her head was flat, though, and had probably been so for some time.

Three days later there was a funeral at the Long Shan cemetery. Ziwei sat in the hearse at the head of the entourage of official black cars. In front of her she could see the flashing lights of a police car and three motorcycle outriders. Her mother's last journey was accompanied by the scream of sirens. The crematorium was packed with men in smart Mao suits, none of whom Ziwei knew. She presumed they were representatives of the state leaders, whose huge presentations of flowers, with their names written on red ribbon, lined the walls. The mayor of the city, blinking behind thick black spectacles, read an oration in a solemn, literary manner. Again, there were references to a hero and revolutionary martyr. To Ziwei, this was more surreal than anything she had experienced in the Cultural Revolution. The only thing that was tangible and real was the pinewood box in which lay the remains of Fu-kuei, and she thought how, only an hour ago, she had kissed the cold forehead of her mother, who was leaving her for ever. Ziwei was the only one weeping when the clanking began, and the coffin moved towards the furnace, disappearing behind velvet curtains, which closed with an air of finality while the national anthem played from loudspeakers on the wall.

Later she was allowed to place the urn with her mother's ashes in the alcove of the wall in the closed-off section of the cemetery for revolutionaries and martyrs. After she had done so, the men in Mao suits dispersed to their parked cars, leaving her alone.

Or not quite alone, she discovered. A man was waiting by the gate. He was grey-haired and wearing the uniform that had been restored to the military after the Cultural Revolution. There were two stars on each of his wide shoulder boards. He was a general.

'Comrade Peng,' he said, when she was leaving, 'allow me to offer my condolences at this sad time for you. My name is Wei. It does not matter from which section of the military I come but, as you see, I have a senior rank, and it has been left to me to explain to you one or two things.'

'You can explain first why my mother has just received the equivalent of a state funeral.' She could not hide the anger in her tone.

'It was not a state funeral. It was a private ceremony. As you may also have observed, there were no press in attendance. We would like to keep this discreet. Your mother was a noble revolutionary who served the state, but it was in an unofficial capacity, and it has not yet been judged appropriate to make any public notice of the honour she has received.'

'I don't care about publicity. I just want to know what she did to merit such attention from the government.'

'As our mayor said in his oration, your mother was a hero and martyr, Comrade Peng. It should be enough for you to know that, and be proud. You should be grateful, too, that the state has recognised her contribution, which would never have happened in the years of turmoil. You can be comforted that her patriotism has been rewarded. Savour the honour, Comrade, that your family has been given – and keep it to yourself.'

'So you're not going to tell me?'

'It is unpleasant for me that I have to remind you of your status, Comrade. You are a released convict from Reform through Labour. Your record since your release has been exemplary, but we are still monitoring your actions. I do not think that you wish to jeopardise the business you have created in your place of domicile, or your daughter's good prospects, with another term in the Laogai.'

'So you're threatening me on the day of my mother's funeral?'

'It is no threat, Comrade. I have merely stated facts. All I want is your personal guarantee that you will inform no one of what you saw and heard today, nor tell anybody of your mother's revolutionary background.'

'Since I know nothing about my mother's revolutionary background, I can hardly tell anybody, can I?'

'Your guarantee, please. A verbal one will be enough.'

'All right,' she said. 'You have it. Can I go now, please? I wish to mourn in peace.'

'Certainly,' he said. 'You are free to remain in Shanghai for the term of your pass. Then you must return to Shishan. In the meanwhile, do you have transport to return to the city? I would be happy to offer you a lift.'

'I'd rather take a bus,' she said.

'As you please. If by any chance you have a problem, or need an extension for your travel permit, here is my number and a post-box address, but it would be better if you completed the clearing of your mother's effects in the allotted time.' He saluted, then departed, leaving her breathing heavily and pummelling the cemetery wall.

She had to spend an unbearable day receiving calls from the neighbours, whose hypocritical condolences hid feverish curiosity. To allay suspicion, she was polite to them although they went away disappointed, having learnt nothing. That was hardly surprising. She had nothing to tell them.

It was late in the evening before she was alone. Immediately she went to her mother's study, where the shelves were still empty except for a pathetic line of books that consisted mainly of the Shakespeare and other works Ziwei had given Fu-kuei on her last visit. Kneeling down at the shelf where her mother had once kept her eighteenth-century collections, including the Johnson, she tapped on the wall. It was hollow.

It took her a little time, but with a kitchen knife she scraped off the wallpaper, revealing neatly aligned planks of soft board. They were easy enough to cut through, but it took all her strength to pull the rusting metal trunk she found behind them into the room.

She broke two knives before she could lever open the lid. Inside she saw . . .

Ballgowns, in the Western style, with taffeta skirts and lace hems. Cheongsams, one on top of another, neatly folded: green silk with a golden butterfly design, pearl grey adorned with pearl buttons, one of deep blue velvet, another cut in traditional style but the cloth was a zigzag art-deco pattern of oranges and browns; there were pink ones, red ones, black ones, some embroidered sumptuously with flowers, others plain. The silk rippled through her fingers. There were black and white silk slacks. A mink coat. A leopardskin jacket. A boxful of shoes. Another box containing . . .

Gold bracelets and bangles, pearl and topaz necklaces, ruby and jade pendants, diamond rings and earrings, emerald necklaces and brooches, horn and ivory hairclips . . . It was like dipping her hands into a treasure trove.

She was beginning to wonder what sort of revolutionary her mother could have been when she came across the photographs, some in envelopes, some in boxes, and nearly all of her mother, when she was young. The background and style of clothing showed that they had been taken in the 1920s. In many Fu-kuei was wearing dresses Ziwei had just touched. Usually she was arm in arm with a handsome officer, wearing the belted and jackbooted uniform of the time, presumably of a warlord faction, although in some of the later pictures it was clearly a Kuomintang uniform. Even a child would have recognised it: it was the uniform worn by the villains in all the movies. In one picture, the couple were standing in front of a portrait of Sun Yat-sen, flanked by a Nationalist flag. Her mother was in a simple wedding dress, and the two were posing stiffly for the photographer. This must have been Fu-kuei's first husband, Ziwei realised, the one she had never spoken about but whose name, Ziwei knew, had been Yang Yiliang.

There were pictures of her mother with other people of varying ages – either military, like her husband, or wearing the long gowns of a merchant or an official, or the white ducks and blazers of the man about town, but they all looked wealthy and important. One sequence of photographs appeared to have been taken on a ship. In these her mother wore a cotton shirt and pleated skirt with an elegant straw hat and her husband a white suit. Some of the backgrounds were of palm trees and mountains, which reminded Ziwei of pictures she had seen of South Sea islands. At the very bottom of the last box she came across a photograph of her mother taken as a university student in Oxford. Behind her were the spires of a church or college, and she was arm in arm with an English girl, dazzlingly beautiful, with a shock of hair that might have been auburn. Ziwei wondered if this was Ha Li's mother. She looked for a while to see if she could spot a resemblance, but gave up.

And she was more intrigued, anyway, by what she had seen at the bottom of the trunk. Rows of notebooks, and bundles of letters tied with string. If she was to discover the secrets of her mother's past, it must certainly be from these.

She removed them all, took them to her bedroom and read through the night.

They were more a collection of jottings and *aides-mémoire* than a fully fledged diary, and written in English. On the surface the notes described the life of a socialite, but there were tantalising clues. In the early years there were constant references to a dress shop, all couched in tailoring terms, but as Ziwei read on she had the distinct impression that such itemised accounts of how Fu-kuei had taken this or that fabric to Barkowitz's shop were actually some sort of code. Later on in the diary sequence, there was a similar accounting of how much she had given to beggars and what they had offered in return. Also, throughout, there were references to 'YYL', usually in the context of his offering an opinion, but why would Yang Yiliang, an intelligence officer, offer 'opinions' to dressmakers or beggars? It did not make sense.

The idea dawned on her gradually – it seemed ludicrous at first, but she remembered the spy novels she had read as a girl and wondered if her mother had described an exchange of information through intermediaries. Had she been a spy?

The entries in the turbulent years of 1925 to 1927 during which Shanghai had seen a general strike, occupation by warlord armies, a

Communist uprising and a ruthless crackdown by Chiang Kai-shek and the Nationalists (called ever since 'The Great Massacre' and commemorated in Party folklore as a tragic turning-point of the revolution) were full of obscure references. 'Meeting C Park', 'Meeting C Tea Room', 'Meeting C Cinema' were typical 1925 entries. This sequence ended suddenly after the ominous 'Barkowitz dress shop burnt. YYL knows of B. All over.'

The more closely Ziwei read the entries, the more she suspected that what at first had seemed a fanciful impression was in fact the truth: her mother had been involved in espionage. But for whom? And why? In the March 1927 entries, YYL's 'opinions' and 'ideas' comprised lists of Shanghai districts with numbers against them, which led Ziwei to believe that her mother was passing on information about warlord militia strength or numbers of weapons. None of it was spelt out but the coincidence of the dates alone made that assumption plausible. On the day of the Communist uprising there was a triumphant 'It is accomplished. YYL and I together. There is no longer a need to hide. Together we went to CPHQ flying openly the flag.'

Then, shortly before the massacre, the pages were covered with what seemed to be recriminations. 'B dead. YYL betrayed C', 'I have brought a wolf into the fold', 'Green and red the instrument. Must warn CP, but how? I am a prisoner.' Had her mother found out that the Nationalists were to use the Shanghai criminal brotherhoods, the Red and the Green Gangs, to slaughter the Communists, and had Yang Yiliang betrayed her?

The last entry in the diary was the most tantalising. It was written on 13 April, the day after the massacre: 'YYL saved us from the fire. It is ironic I must thank him for what he belatedly did, even more ironic that I love him, and will for ever more. But he did in the end listen to me, and was merciful. Many have perished but the leaders are saved. Chou and others escaped. YYL paid the gangs to see them out of the city safely. He did this for me. Can I believe that I am redeemed? Time will tell, and eventual victory. But my work is done.'

Ziwei threw down the notebooks. There were hints and clues but nothing solid. She wondered what message her mother had been trying to pass to her. There was only material for conjecture here, and nothing that, on the surface, accounted for the interest the state had shown in her. She must have missed something – but she had not slept for more than twenty-four hours, and her brain was too tired to think any more.

She went to bed, but could not sleep for a long while. The puzzle went round and round in her head. Her mother had been a spy for the Communists, she was sure of that now, but in those confused times there had been many spies, and few had ever been hailed as heroes. She had to have done something extraordinary to merit the state leaders' attention. The answer was probably hidden in that material. She had the code, but not the key. The key? Where could her mother have hidden it? Sleep, when it came, brought no rest, only nightmares, of her mother, the younger version in the photographs, dressed in a beautiful cheongsam, surrounded by sinister Nationalist officers, clutching a box of jewellery to her breast, and moving away from Ziwei with a smile and in the background a mass rally was taking place, while Chairman Mao, flanked by Lin Biao and his officials, silently clapped.

Afterwards she wondered whether the shade of her mother had come in the night to help her because when she woke she remembered the dream and the jewellery box. Later, she acknowledged, it was frustration rather than any process of deduction that caused her, in a fit of temper after she had looked through the notebooks and letters again, to upend the box of jewellery on to the floor. A letter fluttered out, addressed to her. Like the notebooks, it was written in English.

My darling,

I know I do not have long to live, and I am more and more conscious of what has been unspoken between us. I am in two minds whether to tell you this because information is always dangerous and all I want is to protect you and dear Yanqing. But you have a right to know what your mother has done in her life: the evil and, perhaps, the good. I have come to know you over the last few years. I am proud of you, and I love you, and I have realised belatedly what a strong, wise person you are – a credit to your dear father. And who knows? One day you may find a positive use for the disreputable secret your wretched mother would otherwise have taken with her to the grave.

In the trunk you will find my youth, which I have buried. The diaries, when you read them, will reveal to you that your mother, whom you thought was only a university teacher, was once a revolutionary and a spy. I am not proud of anything I have done. The secret life is one of betrayal and counter-betrayal. I spied for what I thought was a noble cause, but my efforts did more harm than good, and the victory for which I fought proved worthless. The Communist state killed your father. It subjected you to years of suffering and humiliation. It all but destroyed me, and it put our beloved country through decades of monstrous tyranny – so I have no qualms about revealing its secrets.

I do not know why I kept the notebooks. It was not a professional or safe thing for a spy to do. I suppose that always, at the back of my mind, I distrusted my masters, originally the Russians whom I fondly thought were our allies, and these coded notes of my operations were a form of insurance. Those were confusing times. They will not mean much to you, but they will to the secret intelligence services of our country, who will be embarrassed if ever their contents are made known. They constitute a sorry story. I was spying on the man I loved, and who loved me. Eventually I found happiness with him, before he was assassinated and I was wounded. At the time I suffered more in my heart than I did in my body, because the very people we had helped committed the murder. But now I think it was perhaps just, if such a thing as justice exists, because we, too, had on our conscience crimes of betrayal and murder. My life since has been a long, long expiation.

We did do one thing, however, of which I am proud, and this is the great secret I am passing on to you. On 12 April 1927, when Chiang Kai-shek and his gangsters were massacring members of the Communist Party in Shanghai, I persuaded my lover, later my husband, to rescue the man who eventually became the prime minister of our country, a good man, who did his best during the madness of the Cultural Revolution to help the people of China as much as he could. Of course I refer to Chou En-lai (or Zhou Enlai as we have been taught to spell him nowadays). On that terrible night, Yang Yiliang helped him do a deal with the gangs, and he was spirited out of the city. That is a secret that the leaders of the country would wish never to be revealed, because it is shameful that a people's leader, even one as venerated as Chou, should have made an accommodation with gangsters to save his hide. Nevertheless the Party was grateful, and although my role could never be publicly acknowledged, it saved me on two occasions when I faced death. They even told me I was a revolutionary hero – much good that ever did me: I do not count the title an honour, and on each of the two occasions it preserved me, I wanted only to die.

Now I am grateful that I did not die, because since then I have come to know you and Yanqing, and learnt to love again. That – and only that – has made it all worthwhile.

I am an atheist. That is the one thing left in the Communist creed with which I concur. There is no God who would allow the misery I have seen through my lifetime. I do not believe, therefore, in an afterlife. That saddens me now, because if there had been, I would have hoped to look down on you and Yanqing, to see how you develop and, hopefully, prosper. You of course have my blessing, for what that is worth. You have never disappointed me, my darling, although my bitterness may have given that impression. It seems a savage irony that the only concrete token of my love that I can leave you is my secrets. Use the evidence wisely.

Your mother, Yu Fu-kuei.

Ziwei read the letter over and over again, then broke down and wept.

Later she found it difficult to reconcile the image of Fu-kuei the revolutionary spy with the woman she had known all her life. It hurt that her mother had never trusted her enough to tell her before. It was only when she transposed herself into her mother's position, wondering whether in her place she would have told Yanqing, that she realised how much Fu-kuei had loved her. Such knowledge would have been dangerous under Mao, and she had wanted to protect her daughter. Gradually, Ziwei began to see that this other life was not so out of character in the woman she had known. It explained her courage, her idealism, and the strength of purpose she had always displayed. Earlier Ziwei had felt only a sense of loss, but gradually it became tinged with pride as she celebrated the life of an extraordinary woman. Fukuei, she realised, had been what every young child imagines their parents to be, a heroine and unique.

And with that realisation came anger. Her mother had given her life for her country. She had accepted a dangerous, humiliating role so that she could pass information to the Party. She had saved one of the country's leaders – and how had China rewarded her? It had sent her into obscurity as a potential embarrassment. It had murdered her second husband, then cynically used her daughter, first prostituting and then sending Ziwei into perpetual exile. It had consistently humiliated and punished Fu-kuei, twice nearly taking her life – and, such was her sense of duty, she had never once spoken out or revealed her secret. Only at the end of her life had the government thought it fit to send her some letters and flowers.

This put Ziwei's own sufferings into a new light. She was not the nobody she had thought she was. She was the daughter of a revolutionary martyr. She recalled the general who had bullied her a few days ago, and felt outraged. The state had destroyed her identity, imprisoned her, expelled her to the borders of the country, brought her back when it was convenient, and was now exiling her again to obscurity and the tentative rehabilitation of a 'Released Convict from Reform through Labour' after she had played her role in their conscience-salving ceremony.

Then and there she decided two things: one, that she would never return to her life in Shishan; the other, that she was free – so free, in fact, that nobody in the country could touch her. She possessed a secret now that the government, even today, would not wish to be known. Their beloved and venerated prime minister owed his life to a Nationalist secret policeman after an accommodation had been made with gangsters.

All her life Ziwei had been the cat's paw of others. She thought of Mao's slogan: 'To make revolution is no crime. To rebel is justified.' Well, it was her turn now.

And she knew that if she played this cleverly, she might – just might – be invulnerable.

Ziwei's rebellion was a quirky one.

The first thing she did was to make an appointment with Zhang Hong, who was, as she had known she would be, reluctant to see her, but this time Ziwei did not play on their old friendship. Instead she came as a businesswoman with a proposal. First, very delicately, she pricked Zhang Hong's self-esteem, implying gently that her role in the foreign bank that employed her was only that of a junior clerk, with little prospect of promotion. Naturally Zhang Hong smarted, and blustered, but Ziwei smiled inwardly: she had assessed the woman's shallow character correctly. The idealism that had made her so impressive as a Red Guard had been corrupted into greed and vanity.

Ziwei changed tack and flattered her, congratulating her on her sophistication and knowledge, telling her she thought her talents were being wasted. How could a foreign company be aware of the qualities of leadership that Ziwei had seen Zhang Hong display in Iron Man's Glade? The young woman preened.

'I'd like to help you, as you once helped me,' Ziwei said.

Zhang Hong eyed her sceptically. 'And how would you do that?' she asked.

Ziwei explained her market garden and retail business, going over the figures, which were impressive. Zhang Hong's eyes widened. It was now time to bring the Heavenly Pleasure brand into a bigger market, Ziwei said. She paused. If Zhang Hong would agree to be a partner and managing director of their Shanghai branch, Ziwei would give her thirty per cent of the profits of the whole company, and she could keep fifty per cent of the profits of East China sales. She had the forecasts prepared. Zhang Hong's jaw dropped. 'You're making millions,' she said suspiciously. 'Why would you want to share it with me?'

'I'm tired,' said Ziwei. 'Perhaps all my years in the Laogai have taken too much of a toll on me. I have a plan, once my daughter has finished her studies, to emigrate abroad and I want to make sure my business is left in capable hands.'

'But how can you do that?' asked Zhang Hong. 'You're a . . .'

'Released criminal?' Ziwei laughed. 'Come on, you're a businesswoman. You know how things are done. Favours here, favours there.' She winked conspiratorially.

'Yes, of course,' said Zhang Hong.

'In fact, I'm beginning to make my preparations now. Moving things abroad.' She half opened her handbag and revealed Fu-kuei's emerald necklace. Zhang Hong gasped. 'You know – family keepsakes that you wouldn't want the government to know about in case they try to tax you.' She paused, as if she had had a brainwave. 'Why didn't I think of it before? I'd need to set up a bank account abroad. Could your bank help me?'

'There are rules,' muttered Zhang Hong. 'Under our licence we aren't allowed to help Chinese nationals.'

Ziwei laughed. 'Oh, there must be back doors, and I'd only want a small account to start with, and use of a security deposit facility. It needn't be in my name. It could be that of a foreigner, a surrogate. Somebody as clever as you, and with so many contacts, could work that out for me. After all, it's because of your skills that I'm considering asking you to become my partner.'

'Considering?' asked Zhang Hong.

'Yes. I'd have to be certain of your full commitment first.'

'I think I can find a way to help you,' said Zhang Hong hurriedly. Ziwei was amused to see how quickly she had overcome her scruples. 'Where would you want this account?'

'Switzerland, perhaps,' said Ziwei. 'I have one or two boxes I'll get round to you now, if you don't mind. Some of my mother's effects: family mementoes, photo albums, that sort of thing. And these jewels, of course. I'd like them kept safe.'

'You want me to get this out of the country for you? That's illegal.'

'I'm sure your foreign colleagues would assist,' said Ziwei. 'If you're not interested in my proposal, of course . . .'

'No, I can do that for you,' said Zhang Hong. 'Our deputy manager, a German, he and I . . .' She blushed.

Ziwei pressed her hand to Zhang Hong's. 'Oh, I'm so pleased for you, but . . . such a relationship . . . If this man were to be transferred back to his country, what about my proposal?'

'It's all right. He's married,' said Zhang Hong, 'and – and I'm more interested in my career.'

'Excellent,' said Ziwei. 'That's settled, then. Let's seal our new partnership with a small token of friendship.' And she passed the necklace to Zhang Hong under the table.

She spent her last two days in Shanghai clearing out her mother's flat, which involved a certain amount of wallpapering and redecorating.

Back in Shishan, she called a meeting of her managers, explaining to them her desire to take a less active role in the running of the business, telling them about the new Shanghai partner, and outlining the share scheme she had devised so that they would all have a stake in future profits. Then she waited for Zhang Hong's phone call.

When it came, and Ziwei was satisfied that the packages were out of the country, she sent the letter she had written three weeks before to the general she had met in Shanghai. She also told Yanqing that she had to be away on business and apologised that for the next month or two Yanqing must return to Iron's Man Glade to stay with her father. Yanqing was furious, but Ziwei laughed. 'Just look at your face, and I haven't even finished yet. Would it make it easier for you to put up with a short spell in the countryside if I told you that when I get back it will be to take you to Beijing, which will be our home from then on?'

'Beijing? But I'm not due to start college for another seven months.'

'I said *we* would be living in Beijing. You and I together. Don't you think it'd be a good idea for you to settle in where you're going to study? I'll buy a house there. An old courtyard house, perhaps. What do you think of that?'

The girl was still looking at her suspiciously. 'But your *hukou*? How can we move cities? It's not allowed.'

'Oh, I don't think we need worry about that sort of thing any more,' said Ziwei.

The next day Ziwei accompanied Yanqing in one of her trucks to the village. She did not stay long. Once she had made arrangements with the housekeeper, who was looking after Gao, she climbed the old path to Xing's grave where she made a promise. Then, kissing Yanqing, she returned to Shishan with a light heart. The following morning, she took the train to Beijing, where she transferred immediately to a sleeper that in two days would bring her to Chongqing, which was the city in Sichuan province in which Xing had lived.

Ziwei spent much of her time with poets and artists – she found them in Chongging's bars and teahouses, where she quickly established herself, flaunting her wealth, as an eccentric patron. Naturally political events were widely discussed in such circles.

That winter, all the tensions that had been building up in the country during the period of Deng's reforms blew up into student protests in Shanghai. Ostensibly about inflation and living conditions, the protests had a new element, stirred by the astrophysics professor at the Science and Technology University in Hefei, Fang Lizhi, whose writings about human rights and democracy had struck a chord: the foreign press dubbed him the Chinese Sakharov, and speculated about growing dissent among Chinese intellectuals. The rioting was violent but brief, and the authorities soon regained control. However, the result was the dismissal from office of the country's Liberal Party secretary, Hu Yaobang.

But the thawing process had accelerated in China's intellectual community. For the first time since the Cultural Revolution, Chinese intellectuals were gaining easier access to Western writings and ideas. On the economic front, factories were absorbing the technology of

Western companies, and in cultural areas artists were breaking out of the straitjacket of socialist realism to try abstract and other modern forms of expression. Cautiously at first, but with increasing confidence, they were also experimenting with Western political ideas, which they imbibed as readily as the sixties pop music that blared during their 'black-light parties' – the euphemism for their free coupling sessions: sexual liberation in those circles had also become the vogue.

Ziwei was interested in neither the politics nor the sex, but she found the explosion of ideas and culture invigorating. Besides, it fitted neatly with her own plans, and soon she had gathered a diverse group of *liumang* – literally 'vagabonds', as students back from the countryside but lacking jobs liked to describe themselves – who had expressed an interest in her project. They included cooks, minstrels, dancers, and painters.

When she was ready, she returned to Beijing. The reports from her managers in Shishan confirmed that the company had done well in her absence, and the transport business that Zhang Hong had established in Shanghai was taking off – so Ziwei had the money to buy the venue she had in mind.

It had originally been Xing's dream, but Ziwei was doing it for all of them – for Lan Ying, Xiao, Guimei and others who had died while she survived. This would be a memorial to them that would recall what they had talked about when they were starving. It was going to be a Sichuan restaurant, as Xing had wanted.

And, if she had her way, it would be unlike any restaurant the capital had seen before.

The first Yangtze Gorges restaurant opened quietly in a suburb in the south of the city. At this stage, Ziwei was concentrating only on acquiring a reputation for the quality of the food. She was not overly worried because she had found a master chef, who had also spent time in a Laogai and knew exactly what she wanted. On the first night, journalists from all the major newspapers and magazines sat down to a feast. The names of the dishes might have been familiar to *aficionados* of the hot, spicy cuisine to which Sichuan had given its name, but none had eaten anything prepared with such bravura and style.

The starter was Candlewick Beef, threads of meat marinated in red spice and moulded together with oil, that melted in the mouth. The Fish-flavoured Eggplant was a vision to the eye, each slice of aubergine and pork diced, then mingled with herbs and chillies so it resembled fish scales flashing in a river. Husband and Wife's Breath was a *tromperie* to tongue and eye. Even though it was made of vegetables, it looked like slices of tender beef folded in a rich red sauce, and the cook had managed to capture the taste of meat. There was Fish Head and Green Pepper, where the fish eye on the plate gazed at each diner from the greens, like a pike in river grass. The Sizzling Mutton was just that, but served in a yellow broth, flavoured with chillies and beanshoots. There was Sweet Meat Tang Yuan, Fish and Beancurd, there were Pearl Shrimps – another trick with vegetables in which the breaded beetroot looked and tasted like prawns – and to finish, so that her customers were exposed to the true Sichuan experience in which the food is not only spicy but numbs the mouth, she served a hotpot, with red chillies floating in an offal and meat stew. Everything was washed down with copious quantities of Wu Liang Ye spirit, and hot rice wine.

Next day the newspapers that praised this 'feast of the senses', 'this excursion into ancient rural Sichuan', this 'experimental palate of tastes' arrived at the same time as the police, who put a no-entry poster on the door and led Ziwei away in handcuffs.

She had been expecting this to happen. She had not bothered to apply for a licence because she had known it would be refused. No private restaurants were allowed, since eating, like almost anything else, was a state monopoly. She sat contentedly in her cell in the district gaol – it was luxurious compared to what she had been used to – and waited for the letter to arrive, ordering her release. It duly did. The policemen looked at her with new respect. It was not every day that an instruction from the Zhong Nan Hai reached their neck of the woods.

It took a month to find a new venue, this time in Haidian, to the west of the city, but well located in the student quarter of the town. Again, it was a modest establishment. Ziwei knew that it, too, would be closed. Yet this time she spent a month decorating it. The walls were covered with art, mostly modern – big, shocking oils, and several nudes – but they were interspersed with hangings in the blue and white speckled broadcloth traditional in Sichuan. A primitive carving was placed near every table to delight or, perhaps, astound the eye. And the food was as good as before. New journalists came, and wrote even more excited reviews, before the police appeared with the handcuffs, and Ziwei found herself once more in gaol.

This time she was inside for less than twenty-four hours, but it was another general who came personally to ensure her release. This one had three stars on his shoulder boards, and she knew him. He was waiting outside for her by his car as she was ushered out of the police station by the superintendent. 'You?' she said. 'I was hoping you were dead. I wasted my squirrel on you.'

He laughed. Chen Tao had regained his former weight, although his face was lined and his hair was peppered with grey. 'Was that what the meat was? I never knew. Anyway, it saved my life. I owe you for that.'

'You owe me a lot more than for the squirrel,' she said. 'You destroyed my life. And you tried to murder my mother.'

'Yet you helped me when I was dying.' He was still smiling, but his bulging eyes contemplated her curiously. 'I've always wondered why you did that.'

'We all make mistakes,' she said.

'Was it a mistake?' he asked quietly. 'In those camps, you learn many things about yourself and others. None of us comes out unchanged.'

'You seem to be right back where you were before you went in. Promoted, even. What murky plans are you concocting now to destroy other innocents' lives?'

Again, he laughed. 'I am a little more reluctant to play God than I was. My objectives are modest, these days. I have been humbled, perhaps, by you and others.'

'I'm supposed to forget the past, am I, because you have discovered virtue?'

'No, the past will always be there. Its chains and manacles remain even after you leave the Laogai. You were right to say I owe you. Perhaps you will accept a first down-payment and have lunch with me. Sorry, this is an official invitation. I have messages to pass to you.'

He drove her to the Peking Hotel where he had booked a table in the Sichuan restaurant.

'No private room? I thought that was more your style?'

'You're not an enemy agent,' he said. 'They're the ones who get the top-level treatment. Or perhaps you are – but in a rather more subtle way. Anyway, we're here. Why don't you order? You're the one who knows Sichuan food.'

When the dishes were on the table, she asked, 'So, what do you want?'

He sighed, as he chewed a prawn. 'What we would like is for you

418

to disappear back to Shishan,' he said, 'but we all know that isn't going to happen. We would also like you to stop opening these subversive restaurants, but I know you're planning even now to open another. I suppose we could send you back to the Laogai.'

'You're welcome to,' she said, 'but if you do certain documents in a foreign bank will be released, and an article will appear in the foreign press that will embarrass you.'

'Oh, yes, and it would be a big scandal, and we'd deny it, and historians would burrow away at whatever the truth was until the end of time, but as far as the rest of the world is concerned, it would soon be forgotten. At the end of the day you can't blackmail a government, Ziwei.'

'Well, go ahead. Lock me up. Liquidate me.'

'I don't think there's any necessity for that. It would be uncivilised and ungrateful. I never knew it at the time, or I certainly wouldn't have gone near either of you, but your mother was a revolutionary hero, even if her daughter is showing all the signs of becoming an accomplished dissident. I think, actually, what is worrying us most is how far you're prepared to go in working off this tantrum of yours. Where will it end?' He helped himself to another morsel of food. 'You've chosen well, by the way. This beef is excellent.'

'It's nothing compared to what I serve in my restaurants. That's what I am: a restaurateur, no more, no less. Only I live in a country where I'm not allowed to open a restaurant. I think it's you who are throwing the tantrums.'

'All right,' he said. 'What if I were to tell you that effective from this morning, you are no longer in the category of 'Released Convict from Reform through Labour', that you've been exonerated, pardoned, whatever you like to call it, and all record of your detention, as well as such old-fashioned labels as *hei wu lei* and others have been removed from your Party record?'

'I'd say thank you very much.'

'You should thank me. I spent hours doing all the paperwork, more than I did when I put you inside. Oh, by the way, that includes your *hukou*. It can be changed to wherever you want it to be in China.'

'Again, thank you, but I'm still a restaurateur. In Beijing,' she added.

'I was afraid you'd say that. It means I'll have to go outside my brief. What if we allowed you to open your restaurant?'

'In a place of my choosing? In the style and fashion I want?'

'Absolutely. I've read all the articles. I can't wait to be a customer.'

'With no attempt at state control?'

'Who would have the temerity to try to control you, Ziwei?'

'And the condition, presumably, is that certain boxes of diaries, now in a Swiss bank vault, are returned to China?'

He raised his hands and bowed his head in acknowledgement. 'Let us say that you agree voluntarily to offer historical records in your family possession to the care of the state archives for them to keep in perpetuity.'

'And what guarantee do I have that, once they are with you, you will not go back on the deal?'

For the first time he looked serious. The bulbous eyes stared directly into hers. 'Because I am in your debt, Ziwei, also in perpetuity. Put it down to a shared taste in . . . squirrel meat.'

She leant back in her chair and contemplated him. She remembered how he had terrorised her and her mother in Fu-kuei's flat, how he had beaten her, and how she had pleaded with him in his car to spare her mother, and his cruel, rejecting laughter. Then she saw him as he had been by the latrine, in the snow, dying, a bucket of excrement at either side of him, one more broken human being, like all the others in the camp, including her.

'I mean it,' he said. 'And not just because of the squirrel. It will take a lifetime to repay the debt I owe you for having taken your life away from you.'

Suddenly she remembered Ha Li, and his affection for this man, who had once been – before he became a secret policeman – an ordinary boy, the son of a cook, playing on a mountainside.

Was it true? she wondered. Was it possible to regain basic human decency, with which everybody is born but which society and systems use, pervert and strip away?

She looked into the face of her old tormentor. Not with Chen Tao, she thought. No, that would be too much to expect. He would never change, whatever he said. He was not a man she could ever trust – but he was a man with whom she could bargain because their interests were temporarily aligned. 'All right,' she said finally.

'Thank you,' he said, and visibly relaxed.

'I have more terms,' she added,

His eyes widened – she could not tell if it was with amusement or alarm.

'I want a *hutong* house, a large one, with at least three courtyards. It has to be in the centre of town. Off Wangfujing would be best, where the foreigners and tourists go. I'll pay good money for it, but I want you to secure all the permissions.'

'Wangfujing?' He shook his head. 'Why so modest? Why not demand a subsidiary palace of the Forbidden City?'

'Wangfujing will be fine. Can you help me?'

'I suppose I'll have to if I'm going to eat any of the fabulous dishes the newspapers are raving about. I take it you want this place tomorrow?'

'Yesterday would be better,' she said.

Chen Tao nodded, smiled and bent his grizzled head over his food.

The new Yangtze Gorges caused a sensation when it opened. It was her most ambitious establishment yet. In the courtyards of the old temple that Chen Tao had secured for her, there were food stalls, acrobats, conjurers, folk-singers and dancers. The act the foreigners enjoyed most was that of the Sichuan face-changer who, dancing in full operatic costume, as if by magic slipped one garishly painted mask after another on to his face without anybody perceiving his sleight of hand, and then, at the end of the act, bowed with his own very human face – although by that stage none of his audience was quite sure if it really was.

As with her second restaurant, but on a much grander scale, every room was decorated in a unique and stylish way, with risqué modern paintings or the handicraft tapestries from the south-west.

The dishes were even more exotic and varied than before. The waiters wore old-fashioned Sichuan costumes and poured tea from long copper spouts so that an arc of steaming liquid descended with remarkable accuracy from a distance of two yards, like a waterfall over one's head, straight into the tiny cup and not a drop spilt; this was accompanied by a triumphant shout and claps from smiling waitresses who, as a change from the surly service that people had become used to in state-run restaurants, were actually attentive to the guests.

Local and foreign journalists covered pages with florid prose describing its style, its extravagance, its idiosyncrasies, its humour, its deep roots in ancient folk culture, the sense of excitement, unconventionality, sheer audacity and breathtaking chutzpah. 'Every evening is a carnival – a thumb on the nose to conformity,' wrote the *New York*

Times, then went on: 'These are early days in China's reform – it is still the monochrome society of blue work jackets and bicycles, and anything smacking of originality or colour challenges the rigid autocracy that still rules people's minds. The Yangtze Gorges restaurant is unique. It is an emblem of the new entrepreneurial spirit that is blossoming in China. At the same time it challenges the whole Communist system.'

Sometimes they would even write about the thin, bird-like woman, with leathery, weatherbeaten skin and worker's fingers, who would on any given night be seen hovering in the background, eyes narrowed as she observed the waiters through the smoke of a cigarette that seemed to hang permanently from her lips. Invariably dressed in a black leather jacket and jeans, her tomboy fringe flopping over her brow, her cheeks and lips made-up delicately to hide her age, she made an unlikely rebel. There was speculation as to the identity of the woman who had taken on the establishment and won.

Nobody could explain why she was given such privileged treatment. Gradually she took on a reputation for being untouchable and, among a certain group of the populace, she became a heroine – the underdog who had challenged the government.

It became common practice for the foreigners who dined there to try to spot the security men, who must be keeping her under observation. Ambassadors told the Ministry of Foreign Affairs how wonderful it was to see free enterprise being given free rein, always mentioning the Yangtze Gorges in this context, in the hope that a bland official would let slip an indiscreet remark, or an indication that the Yangtze Gorges would be closed down. It had become a litmus paper by which the progress of reform could be gauged. Yet the restaurant only became busier.

Ziwei was aware of the chatter, but she didn't care. All she was concerned about was that a night at the Yangtze Gorges was an experience that nobody would forget, that they would enjoy themselves and have a good meal.

In the league of rebellions, it was small, but it was meaningful to many Chinese, who gathered there to talk, in total freedom, about life, politics, art, culture, society and any other subject under the sun. After more than thirty years of greyness, the spontaneity of the Yangtze Gorges had brought colour to people's lives, and something else, perhaps even more subversive: a degree of normality. It reminded people that, after thirty years of revolution, they had forgotten how to live.

And as for Ziwei, whenever she thought about it, she realised she was content. Her daughter was settled at her university. Her business in Shishan gave her an income. The restaurant was her pleasure, a debt repaid every day to her lost friends. She was no longer bitter. She had no particular desires. She enjoyed each day as it came.

She was free.

PART THREE
Tiananmen

18

The Fisherman

Vancouver, September 1988

Harry's fishing boat, on which he worked and slept, was the smallest, ugliest and rustiest vessel in the Fraser river. Perversely, he had named it the *Whale*. The bridge was narrow and top-heavy – the boat had no aesthetic lines – but it accommodated the wheel, the controls, the radio, the sonar and, somehow, when the boat was sailing, the towering bulk of Harry himself, even though he had to squeeze past a huge cupboard of fishing gear to get there. At the stern, no allowance had been made for the comfort of his clients: there was a hearthrug-sized deck above the hold, with three peeling plastic seats and rests for the rods.

On hot days, other boats tended to moor upwind to avoid the stench of fish and oil. Nobody had come up with an epithet that came near to describing the squalor of the forward cabin. The charitable might have said the tiny compartment resembled a polar explorer's tent, stripped of anything but the most essential gear, while a professor from McGill university, who had gone fishing with him, had once regaled an attentive audience in Sally's Bar with a description of how he had had to wade through piles of unwashed clothes, dirty plates, books, ropes and tools in the narrow space between the mattress and the makeshift galley before he could get to the heads. 'It was worse than any student digs,' he said, 'and they can be horrible. It was a veritable cloaca.'

No one knew what a 'cloaca' was, but when the professor translated the classical term, the fishing fraternity agreed that 'cesspit' was as good a description as any. Later that night someone crept aboard the *Whale* and pinned a misspelled cardboard sign on the door. It must have struck a chord because a week afterwards a proper wooden plaque could be seen hanging on a nail with the correct Greek letters for 'cloaca' carved in a neat frame. This surprised them. It was the first

427

time they realised that the man they had dismissed as a maritime hobo was educated. It was Al the barman's opinion – he knew Harry better than most – that perhaps Harry believed the epithet applied as much to himself as his cabin. 'People who live like that have no self-respect,' Al pontificated. 'This is a guy who's hiding from something.'

'You think he's some kind of criminal?' asked Gerry Bowens, who had the smartest boat on the pier.

'Could be,' said Al. 'He's done something in his past he ain't proud of, I'd bet on it.'

'It must have been a damned small bank he robbed, if all he could afford to buy was a boat like that,' said Stan, who ran the fishing shop.

'Maybe he wasn't a very good bank robber,' said Gerry, 'and that's what riles him.'

They might laugh at him, but it was always with wary respect, for Harry had a way of impressing people. For all his years, he maintained a tight belly and projected a powerful physique. His stern features were those of a craggy movie star, although his bushy grey beard and his shock of black and silver hair, which hung loose over his shoulders, were more reminiscent of a trapper or hillbilly than any handsome hero of the silver screen. It was the talk of the pier that Harry, despite his wretched boat, was often booked by the best-looking female clients, especially single ones. The joke in the bars was that if any rod was brought out on those outings it certainly wasn't for fishing. Over their beers, the fishermen would describe how if, before dawn, you happened to be in the marina, you might see a dazed rumple of fashion labels and sunglasses chic stumbling in inappropriate heels down the gangplank into the pool of the street-lamp, attempting to hail a taxi, while Harry, tall, barechested, leant against the radio mast, watching impassively as he lit a cigarette. The fishermen would shake their heads in envy and disbelief, and wonder how he achieved his conquests in a cabin so squalid. It was a new definition of slumming.

Nevertheless, the more discerning tourists, those actually interested in the salmon, booked well in advance for a half-day with Harry in the strait. The *Whale* might not have been beautiful or comfortable, but its captain directed it unerringly to where the fish were. Harry used his sonar, as they all did, but those who watched him realised he was heading in the direction of the shoals long before the green blips appeared on the screen. He had read the tides and currents. In the evening when the boat returned to its moorings in Steveston, not far from the picturesque Gulf of Georgia cannery, it was only rarely that the salt-water containers strapped to the side of the boat were not full of thrashing tails. There was hardly a bar on Chatham Street that did not have a framed photograph of some happy tourist grinning by the side of his record catch, with the hulking figure of Harry scowling somewhere in the background.

The other fishermen called him the 'Scotsman', 'Big Harry' or, rather obscurely, the 'Chinaman', for nowadays nobody knew the origin of the latter appellation. If he had another name, no one was aware of it. He had always been plain Harry, and only the oldest remembered a time when he had not been fishing there. He was obviously not a native Canadian because he retained a broad Scottish accent, and his background was a mystery. He never told anybody anything about himself. He hardly ever spoke to anybody, except to shopkeepers when he was buying his provisions, or to the old German clerk in Jumping Jack Fish, the tour agency from which he got most of his bookings, or to the barman in Sally's and only then to order his solitary whisky. At the end of the fishing season he disappeared. Some said he had a cabin way up north of Fort St John, where he spent the winter, hibernating with the grizzly bears, but nobody knew for sure.

There were stories that, in earlier times, some members of the fishing fraternity had resented his unsociable demeanour. It was a profession in which yarning to the tourists was as much of a requisite as the ability to find the fish, and it was galling that this monosyllabic recluse was stealing their custom. One night four of the larger fishermen decided to remonstrate with him gently in Sally's. Argument seemed to have little effect, so one kicked his bar stool from under him. Witnesses of the subsequent brawl, if such it could be called, maintained that it was over in thirty seconds and most had not even seen Big Harry move. After that Harry spent six months in gaol, but three of his attackers were still in hospital when he came out, and the fourth had only escaped more serious injury by hiding behind the bar, where he had scuttled at the first rabbit-chop. After that, people kept their distance.

But he was no longer disliked. In a strange way, he had become a mascot in the community, adding to rather than detracting from their professional mystique. They had become proud of the loner who could read the waters. Although they would never have admitted it, they tended to look at what Harry's boat was doing when the weather or the tides changed. They had all done well by following surreptitiously in his wake, and once when, mysteriously, Harry's boat had suddenly headed back to shore on a calm sea under a picture-postcard summer sky, those who had followed him thanked their stars because that had been the day the hurricane had struck. Later that afternoon Harry, having deposited his passengers, steered back into the storm and rescued five men – three fishermen and two yachtsmen – whose boats were sinking. That had certainly been the act of a hero (some said a madman). Next day, when three reporters climbed on to the *Whale* to interview him, he smashed their cameras and threw one man into the water. He got away with a fine, but maintained his privacy – heroism combined with assault and battery did not make the easiest headline.

Shortly after his court case, and with some nervousness – they weren't sure how he would react – a delegation of fishermen approached his boat. It was evening. He had anchored but not yet set off for Sally's. They found him sitting cross-legged on his mattress, with thick-framed spectacles on his nose, immersed in a book. He frowned at them.

Old Tom Honeycotton – so-called for his white hairs – had been elected as their spokesman. 'Boys think it's unfair, Harry, you going out in the storm and all and saving the Brandt boys, that they come at you afterwards and fine you for it.'

Harry said nothing, continuing to stare at them impassively.

'Well, we decided, if it hadn't been the Brandts, it might have been any of us out there and you'd have done the same. So, long and short of it, the boats have clubbed together and, hell, we've decided to pay your fine for you.'

'I've already paid it,' said Harry.

'Figured we could compensate you all the same. Least we could do.'

Harry nodded slowly. 'It's not that I don't appreciate the generosity but it's misplaced. I don't need the money. The Brandts do. They haven't got a boat now, and I heard they didn't keep up the insurance on their last one. So what I'll do is this. If you put the money you collected for me towards buying a new boat for them, I'll match that sum. Was there anything else?' he asked, and turned back to the book.

'No,' said Tom. 'I think we're all a little speechless, Harry, but we'll do what you say. Thank you.'

'Aye, that's fine, then,' muttered Harry, absently, running his finger down the page.

Afterwards respect for him increased, not only for his magnanimity but also because Tom and the others had noticed what book he had been reading. The short lines on the pages indicated that it was poetry, which would have been impressive enough. What they couldn't get over was that it was printed in Chinese characters. Now they knew why at some time in the past he had been called The 'Chinaman' but that only deepened the mystery that surrounded him.

For a while, never to his face, a new nickname came into circulation, but 'The Professor' didn't catch on. 'Big Harry' seemed more appropriate, so they went back to calling him that. Wiser heads, like Tom Honeycotton, began to suspect that the epithet did not go far enough. Big he certainly was in his limbs and his chest, and clearly in generosity and character, but, if they only knew his secret, Tom suspected, they would find out that Harry, whoever he was, had once played his part in a world of affairs much bigger than theirs.

And that made him more intimidating than ever.

That year the sock-eyes were late running, which was good for the fishermen because there were bookings well into September, even though the winds blowing from Alaska were cold and the water in the Georgia strait sometimes turbulent. Harry had gone to Jumping Jack's as usual to fill up his week's card. Johann, the elderly Panzer Corps commander from Pomerania who had arrived in Vancouver just after the Second World War and had remained in menial employment ever since, was as much of a loner as Harry. In all their many years of distant friendship, neither had asked the other about his past, but that reticence was an unconscious bond and perhaps explained their mutual respect and why, from the very beginning, Harry had been favoured with first choice of clientele.

'That woman's asking to go out with you again,' said Johann, wrinkling his nose scornfully.

'Which one?'

'The rich one. The actress. From Hollywood.' He pronounced the word with distaste.

'The fish are running,' said Harry. 'I'm not in the mood. Who else do you have?'

'There's an energy convention at the Pan Pacific. Oilmen. Three want to go out this afternoon. They'll pay well. Give you a good tip. Hope your refrigerator's full of beer. They'll be drinking more than fishing.'

'Who else?'

'The usual. Individual tourists. None of your regulars this week, although there's one who must have heard of your reputation. Englishman, staying at the Sutton. Asked for you specifically. Tuesday, Wednesday, Thursday, Friday. Ten a.m. to six o'clock.'

'I don't take out Englishmen.'

Johann shrugged and moved the order form aside. 'Then he will be disappointed. Poor Mr Pritchett.'

'What did you say his name was?'

Johann raised his eyebrows at the vehemence with which Harry had asked this question. 'Pritchett. Initial J.'

'Initial J?'

'Yes, initial J. It is not uncommon. Even I have the initial J. It is the only one remaining of my many others, including once a "von".' He observed the fisherman curiously. 'Are you unwell, Harry?' he asked. 'Please be careful with those big hands. They look as if they wish to snap off the edge of my desk – in which case my salary will be docked by Jack, who has an unaccountable affection for this cheap plywood.'

'Sorry.' Slowly Harry unbent. He smiled. 'Stupid of me. I was reminded of a ghost from the past.'

Johann shook his head sadly. 'Ah, ghosts. But that is something I understand, Harry. My refuge is music, Mozart or Bach. It is usually enough to drive away the spectres – at least for a while. And work, of course. That helps too. Which brings me back to the oilmen. You will take them this afternoon?'

'Aye,' said Harry.

'But the Englishman – no? Despite his interesting initial?'

'Put him down too,' said Harry, curtly. 'If he's staying at the Sutton, he must be rich.'

Johann shrugged, and scrawled a signature on the order forms, then noted the times of the bookings. Harry stuffed them into his shirt pocket, nodded at Johann and strode out.

Johann watched through the dusty windowpane, as his friend, the big fisherman from Scotland with a past as haunted as his own, angrily kicked a tin can off the pavement, then sloped off in the direction of the marina, his hands in the pockets of his jeans, scowling at the passers-by.

Johann smiled sadly. Nobody else had come into the office so he sat down in the leather chair next to the cubbyhole where he kept his gramophone. He sifted through his records, drew Bach's Goldberg Variations from its sleeve, and gently placed the needle in the groove.

Harry was brusque. He ignored the outstretched hand and the slow, amused smile, merely telling Julian to sit at the rear of the boat while he edged it out of the marina. He kept his broad back to him as he steered into the grey waters to the south that lay outside the mouth of the Fraser. He was heading towards the airport runway that broke the flatness of the horizon. It was less picturesque for the tourists in that quarter than it was in the western and northern fishing grounds close to the islands, so fewer boats ventured there. He suspected that Julian intended to talk rather than fish, but he was not ready for that yet. He was still trying to bring his conflicting emotions under control.

Even though his back was turned, he was acutely conscious of Julian lounging on one of the seats behind him in his Home Counties shooting jacket and trilby and, no doubt, grinning at him as ironically as he had done when, decades ago, he was his controller. Julian had always been able to see through him, Harry remembered. He was irritated with himself, because superior, upper-class mannerisms were still as challenging to him today as they had been when he was a raw squaddy in Korea.

So he pulled roughly at the wheel, heading into the biggest waves. He was aware that he was behaving badly – rocking and battering the boat to make the ride uncomfortable for his passenger was childish – but he was angry and confused.

Julian's appearance had shocked him. Harry was fifty-eight, so he had been expecting a frail creature in his mid-seventies. He'd thought he would be able to handle an old man – and Julian was certainly white-haired, wrinkled and with more prominent blood vessels on his cheeks and nose, but he walked erect, with the same languid gait, and his blue eyes were as penetrating and mocking as they had been when he was in his thirties. That was unnerving, because it meant he hadn't changed.

And just seeing him had opened the floodgates to the memories Harry had thought buried, as well as the bitterness and rage. It was as if the intervening years had never been, and they were back in the Wendy Room at the legation, watching the flickering film that had destroyed his life.

He needed all of the forty-five minutes it took to reach the fishing point, a knot off the runway, to calm down. He turned off the engine, and the boat began to rock on the swell. He went forward, let down the anchor chain, then leant into the cabin and retrieved two beers from the refrigerator. He lobbed one at Julian, who caught it easily. 'Sorry, the price of your charter doesn't run to champagne,' he said.

'Beer is very acceptable. I can't afford to indulge myself as I used to,' said Julian. 'I'm an old man, Harry, slowing down. I lead a sedentary life now.'

'Not that sedentary. You've just flown five thousand miles across the world. I've never known you go anywhere without some devious purpose. Or are you still going to pretend you're here for the fishing?'

'No, I've come to see you, Harry, but I'm happy to fish for form's sake, if you think it's necessary. Are the sock-eye down there?'

'Thousands of them,' said Harry. He lifted himself out of his seat. 'All right, I'll set out a couple of lines, then. For cover,' he added caustically. 'If you want, you can make yourself useful. There's a tail of tuna in that bucket. Cut it into inch-size gobbets so we can use it as bait. Excuse me while I weight the lines.'

For a while, both men busied themselves, the one expertly tying the lines, the other clumsily cutting shreds of fish.

'Well, for all your hirsuteness and your positively bear-like frame, you're still very much the angry young man I remember, Harry,' said Julian as, ten minutes later, he reclined on his seat, the line twisted against an elegant finger, the wind blowing his white hair. 'Yet you live in such a paradise. Are those the Rockies? Quite spectacular. And, of course, this fine stretch of ocean under the dome of the sky – I'd say your situation was enviable. But, clearly, the great heart still beats with passion in the manly breast. I take it that none of us is forgiven, despite the passing of time?'

'Is that why you've come all this way? To seek my forgiveness?'

'No, Harry. It was a long time ago and we were both doing our jobs. Anyway, it's a different world now. Same enemies, I suppose, but in different guises. Thank God I'm out of it.'

'You're retired?'

'Long ago.'

'Then how did you find me?'

'One still has contacts, friends, who'll remember a favour. You weren't difficult to track down.'

'And why would you want to track me down? Isn't the past best left alone? There's nothing anybody can do about it, so what's the point of going back there?'

'Oh, I think the past is always worth reviewing. I've become a bit of a historian in my old age, Harry. I'm not allowed to write my own memoirs – official secrets and all that – but of course I have, and my son may have a look at them one day, as I have been looking at the memoirs of my own father, who also, it might interest you to know, was involved in the intelligence business in China.'

'Fascinating,' said Harry, draining his beer can.

'It *is* fascinating. What is most fascinating is the element of continuity that one discovers. The forgotten wars and intrigues of yesterday have reverberations that echo into our own times, sometimes in the most remarkable ways. I find that encouraging. We begin to understand ourselves better in the prism of the past, where all the uncertainties and loose threads that bedevil our own work suddenly become neat and tidy when put into a wider perspective. I suppose what one is hoping to find is resolution.'

'Very philosophical. But nothing much was resolved about our own little adventure, was it? It was a tragedy that broke several people's lives. For nothing.'

'I would argue by quoting the late Chinese premier Zhou Enlai, who, when asked what he thought of the French Revolution, said it was too early to tell.'

'Would you?' Harry stood up and went to the cabin for more beer. When he came back, he jutted his beard at Julian. 'Unless you have any more philosophy for me, I'd have a look at your line. It's either your fingers twitching or a fish.'

'My, my, how thrilling,' said Julian, 'but perhaps you'd do the honours. You're much more experienced at this sort of thing than I am.'

Harry helped him pull in a twelve-pound sock-eye. 'Do you want to keep this? Or be photographed with it? Or shall I throw it back?'

Julian shuddered. 'Oh, please do. Appearances are more than satisfied. I feel blooded. Is that the word? It'll give me an excuse to order salmon from the chef in the hotel tonight and think back on my triumph with a fond memory. But, if you don't mind, I'd just as soon sit back and enjoy the scenery while we continue our little chat.'

'As you please,' said Harry, pulling the hook from the fish's jaw, and throwing it back into the sea. It lay stunned on the surface, then twitched into life and disappeared.

He gazed out over the water. There was a splash and a large salmon jumped, its fins gleaming briefly in the sunlight. Far away, on the other side of the boat, he spotted another splash, and another sleek, dark shape plunged back into the sea. 'Why've you come here, Julian?' he asked softly. 'I'm a fisherman now. That's what I was as a boy. That's what I should have stayed. I'm done with China, family, memories.'

'If you like, we can say no more about it. You can drive this boat home and go back to your half-life, or whatever it is, leaving me on the pier with all the other might-have-beens that haunt your existence.'

Harry's temper was on the edge of boiling over. 'There were no might-have-beens, Julian. We saw to that, you and I, when we condemned an innocent girl to slave labour.'

'The girl, yes – she was the essence of it, wasn't she? I was wondering whether you would bring her up. So, you still think of her?'

Harry crushed his can. 'Every hour of my life.' He turned his back on Julian, and leant against the wheel. The sonar was spotted with shoals, and everywhere he looked on the horizon there were scattered splashes of jumping salmon, but he was thinking of two brown eyes, a pink hair ribbon and a pair of buckled shoes.

'I was sharing with you some family history,' said Julian. 'Earlier I mentioned resolution. Perhaps I should also have added redemption.'

'Your point?'

'Sometimes life gives us a second chance – if we're prepared to take a risk.'

'Are you speaking for yourself or me?'

'Both, as it happens,' said Julian. 'By the way, there seem to be a lot of fish jumping in the sea. Is this usual?'

'It sometimes happens. Nobody really knows why. It's a sort of ecstatic madness that comes over them during the running.'

'Ah, madness. We've seen a lot of that in this dismal century of ours. Especially in the China we hate and love. Like human, like salmon, eh? No, Harry. Redemption, if it comes, comes for all.'

Harry had had enough. He was tired of Julian's innuendo. He

switched on the engine and steered the boat into an easier position against the waves that were battering its side. He turned to face his old colleague. 'It's too late, Julian. There's no redemption, no forgiveness. We're who we are, and we must live with it. Let's leave it at that, shall we? Ziwei's dead, and nothing can be done about it. I'm not going to soothe your conscience. I've a hard enough time dealing with my own. So, let's pretend I'm a fisherman and you're my client. If you don't want to fish, I'm taking you back.'

'You're sure she's dead?' Julian was peering at him intently. 'What if I were to tell you Ziwei is alive? Would you remain so . . . phlegmatic?'

Harry clenched his fists and threw back his head, taking a gasp of air to control his mounting rage. 'You're trying my patience, Julian. That's enough or, by God, you go overboard and you can swim back.'

Julian nodded. 'I had to know, Harry. I made you a promise once, many years ago. Belatedly, I have the information you wanted, but I was in two minds whether to deliver it. People change over the years. They get over their anguish and traumas, and achieve a kind of equilibrium with themselves, putting the past behind them. For such people, reminders can be damaging. I had to ascertain that you still loved her or I would have kept silent. Turn off the engine, please. I have something to show you.'

He reached inside his Barbour jacket, and pulled out an envelope, from which he retrieved a newspaper cutting. 'This is small amends for a wasted life, but I think you still have the passion to do something about it, and take the risk, for that's what it will be. If I can help, I will. I can still pull a few strings with the Office should you require passports, contacts, little things like that. I would like to think that at the end of my life I was responsible, in a small way, for a resolution of one of the botches I made.'

Harry took the fluttering pink sheet, a cutting from the *Financial Times*, and read the small print about a restaurant in Beijing, called the Yangtze Gorges, and its remarkable proprietor. She was rumoured to be an ex-convict, the journalist claimed, although nothing much was known about her other than that she was Shanghainese, had single-handedly challenged the government and her name was Peng Ziwei. Of course, there were millions of Pengs in China, and many women by the name of Ziwei, but there was a photograph of this one. She was a small woman, standing next to an acrobat. She had tight, lined skin, and looked older than the fifty years the article claimed was her age, despite her neat, fashionable haircut and the care with which she had made up her face. However, there was no mistaking the shape of the nose, the curve of the eyebrows or the mole on the chin, and the quizzical eyes were the ones that had haunted Harry for twenty-five years.

For a full ten minutes neither man spoke. The only sounds were the whine of the radio mast in the wind, and the slapping of the waves on the side of the boat. The top of the huge white cumulus that had been growing above the mountains was flattening into a black anvil, its tendrils moving over the sky towards them, threatening a storm. As far as the eye could see, the surface of the olive grey water was turbulent, but less with white horses than with the splashes of long dark shapes leaping out and falling back. The ocean had become as densely tumescent as an over-packed fish tank. Oblivious of the worsening weather, the salmon revelled in their last play of freedom before they climbed the mountain streams to breed. The sky darkened and gusts of breeze whipped at the paper in Harry's hand. The first raindrops blurred the print, but he continued to stare at the photograph, his mind churning with conflicting hopes and fears, quite as elemental as the forces of nature being released around the frail craft illumined in the failing sunlight.

'It's getting a mite choppy, old fellow.' He heard Julian's patrician drawl faintly. 'Might it be time to return?'

'Return?' Harry repeated. It took him a moment to grasp what Julian meant. 'Yes,' he said, swaying as the boat rocked in the mounting swell. 'Perhaps it's not too late to get to safe harbour.'

Julian had pulled the hood of his Barbour over his head. In the white, electric light, his face resembled that of a wise old monk. His eyes were gleaming. He had to raise his voice over the wind. 'Oh, I hope so, Harry. For your sake and mine – maybe hers too.'

When the storm hit, Julian took shelter below while Harry stood broad-shouldered against the wheel. The *Whale* plunged through the foam and the leaping salmon, making for the small point of safety on the obscured horizon.

Harry lasted out the fishing season. He needed the money. In late October he locked up his boat and put it into winter moorings, packed a few clothes and books in his gunny bag, then took a bus to the freeway and spent two days hitchhiking north to his cabin in the mountains.

He spent two weeks fishing the lake, storing his catch in his freezer, and another fortnight with his gun, stalking in the woods. In his half-truck, he drove the twenty miles to Fort St John, where he bought the rest of the provisions he would need for the winter. He also checked his account at the bank, satisfying himself that the remains of his savings from the days when he had worked at the power station and the income he had since earned fishing would provide him with enough for his project, should he decide to go through with it.

He was still in two minds. His first impulse, after Julian had left, had been to take a flight directly to Beijing, but he had become cautious over the years. He had forgotten what it was like to talk to a woman. Sex had become a business transaction: it never touched his emotions.

There had been only one woman in his past – he did not count Audrey. He had fashioned his life into a memorial for her. But now Ziwei had miraculously come alive again, and challenged him on every level. He was scared that when it came to meeting her he would not know what to say. He loved her, he always had, but reason told him that, after so many years, she would no longer hold any tender feelings for him. If she felt anything, it was probably hatred. He had been responsible for her incarceration. The last time they had met he had abused her.

The coward in him said that it was too late, that no purpose would be served except to bring further anguish to them both.

What good was an apology, he asked himself, to a woman who had suffered for years in a concentration camp? If he pleaded for forgiveness, he would sound pathetic.

It would be better to leave things as they were.

Yet against that was his desire to see her. Just one more time, he told himself, to settle accounts, to resolve all the hanging questions of the past. He tried to persuade himself that she might even be glad to see him. She must be curious to know what had happened to him. Establishing that each other was all right would take a weight off their minds. Or so he argued, and gradually, as he did so, he became prey to wishful thinking, even though part of him knew it was foolhardy.

It was possible even that she had retained some of her old affection for him, as he had for her. They were both older now. Probably it would be difficult to rekindle the passion of the past, but that was not important at this stage of their lives. Then again, Harry was not that old. Other women found him appealing, and the more he pored over the photograph in the *Financial Times* article, the more the older Ziwei reminded him of the girl who had taken his heart. The inner beauty remained. They could live quietly together in China or Canada. It might initially be friendship, but the old love would return if they were patient with each other, and helped each other get over the pain of the intervening years . . .

His fantasies grew wilder. Perhaps she still needed him. He had no idea why she had opened a restaurant, but the commentary in the article disturbed him, suggesting that this was a provocative, possibly dangerous, action. China was still a totalitarian country, with absolute power over its citizens. Perhaps she was in trouble. If so, he would be her white knight and redeem himself in her eyes . . .

As soon as he thought that he knew how stupid it was.

At the end of the day, there was only one reason that he wanted to see her. He loved her and, however selfish, however irresponsible, however stupid it was, he knew that if he did not pursue this one chance, he would spend the rest of his life regretting it, and this time there would be no Chen Tao, no Julian, no malign Fate with whom to share his guilt. This time the decision was in his hands. If he did not act now, he might as well take the shotgun that, through many long winter months, had beckoned from the rack on the wall of his cabin, slot in a couple of shells and blow his brains out.

On the other hand, the last thing he wanted to do was to hurt her any more than he had already . . .

By the time the snows began to melt, Harry had still not come to a decision.

In mid-April, when he drove his half-truck through the fir woods towards Fort St John, he was changing his mind with every shift in gear. Bumping along the track, he was brought up short by the sight of a stag, antlers held high, standing alone in a clearing on the slope that rose to the north. There was nothing remarkable about spotting a red deer in the woods, but it gave him an idea. If he couldn't make up his mind, he would look for a sign.

He parked the half-truck in Don's Yard, tarpaulined it and went to the bank. This time, he decided not to hitchhike. He bought a bus ticket to Vancouver. On arrival, he took a taxi to the marina, and began immediately to overhaul his boat.

Next morning, before dawn, he set off into the Georgia Strait. By mid-morning he had skirted the Juan de Foca channel and the southern tip of Vancouver Island and was heading into open sea. Just out of sight of land, he turned off the engine, allowing the boat to drift in the slow swell. By four o'clock he had seen nothing except a tanker and two ocean-going yachts. By five, the sky was pink with the sunset. Wearily, he checked his position on the compass and charted a course for home. It was not to be.

He tried to persuade himself it was for the best. His heart was breaking – but he had sworn that he would abide by whatever Fortune decided, and he was not a man to go back on his word. As he was nearing the Broken Group islands and Pachena Bay, he was no longer concentrating on his course. His eyes had misted with regret. He was vaguely aware of the green blips on his sonar, but it was only when he was upon them that he realised what they were.

Half a mile off the wooded shore, already dim in the twilight, he saw darker shapes in the water. Flippers, tails, and then an enormous splash as two orcas breached not a hundred yards from his bow. Even in the twilight, he could make out the black and white markings, the coal eyes in their white rings, the water cascading off the dorsals as, for a moment, they seemed to hang, frozen, in the air.

He rested his head on the wheel, remembering the fishermen's prayers in the kirk after he and his uncle had returned from a long haul in the forbidding Atlantic, words of praise he had forgotten for nearly forty years. If he was honest with himself, he had been envisaging the spout of sperm whale. But a whale was a whale, whatever its size, and he had discovered a pod.

He had his sign.

19

Sacrificial Offerings

Beijing, 17 May 1989

In April, students from Beijing's universities defied a government ban and gathered in Tiananmen Square to pay public tribute to the dismissed, and now deceased, Party secretary, Hu Yaobang. The protests escalated, and so did the rhetoric. The government responded to the demands for democracy with stern editorials, which had the effect of pouring oil on a fire. By mid-May, the central square in China's capital had become a shantytown of tents, with hundreds of thousands of students pouring in from universities all over the country. When the workers 'came out' to support them, up to a million people might be seen marching along Chang An Avenue on any given day.

In the centre of the city the protests brought normal life to a standstill – but for some it was good for trade. The canny Beijing pedicab drivers, who usually eked out an existence giving rides to citizens too poor to take a taxi, suddenly realised they had a monopoly on access to the square because no motor-car could go near it – and charged accordingly.

The Yangtze Gorges restaurant had more custom than it had ever attracted before. At lunch- and dinnertime, people queued sometimes for as long as an hour. In addition to her normal clientele, Ziwei had to accommodate the foreign journalists who had arrived in Beijing in huge numbers to cover the protests.

The famous restaurant was a convenient watering-hole for them since it was only half a mile from Tiananmen Square, but the more perspicacious realised that it was also a place where dissident intellectuals gathered, and occasionally the student leaders. While they enjoyed the excellent food and watched the jugglers and mime artists, they kept their eyes peeled for familiar faces.

Ziwei tried to ensure that they were disappointed, directing the dissidents, when they arrived, to take the north door through the

442

kitchens, straight to the private hall at the back where, for several years, she had run her salon. She spent more and more of her time there, leaving the running of the main restaurant to her staff. There was always the hope that Yanqing, one of the student leaders, might come with her friends from the square. In her absence Ziwei perched on a stool beside a big round table, chain-smoking while she listened to the free-ranging conversation, hoping to glean some snippet of information that might ease her gnawing worry.

Usually the intellectuals blathered on about history and society, about ideal government and what it meant to be Chinese. Ziwei suspected that they frequented the restaurant for the same reason as the journalists. The students, who had a different perspective from theirs, barely tolerated these passed-over warriors who wanted to be close to the action.

The only students who had turned up today were a contingent of Yanqing's runners, who came each morning, with a column of pedi-cabs, to collect the packed lunches Ziwei had been providing, at her own expense, since the sit-ins had begun. When they were all stowed on board and she had paid the drivers' exorbitant fares, she had asked the tall spotty youth in charge, Cheng or Chang – she had never estab-lished his name because of his thick Hunanese accent – how Yanqing was.

'Leading Committee Member Gao Yanqing is an inspirational leader,' he told her. 'She is implacable in her support for democracy.'

Ziwei's heart sank as she heard again the vocabulary of the Cultural Revolution. Such was the limit of these youngsters' experience that they were dressing their new revolution in old clothes. Knowing nothing else, they had modelled their organisation on that of the Communist Party they were attacking. They had central committees, politburos, disciplinary commissions and, it seemed to Ziwei, an ideology as straitjacketed as the government's. Once, when she had tried to see her daughter, she had been turned away at a checkpoint a hundred yards away from the leaders' tent. A beatnik in a headband, who in an earlier incarnation would certainly have been a Red Guard, had packed her off with an earful of slogans.

'But how is she?' she responded patiently to Cheng or Chang. 'Is she in good health? I'm not asking about the state of her ideology, child, but as a mother. You also presumably have one.'

The boy blushed, and grinned uncomfortably. 'Sorry, Auntie Peng,

I was being thoughtless. Leading Committee Member Gao is in fine health . . . Well, she is now . . . but—'

'What do you mean she is *now*?' Ziwei snapped in her alarm.

He shifted his feet uncomfortably. 'Gao Yanqing's put her name down to be one of the hunger-strikers. It may not come to that,' he added hurriedly. 'They're debating it.'

'Hunger-strike?' she gasped. 'What utter madness is this?'

'We have to do something after Premier Li rebuffed Wu Er Kai Xi, Gao Yanqing, Chai Ling and our other leaders in the Great Hall of the People the other night.'

Ziwei felt faint. 'You tell her to come and see me. Or ring me. Do you hear?'

'Yes, Auntie Peng,' he said, obviously anxious to leave.

She spent the rest of the morning consuming nearly two packets of cigarettes and four coffees. What she heard over luncheon did nothing to ease her mind.

The usual crowd had gathered for their free meal. There was a historian from the Academy of Social Sciences, a poet and essayist who had been sent to a Laogai during the Anti-rightist Campaign in the late fifties, a renowned architect, who was also a veteran of the Laogai, an economist, prominent in the Democracy Wall Movement of the late seventies, radical scientists and several dissident artists.

'Their hearts are in the right place,' Wang Lei, the historian, was complaining, 'but they're going about it the wrong way. You won't change the Party by needling it with hunger-strikes and posturings. They should be guided by people like us, those who know how to work within the system.'

'And what have you achieved by working within the system?' asked Lin Zhen, the poet. 'We're the compromised generation. Old Mao sent us to the Laogai and we thanked him for it. So brainwashed were we by the Party that we convinced ourselves it was our own fault we were being punished. Now we've been rehabilitated, what's changed? We still cling to the idea that the revolution we grew up believing in was right in almost every respect. We can't face up to the shame that we were so foolish. Or, worse, wrong. Face it, Lao Wang, we're eunuchs, and these young people have recognised that.'

'I'm no eunuch,' said the history professor, bridling. 'Last year my paper on the anti-democratic aspects of Mao's personality cult was praised by Zhao Ziyang.'

'Typical!' The poet banged on the table. 'Don't you see that that's the flaw in every Chinese intellectual? Mao was right to call us weaklings. You should be ashamed of yourself – boasting because the Party secretary has bestowed on you the colourful robe of a scholar official with which you can impress your family. They've neutralised your protest by giving you a high position, and you grovel to them with thanks. At least these students have balls.'

'I'm sorry, Lin Zhen.' It was Ma Renzhi, the economist. 'Though I don't disagree with you about Chinese intellectuals, I think Lao Wang's also got a point. Simply goading the government, without giving them any position of retreat, will inevitably lead to bloody reprisal. We saw that with the Democracy Wall Movement. The daily escalation of this protest worries me. If I could advise the students, I would tell them to withdraw now they've made their point. You can't institute democracy in a vacuum – certainly not in a country like ours. Half of the students don't even know what it is. It's a slogan, that's all, fine words to hide vague feelings of discontent and a yearning for liberalisation. Well, more experienced heads, like ours, know how to work the system, and we will be in a position to guide the government towards real democracy when they agree to reform.'

'You believe that, you'll believe anything.' It was a clear female voice. All heads turned towards the door where a slim girl, in a white cotton frock, sandals and a sun-hat advertising Coca-Cola, was observing them with scorn. Ziwei flushed, partly with sheer relief to see her daughter, partly with concern at her forthrightness in such august company, but also with pride that she could be so bold.

'Don't you wonder sometimes, uncles, why we don't come to such wise men as you for advice?' Yanqing's brown eyes contemplated each figure sitting at the table. Most dropped their gaze. She pulled off her hat, and her hair, cut into the pageboy-type flop known as the "May The Fourth", a style that had come into fashion again after seventy years as a new generation of students commemorated their famous forebears who had protested against imperialism in 1919, fell around her ears. Confidently she sat down at a spare place at the table, and reached out with a pair of chopsticks for a prawn.

'Perhaps you should,' said the history professor. 'You've embarked on a dangerous course.'

'We're doing all right so far,' said Yanqing.

'You're very young.'

'We are,' she said, 'and, I admit, none of us has your experience, Uncle Wang, or your knowledge. We have passion, however, and that is something that you, with your wisdom, have forgotten. It is our strength and unity, and it prevents us going into long, self-justifying arguments about the best ways of doing nothing.'

'*Hao!* Bravo!' The poet banged on the table again, grinning broadly. 'My point exactly.'

'Yanqing, deeds rather than words are all very noble, but may I ask what exactly you hope to achieve?' asked the architect, a widower and long-time suitor of Ziwei. He considered himself a family friend. 'I'm not sure if you've thought through the consequences. Your mother and I know what it's like to be cast into the Chinese penal system. We wasted our youth there without changing anything. That was the result of our passion when we were young.'

'Have you been out in the streets lately, Uncle Cheng?' asked the girl. 'Have you been to the square? Have you not seen the support we have from the people? Do you think that any government – even this one – can ignore such numbers? All we're asking for is dialogue so we can present our just demands. We're no longer the cowed nation that crawled to Mao. We have no fear of the government or the Party because at the end of the day they must acknowledge that we represent the people.'

'I don't think Premier Li Peng agrees with you, or the Party elders, and they control the People's Liberation Army.'

'The PLA loves the people,' said Yanqing. 'Isn't that its slogan? We're not blind, Uncle. We know we're playing a high-stakes game and we're aware of the symbolism of our actions – but so is Li Peng. He cannot hold out indefinitely against our petitions because they're based on the law and the founding constitution of our country. Is it not shameful that the government of China, in the eyes of the whole world, is spitting on the very freedoms it's their duty to uphold, and to which the Communist Party itself pays lip service? Some of you are advising us to get out while the going's good. Didn't I overhear Uncle Ma say we'd made our point? We haven't made our point, and won't until Li Peng and the others acknowledge that our demands are just. Then, and only then, will it be time for you wise heads to come in and draw up constitutions. For now, we hold firm.'

'And this hunger-strike you're planning? Is that also symbolic?' asked the history professor.

Yanqing's lips trembled. 'No. They must understand how serious we are. We're prepared to die for what is right. I – I've come to tell my mother. This is my last meal before we start our hunger-strike this afternoon.'

Ziwei gasped. Yanqing leapt to her feet and put her arms around her. A shocked silence had descended.

Lin Zhen, the poet, stood up. 'Gentlemen,' he said, 'we should leave mother and daughter alone. However diverse our opinions, I believe we can all unite in a toast to the bravery and patriotism of these young Chinese men and women.' He drained his glass, nodded at Ziwei and Yanqing, then made for the door, followed in uneasy succession by the others.

'Don't worry, Mama,' Yanqing whispered, as she stroked Ziwei's brow. 'The government won't allow it to go too far. The whole of the world's press will be there. I've been talking to them in the restaurant. Can't you imagine the humiliation for those bastards if they stand by and allow their young to die in Tiananmen? The whole world is watching us and them.'

'You don't know them!' cried Ziwei. 'How ruthless they are!'

'It's a different world now, Mama. Look at Russia and Poland. Communism's so rotten it's on the point of collapse. And China's no different. You think Mao or Stalin would have let us go so far? They'll give in. All we're asking is to talk to them.'

'Those men talk with guns, Yanqing, and brute force. That's all they understand.'

Yanqing laughed. 'Since when were you afraid of guns? You're more revolutionary than I am.'

Ziwei stared at her daughter, trying to see in this obsessed firebrand the sweet girl she had raised. She remembered how, during the early days of the protests, she herself had gone to the square and stood among the excited university students, wearing headbands, waving banners and shouting slogans about democracy. These are children – children, she had thought, seeing the grim ranks of policemen on the steps of the Great Hall of the People. They don't know what they're doing.

Suddenly there had been a roar of cheers, and all eyes had turned to the Martyrs' Memorial, where a slight young girl in a sun-hat with a megaphone in her hands was bounding up the steps. She raised both arms and that simple gesture had the authority to still the crowd. For a long moment, while her eyes shone with apparent amusement, she surveyed the faces gazing up at her. Then she began to speak into the microphone, her voice dripping with sarcasm: 'We've been privileged, fellow students. I've just been talking to an emissary from the Zhong Nan Hai.' She waved her hand at the banners and the ranks of protesters that filled almost every inch of the square. 'They've apparently just noticed we're here.' There was a ripple of laughter. Her smile widened. 'And they're concerned. They're worried about us.' She paused. 'They seem to think we're in trouble. We might be arrested, they said. Did we know, they asked, that we were breaking the law?' There was an expectant titter. 'Fellow students, I'll be honest. My heart fluttered with fear when I heard that. Did they think we were an illegal assembly? Were we challenging the Party? Were we counter-revolutionaries?' Her voice lowered. 'But it wasn't anything so mundane as that. No, fellow students, the political aspects of what we're doing don't seem to alarm our wise leaders. We're guilty of something much worse. We've been told to go home – pack up – not because we're exercising our right to bring our grievances to the attention of the state, not because, as patriots, we are trying to do something about the injustice, corruption and nepotism in our country, not because we are demanding the democracy that is enshrined in the constitution. We're being told to stand down because our presence here is disturbing the traffic.'

Ziwei had been deafened by the angry shouts of protest, but her daughter raised her hands again. 'Yes, fellow students, that's the level of scorn in which they hold us. We're not protesters in the honourable tradition of May the Fourth. We're not the young people of China, saying, 'That's enough.' No, we're street hooligans, disobeying the municipal health and safety regulations.' Suddenly she raised her voice, and the amplified screech echoed around the buildings surrounding the square. 'Are we going to allow them to treat us with such contempt?'

'No!' the crowd roared.

'Are we going to go home meekly, as they ask, without making them hear our petitions?'

'No!' The expression on the face of the boy standing next to Ziwei was one of fury.

'Are we going to stay here until our demands are met?'

'Yes!'

Ziwei was jostled as the crowd pressed forward.

'What are we fighting for?'

'Democracy!'

'What are we prepared to give our lives for?'

'Democracy!'

Yanqing had gone on to raise the passions in her audience to fever pitch. She was carried on the shoulders of her fellow students in an impromptu march to the gates of the Zhong Nan Hai compound, where she harangued the crowd again. The policemen standing at the gates backed away in confusion. Ziwei, at the edge of the throng, had watched the stranger who was also her daughter with a mixture of awe and fear. A terrible premonition came over her that Yanqing's idealism would end in disaster.

Now, a month later she felt the same.

As her daughter challenged her, the old anger rose in her breast. 'No, Yanqing, you're wrong. I was no revolutionary. I made the system accommodate itself to what I wanted, never challenged it. And it was only because I had a lever that I could get away with it. You are spitting in their faces.'

'We have a lever too. The people. The whole of China is behind us.'

'Oh, you *are* young. You think the people really care? Don't you remember your childhood in Iron Man's Glade? Peasants aren't interested in democracy. They despise you and your friends. They see you as privileged intellectuals who are threatening stability. When Li Peng sends in the army to stamp you out, they'll support him.'

Yanqing stood up and spoke coldly: 'Then the peasants will have to be guided so that they understand. We're not going to back down. And I will pursue this hunger-strike to the bitter end.'

Ziwei clutched her. She saw the beast that Yanqing fondly thought she could tame with protests tearing her to pieces with its claws. 'Oh, my darling, why you? Aren't there others who can do this stupid thing, if it has to be done?'

Yanqing's eyes were shining. 'I'm Yu Fu-kuei's granddaughter and Peng Ziwei's daughter. Could you see yourself standing by while your comrades sacrificed themselves?'

Ziwei knew there was nothing she could say to dissuade her child.

Yanqing kissed her. 'Give me your blessing, Mama. I'll need your strength and support. You know I love you and I couldn't bear it if you were angry with me.'

Ziwei embraced her, brushed aside her tears and stood up. 'Well, if you're going to do this crazy thing, at least I can make sure you have a good meal before you leave.'

'Yes, Mama,' said Yanqing.

'And you'll eat everything the cook's made. I'm going to stuff you with so much protein you won't be hungry for a week.'

'Yes, Mama. Look,' she said, sitting at the table and shovelling half a plateful of abalones into her bowl. For a few minutes she made a good pretence of gorging herself, then put down her chopsticks. 'You should know, Mama, that you're my inspiration. You always wanted me to be free. You once told me I'd become a wild goose who would fly to the ends of the earth. Well, I'm about to fly now. You should come down to the square some time. I cannot describe the feeling of liberation.'

'I did go to the square. I was sent away with a lecture.'

'I'll make sure you get a pass. You can visit me. I'd like to have you near me.'

'I'm not sure I want to be associated with such foolishness.'

Yanqing laughed. 'Yet once you bit the head of an eel even though you thought it was a water snake that might poison you. We're doing the same now, Mama, because we have to show the people that the snake they're so scared of is only a harmless eel. I'll be all right, I promise.'

'Will you stop talking and eat? Please.'

Yanqing ate, not as much as Ziwei wanted, but both women knew it was only an expression of love. At three she left, loaded with the pillows and blankets her mother insisted she take. She waved from the back of the pedicab, eyes sparkling and white teeth shining in the sunlight. Ziwei watched the creaking vehicle turn into Wangfujing, then, with a heavy heart, made her way back through the kitchens to the empty salon, where she rested her head on her folded arms.

'*Laoban*. Boss.' It was Tan Ming, the head waiter, whom she had recruited in Chongqing and who had been with her from the opening of her first restaurant.

'What is it? I don't want to be disturbed now.'

'One of the guests won't leave. A *laowai*. He's asking to see you.'

'Tell him I don't give interviews.'

'I don't think this one's a journalist. He's – strange. The waitresses are scared of him.'

'Is he drunk?'

'No, he's only taking tea. Pot after pot, but there's something about him. He's very big, and from his expression I think he could become violent. He's been polite so far, speaks very good Chinese, but . . .'

'I really don't want to see anyone right now.'

'If you could just talk to him. It would only take a minute of your time.'

She stubbed out her cigarette and followed him into the courtyard where tables had been set out under umbrellas. The waitresses were standing in a knot at the door of the main hall, whispering to each other, and two jugglers were tidying their equipment after their act, casting sidelong glances at a table in the centre. She saw neatly cut peppery hair and the broad back of a man dressed in a light fawn suit that seemed to strain at his wide shoulders. She could not make out his face since he was leaning over the table. The teacup looked tiny in his massive hand. A bouquet of white lilies leant against one of the chairs beside him.

She adjusted her lips into her *patronne*'s smile, and moved towards him, ready to charm him, as she had done with a hundred difficult customers, but he sensed her presence and rose from his chair, towering above her. He had dark, craggy features. His chin was stubbled and raw, with the pockmarks you sometimes see just after a man has removed a beard. His tie appeared to constrict his neck, and he was sweating in the heat. He stared at her with piercing blue eyes. She had the impression that he had begun to say something and frozen in the act. The deep lines on his tanned forehead looked like whorls on an oak plank.

'Can I help you? My name is Peng Ziwei. I am the owner of this restaurant.'

He continued to stare at her.

Disconcerted, she spoke more curtly: 'My head waiter told me you had something urgent to discuss with me. I cannot give you much time. We're closed now and the staff need to get away.'

He spoke, so quietly that he might have been addressing himself: 'You haven't changed in all these years. Well, you have, but you're still the same.'

There was something familiar about his voice, the modulation of his Chinese. 'Have we met before? Do I know you?' she asked.

'It was a long time ago – too long.' Clumsily he picked up the lilies, and proffered them. 'I brought these for you, Ziwei. I couldn't think of anything else.'

She felt a drumming in her ears and a chill ran down her spine. 'Ha Li?' she whispered, and swayed.

He threw the bouquet on to the table, caught her arm and guided her into a seat. 'I'm sorry,' he said. 'I should have written to you. I didn't mean to shock you.'

She reached into the pocket of her shirt and fumbled out a cigarette. He produced a lighter and lit it. He sat down opposite her, allowing her to draw in the smoke several times before he spoke again. 'I read about you in a newspaper. You're famous.'

She nodded. 'I've been fortunate,' she mumbled. It was the automatic response she gave to journalists. She had still not got over her disbelief.

'Fortunate?' After a moment's uneasy silence, he, too, nodded. 'Yes, I see that. It's an impressive establishment.'

'Thank you,' she said.

He seemed tongue-tied. He rubbed his hands together – she remembered vaguely that he did so when he was nervous. 'There was a girl here earlier,' he muttered. 'Pretty, in a white dress, talking to the reporters. I overheard one of the waiters say she was the daughter of the *laoban*.'

Calmer now, she was feeling angry. How dare he descend on her like this, out of a past she had forgotten, on this of all days, with flowers? 'Yes, Ha Li, Gao Yanqing is my daughter. I have been married for twenty years.'

'Congratulations,' he said, after another uncomfortable pause. 'She's a fine-looking young woman. A credit to you. Why were the reporters paying court to her?'

'She's one of the leaders of the students in the square.' She had meant to leave it at that, and she did not know why she added, with a catch in her voice, 'She's starting a hunger-strike this afternoon.'

He leant back in his chair, eyes half closed, then slowly shook his head. 'I'm sorry, Ziwei. This is a lousy day for me to come calling. I'll go – come back another time when you have less on your mind. Forgive me.' He put his hands on the table to lift himself from his seat.

A moment before she had been willing him to do just that: go, leave her, return to the blank in her memory from which he had erupted, but she reached out and laid her hands on his. 'No,' she said. 'Stay. I could do with the companionship of an old friend this afternoon.' She sat back. Touching him had confused her.

'Thank you,' he said. 'Ziwei, I'm glad you can still call me a friend. I was not sure how you'd react when you saw me.'

She half panicked. She didn't want to think about the past. Not today, when she was worrying about her daughter. She had no idea why she had asked him to stay, only that his presence was familiar, and his offer to leave her to her private anguish had touched her. She became aware of Tan Min and her other staff hovering by the door, observing them curiously. 'Ha Li.' She raised her voice for their benefit. 'Let us go inside to one of the banqueting rooms out of the sun, where we can – catch up on all our news.'

'Whatever you say.'

She shouted to Tan to bring some tea into the salon, and hurried in that direction, followed by Ha Li, who had picked up the ridiculous flowers. Inside, she gestured him towards an armchair, while she sat on the sofa. They were both silent until Tan had brought in the jasmine tea and left. Her hand shaking, she poured it into the little cups. She attempted a bright smile. 'Ha Li, it's been so long since we last saw each other. You must tell me what you're doing now.'

'Nothing much. I moved to Canada. Had several jobs. I worked for a while in a power station. Now I'm a fisherman.'

'A fisherman?' It struck her as incongruous, almost banal. Fishing was too ordinary and innocent a pursuit for a man who had been the cause, unwitting or otherwise, of all the tragedies in her life – yet looking into the steady eyes in the weathered face confronting her, she felt it was strangely reassuring. She remembered a half-forgotten conversation on a boat on the Yangtze when he had told her that he had been a fisherman in his youth. It had sounded incongruously innocent then, too, but, she recalled, it had been that side of the man she had been told was a spy, which had caused her to fall in love with him. She had no such feelings for him now, but his presence was oddly comforting. Despite his foreignness and his outlandish appearance, there was still something appealing about him. His size and strength were palpably masculine. She tried to remember how it had felt to love him, when she, too, had been innocent, idealistic and naïve – her daughter's age, or only slightly older.

Suddenly she felt choked, and saw in her mind's eye Yanqing heading off to Tiananmen Square, also innocent, idealistic, believing, with equal naïvety, that there was justice in this world, and that a hunger-strike might make a difference. All her fears returned and she found it difficult to concentrate on what the man from her past was saying.

'Yes, I'm just a fisherman, taking out tourists to catch the salmon. I told you once how I loved being on the ocean.' He laughed. 'You said I reminded you of *Captains Courageous*, though that wouldn't describe me very well now.'

She was hardly aware of his words. She had a vision of Yanqing lying in a tent, with Red Cross staff in white uniforms adjusting tubes of liquid, the great noisy crush of the crowd in the square outside, chanting, singing, loudspeakers blaring, and her daughter, with a pale, set face, determined to die for China's stupid, stupid politics. Her shoulders began to shake.

He was observing her curiously. 'Are you all right, Ziwei?' he asked.

'I'm fine,' she said.

His blue eyes seemed to search into her soul. 'You love her very much, don't you?' he asked softly.

She couldn't understand it. She prided herself on her self-control. She had trained herself throughout a bitter life to handle anything, yet this man, whom she hadn't seen for decades – had penetrated her thoughts and defences – and wrung her heart.

'Yes,' she said weakly. She crossed her arms around her shoulders, hugging herself in her misery.

In a moment she felt Ha Li's arms around her, cradling her against his chest, stroking her hair and murmuring, 'Cry, my love. That's best. Just cry. I know how you're feeling, but she's a brave, resourceful girl like her mother. She'll be all right. It's a gutsy thing she's doing, and you know you're proud of her. For now just cry. That's what a mother should do, and I'll be here as long as you need me.'

For a while, she allowed it to happen. Those strong arms were so familiar – even his smell was the same, and his voice. She rested her head on his shoulder, letting herself be comforted. Gradually, her sobs subsided. She sat up and wiped her eyes. He had a cigarette ready for her.

'I never cried like that before,' she said hoarsely. 'In all those years, I never cried.'

'It's easier to be strong if it's only for yourself,' he said. 'You can learn to bear anything. It's tough when your concern is for somebody you love and you can't do anything to help them.'

'You know that?' she murmured.

'Yes,' he said. 'That's how I felt when they took you away.'

'You knew what happened to me? Chen Tao told you?'

'No, but I found out – too late. I've never forgiven myself, Ziwei. I came here to apologise,' he said.

'Let's not talk about those things, Ha Li. They don't mean anything now. Just let me lean on you a while longer.' She made an attempt to laugh. 'You're still comfortable, you big fisherman.' She began to cry again.

'She'll be all right, Ziwei, you've got to believe that. I observed her only fleetingly, but she impressed me, the way she handled herself with those newshounds. She showed strength of character, honesty and courage. I could see she's your daughter, Ziwei.'

'She's so young, Ha Li, so young, my baby.'

'I know,' he murmured, kissing her hair. 'I know.'

She leant against him for a while longer, until sunlight began to slant through the windows. 'I've got to prepare for this evening's dinners,' she said.

'I'll leave you, then,' he said. 'I'm staying at the Great Wall Sheraton. You can always call me there, although I've booked under another name, Henry Manners. Just in case anybody in China's security departments remembers there was once a diplomat called Harry Airton who was deported.'

'Perhaps tomorrow,' she said.

'See how it goes,' he said. 'See how you feel. I've waited a quarter of a century. I can wait a while longer.'

'Ha Li,' she said, 'what happened just now. It doesn't mean . . . It doesn't mean that we can . . . So many years have passed. We can't go back . . . It's too late.'

'I know,' he said, 'but earlier you called me a friend. That's a start. It's more than I deserve.'

'Perhaps – perhaps we can be friends,' she said.

'Let's see how it goes,' he replied. 'For now, what's important is your daughter, and that's who you should be thinking about. If I can help in any way I will. Ziwei?' The blue eyes were gazing intently at her. 'I'm glad to see you again.'

'I – I think I am also glad to see you, Ha Li.'

That evening she left the intellectuals to themselves. She could not bear to sit through their self-pitying recriminations. She busied herself supervising the cooks, observed the service in the public dining rooms with a severe eye, criticised Tan, and made a nuisance of herself lecturing the conjurers. The staff, who knew why she was upset, nodded and did as they were told. Tan hovered behind after he had locked up the dining halls and asked her if she would like him to stay. He could sleep in one of the small rooms off the kitchens, he offered. She snapped at him, telling him she was fine, perfectly fine, and regretted her rudeness after he had left to cycle home.

She sat for a long time in her small apartment, which felt empty without Yanqing. At two, too restless to go to bed, she walked to the square. It was spitting half-heartedly with rain, but that did nothing to alleviate the last of the heat from a burning summer day. She did not cross Chang An, but stood in the shadow of the trees by the red walls of the Forbidden City, gazing at the flapping canvas and plastic sheets that filled the space between the Martyrs' Memorial and the road. Their green and grey shadows glinted eerily in the orange glare of the street-lamps. The Great Hall of the People was shrouded, like some great castle, in haze. Perhaps that was how the students saw themselves, she mused: as a rebel army of old, investing the bastions of a dynasty in decline – but despite the ragged red flags and slogan-covered banners that drooped above some of the tents there was nothing ordered or military about the layout of this army's camp. It was as chaotic as a country vegetable market, and as shabby. In the dampness of the night, she could smell the sweat of thousands of bodies, mixed with the acid stink of human waste. A discordant hum of activity assailed her ears. There was the usual milling crowd of people, despite the late hour. She could hear laughter, drunken shouting, the twang of an electric guitar and voices raised above howling amplifiers as they chanted some foreign protest song – the Beatles or the Rolling Stones, perhaps. She tried to remember the names of the noisy singers Yanqing so admired. It was not music Ziwei understood, and it sounded alien in the heart of the city.

She caught herself. Would she have preferred an anthem to Mao? Twenty years ago millions of youths, these children's age, had screamed here in the ecstasy of the Cultural Revolution. She herself had been a victim of their havoc, as had her mother. Hovering at the edge of the square, she realised how distant she had become from this new generation, which still preserved some sort of hope, but at the same time her heart was breaking because she saw also the dreadful continuity.

Seventy years ago her mother had taken part in the May the Fourth demonstrations, and had marched from her university to this square. That generation's idealism had led to the founding of the Communist Party, all the subsequent miseries and bloodshed. She looked at the great monuments with loathing. It had been in this place nearly forty years later that Mao had launched the Cultural Revolution, gulling a new generation of idealists like her friend Zhang Hong, who had returned as a Red Guard to Shanghai to persecute Ziwei's mother. Throughout this horrific century, innocents had paraded here, impelled by the same youthful ideals as Yanqing today, and each time with horrible consequences. Ziwei turned her eyes to the great Tiananmen Gate, where Mao's sardonic face still hung in the orange glare of the lamps. On the podium above the gaping arch, Chinese leaders – Nationalists, warlords, Communists – had in turn shouted their high-sounding slogans, bringing calamity and death to those who cheered them. This was not a national monument, she thought, with disgust. It was a blood-soaked temple, an Aztec pyramid, where the hearts of China's young were hacked out, generation by generation, in useless sacrifice.

And she was powerless to save her daughter from the same fate. She felt a sudden urge to cross the road, storm past the pathetic security committees into the leaders' tents and drag her daughter away – but she knew she was unlikely even to find her. Yanqing was probably still up and about, taking part in one of her endless meetings, or haranguing an admiring throng of fellow students. Ominously, Ziwei could make out the red crosses on the ambulances, parked among the tents. The doctors and nurses were making their preparations – but she knew too well how long the body could survive in the extremes of hunger. There would be no effects for at least a couple of days. Ziwei could imagine how Yanqing and the others must be feeling now, buoyed up by each other's example, in some rarefied state of exultation. It was pitiable.

She jumped, startled by a sudden ear-splitting roar. Motorcycles were pouring past. Youths in leather jackets, with brightly painted helmets or dark glasses and headbands, gunned the engines of their army-surplus bikes to make the maximum amount of noise and waved arrogantly at the applauding passers-by, while the girls in short skirts who were clinging to their waists smiled dreamily. Some were holding aloft banners. The characters for 'Democracy' and 'Support the

Hunger-strikers' cracked in the breeze. Ziwei had heard of this group of bikers who called themselves the Flying Tigers, or sometimes the Dare to Die Brigade. The student leaders used them as messengers. Now they were triumphantly circling the square. Oh, heaven, Ziwei thought, they think the hunger-strike is cause for a celebration.

Angrily she walked on, skirting the empty benches that stretched along Chang An Avenue. They were used only for National Day reviews, like the one Deng Xiaoping had organised five years ago on the thirty-fifth anniversary of the founding of the People's Republic. He had stood on the same podium, waving and grinning, while the massed ranks of troops, rockets and tanks had passed . . . She stopped.

They couldn't. They wouldn't . . . She tried to push away the terrifying vision because, deep inside, she knew that hardened revolutionaries, men like Deng who had been trained in the days of Stalin and Mao, could and would. She remembered newsreels of Russian tanks in Budapest and Prague. They had used the same terms in those days, too, to describe the peaceful protests: Prague Spring, Hungarian Spring – on the BBC she had already heard a correspondent describe what was going on here as the Beijing Spring.

Now she was close to the Tiananmen Gate directly facing the square and the stench was overwhelming. She looked at the shantytown in front of her. What government in the world would tolerate such a disgusting spectacle in the centre of their capital city? As she stood there in the gloom, the face of Mao behind her, she could imagine it – the crunching sound of the tank treads on the asphalt, the screams as they turned in to crush the tents, lines of helmeted soldiers with their guns moving forward under the orange glare of the street-lamps . . .

Ahead she saw a tall figure standing motionless by the marble balustrades of the ornamental bridge that led to the Tiananmen Gate. He was indistinct in the haze, but she recognised the fawn suit and the neatly trimmed grey hair. Ha Li! What was he doing here? Had he been following her? She was both irritated and embarrassed. She already regretted their earlier intimacy. She acknowledged that she had found his presence comforting, but he had come upon her in a moment of weakness. She had determined that it would not happen again. She had actually been in two minds about whether or not she would call him. It was outrageous if he was *following* her.

Then she realised he was unaware of her presence. He was gazing fixedly at the square. Moving closer, she saw that he had half unbuttoned his shirt and replaced the black leather brogues with comfortable running shoes. Tiny raindrops gleamed on his chest. His features were impassive. His brow was set in a frown, and his lips were clenched above his raised jaw. He was standing on the hump of the bridge, whose height made him look like a giant.

Ziwei ducked into the shadow of the steps in case he turned and saw her. She was fascinated. On the rare occasions that she had thought of him over the last twenty-five years, she had recalled his kindness. She imagined him as her big, gentle lover. She remembered how, when they had been briefly together, so many years ago, she had pitied him because Chen Tao was using him and she had wanted to protect him. That impression had survived even their last terrible night together, when he had used her cruelly – but over the years she had justified even that, believing that somehow he had seen through her own falsity or that subconsciously he, too, had been manipulated by Chen Tao, who had dressed her as a whore. It had been easier to believe in the man she had wanted him to be. Even earlier today it had been his sensitivity that had moved her. What she saw now made her reappraise him. There *was* hardness, and perhaps cruelty in him. Surprisingly, that made him more attractive. She realised, with some shame, that there had been occasions on the lonely nights in the Laogai when, fantasizing about making love to him, she had thought about their last night. After all, she had responded to him even then. These thoughts confused her, stirring feelings of which she had no longer thought herself capable.

And this was no longer the sensitive, ungainly man who had comforted her that afternoon. The Ha Li standing before her resembled a statue carved from granite. His silent tension made him appear formidable. He was gazing at the square with deliberation, as if he was imprinting what he saw on his memory. He looked like one of the heroic generals in the Communist movies, standing on the brow of a hill, planning his campaign. He exuded resolution and strength. She began to wonder if, in the past, she had ever really known him.

Still he did not move. For the first time that day she wondered whether it was possible that this new Ha Li could still hold tender feelings for her. She had been so preoccupied with Yanqing that she had taken his reappearance for granted, as someone in a shipwreck clings to any driftwood available. Did he still love her after all these years? Did he really think that she could still love him? The feelings that he had disturbed frightened her. One couldn't resurrect the past, she told herself. Not after twenty-five years. Until today she had brushed him out of her mind. Nor had she desired any man since – since she had last seen Ha Li. Could desire be rekindled after so long, after everything that had happened? Impossible. For a start they were old. Not really, she found herself arguing, and even though he was grey-haired, he was undeniably attractive. In fact, he exuded sexuality, especially now, and she . . . she was only fifty, young enough biologically to . . . Her cheeks were flushed and hot. She was not herself today, she thought. Her fear for her daughter had disoriented her. Yet she could not take her eyes off Ha Li, standing like a rock in the rain, or deny how handsome she still found him.

She started as he moved in her direction, then ducked further into the shadows, but he was making for the road, which he crossed with deliberate strides. She stared after his erect back as he towered above the students crowding at the edge of the square and watched until he disappeared among the tents.

On her way home, she told herself she was being ridiculous. Hundreds of foreigners were interested in what was going on in the square, and visited at any time of day or night. Perhaps, like herself, Ha Li could not sleep and had gone there to indulge his curiosity – but she could not rid herself of the suspicion that his purpose had something to do with her and Yanqing, which disturbed her – but strangely, pleased her too. Did this strong man who had come back into her life intend to protect them? Was he checking out the situation in the square so he could come up with a plan to rescue Yanqing if something went wrong? That was so foolish – what could he, a single foreigner, do against the Chinese state? – but it was also incredibly romantic and rather sweet. She began to laugh – so hard, in fact, that she had to support herself against a tree. She knew she was behaving oddly, but the mystery of his presence in the square had taken her mind off her worries about her daughter. For the second time that day, Ha Li had cheered her up. As she unlocked the door that led into the restaurant compound, she thought she might phone him tomorrow after all.

20

The Dare To Die Brigade
Beijing, 19 May 1989

Two days later she and Ha Li had lunch together. For some reason, he had cried off a meeting on the previous day, saying he had an appointment with somebody from the British Embassy. They met in the almost empty dining room at the Great Wall Sheraton Hotel. There was a Spanish food promotion on, and she ordered octopus soaked in ink. It tasted good, but she was unaccustomed to using a knife and fork, while the dark green hangings and plush furniture intimidated her. She refused the glass of wine he offered her, but he drank steadily. Again, he was tongue-tied, and so was she. The gulf between them was too great to cover with small talk and, equally, neither was eager to broach the subject on their minds.

When the bottle of wine was finished, Ha Li raised his arm to summon another but thought better of it. 'I shouldn't be looking for Dutch courage,' he said. 'I should come straight out with it. I've got a confession to make to you that's long overdue.'

'If it's about the past, Ha Li, I'd prefer you to leave it alone. Better to forget.'

'No, Ziwei. This is something I have to say. Our – our affair, Chen Tao's honey trap, it was all planned. I knew about it.'

'I know that, Ha Li. You suspected something was wrong, which was why on that last night you acted so strangely, as if you were punishing me. Do you think I have ever forgiven myself for deceiving you? I had to, even though by then I loved you. Chen Tao was threatening my mother. Why do you bring this up now? We can't change our fate. Chen Tao told me you escaped his trap. I was pleased about that.'

'He told you that? When? I thought he'd sent you off already to the camps.' He looked confused.

'Oh, not then. Recently. I see him from time to time. He helps to

461

protect my restaurant. Why can't we forget these things? You were saved, Ha Li. Chen's conspiracy failed. Isn't that enough?'

He had sat back in his chair, his face showing his shock. 'You see Chen? After everything he did to you?'

'You can never understand, Ha Li, what happened in this country after you left. Each of us had to do terrible things to survive. We all became victims. We've learnt how to forgive. Even Chen Tao is different now. He's not a bad man. If you wanted, I could arrange for him to meet you. He has become a general, in a secret part of the military. He is probably busy spying on my daughter and the other students, but if you wanted, I could find him. Were you not childhood friends?'

'Ziwei, if I ever see Chen Tao again, I'll strangle him with my bare hands for what he did to you.'

Suddenly she remembered him standing in grim contemplation of the square. She felt a well of sympathy for him in his loneliness, reached across the table and clasped the back of his hand. 'Is that what you do when you're alone on your fishing-boat, Ha Li? Do you torture yourself with dreams of revenge? Is that why you have come back? If so, I plead with you, forget. Just forget. Forget Chen Tao. Forget me. Forget anything ever happened.'

'That's impossible, Ziwei. I told you I had a confession to make. Perhaps you're right not to blame Chen entirely for what happened to you because I was equally to blame. I set him up in the first place. I was responsible for the honey trap. I'd planned it for years. I wasn't the scientist you thought me, I was a British spy, and I was using myself as bait. I *wanted* Chen to recruit me so that I could spy on China. I was never honest with you, Ziwei. I'm the cause of all your sufferings, because it was I who initiated the chain of events that sucked you and your mother into a trap.'

Slowly she withdrew her hand. It was her turn to be stunned. 'You're saying you knew all along what Chen Tao and I were attempting to do?'

'Yes.'

'And you let me seduce you, knowing I was doing it on his orders?'

'Yes.'

She stared at him, her mind turning over the implications. 'So you never truly loved me?' she said, in a tiny voice.

He closed his eyes. 'That was where it all went wrong. It was the one thing I never calculated. I fell in love with you the moment I first saw you, when you came into your mother's flat with a bag of biscuits, wearing a ribbon in your hair. I've never stopped loving you. When I saw the film of you being bundled into the truck, my heart broke and it's never recovered.'

'The film?'

'Yes, we were monitoring Chen's club with a spy plane.'

'A spy plane? You filmed me on a spy plane?'

'I'm sorry, Ziwei – so sorry.' He cleared his throat. His face was set in the grim expression she had seen in the square. 'I know that's a useless thing to say. If you like, you can get up now and walk out, and I promise I'll never bother you again.'

Ziwei leant back in her chair. The events of her life rushed through her mind in jagged memories. It was as if Harry had shaken a child's kaleidoscope, and all the patterns that she had accepted as true had been distorted into new shapes. She began to laugh, quietly at first, but the surreal humour overwhelmed her, and soon she was in hysterics, with tears in her eyes, having to clutch at the table to support herself. For some reason, she remembered Technician Li, and the hand that had touched the mango, how solemnly he had offered his knuckle to everybody to kiss, and how she had so wanted to tell Lan Ying about it because she had known how funny she would find it. She wished Lan Ying were here now. She would be bawling with laughter, as Ziwei was, and little Xiao, poor little Xiao, would be looking at them with a frown, wondering what had set them off.

With an effort, she brought herself under control. In the mirror she caught sight of the two of them, a plain woman in a leather jacket across the table from an ageing man with a businessman's haircut, staring at her as if she had gone mad, and an alarmed waiter, hovering, not knowing what to do. That almost set her off again but, panting, she grasped her glass of water, drained it and refilled it.

'"As flies to wanton boys, are we to the gods, They kill us for their sport,"' she quoted, in English, between gulps.

'What?'

'Shakespeare. *King Lear*. My mother used to recite that whenever there was a new political campaign.'

'I don't understand. You can laugh at this?'

'You must admit it's all very ironic. You filming Chen Tao while he was filming you and me. Me trying to trap you. You trying to trap me. Your big Cold War plans coming to nothing, because you fell in love with a girl in a pink ribbon – and she with you. Isn't that funny?'

'The results were tragic. When I think of you going through hell on earth in a concentration camp, a life thrown away, because I . . . because I . . .'

'It's all right, Ha Li. I survived. Life went on. You were doing your duty, as I was, as Chen Tao was. It was the times, that's all. Blame Mao, if you have to blame anybody. That's what we do now. If you heard the conversations that go on in my restaurant you'd believe that the whole Chinese population, all one billion of us, were innocents. And in a way it's true, even in our little comedy of errors.'

His weathered face quivered. 'Are you saying you can forgive me?'

'What's to forgive? You've just told me you loved me.' She had to drain the glass again, to prevent a renewed bout of laughter.

He stared at her.

'Don't you see, Ha Li? It doesn't matter. Perhaps if you'd been through the Cultural Revolution you'd understand.'

'I can't look at life as if it were some sort of cosmic joke. I see actions and consequences and, inevitably, retribution. I treated you cruelly. I suppose I deserve your scorn.'

'If old Mao were listening to us now, I assure you he'd be laughing,' she said. 'Don't you see? We were all pawns, you, me, Chen Tao. Politics, fate, history, call it what you will. We were the little people, washed by the foaming tides. The one bright thing in all this is that, despite it, we came to love each other. There was never a chance it could be permanent. I think we should be thankful we had those few days. It should be a happy memory, not a sad one, and it had good results, at least for me. The farmer I married gave me a beautiful daughter. That would never have happened if you had not come to China to set up a honey trap.'

'And isn't Yanqing adrift on those same foaming tides now?' Ha Li said bitterly. 'Are we supposed to laugh at that too? You weren't so amused the other day.'

She looked at him fondly. 'You're a kind man, Ha Li. I don't regret once loving you. I think you're stronger now than when I knew you before. I see your concern for the weak and the innocent, and you're right to rebuke me. No, life's bitter joke only applies to ourselves. Of course, I'm deeply worried about Yanqing and would do anything to protect her.'

He leant forward, dark brows knitted with urgency. 'Then let's do something about it. It may be too late for us, but if what you said the other day is true, that we can be friends even after what I've told you, let's find a way to get her out of that square before something terrible happens to her.'

'My daughter does not believe that anything terrible will happen – even though at this moment she's intent on starving herself to death.'

'Listen,' said Ha Li, 'I've been to the square several times. I haven't gone near Yanqing but I know where she is. Those children seem to think they're taking part in a carnival. It's an even bigger one now all the workers are trooping in. It's peace and love, and everybody smiling at each other, like some sort of rock festival – but the government is making its preparations. Every few yards you can spot a goon watching them. You can tell them by their cropped hair and their sunglasses, pretending they're protesters too, but they stick out like a sore thumb.'

'You think my daughter and her fellow students aren't aware of that?'

'Maybe they are. I'm not saying they're stupid, but they aren't experienced and maybe don't realise the full extent of the threat. There was a reason why I didn't come to see you yesterday. I went to the embassy in the morning. I was given a contact there by an old friend – my controller when I was here twenty-five years ago. The man he introduced me to works on the intelligence side. He took me into the safe room, unofficial favour for his old boss, and showed me satellite photos that turned my stomach. The whole city's ringed by troops.'

'Yanqing knows that too,' said Ziwei. 'The students have sent out parties to talk to the soldiers on the approach roads, reminding them that "The PLA Loves the People".'

'I saw them,' said Ha Li. 'I hired a taxi in the afternoon and drove to the outskirts, west, south and east. Yes, it's all sweetness and light, students pinning badges on the soldiers' uniforms, speeches and cheers. Carnival again. But that doesn't alter the fact that the lorries are parked along the road as far as the eye can see. Anyway, it's what you can't see that's worrying, and that's what the satellite photos picked up. Troops are massing all over China. Several military airports are covered with army tents, big transport planes standing on the runways. There are columns of tanks heading this way from Shanxi, Hebei and Liaoning. There are probably four divisions camping in the counties around Beijing. This morning I went to the station and wandered round the sidings until I was sent away, but I'd already seen the helmets in some of the parked carriages. This is a major deployment, Ziwei.'

She felt a chill as he was speaking, remembering her vision of the tanks in the square. She found herself clinging to what Yanqing had said to her. The government wouldn't dare use the army. The hunger-strikers would force a political compromise. It was a symbolic game of risk the student leaders were playing. She felt Ha Li's hand on hers, squeezing a knuckle.

'How is she, Ziwei? I should have asked you earlier. Have you seen her?'

'I went to the square this morning. I had a pass. She's a little weak, lying down in a tent, but the nurses were attentive. They've taken some of the other hunger-strikers to the hospital, but they told me Yanqing is strong. She was so sweet, smiling at me, holding my hand. Her eyes were shining with confidence and she was reading a document when I came in, which apparently was a copy of a report leaked from Zhao Ziyang's office. He's arguing for moderation ... Oh, Ha Li, I'm so worried.'

He squeezed her hand again. 'She'll be fine. I've never been worried that she or anybody else would die of hunger. Your daughter's a politician, not a martyr. No, it's brinkmanship they're playing. Either the government comes to the table – I suppose that's still a possibility – or—'

'The army will come in,' said Ziwei, flatly. 'That's what you believe, isn't it?'

'That's the worst case scenario,' he said. 'If they do, we'll have to get her out of the square.'

Ziwei was feeling the same sense of surreality she had experienced earlier. At another table, some American businessmen were noisily making their farewells. In front of her, a waiter had just deposited an enormous sorbet. 'Do you really believe it will come to that?' she whispered.

'No,' said Ha Li. 'I think it'd be a last resort. If they wanted to keep good ties with foreign countries, it would be madness. That, by the way, is the official British Embassy view. They see, quote, 'no grounds for alarm', unquote – but the PLA is mobilising, and my experience of soldiers is that they don't love the People or anybody else. They obey orders. We should be prepared.'

'And how do you intend to – what did you say? – get her out of the square, in the worst of circumstances?'

'I'll think of something,' said Ha Li.

And as he said it, she realised he was still holding her hand. He grinned, and she felt a flush of warmth in her belly, as well as a shaft of alarm – and this time not for her daughter. She had realised that holding Ha Li's hand came naturally to her, and was not merely comforting . . .

It was also natural that he took her arm as he walked her out of the restaurant. Instead of flinching at the intimacy, she curled hers closer round his and leant into his side. They passed the lift, and Ha Li paused. For a moment his eyes flickered upwards, then turned to hers. Did she imagine a questioning look? She gave a slight shake of her head. He smiled and nodded, but his arm had moved round her waist.

When she was about to get into her taxi, he put his hands on her shoulders and kissed her lips, and that, too, seemed the most natural thing in the world.

She did not return to the Yangtze Gorges. She told the taxi driver to take her as near to the Peking Hotel as he could get, and from the side road where he had dropped her she started to walk towards the square. She had managed to restore her self-control during the drive, pushing aside the uneasy implications of their increased intimacy to review the more pressing problem of her daughter. Her mind churned as she went over her conversation with Ha Li. What he had told her troubled her – not the revelation that he had been a spy: if anything, that was reassuring. When it came to practical matters, this new Ha Li seemed to know what he was talking about, and he might be able to help her – but the news of troop movements across China could not be ignored.

She had to tell her daughter, but how would she disguise the source of the information? Now was not the time to load Yanqing with stories about old lovers, still less that Ziwei had been involved in a humiliating honey trap. She decided she would pretend the information had come from an informant among the intellectuals who visited her salon.

She could not get near to Chang An Avenue. The fifty-yard width of the road was covered with a demonstration that stretched back a mile to Dabeiyao. There must be a half a million people here, she thought, marching to the square. From the top of the steps of the Peking Hotel, she looked down on their heads. The column was a vast, undulating snake. It was almost impossible to distinguish individual faces.

Floating above it, banners named each of the contingents that had rallied in support of the hunger-striker. Most of the student groups came from universities outside Beijing. They had travelled from all over the country to support the cause, and almost as many flags bore the names of Beijing factories and institutions. There were steel workers in safety helmets, department-store workers in green overalls. A white patch in the mass could be identified as nurses from 317 Hospital. That amazed her: it was the hospital for party leaders. Other banners proclaimed that the State Planning Commission, the Science and Technology Commission, the Coal Ministry, the Ministry of Railways, the Ministry of Foreign Affairs, even the Central Party School were represented. These were bastions of government. There were military uniforms in the throng. One sign read the 'People's Armed Police' and another 'Ministry of Public Security', which was ironic because that organisation was responsible for the plain-clothed goons who, according to Ha Li, were infiltrating the square. Yet they, too, were roaring the anthem the student demonstrators had adapted from the old workers' hymn, the 'Internationale': 'Rise up, you oppressed people, Let us build our flesh and blood into a new Great Wall . . .'

The bald doorman of the Peking Hotel was standing beside her, fists on his hips. In his thick Beijing accent, he swore: '*Tamade*! Just look at them! They strut like rebels but they're goats trotting to slaughter.'

'What do you mean?'

'Haven't you heard? The Party secretary, Zhao Ziyang, went down to the square this morning, weeping and wailing, "I've come too late. Too late."' The doorman adopted the manner of an operatic clown, over-emphasising the words for dramatic effect. The porters giggled. 'Disgusting behaviour.' He spat. 'It shows he and the moderates are out. You can bet Li Peng and the hard-liners are in charge now, and they won't allow this sorry state of affairs to go on much longer. And you can be sure old Deng's behind them too. I wouldn't go anywhere near the square tonight, lady. Expect fireworks – and not of the Spring Festival kind.'

She hurried away. This morning? She had been in the square in the morning. The students had been so confident they were winning, but in just a few hours their only sympathiser in the Central Committee of the Politburo had apparently been overthrown. She realised that Zhao must have visited the square just after she had left to join Ha Li for lunch.

Stunned, she pushed through the equally large crowd of spectators on the pavement. She was being jostled from shoulder to shoulder. She did a little dance with a young student, he stepping to the right as she stepped to the left and vice versa. He had the laughing face of a child but wore a headband on which he had scrawled in Chinese, 'Dare to Die', and a cloth placard wrapped round his stomach which proclaimed in English, 'My life is ours. My love is yours.' Suddenly he embraced her. 'Thank you, Auntie, for coming to support us.' She pushed on, sweaty and light-headed in the heat.

The undulating snake of protesters was even thicker at the entrance to the square. It would be impossible to cross the road. She backtracked to the underpass, which was open. At last she emerged into the square, and found herself facing rows and rows of seated students raising their fists and shouting slogans. They made an impenetrable obstacle. To get to the tents she had to skirt round the side of the square. She shoved her way through knots of laughing students and workers brandishing placards that caricatured the country's leaders. There was even a cartoon of Deng Xiaoping, his wrinkled face grinning over a cigarette as he spat into a spittoon. This was another ratcheting up of the stakes, she saw, and her heart sank. Until now nobody had dared insult the Party so flagrantly.

The tide of people pushed her almost to the steps of the History Museum. There, she came across a path that was being kept clear to allow ambulances access to the hunger-strikers. She started to walk along it – but suspicious students wearing red armbands surrounded her.

'Thank you for coming, Granny,' said a boy, wearing sunglasses and a baseball cap. 'We appreciate your support, but you can't go further without a pass.'

'I have a pass,' she said. 'I'm Gao Yanqing's mother.' She fumbled in her pockets for the document and handed it to them. The students retired into a knot to examine it.

'Is she still here?' one of the female guards asked. 'I thought she was taken away by the ambulances.'

Ziwei clutched her arm. 'When? Which hospital?'

'I don't know which hospital but it was yesterday, I think,' said the girl.

Ziwei felt a rush of relief. 'You must be thinking of somebody else,' she said. 'I was with Yanqing here this morning. Please will you let me pass?'

The boy in the baseball cap was smiling. 'All right, Granny. That's in order. Do you want one of us to take you inside?'

'Thank you, but I can find my own way.'

She had to show her pass again at the entrance to the hunger-strikers' tent. As she waited there were shouts from inside, and the door flaps were flung open. Masked doctors in white coats were pressing an oxygen mask over the face of a hunger-striker wrapped in a silver space blanket on a stretcher carried by four students. Nurses hovered in their wake, one stumbling under the weight of the apparatus. Ziwei felt a flutter of fear, but relaxed when she saw that the pale face on the stretcher was that of a boy.

Inside, it took a moment for her eyes to adjust to the gloom. Rows of bodies lay against the canvas walls, moving listlessly. Some had tubes attached to their arms, and nurses were kneeling beside others taking temperatures or adjusting blankets. She moved down the line until she recognised her daughter. She had on her reading glasses but her book lay on her chest. She was asleep. Her face was the colour of parchment and her lips were pinched and dry. As Ziwei watched, Yanqing stirred and mumbled something. Ziwei knelt beside her, wondering if she would be allowed to stroke her hair.

A nurse in a facemask told her, 'It's all right. You can wake her. She's had a good two hours' sleep and I was going to check on her soon, anyway. You're her mother, aren't you? You probably heard what happened this morning. She insisted on going out to meet the Party secretary with the others, but it tired her out, poor thing.'

'Is she all right?' Ziwei asked.

'None of them is all right,' said the nurse, 'but your daughter's strong, and she's taking plenty of fluids. She'll last the course.'

'You know how long the course will be?' asked Ziwei.

'Well, the government must give in soon surely?' said the woman. 'After all, the Party secretary himself was here this morning. That speaks for itself.'

There is another interpretation of that, Ziwei wanted to say, but at that moment Yanqing opened her eyes. 'Mama? Is that you?' she said weakly. 'I didn't expect to see you again today.'

'How are you, my darling?' whispered Ziwei, kissing her.

Yanqing gave a mischievous smile. 'Hungry,' she said, and coughed.

'You don't have to do this.'

Yanqing's eyes gleamed. 'We're winning, Mama. Didn't you hear what happened? Zhao Ziyang came, and he wept. The government's falling apart.'

'But aren't you afraid now that the hard-liners seem to be in charge?'

'That's good,' said Yanqing, with effort. 'They may be tempted to use force. Then they will find not only the People but the PLA turning against them. They'll never survive that humiliation.'

'But if they order the army in, darling, there can be only one result. Listen, I heard some terrible news. You have to tell your colleagues and persuade them to leave. It's not just the soldiers on the outskirts of the city. They're massing troops in other cities. Tanks are coming . . .'

Yanqing was laughing and clutched her mother's hand feebly. 'I so love you, Mama, but I don't think you understand politics. Your generation were victims. You never learnt how to stand up to them and play them, as we're doing. We're aware of every detail about the mobilisation. It's good. It's what we want. They want to scare us but they can't because we know they can only risk going so far. At the last minute they will turn back.' Exhausted, she closed her eyes, murmuring something about 'paper tigers'.

Ziwei's head throbbed.

The nurse suggested she leave. She wanted to check Yanqing's fluids; Ziwei could come back in half an hour.

She went outside, stumbling past the students on guard. She saw a group come out of the headquarters tents, at least twenty boys and girls with set lips and determined frowns. They were carrying bundles of cloth in their hands. New placards. One dropped on to the ground where it unfurled in the breeze. Ziwei read, 'The People love the PLA and the PLA loves the People.'

Over the immediate sounds around her – shouting, laughter, loud-speakers, ambulance sirens – she became aware of the steady background roar of hundreds of thousands of voices chanting the 'Internationale'. Beyond the tents she could see the seated lines of students, raising their fists towards the snake that undulated along the road. Behind it, the walls of the Forbidden City and the towering eaves of Tiananmen Gate, with its portrait of Mao, were tinged blood red in the sharper light of the late afternoon. The high priest was smiling on his sacrifical pyramid.

* * *

471

That night only a few intellectuals gathered in the Yangtze Gorges. The courtyards shone with puddles. The tables were abandoned and the dripping umbrellas were folded. The weather had broken after the hot day, and earlier there had been lightning, thunder and a violent downpour. Now dense grey cloud blanketed the sky, obscuring the stars.

As her guests arrived, each commented on the weird atmosphere in the city. 'It's as if everybody knows something's going to happen, but nobody is certain what,' said the poet, Lin Zhen. 'As I came here the streets were empty. The only sound was ambulances, screaming to and from the hunger-strikers – sorry, Ziwei,' he muttered, nodding at his hostess.

'I'm not made of eggshell,' she snapped. 'What else did you see?'

'Nothing much. That's what was so strange. Well, some of the townspeople were about, gathered at road junctions, ready for anything, but everywhere's so quiet. It's as if Beijing has become a ghost city.'

'I think we're overreacting,' said Ma, the economist. 'It's a wet night, that's all, and everybody's staying at home.'

'Come on, Lao Ma. The Party secretary is under house arrest. People are scared. Even I'm scared.' Lin Zhen smiled round the table, cooling himself with his fan.

'The students believe they're winning,' said Ziwei. 'That's what my daughter told me this afternoon. She believes the government is a paper tiger.'

The intellectuals looked at each other nervously. Clearly none agreed.

'If only they would take our advice and withdraw,' said Ma, after an uncomfortable pause. 'If they did so now, that would be a victory. It's all in Sunzi's *Art of War*. Reveal your strength, then allow the enemy to come to terms.'

'Why don't you misquote Mao while you're at it?' said Lin Zhen. '"All the guiding principles of military operations grow out of one basic principle: to strive to the utmost to preserve one's own strength." He, too, was a master in justifying how to do nothing.'

'Listen to yourselves, talking and talking to hear the sound of your own voices,' said Ziwei, angrily. 'These are not politicians or guerrillas out there. They're our children, and now, it seems, the government is ready to send in the army.'

Feet shuffled, and chopsticks were temporarily lowered.

'We don't know that the government is planning to take a hard line,' said Ma, quietly. 'Objectively, it would be foolish for them to cross that moral boundary. It would be equivalent to admitting they had lost the political argument.'

'There you are, turning reality into a comfortable debate again,' said Ziwei. 'You're worse than my daughter. She's blind because she has revolution in her blood. Yours has been turned to water – or ink for your useless articles.'

There was a shocked silence, until Lin said, 'Eunuchs. I said it. That's what we are.' He dipped his chopsticks into the hotpot and brought out a piece of tripe.

When the telephone rang everybody jumped. Ziwei picked up the receiver. It was Ha Li. 'Have you seen what's on television?' he said urgently. 'It's on all the channels.'

'Wait, Ha Li.' She pulled off the brocade that covered the set by the window, and clicked the dial. The black-and-white screen showed what must be a meeting of the Central Committee. She saw ranks of cadaverous old men clapping mechanically, some in Mao jackets, many in uniform. The camera turned to the speaker. It was the prime minister, Li Peng. The black-rimmed glasses merged with the line of his heavy eyebrows in the tightly buttoned face, and his pursed, feminine lips mouthed the slogans to which his audience was clapping. She fumbled for the volume control and heard Li Peng's high-pitched voice: 'We don't blame the students, who have been led astray by the malicious propaganda of a small group of conspirators with plans to overthrow the legal Government of the People – but now is the time to nip this evil in the bud.' The old men applauded. 'That is why we have called upon the PLA to save the country and declared martial law.'

The intellectuals round the table had frozen, staring at the screen. There was a plop as the morsel on Lin's chopsticks fell back into the pot. She heard Ha Li's voice buzzing in the receiver and picked it up. 'Did you hear?' he was saying.

'Yes . . . yes.'

'I'm going to the square. I'll find Yanqing and make sure she's all right. Stay where you are and wait for my call.'

'I'm going there too, Ha Li,' she said.

'That's not wise.'

'She's my daughter.'

There was silence at the other end of the line. 'All right,' he said. 'I'll meet you by the Martyr's Memorial in an hour.'

473

'Ha Li—' But he had gone.

She turned towards the intellectuals, who were gaping at her. 'If you want anything, call Tan,' she told them. 'There's plenty of food, plenty of wine. Enjoy what you see on the television. I'm sure it will give you much more to debate.'

The streets might have been empty earlier, but now they were full of people. It took Ziwei almost an hour to get to the square, which was as crowded as it had been that afternoon, but this time there were no marchers singing the 'Internationale'. The deafening sound that carried over the voices shouting defiance was the speech of Li Peng, which the government had somehow found a way to loop into the loudspeaker system. If it was designed to intimidate the students, it had the opposite effect. The crowds on Chang An Avenue were cheering the Flying Tigers. The leather-suited bikers in the Dare to Die Brigade, driving back and forth in front of the Tiananmen Gate, scowled grimly as they gunned their motors and there were fewer girls riding pillion. They were warriors now, the cavalry of the student protesters, gathering before battle. Trucks of workers were entering the square, too, mobbed by ecstatic students running beside them.

As Ziwei pressed towards the tents, she saw knots of students gathered by each loudspeaker, jeering the prime minister's every word. A man with a megaphone was shouting news that had just come from the Muxudi suburbs: 'Brothers, have you heard? We have had our first victory. Our worker allies have stopped the troops coming in from the west. They have punctured the oil tanks of their transport.' This time, the continuous cheering that followed drowned Li Peng.

But Ziwei did not believe it because she had heard the counter-rumours, as she passed through the crowds. A tank column had been seen coming down the road from Tianjin. The Great Hall of the People and the Forbidden City were full of troops smuggled in through the Metro and the underground tunnels of the old 1950s nuclear-shelter system.

She suspected that nobody knew what was happening. She saw several students who were not sharing the euphoria. One boy was slumped in front of a tent, staring dejectedly at the ground, a banner proclaiming democracy wrapped round his waist. A small group of girls were hugging each other and weeping. An old pedicab driver was shaking his fists at the loudspeakers, tears running down his face, as he shouted: 'Those cock-suckers! Those cocksuckers in the government have betrayed us.'

She forced her way to the Martyrs' Memorial, on whose steps one of the student leaders was screaming that it was their duty to stay and spill their blood if necessary to protect their sacred cause. She was shocked by the vehemence, then recalled that her own daughter had made similar speeches. She circled the monument twice, but could not see Ha Li. She looked at her watch. She determined to visit the hunger-strikers' tent to see Yanqing. She would find Ha Li later.

'I demand to be let in,' she yelled at the grim-faced boy who stopped her. 'I have a pass. I'm Gao Yanqing's mother.'

'I don't care who you are,' he said. 'Nobody goes near our martyrs tonight. Don't you know the government has declared war on us?'

The word 'martyrs' struck her like a blow. 'But she's my daughter. I must see her.'

He shook his head, not unkindly, and began to turn away.

'I have information,' she said, 'vital information for her and the other leaders.'

'What information?' He looked sceptical. Then he grinned, because he must have realised, from her expression, that she was bluffing. He took pity on her. 'All right, Auntie,' he said. 'I'll tell you. She isn't in the hunger-strikers' tent. She's been carried to the leaders' tent with Wu Er Kai Xi, Chai Ling and the other committee heads. As you can imagine they're a little busy now, so nobody's being allowed in, but I can tell you she's fine – weak but fine. I saw her myself just an hour ago. So don't worry, OK? If I get a chance I'll tell her you're here.'

She stood there impotent and despairing. Suddenly a pair of strong arms encircled her and she was clasped in Ha Li's embrace. 'It's OK,' he murmured, a loose strand of his hair brushing her forehead. 'She's safe enough for now. What that young man told you is correct. I saw them move her. She was walking on her own.'

'What are we going to do, Ha Li?' she whimpered.

'We've hours to think of something,' he said. 'We don't know yet what the government intends. From what I've been hearing the workers really have been able to halt some of the army's columns.'

'But if they bring in tanks?'

'I don't think they will,' he said. 'They're still playing a game of bluff, threatening force but not necessarily prepared to go the whole way. They must be thinking twice now they can see that instead of terrifying the students into submission their speeches have brought the whole city out in support.'

But even as he spoke, there was a cry from the the square, which intensified in volume as it was picked up by new voices: 'The army's at Dabeiyao.'

Ziwei froze. That was only three kilometres away, on the straight road that led directly to the square from the east.

There was a flurry of activity in the space before the Tiananmen Gate. The Flying Tigers were accelerating in that direction. The workers were pulling students on to the overloaded lorries, and red flags were unfurling as they edged out to follow the motorbikes. There was a great roar. 'Defend the Dabeiyao junction with our lives!' Students and workers were raising their fists, shouting, 'Rise up! Rise up!' Waves of cheers again drowned the loudspeakers.

'It's like those old newsreels,' murmured Ha Li, 'the workers going off to defend Madrid.'

'I don't understand,' said Ziwei.

'Nor do I, but I ought to check it out,' said Ha Li. 'You stay here. I won't be long.'

She clutched his arm. 'No – I'm coming with you.'

She could see the conflicting emotions on his face. He seemed to be weighing various options. 'No point in telling you it might be dangerous?' he said at last.

'There's nothing I can do for Yanqing,' she said, 'and I want to know what's going on.'

As she said it, she realised she had been affected by the great cry and the passion of the students heading off to the barricades. 'It may sound silly, but I'm in the mood to rise up myself,' she said.

He kissed her quickly, and held her shoulders, smiling at her. 'Come on, then,' he said. 'Somewhere round the back of the History Museum I should have my own pedicab. I've paid him half a year's salary already and promised him the other half if he stays with me for the whole night so he shouldn't have run off.'

Taking her hand, he pushed through the crowd, which divided easily as his giant figure approached.

In ten minutes they were in the back of a pedicab, heading east along Chang An Avenue towards Dabeiyao. They passed the Jesuits' Observatory and on into Jianguomenwai. On their left towered the blocks that housed diplomats. They passed the Jianguo Hotel, whose forecourt was full of westerners, staring at the streams of workers and students on bicycles, motorbikes and trucks heading east. Where the new World Trade Centre marked the entrance to the Third Ring Road they had to stop because of the crowds.

The Dabeiyao Bridge was half constructed. Some of the lorries that had driven from the square had parked crossways on its rim to form a makeshift barricade, with rubber tyres, wastebins, concrete slabs and any other solid material the students could lay their hands to complete their line of defence. Ha Li pushed through the throng. At the barrier, students armed with poles and workers holding spades and hoes gazed out into the gloomy night.

A short girl was pulling at her boyfriend's shirt. 'Are they coming? Are they coming?' she was whimpering. His answer was drowned in a chant that started from the students on the back of the trucks and spread to the others: 'The People love the PLA and the PLA loves the People.' It rose to a crescendo, then died. There was a short burst of the 'Internationale', and silence. Mist swirled over the bridgeworks.

Ha Li scrambled up the tyres and peered over a concrete slab.

'What can you see?' called Ziwei, anxiously.

'Damned difficult to see anything.'

The student whose girlfriend had been pulling his shirt, was staring at Ha Li admiringly. 'Even *laowai* have come to join us.' He grinned, and slapped Ha Li on the back.

'Can you tell us what's happening?' asked Ziwei. She had scrambled up beside them.

'Earlier a column of trucks was advancing,' said the boy. 'We could see their headlights, hundreds of them, but they stopped when they saw us building the barricade. Some of our comrades in the workers' trucks have driven down to negotiate with them. Now we're waiting.'

'For what?' asked Ha Li.

'For our delegation to return – or soldiers with guns.' He looked ahead grimly, adjusting his grasp on what looked like a snooker cue.

'You plan to fight them with that?' said Ha Li.

The boy turned his eyes towards him, and said simply, 'Yes, until they kill me.'

'And what will that achieve?' asked Ha Li.

The boy's eyes had misted. 'It will show them I'm free,' he said.

Ha Li nodded. 'You're a brave man. Where do you come from? That's a Shandong accent, isn't it?'

'Yes,' said the boy, surprised. 'I come from Yantai and I study at Jinan University. I want to be a civil engineer.'

'I was once a sort of engineer,' said Ha Li, 'and I was born in Shandong. I grew up in a small village under Mount Tai.'

The boy was grinning again. 'Some Shandong people are very tall, but they don't usually look like *laowai*.'

'I'm Canadian,' said Ha Li. 'I was once British.'

'You're Chinese tonight if you're standing with us here,' said the boy.

There was a great roar of 'Democracy!' Ziwei, who had been staring ahead, saw the two round orbs of a headlight, blinking in the mist. As she watched, others flashed on behind them. They looked like tigers' eyes. She had a vision of wild animals padding towards them.

There was a tense rustle as the students and workers on the barricade raised their useless weapons. She heard a girl scream behind her: 'Have they guns? Have they guns?'

Ziwei felt her arm in Ha Li's firm grasp. 'We'd better get out of here,' he was shouting above hundreds of voices yelling 'Rise up! Rise up!'

Suddenly she knew she couldn't leave. Until this moment, the student protests had not been her struggle. In fact, if anything, she had disapproved of them, terrified for her daughter – but now she felt disgust and growing anger. The government was sending soldiers against unarmed children. Strangely, she felt exhilarated too, as if her whole life had led to this moment. She had a sudden vision of Lan Ying and Xiao standing beside her. Xing had been no older than this boy with his pathetic snooker cue. This monstrous machine had crushed their lives. Now it looked as if Ziwei, too, was about to face its wrath, and most likely her own extinction, because she knew the flimsy barricade would not hold, and the machine would be as merciless as it had always been, but that was fine, because this *was* her struggle. She had been resisting it, one way or another, since she and her friends had become the Three Crows in the Laogai.

She shook away Ha Li's hand, and gazed at his craggy features. 'No, Ha Li.' She waved at the boy he had been talking to, who was leaning over the barricade, screaming, 'Democracy.' 'These are also our children,' she said. 'I don't know how to explain it, but I can't leave them.'

'And what about your daughter?'

'I'm with my daughter,' she said. Her brow furrowed. 'But you go, Ha Li, while there's time.'

The affection in his calm gaze fired her heart. 'No, Ziwei,' he said. 'I left you once before. Never again.'

And she knew that that was right too, that it should be Ha Li who stood beside her, with the shades of her other friends, on this last barricade. It was a closing of the circle of her life. 'Oh, Ha Li,' she whispered, then louder, so he could hear her over the rumble of the approaching vehicles, 'We've been so foolish.'

Suddenly she was in his arms and responding as he kissed her mouth, her cheeks and chin. 'I'm sorry,' he was murmuring. 'That last night, when I hurt you . . .'

'No, Ha Li, it doesn't matter because we've found each other again.' She closed her mouth on his – and suddenly nothing mattered any more.

'They're coming!' somebody was yelling. 'Get ready!'

'I love you,' said Ha Li.

The girl below was still screaming, 'Have they guns?'

'I know,' she said, and put her arm round his waist. Together, from the top of the barricade, they watched the headlights advancing through the haze. She felt a flutter in her stomach, looked at Ha Li for reassurance, and he smiled.

The front of the first lorry came into view. The students on the barricade fell silent. At any moment, men in green uniforms with helmets would leap off the back. She tightened her grip on his waist. Ha Li's face was grim now. Gently disengaging himself, he reached down and heaved an iron support out of its concrete base. He looked like a warrior of old.

She could see the figures of their attackers clearly. They were waving and gesticulating from the back of the truck.

'Stay behind me, whatever happens,' said Ha Li. The tension on the barricade was like stretched cloth about to tear.

A shout broke the silence: 'They're ours.' There was a second of stunned disbelief, then everyone on the barricade broke into cheers. Ziwei stared in incomprehension at the grinning faces.

'Well, I'm damned,' Ha Li was whispering, in English. 'They've turned them back.'

She saw the delighted face of the boy as he scrambled down to embrace his girlfriend, who was weeping. The others on the barricade were pouring down the other way to mob the returning workers and students, leaving Ha Li and Ziwei alone on top of the barricade. She raised her chin, closed her eyes and felt his lips again on hers.

When they returned to the square, the student leaders were addressing a huge crowd from the steps of the Martyrs' Memorial. Ziwei could see Yanqing among them, sitting at the feet of the speaker, who was announcing victory and the end of the hunger-strike.

Ha Li let her go and she pushed forward to the front of the delirious crowd. Yanqing saw her and waved. Ziwei, sobbing and laughing, mimed for her to come down so she could take her home. Yanqing, grinning, circled her watch with her hand, indicating she would come tomorrow. Ziwei did not mind. Her daughter had won a victory. Tonight her place was with her celebrating comrades.

Later, Ha Li took her in his hired pedicab back to the Yangtze Gorges. They nestled close to each other on the leather seat, her head resting on his shoulder. At the door of the restaurant, Ha Li got out first and gave her his hand to help her down. He was looking at her questioningly. She smiled and pulled his arm. Mock-impatiently, she waited as he took wads of money from his pocket to pay the driver.

She pulled him through the damp, misty courtyards to the salon and her rooms behind. In her bedroom, she kissed him, then began to unbutton his shirt.

There was a moment of sorrow when they gazed at the ravages of time and hardship on each other's bodies. Ziwei touched the great scar on Ha Li's side, which he said had resulted from a fishing accident aboard his boat. Ha Li, with tears in his eyes, kissed the marks of Ziwei's years in the Laogai: the white cicatrices of insect bites on her sun-hardened skin, the knotted muscle, the discoloration on her calves from immersion in paddies; her ribs and bony hips in a body that had never, to this day, recovered from extended malnutrition. She was sensitive about her shrunken breasts, but he removed her hands and kissed them. 'I'm so ugly, Ha Li,' she said.

'No, you're beautiful,' he murmured. 'You're my Ziwei, and I've found you again.'

Later, he covered her cheeks, nose, eyes, ears and the mole under her lip with kisses, his big hand smoothing the hair from her forehead, and then they were aware only of hot skin on hot skin, the scent of each other and the comfort of their touch. When they made love, it was as if none of the wasted years had ever been. They were again the two young lovers who – many years and many miles ago – had first explored each other in a bathhouse on a mountain, then, as now, losing themselves in the moment, where neither the sufferings of the past nor the complexity of the present nor the uncertainty of the future mattered any more.

21

The Goddess of Freedom and Democracy

Beijing, 20–28 May 1989

She contemplated his naked body, only partly covered by the eider-down. 'Ha Li, you must get up. It's seven o'clock.'

His lips curved and she wondered if he was dreaming about their lovemaking. It had been subtly different from what she remembered so many years before, when the desperation of their situation and their youth had exploded in hungry passion. It had been better, gentler, surer. It had been beautiful, she acknowledged, and it had exorcised the nightmare memories of the last time they had coupled for Chen Tao's camera.

Now, as she sat on a stool at the end of the bed, fully dressed, she was stirred by his ruggedness. As she looked at his broad chest, and the arm that stretched over the side of the bed in which she had been lying, she wondered if she could go through with what she knew she had to do.

She felt a wave of sadness that seemed to numb her limbs. This morning she had woken with a start, feeling the warmth of his body next to hers, and the weight of his hand on her shoulder. For a long while she lay there, luxuriating in it, experiencing a contentment she had never known before. She was waking in a shared bed with the man she loved. Dreamily, she had sketched out a life they might have together. Ha Li would move into her restaurant. He would entertain the foreign guests with his stories. One day she might travel with him to Canada. They would go out on his boat and fish. Perhaps Yanqing, when she graduated, would find a good job with a Western company and come out to visit them . . .

But even as she fantasised, the chill realisation came upon her that this could never be. How could she think selfishly of a life for herself when her daughter even now was leading a revolution? Suddenly all the lost years that had telescoped during their lovemaking stretched out starkly in her mind. Yanqing would never understand or accept it. Nobody would. And what, anyway, did she have in common with this foreigner from her past? He had had no part in the sufferings of China over the last quarter-century. He had been living the easy life of a fisherman while she had experienced hell. They came from different worlds. Was a night of passion, caused by the momentary exhilaration of the barricades, enough on which to build a new life or to throw away the one she had? She had a duty to Yanqing, to protect her as far as she could, whatever the outcome of the demonstrations – and to survive, as she had done all her life, the changes they might bring to the country, her country. What place for Ha Li could there be in that?

Slowly, her confusion and fear had turned to resentment. She had sprung out of bed, and looked in horror at the intruder lying naked on her sheets. At that moment he *was* a stranger to her. She hated him because she had allowed him to stir feelings inside her that she had buried long ago. He had brought complication to a life that had been, for these last few years, one of order and contentment. She felt defiled, like the errant Buddhist nuns in the stories who betrayed the vows of their celibate existence in the arms of a mendicant priest.

Yet even then she remembered his kindness and strength, and appreciated his beauty. Even now she felt the urge to cut out the white strands from his hair, to run her hand over that smooth back, to link her fingers with his . . . She had sat on her stool for more than an hour, chain-smoking while he slept, trying to sort out her conflicting emotions.

She steeled herself, and said peremptorily, 'Ha Li. Wake up. The restaurant cleaners will be arriving soon.'

His eyes flickered and opened. For a moment, Ha Li seemed puzzled, as if he was wondering where was this strange room, with its old beamed ceiling, and the morning light slanting through the windows. His head turned to her empty pillow, and a flash of disappointment crossed his brow. Then he raised himself on his elbow and grinned at her. He looked boyish – heartbreakingly so. 'Oh, you're already dressed,' he murmured. 'I wanted to see you naked in the daylight.'

'You have to go, Ha Li. People will be coming soon. Yanqing might arrive from the square.'

He nodded slowly and sat up, patting the bed. 'I know, my love, but let me hold you in my arms one more time before I go. You're so beautiful.'

Part of her wanted to throw herself into his embrace, and the immediate self-reproach fuelled her anger. She knew it had not been his fault. She had led him into her home and given herself to him. But the other half of her told her it had been a mistake, foolishness brought on only by the emotion on the barricade and afterwards in the square.

'No,' she said, 'I don't think that would be a good idea. We've already allowed the events of last night to cloud our judgement. What we did was madness, Ha Li, madness. We're old enough to know better. Copulating like rabbits – we behaved no better than some of the students in the square.'

For a moment he looked shocked, then he laughed, a warm, comforting sound that irritated her because she thought he was mocking her. 'Well, my dear, love and death, sex and war have paired themselves through history. It's what almost every romance that's ever been written is all about. But don't you think that what happened between us last night was natural, that maybe it was because we both realised we still loved each other?'

'I don't know, Ha Li. I'd like some time to myself to think it through. All I want is for you to go now, before anybody comes.'

He nodded thoughtfully. 'I didn't mean to make light of it. I know I've come back into your life like a thunderbolt. Of course, we must both think it through.'

He lifted the eiderdown aside and stood up in an easy motion by the bed. He was unconscious of his nakedness, and stretched. Again, she felt a stirring inside her. This stranger, whom once she had loved, was perfectly formed despite his age. He reminded her of a statue she had once seen of Olympian Zeus. He bent down to pick up his clothes, his muscles moving under his skin, then stepped forward to kiss her.

She turned her head away. 'Please go,' she murmured, agonisingly aware of the powerful shoulders so close to her. 'I'll call you at your hotel.'

She kept her eyes averted as he dressed, but she pictured his every movement as she heard the rustle of his clothes. He was tying his shoelaces when she turned. He looked up at her with such sadness in his eyes. 'I love you,' he said. He straightened, then leant over and kissed her forehead.

Somehow, she resisted the temptation to cling to him. 'Go,' she said, her voice breaking.

'You will call?' he asked.

'Yes,' she said. 'Later today. Tomorrow.'

'All right,' he said, and picked up his jacket.

'Go out through the kitchens. There's a door into the alley. Nobody should see you,' she said.

'I'll make sure I'm invisible.' He paused by the door. 'And take your time. I know this is hard for you. I can wait. I do understand.'

He turned the handle and slipped out. She felt a moment of bitter loss, and nearly ran after him. She could still hear his footsteps on the flagstones outside, becoming fainter. She drew out her last cigarette, but did not light it. It hung limply between her lips, while her hands clutched the edge of the stool. She saw her reflection in the mirror – a thin, drawn woman with dishevelled hair. The picture blurred as tears filled her eyes.

Yanqing did not come to the restaurant that day or the next. Neither did the intellectuals appear in her salon. They were probably with the rest of the population, she thought, flocking to the square, or to the student barricades that had been set up on every access road. Or perhaps her hostility at their last meeting had put them off. She did not care either way.

She sat in her room listening to the BBC and Voice of America reports on her radio. Describing the emotion in the square, the BBC correspondent could not disguise his wonder, speculating that there must be two million people celebrating the ignominious retreat of the army. He allowed himself to get carried away and announced in stirring tones that the city now belonged to the people. He compared the events of the other evening to the overthrow of a dynasty. 'The mandate of heaven has been withdrawn from the Communist Party,' he declared, in ringing tones.

It would take a lot more than popular euphoria to overthrow the Communist Party, she thought. What was more worrying was what was not reported. There was nothing on any of the Chinese channels except for bleak propaganda, interspersed with PLA concerts. There was no mention of the government considering further talks with the students, and what bulletins there were still emphasised that the city was under martial law. That could only mean that the hardliners were regrouping and considering their next move. Her fears for Yanqing returned with even greater force than before.

And on top of that there was her guilt about Ha Li. She had not phoned him – she did not know what to say – but she could not prevent herself thinking about him. Sometimes she was disgusted with herself. Sometimes she was angry with him. Alone in her room, she relived every moment of their lovemaking, sometimes with dreamy pleasure, sometimes with fear: the fact that it had happened meant she had deep feelings still for the lover of her youth.

It scared her. Ha Li was drawing her back into a world of passions she had put behind her. She did not think she was strong enough to begin another new life. She had neither the will nor the desire.

She lay fully clothed on her bed, smoking. The prospect of talking to customers, even to her own staff, repelled her. When Tan brought her meals she saw concern in his features. She had told him she was unwell. He said nothing but she knew he did not believe her.

And all the time the green telephone, on its stool in the corner, accused her of cowardice. She realised Ha Li must be waiting by the telephone in his hotel room, and there were times when she felt sorry for him, imagining his anguish and disappointment – but she could not bring herself to call him.

Long days passed into long nights. On the fourth day Yanqing came and Ziwei got up. The two ate a meal together in the salon. Ziwei was pleased to see that the girl had recovered her colour after the fasting, but it was not a happy meeting. Her daughter was preoccupied, and her attempt at cheerfulness was hollow. She described how a student had thrown a pot of paint at the portrait of Mao, couching the incident in comical terms, but Ziwei could see that Yanqing was concerned by the implications. Clearly the student leaders, despite all the mass support they were receiving, were as worried as Ziwei by the government's ominous silence. Ziwei pleaded with Yanqing to leave the square: 'You've achieved a victory. Isn't that enough?'

'You don't understand, Mama,' was the surly reply.

'I think I understand these people better than you. What possible point is there in waiting for the inevitable retaliation?'

Yanqing became angry. 'I had thought better of you, Mama,' she said coldly. 'You've been listening too long to your lily-livered coterie of has-been intellectuals. I see no purpose in talking to you about it.'

Shortly afterwards she left, still fuming, and Ziwei retired to her room, more depressed than she had been before.

On the sixth day, Tan came in to announce a visitor.

'Is it that foreigner again?' asked Ziwei, feeling a mixture of both alarm and excitement.

'No, a military officer – a general. He said his name was Chen and that he knows you.'

She found Chen Tao sitting alone over a meal in one of the private banqueting rooms. He smiled when she came in and waved her to a seat. 'You look pale,' he said.

'I haven't been well.'

'So much excitement lately,' he said. 'It's getting all of us down.'

'You've been busy, I suppose?'

'Of course.' He grinned. 'Somebody has to look after the interests of the state. I must say, your food only gets better. This stew is delicious. Won't you have some?'

'Why have you come, Chen Tao? Shouldn't you be in the square, spying on my daughter and the other students?'

'Oh, my men do that and, besides, nowadays we have such sophisticated instruments of surveillance we hardly need agents on the ground. Did you know that we have hidden cameras in every light fitting in the square and throughout the city? And there are listening devices almost everywhere. I can monitor what anybody's been doing without leaving my desk. Who meets whom, what they say to each other when they think they're most private. There's very little happening that we don't know about.'

'Yet you didn't make a very impressive job of it when you tried to clear the square. A little humiliating, don't you think, that the PLA could be turned back by students and workers?'

He laughed. 'I wouldn't dismiss the PLA too quickly. On the nineteenth of May their orders were unclear. When you have confusion in the top ranks of the government, how do you expect simple soldiers to interpret their orders? How can you march in and hold the square if you're under instruction not to use too much force? It was all far too hasty. Politicians wanting to make a point.' He spooned some green bean curd on to his rice. 'I was one of those who advised delay. My old boss Kang Sheng, may he burn in hell, taught me that there are no half-measures. Exemplary action of any kind will be doomed to failure unless there is political weight behind it and the willingness to bear all consequences. And it was because there was not that political will, my dear Ziwei, that you were able to have your little moment of triumph on top of the barricade at Dabeiyao.'

She felt a chill in her spine, 'Cameras in street-lamps?' she said.

'Suffice to say that you were observed,' said Chen. 'You and your foreign friend.' He allowed the words to sink in. 'Our foreign friend, perhaps I should say. It *was* Ha Li Aitun, wasn't it? This bean curd is excellent.'

She stared at him, lost for words.

'Oh, I've seen to it that the relevant pieces of film were "lost", as well as the strange report that he apparently stayed the night with you afterwards. It's charming that the two of you have rediscovered your old passion, but wasn't it a bit foolhardy? Everybody's watching everybody these days, and a liaison with a dubious foreigner on the part of the mother will hardly be seen in a positive light when the daughter is manifesting dangerous counter-revolutionary proclivities.' Ignoring her shock and mortification, he continued, 'Mind you, I would like to see Ha Li again myself. I've often thought of him affectionately over the years.'

'He told me that if he ever came across you again he would strangle you with his bare hands.' At that moment, she was so angry she almost felt the urge to do it herself.

Chen grinned. 'That's the Ha Li I remember. Honest, honourable and a little naïve. You know, what galls me most about the failure of our honey trap was that in so many ways our profilers had read him perfectly. We'd spotted his old-fashioned chivalrous streak, and worked our approach around it. The only thing we didn't know was that he was also a British intelligence agent. It was so out of character it never even occurred to us. In the end, of course, it was his nobility that led to his downfall, as well as ours.'

'I don't know what you're talking about,' she said.

'Yes, you do. He told you about it over lunch at the Great Wall Sheraton. That's another tape I've ensured was "lost", by the way. Can't afford to have my name bandied about in conversation by the mother of a student protester and an ex-imperialist spy. Luckily Ha Li's file is so buried that nobody besides myself has yet made a connection with his former activities in this country, or he would certainly have been arrested, if for no other reason than that he travelled here using a false passport.'

'You bug restaurants too?'

He shrugged. 'Of course. They're where people usually go to talk.'

'And my restaurant? Is somebody recording us talking now?'

'No. When the tapes are played back tomorrow, the listeners will discover some inexplicable interference.' He pulled from his pocket an instrument that looked like a transistor radio with a flashing red light. 'This is what we call a jammer – but you're the mother of a leading student protester, Ziwei,' he continued, 'and you entertain known dissidents. I can prevent some things happening but not everything. Certainly not in the present political climate, but again, don't be too concerned. Every conversation in your salon has been tediously predictable, and the 'lily-livered coterie of has-been intellectuals', as I overheard your daughter so aptly describe them the other day, is of little interest to us. Yanqing is another matter, of course, but she has said enough publicly in the square to hang herself many times over without us needing to seek evidence of sedition here.'

'I hope you're not speaking literally,' said Ziwei.

Chen frowned. When he spoke again, his tone was no longer ironic. 'This situation cannot be allowed to continue, Ziwei. I spoke earlier of political will. I assure you it's there now. When the army goes in again, I promise you its orders will be clear-cut, and they will not fail. When that happens – and I can't tell you when it will be because it's not yet been decided – it would be better if your daughter was not around to be caught with the others.'

Ziwei clutched the table. Chen had put down his chopsticks and was looking at her earnestly. 'I'm your friend, Ziwei. I owe you my life, so please consider what I say seriously.'

'She won't listen to me, Chen Tao.' It came out as a whisper.

'I know that, but you have time. Many preparations have to be made before the government is ready to move in. Perhaps we can find a way to convince her, or otherwise extricate her in time.'

'What preparations? What are you planning?'

'Don't ask me that. I can only reveal so much. Also, please don't let on to your daughter what I've been telling you. If you do, you will compromise me and then I will never be able to help you – or her. Please, I need your promise on this.'

She saw the logic, and nodded.

'As I told you,' he continued, 'I know something of your situation, but not everything that passed between you and Ha Li the other night.

You might be relieved to hear we haven't bugged your private rooms. I'd never do that to you again, Ziwei. When I said earlier you were lovers, I had inferred it, although you appeared to confirm it. What I do know, however, is that you have not been in contact with him since. Perhaps you have had a falling-out. It's not my business. But I would be relieved if it were so. In this political climate, and with your connection to a student leader, a liaison with a foreigner could only be compromising. I hope you can see that.'

'I'd say you're correct. It's none of your business.'

'Call it off, Ziwei. Do it as gently as you like, but cut your ties with this man, at least until this is over. It will be difficult for me to help you if it becomes known – and it may be, despite my precautions – that your lover is a foreigner and a former spy. He's better out of your life.'

'If the government plans to take Tiananmen Square by storm, and my daughter's there, how can you possibly help me?'

'Assume for the moment that I can. Will you do as I ask?'

'And break off my liaison, as you call it, with Ha Li? That seems to be a minor matter for such an important official as you to be concerned about.'

'I'm here in a personal rather than an official capacity. I'm worried for you, Ziwei, and maybe also for him. It'd certainly be a weight off my mind if he left the country. It's dangerous for him, too. Tell him that. Use my name to threaten him if you like. Meet him discreetly one last time. I think you'll have to do that. You can't say all this in a letter or over the phone. I don't care how you do it, but persuade him to leave you and China.'

She had been agonising about how she would tell Ha Li she wanted him to leave – but she resented Chen ordering her to do so, and now the prospect had become concrete she felt an intense pang of regret. On the other hand, everything Chen had said made sense. And at the same time he was promising to help Yanqing. To Ziwei, as a mother, that counted for more than anything else.

He seemed to sense her indecision. 'Think about it, Ziwei. What other motive could I have in coming here if it were not goodwill towards you and your daughter? I'm certainly not doing my duty as a secret policeman, which would be to arrest the lot of you. In covering up for you, I'm risking a life sentence. You're a harbourer of dissidents, Ha Li's a foreign agent and Yanqing's leading a revolt against the government. What does that make me?'

'You really will find a way to protect my daughter?'

'Yes.'

She stared into those searching, protuberant eyes, wondering if she could trust him. 'You know she despises you? You're the enemy as far as she's concerned.'

'She's the daughter of my friend,' he said.

This was the second time he had called himself her 'friend'. 'I'll consider it,' she said.

'Thank you.' He picked up his cup of Wuliangye and drained it.

Somehow it was easier after that. Chen Tao's warning had hardened her resolve. She already believed their lovemaking had been irresponsible. Chen had made clear that it was also dangerous, particularly for her daughter. Yanqing must be her only concern.

She felt sad about it. She loved Ha Li. Even now she could not get him out of her mind. She knew it would be a long time before her feelings for him faded, if they ever did – but now her daughter's safety was at issue, and she saw clearly that he could play no further part in her life. She would put it to him gently, as Chen had suggested. She owed him that kindness, but she would be firm and leave him no room for doubt.

Of course she was tempted to soften the message with promises that the day might come when they could take stock, test their love again – but she knew that if she left even the slightest hope, she would never convince him or herself of her seriousness. Unconsciously she had adopted the philosophy of the Laogai, which had preserved her through years of torment: abandon the future, abandon hope, and live for the present because that is the only reality. She was fighting for survival again – not for herself, this time, but for her daughter. There were no half-measures. If she was to bring herself to break off with Ha Li, she would have to make clear to him that it was permanent – even if it broke their hearts. Those were the stakes.

Having decided what she would say, she called his hotel.

They met on the following Sunday in the Jietaisi monastery in the Western Hills.

Ha Li had already arrived when Ziwei's taxi drew up. As she paid the driver she could see his tall figure standing immobile by a stone pagoda in the garden at the bottom of the hill. She was reminded of the time she had observed him in the square, a figure of impassive strength and powerful determination.

When she approached him, he smiled. 'How are you?' he asked.

'I'm fine, Ha Li,' she said.

'And Yanqing?'

'I haven't seen much of her. She's still in the square. We quarrelled when I tried to persuade her to leave.'

'I'm sorry to hear that.' She noticed that he was rubbing his hands, the sign that he was nervous.

It was a hot blue day. Above them, the pines and firs on the mountain were etched in stark clarity in the sunlight. A prayer walk wound up to the monastery from the pagoda garden. In the shadow of the trees, statues of the Buddha and Guanyin, worn with age and weather, looked down on the transient world with blank serenity.

'You've chosen a beautiful place for us to meet,' said Ha Li. 'The Western Hills were off limits to foreigners when I was a diplomat here in the sixties.'

'When you were a spy, Ha Li,' said Ziwei, gently.

'Yes, when I was a spy,' he said.

'Shall we walk up to the monastery?' she suggested. 'We went up a mountain to a temple once before. Do you remember?'

'It was raining then,' he said.

'Yes. Fate has never been kind to us.'

They walked slowly up the path. Once, at a steep step leading to a stone bridge, Ha Li gave Ziwei his hand to help her up, but they put their arms by their sides again afterwards, walking some metres apart, their silence wrapped in the greater silence of the mountain.

They reached the temple and bought entry tickets from a monk in a kiosk dwarfed by a huge stone lion under an ancient cypress tree. They walked through the entrance hall, past the statues of the four giant guardian spirits, clad in armour and rolling their eyes in choleric red faces as they brandished their clubs and swords. They entered a tranquil courtyard. Ornamental rock formations surrounded the temple pool, and on either side two bronze pavilions contained a drum and gong. Hanging over them were the twisted branches of the pine trees that had stood there for hundreds of years.

'Do you want to see the temple, Ha Li?' asked Ziwei. She looked at the brochure the monk had given her. 'It was built in 622 during the Tang Dynasty, but thirteen hundred years ago a monk called Fajun made an altar here.' She ran her eyes down the page. 'That tree over there is called the Sensitive Pine. If you touch one of its branches the whole tree shakes.'

'How appropriate,' said Ha Li. 'That's rather how I feel at the moment. But no, Ziwei, if you don't mind, I'd rather sit here with you on this bench. We haven't had a chance to talk properly with everything that's been going on.'

They were silent as an old monk with a broomstick crossed the courtyard and made his way slowly up the steps towards the temples that climbed the hill above them.

'What do you think we should say to each other, Ha Li? What is there to say?'

'You could tell me why you don't want to see me any more,' he said quietly. 'I presume you have brought me here to say goodbye.'

She felt the sting of a tear. She leant forward, head bowed over her clasped hands. After a few moments, she sighed and reached into her bag for her cigarettes. Ha Li had his lighter out, anticipating her. She turned towards him, and spoke coldly. 'I wanted to tell you what my life has been like since Chen Tao separated us so long ago, but I don't think a foreigner, even one as knowledgeable about China as you, Ha Li, could ever understand what sort of experience it was to be sent to the Laogai.'

'Don't try,' said Ha Li. 'I think I can imagine.'

'Yes, I'm sure you can understand the physical hardships we suffered. Even in the West you will have heard about the agricultural slave camps, the starvation conditions, the cruelties, the hopelessness. You'll have heard about the Cultural Revolution too, the madness that descended on the country and even affected us in our prisons – but that doesn't even begin to describe the Laogai, its full horror and beauty.'

'Beauty?' Ha Li looked shocked.

She contemplated him as she drew on her cigarette. 'That surprises you, Ha Li. There was beauty there, you know, and when we found it, we cherished it all the more because we had nothing else.'

'You'll have to explain that to me,' he said.

'Slave labour is not unique to China, nor are physical abuse and cruelty, but there was an additional refinement in the Laogai that we Chinese can claim credit for. They stripped us, Ha Li, not only of our freedom and dignity but of our very humanity, our identities, even our souls. Do you know who inflicted the worst cruelties on us when we were undergoing Reform through Labour? It wasn't the capos. It was ourselves. Would you believe it, Ha Li, if I told you that when I was an inmate of those camps, I stole, I lied, I reported others – once my best friend, who was shot because of it? I even murdered, Ha Li.' Her hand was shaking. The stub of her cigarette slipped from her fingers.

'You had to survive in intolerable circumstances,' muttered Ha Li.

'Yes, that's true,' she said, 'but many didn't. They were the good ones, Ha Li. The ones who resisted becoming monsters.'

'You can't carry this guilt,' he said. 'It was the system, not you.'

'You still don't understand. We *were* the system. All of us. We made it work.'

'You're just saying this, Ziwei. I know you. You're not like that.'

She pulled out another cigarette. He lit it for her.

'I was,' she said. 'The system broke me and I turned into the sort of creature they wanted me to be. But I was fortunate.' She smiled. 'I had friends, an actress and a thief, and they saved me. Slowly, over the years, I managed to rediscover my humanity – or, rather, from being nothing I built myself into a new person. I'm not the girl you knew, Ha Li. The innocent naïve, who could lose herself in the passion of love. That Ziwei was destroyed. I'm somebody else now. Older, maybe wiser, somebody who sees more clearly the implications of thoughtless actions.'

'You talked of beauty,' said Ha Li.

'Yes, I did. That's the strangest thing you discover, that when a person is broken down to nothing, a residue remains of something good. Do you know what I remember now about the Laogai? It's not the horrors I've been describing but the friendships, the self-sacrifice, the generosity of people who have nothing to give but give it all the same. Perhaps you need to see the very worst that others, and even yourself, can do before you can begin to appreciate what is beautiful about ordinary people. Only then can you learn to forgive, Ha Li – others, and maybe, one day, yourself.'

'That all sounds very noble,' he said bitterly, 'but I doubt I'll ever find a way to forgive myself for being the cause of your sufferings.'

'Then you haven't been listening to what I've been telling you. Good comes out of bad. I don't regret what happened to me. I wouldn't be the person I am today if it had not happened. I never told you about my husband. I married him because I had to. He was a brute, one of the worst of the peasant cadres who preyed on others during the Maoist period. For years I hated him, but now I'm grateful to him. He gave me Yanqing. Now I feel sorry for him.'

'You're still married to him?'

'Only because I never saw the need to divorce him. He is an invalid, almost a vegetable, after a stroke – but, Ha Li, don't have any wild hopes. He is still more part of my life than you are.' She put a hand on his. 'That's what I've been trying to make you understand. I have made my peace. We belong to different worlds, Ha Li. We always did. We never got to know each other before calamity overcame us. If we had allowed reason rather than passion to rule us, we would have realised we were fooling ourselves. What real future existed for us then – or now?' She sighed. 'We're older today, Ha Li, and should be able to see more clearly.'

'I don't think I've ever been clearer,' he said coldly. 'I love you. I'd thought it might be mutual.'

'Don't be bitter, Ha Li,' she said, brushing his cheek with her palm. 'Of course I'm fond of you. We shared one last beautiful evening of passion, but it was the exhilaration of what had been happening in the square that made us forget ourselves – that made me forget myself – and perhaps some nostalgia for when we were young, and because . . . because you're still a handsome man, Ha Li.'

'Then if something's there why don't we try to make a go of it?' he said. 'For God's sake, Ziwei, neither of us is young now, as you say, but after all the misery we've lived through, can't we try to see if we might find some happiness together in the time remaining to us?' He put his arm around her shoulder, and tried to turn her face towards him. She remained rigid, and he released her.

'I *am* happy, Ha Li,' she said. 'That's what I've been telling you.'

'I love you, Ziwei. I always have. I always will.'

'Then I'm sorry,' she said. Again, she felt a sting in her eyes. She got up and began to pace beneath the drooping pine. Absently she touched one of its branches. The tree shook infinitesimally. She let out a half-sob, but controlled herself immediately. She turned back to Ha Li, who was still on the seat, watching her with agony on his face. 'If you love me, you'll leave Beijing,' she said harshly.

'I thought we were still friends at least,' he said.

'Not now. You're only a pressure on me. This situation in the square – my daughter . . .'

'I can help there,' he said. 'Remember? We talked about it . . . If the army comes in again, I can—'

She almost screamed: 'Don't you understand? You're a foreigner, Ha Li. Your very presence is dangerous for me and Yanqing. The army *is* coming in, very soon, and I don't want you anywhere near.'

He froze. 'What do you mean "dangerous"? And how do you know the army's coming in? Who told you? Was it Chen Tao?'

His mention of his old friend startled her. 'Yes, it was,' she admitted. 'Oh, Ha Li, I know what you think of him, but he promised me he would protect Yanqing. He also warned me about you, Ha Li. The Chinese security services know you're here and that you were once a spy. Chen Tao says you should leave on the first available flight.'

'That bastard! I wouldn't believe a word he tells you.'

'Don't call him that. He's my friend and has proved it.'

'Friend?'

'Ha Li, I told you. We make accommodations to survive. All right, if you prefer it, he's not my friend – I can never forget what he did to us – but he belongs to my world, and you don't. I trust him more than I do you.' Again, she regretted the hurt she knew she was inflicting on him. 'Oh, don't misunderstand me. I know you mean well for Yanqing and myself, but your very presence is a threat to us. Chen Tao is trying to cover up, but if others found out that Yanqing's mother had been consorting with a foreign spy, it would give the government grounds to have her and me tried for treason. You compromise us, Ha Li.'

'I see.' He slumped on the seat, as if all the energy had drained from his body.

Her heart went out to him. 'Ha Li, this is China. There's nothing you can do to help me. Please, please understand – and I say this with gratitude for what you have offered to do for me – this is not your concern. This is not your country, and we are not your family. I beg you, go to the airport and fly home.'

He was scowling. 'I'm not sure I'm prepared to leave anywhere because Chen Tao tells me to.'

'It's not Chen Tao, it's me. For all sorts of reasons, Ha Li, I want you to leave me in peace. Perhaps we can be friends one day, but nothing more, and not now. Oh, Ha Li, is there not some woman in Canada you can go to? Somebody better than me, who can make you happy, as you said? I am concerned for you.'

'I think you've made your feelings perfectly clear,' he said.

His bitterness struck to her heart. 'This has not been easy for me,' she said.

'I appreciate that,' he answered. He bowed his head. 'I do understand, you know.'

She leant forward. He turned and saw the emptiness in his expression, and she felt a pain in her chest. 'Do you?' she said. 'Do you? You're not just saying that?'

Suddenly he grinned, and his clear blue eyes looked at her steadily. 'Yes I do, Ziwei, and I don't blame you, not in the slightest.' His lip quivered, and again he hung his head, but when he looked up the brave smile was back again. 'This won't stop me loving you. It'll probably take me some time to get over that, but don't concern yourself about me because I'll be fine.' He was rubbing his hands together. 'I see now it was a fool's errand that brought me here, so I apologise for the anguish I've caused you. I only wish there was something I could do to help you with your daughter, but I hear what you say on that score as well and I won't stay where I'm not wanted. I suppose I still have some pride left in me, after all.'

'Oh, Ha Li?' Ziwei wanted to put her arms round him to comfort him, and it took an effort to control herself. 'Then you will leave Beijing?' she asked, hesitantly.

The blue eyes were still contemplating her calmly. 'Tonight, if I can get a flight. If that's what you want?'

'I do, Ha Li,' she said in a small voice, feeling her heart breaking.

'Then that's what I'll do,' he said. 'What's to make me stay?'

'You're a good man, Ha Li. I will always remember you with affection.'

He stood up, towering over her, and kissed her. 'You're a magnificent woman, Ziwei. You always were and you are today. Who knows? In a different political system or different times, we might have made it work, you and I. Guess it's malignant old Fate again.'

'What are you going to do now, Ha Li? I'm worried about you.'

'Now? Oh, I don't know. Perhaps, since I'm here, I might stay and see the rest of this monastery. I could do with some tranquil reflection before I leave. I take it you're heading back to town straight away?'

'Yes, Ha Li, I think that would be best.'

'That's fine then,' he said. He looked like the boy who had kissed her when they made love. She knew the grief he must be feeling inside, but all she could see was kindness.

'I'm not one for long-drawn-out partings,' he said. He stroked her cheek, then leant forward to kiss her forehead and, briefly, her lips. 'Here, take this,' he said, reaching into his pocket and withdrawing a crumpled piece of paper. 'This is my address in Vancouver, just in case you—'

'No, Ha Li, I won't change my mind,' she said, her heart thumping at the finality of her own words.

He nodded. 'I know, but take it anyway,' he said. 'Goodbye, my love,' he added. She heard the choke in his voice, as he thrust the paper into her hands. Then he was striding up the steps towards the temple terrace, his coat hanging over his shoulder.

Tears in her eyes, she watched him until he became indistinct in the smoke of the bronze incense-burner in front of the temple door, and disappeared within.

Slowly she made her way down the path. When she came to a dustbin, she paused, determined to throw away the address he had given her, but she could not bring herself to do so. She stuffed it into her bag and strode on.

Again she paused. In the distance she could make out the Capital Iron and Steel Works and beyond it the expanse of the city. From this height the metropolis looked as tranquil as the temple surroundings, showing no signs of the turbulence within. In the same way she was sure that the few passers-by, glancing at her as she stood there, could see no sign of her breaking heart.

There was another great march the length of Chang An Avenue, so the taxi-driver had to divert to the Southern Ring Road. They passed northwards along the eastern side of the great park that contained the Temple of Heaven. The blue tiles on the conical roof of the Hall of the Prayer for Great Harvests gleamed almost purple in the bright sunshine. The driver would have turned right towards the station but on a whim she asked him to turn north through the old legation quarter towards the Peking Hotel. She paid him off, then made her way through the crowds cheering the marchers in the direction of the square. Again, she pushed and shoved against the stream. She wanted to see Yanqing, to be with somebody she loved.

She skirted the huge edifice of the History Museum, passing the large framed portraits of Marx, Engels, Lenin, Stalin and Mao. She remembered laughing when Yanqing had told her, at an early stage of the protests, that one of the students had rechristened this decreasingly hirsute gallery of the founders of Communism 'The History of Shaving' and pasted a Gillette logo under the clean-cut face of Mao, with a label: 'Mao Tse-tung Thought: The ultimate in Communism – no more beards or moustaches.' The final touch had been a photograph of the bald reformist Russian president, Gorbachev: 'Is this the future?'

With Chen Tao's warning of what was to come, such irreverence no longer seemed funny.

The square stank under the hot sun and, when she neared the tents, she heard the buzz of insects swarming over the Portakabin latrines and the piles of rubbish. She walked into a cloud of flies and mosquitoes. It reminded her of the Laogai.

It was with relief that she neared the first student checkpoint. A skinny boy in shorts and a baseball cap studied her pass, then checked a clipboard hanging round his neck. 'This has been cancelled,' he said.

'There must be a mistake. I'm Gao Yanqing's mother.'

'I'm sorry. See for yourself.' He showed her the board to which was clipped a list of names and pass numbers. He pointed and she saw her name, but it was crossed out. She recognised Yanqing's signature. Next to it was a date: the day on which Yanqing had come to the restaurant and they had argued.

She felt numbed with sorrow and disbelief. 'Can you check with her? Or get a message to her?' she pleaded.

He conferred with his colleagues. 'All right, it's quiet now. I'll see if she's around.'

She waited. Flies buzzed around her head.

Yanqing was with him when he came back. She looked tired and sweaty and it was clear that she had not washed for days. Dust ringed her eyes. She took her mother's arm peremptorily, and guided her to an empty alley between two tents, then turned to her with a frown. 'You mustn't come here, Mama. The situation is tense, and we're discouraging personal visitors. Only those who have business with the committees are allowed in. We student leaders must set an example.'

'My darling, I only wanted to see you. It's been days. But, Yanqing, look at you – you're so thin, and your eyes are red. Haven't you been sleeping?'

Yanqing looked rather obviously at her watch. 'If you have anything urgent to tell me, please do so. I have little time.'

'I'm worried about you, that's all, and I miss you.'

Yanqing's answer was cold: 'Don't you think all of us have parents? Do you realise what's happening now? We're in open conflict with a government that has tried once, and probably will again, to use force against its own people. We cannot afford to allow sentimentality in our decision-making. We have a responsibility to the people of China that must override personal feelings. And we are busy. I think it would be best if you left.'

Ziwei stared at her. She did not recognise her daughter in this fierce activist. She had a sudden memory of Zhang Hong, when she had first met her in Iron Man's Glade. 'Oh, Yanqing, this is taking you over,' she murmured.

'It's politics, Mama. You wouldn't understand.' She put on an artificial smile, and patted Ziwei's arm. 'Don't worry about us. We know what we're doing and what our enemies are planning. We'll be victorious. I'll come and see you when it's all over – but please, Mama, if you have any sympathy with the Democracy Movement, you must allow us to do what we have to do.'

She shook her mother's arm and smiled again. 'Thank you for coming to the square,' she said. 'We appreciate your support.'

She turned abruptly and hurried off, pulling a sheaf of papers from her pocket and studying them as she went.

Lonelier than she had ever been, Ziwei stumbled through the crowds. She had lost Ha Li and her daughter in a single day.

There were shouts and laughter and a bustle of activity at the Chang An Avenue side of the square. Unconsciously, she found herself wandering in that direction. There seemed to be a new structure of some kind in front of Mao's portrait. It looked like an enormous upended crate, but twenty feet tall. As she watched, she saw excited students straining at ropes. The wooden sides fell away to reveal an enormous white statue. It bore a resemblance to the pictures she had seen of the Statue of Liberty in New York: the woman wore a loose, Grecian dress and her raised arm pointed mockingly at the paint-spattered chairman.

A great shout rose up above the cheers. 'Long live the Goddess of Freedom and Democracy!'

They've gone mad, she thought. This was blatant provocation – as near as they could come to a declaration of war. She shivered, despite the heat of the sun. They're no longer seeking a compromise, she thought. They've given up all attempts to open dialogue with the government. They've gone beyond that. They're daring the authorities to do their worst – and they will.

Laughing boys and girls were streaming past her in the direction of the statue, singing the 'Internationale'.

She tried to stumble away, but found herself on the western side of the square. Here she saw something that terrified her even more. It was not students gathered there, but workers, thousands of them, listening to a man with a megaphone who was standing under a bright red banner on which white characters were stencilled: 'Celebrate the Founding of the Independent Trade Unions of Workers.'

'No longer will we allow the Communist Party to manipulate our rights,' the man was shouting. 'From now on all workers in China are free.'

She felt dazed with the heat, anguish and a new sensation: cold, dripping fear. This was no longer peaceful protest.

She looked down Chang An Avenue at the procession of marchers that disappeared in the direction of the distant Western Hills. Her vision returned of tanks and advancing soldiers.

'Yanqing,' she murmured, 'My baby.'

She tried desperately to comfort herself: Chen Tao had promised to save Yanqing – but could she trust him? What could even he do in the light of this?

Then she thought of Ha Li, his strength, determination, and confidence that he would find a way to rescue her daughter. She remembered leaning on his shoulder in despair and how he had comforted her. She remembered their lovemaking and how secure she had felt in his arms.

It may not be too late, she told herself. He might not have left. There may be time.

It took her an hour to get to the Peking Hotel, where she knew there was a public telephone. Frantically she dialled the Great Wall Sheraton and asked for Ha Li's room, using the alias he had earlier given her.

'Mr Henry Manners? He's checked out,' the receptionist told her.

'When? Where did he go?'

'I can't tell you that,' said the receptionist.

'Please,' begged Ziwei. 'It's very important.' She racked her brains to think of a way to learn more. 'I'm from the aviation ministry,' she said, putting as much authority into her voice as she could. 'Mr Manners was negotiating a contract with us. It is a large deal for our country and we would like to get a message to him. Please can you check when he left?'

'I'll have to ask the duty manager,' said the girl.

Ziwei waited for two frustrating minutes listening to a foreign jingle on the line. Eventually a man's voice answered her: 'Can you tell me who I'm talking to?' he asked. 'For the record, please.'

'My name is Lan Ying, and I work for the Ministry of Aviation. You can check that later,' she said. 'Please, it's vitally important we contact Mr Manners. Can you tell me where he is now?'

'Wait a minute,' he said. There was more jingle on the phone. When he came on the line again, he told her, 'Mr Manners left more than an hour ago. He's taking the five o'clock flight to Hong Kong, and from there to Vancouver tonight. We helped him book his ticket. It's four fifteen so I imagine he must have passed through Immigration. You'll probably have to contact the airport authorities if you want to talk to him now.'

She hung up, knowing there was nothing she could do. She walked home slowly and, ignoring Tan and her staff, went to her room and lay on the bed. There she cried a little, for Yanqing, for herself, for the man who loved her and whom she had sent away.

Afterwards she stared at the ceiling beams. It was a clean, snug room, nothing like a solitary cell in the Laogai, but she felt as isolated and as hopeless as she had all those years ago. In a way it was worse. In the Laogai she had found strength to go on, merely by willing herself to survive. Then she had still been fractionally in control of her fate – but now events were in motion that affected the people she loved, and she was powerless to do anything but wait. The shred of hope that kept her from utter despair was that Chen Tao had said he would help. She tried to cling to that – but in her heart of hearts she did not trust him, and the one man she did trust was in the air, flying away from China, and she had only herself to blame.

Harry was not in the air but that would have been no comfort to Ziwei, had she known it. Shortly after he had passed through Customs and Immigration, and was waiting in the departure hall for the Hong

Kong flight, he had been approached by two policemen in green uniforms and told there was an irregularity. They took him into a small office where there were more policemen. Chen Tao was sitting behind the desk. He grinned broadly as Harry was shoved into a chair in front of him.

'I'm very sorry, Ha Li,' he said, 'but you're now under arrest. Coming into the country illegally under the false name of this Mr Manners will be the given reason for detaining you, but I'm sure we'll be able to think of other charges as we delve further.'

'Ever the bastard you always were, Chen Tao,' said Harry. 'I don't suppose there's any point in my asking to talk to a representative of the Canadian Embassy?'

'None at all,' said Chen, cheerfully. 'As far as they will know, you have already left the country. A Mr Manners will take your flight to Hong Kong. We can forge passports too. But you, my old friend, will remain here. It has been such a long time since the two of us had a chance to talk. I think I will enjoy renewing our acquaintance.'

For form's sake, Harry protested, and even struggled when they showed they intended to handcuff him, but he knew it would be to no avail, and as the plane that would have taken him out of China was taxiing down the runway, he found himself sitting in the back of a limousine with tinted windows and Public Security Bureau number plates. There were policemen on either side of him, and Chen Tao was sitting next to the driver, whistling.

'Where are you taking me?' he asked.

'Oh, somewhere safe and quiet. Very quiet. Don't worry, my old friend. I will personally be looking after your every comfort.'

22

Circling the Square

Beijing, 4 June 1989

The ceiling mirror above the big double bed almost certainly contained a camera. It amused Chen, no doubt, to hold him in a safe-house that the Chinese intelligence services used for their honey-trap operations. It was a not-so-subtle message that personal scores remained to be settled between them.

At least it was not the concrete gaol cell that might equally have appealed to the secret policeman's sardonic sense of humour. There was a desk, a silk carpet, two artificial-leather armchairs, a well-stocked mini-bar and an *ensuite* bathroom. In addition, there was a television and an old-fashioned wireless in a walnut case, which, he was pleased to discover, when he twiddled the knobs, had short-wave reception so he could pick up the BBC and Voice of America. Except when Chen came for what he ironically called his 'interrogation sessions', Harry spent the next six days listening to the reports of the foreign correspondents.

At first it was just more of the same: daily marches to the square; increasingly impassioned interviews with student leaders (once he heard Yanqing shrilly articulating the new student demand for a nationwide general strike), and sometimes farcical reports of army movements, based on guesswork and rumour, and exemplified by one female correspondent's assertion – obviously she had no access to an atlas – that 'the army of Manchuria is marching in from the south'.

Only towards the end of the week had the rumours and counter-rumours coalesced into some semblance of factual reporting, as the pace of events accelerated, both in the square and outside. Two days ago there had been an intensification of student protest when a famous Taiwanese pop singer and an eminent essayist announced publicly that they were renewing the hunger-strike. That day, a journalist made his way into Nanyuan airport in the south of the city, and discovered that the landing strip was covered with tents of the prestigious Paratroop Regiment from Nanchang. Ominously, the Forbidden City was closed, fuelling rumours that troops were being infiltrated into the centre of the city and that all access roads to the Western Hills were blocked by heavily armed checkpoints. This suggested an intensification of military preparation in the bases. Harry wondered for how much longer the precarious status quo could be maintained.

The next afternoon, 2 June, a column of lorries, full of burly navvies sporting uniform crew-cuts, drove into the city and was surrounded by a mob. When it was discovered that each vehicle concealed a cache of weapons, many of the so-called workers were beaten up. At about the same time, close by Tiananmen Square, a speeding army jeep knocked over and killed three students. There had been a furious response, and a public funeral of the first 'martyrs' of the Democracy Movement was to be held the next day.

Harry, like everybody else in the city, was on tenterhooks. How would the government react?

At midnight, they sent in a column of unarmed soldiers. At Dabeiyao, jeering crowds surrounded them, confiscated their boots and sent them packing. Incompetent as this incursion was, it angered the populace.

At ten o'clock this morning – it was 3 June and he had been incarcerated for five days – Harry heard how linked phalanxes of policemen in front of the Peking Hotel were trying to prevent angry townspeople entering the square to protest. They were pushed aside, and the mob flooded through. In the afternoon the bodies of the three traffic-accident victims were brought, amid great emotion, to the steps of the Martyrs' Memorial. Later, there were clashes between students and troops guarding the Great Hall of the People, with injuries on both sides. The *Voice of America* correspondent said you could cut the air with a knife.

And now it had begun. At six o'clock, all Chinese networks switched to the same programme and two severely dressed announcers, a man and a woman, began to read the new government orders. It was a simple message, repeated over and over again: a dangerous criminal minority had occupied the central square of Beijing. This amounted to counter-revolutionary rebellion. A curfew had been imposed with immediate effect. Anybody found on the street would face the consequences. The news announcement was followed by mournful classical music, which had continued ever since.

Harry was not surprised. The situation had reached breaking-point.

As he paced the room, Harry was no longer attending to the excited voices on the radio. He was thinking of Ziwei, who must be waiting in a state of terror at her restaurant, probably listening to the same radio reports as he was. He felt the urge to call her. There was a phone in the room that he had deliberately not used, for he knew he must resist the impulse to dial her number. If he was to get through this, he must allow no emotion to distract him.

It was now eleven o'clock and the first news was coming in of clashes between army convoys and barricades manned by students and workers in the far west of the city. He was still gnawed by the fear that Ziwei might allow her maternal feelings to get the better of her and attempt to join her daughter. He had Chen's assurance that he had placed men round the Yangtze Gorges to stop her if she attempted to leave – but he knew how resourceful Ziwei could be when she was determined. She had survived the Laogai and built a business for herself against all the odds. That had taken resolution and courage. In any case, there was nothing he could do about it. It was out of his hands. Like her, he had to trust Chen. What other choice was there?

He thought back to the days following their lovemaking when he had made up his mind on his course of action. He had waited three days by the telephone, ordering his meals in his hotel room. On the fourth day, he had accepted that Ziwei had rejected him. He had tried to take it philosophically, although it had broken his heart. He had been expecting it: her cold manner when she had thrown him out of her room had been clear enough. He would have the rest of his life for regrets, but now he had something important to do.

He had dressed, shaved and made his way to the British Embassy, where Julian's contact had given him all the information he required. Then he made the phone call that set things in motion.

Now the time had come for action. Again Harry checked his watch. If the troops were already in Muxudi, it would be a matter of hours before they reached the square. He expected Chen to arrive imminently. He stripped to his underpants, then checked the clothes that had been provided for him and which were now laid on the bed. Carefully he began to dress. When he heard the knock on the door, he was in the bathroom, balaclava over his face, applying boot polish to the flesh that was still visible round his eyes.

Chen was alone. He looked up at the big man dressed in black. 'Ha Li,' he said, 'this takes me back, but you look so terrifying that I think even our dear old Hong Huzis would be wary of you if they could see you today.'

'I don't intend to be seen, Chen Tao,' he said, pulling off the mask. 'Is everything ready?' He glanced briefly at the mirror. With the black rings around his eyes, he looked like a clown, but he was reasonably confident that dark glasses would cover the camouflage when he was not masked.

Chen Tao threw himself into one of the armchairs and lit a cigarette. 'We still have some time. The army's making slow progress against the barricades.'

'What's happening in the square?'

'The citizens are literally playing with fire,' was the caustic reply. 'Molotov cocktails, to be exact. As we speak, a pillar of flame from a blazing armoured car is illuminating the Tiananmen Gate. The crew, who – rather foolishly, in my view – decided to reconnoitre the square, are probably regretting their impetuosity. The last report I received, just before I arrived, was that your peace-loving student friends had pulled the survivors out of the burning vehicle and are now in the process of beating them to death.'

Harry shook his head. 'Stupid. When the other troops hear about that they'll want retribution.'

'Oh, we're a long way down that road,' said Chen. 'Muxudi is a bloodbath already. These soldiers are young men from the provinces. Detachments from one regiment are mingled with another, and they've been secluded for nearly a fortnight, receiving daily propaganda that the homeland is in danger from well-armed insurgents and Enemies of the People. It only took a few bricks thrown at their heads to scare them into firing directly at the students and workers, and now, as they progress down Chang An Avenue, I gather that they're shooting happily at the buildings on either side of the road, knocking old biddies off their balconies. It's all very regrettable, but I suppose old Deng knows what he's doing. Nothing like a bit of terror to bring order and control.'

'Is that what you call it?' said Harry.

'Be careful, Ha Li. I told you that the two of us stand on opposite

sides of a political divide. I'm helping you and Ziwei out of friendship, because we were once Hong Huzi together, and you and I have
reached an age when it is time to put behind us old scores. We did
our best in our youth to damage each other, and life has taught us a
lesson or two on how to live and let live.'

'Those were my words.'

'And I agreed with you.'

After much fencing, thought Harry, recalling their first tentative
contact.

Chen had been disbelieving on the phone, demanding to know how
Harry had got his number. One up for British Intelligence, thought
Harry. To be jumped like that had clearly infuriated his old enemy. Yet
Harry's mention of blue flags had convinced the suspicious secret
policeman that he was who he said he was. Anyway, he had agreed to
meet him in Ritan Park by the ornamental rocks.

Harry had allowed Chen to arrive first, and only approached him
after he had satisfied himself that he was alone. Also he had to calm
himself to the point at which he felt he could talk to the man without
attempting to throttle him. It had taken only a few seconds to realise
that the hatred was mutual – but that, strangely, had been their bond,
for there was no need to pretend any more. They knew each other too
well.

Chen had glared at him. 'So, what game is it this time? Why is
British Intelligence using a superannuated spy like you?'

'They're not. It's private business. I've used old contacts to find you,
but there's no secret operation. They retired me twenty-five years ago.'

'Private business,' Chen scoffed. 'What? Come for your revenge at
last, have you, Ha Li? Isn't it a bit late for such childishness? We're
no longer little boys.'

'My sentiment entirely. It's time we got over our childhood. Life's
moved on, Chen Tao.'

'Meaning?'

'That we should get the poison out of our systems. Wipe the slate.
We'll never be the friends we once were, but we can co-operate instead
of tearing each other apart over grievances that date back fifty years
and don't mean a damn thing any more anyway.'

'And how – or, rather, why – do you expect me to co-operate with
you?'

'Because we have a mutual obligation.'

Chen's eyes narrowed in suspicion. 'And what's that?'

'Ziwei.'

There was no mistaking the surprise. 'Ziwei?'

'Yes, And her daughter. I think you want to protect them, as I do.'

As he said the words, Harry's heart was in his mouth and, for a moment, as Chen stared at him, he thought he had miscalculated. After all, it had only been a hunch, based on a few words Ziwei had said over lunch: Chen Tao was not a bad man, she had told him. He was a victim of the system, like everybody else. She had even offered to introduce them. Why would she do that if she didn't believe he had changed?

Harry had thought long and hard about it. Nobody had suffered more at the hands of Chen than her – she knew him as well as anyone – and he doubted that after what she had been through she was the sort of person to absolve a tormentor lightly. So something in the man had changed or, at the very least, Chen wanted Ziwei to believe he had changed, for whatever reasons of guilt, conscience, obligation or self-esteem that complicated his proud nature. Harry, too, knew his childhood friend, and that he was capable of the most devilish decep- tion, but he had never been able to disguise his arrogance. For Ziwei to have said that, she must have seen him humbled. Something – perhaps his own downfall during the Cultural Revolution – had chastened him, or perhaps she had a hold on him. She said she had met him in the Laogai. It was light straw with which to build a castle, but Harry saw no alternative. He needed somebody on the inside. Anyway, once Ziwei had rejected him, he felt he had nothing to lose. Or so he had steeled himself to believe.

He had made his proposal, and Chen had stared at him as if he was mad.

Iacta alea est. Suddenly recalling Julian's Latin tag, Harry felt a chill in his stomach. Once before he had gambled to save Ziwei and her mother, and on that occasion he had lost everything. The frown on Chen's face was not encouraging. Harry wondered if again he had made a terrible mistake.

Then Chen's eyebrows had risen. He patted his pockets for his cigar- ettes. 'Go on,' he muttered, as his fingers trembled over his lighter. Harry began to breathe again. He did not need his fisherman's instincts to tell him that the bait had been snatched.

Yet it had taken an hour of patient trawling before Chen agreed to his plan.

He was still unsure how committed Chen Tao was, but, looking at him now, lounging in his chair, he only said, 'Good. So our understanding holds?'

'Only so far, Ha Li. Yes, I have gone along with you and done everything you requested. I visited Ziwei and put the fear of God into her, persuading her to order you to leave. I made sure your disappearance from the city would be convincing in case she checked, and now, this evening, I intend to uphold my part of the bargain. But don't push me too far, or criticise what my government is doing, because I believe this exemplary action is correct. The students in the square are our enemies and, I might remind you, so are you. So be careful in case I change my mind.'

'I hear you, Chen Tao, and I'm grateful. Let's drop the subject. Have you got the maps?'

'You realise that by showing you our troop deployment I'm committing treason?'

Harry grinned, feeling the dried boot polish crack on his face. 'But what fun, eh? Just like old times, when we campaigned against the Aizi. Aren't we still playing all sides against the middle, as we did on our hillside?'

Chen smiled too. 'Do you know one thing I am eternally grateful for? In retrospect, of course. I am so very glad that our mutual honeytrap failed. Trying to control such an agent as you, whether you were a double, a triple or a quadruple, would have been a nightmare. Yes, let us pretend tonight that we're on the same side. I think I'll feel safer.'

'Then it's a blue flag? Blue for go?'

'Yes.' He chuckled, then his brows frowned over his bulbous eyes. 'Let me ask you one thing in return, Ha Li. After everything, do you really believe that one day we can see ourselves again as blood brothers? Is that possible?'

Harry studied his old enemy. There was no trace of Chen's usual cynicism in the features that peered back at him. He saw grizzled hair and an ageing face whose lines revealed the suffering he had endured. There was nervous appeal in the intensity of his stare, which suggested that whatever devils haunted the proud, secretive man, this question came to the nub of the matter. He knew he had to answer carefully, at least with an impression of honesty.

He thought of Ziwei being bundled into a truck on her way to hell on earth, and for a moment his fists clenched. Then he saw her in the restaurant and recalled her composed smile as she told him that Chen could be trusted. So far, she had been proved right.

He picked his words. 'For a long time, I thought of nothing but having your throat between my hands and tearing you apart. I don't know even now if I can ever forgive you for what you did to Ziwei, but recently I've accepted that perhaps that's something between you and her and not my business, as my own role in the whole sorry affair is between her and me and none of yours. As for the score between the two of us, I reckon we're pretty even. I attempted to trap you as you did me. But, as Ziwei told me, good can come out of bad. So, yes, I will try to forget the past because that is her wish. And if you want it too, Chen Tao, then I'll make every effort to see you again as the friend of my happy childhood, my blood brother. A lot depends on what happens tonight, of course.'

Chen sighed as, visibly, he relaxed. 'Thank you,' he said. 'I feel the same. That would be a good result of our – co-operation.' He cleared his throat. 'I was going to show you a map.'

For the next half-hour, the two men pored over the chart Chen produced from his inside jacket pocket. It was covered with arrows, converging from varying directions on to the square, with numbers of regiments and anticipated times.

Finally Harry put his finger on the map at the point marking the south-west corner of the Great Hall of the People. 'Here,' he said.

'Yes, I think that would be the most likely escape route.'

'An hour after the troops move in?'

'Maybe less, depending on what course of action the student leaders take. But I will try to be there.'

'Good,' said Harry. 'It's probably time to go, isn't it?'

'Yes,' said Chen. He looked at Harry uncertainly. 'It's a long time since we trusted each other, Ha Li,' he said. 'It's a pleasant and familiar feeling. How sad that things ever changed between us.'

Harry was startled. The man looked emotional. 'We can't change the past, Chen Tao,' he said.

'No, we can't, and nor would apologies convince either of us – but we can express regret for what happened, while preserving our dignity.'

He proffered a hand. 'Do you remember our old oath? Under the waterfall? "Your life is mine, mine is yours. We swear to live and die together."'

'Hell, it's been a long time,' said Harry. Quickly, but fiercely, he embraced him, then put on his gloves and pulled the balaclava over his head.

Keeping to the shadows, even in the corridors of the safe-house, he followed the secret policeman into the forecourt of the building. When the sentry was not looking, he slipped into the back of Chen's jeep, and covered himself with the blanket waiting for him on the seat.

It might have been another conscious irony on Chen Tao's part: he dropped Harry at the same junction on Nanchizi that he had used twenty-six years ago as the pick-up point when he was taking Harry and Ziwei to the other safe-house in the west of the city. Harry slipped out of the car into the shadow of the trees.

It was the noise that hit him first. Incoherent shouts and screams were drowned in the occasional burst of gunfire. In the background he heard the wail of ambulances or police sirens, and sometimes the crump of an explosion, which echoed and rustled the leaves. It might have been artillery or tank fire or, alternatively, the sound of petrol tanks going up in flames: Chen had told him the students were pulling buses and trucks across the road and setting light to them to make barriers against the advancing troops.

He heard whistling and, looking up over the trees, saw arcs of tracer rising into the air.

Beyond the gate that opened on to Chang An Avenue, milling people were silhouetted against the orange glare of street-lights, and a redder, flickering glow that he thought must be the bonfire they had made of the armoured car. He pulled his scope out of one of the pouches hanging from his webbing, and examined the scene framed in the arch.

It was bedlam. Students and townspeople were running this way and that in confusion or fear. Others, frozen to the spot with terror, were jostled by those attempting to flee. Briefly, he focused on the face of a young woman who had tears running down her cheeks and was obviously screaming though he could not hear her. In a moment she was pushed aside, and he saw the face of a boy, a Dare to Die headband crowning his tousled hair, also weeping as he pressed a handkerchief to the side of his face, trying to staunch the blood from some wound on his cheek. He, too, was pushed aside. Shouting youths were trying to clear a path for two pedicabs, which were loaded with bodies. Harry winced when he saw the bloody patches on the fronts of white shirts, the limp, hanging arms.

What he could not see yet were helmets. The violence had not reached the square, he decided, although the advancing column must be close now. The dead and wounded being evacuated must have been brought from the barricades in the west, the direction from which the army was approaching. If he hurried, he thought, he could reach the square before the soldiers.

He pulled off the balaclava – it would make him too conspicuous – and stowed it in the pouch with the scope. He put on dark glasses to cover the camouflage round his eyes, and ran towards the junction with Chang An Avenue. In a moment he was in the middle of the crowd. His nostrils were assailed by smoke, sweat and an odour, long-forgotten, that he remembered from the battlefields in Korea: that of panic and fear.

While scared people pushed past him, he paused to get his bearings. His extra height gave him a view over the bobbing heads. The bulk of the Peking Hotel towered over the trees on the left side of the boulevard. He noticed that the balconies were full of foreigners. Several held film crews, leaning over the railings with their cameras and booms. Clearly the Chinese authorities no longer cared that what they were doing was being reported to the world. He could make out red crosses on white vehicles parked on the road in front of the hotel. It was to these that the pedicab drivers were heading with their grisly loads. Sirens screamed and flashed as full ambulances set off to the hospital in Wangfujing, and empty ones arrived to take their places. The casualties kept coming.

Harry pushed his way against the flow of people fleeing from the square. Ahead, he could make out the roofs of the Tiananmen Gate, its top indistinct in the night haze and smoke. Wraithlike, the Goddess of Liberty and Democracy shimmered in her white robes, her smile serene despite the chaos around her. There was a blood-like sheen on her defiant, upstretched arm, reflections of the dying embers of the flames that still played half-heartedly on the blackened hump of the armoured car.

It was slow going, partly because many of the students stopped when they saw him and wanted to talk to him. It was no longer the patronising 'Thank you for your support' of the demonstration days. Boys and girls were now pulling his arms, and urging him fervently, 'Tell the world. Make known what the Chinese government is doing to its people!'

'I will,' said Harry patiently, and pressed on. The scene was becoming more and more surreal. Tracer flew overhead, gunfire moved ever closer, young men and women fled for their lives and grim-faced pedi-cab drivers pedalled the wounded to the dressing station – yet he saw several Beijing residents calmly taking a stroll. As two agonised students shouted for the way to be cleared, while a third lolled between them, his face and shirt crimson with blood, unbelievably, a young man was pointing out the tracer arcs to his delighted child, swaddled in a quilt on a baby seat at the back of his bicycle . . .

Just before he reached the entrance to the square, Harry was waylaid by a madwoman. She had whitened her face with ashes and her clothes were torn, revealing her breasts. Her lank hair was festooned with strips of paper on which were scratched incomprehensible characters. She was chanting nonsensical doggerel: 'Oh, why did you have to head-butt Mount Buzhou, Uncle? Can't you see that the ties of earth and the pillars of heaven are tumbling, tumbling, tumbling down . . .' Seeing Harry she burst into laughter, pointing at his sunglasses: 'CIA!' she shrieked. 'CIA!' Harry shoved her aside.

And found himself face to face with a platoon of soldiers.

There were two rows of them, fifteen men in each, marching forward with parade-ground discipline, their helmets reflecting the flames. Their faces were set and expressionless, and they were holding their AK47s at an angle to their chests. Students and workers scur-ried out of their way. An officer shouted an order and, while they maintained their blank expressions, their rifles, still pointing upwards, stuttered with flame. The tracer arced over their heads. Harry had to use all his strength not to be thrown backwards by the fleeing tide. He was jammed into the crowd and neither he nor the soldiers could advance.

The officer barked another order. The automatic rifles lowered, and Harry felt a moment of dreadful calm. Time stopped and everything went into slow motion. It was not death that worried him – after Ziwei's rejection, he had nothing to live for – but he felt an intense regret that he would no longer be able to make the amends he had planned tonight. The eyes of the young soldier in front of him narrowed. Harry readied himself. He knew that the gun pointing at his chest was about to fire. So this was how it would end.

He saw the flames, and heard, as if from far away, the popping sounds. The press around him parted and, dumbly, he looked down at the bodies of the two men who, a moment before, had stood at either side of him, one a young student, one a middle-aged worker. Their faces bore the same surprised expression as they lay empty-eyed on their backs, red stains spreading on their white shirts.

Harry started as the noise around him swelled. Wounded people were moaning as their fellows tried to pull them away. Others were running for their lives. A girl was screaming. A boy was cursing. There was bustle, chaos and confusion. The soldiers were motionless, their rifles again pointing upwards. There was not a flicker of expression on their faces. The officer shouted a new order, and the helmeted line, as one, stepped forward with the inhuman precision of robots or mechanical toys.

As quickly as he could, he edged round their flank. The soldier at the end of the line turned a curious face towards him, then looked forward again, and marched on with his fellows to take a position under the trees.

Shaking, he wondered where they had come from. They had materialised from nowhere. Gazing over the crowd, he saw more and more knots of helmets, making a steady progress through the throng, firing and scattering the people in front of them.

His ears ringing, dazed and horrified, he pushed on. Once, he nearly tripped over the body of a girl. She looked as if she was posing for a fashion photograph, her head resting coyly on an outstretched arm, a knee raised, showing a provocative expanse of thigh, but her face was bloody mush and bone.

Eventually he found himself alone by the now deserted Goddess of Liberty and Democracy, who was still smiling amiably at Mao Tse-tung's portrait across the road. Looking up at the calm white face, he had the strangest feeling that the two immortals were holding a mute dialogue, and were above the disturbances going on at their feet. This area had claimed at least three sacrifices. He turned his eyes away from the contorted bodies as he stumbled across the flagstones towards the tents.

They, too, had been deserted. Eerily lit by the street-lamps they

slumped like a herd of sleeping elephants. He made his way past abandoned banners and posters, his feet cracking plastic bottles and
crunching Coca-Cola cans. Tent flaps rustled in the breeze. He was
startled by the booming twang as he kicked a guitar somebody had
dropped during a hurried exit. It was a ghost town now, or a refuse
dump of high hopes and ideals. Above him the air still whistled with
tracer, as if banshees were mocking those they had come to destroy.

Half-way across the square, he heard from behind him the grinding
of machinery, the whine of engines and another sound that he found
obscene: the ploughing scrape of tank treads on the asphalt of a
civilian city. He pulled himself up one of the sturdier-looking tent
poles, and saw long black shapes moving east along Chang An Avenue.
The armour had arrived.

Their first target was the Goddess. A tank pushed its weight against
the pedestal. She withstood for a few seconds, her arm flapping at
Mao, then toppled over with a crash. The dialogue was over. One by
one the armoured vehicles began to turn so they were facing into the
square. Harry saw that the soldiers had cleared the area in front of
Tiananmen Gate of people, though he heard shooting continuing east-
wards, behind the History Museum towards the Peking Hotel. As he
watched, some companies of soldiers, who had been corralling the
crowds, formed into long lines the width of the square and advanced
in front of the armour.

Harry had heard the sound of voices near the Martyrs' Memorial
ahead, somebody speaking through a megaphone and others cheering,
with occasional bursts of defiant song. He hurried in that direction.

The tall white column was lit by arc-lamps. A group of student
leaders was standing in front of the frieze on the pedestal. Students
in Dare to Die headbands were sitting with folded arms on the steps,
gazing with stern faces at the advancing military, who were clearly
visible to them from their elevated viewpoint.

The woman with the megaphone was screeching, 'Here we will
stand. We will not allow them to move us, if we have to defend this
monument to the last drop of our blood.' It took Harry a few moments
to recognise Yanqing.

After the reality of the casual murders he had seen, her rhetoric
sounded unreal. Quietly he joined the larger group of students who
were standing at the foot of the steps. One or two looked up with
surprise at the big foreigner who had materialised beside them, but as

quickly they forgot him, too intent on what was being said on the platform.

As Yanqing ranted on, he calmed down, remembering why he was there. He breathed a sigh of relief that she was safe – but her fixed expression and the glazed look in her eyes worried him, as did the vehemence of her rhetoric. She looked as if she was drugged. The gesticulating arms seemed to operate independently of her body, which was unnaturally rigid. Harry realised that she had determined to commit the ultimate sacrifice in the square.

Yanqing finished her speech on a crescendo: 'Victory or death! For democracy, we are prepared to lay down our lives!' There were cheers and a repeated chant of her slogan from a substantial part of the audience, as well as those sitting on the steps, who shook their fists in the air and screamed defiance. They were obviously the faithful, but Harry noticed that many of the students immediately around him seemed distinctly undecided about the prospect of sacrifice. Many were glancing surreptitiously behind them to where the sound of the approaching armour was growing louder. From the crunching he could hear, Harry assumed that the vehicles were in the process of crushing the abandoned tents.

A tall, bespectacled man in his thirties had the megaphone now. His wild hair was bunched above a headband. From the excited mutters of those nearest to him, Harry picked up that this was the Taiwanese pop star who had recently gone on hunger-strike. Harry remembered that his dirge-like but haunting song had been a subsidiary anthem of the student movement from the beginning.

'Student Leader Gao has urged that we die here, fellow students,' he began, in a conversational tone. 'That is courageous, noble, committed but also – if you'll excuse my bluntness – stupid, for there is no reason that anybody should die here. If we retreat we can fight another day.'

Thank God, thought Harry. It was the first piece of sense he had heard all evening.

But there was an angry murmur from those sitting on the steps, and much confused shouting. Suddenly Yanqing seemed to wake from the trance into which she had settled after her impassioned speech. 'With all respect to this great composer and singer, this superstar who has allied himself to our struggle, he is not one of our elected leaders and he is offering the counsel of cowardice.' Her voice shook with passion. 'My colleagues and I in the Leading Committee have spoken what is in our hearts. We cannot, must not surrender. We have sworn to die for our cause. Are we to abandon everything in which we believe? Brothers, sisters, fellow students, listen to me . . .'

'Hear him out,' called a voice from the audience, followed by others. 'Let him have his say.' Yanqing faltered to a halt. Her face had gone pink with rage. What a little commissar, thought Harry, appalled by her entrenched attitude, but he admired her pluck. She was her mother's daughter.

All this time, the pop star had been watching her with a smile. He raised both arms in the air and his commanding presence secured silence. 'It is not cowardly to wish to preserve your life. It takes even more courage to live on. A martyr's death may be attractive, but it is a cop-out. It is as opposed to reason as the brute military that is coming against us. I vote we leave if we can.'

'Don't you see their guns?' Yanqing screamed through her megaphone. 'You think the military will let us leave, with our heads high, as if nothing's happened?'

'Frankly, I don't care if we leave with our tails between our legs, anything to avoid unnecessary bloodshed,' he said, 'but my honest answer is I don't know. It seems sensible to ask what they intend. Will you come with me, Yanqing, if I go to the army under a white flag to negotiate?'

There was a murmur of support from the ranks. His suggestion seemed to offer a straw of hope. Yanqing and her radical colleagues exchanged a perplexed glance. They were not unaware that the pop star had presented her with an implicit challenge. Another of the leaders took the megaphone. Harry did not know his name but recognised him. He had been one of the students who had bearded the premier in the Great Hall of the People and precipitated the hunger-strike. 'I will go with you,' he said, 'although I think it's a fool's errand. With respect, Yanqing, it's better if you stay here, in case the military are not so friendly as our comrade seems to think they will be.' The crowd cheered him, and he gave them a cocky bow. Harry, meanwhile, was breathing a sigh of relief that Yanqing had not taken up the challenge. He wanted her where he could see her – and he didn't trust the military either.

A white flag was produced and the crowd clapped them on the back as the pop star, the young man who had just spoken and two other leaders walked boldly towards the soldiers, who were now visible to all, having moved past the tent lines. There was a tense moment of confrontation, then the ranks parted to let them through – but they continued to advance when the gap had closed behind them.

A murmur of fear rippled through the student ranks, and they edged backwards, closer to the monument. Yanqing stepped forward and shouted through her megaphone, 'Brothers, sisters, let us show them that we're not afraid.' In a strong voice, she began to sing the first bars of the 'Internationale'. Falteringly, the other students joined in. As the song swelled the troops, now so close that everybody could make out quite clearly the buckles and webbing of their uniforms, stopped in their tracks. Rifles still raised, bayonets glinting in the orange lamp-light, they observed the students dispassionately. They presented an ominous wall of steel, and behind them loomed the hulking shadows of the armoured vehicles, but the students, emboldened, sang louder.

Good girl, thought Harry, admiring the way she had restored morale. He edged towards the other side of the square, over which bulked the Great Hall of the People. In the shadows away from the students, he would have more freedom of movement, and still be close enough to hear what was going on. If the worst came to the worst – the truce was not upheld or the negotiations failed and the army moved in – he might still be able to get to the Martyrs' Memorial in time. In that event, his chance of success, let alone escape, would be slim. But Chen had been trustworthy so far. 'We don't want to turn the square into a slaughterhouse if we can avoid it, Ha Li,' he had told him, with his throaty laugh. 'That would be terrible propaganda. Much more sensible to let them leave and pick them up afterwards so we can deal with them at leisure. We know who they are.' It had been Chen at his most cynical and callous, but it made sense to Harry, and it was on this basis that they had made their plan.

A lot depended now, he realised, on the pop star and whether he could continue to sway the crowd.

There was a cheer. The white-flag party had returned. The pop star took the megaphone first. 'I have good news, fellow students,' he cried. 'We met four generals and they've agreed to let us leave the square.' He turned, with a mock-bow to Yanqing, and added: 'With our heads high.'

Before the audience could respond, Yanqing was shouting into the megaphone: 'You do not represent us students, and what you're preaching is still cowardice. I don't know what took place in your meeting but it is we who represent the student body. We should first listen to our own representatives.'

'By all means,' he said.

She turned to the young man who had been the first to volunteer to go with him. 'Did they give us this amnesty, Student Leader Wu?'

The young man shrugged. He took the megaphone. 'They said we could leave,' he said. 'I didn't hear any guarantees. They said they'd let us leave but not what they'd do to us afterwards.'

Yanqing snatched back the megaphone. She tossed her hair out of her eyes, then ran them over the audience until she had everybody's attention. She spoke with quiet deliberation. 'As I thought,' she said softly. 'They gave us words of honey.' She raised her voice to a screech. 'Sweet words coating the dung in their hearts. Fellow students, you know me. I have always striven to think clearly on your behalf. And I am less trusting of those bastards than our idealistic friend. They offered us no guarantees for our safety afterwards. You heard Student Leader Wu. I believe they want to divide us so they can deal with us more easily one by one. On this basis I reject their so-called amnesty, and I think you should do the same. Our strength is in our unity. I defy them to do their worst. Think about it, fellow students. Look what we have achieved. We, the young people of China, have created democracy in the heart of the capital of our country. Are we going to run away? Are we going to abandon every gain we have achieved? How, in future, even if we do survive, would we ever be able to look anybody in the face if we retreated ignominiously and, yes,' here she turned to the pop star with the same mocking smile he had given her, 'in a cowardly fashion? Where would be our self-respect? No, fellow students, I have not wavered, and neither, I believe, have you. This will be where we stand and, if necessary, this will be where we die, as free citizens not slaves. Let our blood be a permanent memorial to our movement.'

The response was deafening. Harry felt a sinking in his stomach, particularly when he saw Yanqing's face, wreathed in smiles, her eyes glinting as she clapped with those supporting her. She had been clever. She had appealed to the students' sense of shame. She had thrown back the Taiwanese upstart's challenge. Which of these naïve young men and women would be able to resist the peer pressure? Yanqing would have made a good army sergeant, Harry thought ruefully. She knew how to inspire lunatic bravery with moral blackmail when her arguments failed.

After some of the other student leaders had had their say, mostly supporting Yanqing, the pop star again had the floor. He spoke in the same relaxed voice as before. 'There you have it, fellow students. Option A, an honourable retreat. Option B, a blood sacrifice. I know which one appeals to me but, as Gao Yanqing has pointed out, it is democracy we have established here, not demagoguery, or a dictatorship. So, what do we do in a democracy? We take a vote. No time for a secret ballot, so we'll do it in the old-fashioned way, by a raising of hands. Now, who will vote with me that we should leave?' He raised his own arm high, very much in the manner of a pop idol who has twanged the last chord of a song. His eyes twinkled behind his spectacles as he smiled at the crowd. He exuded confidence.

Slowly hands rose, few and hesitantly at first, then more and more, as those who wanted to live felt the confidence of numbers. Harry began to hope again but, substantial as the vote was, he saw that many more students had hung their heads and folded their arms.

'Excellent,' cried the pop star, unabashed. 'And who's for the death vote?'

'For democracy,' shouted a leader, raising his hand. Yanqing lifted hers too, her eyes shining. All the diehards sitting on the steps had their fists outstretched. One by one, arms were rising in the audience. Some who had voted to leave had now apparently changed their minds. There were tears on many faces, and a few abstentions, but any objective count would show that the majority had voted to stay.

So that's the way it's to be, then, thought Harry, philosophically. He took out his balaclava, put it over his head, then unbuttoned the clasp that held his knife in its sheath. If he was going to fail, he would do so fighting. He began slowly to walk back towards the monument, then stopped in surprise. The Taiwanese was speaking authoritatively into the megaphone. 'A clear vote for life,' he shouted. 'The majority wants to leave.' He started to bark orders. 'We'll do this in an orderly fashion. Those at the front move first. Try your best to make a column four abreast. Head for the south-west corner of the Great Hall of the People. Don't deviate from the route or they'll shoot you,' he added jovially. 'That's it. Don't panic or run. A slow, steady walk is safest. Well done. Those on the steps, get ready too.'

At first they had stared at him, stunned, but the command that emanated from his voice brooked no argument, and faces that had become resigned to martyrdom brightened at this unexpected reprieve. Those nearest the Great Hall began to move, followed by the others.

'Recount! Rigged vote!' Yanqing and others were screaming, their faces livid with anger, but the singer ignored them. 'That's it. Slow and easy, and remember, heads held high. Don't let them think we're defeated because we're not. Come on, fellow students, where's your spirit? You were singing earlier.' In his deep, haunting voice he launched into the 'Internationale,' which effectively drowned any further complaint Yanqing and her diehards could make.

What a man, thought Harry. He's done it. Stepping back into the shadows, he began to run ahead of the retreating column towards the point on the map that he and Chen had selected. Behind him the 'Internationale' swelled as, indeed with heads high, the students began their retreat. At the same moment, all the lights in the square were extinguished, but the anthem continued to echo in the darkness.

'Rise up, you oppressed people, let us build our flesh and blood into a new Great Wall . . .'

Harry was crouched behind a bush at the corner of the Great Hall. He had been just in time because phalanxes of soldiers were already moving in to take positions along the route the retreating students would have to take. It was now pitch black, the only faint light coming from flames at the other end of the square, where the army was setting fire to the tents. He reached into another pouch on his webbing and extracted the Cat's Eyes he had borrowed from Julian's contact at the embassy. Adjusting the headband over his balaclava, he lowered the night-vision goggles, and the scene was illuminated in ghostly green.

The first students were filing by. They had stopped singing and were now plodding along, their heads bowed or glancing nervously at the stony-faced soldiers lining their route. They had ceased to be indomitable protesters, and looked like a bunch of scared boys and girls. The column extended back to the square.

It should be easy enough, he thought. As they turned the corner the students were tending to bunch, obscuring the view of the soldiers on the other side of the road. It would take him ten strides to be among them, make his snatch, then retreat to his hiding-place. Later, when the opportunity presented itself, he should be able to pass unobserved across the road to find Chen, who, according to their plan, would be waiting for him, parked in an alley behind the Bank of China. All he had to do was wait. She was bound to be one of the last to leave.

His heart jumped when he heard firing from within the square. Quickly he turned his Cat's Eyes towards the Martyrs' Memorial. The angle of the tracer told him that the soldiers were firing into the air, above the students' heads. They were probably trying to hurry them, or persuade any reluctant Dare to Dies to leave with the others. That was a good thing, he told himself, and forced himself to calm down.

It took the column nearly half an hour to file past. The ranks were thinning. He peered carefully through the night-vision goggles, scanning the faces. He saw the Taiwanese pop star pass, his head in a hood so he would not easily be identified. Other student leaders strode forward defiantly, their chins raised and their eyes spitting anger – but where was Yanqing?

Suddenly a white flash blinded him. He lifted the goggles and found himself staring into blazing headlights. At the same moment he became aware of grinding engine sounds and the crunch of treads on asphalt. Three tanks were heading up the road, straight for the students. There was a cry of alarm and the tail of the column scattered and ran. There was a high-pitched scream as a girl found herself caught in the path of the first tank. It blundered on and Harry saw her disappear beneath it.

He stood up, aghast. All order had broken down in the column. Screaming students were jostling each other in panic. Others were breaking away. Soldiers, guns raised, were trying to waylay them. The tank was skewing round, its gears roaring, as it tried to back up and turn. Another student fell under its treads. The boy still had life in him when it passed on. He was sitting on the pavement staring in bemusement at his flattened legs. His fellows ran past him, ignoring him in their terror. It was impossible to identify anybody now. Harry threw caution to the winds and ran forward. There were no more students coming from the square. She must be among this rabble somewhere. He tried to put aside the horrific fear that Yanqing had been the girl who had fallen under the tank.

He heard shots, and saw a soldier deliberately aim at the back of a running student and cut him in half with a burst from his AK47. Moving like a dark shadow among them, Harry saw a girl whose pageboy haircut resembled Yanqing's. Roughly, he turned her shoulder. It was a stranger. She saw his mask and screamed. Releasing her he moved on, knowing that everything had gone wrong.

The tanks switched off their lights and the blackness added to the confusion. Harry lowered the Cat's Eyes, and saw green faces around him, the eyes panicked and the mouths open in silent screams. It was as if he had found himself in some sort of Munchian nightmare. And none of the faces belonged to Yanqing.

He heard shots behind him. A soldier was firing into the bushes where he had recently been hiding. Obviously some students had gone to ground there. He pushed his way towards him. The man had raised his AK47 and was aiming at a girl, whose scared face peered up at him from the leaves. This time Harry did recognise her. It was Yanqing, and in perhaps half a second the man would fire. It took two strides to come up behind him. Harry pulled his shoulder and the flames arced upwards. He had no time to pull out his knife so he put his big hands on either side of the man's cheeks, and gave a sharp twist, snapping the neck as, in another life, he despatched a fish. Then, without letting go, he dragged the limp body into the bushes.

The girl was standing up, staring at him, her hands over her mouth, her eyes dilating with shock. For a second, Harry thought he was looking again at the young Ziwei. He put a hand gently on her shoulder. She shivered with fear, but probably did not notice the other hand that rose, then fell in an efficient rabbit-chop that dropped her senseless to her knees. Harry threw her over his shoulder, and plunged into the bushes. Behind their screen, he began to run, leaving the mayhem behind.

He came to the end of the wall. Two soldiers were standing with their backs to him, blocking any chance of crossing the road to the safety of the alleys. There was no chance of passing them unobserved. Through his goggles, he could see an advancing platoon three hundred yards further up the road. At the mouth of every alley they passed, they were leaving behind two or three sentries. He realised that unless he moved now every escape route would be closed to him.

Silently, he cursed his luck. He laid Yanqing on the ground, took a deep breath and drew out his knife. He searched the pavement at his feet for something metallic he might throw. Nothing. In this most littered of cities, there was not even an empty Coca-Cola can. He would have to sacrifice his scope.

It landed with a tinkle on the pavement a few feet away from the soldiers. Both turned, startled, and raised their rifles. Harry took two strides to reach them. It had been thirty years since he had last rehearsed these movements at the Office's training school, and he was clumsy. He couldn't prevent the cry of alarm before he sliced the knife through the first man's jugular. The other turned and raised his gun. Harry had a glimpse of a terrified, boy's face, as, dropping the first man, he reached out his arm and pulled aside the barrel of the AK47, just as it fired. He kicked the boy's crotch and, as he bent forward, stabbed the knife upwards through his throat. He picked up the AK47, expecting that the advancing platoon would have heard the firing, but they had not even turned their heads. There was too much random shooting going on for it to have been noticeable.

He pulled the two bodies into the bushes, picked up Yanqing and ran across the road into the darkness of the alley opposite.

He felt acid rising in his throat. Trembling, he leant against a wall. He had just enough time to lay Yanqing down again and pull up the front of his balaclava. He vomited, the face of the boy he had killed in his mind. When he looked up, three old ladies and a small child were staring at him curiously. He nodded at them, forcing a smile. One offered him a glass jar containing tea.

Not knowing what else to do, he sipped. With an increasing sense of unreality, he noticed that the jar had once contained Maxwell House coffee. 'Thank you,' he murmured.

'Don't mention it,' she said.

The exchange of courtesies in a war zone was bizarre.

'Where are you taking your friend?' she asked, nodding at Yanqing.

'To the Bank of China,' he said. He half expected her to tell him in a friendly fashion that it was closed at this time of night, but she nodded. 'You'll have to pass a tank to get there,' she said. 'It's parked at the end of our *hutong*. We'll accompany you and catch the attention of the driver while you slip behind the back.'

'That would be very kind,' he said.

'It's our pleasure,' she replied. 'It's terrible what the army's doing tonight, and we'd like to help the students. My own son is at university in America or he might have been among them. Shall we go now?'

Picking up Yanqing, he followed the hobbling procession. They came to an abrupt halt at the end of the alley. Through the gaps in the brick, they could see a dull, metal flank on which were stencilled numbers. The silhouette of a soldier protruded from the turret.

'Goodbye.' The old lady bowed politely. With her companions, she turned to the right, the direction in which the barrel of the cannon was pointing. Harry heard angry shouts. The tank commander was warning them to get back to their homes or suffer the consequences of the curfew. As the old lady, complaining of deafness, asked the man to repeat what he had said, Harry slipped round the back of the tank and into the mouth of the next *hutong*.

He had not gone ten yards before he was dazzled again by the blinding light of headlights. He despaired. This time he was trapped. Then he heard a familiar laugh. 'My old Hong Huzi friend, I am so very pleased to see you, and with the girl as well. But look at your bloodstained clothes. Have you been adding new martyrs to our government's noble cause, Ha Li? You make my life very difficult.'

'Are you sure you haven't killed her?' murmured Chen, as Harry placed Yanqing's limp body on the back seat. 'Those big hands of yours terrify me.'

'She'll be fine,' muttered Harry.

'I hope Ziwei will forgive you for so mistreating her daughter.'

'Ziwei will never know it was me. I have your promise that you won't tell her.' He slammed the back door and clambered in beside Chen on the front seat.

'I won't,' said Chen, flicking a thumb behind him, 'but will she?'

'All she saw was a black figure in a face mask. It could have been anybody.'

'Are you sure? A giant like you?'

'She won't remember,' said Harry. 'She was already in shock. Are we getting out of here or not? The sky will be lightening soon, and we've still much to do.'

Chen switched on the engine and backed out of the alley. 'Damn,' he muttered. The side road was full of soldiers.

'I thought you were on their side.'

'I am, and this is a car with an official number plate, but on a night like this you never know what people's reactions are going to be until you try them.'

A torch flashed and a helmeted head appeared in the side window next to Chen. The barrel of the AK47 swinging on the soldier's shoulder was pointing directly at Harry. Chen had his identification card ready.

'And who is that?' asked the soldier.

'He is from Special Forces, assigned to Politburo protection,' said Chen. 'You notice that this card has been issued by the chief of Security at the Zhong Nan Hai. Please do not impede us, unless you want a reprimand for interfering in state business.'

The head ducked away. Someone shouted an order and the column divided. Harry found himself being driven through two ranks of saluting soldiers.

Chen turned left along the road ringing Tiananmen. In the dim grey light, Harry saw that it had become an armed camp. There were tanks parked where the tents had been, and rows of kneeling soldiers facing outwards in all directions reminded him of some battle print of one of Britain's colonial wars. The comparison was apt, he thought bitterly. The engagement in the night against unarmed students and towns-people had been as one-sided. As they drove past the Great Hall of the People, its pillars pink in the light of dawn, Harry saw a helicopter descend. Four or five elderly generals stepped out of it.

'A beautiful sight, isn't it, Ha Li? Law and order restored.'

'Only a bastard like you could say that,' retorted Harry.

They heard groans from the back of the car. Yanqing was coming to.

'Deal with her, Ha Li,' murmured Chen. 'We could hardly be in a more inappropriate place for her to make a scene.'

Hating himself, Harry leant over the back and punched the dazed girl's chin. She slumped back on the seat.

'Poor Ha Li,' said Chen. 'And you so chivalrous.'

They were approaching the Tiananmen Gate, and Harry could make out Mao's portrait Chen had to wait while a tank rumbled past. Harry turned his head towards the east where, faintly, he could make out the Peking Hotel. In front of it a bus was burning. A crowd seemed to be gathering there. As he watched, a troop of soldiers ran forward and fired. The people ran, like a flock of disturbed starlings, leaving their bicycles and one or two bodies lying in the road. 'It doesn't look as if law and order is restored yet,' he said angrily.

'No, Ha Li, you are confusing the establishment of order with the beginnings of retribution. Beijing people are thick-headed and need the lesson to be drummed into them.' He yawned. 'After I have dispensed with my obligation to you and Ziwei, I imagine I'll be very busy over the next few months. All those files and films we've collected.

Punishing the guilty so that honest citizens can sleep easily in their beds.'

He turned right, and Harry saw the arm of the Goddess of Liberty and Democracy pointing out of the rubble. Chen had to dodge two tanks trying clumsily to negotiate their way round a traffic policeman's stand before they could turn into Nanchizi. Half-way along, they had to stop once more. Doctors and nurses were marching at funereal pace across the road. Four were carrying a bier on their shoulders. An arm in a white doctor's coat hung limply from under a red blanket. Then Harry saw that it wasn't a blanket but the dead man's blood-soaked coat. 'Your law and order comes at some cost,' he said.

'When I stood in this same square and heard Chairman Mao announce the establishment of our new nation, he said something I've never forgotten. 'Things develop ceaselessly. It is not fifty years since the revolution of 1911, but the face of China today is completely changed. In another fifty years, that is, in the year 2000, the start of the twenty-first century, China will have undergone even greater changes. She will have become a powerful socialist industrial country.' That's our goal, Ha Li, and to achieve it we have to be ruthless and determined. A few lives lost on the way are a small price to pay, don't you think?'

'No, Chen Tao, I don't. All I see is old men clinging to power by whatever means they can, and the whole bloody cycle revolving over and over again to the misery of all.'

'Then we'll have to agree to differ, won't we, Ha Li?'

They drove in silence past the British Embassy. Chen parked a hundred yards beyond it under the shadow of some trees. 'I'll be back in an hour with Ziwei.'

'Is that necessary?'

'We've been through this before. I suspect we'll be ordered to arrest everybody remotely connected with these events, Ha Li, and she's compromised enough through her associations with dissidents even if she didn't have a daughter who is a student ringleader. Anyway, she won't be able to keep her restaurant. It's goaded the government long enough, and now even I won't be able to protect her. Better she seeks asylum too. Don't worry about her. She's rich enough, with all her money from her Shishan business. Anyway, don't you think, after we've gone to all this trouble, she'll want to be with her precious daughter? And Yanqing certainly can't stay here.'

'I'm just sorry. She said she had found peace in the Yangtze Gorges.'

Chen grunted disinterestedly. 'I hope you have a plan to get her inside the embassy,' he said. 'I won't be able to bring her in myself.'

'I'll make sure somebody's waiting for her.'

'Not you?'

'No. Better she forgets me.'

Chen shrugged. 'If you say so. Although I don't remotely understand why you've gone to all the trouble of saving the daughter if you don't wish to reap the reward from a grateful mother.'

'I don't expect you to understand. You can't buy love back once you've lost it.'

'Really? My experience is you can buy anything if you're prepared to pay enough. But, then, you're honourable while I'm pragmatic. That's the difference between us. Maybe we'll have a chance to debate it one day.'

'I doubt there'd be any point. Shall we just get on with what we have to do?'

Chen chuckled quietly. 'Are you sure this noble sacrifice isn't just a way to salve your hurt pride, my friend?' Harry glared at him and Chen's smile widened. Then he shrugged. 'But have it your own way. I'll see you in about an hour.'

'All right. When she's safely inside.'

The street was still dark enough for him not to be observed too closely, but he wrapped Yanqing in the blanket all the same. Its red colour reminded him of the funeral procession they had seen earlier. He walked towards the embassy gates, wondering how Johnny Millar, his SIS contact, would deal with the Chinese armed policemen on guard, the silhouettes of whose peaked caps and rifles he could see quite clearly in the lamplight.

There was the flicker of a headlight in one of the parked cars ahead. A short man stepped out and opened the boot.

'I was giving up on you,' said Johnny, as Harry deposited Yanqing on the cushions that the SIS man had thoughtfully provided.

'It's been a little busy out there,' said Harry.

'Tell me about it,' said Johnny, clicking the boot closed. 'Now, let's see if these boys in green decide to be heroes and stop an official embassy car. My guess is they'll deliberately not notice a thing. It's the sort of night when "See no evil, hear no evil, speak no evil" makes practical sense for the simple reason of self-preservation.'

Nevertheless, Harry tensed on his seat as Johnny stopped the car and unlocked the gates. Johnny, too, was grim-faced as he got back in and put the car into gear – but he had read the guards correctly. They drove through the gates without attracting a single glance.

When they were inside the main embassy building, Harry laid Yanqing on a sofa under a portrait of the Queen. He checked her pulse. 'I had to knock her out,' he said, 'but she'll come to soon. Can you handle her from here?'

'Yes, I've made all the arrangements. The ambassador's cool about it. It may take a few months but we'll get her out of the country without anybody being the wiser. We've done it before.'

'And her mother?'

Johnny laughed. He had the same languid elegance as Julian, on whom Harry guessed he had based several of his mannerisms. 'The ambo wasn't so cool about her when I told him, but he's a regular at the Yangtze Gorges and I promised she'd cook for him from time to time during her confinement. I assume she's picked up some of the recipes from that magnificent chef of hers. You'll be glad to hear that self-interest overcame his scruples. Yes, we'll get her out too. I don't think we need to be so cloak-and-dagger with her. I've forged a few impressive-looking papers in case she's stopped when she arrives.' He grinned. 'New embassy cleaner approved by the Public Security Bureau. Do you think she'll mind?'

Meanwhile he was staring down at Yanqing's white features. 'So this is the famous Gao Yanqing. For such a firebrand, she looks like a child. A rather dirty one.' He wrinkled his nose. 'She needs a bath. Anyway, hats off to her, and to you for getting her away safely.'

'Johnny, you will remember your promise?'

'Mum's the word. I'll invent some story when she wakes. You never existed.'

Harry showered and changed in the small bathroom downstairs. He remembered the chipped tiles from when he had been there twenty-six years before. Johnny was waiting for him in the lobby when he emerged in a dark blue suit. The SIS man raised his eyebrows. 'Very sartorial,' he said. 'She's awake, by the way.'

'How is she?'

'Confused. Scared. Angry. I left her with the embassy nurse. She'll be okay.'

'I'll be off, then. You'll be there when the mother arrives?' He looked at his watch. 'In twenty minutes.'

'Don't worry, Harry. They'll be fine.'

'Thanks.' Suddenly Harry felt uncomfortable. 'I don't know how to thank you.'

'Just tell Julian he owes me one,' grinned Johnny. 'Off you go before Madam Peng Ziwei arrives.'

Harry waited behind a tree so he had sight of the embassy gates.

When Ziwei stepped out of Chen's jeep, he wanted only to cross the road and take her in his arms. She was wearing her leather jacket and holding a small suitcase as she walked with heart-rending dignity towards Johnny, who was standing outside the gates. He felt he had never seen anybody so beautiful.

It was better this way, he told himself. She would soon be starting a new life. He would not inflict on her any more baggage from the past. It was better that the slate was wiped clean.

He watched as Johnny took her arm, and they disappeared inside. The embassy door closed behind them.

As he walked to Chen's parked car, he thought it might as well have been closing on his life.

Chen observed him closely. 'Are you all right, Ha Li?' he asked.

'I'm fine.'

'I've got you a seat on the Cathay flight that leaves in just over an hour. The airport's chaotic but still functioning, although nobody's bothering with Customs or Immigration any more. You should be able to get on the plane unspotted.'

'Thank you,' said Harry.

They were silent as they drove out of the city and up the airport road, past the columns of troops parked by the side.

Just before they reached the terminal, they had to stop to allow an old shepherd to take his sheep across the road. Chen beeped his horn but it was to no avail. 'Look at that, Ha Li. Rural China. Some things never change. Peasants are peasants. They were like that during our boyhood, and they're still the same, despite all these decades of revolution. Depressing, isn't it? By the way, I hope you have no intention of coming back here soon. Much as I would enjoy seeing you again, I fear I would have to greet you in my official capacity, and you know how unpleasant that can be.'

'I won't be coming back, Chen Tao.'

'No more China nostalgia?'

'No, that's over. Everything's over, I guess.'

Chen laughed. 'You always were morbid. We had that right in your profile. But cheer up. Look what you've achieved today.'

'What?'

'You've cocked a snook at Chinese authority, something you've always wanted to do. And you've saved the life of the daughter of the woman you say you love, even though you're abandoning her for reasons I still don't entirely understand. Not bad for a morning's work, is it?'

'I suppose not,' said Harry. Chen's earlier taunt about hurt pride was still smarting.

'There you are,' said Chen, honking his horn again. 'You've got away with it. Ha Li takes on the world and wins. In my book that makes you a lucky man.'

'I'm not lucky in love, Chen Tao.'

'Love!' Chen spat out of the open window. 'What does love do for you?' He spoke bitterly. 'Doesn't the world throw enough calamities at us without us inflicting them on ourselves? Love, honour, all those stupidities. They're the inadequate compensations of those who don't understand the realities of existence, which are survival and power.'

You poor, poor man, thought Harry, looking sadly at the friend he would never see again. He thought of Ziwei's proud face as she handed Johnny her bag and entered the new life he had made possible for her and her daughter, and he realised it had not been hurt pride. He had done the right thing. He had made amends for the injuries he had inflicted on the woman he loved, and he had freed her to live with her daughter in a world where she need not worry about the present or be pressured by the past, which included himself. He had nothing to regret. It was worth the price of his happiness, although that would hardly make the prospect of living without her easier to bear.

Chen had to concentrate as they neared the terminal to avoid cars abandoned at the side of the road. He drove up the ramp to the departure hall, inching behind buses and taxis, which were parking where they could. White-faced Europeans, loaded with suitcases, were milling on the pavement. Panicked mothers dragged their children by the hand. There were no police, porters or airport officials in sight. Flustered foreign representatives were holding up pieces of cardboard with the name of their airline, trying to get the heaving mass into orderly lines. 'We have ten more places on the flight for Helsinki,' one was shouting.

'Cash only.' Immediately he was swamped by a mob of businessmen waving banknotes.

Chen turned off the engine. 'Think you can manage? You, unlike these poor fools, have a ticket. As you can see, the foreigners are rushing to leave the sinking ship. I don't think you'll be conspicuous.'

'I'll be fine,' said Harry.

Chen leant back in his seat. 'Well, then, my old friend, this is where we go our separate ways. We're square now. No more debts on either side.'

'That's how I see it.'

'We part as friends? Blood brothers? You were serious?'

Harry paused. Eventually he sighed. 'Yes. Though somehow I doubt we'll meet again.'

'No. There are still shadows.'

'I'm afraid there always will be.'

Chen gripped the steering-wheel. 'Ha Li, there is something I need to tell you. My conscience is troubling me.'

'It's not necessary. We're even.'

'This relates to the past. You were wrong, Ha Li, about one thing. You should not have tortured yourself with guilt for so many years about my capture by the Japanese.'

'I don't feel any guilt now. Sorry, but that's all past too.'

'No, you don't understand. It was I who betrayed you.' His lip twisted. 'I was working for the Japanese, Ha Li. I led you into the trap. The purpose was to catch you in a crime so they could blackmail your father. I shouted a warning so that the Japanese would know where you were. You surprised me by escaping, and I was punished for it afterwards. Perhaps you guessed.'

Harry was silent. 'No, I never did.' He reached for his bag.

'I'm sorry, Ha Li.'

Harry turned to him. Suddenly he had a memory of the boy he had first met, offering ducklings. 'It's not important any more. Too much has happened. The slate's clean. Let's leave it at that.'

'Thank you,' said Chen. He held out his hand.

Harry shook it briefly. 'I have to go,' he said.

'Good luck,' said Chen.

'And to you.'

Harry clicked the door shut and strode into the terminal, the bag over his shoulder. He wondered why Chen's revelation had left him so cold. Perhaps he would think it over later – but then he realised that what he had said was the simple truth. It wasn't important any more. Nothing was important any more. Everything that had been done was done. In a small way he had made amends. He would spend the rest of his life wondering if it had been enough.

A year ago Big Harry's disappearance had been the talk of Sally's. All the old speculation that he had been hiding from a criminal past emerged again. Half the bar decided he had rejoined the Mob, the other that the law had finally caught up with him and put him away. Al the barman, who felt he had to defend Harry's moral reputation if for no other reason than that he was a regular customer, wondered whether the police should be informed. He might have had an accident in that far-away cabin of his in the mountains, he said. This went down well and, in their imaginations, Harry became a meal for grizzlies, wolves and vultures, before somebody spoilt the gruesome fun by remembering he had been seen in the spring, taking out his boat alone for a day. Al changed tack and said in that case a woman must have lured him away, one of his Hollywood film stars, perhaps – she had been so impressed by his services that she had taken him to Malibu as her kept man – but that idea strained credulity even in Sally's.

When he reappeared in time for the late-summer fishing season it had been anticlimactic in one respect but even more intriguing in another, because it soon became clear that wherever he had been and whatever he had done in his months away the experience had changed him.

For a start, the beard and shaggy mane had gone, apparently for good. A bigger surprise was that he had cleaned his boat and taken down the 'cloaca' sign from his forward cabin, which, as one of his regular clients had reported, was now as tidy and ship-shape as anybody would wish. Later it transpired that Harry no longer slept on his boat but had taken rooms in a boarding-house.

Also, his demeanour was different. He was as monosyllabic as ever, but he was no longer the morose, brooding presence that had once intimidated them. He had become curiously gentle, smiling and nodding when he came for his whisky at Sally's, and even, on one extraordinary occasion, joining a conversation. It had only been about the weather, but it set a precedent that made him more human, and even, in a strange way, vulnerable – because physically he appeared to have shrunk. He walked with bowed shoulders, and his forbidding scowl had been replaced by a meek, if distant, smile.

This led Al back to his theory that a woman was at the bottom of it. When he wanted to impress, he liked to show off his familiarity with the Bible. He was not a churchgoer or a book reader so his knowledge was culled from his video collection of cinematic epics of the fifties and sixties, in this case the 1949 movie version of the Samson story. 'It was like when Hedy Lamarr cut off Victor Mature's hair when he was sleeping,' he announced. 'She emasculated him. He was never the same again. You mark my words. There's a Delilah out there somewhere who's done her worst on him.'

This led to a resounding chorus of Tom Jones's hit song, which ceased when Big Harry himself entered the bar quietly, and sat on his stool to order his whisky.

Harry fished as conscientiously as ever, but there were no more bookings from women, or if there were, he refused them. Johann, the old German clerk in Jumping Jack's, would never be drawn on the subject, telling his questioners in that infuriating accent of his that a fishing clerk's duty, no less than a lawyer's, was to keep his clients' affairs confidential. It was all the more infuriating because they could never be sure, with his poker face, whether he was laughing at them or keeping something back. Certainly Harry seemed to be spending more time with the old man than he had before, although once, when the two had been seen in a restaurant together, it had been disappointing because during the meal neither had said a word to the other.

If Johann had chosen to say what was in his mind, the fishermen might have been surprised by his concern for his old friend, who would often now, of an evening, go round to his lodgings to listen to one of his Bach or Mozart recordings. During those sessions, Harry never spoke of what was troubling him, and Johann never asked, because reticence had been the basis of their friendship from the beginning. When the concerto or symphony was over, Johann might ask him, 'Did you enjoy it, Harry?' and Harry would reply, 'Aye, it was beautiful.'

'Is there anything else you would like to listen to, or would you like some of my schnapps?'

'No, that's kind of you,' he would say, 'but I think I'd better go.'

Johann was deeply saddened. He knew that he himself had long ago given up on life. The memories of what he had been made to do in Poland and Russia haunted him, and had anaesthetised in him the desire, even after fifty years, to take up any challenge life might offer. He had known instinctively that Harry too, was escaping from terrible, probably guilty memories, but his burning anger had been an inspiration to the old German. Harry had been spiritually wounded, he believed, as he had been, but unlike him, Harry had not lost the will to fight. That accounted for his violent, moody behaviour in all the years he had known him. They were positive qualities, Johann convinced himself, because they meant there was still hope for Harry, if there was not for himself.

After Harry had taken the charter of the Englishman with the interesting initial, Johann had noticed a change in his old friend during the few weeks' fishing that followed. He seemed to have purpose and determination. Life had been calling him again. In the entire marina, Johann had been the only one who had not been surprised when Harry disappeared, and he was pleased for him. He harboured a hope that one day he would hear that Harry had conquered his devils.

The man who returned, however, had, to Johann's discerning eyes, lost the will to live. He was no longer a fighter. He had despaired. In other words, he had become like Johann. Harry's new amiability, his neatness, his conscientiousness to his clients – all virtues, according to society's conventions – were telltale signs to the old man that his friend had given up the struggle, which depressed Johann immeasurably and led, among other things, to a resurgence of his own nightmares. For weeks he had been unwell since his dreams of burning villages and mass slaughter had returned. When he recovered, he had come to terms with his disappointment, and that was when he first invited Harry to listen to music with him. It did not deepen their friendship or bring either much comfort, he suspected. It was as if each had acknowledged a shared state of mind, and like old men who have nothing in common but sit together anyway to wile away an afternoon on a park bench, it was acceptance that, for both of them, their active lives were over, in their cases prematurely, because they still had jobs.

Such had been the situation for a year when one day, in the post, Johann found a letter for Harry, care of Jumping Jack Fish. Idly he looked at the postmark. It had been sent from Anchorage in Alaska. He thought little of it, imagining it must be a letter of appreciation from a fishing client. These were rare but not unknown.

Three days later, when Harry came into his office and, with his new courteous manner, asked if there were any bookings, Johann remembered the letter. 'From one of your fans, Harry,' he said.

Harry gave him a kindly smile.

While Johann was sorting through his booking register, he cast a glance at the big man who was looking at the postscript without any sign of curiosity. 'Aren't you going to open it?' he asked. 'It will give you something to do instead of just towering over me blocking the light while I sort the bookings.'

Harry moved to the seat under the window, and without any apparent interest, slit the side of the envelope with his nail. Johann started to sift through the phone messages. Suddenly he heard Harry exclaim. He looked up. The other man was on his feet, staring at what appeared to be a postcard. Johann could see the back and noticed that there was no writing on it. It was just a plain picture postcard.

'What is it, Harry?' he asked. 'You look as if you've seen one of your ghosts again.'

Harry turned the card. The photograph on the front was a typical *National Geographic* nature scene. It showed a flat blue sea and, rising from it, the perfectly formed tail of a sperm whale making a dive. To Johann, it was unremarkable, but the progression of expressions on Harry's face was extraordinary. His brow had knitted in concentration, while his mouth twitched in what might be confusion, puzzlement, anger, or a mixture of the three.

'You are a strange man, Harry,' said Johann. 'What's so interesting about this postcard? Ever since you've come back, the new you, without your beard and shaggy hair, has been puzzling your friends, but is this reaction to a postcard not going over the top a little?'

Harry's face was suddenly rigid. His blue eyes stared at Johann. 'I've got to go.'

'I've got to go,' he says. As if I'm to understand what that means.'

Harry's eyes were gleaming with excitement, and the hand holding the card was shaking. His lips were curving into a wide smile. 'Cancel all my bookings. I'm taking out my boat this afternoon on my own.' He was grinning, like a boy. 'I'm going on a journey, Johann.'

'A journey? Where?'

'Oh, north,' said Harry.

'"North", he says.' Then Johann began to feel excited – he had worked out what had happened. 'Oh, Harry,' he said, 'you are going to Anchorage in Alaska. This is a summons, isn't it?'

Harry smiled, rubbing his hands. The postcard of the whale was already in his pocket.

'You're going to Anchorage in that little boat of yours, which is hardly even seaworthy. Are you sure you can get there?'

'Oh, aye,' said Harry. 'I'll get there, all right.' He frowned a little. He looked embarrassed. 'I don't know when I'll see you again, Johann. You've been a good friend.' He turned on his heels and the doorbell tinkled as he pulled it open with gleeful force.

'Send a postcard,' called Johann after him. He, too, was grinning now.

Through the window he watched Harry stride down the pavement. His shoulders were thrown back. His arms were swinging. He was a picture of purpose, energy and determination. He was even whistling.

Johann, shaking his head, moved back to his cubbyhole. He was about to reach for his Bach when he changed his mind. Instead he leant back in his armchair and began to laugh. How arrogant, he thought, that a man could think he might give up on life, when life itself was always waiting to surprise you. Yes, he thought. There is hope, after all.

AFTERWORD

U *nlike my previous two novels, which I based loosely on the history*
of my family in China in the 1900s and 1920s, the events that I
have described in The Dragon's Tail *occurred in my own lifetime.*

I was born and grew up in Hong Kong. China was therefore ever
present, looming over the border behind the hills of Kowloon, often
menacing but also enticing. As a small boy I'd be taken to the Chinese
cinema by our cook, and besides the fantastic stories of gods and
Kung Fu warriors, I would sometimes see a communist propaganda
film and my vision was formed of a country where teeming millions
of shiny-faced peasant girls were building something wonderful in the
fields. Later, during the Cultural Revolution I was taken on a
schoolboy's outing to visit an army post on the border, and there
through a high-powered telescope we looked into the farmland of
Shenzhen (no skyscrapers then) and watched Red Guards waving their
books of Mao's thoughts and throwing hand grenades (actually stones)
at a river bed. It was by then the radical end of the sixties, so I was
excited by the idea of revolution, and went to China Products Stores,
and bought my own copy of the Little Red Book, and a scroll portrait
of Mao to hang on the study wall of my public school. I think I even
took up ping pong . . .

In the seventies, as a journalist in Hong Kong I met people coming
out of China after the fall of the Gang of Four. They had horrific
tales to tell of that Cultural Revolution, which had so bewitched
students of my idealistic generation. I remember one man telling me
about his girlfriend's most phenomenal act of bravery. He and his
flatmates in 1971 were cutting up squares of newsprint for lavatory
paper in their tenement in Shanghai. Suddenly he realised that he had
in his hand a full square portrait of Mao Tse-tung – that day's front
page from the People's Daily. *They all looked at each other in fear.*
Then his girlfriend grabbed the photo of Mao from his hands, and

540

deliberately and defiantly hung it on the spike with all the other pieces of lavatory paper . . . I have slightly twisted that scene in the pages of this book, but what courage it implies! Imagine living in that atmosphere of paranoia, where the most harmless activity could be interpreted as revisionist or worse, and you were in constant danger of being reported by your neighbours, friends, even family . . . yet that was once the daily reality for every person above forty you meet in China today. How can we even conceive of that sort of existence, brought up in our liberal certainties? You would have to go to North Korea nowadays to get an impression of how intrusive and all-embracing totalitarianism was under Mao.

Eventually China became my profession, and in the early eighties I went to work there and have lived in Beijing ever since. From the beginning of the eighties I have witnessed an economic revolution, an industrial revolution, an agricultural revolution, a social revolution. Few human societies in history have developed so rapidly as China has over the last quarter century. When I first visited in 1979 the cities were blacked out at night, there was nothing to buy (only queues for vegetables at scattered co-ops), there were hardly any cars on the roads, clothes were uniformly drab, worse, the thought police were everywhere. Every conversation with a Chinese was guarded. Everybody was poor. and nothing worked. I remember once retiring to my bed in the old Dongfang Hotel in Guangzhou during the Trade Fair, glowing with the satisfaction of having had a really productive day – and then I realised that all I had done was to make one long distance telephone call. Believe me, in those days, that was an achievement! And it wasn't so long ago.

Yet now it seems like a distant memory. Today China has a GDP growth rate of 10%. It boasts some of the most modern and bustling cities in Asia. More hand-held phones are sold each year than in America. Prosperity shouts at you from the streets and restaurants. A hungry consumer society has grown from nothing, a middle class with the same interests and aspirations as our own. China embraces the new with a boldness that we have not witnessed since the age of Brunel: the world's fastest train in operation in Shanghai; the longest bridge in the world about to link the Hangzhou and Shanghai shores; the Three Gorges Project, which may raise ecological eyebrows but which will bring ocean-going vessels thousands of miles into the hinterland and provide hydro-energy for a significant fraction of the human population. We are a long way from the Ground Zero of the sixties and seventies. Only a blindfolded churl would not pay homage to China's material achievements, and acknowledge the freedoms that come with them.

Yet I have never forgotten the China I first saw – the scarred, numbed society trying to find normality after a holocaust induced by its own leaders. The contradictions of those early years of Deng Xiaoping's reforms eventually led to the bloodbath at Tiananmen on 3 June 1989, which I witnessed from my office in the Peking Hotel and which provides the denouement of this novel. I thought it would be a fitting end to a trilogy where the historical backdrop is the story of China's revolutions through the 20th Century, but the heart of this novel, which spans the period from the Cold War to the beginnings of the society we know today, is the Cultural Revolution, which was a communal madness that it is difficult to find an equivalent of anywhere in human history – except in the pages of George Orwell. It is just one of Mao's achievements that he brought unthinkable fiction to reality.

Mao does not appear in person in the pages of The Dragon's Tail, *yet his presence is palpable throughout. Jung Chang and Jon Halliday's extensively researched biography,* Mao – The Untold Story, *is not published in China. The events it describes are too raw – yet a Chinese edition printed in Hong Kong circulates in samisdat. Its message, that China's leader was an inhuman monster with hardly a redeeming feature is not accepted, however, by the mass of the Chinese people or its government. Yes, they recall the hideous events of the Cultural Revolution with horror and ninety per cent of intellectuals acknowledge that Mao was the author of their misery. Yet there are few Chinese who forget that, despite the 'mistakes' of his later years, in 1949 he united the country and they still give him credit for that; and certainly in the countryside, there are millions of peasants who love this man and revere his memory. His portrait still hangs in Tiananmen Square. Last year I visited his birthplace in Shaoshan along with thousands of pilgrims. Only a month ago, I dined at a popular restaurant in Beijing, which enacts every night the songs and dances of the Cultural Revolution. It was packed, and there were tears in people's eyes as they sang the old hymns to Mao, conducted by waitresses dressed as Red Guards. For many peasants, he was a god. In a village in Shaanxi, a large statue of him is worshipped with incense sticks. He is flanked* on the altar by his two wise counsellors, Zhou Enlai and Zhu De, who are smaller in size, like the disciples in an equivalent Confucian temple. As far as taxi drivers are concerned, he is a tutelary spirit: a portrait of him hanging from the driving mirror will protect them from car crashes.

It will be many years, if ever, before there will be a universally accepted verdict about who exactly this man was, what was the significance of his actions, and, bafflingly, what motivated him to do them. Jung Chang's book has reinvigorated academic debate in the West. Roderick MacFarquar last year published the first comprehensive narrative history of the Cultural Revolution, and in universities there is increasingly valuable research. In China, however, the subject is not officially mentioned. In the early eighties, Deng Xiaoping had the People's Congress pronounce that Mao was 70 per cent good and 30 per cent bad. Today the most inveterate opponents of Mao will acknowledge the verity of those proportions, albeit the other way round. Clearly, there is a reluctance to damn him completely, for where then does the finger point? How then to justify the people's complicity in the actions he unleashed? The full horror of the Cultural Revolution – and I have attempted to describe this in these pages – is that it was a communal activity. As in the Laogai (the Gulag system perfected by Mao's regime) everybody was victim and everybody was also persecutor. That is what distinguishes China's totalitarian nightmare from its equivalents in Nazi Germany and Soviet Russia. The idea of perpetual revolution became a mass, self-induced delusion, of which the Mao worship was only a bizarre part.

I have the art historian, Alfreda Murck, to thank for putting me on to the story of the Mango Cult, which seemed to me a perfect symbol of the madness of that period, and which I have used in my novel. What I have not written was that when Mao heard about the extraordinary results of his whimsical gift to the workers, he, in the account of his doctor, "merely chuckled". He may have been the instrument by which the holy mangos reached the hands of the faithful, but it was they who created the hysteria that followed. In writing this book, I have with gratitude thought back to the great Sinologist, Jonathan Spence's, conclusion in his own biography of Mao, that the Chinese leader was a "Lord of Misrule", like the jester in our medieval Twelfth Night celebrations. From Mao's writings as early as the 1920s it is evident that the future Chairman seemed to have believed in the virtue of chaos for its own sake, that society needed to be upturned for it *to become healthy, that one only had to unleash revolution and the people would do the rest. In his septuagenarian megalomania did he merely have the means to put his anarchistic credo cynically into practice? Was the Great Proletarian Cultural Revolution for its author something akin to a Cosmic Joke? If so it was one that destroyed millions of lives, with repercussions that reverberate to this day.*

Thankfully, for the writer of historical adventure romance, the causes of shattering events are of less concern than the recreation, in fictional form, of the effects on the individuals who experienced them – and I hope, as with The Palace of Heavenly Pleasure *and* The Emperor's Bones *that preceded this final volume of my China trilogy, readers will be moved by the loves, trials and agonies of my characters involved in the maelstrom of events in this tale, and that they become as real in the imaginations as they certainly were for me when I was writing about them – all too horribly so at times.*

I have many people to thank. I have mentioned some of the books that were my sources. To find out more about the Cold War as it affected China I would recommend Max Hastings' history of the Korean War; the novels War Trash *by Ha Jin and* Cry Peace *by Robert Elegant, about the UN prison camps in that war that anticipated Guantanamo and Abu Ghraib; Robert Byron's biography of the Chinese spy chief, Kang Sheng,* The Claws of the Dragon; *and Robert Lewis's and Litai Xue's* China Builds The Bomb. *There is a body of factual information about the Laogai of which Harry Wu's* Laogai: The Chinese Gulag *is the most comprehensive, but I also found inspiration in Chinese former prisoners' memoirs and fictional accounts, for example Bao Ruo-wang's* Prisoner of Mao *and Zhang Xinliang's* Grass Soup, *which are monuments to the tenacity of the human spirit, as moving as Primo Levi's account of Auschwitz,* If This Is A Man. *As mentioned, there are few comprehensive accounts of the Cultural Revolution, but I have found many books helpful, some fictional, some fact, including Simon Leys'* The Emperor's New Clothes; *Chen Juohsi's* The Execution of Mayor Lin; The Cambridge History of China *Volume 15, edited by Roderick MacFarquar; and Li Zhenshang's extraordinary photographs in* Red Color News Soldier; *not to mention recollections of several friends in China who experienced it all.*

Others who have helped me were former British diplomats who were present through these times in China, including Sir Anthony Galsworthy (who also advised me on naturalistic aspects of this book) and Lord Wilson of Tillyorn (who provided me with wonderful anecdotes of what it was like to live in the Beijing of the early sixties, including a hilarious account of how he went duck shooting with the Swiss Ambassador at Marco Polo Bridge); academics like Freda Murck (I have mentioned her in connection with the mango, but she also photocopied for me a wonderful handbook for Red Guards, printed in English, on which I could draw on accurately for slogans and songs); and long term 'China Hands' whose knowledge has saved me many errors. These include Peter Batey, Andy Browne, Gerry Clarke, John and Isabelle Holden, David and Isabelle Mahon, Jim McGregor, Robin Munro, Edward Radcliffe, Peter Wood and Geoffrey Ziebart. Thanks to Helen Callendar, Humphrey Hawksley, Hua Shan, Hong Ying, Tessa Keswick, Eugene Liu and Mdm Liu Lu for their support, advice and ideas, and I am deeply grateful, as always, to my agent, Araminta Whitley, editors Peta Nightingale and Hazel Orme, and my publisher, Carolyn Mays, for their unflagging encouragement, and always positive criticism: it has to be a vain author who does not acknowledge his debt to the professionals!

Adam Charles Newmarch Williams
Hotel Paradiso, Amandola, Italy
21 February 2007